BRUTAL BOYS OF EVERLAKE PREP BOOK 4

QUEEN OF QUARANTINE

CAROLINE PECKHAM   SUSANNE VALENTI

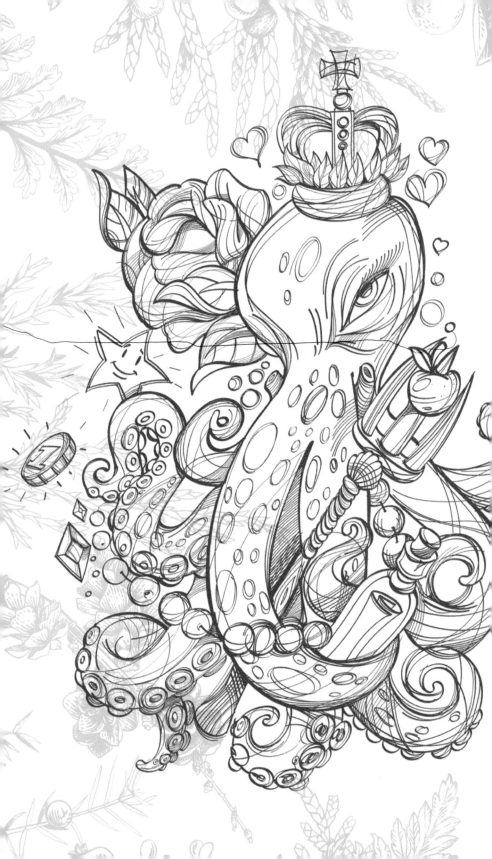

Queen of Quarantine
Copyright © 2021 Caroline Peckham & Susanne Valenti

Interior Formatting & Design by Wild Elegance Formatting

All rights reserved.
No part of this publication may be reproduced or transmitted by any means, electronic, mechanical, photocopying or otherwise, without the prior permission of the copyright owner.

Queen of Quarantine/Caroline Peckham & Susanne Valenti – 1st ed.
ISBN-13 - 978-1-914425-47-9

This book is dedicated to Lord Squidington who's been in quarantine because of Co-squid 19. We know it's been a struggle, buddy, especially when your girl got squidnapped during the clamdemic.

You went through so many em-oceans and had to really ink about how to save her. It was turtley stressful. Especially when you swam down to the seabed on a rescue mission, but when you saw the bottom of the ocean, you blushed. Life's a beach like that. But you shore made it through anyway! You swam into that shark's sea-cret hideaway and rescued your bay. It was inkredible.

Hopefully next year won't be so cra-sea!

TITANS FOOTBALL GROUNDS

ACACIA SPORTS HALL

THE TEM[PLE]

REDWOOD DINING HALL

ASPEN HALLS

PINE AUDITORIUM

HAZEL HOUSE

BEECH H[OUSE]

EVERLAKE

Cypress Gym

Maple Lodge

Tahoma Mountain

Oak Common House

The Sacred Stone

Catacombs

Sycamore Beach

Boathouse

The Hemlock Library

CHAPTER ONE

Of all the torturous moments I'd endured in this lab, nothing compared to when the earpiece died. Losing contact with the Night Keepers had driven fear into my heart and made me question for a few hopeless seconds whether I was ever going to be found.

But then I'd replayed all of their promises in my mind. They were spending every day hunting for me and they wouldn't stop until I was free. The problem was, I'd been hidden by a monster as calculating as his son. And I knew in my heart that if Saint had wanted to keep me locked away forever, he could have pulled it off. So why should I expect any less from his father?

But Saint was still Saint. If anyone could find a way to the centre of his father's labyrinth, it was him. I'd given him every scrap of information I could. Everything from the colour of the walls, to the details of each face I saw, even though they were always hidden behind masks and visors. They only wore name badges with their first names and the Night Keepers couldn't track anyone down from that alone. So I had no substantial clues to my whereabouts. Nothing to go on at all. Just faith that my boys would somehow pull through for me.

A hacking cough tore at my throat and I grasped my neck, wincing against the pain. I brought my knees to my chest, my back to the wall in the glass box of an isolation room which I spent all of my time in. It was cold and bare and smelled like chemicals.

I may have been immune to the Hades Virus, but the amount of it that I was being exposed to regularly meant that I was sick all the same, my body being forced to create antibodies as fast and as much as possible just so that they could harvest them from my blood and create their own version of the vaccine.

I scrunched my eyes up and thought of my boys, missing them with all my heart. They were going to find me. I had complete faith in them. If anyone could track this place down, it was Saint Memphis. And if there was an army fit to break down the doors of hell and face what lay in the hottest part of the fire, it was the Night Keepers. But it was on me to survive until then. Which I damn well would. I'd faced demons bigger than the Hades Virus. I'd gone up against the most ruthless of beasts and had them purring in my arms by the end of it. I would not be destroyed by this monster, even when it clawed its way deep inside me and built a home in my body. I would drive it out and be strong for when the time came to run.

A shiver wracked through me and I clenched my jaw against the biting cold. Pills were waiting for me beside my bed. But the painkillers made me sleep, hours slipped by until I was disorientated and confused. That was when they took my blood, harvesting what they wanted from me. If they tried it when I wasn't sedated, more than one of the nurses ended up injured from how hard I fought them. There were still scratches on one bitch's arms that hadn't healed yet, and I relished seeing them. It was a small blow to have struck against them, but I'd take each and every win I could get right now.

Eventually, I would have to give in and take my meds. I needed to keep my temperature down and ensure I had every chance of surviving this. But I only ever took half of what they left for me. If I took nothing, they'd just inject me with it anyway. They weren't going to let me die unless there was nothing they could do to stop it. I was their little vaccine farm after all.

I pressed my face against my knees, picturing each of my Night Keepers as they hunted for me. Saint and his dark soul, plotting the cruellest of fates for my enemies; Kyan thirsting for blood with vengeance written into his flesh as if it were inked there alongside his tattoos; Blake preparing to fight for me with all the strength he'd built from his pain and suffering; Monroe waiting to charge in and save me like a dark knight with fury and justice in his heart.

So help everyone in this building when they came for me. The four horsemen were going to collect their queen. And when they arrived, there would be blood to pay.

I held out a while longer before I took half my pain meds and stuffed the rest under the mattress. I curled up beneath the blanket on the bed and shivered myself into sleep as the sedative dragged me away. It wasn't all bad. In the darkness, I always seemed to return to one place. A time when life was simple and good and nothing bad ever happened. So at least there I could escape this agony, for a little while.

"What's the point of this?" I huffed as I tried to climb up onto the lowest branch of a large tree. Jess was already high up in the canopy, her whoops of excitement occasionally carrying back to me.

"It's to make you strong," Dad called from the ground as I managed to heave myself up onto the next branch. Jess was thirteen and had stronger arms than me. I still had beanstalks that could barely hold my weight, let alone drag me up a stupid tree.

"Why do I have to be strong?" I groaned as my palm rubbed against a spiky knot and I gave up, dropping down to sit with my back to the trunk and pouting at my dad.

He pushed his glasses up his nose before folding his muscular arms. "Because you never know what life is going to throw at you, Tater-tot. You need to prepare for every outcome so you can weather anything. You have to be ready to fight, just in case you ever need to."

"Well, if I didn't climb trees then there wouldn't be anything to weather. What if I fall?" I tossed at him. I was in a bad mood today. We were staying on a farm and there was a rooster who always made a horrible noise at stupid o'clock. I'd give him a cock-a-doodle-doo to remember if I got my hands on him.

"What's the alternative, kiddo? Are you gonna stay at home hiding from life forever?"

"That's the safest thing to do, isn't it?" I insisted. Sometimes I got so tired of moving around the country, never staying anywhere too long, never having fun that didn't involve being stuck in the middle of nowhere. I liked campfires and scavenger hunts, but I also liked sleeping 'til noon and hanging out with Elle Tompkins.

Okay, so maybe I wasn't just mad about the rooster. Dad had made us move again. I'd known it was coming. But I'd really, really liked the last place in Virginia. And Elle had been cool. She enjoyed dancing and singing and had promised to teach me a routine we could do together. I'd been dumb enough to think I could convince Dad to finally stay in one place. But he'd said no again and again. I just hadn't wanted to hear it. Now I was up a tree on a drizzly day in nowheresville and I'd never see Elle again. It sucked.

"Life can't be lived in one place, kiddo," Dad said with a taut frown on his brow.

"Why not? I liked the last town, why can't we live there like normal people?" I pushed my lower lip out.

"I don't mean physically, I mean everything is always changing, you'll always be moving forward, time will keep passing, stuff will forever happen to you. So you have to go out there and experience the world and make the most of it, because if you don't, life will one day come knocking on your door and you won't like what it has to say."

I eyed him suspiciously. "But what if I do that and life is bad? Like falling out of a tree bad."

"Then you've gotta fight, kiddo," he said fiercely. "Because life will be bad sometimes. It'll test you and push you and you'll want to give up, but if you do it'll suck every drop of happiness out of you until there's nothing left."

"I don't want that," I murmured.

"So fight," he growled, his eyes flaring. "Fight with the spirit of the warrior I know lives in you. Fight for the good days. Fight to be stronger than anything the world hurls at you, fight for what you want. Always, Tatum, always. Because no one but you can make your life what you want it to be."

"But how do I know what I want?" I asked in a small voice. The world felt too large sometimes, like there were too many doors and windows and I didn't know which ones to go through.

I liked the sun and the sea and playing with my sister. I liked burgers without pickles and silly emojis like squids and potatoes. But I didn't know what I wanted from life. The question was too big. There were too many answers. And I didn't have any.

Dad gave me a knowing smile. "You'll know it when you find it."

"But what if I don't know it?" I asked sheepishly.

His smile dropped away. "Then you'll know it when you lose it."

"Oh," I breathed.

"But the world is full of second chances, kiddo," he promised. "You can make things good. Any situation. No matter how bad. It can be good again. I swear it. You've just gotta be brave enough to give life hell. Don't settle for less. You're not here to bow to the world, beautiful girl, you're here to make the world bow to you."

I woke like I was rising out of the deepest, darkest of waters. My eyelids were too heavy to lift and the familiar rattle of the air conditioning unit sounded as a wave of cool air gusted against my cheek. My lips were bone dry and I tried to move my tongue to wet them, but the sedatives still held me in their grip.

A buzz sounded then the door opened and voices moved into the room.

"I feel sorry for her," a man muttered.

"I don't," another replied. "The world has gone to shit, Alan, and I want it back. I want my damn life back."

"I know, I do too, Jonas. I just…" Alan sighed.

"Don't be an idiot, she's just one girl. Thousands of people are dying every day because of the Hades Virus. What's one more to save the whole world?"

"I guess," Alan gave in and my pulse beat out a grim tune. "How much longer do you think she'll last?"

"As long as we can make her live." A thermometer was pushed into my mouth and the cold metal bit my tongue. A beep sounded a minute later. "Jesus. Get the heating up in here. Who the hell was on the last shift?" Jonas snarled.

The air conditioning soon switched to a warm rush of air and I realised how numb I was as my fingers began to tingle with sensation again.

"I bet it was fucking Gary, he couldn't keep a goldfish alive for an hour, let alone a girl," Alan muttered.

"He'll be fired before noon," Jonas said under his breath, taking hold of my arm then a needle slid firmly into my skin.

More strength began to curl through my body, and I managed to crack my eyes open and take in the guy whose face was hidden behind a visor and a face mask beneath it. His attention was on the needle in my arm as he drew out a vial of blood. Alan was across the room gathering more vials and I clenched my jaw determinedly as I saw a small window of opportunity.

I flexed my toes, assessing the strength in my right leg as I glared at this asswipe of a human being beside me. Dad had taught me to fight no matter what. Fight for the good. *Make it good, Tatum.*

I lifted my leg fast and slammed the heel of my bare foot into Jonas's groin, knocking his arm away from the syringe in the same movement. He roared in pain, stumbling back and clutching his junk.

I shoved myself up, my head spinning as I tugged the needle out of my arm then I lunged at him with the last of my strength, grabbing his white coat in my fist and knocking his visor aside as I fought to see the face of one of my captors. I coughed heavily and he shoved me to the ground with a panicked yell and my head impacted with the floor, making my skull ring like a gong.

"Stupid bitch," Jonas spat, slamming his visor back into place while Alan looked between us in alarm, two empty glass vials still clutched in his grip.

"I'll get the doctor." Alan ran for the door, but Jonas caught his arm to stop him, his dark eyes swirling.

"No. We have a job to do." He took a syringe from a tray beside him and stalked forward with murder in his eyes.

I coughed again, scrambling backwards as my strength failed me. My coughing grew heavier and I tasted blood in my mouth, swilling over my tongue like poison. Fear pulled at my heart and whispered deadly promises in my ear. I dabbed my lips with shaking fingers, my death staring back at me more keenly than ever before as they came away wet and red.

"She's in the final stages," Alan gasped.

"Then we'd better take what we can get." Jonas sneered, dropping down and jamming the needle into my thigh. The sedative washed through my veins fast and my eyes locked with Jonas's as darkness grabbed me and tried to pull me into oblivion.

Spots of blood speckled the mask he wore beneath his visor and I managed to paint on a mocking smile, aware it might be my last. If I was going to die soon, I wouldn't let these motherfuckers see my spirit break.

"It looks like you're coming with me to hell, Jonas," I rasped and terror swirled in his eyes before I fell away into an endless abyss.

CHAPTER TWO

Four weeks. Four fucking hellish, unbearable weeks without my baby in my arms and her soul in my keeping.

I crouched behind a parked car a block away from the private research lab we were all focused on, flexing my busted knuckles and relishing the twinge of pain as the scabs cracked open across them. I probably would have broken my hand punching that damn wall if Saint hadn't stopped me, though he was sporting the mother of all bruises on his ribs in thanks for his help. I was enough of an asshole that I hadn't even apologised for that move and he was enough of a man to understand that I was sorry all the same.

I didn't deserve him. Didn't deserve any of them. But they were stuck with me and I'd do whatever I could to make my place amongst them count.

I owed Saint an apology for smacking him, I just didn't have enough good in me right now to give him one. I was blinded by the loss of our girl, just like we all were. Until she was back in our arms, I knew this violence, this tension, this unrelenting anger wouldn't do anything other than fester and spread like rot.

It was hard to feel anything other than fury and fear right now. And I hadn't felt fear in a long damn time. I'd even begun to believe that I wasn't capable of feeling it anymore. But then Tatum Rivers had made me feel a lot of things I'd never thought I could feel.

She was the light to my dark, the hope in a world without any, the reason for my shackled soul to crave freedom. She'd given me dreams of a life with something more. So much fucking more. It was beyond anything I ever could have claimed to deserve but she'd given it to me anyway. Even after all the things we'd put her through when she'd first fallen into our lives.

But I should have known then what I did now. She was never just some girl, never a victim or a means to an end. She was the centre of us. The heart we never believed we had. She'd drawn four lost and hopeless souls into her orbit and claimed each and every one of us as her own, despite the dark and depraved beasts she knew us to be. Without her, we were nothing. I was nothing. Cast adrift without purpose or meaning. But that wasn't going to be my fate, because I refused to even consider the idea of it being hers.

I was terrified at the thought of her being taken from this world and while that could have been crippling, it was actually liberating. I had no limits left on me now. There were no depths I wouldn't stoop to. Nothing I wouldn't do and nothing I wouldn't sacrifice for her. So now that fear was my fuel, I was going to use every last drop of it in the quest for her safe return to us.

"Is everyone in position?" Saint's cool, level voice came through the earpiece as I looked towards the innocuous building we'd surrounded.

Unlike me with my emotions untethered and the constant edge I balanced on, Saint had lost every scrap of emotion since it had happened. He was a cold, hard machine of a man with one single goal only and I had no doubt that he would achieve it.

"I'm at the rear entrance," Monroe confirmed, his voice gruff and low. "It's locked up tight by the looks of things."

"Fire escape looks the same," Blake confirmed.

"On it," I growled, rolling the ski mask I had perched on top of my head down to obscure my features.

I didn't really give a shit about being seen and I'd told Saint as much, but he'd insisted we keep our identities hidden, not wanting his asshole of a father to realise that we were the ones on the hunt. We'd covered up our break ins to the other four labs and hospitals owned by Serenity Pharmaceuticals under the guise of stealing medicines. We'd also paid off contacts via my family to break into other similar places around the city to make it seem like a widespread series of attacks based on a need for antibiotics and the like in the face of the Hades Virus. Saint didn't want it getting out that we were the ones orchestrating it until it was too late and we'd rescued our girl.

I'd argued at first, having no reservations at all over the idea of letting Troy Memphis know that a member of the biggest and most ruthless crime family in the state was hunting him like the dog he was, but Saint had disagreed. He wanted us to use the element of surprise and keep our plan smart. If he hadn't pointed out the fact that his father could easily move Tatum out of the state or even out of the country at the slightest hint of a rescue attempt, then I'd have been more inclined to argue my point. As it was, I trusted Saint to know the best way to go up against his crazy fuck of a father, and if he was sure that this was it then I wasn't going to argue.

But my temper was running very thin. I wasn't coping. I knew for a fact that I was unravelling fast. On the days that I was forced to spend waiting for Saint to come up with our next target to hit, I was drinking heavily and chain smoking and basically falling into a pattern of self-destruction which I had no reason to fight against. But tonight wasn't like the others where I roared my agony and the loss of my girl to the sky and drowned my sorrows in a bottle of Jack until I passed out, murmuring apologies to the girl I was failing. No, tonight was one of the few nights where I could actually do something to help her.

In fact, I felt certain I was about to find her at last and pull her into the safety of my arms, never to let go again.

There wasn't a drop of liquor in my system. There wasn't a single, errant, distracting thought in my mind. I was embodying the monster I'd been raised to be. Every fucked up, horrific moment of my childhood had been specifically designed to mould me into the perfect kind of beast to get this job done. I was lethal, bloodthirsty and entirely focused on one goal.

I was getting my girl back. Come hell or high water she would be returned to my arms by the time the sun rose, and I'd worship her for the rest of my days like only a demon knew how.

I tugged the pair of black gloves on, concealing the last of my flesh within the dark fabric and flexing my fingers to make sure I could still use my hands properly inside them.

I slipped down a side alley to the right of the building, using the dark spots between streetlamps to creep closer to the research centre in the shadows.

The place was well guarded but only against people who didn't know what they were doing. I had no intention of heading in via the front door where the guards were waiting. I wasn't a fucking amateur. I'd been trained in the art of criminal behaviour since I was a boy and I was a damn good study.

I crept quickly down the narrow alley, inhaling the scent of smoke on the air and glancing up at a vent which was churning it out from the third floor. The scent was slightly clinical, and I frowned towards the rising smoke for a moment before continuing on with the plan.

I had no time to hesitate, no moments to spare. My girl was inside this building. I could feel it in the depths of my darkened soul. My heart was thumping to a deep and sultry rhythm which could only be in answer to hers. She was close. She had to be.

I paused in the shadows as I looked up at the smooth wall beside me, spotting the air conditioning vent just where Saint had said it would be after he'd managed to get his hands on the blueprints to this place. Two floors up and bolted down as tight as fuck. Not that that would stop me.

When I was fourteen, my uncle Niall had started taking me with him when he went on jobs that required a bit of stealth. That fucker was the grand master of breaking and entering. He even had a reputation in some circles which claimed he could walk through walls. Everyone knew if Niall O'Brien wanted you dead, there was no escape. You'd wake up in the night with him looming over your bed - a garrotte or axe or sledgehammer in hand depending on his mood - and you'd leave this life bloody and screaming for a mercy which would never come.

Suffice to say, after having a teacher like him, I could break into this place no bother.

"The guards should be finishing up their patrol in seventeen seconds," Saint's voice informed me via the speaker in my ear.

"Most people don't actually stick to your anal as fuck routines, you know," Blake muttered over the comm too and I almost smirked as Saint bit back at him. Almost. But there wasn't enough good left in me for smiles while my girl was gone.

It took a bit of doing to scramble up to the vent, but I made quick work of breaking in once I was there.

I grunted as I hauled myself into the shaft, my shoulders brushing up against the cool metal as I forced my broad frame into the tight space.

"I'm in," I murmured, pushing my tools back into my pocket and starting to wriggle forward on my stomach.

"No theatrics," Saint growled, a command more than a warning and I growled right back at him like the animal I was.

"Stick to the research part of this plan," I muttered. "And leave the heavy lifting to the career criminal."

"There's a delivery truck approaching the rear entrance," Monroe interrupted us and I could practically see his stern teacher face as his jaw ticked over our bickering.

I tuned them out as the others kept watch on the building, all of them moving towards the emergency escape as they waited for me.

I didn't have to take the vents very far, pausing at the first grate which looked down into one of the white corridors inside the building. The lights were low due to the late hour, but the place wouldn't be entirely deserted even in the dead of night. They had workers here around the clock, desperately trying to create the vaccine the world was waiting for. And we had a damn good idea on what - or rather *who* - they were using to create it.

But fuck that. Fuck the world if the price of saving it was her. She was worth more than every other fucker on this miserable planet and I wasn't ever going to apologise for believing that. She was it for me. It might have been selfish and greedy, but I didn't care because my love for her was those things and more. If the creation of this vaccine required a sacrifice, then let it be anyone at all besides her. Let it be *everyone* besides her. Because without her, as far as I was concerned there was no world. At least not one I had any desire to exist in.

I yanked the grate covering the vent free and dropped down into the darkened corridor as silent as a wraith.

There was a distant bleeping which continued in a repetitive tone from somewhere further down the corridor, but aside from that this floor seemed silent.

A CCTV camera looked down at me from the far end of the hallway but I ignored it - Saint had already taken care of the surveillance systems for us and I was concealed all in black anyway.

My fingers twitched with the desire to start hunting the rooms on this level of the building for any sign of my girl and I gritted my jaw against my need to do that. I had to stick to the plan. I blew out a frustrated breath as I forced myself to turn away and headed for the door that led to the emergency escape stairs at the rear of the building.

I slipped inside the darkened stairway, the dim, red lighting just letting me see the stone steps as I headed down them at a fast pace.

My footsteps were silent as I descended, my breathing controlled, just the way Niall had taught me. Even with my girl's life on the line, I wasn't going to get sloppy. *Especially* with her life on the line. The skills I'd earned in blood and bone were worth every moment of suffering on my part if they equalled her life now and I wouldn't let her down.

The acrid scent of cigarette smoke twisted into my nostrils as I made it to the top of the final flight of stairs and I fell still as I noticed a faint blue light mixing with the red coming from somewhere below me.

A half-hearted snort of laugher came next and my pulse leapt as I realised there was someone down there, taking a smoke break and checking out their TikTok feed if I had to guess.

The smart choice would have been for me to hold my ground, wait for him to finish up and fuck off.

But I never had been praised for making smart choices.

My blood was pumping with heat and the desire for violence and I was helpless to resist its call.

With a shiver of anticipation, I continued down the stairs.

I moved silently, my back to the wall and my bulk hidden in the shadows as I closed in on my prey.

When I finally spotted them standing at the foot of the stairs right by the emergency exit, my heart leapt. Not one asshole. Two.

All the better to feed the demon in me.

A grim smile captured my lips as I thought of my girl being held here by these thugs and before I could even consider second guessing my choice, I pounced.

My fist collided with the closest guy's face hard enough to send his skull crashing into the wall beside him and he crumpled to the ground with a cry of pain, the cigarette and cell phone falling to the floor.

The second guard had time to wrench his pistol from his waistband, but my hand closed around his on the butt of the gun before he could even aim it my way.

I used my momentum to slam the gun into his face, locking his fingers in place so he couldn't reach the trigger and spilling blood which made him yell as something most definitely cracked. But before he could get another sound out, I was whirling him around, wrenching the gun from his grip and throwing him face first into the wall.

He staggered away from it, his back to me for the briefest moment, giving me the opportunity I needed to throw an arm around his neck and lock it in place by grasping my wrist in my other hand and exerting enough pressure to cut off his airway.

The guy kicked and flailed, clawing at my arm as he struggled for a breath I wouldn't allow him to take and I just smiled as I thought of my girl, of laying his body at her feet and showing her what depths I'd fall to just to ensure she was safe.

Movement in the shadows to my left drew my attention to the asshole I'd first hit as he scrambled for the radio at his belt and I grunted a curse as I dragged the guy I was strangling towards him and threw a boot into the side of his head.

He fell still just as the fucker I was holding gave in to oblivion too and I dropped his unconscious body on top of his friend, panting with exertion and smiling like a demon.

I wanted more. Wanted to spill their blood across the ground and paint myself in it. But I forced my attention back to the door instead, ignoring Saint's demands to know what was going on as he hissed them through my earpiece and I pushed it open.

Blake slipped inside first, his features fully concealed by a ski mask too, and he had the addition of a military grade gas mask as well, but I knew my brothers by aura alone. There was something tangible about this connection between the four of us and I didn't need to ask to know which of them was close to me at any given moment.

"Shit," he murmured, looking down at the two guys I'd taken out as Monroe and finally Saint moved inside too, closing the door behind them.

"Are they dead?" Monroe asked, the lack of emotion in his voice saying he didn't much care either way.

"Not yet," I replied just as Saint threw a solid punch into my gut and got up in my face.

He really did look like a devil with nothing but his eyes on show beneath that mask, the red emergency lighting glowing in his pupils as he glared at me.

"What did I tell you about keeping a low profile?" he snarled.

"I didn't cut their throats," I pointed out. "I didn't fill them with holes like I ached to. So maybe you should stop freaking out over a few pricks getting their asses handed to them and focus on what's important."

Saint scoffed angrily then dropped down without another word, pulling a coil of fine, black rope from his pocket and quickly hog tying the two of them before slapping a piece of black tape over their mouths in case they came to.

"Where the fuck is your gas mask?" he growled at me.

"Must have forgotten it in the truck." I shrugged, watching the way his eyes flared with rage and kinda hoping he'd punch me again. The beast in me was desperate for blood and pain tonight and that little tussle with the unconscious men at our feet hadn't even whetted my appetite.

Saint took a moment to decide whether or not he wanted to have this argument. We'd had it every single time we'd come out hunting for our girl and he hadn't won yet, so he had to know it was a waste of time. I'd already caught the Hades Virus and survived; it might have fucking sucked and made me as sick as a dog, but it came with the perk of me being immune now. Though Saint liked to get his panties in a twist over the possibility of my immunity not being all that great. But like I'd told him – I didn't give a shit and I wasn't wearing that fucking mask. It reminded me too much of the skull mask I'd had to wear at Royaume D'élite and the things I'd done there. Now that we'd had to put our vendetta against them to one side, I had no desire to live in those memories.

Saint seemed to realise there was no point arguing this with me, especially as I couldn't exactly go and get the thing now anyway, so he dropped it with a sharp exhale of irritation.

"If you fuck up our chances of rescuing her, I'll personally put a bullet in your skull, you neanderthal," he hissed as he straightened.

"Don't worry your little cotton socks about that, sweetheart," I said, stepping forward and putting out the cigarette that was still burning on the ground with my heel. "If we fail to rescue her, I'll be doing that myself."

Saint looked deep into my eyes, reading the truth of that statement for himself and grunting his approval. There was no me without Tatum anymore. Shit, I didn't think any of us wanted to consider an existence without her in it. So it hadn't been hard to realise that I'd rather eat a bullet than linger on in this life without her.

It wasn't suicidal. Just practical.

Besides, I had no intention of following through on that promise because we were going to get her the fuck back. Tonight.

"Your hot-headed behaviour could fuck this whole thing up," Saint warned. "You need to remember that the entire world doesn't revolve around you and your *emotions*." He said that last word like it was dirty and I snarled at him as I stepped closer, letting him see every dark corner of my soul lurking within my eyes.

"Fuck the world. I don't care. Without her in it, there isn't anything else worth saving anyway. I don't give a shit if it's right or noble or ethical. My love for her isn't any of those things. It's dark, twisted, dangerous and unstoppable. So if saving her means letting the rest of the world burn then pass me the fucking matches and I'll get the gasoline. Because there isn't a thing in this universe that I'm not willing to sacrifice to get my girl back."

"Wrong," Saint snarled, his dark eyes pinning me in his gaze like he seriously thought he had any chance of stopping me now.

"I don't care what you have to say on the matter. I'm going to-"

"You called her *your* girl again,» he growled, cutting me off with a look so toxic it was practically burning me where I stood. «She›s not yours. She›s *ours*."

"Too fucking right she is," Blake agreed, every piece of light that usually shone in him utterly replaced with dark instead as the monsters in us rose to the surface of our skin and scented blood on the air.

There would be death in payment for her being taken from us.

"Then why the fuck are we still standing here?" Monroe demanded, his fury written in every inch of his posture as his muscles flexed with tension. "Let's go and burn the world down for her then."

The rest of us agreed without words as we followed him back up the darkened stairs with the intention of doing just that. I'd tear this place apart brick by brick if I had to, but one thing was for sure, I wasn't leaving here without Tatum Rivers by my side.

Just a little longer, baby. Your monsters are coming for you. And we won't stop until you're safe in our arms once more.

CHAPTER THREE

Monroe strode up the stairs with all the grace of a buffalo in stilettos and I snarled irritably as I shoved past him and took the lead. Honestly, it was like he was *trying* to make noise with those stomping footfalls of his.

"Fucking megalomaniac," Monroe muttered beneath his breath but I didn't call him out on it.

The way I saw it, he was correct and that wasn't an insult. Power was all that mattered in this life and if he hadn't figured that out yet then he needed to pay more attention. Well, power and my siren. But my feelings for her defied all logic and I had given up on trying to analyse them. I just had to accept that I was hopelessly enthralled by her and embrace it because I certainly wasn't going to attempt to give her up. My addiction to her might be my downfall, but if I was going to burn for any reason then I would happily do so for her.

"Try to keep your steps silent," I hissed back at Monroe. "If Kyan can manage it then there's no reason you can't."

Kyan chuckled darkly which really seemed more like an automatic response to my words than a real laugh, but I knew why he wasn't feeling any actual joy and I wasn't going to point it out.

"Fifth floor?" Blake confirmed as we hurried up the dark stairwell and he moved to walk on my left. The gas mask he wore warped the tone of his voice a little, but these things were the best money could buy and I doubted any of the others even noticed the difference. But I had a musician's ear - much to my father's disgust - and the alteration in pitch was quite disconcerting.

"That's where they keep the medical test subjects, so unless they have completely reconfigured the layout of the building in the time it took us to drive here then yes," I said emotionlessly.

"Wow, what crawled up your ass and died?" he muttered and I ground my jaw against the desire to lay into him.

We were all on edge, each of us just trying to find a way to power through this uncertain time and do all we could to bring our girl back to us. His childish comments were a way for him to cope and as irritating as I found them, I was just pleased he hadn't fallen back on the habit of getting himself drunk and chasing adrenaline rushes. In fact, Blake had been perfectly single minded in his determination to get Tatum back into our arms. He had been by my side day and night while I used all of my connections and tactics to dig into my father's businesses and Serenity Pharmaceuticals in pursuit of her, wordlessly carrying out any and every task I'd asked of him to help speed up the process. So I could allow him the odd badly timed, non-amusing joke.

We climbed the stairwell at speed and paused on the top floor as I pressed an ear to the door, listening for any sign of movement beyond it.

Kyan took a pistol from his belt and Monroe drew his too. So far we'd managed to conduct these raids without killing anyone, purely to keep the investigations into the 'robberies' low priority and keep the police off of our tails. But the more places we hit, the higher the security was getting at the new targets. They didn't know we were searching for our girl of course, but stories of the gangs breaking into medical research facilities and private hospitals all over the city to steal medicines were making them up their security.

Ideally we'd leave this place without getting blood on our hands, but if that was what it took then I wasn't against it. Besides, if our girl really was here then I had more than enough motivation to kill every last one of them if we had the time. But until we were certain, I wasn't looking to spill too much blood.

Nothing but the soft sounds of my brothers' breaths reached my ears as I listened intently for a full minute - ignoring Kyan's impatient growl - before cracking the door open.

The corridor was softly lit with night lighting and I spotted a woman in a nurse's uniform at a desk at the far end of the hall. Her back was to us and she was reading a book, seemingly lost in her own world. I took another moment to listen out for other sounds, but it seemed like she was the only member of staff nearby, and from what I'd learned in my research into this place that was to be expected. They kept one nurse on shift overnight and that was it.

Kyan slipped past me as I pushed the door wide and the rest of us waited as he stalked along the corridor, his eyes set on the woman as she stayed lost in her book, completely unaware that she was being stalked by a predator.

When Kyan pounced, it was so fast that I almost missed the move. One of his hands slapped down over the woman's mouth, stifling her cry and his other locked around her neck as he choked her out.

It didn't take him long to render her unconscious and I moved forward to tie her up, hidden beneath her desk where she wouldn't be discovered until we were long gone. My gaze fell on her lanyard for a moment as I memorised her name in case it would be of any use to me in future. *Erica Mortensen. I have you marked.*

Blake picked the paperback up from her desk entitled Warrior Fae, flipped it open to the last page and tore it out before scrunching it up and tossing it in the trash. *Fucking savage.* Not that I was complaining. She deserved to never find out the end of her book. If I had the time, I'd find a way to track down every copy in the world so that she could suffer forevermore without knowing how it ended. I wasn't sure if there was any worse fate than that to bestow on someone.

Monroe, as usual, wasn't waiting for us and was moving along the corridor, cracking open doors and checking on the patients inside them as he hunted for our girl. I was guessing they were either sleeping or in no state to cry out in alarm at the sight of a masked man peering in on them, which was for the best. I quickly disconnected the alarm sitting on the desk in case any of them reached out and hit that red call button by their beds though. We didn't need any of the guards posted downstairs to take it upon themselves to do another sweep of the building before their scheduled rounds in an hour.

I ignored the others and their haphazard methods of checking the place out as I quickly started searching on the computer at the desk, hunting down a list of patient records and frowning as I noticed the title for the clinical trials being conducted here. It appeared that they were working on a new form of cancer treatment, not a vaccine at all. But that couldn't be right. They *had* to be working on the Hades Virus. Tightness filled my chest and my knuckles paled as I gripped the desk. All signs had pointed me here when I'd hacked into my father's servers. It made no sense for that information to have been wrong. Unless he had suspected someone was on to him…

I banished the terrifying thought of what my father might do if he truly had realised someone was searching for Tatum and instead focused on the task at hand. That was a worry for another time. And as the motherfucker in question had managed to conveniently retreat to an unknown location which he wouldn't even share with me, we weren't even able to get our hands on him as a last resort. Which just meant that this had to work. It *had* to. I refused to consider any alternative.

I checked the list of patient names on the list and my upper lip peeled back as I read through them, obviously not finding Tatum's name anywhere but taking note of one patient who was only referred to with a number. If that wasn't suspicious as fuck then I didn't know what was. And it was exactly the kind of dehumanising bullshit my father would choose to entertain. If she didn't even have a name, then he didn't have to admit that she was a real person who he was hurting and possibly killing in pursuit of his own agenda. Not that I was delusional enough to believe he gave a fuck about murdering someone to advance his own interests, but this was precisely his style. Meticulous piece of shit that he was.

"Room thirty-nine," I growled, closing the computer down so that no one realised it had been used to find this information and turning to head that way.

Kyan had joined Monroe in searching the other rooms and I moved away from the two of them as they continued to open and close doors, stalking in the direction of room thirty-nine. Blake stayed tight on my heels, knowing full well I was the most likely to have tracked her down first and wanting to be there when I found her. I couldn't fault him for that. We were all in desperate need of a reunion with our girl.

My heart raced as I closed in on the door at the furthest end of the corridor and I couldn't help but break into a jog at the thought of finding her there, of pulling her into my arms and looking into those bright blue eyes which consumed me. She was my drug of choice and I was hopelessly addicted. I needed my fill of her or I knew I was going to go insane.

Tatum Rivers was the one and only person who had looked upon this heartless monster of a man and somehow found a pulse thumping away beneath the vitriol and poison I wore as a shield. She'd seen the corruption and toxicity of my soul and had found something else there too. Something I'd never believed I even had and yet she'd discovered it all the same. I was her creature now whether she wanted me or not and she was mine too. My Night Bound. And I wasn't ever letting her escape me.

I reached the door and had to fight with every inch of self-control I owned not to throw it open as my fingers curled around the handle and I released a shaky breath. Blake laid a hand on my shoulder in solidarity and I nodded once before pushing it wide.

Inside the room, all was dark. The bed was nothing more than a hulking shadow in the centre of it. The machines which should have been monitoring vital signs deathly quiet.

"No," I breathed as a rock sank into my stomach, growing heavier and heavier, the weight of it threatening to drag to me to the deepest depths of the vastest ocean imaginable. I was drowning. Drowning in my grief and the knowledge of my failure yet again.

Blake wasn't so pessimistic as me and he found the light switch, flicking it on as he raised his weapon and pointed it at the empty bed.

My heart thrashed and pounded within my chest like a wild animal, caged and desperate, doomed and dying.

Above the bed was a whiteboard with various observations noted on it from vital stats to notes on blood extractions and the condition of the patient who had been kept here.

At the very bottom of the board were words that set my whole world alight with a desperate kind of agony as I stared up at them.

Patient deceased: 10:07am.
Resuscitation unsuccessful.

I stared at the clear declaration before me with my pulse spiking and the most debilitating fear rooting me in place for far too long. But my heart refused to accept the words that had been scrawled on that board. I just couldn't.

"No," Blake snarled in refusal, echoing my own thoughts and turning from the room. He was taking much less care than he should have been as he raced along the corridor and started opening other doors, checking the rooms where other patients slept as he continued his hunt, clearly not accepting the facts as they'd been presented to us.

I stepped out of the empty room and stood waiting in the corridor for the other three Night Keepers to finish up their search, but I already knew what they would find.

"She's not here and I don't believe for one fucking second that she's dead either," I snarled, refusing to allow them to even consider panicking or giving into some useless form of grief.

"How can you be certain?" Blake demanded, his eyes wild with concern, a desperation in them that begged me to give him a definite confirmation which I couldn't give.

"Because my father knows she's too valuable to allow her to die so quickly. Besides, I'm not fool enough to believe something I haven't seen with my own two eyes. She isn't dead unless I see a body and if any of you even consider giving up on her then you'll answer to me over it."

None of them voiced any complaint to that. We were all equally determined not to believe in her death, so I forgot about the words which had been scrawled on that board and set my mind to continuing our search.

Our girl wasn't here. But I was certain she had been. She'd been here and she'd been in that room. We could hunt the rest of this place to be sure, but I knew we weren't going to find her here now. Of course, now we'd have to rob the place to cover up this break in just like the others.

She wasn't dead. She couldn't be. If she was, I was sure I'd know it. I'd have felt it as my heart was torn to shreds and my world imploded with the impossibility of it going on without her in it.

She wasn't dead.

But she *was* gone.

And we were going to get her back.

CHAPTER FOUR

My body was breaking. Everything hurt. It felt like there was a fissure rupturing open in my chest every time I took a breath. And when I did, it was with a wheezing rattle that made fear splinter through me. But for every way my body felt weak, my soul was galvanised, refusing to break.

I will not give up.

I was running out of time though. And I had to do something now if I was ever going to survive this. As much as I knew my boys would be hunting for me with the bloody ferocity of hell hounds, I was also starting to accept that Troy Memphis may have just hidden me too damn well for even his own son to find. And as I caught sight of a nurse approaching the glass door and tapping in a code to open it, I knew now was my shot. Possibly my last too. Because I didn't know how much longer I could fight this virus. Its roots were too deep in my flesh, its hunger for my death all too keen.

I feigned sleep as the nurse approached, my meds tucked away under my mattress. I'd taken none today. Every time I took them now, I seemed to sleep longer, deeper. And that frightened me in a way I didn't want to admit to. My dreams were so vivid, and the more time I spent with Dad and Jess in my unconscious state, the closer I actually felt to joining them. And as tempting as it would have been to slip away into their arms once more, it wasn't time for me yet. I had a life I was desperate to live. I had four men waiting for me who I'd never gotten to show the depths of my feelings to.

My monsters, my saviours.

I'd once stood on a beach in the pounding rain and placed my hand against the Sacred Stone before swearing an oath to belong to the Night Keepers. I hadn't believed it and I certainly hadn't wanted it. But fate had bound us and now I knew why. Because through all the pain, the suffering, the way we'd tortured one another, we'd all somehow healed each other too. They were four kings of the dark, and I had become their queen. The girl my father had always wanted me to be, the girl I had always aspired to be. So I needed to return to them and reclaim my position in our tribe.

"I thought you might not make it through another night," the nurse murmured to me even though he must have believed I was out cold, and I recognised Jonas. The motherfucker hadn't gotten sick after I'd coughed on him and I was pissed as all hell about that. "It's a fucking miracle."

You know what's a miracle, assface? You still being healthy and well.

He took hold of my arm, rolling it out to get access to the bruised skin around the crook of my elbow which had been punctured by countless needles. "I'd be more grateful if you hadn't kicked me in the balls though, but I guess I still got one of the first vaccines last week because of you so I can't be totally bitter," he said icily. *Of all the people my blood could save, why this guy?*

I felt his fingers on my face as he pushed my hair away from my forehead and I released a small murmur as if I was coming to, shifting on the bed.

"Shit," he muttered then he moved away and I cracked my eyes open, watching as he drew up some sedative in a syringe just as I'd expected.

As he turned back toward me, I shut my eyes again, my fingers prickling as I mustered my strength. It wasn't much, but all I had was going to be directed at this shit stain.

He gripped my arm again and just as the needle grazed my skin, I whipped my other arm around, catching his wrist and twisting it sharply, plucking the syringe from his hand as his grip loosened. He gasped, but he wasn't fast enough to run as I jammed the needle into his neck and slammed my thumb down on the plunger with a squeeze of satisfaction in my gut. His eyes widened behind his visor and I grinned demonically.

"You little bitch." His hand whipped out, crashing into my face and my head wheeled sideways from the impact. "Help!" he choked out, lurching toward the emergency button beside the door.

But he was stumbling, the sedative already taking affect. I pushed out of bed as his knees hit the floor, staggering toward him as my vision went from dark to light. He crawled toward the door, still reaching for the button then gave up and took his phone from his lab coat pocket instead. I leapt on his back with a grunt of exertion, making him crumple to the floor as I prised the phone from his grip.

"No one's coming for you, so pray to whatever god serves small-dick douches," I rasped.

He growled angrily, trying to fight, but it was no good. He was slipping away second by second and I pushed his face against the floor, hearing his visor crack as I waited for him to pass the hell out. "Goodnight, asshole."

He finally fell still and I drew in a wheezing breath as I slumped down beside him and looked at his phone, finding it needed face ID or a code to unlock it.

I shoved Jonas to roll him over, the effort it took making my vision blacken again for a moment. My muscles shook with the exertion, but I didn't slow as I ripped his visor and mask off, finding a hairy face beneath. Not a real beard, more like that bum fluff teenagers liked to grow when they couldn't actually achieve proper facial hair. *Gross.*

I angled the phone down at him and the screen unlocked just as a cough crashed through my body. The doctor had given me a steroid injection which had slowed the bleeding on my lungs, so I didn't taste blood this time. I was gonna take that as a good omen.

Adrenaline gave me a burst of energy as I dialled Saint's number, my heart hammering madly against my ribs like a tiger trying to break out of a cage. I'd never thought I'd think this, but thank Christ for Saint and his punishments because he'd once had me write out his phone number a thousand times after I told him Kyan had fucked me with the cucumber Saint had eaten in his salad for dinner. Not true, but totally hilarious.

Hope fluttered through me as ringing filled the silence, but a beeping in my ear signalled that the battery was low. I glanced at Jonas's phone seeing it was on two freaking percent. What kind of psychopath diced with fate like that and let their battery life dance on the brink of doom? Trust my fucking luck to pick the one asshole in this place who didn't keep their goddamn phone charged up.

"Pick up," I hissed in desperation. But my hope waned as the call rang on and on.

It was an unknown number. What if Saint didn't pick up to anyone who wasn't in his contacts? He must have hated cold callers with a vengeance. And I knew he didn't have voicemail because he'd once told me voicemails were left by peasants who didn't value their time on Earth.

"Come on, devil boy," I begged and miraculously, the call connected.

"Hello?" Saint asked, suspicion colouring his voice.

"Saint, it's me. It's Tatum." But there was no answer and as I pulled the phone back to look at the screen, I found it was blank. "*No*," I gasped, panic slicing up the centre of my being.

My hand shook and I wet my desperately dry lips as I considered what to do. And there was only one thing for it. I had to fucking run. I abandoned the phone beside Jonas and ripped the lanyard from around his neck which held a key card. I dragged the lab coat off of him next, putting it on before covering my face with his mask and visor. His feet were far too big for me to borrow his shoes, so I just had to hope no one looked too closely at my bare feet.

I stumbled to the door, running on adrenaline alone as my entire body quaked with weakness. I slipped outside and headed down the empty corridor in the direction of an elevator, my pulse thundering in my ears.

The tiles were icily cold against my bare feet as I moved as fast as I could toward the metal doors ahead. Before I reached them, they started to open and chatter sounded from inside. With a jolt of anxiety, I lunged toward a set of double doors beside the elevator and stumbled through into a brightly lit stairwell. I stifled a cough, my lungs feeling like they were about to pop in my chest as I held it back with all my might.

Stay in my damn chest, you explosive cough of doom.

My tongue was thick and heavy in my mouth as I gripped the railing and started moving down level after level, my breaths coming unevenly. *If I can just get outside, get to a road, find help...*

An alarm sounded like a klaxon in my head and I cursed, quickening my pace, nearly falling several times but somehow staying upright as I pushed myself harder and harder. I felt like Bambi on the ice, my legs as brittle as twigs. But the only Thumper I had cheering me on was my pounding heart in my chest.

I made it to the ground floor and shoved my weight against a fire exit door, depressing the bar that secured it. But it didn't budge. *Who the fuck kept fire exits locked??*

"Shit," I growled, pushing it harder, but the thing wasn't opening.

The sound of running footsteps reached me somewhere further up the stairs and panic washed through me.

I have to get out. I can't give up.

I ran for the door next to the stairs, pushing through it and finding myself in a large foyer with two security personnel with fucking guns at their hips staring out of a large, rotating door. My heart leapt as I gazed at the street ahead of them. Rain started tinkling against the floor length windows as I looked around for any other way out. But that was it. My one, single hope.

A reception desk lay empty opposite the doors and I ran boldly toward it, dropping down behind it before I was seen. I'd moved with all the grace of a drunk zombie, but had somehow made it here silently.

I pulled open the bottom drawer, rifling inside it for something I could use as a weapon, but there was nothing aside from a stapler and some equally useless stationary. *Oh come on, gimme a break.*

Static crackled over the guards' radios and a female voice sounded through it. "Security footage shows her heading down the main stairwell. She's – ah! She's behind the reception desk."

Fuck a fucking duck on a truck.

Heavy footfalls sounded, coming my way and I pushed myself to my feet, figuring I had no alternative as I threw the stapler as hard as I could. It bounced off of one of the guard's heads and he grunted angrily.

"Stay back, I'm contagious," I snapped and they slowed their approach.

The one I hadn't struck glared at me as he pulled up a black face mask from his chin to cover his mouth and nose. "On your knees."

"I'm the most valuable person in the world," I blurted, pressing my shoulders back even though all I felt like doing was curling up on the floor and trying to drown the pain in my body. "You can't shoot me."

The guards shared a look that confirmed it and I ran for the door with my heart in my throat. Sure enough, no shots were fired and they clearly didn't want to get too close to me and the Hades Virus either. That dirty cluster of death in my body was suddenly my only friend and I clung onto its hand as it offered me my only chance for freedom.

I wasn't fast or graceful, but I was fucking desperate and the daylight pouring in from outside called to me like a song. I was most likely going to be caught, but maybe someone out there would hear my screams first.

I made it into the rotating door, pushing it around, almost tasting the fresh air. Then it slammed to a halt and I turned back with a snarl on my lips, finding the guards stopping it from moving any further. They started turning it the other way, one of them walking around with it to return me to them. I tried to force it back again with all I had, but my weakened body just couldn't do what I needed it to and I almost heard the Hades Virus laughing maniacally in the back of my head.

I screamed as much as my lungs would allow, making as much noise as I possibly could, banging my hands on the window and hoping someone out there would see or hear, would call the police. It was no hope at all really, but doing nothing wasn't in my nature. I couldn't lie down and take this. And I may not have been able to fight right now, but I still had one weapon at my disposal.

I ripped the visor and mask off of my face as the door rotated back into the foyer and the guard grabbed my arm. I coughed as I tore at his face mask and he cursed, slapping a hand over my mouth and nose as he immobilised me against his chest.

My heart catapulted into my throat as I suddenly couldn't breathe, his meaty palm clasped down too hard as my lungs laboured for air. I jerked in his hold, stamping on his foot and using my elbows to try and escape, but I was too weak.

Darkness curtained my eyes as a bunch of nurses in full biohazard suits ran toward us across the foyer and it was only a few more seconds before a needle was driven into my thigh. Everything went black as the strength of the drug overwhelmed me and I thought of my Night Keepers as the last of my hope faded with my strength.

They weren't going to find me.

I couldn't get free.

I had days left at the very most. My fate was paved, walled in on all sides as it led me to my final destination. And only a grave awaited me at the end.

CHAPTER FIVE

"How fucking long is this going to take, man?" I asked, the impatience in my voice clear as I paced back and forth in front of the dining table in The Temple.

Saint sat there before his laptop, totally still, staring at the screen with his fingers steepled as he waited like a freaking statue and the rest of us tried not to lose our shit.

Well, me and Monroe were trying not to lose our shit - Kyan was currently on the phone to his uncle Niall while clenching his jaw so hard that I was fairly certain he was about to flip out. But he pretty much constantly flipped out these days, so I didn't pay him much attention.

I'd been looking right at Saint when he'd answered that call, the colour draining from his face as the faintest sound of her voice reached me from the speaker for the briefest of seconds before it was cut off. One word was all she'd managed. Saint's name. A plea for help, a single chance at a lifeline and less than a second of connection between them. But it was all he needed. Because this was Saint motherfucking Memphis we were talking about. One word and a call from an unknown number – she might as well have given him a full address and a time for us to swing by and pick her up. Thank fuck. Although the hour that had passed since that one, momentary, fleeting phone call had seemed to drag on into eternity while Saint worked his magic, pulled the right strings, greased the right palms and now we just had to fucking wait until it paid off.

"Good," Kyan ground out, drawing my attention back to him and his phone conversation. "I'll call you about where to meet us when I know the details." Kyan hung up and I wondered if that was really the best way to treat a man who he had declared a criminally insane psychopath on more than one occasion. But apparently he gave no shits about that and I just had to hope that Niall O'Brien was still on our side despite his nephew's rudeness.

"He's in," Kyan said, tossing his cell down on the table so that it slid across the polished wood and smacked into the side of Saint's laptop. "Tell me when we're ready to leave."

He stalked away without another word and headed down into the crypt where a bellow of rage escaped him, echoing off the cold stone walls down there before the predictable sound of him beating the shit out of the punching bag came a moment later. He'd managed to split two of them in the weeks that Tatum had been missing, spilling sand all over the floor while he stood there sweating and panting over the carnage, barely even seeming human anymore as the rage in him burned freely.

"I'd better make sure he puts gloves on," Monroe grunted after a few moments passed of us listening in to Kyan's pain in physical form. "If he fucks his hands up before we head out, he'll be no good to her."

Her.

No need for any of us to mention her name. There was only one woman in our lives. Only one. She was the spider that had lured us all in and bound us to one another within her web. We may have been close without her, but with Tatum at the heart of us, we were an unstoppable force. We only needed a direction to point our fury in and we'd be ready to tear the world apart to return her to her rightful place at the heart of us.

Monroe stalked away to join Kyan and I expelled a hard breath as I tried to contain my own frustrations.

"Anything?" I demanded while Saint just continued to stare at nothing on the fucking laptop screen.

"Yes," he replied scathingly, his voice dripping disdain. "My contact within the FBI already traced that motherfucker's number and sent me over all the details. I chose to continue sitting here and not to react in any way because clearly, I don't give a fuck about the welfare of our queen. Perhaps I'll go and take a nap before opening the email."

His cold gaze slid to me for a single second before he went back to staring at his fucking screen, waiting for that email to come in for real and I felt the weight of that look like a fucking sucker punch.

"Alright, alright," I replied, raising my hands in surrender and apology. "I'm just desperate to get out there and find her."

Saint exhaled slowly and nodded once. "We are all equally shattered by our separation from her. Our enthralment with the girl we made our own is something quite astounding, wouldn't you agree?"

"Not really," I replied. "You only have to take one look at the girl - a real look, beyond the fucking stunning exterior to the richness of her soul beneath it and the power she commands without even trying. Once you see that, I don't think anyone would be surprised that she caught the four of us under her spell. I mean, shit, that girl deserves a whole hell of a lot from this life and if we can even begin to give it to her then I'm all in."

The sound of Kyan and Monroe arguing about his lack of gloves called up to us, quickly followed by the sound of the two of them fighting each other. I wasn't worried about them injuring themselves in any lasting way though. Neither of them would want to render the other useless once we found out where we needed to go. The four of us would need to be on top form to rescue her.

"She's the light to our dark," Saint said when I'd just about given up on getting a reply from him. "I just hope our corruption doesn't taint her soul too much."

I scoffed dismissively and he raised an eyebrow, deigning to look at me once more.

"That's not the way this works, dude, haven't you figured that out yet?" I asked him.

"What?"

"The corruption. It's not us darkening her soul, it's her lightening ours. She's more powerful than any of us and the deeper we let her into our hearts, the closer I think we move to salvation."

"Salvation?" Saint asked before shaking his head. "No, I don't believe we are about to become reformed citizens, Blake. I think we have become her creatures. We are still the dogs of war, dark, desperate and ruined as we are, but she is our master. She won't remove that stain upon our natures, but she will show us where best to aim it. And I for one am ready to let her."

I swallowed thickly as I considered his words. Had I hoped that being with her might reform me? Mould me into a better man than the one I was? Perhaps. But maybe he was right. Maybe I shouldn't have been trying to use her to drag myself up out of the dark. Maybe I should just embrace my shadows and use her as a guiding light for where I should aim them.

Saint somehow managed to straighten further even though his spine was ramrod straight to begin with and he quickly leaned towards the laptop, tapping a few keys before his eyes scanned back and forth across the screen. I watched with my heart pounding, hoping against hope that Saint's contact had come through for us. That that number Tatum had called us from was the breadcrumb we'd needed and not another loose end.

"Got him," Saint purred, pushing to his feet and stalking away from the laptop.

I leaned in instantly, needing to see it for myself and I smiled as I found the registered owner of the cellphone we'd received that call from. Jonas Barrow, thirty-nine, single, clinical assistant at Serenity Pharmaceuticals. His address was listed too alongside a recent photograph which I guessed was from his driver's license. Tatum had given us the name Jonas before her earpiece had died but we'd had no other leads to go on until now. I hated him on sight, from his wispy brown hair to his patchy attempt at a beard which looked more like someone had glued clumps of pubes to his face in random places.

"Wait," I called, just as Saint made it to the foot of the stairs which led up to his bedroom. "There's no address here for his place of work. We already knew Serenity Pharmaceuticals were the ones holding her, but they have countless buildings and offices around the city, so how-"

"We're going to pack up our shit and head to Mr Barrow's house," Saint said, an evil glint in his eye. "And then we're going to wait for him to head into work and follow him."

"Just like that?" I asked, wondering if there weren't more layers to his not-so-diabolical plan.

"Never forget, Blake, if you have a vermin problem there is no point taking out a single rat. You need to lie in wait, watch it return to its nest then you can strike at the whole lot of them. Complete annihilation. True victory."

He turned and continued up the stairs and a slow smile spread across my face. This was it. Finally. We were really going to get her back.

Jonas Barrow's home turned out to be a nice new house out in the suburbs with pink roses growing in the garden and kids playing loudly within the neighbouring houses, no doubt sending their parents batshit after months of lockdown with no end in sight. Still, better safe than sorry I guessed. I certainly would rather have been locked in a house with my mom for months than to have lost her like I did.

It was a bright and unseasonably warm day and it seemed like almost everyone on this cosy little nowhere street had decided to open their curtains wide and sit by their windows to enjoy it.

We sat in Saint's mom-mobile with its blacked-out windows, comfy seats and cup holders and watched Jonas's home with the eyes of a hoard of bloodthirsty men.

"I still say I could just beat the information out of him," Kyan grumbled, not for the first time.

We'd been camped out here for hours - though of course Saint had planned for that and we had plenty of food, drinks, blankets (because he didn't want the engine running and drawing attention) and even our own personal bottles to pee in. Of course, I'd made a smartass comment about what we were supposed to do if one of us needed a shit and he'd just casually lifted a Tupperware box from the space beneath his seat in answer. Luckily none of us had felt the need to make use of it, but I was pretty certain he really expected us to rather than risk getting out of the car and alerting our target to our presence.

The only time any of us had gotten out was when we'd first shown up here. Saint had dropped Kyan off on a side street where no one would see him then he'd snuck through backyards until he reached Jonas's house. He'd managed to confirm that the bastard in question was currently asleep in his bed and had seen a work schedule stuck to the fridge which confirmed he was back on shift tonight.

Niall had come through for us, meeting Kyan to give us the weapons we needed, and my gut twisted uncomfortably as I wondered what he was going to have to do to pay his family back for all the help they'd been giving us recently. I knew he was more than willing to pay the price, but I also wished for a better life for my brother. One that he could choose for himself. But now wasn't the time to worry about the future. We needed to get Tatum back if we wanted any chance of one anyway.

Ever since Kyan had returned to us he'd been chomping at the bit, wanting to beat the answers from that fucker. But Saint had overruled him, not wanting to do anything that might alert the people holding Tatum to our approach. With his dad pulling the strings here, he was adamant we needed to be careful and I had to agree. As much as I ached to move now, the main focus had to be on getting our girl back.

So we sat there all fucking day and just waited him out.

Hours later, I shifted in my seat, trying to alleviate some of the numbness in my ass as the gun at my hip dug into my side.

Night had fallen and the tension in the car was palpable as we waited on Jonas to appear.

When he finally did, I straightened in my seat beside Saint who barely even reacted to our prey emerging at last.

We watched as Jonas headed out of his house with a medical mask covering his lower face like a good little citizen, before he slipped into the blue sedan parked on his drive.

He started up the engine and backed out into the street before heading away from us at a steady speed.

"Come on," I urged when Saint just remained seated behind the wheel, the engine silent and desperation filling the car. "We need to follow him."

"I'm perfectly capable of tailing that asshole," Saint gritted out, not taking his eyes from the now distant taillights. "But I'm also capable of subtlety. Something you lack considerably."

"Start driving or I'll rip you out of that seat and take over," Kyan growled while Monroe muttered insults at our self-appointed leader.

Saint slowly slid his seatbelt on and sighed like we were testing his patience before starting up the engine and pulling away from the curb.

He stuck to the motherfucking speed limit as he followed Jonas at far too great of a distance for my liking and I bit down my own complaints as I just kept my gaze fixed on the car which was now several blocks away from us.

With the lockdown still in full force, there weren't many cars on the street as there weren't that many essential workers still allowed to leave their homes for work. And as much as it frustrated me, I guessed Saint had a point about us not riding the sedan's ass the whole way there, but it still made me nervous as fuck in case we lost him.

Predictably, we headed into the depths of Hemlock City and Saint begrudgingly drew closer to the sedan as Jonas took various turns, the chance of us losing sight of him increasing.

Eventually, Jonas pulled off of a darkened street into an underground parking lot beneath an innocuous looking office building which towered overhead and didn't even have any signage on the front of it. There was just a glass front to a barren looking reception area where four armed guards lingered far enough away from the doors not to draw notice, but they were easy enough to see if you knew what you were looking for.

"What is this place?" Monroe asked, leaning forward between the chairs so that he could peer out of the windshield as Saint took a turn around the block and parked up in a shadowy side street.

We definitely weren't supposed to park here, but Saint had put fake plates on the car and he couldn't give a fuck about getting a fine.

"I researched every single building that was listed in the Serenity Pharmaceuticals repertoire," Saint replied with a faint frown on his brow. "This one wasn't on that list. So I'd say it's the place they don't want anyone to know about. The place where their ethical standpoint takes a backseat and they conduct the kind of research they don't want the media to find out about."

"Great. So it's an evil lab?" Kyan asked casually, like he came across evil labs every other day.

"Why must you always reduce everything to a crass, layman's description?" Saint tossed at him, but Kyan didn't bother to reply.

I glanced back at him and found him gripping his baseball bat tightly as he stared up at the building in question. My gaze lingered on the tattoo which wrapped around the ring finger on his left hand, the wedding ring he could never take off, and my chest tightened as I considered it. I'd made my peace with the idea of the two of them being married for the most part, but I couldn't deny it awoke a level of jealousy in me that I struggled to banish entirely sometimes.

"What now?" I asked, happy to follow Saint's lead in this. He was the man with the plan after all and I knew if anyone could figure out how to get Tatum back into our arms against the odds, then it was him.

"Now we mask up, cut the power to that building, and go get our girl," he replied simply. We all knew this was going to be anything but simple, but we also wouldn't turn back now for all the treasure in the world.

"They'll have a back-up generator in a place this important to them," Monroe pointed out, drumming his fingers against his knee as he assessed the different ways this might go.

"So we'll cut the power from that too," Saint said simply. "And once they're cowering in the dark, we'll strike. They won't even know what hit them."

I smirked as I accepted the ski and gas masks from him and deftly strapped them on. We looked like monsters wearing this shit, but that was okay by me. Because I got the feeling that monsters were exactly what we needed to be if we were going to get our girl back.

CHAPTER SIX

I sat in bed, draining a cup of hot tea as I avoided looking my pain meds in the eye. I'd been given some sort of drug cocktail which had perked me up overnight and I had a fierce resolve to take nothing more until I absolutely had to. The drugs were cutting edge and no doubt had been given to me just in time to save my freaking life because I'd been close to puking up a lung last night. Now I just felt weak, dizzy. But the pain had eased and death didn't feel like it was breathing down my neck today.

"-a week, then we can expose her to it again," an anxious female voice sounded out in the corridor and I strained my ears to listen.

"Every day of recovery she has, the more American lives that are lost. The doctor has given me the go ahead on this, so you need to stop fighting it," my old friend Jonas replied and I craned my head to try and see them out in the corridor, but they must have been standing just beyond the door.

As far as I knew, no one knew I'd made that call from Jonas's phone. It still infuriated me that I'd managed to get a phone off of the only prick in this place who apparently didn't keep his charged up. Had Saint heard me? Did he know it had been me at all? I'd tortured myself thinking about it, hoping he'd known, hoping he'd at least think to look into the mysterious call. It was something he might have done, so maybe there was still a chance he'd gotten something useful out of it.

"She needs time to recover, why are you so determined to push this?" the woman hissed. "Is it about revenge because she gave you that sedative?"

Jonas tutted. "No," he clipped. "Stop questioning me, Darla."

They walked to the door and opened it, striding in as Jonas glared at me through his visor. I placed my empty cup down beside me and levelled him with a cold look right back.

"We meet again, Jon*ass*," I said airily, like I gave no shits what they did to me, even though fear was trickling into my chest again at the way he was staring at me.

"We're going down to the lab," he announced and my blood ran cold. They really were planning to expose me to the Hades Virus again so soon. "We need to make more of the vaccine to replenish our supplies," he continued as Darla threw him a frown.

"Well maybe we wouldn't have to if the batch we already have wasn't going to be given to the founders and the rest being auctioned off to the highest bidder today," Darla muttered and my pulse rate spiked.

"Stop questioning me," Jonas snapped at her then approached me with cruelty in his eyes. He wanted to make me pay for humiliating him. And he had the chance to do so because of this sick company and Troy Memphis giving them the green light to do anything they had to to create as much of the vaccine as possible before I succumbed to the virus. "Get up."

"Make me," I growled.

I wasn't fit to fight or do much at all with how shaky my body felt. It wasn't just because of the virus either, so much blood had been harvested from me yesterday, I was running on fumes.

Jonas grabbed my arm in a vice like hold, his eyes blazing with rage and I tried to pull free.

We were suddenly plunged into darkness as all the lights went out and my heart jolted. Silence fell eerily as the sounds of all the machines in the building faded away with the loss of power and my skin prickled as I strained my eyes to see in the dark. There was just something about a power cut that made you feel vulnerable somehow, like all of the electronic crutches you leaned on every day were ripped away with no warning and you were left wondering, can I even survive without them? If they never came back on, what would I do?

Of course, I'd be just fine if that happened. Dad had made certain of that. I could live in the wild like a beast if the need ever truly arose, but for most people, the loss of electricity would be like the loss of a limb.

Jonas released me in surprise but the lights all flooded back on a beat later.

"I swear the whole world is going to shit," he muttered as he shared a confused look with Darla. "Thank fuck for back-up generators though, am I right?"

She offered a slightly nervous laugh, parting her lips to speak, but just as suddenly, they all went off again, the silence in the building becoming thick. *Holy shit.*

Then realisation hit me like a hurricane. Because this was no normal power cut. A laugh bubbled up in my chest as I realised what was going on. Relief and hope and excitement twisted together inside me until I was laughing like a maniac and Jonas was demanding to know what was wrong with me.

He grabbed hold of me, just a shadow in the dark as my laughter grew out of control. "Stop it, you crazy bitch," he commanded, but I didn't give a damn about listening to him. I didn't give a damn about anything at all in this fucking hell of a place. It could burn for all I cared, and I was starting to think it just might.

"What's wrong with her?" Darla asked in alarm and I was glad that I was creeping them out. I hoped they were scared. I hoped they were freaking terrified and quaking in their damn boots. Because they should be. In fact, if they were smart, they'd turn tail and run for the goddamn hills before it was too late.

"Just go downstairs, find out what's going on. I'll watch her," Jonas growled, and a flashlight on his phone illuminated as she hurried out of the room.

He swung it down to flare in my eyes and I scrunched them up against the punishing light. "Why are you laughing?" he demanded again, his features cast in shadow beyond the light and making him seem like a monster in the dark. But he was no monster, not in comparison to what was coming.

I let a wide smile pull at my lips as triumph pumped through my chest.

"Because the reapers of hell are here, Jonas," I told him in a deadly whisper. "And they've come to collect your soul."

CHAPTER SEVEN

The funny thing about buildings which are locked down as tight as a duck's ass against intruders, is that all you have to do to breach the security is set the fire alarm off. I always thought that was dumb as fuck. I mean, yeah, someone could be trapped inside and need to get out or the firefighters could need to get in and all that shit. No one wants to burn to death, blah, blah, blah. But it seemed to me like they needed more counter measures in place against the prospect of some psychopath strolling up to their place of work and letting themselves in via the auto unlock system. I mean, honestly, they might as well have sent me an invitation and just opened up the front doors.

Sure, it wasn't a total guarantee that the door locks would be hooked up to the alarm. But in all the times Niall had taken me to break in to an office building or even an apartment block in the city, it had worked. It had to be a real fire though mind, not just some half-assed attempt at tripping the drill alarm. Real flames and real smoke and a real reaction from the security system to the threat. Then Bob's your uncle, Fanny's your aunt and I'd be strolling right on in to their super secret evil lab. Because yeah, I was calling it an evil lab and if Saint had a problem with it, he could suck my balls.

So we required an honest to shit fire. And that was just fine by me.

"What's taking so long?" Monroe grumbled in my ear and I had half a mind to just tug the earpiece out and toss it aside.

Honestly, these assholes acted like Saint was the only reason we were going to be getting our girl back today, but who was the motherfucker currently rigging a car to blow? I'd like to see Sainty boy flat on his back in a parking lot, half wedged beneath a car while he cut the fuel lines. He'd be all like *'for the love of all that is holy, I just got dust on my posterior.'* Yeah, that wasn't going to fly for this job. Sometimes getting your hands dirty literally meant crawling around in the muck and blood and piss before rising up victorious, and I was down with that. Saint could lord it over us from afar with his plans and commands but when it came down to it, our team of hooligans needed all varieties of fucked up and if my role was to be the guy who got the job done, then great.

"If you think you're better equipped to handle this part of the plan then why don't you come down here and do it?" I muttered back, forcing my way further beneath the car before taking my hunting knife from my belt and reaching up to sever the fuel line.

The sharp blade cut through the plastic with a jerk of my muscles and the heady scent of gasoline assaulted me as the fuel began to piss out onto the concrete.

"Incoming," Blake's voice reached me as I wriggled back out from beneath the BMW and rolled over onto my front as I stayed hidden in the shadows behind the parked cars.

Headlights swept into the space and I remained unmoving as the new arrival parked up on the far side of the underground lot.

I stayed silent, a wolf in the shadows, ready to pounce if need be and hoping that the woman wouldn't smell the gasoline on the air as she got out of her car. She paused, looking around at the dimly lit lot and frowning at the glow of red emergency lighting before carrying on to the stairs which led up into the building as she decided to dismiss her concerns. *Bad call, Veronica. I didn't know if her name actually was Veronica, but she looked like a total bitch with a stick up her ass so it seemed to fit. I had an aunt called Veronica and she was an asshole of mass proportions.*

It wouldn't be long before she figured out that heading into that building was a bad fucking idea, but I wasn't inclined to warn her. I just needed to finish up my part in this then make it back to the others in time to head inside via the fire escape to fuck this place right up.

I waited in the dark until the door to the stairs closed and the woman headed up into the building. I'd only managed to cut the lines on four of the cars, but that would have to do. We couldn't wait any longer.

"You good to go?" I checked as I pulled a pack of cigarettes from my back pocket and planted two in my mouth.

"Hang on, I want to scramble the emergency signal hooked up to the fire alarm to delay the fire service's response time," Saint muttered, his attention clearly on whatever he was doing with his laptop to make that happen.

Tippy, tap, tap, tap. I listened to him hitting the keys as he worked furiously to achieve that, fighting off the urge to mock him for making me wait. It was seriously tempting, but on reflection it made more sense to let him concentrate than it did to bait him right now. *Look at me, being all grown up and rational.* I'd make a mental note to mock him tirelessly for it later though. Saint bait this good couldn't be ignored.

I backed up a few steps, shoving the box of smokes in my pocket before bringing the lighter to my lips and flicking my thumb down on it to spark it up.

I'd been smoking almost constantly since Tatum had gone, using that familiar scent and taste to torture myself with all the memories it awoke in me of my fucked-up childhood. I'd needed to hurt like that, needed to punish myself for failing her. To hate myself for being such a fuck up. But I was going to make it right. I'd made my girl a vow, to have and to hold, honour and protect. I was failing in all of that right now but I was going to fix it, no matter the consequences.

I glanced at the wedding ring I'd tattooed around my left ring finger and almost smiled. *I'm coming, baby.*

I inhaled deeply as the two cigarettes lit up, taking a heady toke of nicotine down into my lungs. It was an awful fucking habit, but I'd worry about quitting again once I had my baby back in my arms. She was the only vice I needed anyway.

The gas mask Saint had insisted I wear was currently hanging from my belt and no doubt he'd flip out when he realised I wasn't wearing it. But unlike the others, I'd already caught the Hades Virus and survived. Kyan Roscoe was just too damn hard to kill. And that was the way I liked it. I didn't care if Saint seemed to think I might not have full immunity or whatever the crap he kept harping on about. I was as strong as a bull and didn't like wearing that damn thing over my face.

The ski mask I could live with for anonymity's sake, but fuck that ventilator shit. I never had liked sci-fi movies anyway.

"Got it," Saint said over the earpiece, that underlying current of smug to his tone which I loved and hated equally. "I'm on my way to meet you at the fire escape now."

"The coast is clear," Monroe confirmed.

"Anyone wanna give me a countdown?" I asked, a smirk lifting the corner of my lips as I backed up further, taking one of the cigarettes from my mouth and preparing to flick it towards the puddles of fuel beneath the cars I'd sabotaged.

It was like car dominoes. I'd lined them all up, primed them to blast and now they were gonna go boom one after another. The fire alarms would automatically activate, the doors would pop open and hey presto - four demons would be granted entry into the tower that held our queen. So help anyone who tried to stand between us and her then.

"Three," Blake obliged, sounding excited. "Two. One-"

I flicked the cigarette towards the puddle of gasoline and turned to run, keeping my head low as I expected the explosion to tear through the cars in a matter of moments.

I sprinted to the bottom of the exit ramp and paused as the deadly ring of silence told me I'd managed to fuck that up. *Nice work, asshole.*

"What's going on?" Monroe asked over the comm.

"Did you fuck it up?" Saint snarled.

"Fuck you," I tossed back, tilting my head to one side and seeing the lit cigarette on the ground a few inches away from the puddle of fuel. "Give me a sec, my aim was off."

I started back towards the row of cars, my boots heavy across the concrete as I raised a hand to my lips for the second cigarette. But before I could take hold of it, the one on the ground began to roll and my eyes widened in alarm a second before it managed to find the puddle of fuel.

A whoosh of heat swept over me before I even heard the almighty boom of the car exploding and I was thrown right off of my feet and hurled back towards the exit ramp.

My back collided with the concrete and by some miracle, I managed not to hit my head as I kept my hands locked over it. Three more explosions rocked the building as the other cars I'd sabotaged followed the first into a fiery death and I rolled over, shielding my head as best I could as lumps of mangled metal slammed down all around me and agony spilled through my body.

"Fuck," I groaned, the cigarette falling from my lips as I pushed myself to my hands and knees. That had hurt like a motherfucker, but I was alive which meant I had more important things to do than lay here crying about a few cuts and bruises.

The fire alarm burst to life, ringing loudly as the sprinklers suspended above the cars kicked into action too and I forced myself up to my feet.

My head spun and my back flared with agony, but I was up which meant I was going to keep moving.

The others were all speaking over the comm, but my ears were ringing so much from the explosion that they were nothing more than a jumble of noise to me. They were probably freaking out over me, but I wasn't the one who they needed to focus on.

I grunted something which I wasn't even certain formed words as I started moving as fast as my battered body would take me. I needed to meet them at the fire escape and get inside that building. Nothing else mattered. Nothing.

Just my girl who was waiting up there for me to prove my worth to her. And I'd do it. Even if it killed me.

CHAPTER EIGHT

The fire alarm blared in my ears after an explosion had rocked the entire foundations of the building. Excitement rushed through me and made me as happy as a damn rainbow. There was only one explanation for it. Well, four actually. Four devils whose souls were linked to mine so deeply that it defied all logic. I thumbed the wedding band on my finger, sensing my connection to Kyan in the depths of the gleaming skull's eyes. It was the ring of a heathen's wife and the bastards in this lab should have thought to run for their lives the moment they saw it. It had been their one and only warning. And now time had run out and they were all marked by the creatures of the night creeping in their back door.

Jonas guarded me like a dog, pacing back and forth as he texted his colleagues and got no answers. The light on his phone swung across the floor as he walked, paying me no attention while I eyed his creepy facial hair with my upper lip peeling back.

"If you can't grow a beard, you shouldn't try," I told him lightly and he shot me a sneer as he continued his pacing.

"Keep your whore mouth shut," he barked.

"Keep your pube face shaved," I tossed back and he ignored me, shaking his head in irritation.

I slipped out of bed into the cool air, the bland white sweats they gave me to wear not nearly thick enough for this place.

"Get back in the bed," Jonas snarled, pointing a finger at me in warning.

"No," I said evenly. "Did you know I have four boyfriends?" I questioned lightly.

He sniggered. "Doesn't surprise me. I could tell you were a slut the moment they brought you here."

"Oh Jonas, you poor, sad little dead man," I purred and his eyes flickered with uncertainty for a moment as I slowly approached him. "On a healthier day, I could gut you myself, but I'm quite looking forward to watching them do it for me."

"Get back in the bed or I'll make you," he warned and I ignored him, continuing on.

"Saint's the brains, he's the one who will have found you. He was who I called from your phone by the way." I smirked as his brows pinched together.

"You fucking-"

"He's got a real psycho streak too," I spoke over him. "Then there's Nash, my beautiful knight looks like an angel but he will have left his heart at home for this job. And Blake? You don't wanna see him scorned, Jonas. I've seen him kill and he goes to a dark, dark place that still surprises me every time. And Kyan, oh Lord, you don't wanna meet Kyan."

"Who's that?" he murmured, like he just couldn't help but ask.

"Kyan's vengeance embodied," I breathed. "He makes men far bigger than you bleed just for fun."

Jonas swallowed hard, then straightened his spine and fixed on a mask to hide his fear. "So which one pimps you out to the others then?"

I laughed coldly even as my head started to spin with dizziness. "If I'm a whore, I'm the whore of four demons. And they *really* don't like when people try to take me from them. I wonder what they'll do when I tell them how *nicely* you've been treating me."

A buzz sounded and the door unlocked behind him, making him nearly jump out of his skin but no one came in. He wheeled the flashlight toward it and I gazed out into the corridor where the lights were turning green on all of the keypads beside the other rooms.

My Night Keepers were close, I knew it. I could feel my connection to them thrumming in my chest like the wings of a dragon. They were coming for me. They'd found the viper's nest and were no doubt cutting off the heads of every snake they found to get to me.

My limbs prickled with anticipation and my breathing laboured as I moved toward the unlocked door.

Jonas stepped in front of it, barring my way forward and angling the flashlight on his phone at me.

"Your best bet is to let me go," I reasoned. "If you want to live, let me walk out that door."

"Ha," he spat. "Get back into your bed, bitch. And keep your mouth shut."

I stepped closer to him, ignoring his words. "They're going to gut you," I warned. "I'm going to see the whites of your eyes as they roll up into your head."

"Get. Back," he snarled.

"I'm giving you an out," I said, lifting my chin as my legs shook beneath me. My mouth was parched and my lungs felt bruised from so many days of coughing. But I'd find the strength to run today. I would be leaving with my men.

"Shut up," he snapped, lunging forward and shoving me back.

My legs gave out and I hit the floor with an oomph, cursing as I fought to get up. Fuck I hated feeling like this. This weakness that gripped my muscles was insufferable. But I would get up. I had to get up.

I fought my way back to my feet and Jonas shoved me again, a rumble of amusement in his chest.

"You're dead," I laughed. Screw this asshole. I'd given him a chance. Which was more than he deserved. "They're going to make you scream and bleed and-"

"Shut up!" he threw a kick at my side and I doubled in on myself with a groan of pain.

Heavy footsteps pounded into the room and I looked up with my heart jumping hopefully. Jonas whipped around in fear, but it wasn't my boys. It was four armed guards and the lead doctor in his long white coat.

"We have to evacuate the asset," the doctor spoke, his gaze skimming down to me on the floor before he clearly decided not to comment on it. "*Now.*"

Two of the guards stepped forward, lifting me off of the ground and pushing me down onto the hospital bed. I thrashed with all the strength I had as fear took hold of me. I bit and kicked but in my weakened state, my blows felt as hard as feathers and exhaustion crept up on me like a beast in the night. They forced me down beneath them, pinning me in place before one of them pulled strong straps over my body, securing me to the bed.

My heart sank into the depths of my stomach as panic found me. They couldn't take me from my boys. Not again.

Jonas started wheeling me out of the room and the guards clustered around me with face masks in place and guns in hand.

I did the only thing I could do and started screaming, crying the names of my boys in hopes that they could hear me and find their way here. I couldn't let these assholes take me. I couldn't come too close to salvation only to be stolen away into the night once more. My men were so near I could taste them on the air. I refused to be torn away from them again without so much as seeing their beautiful faces.

"Get her to the roof," the doctor barked, directing us down the corridor. "The emergency generator on this level will have kept this elevator operational. A helicopter is on the way."

Dread seeped into every inch of my flesh and I bucked against my restraints, screaming louder even though it pained my insides to do so, scorching my lungs like fire.

"Nash!" I yelled. "Blake, Kyan, Saint!"

I was wheeled into the elevator and planted at the back of it as the guards all took up position in front of me.

Jonas pulled his face mask down under his visor to smirk at me. "What was that about me bleeding?" he mocked in a quiet voice.

This fucking guy. I wriggled a hand free of my binds, reaching out and snatching a tactical knife from one of the guard's belts with a surge of adrenaline. I twisted it around and stabbed at Jonas, missing his gut as he lurched away, but it drove deep into his forearm instead, spilling blood everywhere. He shrieked like a new-born baby, clutching the wound as one of the guards grabbed the blade from my hand and strapped me down tighter on the bed so I could barely move my arms at all.

"Calm down, put pressure on it," a guard barked at Jonas as he leaned against the wall whimpering and the elevator soared.

"If they don't kill you, I will," I promised Jonas and he had the good sense to finally look afraid of me.

Because I refused to believe they wouldn't get here on time. I had faith in them. They had my scent and they wouldn't stop tracking me until we were reunited.

I was a ruler of the most ruthless beasts to walk the earth. And they were hunting me down with vengeance in their hearts and bloodlust in their souls. So help anyone who tried to keep me from them.

Kyan

CHAPTER NINE

It had taken me a little longer than it should have to get back out of the parking lot and make my way around to the emergency exit where the others were waiting by the door. Saint had laid into me the moment I arrived about my unused gas mask hanging from my belt, his face scrunching up with fury at the idea of someone defying him. Luckily for me, I'd still been mostly deaf from the explosion at that point, so I hadn't caught much of his tirade aside from the angry look in his eyes.

I hadn't wasted much time standing about there for him to go off on one though and we were all in agreement that there was no time for that shit, so we'd taken off into the building via the handily unlocked emergency exit. The door opened into a dark corridor and the sounds of people racing our way in a bid to escape reached our ears. Monroe ran across the space to another door and shoved it open as we hurried to follow, my heart beating hard as adrenaline surged in my veins.

The moment we stepped out into the reception, shots were fired in our direction and it was only through luck or chance that we all managed to dive into the relative safety behind the reception desk before any of us were gunned down.

Blake released a shaky laugh as our gazes met, but I was already in attack mode, needing to remove these assholes as they blocked my way to my girl. That was all they were, an obstacle in my path which I would gladly mow down.

I yanked a pistol from the holster at my hip and started firing without so much as blinking. This was where the beast in me thrived, deep in the heart of the fight. Where life and death hung in the balance and the only clear-cut payment for making it out was blood.

Saint ignored me totally, reaching up and yanking the monitor off of the desk as he booted up the computer and began typing. I'd never paid a whole hell of a lot of attention to his nerd habits when he set to work preparing to take over the world on his laptop every evening, but it was becoming more than clear that he could pretty much hack his way into anything when he set his mind to it.

"Keep them busy while I figure out where they're holding her," he commanded as Monroe leaned around the side of the desk to take a shot and almost got his head blown off, a chunk of desk shattering beside him instead.

"Holy fuck," he breathed, half laughing as a wild look filled his eyes from the rush of coming so close to death. This feeling right here was damn addictive, but I slapped a hand down on his shoulder for a moment to let him know I was glad he hadn't died.

I drew in a breath and leapt up, taking four shots in a row, hitting two assholes square between the eyes, one in the chest and missing the fourth. I wasted an additional second taking count of our opponents and was rewarded with a flash of burning pain scoring across my bicep half a second before I dropped down out of sight again. But at least now I knew there were only three of them left. At least until their backup arrived - no way I believed there were only a handful of guards working in a place like this. Not while our girl was here. I might fucking hate it, but Tatum Rivers was currently the most valuable commodity in the world. People would sell their souls to get their hands on a vaccine for the Hades Virus and she was the only key to it. They'd be guarding her heavily and would do anything it took to make sure they kept hold of her.

But that was okay. It just meant I had to be willing to sacrifice even more than them to get her back, which I wholeheartedly was.

I cursed and Blake turned to look at me, his green eyes widening as he took in the blood on my arm, but I just shook my head, dismissing it.

"It's nothing," I growled. "It only skimmed me." But I was willing to bet that had just fucked up some of my ink. *Assholes.*

Blake jerked his head, accepting my words as he pulled a smoke grenade from his pocket, pulled the pin and tossed it over the desk. Niall had really come through for us with all of this shit and I made a mental note to send him a gift basket when we all got out of here alive.

Cries of alarm met the sound of it hitting the floor and I listened to it tinkling across the tiles and hissing as it rolled away, a huge cloud of pink smoke swirling up to engulf the far side of the room.

"Pink?" Saint growled, sounding like he'd just seen someone dick slap his grandma or something.

"What can I say, my uncle is a flashy asshole." I shrugged, not caring if Niall had given me pink smoke, glitter smoke or even smoke that stank of shit, so long as it worked.

No doubt he was laughing his ass off somewhere over this as we spoke though and I just hoped I'd live long enough to tell him the story.

He'd offered to come help us with this rescue mission, but in the end, we'd agreed that he was best occupied keeping my grandpa out of the loop until it was done. The last thing I needed was Liam O'Brien weighing in and fucking everything up for us. He would have agreed to help get Tatum back, I was fairly certain of that. His attachment to the idea of family being the most important thing in the world would have driven him to do that much. But the O'Briens were about as subtle as a porn shoot taking place at a kids' party. And that just wouldn't have worked against Troy Memphis. He was a sneaky bastard and we'd needed to play him at his own game if we wanted to get the jump on him and rescue our girl.

Besides, it was only right that this fight remained our own. The Night Keepers didn't need help from anyone else. We'd made an oath to protect Tatum and we'd keep our damn word on that.

I gave the smoke a couple of seconds to thicken up, yanking the gas mask from where it hung at my belt and pulling it on for the first time as I admitted, in this instance, I actually needed the damn thing.

The moment it was secure, I vaulted over the reception desk and took a pot shot straight at a figure I could just make out moving within the pink smoke. The satisfying sound of a body hitting the ground followed, letting me know we were down to two guards now.

The only light in here was from the streetlamp beyond the glass front of the building, but that was plenty for me. I knew how to move in the dark.

I slipped over to the wall, straining my ears to listen over the lingering ringing in them from the explosion and the sound of a scuffle had me whipping around and shooting another guard straight in the face.

The pink smoke swirled all around me as I dove into it, my grip on my gun tight as I hunted for my prey. I only had two bullets left before I needed to reload, but that was going to be enough.

My heart beat to a solid rhythm, my breaths coming slow and deep as I fell into that primal, base piece of my being. I was nothing more than a beast hunting out enemies in the dark. Just a creature bound to protect its mate beyond all other desires.

I rounded the elevator bank, its doors firmly closed as the fire alarm continued to blare out.

"I need back-up on the ground floor," a voice came from somewhere deeper into the smoke. "Armed assailants. Secure the asset."

A growl spilled from my lips and I ran forward, not caring if I was giving myself away as the crackled response from another voice came over the radio, confirming that there were more guards heading our way.

I fired a shot based on the sound of where I'd heard that voice, but my hearing was still off from the explosion and a moment later the guard returned fire.

A bullet hit me square in the chest, pain ricocheting through my body as I staggered but managed to stay on my feet. My second bullet found the target, but I kept my aim low and the guard screamed in pain as he was hit.

I forced a breath down into my lungs through the burning agony of where the bullet hit and stumbled forward a few steps as my body yelled at me not to move. But fuck that. Tatum needed me.

I found the guard within the smoke, kicking his fallen gun away from him as he tried to grab for it with one hand while pressing down on a seriously bloody wound in his gut with the other.

My second kick caught him in the jaw and I was on top of him the moment his back hit the ground.

"Clear," I called out to the others, ignoring the pain in my own body in favour of inflicting some on the piece of shit beneath me.

I holstered my gun and pulled the hunting knife into my grasp instead.

"Have you found her?" I demanded, looking back towards Saint for my answer.

I wrapped one hand around the guard's throat as my weight pressed down on the bleeding wound in his stomach and he tried to scream.

"The whole thing is coded," Saint growled, the sound of furious typing still coming from beyond the desk.

My gaze fixed on the soon-to-be-dead man beneath me as I squeezed hard enough to cut off his air supply. "We're here for the girl," I said in a rough growl that made it clear I wasn't fucking around. "Tell me where they're keeping her."

I took a good look at the fear in his eyes before loosening my hold enough for him to speak.

"I don't know what you m-"

I slammed my hunting knife down into his bicep and bared my teeth at him as I cut off his air once more.

"Where. Is. The. Girl?" I didn't need to elaborate. He knew which fucking girl.

This time when I let him speak, he looked about ready to piss himself. "T-top floor," he gasped. "Isolation unit. But you'll never-"

I slammed my blade down into his chest just as Blake and Monroe made it to us, stabbing him over and over, purposefully avoiding anything too fatal for the first few blows as I let my beast feed on his pain before finally driving it into his cowardly heart to end it.

I was covered in blood by the time I reared back, and Blake's hand landed on my shoulder as he wrenched me away.

"Were you hit?" he demanded, his eyes widening behind his mask as he looked at the round hole in my shirt right in the centre of my chest.

"Yeah," I grunted. "Hurt like a bitch too."

I reached down to tear the front of my shirt open, using the tip of my bloody knife to pop the bullet out of the Kevlar I was wearing and taking in a deep breath. If I lived to see tomorrow that was gonna leave one hell of a bruise.

"What was it you called that vest when Saint insisted you wear it?" Monroe asked, giving me a look that said 'you would have been dead, idiot' as we headed towards the stairwell.

"A coward's cheat sheet to get out of death," I replied, shrugging as I refused to backtrack on that opinion. "But if I have to cheat death to make it to my girl then fine."

"You're insane," Blake muttered.

"We will be discussing your lack of care for your own mortality in further detail once we get *our* girl back," Saint snapped as he abandoned the computer hacking shit to join us, drawing his own gun. "But as of right now, we need to focus on getting to the top floor."

I shoved the door to the stairs open but flinched back as bullets rained down from above, cursing as the four of us were forced to back up into the reception again. Who knew how many assholes were headed our way? I cursed at the idea of a shootout. Not that I didn't enjoy blowing people's brains out, but we didn't need to be wasting time on these motherfuckers.

The dead guard's radio suddenly crackled to life and I glanced towards him as words came over it that set dread pooling in my gut.

"Chopper inbound, prepare for evac."

"Fuck!" I roared, shoving the huge desk across the room to block off the stairs and looking around.

"We have to get up there before they get her on that helicopter," Saint snarled. "My father won't be this sloppy again. We won't get another chance."

We all looked to the staircase where the sound of the approaching guards was getting loud enough to let us know we were almost out of time. We could fight our way through them, but could we do it before the chopper got here?

"There's gotta be a maintenance ladder in the elevator shaft," Monroe said, turning and running across the room to force the doors open.

"I'll hold them off," I said firmly as he and Blake managed to yank the doors wide. "We can't have them taking pot shots at us on that ladder."

My brothers all looked to me with concern in their eyes and a silent communication spilled between us. We were all equally desperate to get to our girl, but this plan could only work if we were smart about it and played the best game possible. So long as one of us made it to her, that was all that counted.

"I'll stay too," Blake agreed.

"Be careful." Monroe clapped us both on the shoulders before heading into the elevator and climbing up to force the maintenance hatch open.

"Don't get yourselves killed," Saint growled in a command that brokered no negotiation.

"Yeah, yeah, we love you too, you fucking psycho," I teased.

I grabbed an assault rifle from the body of one of the guards I'd already finished off and the door to the stairwell began to rattle as the guards beyond it started trying to batter it down.

In the next breath, Saint was gone, climbing up into the dark elevator shaft behind Monroe, and Blake and I raised our guns. He tossed a couple more pink smoke grenades to fill the rest of the room as we readied to fight for our damn lives.

"For her," he said in a fierce voice and I smiled the only true smile that had crossed my lips since she'd been taken. Because this might be a form of insanity and I could be looking my death in the eyes right now, but so long as it was in aid of that girl, I knew that I'd die with this smile on my face. Though I was seriously hoping it wouldn't come to that and I'd have her in my arms before the night was up. Either way, I was all in and I knew the others were too.

"For her."

CHAPTER TEN

I was wheeled outside onto the roof and the cold night air swirled around us as the crescent moon smiled a crooked smile at me.

I was working on my right leg which felt the loosest of all my limbs, trying to tug it free of the binds even though it wouldn't do me much good. But I wasn't just going to lay down and accept this fate. The Night Keepers were so close. They had to make it to me. Maybe I could buy them a little extra time if nothing else.

"Where the fuck is it?" Jonas barked and I craned my neck to see that the helipad was empty.

Hope sparked in me like fireworks and I screamed once more, the sound echoing everywhere. They had to hear me. They couldn't be far behind now. My skin prickled like I could actually feel them drawing closer and I was certain that if I could buy us even a few more seconds that would be all it took for them to reach me.

"Would someone shut her up?" the doctor snapped, but the guards seemed reluctant to touch me despite the masks covering their faces.

One of them lifted their handgun, aiming it at my forehead.

"Quiet," he growled, but as terrifying as that dark barrel was, I knew my death didn't await me in it.

They weren't going to kill me when they were taking so many measures to get me the hell out of here. So I screamed louder and cried my Night Keepers' names into the wind, praying it would carry my voice to their ears.

"For fuck's sake." A fist cracked against my face and my lip busted as Jonas stood over me, blocking out the light of the moon, his shoulders rising and falling as he glowered at me. My head rang and blood wet my mouth as I glared up at this asshole, silently promising him an agonising death. *"Quiet."*

The thumping sound of a helicopter approaching somewhere off in the sky reached us and Jonas gripped my throat to keep me from screaming again, squeezing tight enough to make my ears pop.

The world grew loud as the helicopter circled overhead and came down to land on the helipad, the wind whipping wildly around us and blowing my hair across my face so that it was hard for me to see what the people surrounding me were doing.

I continued to jerk my leg back and forth to try and get it free, my heart rioting in my chest as time seemed to move too fast. They weren't here. Why weren't they here? Had something happened to them? Were they in trouble right now, needing me just as much as I needed them? I'd never felt so fucking helpless as I did right now, strapped to this goddamn bed and immobilised by the weakness in my body just as much as the men surrounding me. I was a goddamn fighter and I needed to fight. I refused to give up, no matter how hopeless it might have seemed.

Jonas released my throat as he wheeled me toward the helicopter, one of the guards yanking the door open as I was rolled beneath the propellers.

I screamed once more, but the sound of the helicopter stole my voice away and panic ripped through my core. *I'm running out of time.*

The guards collapsed the legs of the hospital gurney so it flattened down beneath me then they lifted me into the back of the helicopter while my heart raced with panic and I thrashed uselessly against my bonds. They all poured in after me and fear spilled through my chest like a vat of poison tipping over.

"Saint!" I screamed. "Nash! Kyan – Blake!" Desperation built in my soul, in every fibre of my flesh.

"What are we waiting for, go!" Jonas snapped, wheeling around to glare at the pilot.

"There's a team coming with the vaccines," the doctor explained sharply. "We can't leave without them."

I twisted my head to try and see back across the roof and the door flew open a beat later, making my heart stutter with my final hope.

But it wasn't my men. Three nurses ran toward us in hazmat suits carrying a large metal box between them.

They started climbing into the helicopter, securing the box of vaccines beside me and I was engulfed by panic. The Night Keepers hadn't made it to me in time. It was too late. My enemies were taking me. And I knew the moment the helicopter took off from this building, I'd never see my boys again. Troy Memphis would put me somewhere I'd never be found in a million years. Even after his work was done, I knew he'd never let me go. If the Hades Virus didn't kill me, my usefulness would expire eventually and he'd have to tie off all the loose ends. My truth could never get out, so he'd ensure it died with me.

CHAPTER ELEVEN

I raced up the last stairs with Saint right on my heels as we headed for the roof exit, the sound of the helicopter making my heart seize in my chest as I threw the door open with a heavy bang.

The wind tore around us as the helicopter began to take off and I spotted Tatum onboard it, strapped to a hospital gurney, her lips moving like she was screaming something though the roar of the engine stole her words from me.

"Tatum!" I bellowed in reply, answering her call and promising her I wouldn't let them take her with that one word alone.

I sprinted forward, running as fast as my years of training allowed, my muscles burning and pumping as I roared her name.

The guards onboard the helicopter began firing at us and I wasn't sure if it was through some miracle or divine intervention that I didn't feel the rip of metal tearing through my flesh.

A flash of motion shot past the corner of my eye and a plume of pink smoke spiralled through the air from the smoke grenade Saint had just thrown at them.

His aim was true and the grenade landed in the midst of the guards on the aircraft, rolling beneath their seats as they all yelled out in alarm.

They stopped firing at us as they fought to get their hands on the grenade that had quickly filled the entire helicopter with pink smoke, and it stopped rising as the pilot was momentarily blinded.

I exchanged a look with Saint and for once there wasn't an ounce of animosity between us. I could only see the burning, desperate desire in him to return our girl to safety and we agreed on that sentiment so wholeheartedly that we were bound as one in that moment. No words needed to pass between us, no bullshit, no communication of any kind. Because we both knew that if that helicopter left here with our girl onboard, we would forever be cast into damnation for it.

This was our one shot and we wouldn't fuck it up.

We didn't slow a beat as we raced towards the helicopter which was now hovering about eight foot above the rooftop and starting to rise again.

The smoke grenade was tossed out over my head and I could see our opportunity sliding through our fingers as we both leapt up beneath the belly of the mechanical beast at the same moment.

My hands gripped the landing skid and I grunted with the effort of heaving myself higher as the helicopter lurched to one side thanks to our weight hanging from it.

I cursed as the thing shot skywards, the rooftop disappearing beneath us as we sped higher. Saint and I hung from the skid with nothing more than the strength of our arms and the power of our bond to the girl they held captive to keep us there.

I managed to swing my leg up and over the landing skid, hanging like a sloth from a tree as I tried to figure out how the fuck I was going to make my way up into the aircraft without getting my brains blown out.

Saint made it into a similar position to mine and caught my eye as he pulled another smoke grenade from the clip on his belt and I nodded once, seeing his plan as clear as day.

He tugged the pin free and reached up, tossing the smoking canister into the helicopter through the open door before they got a chance to close it, causing the guards to yell out in fright.

I didn't give them time to recover from their shock, grasping the edge of the open door above me and heaving myself up and into the helicopter, making sure I didn't look down at the fall below us for a single second.

A gun was levelled at my head the moment I stood and Tatum's alarmed scream sounded through the haze of pink smoke just as I managed to knock the pistol aside before the guard could fire. The loud bang made my ears ring as his bullet sailed out through the open door into the nothing beyond and my heart leapt as I wrestled with him before he could fire again.

I wrapped my arms around him and whirled him around using brute strength, launching him out of the open door behind me before he even got the chance to try and fight me off. He fell with a scream that was drowned out by the roar of the propellors overhead and I forgot about him before he even hit the ground.

I dove at the other three guards who were little more than shadows in the pink smoke as the helicopter tipped sideways and Tatum yelled my name, like even in the murky depths of the smoke she could recognise me.

"We've got you, princess," I promised her just as a heavy fist found my jaw and I was knocked sideways by the force of it.

It was too smoky to be sure who was who within the confines of the belly of the helicopter, but seeing as I was happy to kill each and every one of them, that wasn't much of a problem for me.

I wrenched a knife from my belt, driving it into the chest of one of the guards as he lurched at me then lunged for another before he'd even fallen back into his chair. But just as I swung towards him, the helicopter dipped dramatically and I lost my footing, falling backwards towards the open door with my heart leaping as I dropped my knife and tried to grab anything at all to stop my fall.

My gut plummeted as I fell out of the door, but before I could fall to my death, a hand caught mine in a firm grasp and my gaze lifted from the churning propellors to meet Saint Memphis's cool, dark eyes.

The smoke grenade tumbled over my feet and twirled away into the darkness of the city below as the helicopter lurched the other way again.

"Watch yourself, brother," Saint growled like me almost dying had been a major inconvenience to him as he hauled me back into the belly of the aircraft.

I shoved him aside as one of the guards lunged at him, catching a fist to the jaw for my troubles before I was knocked from my feet and fell hard on my back with the asshole on top of me.

I fought like a demon, using every last drop of power in my limbs as I punched and punched as hard as I fucking could, feeling bone break as my opponent tried to pin me down beneath him.

Three gunshots went off in quick succession and Tatum's scream made my blood run cold as I failed to see anything beyond the beast of a man on top of me.

With a snarl of determination, I managed to get my knees up between us and I kicked out as hard as I could. The guard screamed as he was launched right out of the open door and I swiped blood from my face with the back of my hand as I got to my knees.

"Easy now," warned the asshole we'd been tailing earlier to find the lab, glaring at us from his position beside Tatum where he had a knife pressed to her throat.

Tatum's big blue eyes were wild and furious, not a drop of fear in them, just that burning determination to live which I loved so fucking much.

"I can put a bullet between your eyes before you spill so much as a drop of her blood," Saint threatened, his pistol aimed directly at Jonas as he stood facing off against him.

But the fact that he hadn't taken that shot told me he wasn't certain of that at all.

I rose to my feet slowly and Jonas's tongue darted out to moisten the corner of his lips as he looked between the two of us.

"What's going on back there?" the pilot called in fear and Jonas almost glanced his way before realising that was a bad fucking idea.

The last guard and the doctor were lying dead on the floor in growing pools of blood from Saint's shots and the two nurses were crying and cowering in the far corner, clearly hoping to avoid our attention.

"It's under control," Jonas barked at the pilot as the helicopter continued its route to fuck knew where.

"Is it?" I asked, tilting my head to one side and he tightened his grip in Tatum's hair, making her curse as she scrambled against his hold, a drop of blood spilling along the blade he held. He'd die for that. And I'd make sure it really hurt.

"Toss your guns out," Jonas snapped, raising his chin like he thought he was the man.

My lip peeled back as I did just that, the two pistols on my belt sailing away into the city below. Saint tossed his gun out a beat later and Jonas nodded eagerly.

"Knives too," Jonas added and our blades were quickly tossed out of the helicopter as well, neither of us willing to risk Tatum over a damn weapon. "Now, hold your wrists out."

I bristled as I did what he said and he gingerly reached out to the dead guard closest to him who was slumped in his chair, pulling a pair of thick zip ties from the corpse's pocket and tossing them towards us. He never once took the knife from Tatum's throat, keeping it in place with his other hand.

"Secure your wrists," Jonas snapped, getting cocky now and I was really looking forward to wiping that smug look off of his smarmy face.

We both did as commanded and I used my teeth to pull the zip tie tight around my wrists, though not so tight that I wouldn't be able to escape the hold they had on me. Jonas seemed to realise that and hesitantly moved around the bed, taking the knife from Tatum's throat and pointing it at me as he reached out to yank the zip tie tighter.

He stepped forward to do the same to Saint, but just as he did, Tatum managed to yank her leg free of her restraints and aimed a harsh kick at his back.

Jonas swore, stumbling forward and Saint threw his forehead down onto the bridge of his nose, making him shriek in agony as it shattered and blood spilled.

I charged at him like a raging bull, head down and shoulder catching him straight in the gut, knocking him down beneath me where I fell on him, slamming my bound hands into his face as hard as I could.

The keen sting of his blade swiping across my side sliced into me, but I just bellowed my rage as I hit him again and again.

Saint's heavy boot slammed down on Jonas's hand, immobilising the blade and grinding his fingers beneath his heel as blood poured from Jonas's face beneath me while he screamed.

I didn't stop hitting, striking him again and again as Tatum yelled encouragement, giving me all the motivation I needed to understand that this motherfucker had done something terrible to her.

Jonas fell still beneath me and Saint dragged me back, the knife now in his hand as he swiftly cut through the zip tie binding my wrists and freed me.

Jonas groaned in agony as he came to and I hauled him to his feet before shoving him towards the open door and the terrifying drop below.

"Nash," Tatum gasped and I glanced over at her where she remained strapped to the hospital gurney. For a moment I thought she might have been about to tell me to spare him, but of course she didn't. She wasn't some frightened girl, scared to kill those who hurt her. She was a queen, and she wanted to command her knight into action. "Make it hurt," she snarled.

I smiled darkly at her, accepting the knife that Saint passed me as Jonas tried to fight against my hold on him, stamping on my feet and throwing elbows back at me. But I ignored every attempt he made and every hurt he caused me, focusing on the idea of our girl suffering and the knowledge that I was about to pay him back in kind.

I swept the blade across his throat, spraying an arc of blood out over the streets below and listening to him choke on it for several long seconds before shoving him out to die.

I didn't waste time watching him fall, turning back to Tatum and yanking the restraints off of her as Saint took the knife back from me and made the nurses get to their feet.

They were crying and begging but the coldness in Saint's gaze held no mercy for them. They had been a willing part of this. They'd been onboard with kidnapping Tatum, making her suffer, watching the sickness eat away at her strength bit by bit while stealing her blood until eventually it would have killed her. So fuck them.

"You still need me to fly this thing!" the pilot cried, clearly having seen the way this had gone.

"Shut the fuck up," Saint snapped, his words for all of them. "Or I'll throw you out of the door too."

They miraculously quit their petrified pleading just as I managed to pull Tatum into my arms, my throat tightening with the desire to rip this fucking gas mask off of me and lose myself in the taste of her lips.

"Nash," she murmured, her skin so pale it made my heart race and she sagged against me as I heaved her into my arms. "Where are Blake and Kyan?"

"They're okay," I promised her, hoping I wasn't fucking lying because I had no real idea how that fight had gone back at the lab and the comms had been quiet since we'd parted company.

Tatum sighed in relief before her eyes fluttered shut and my heart leapt as I feared the worst, before she opened them again. She looked seriously weak, her skin pale and drawn and she started coughing as I held her, turning her face from me like she wanted to protect me beyond what the mask was doing. But this thing was the best money could buy and I wasn't worried about that.

"What's wrong with her?" I bellowed, looking around at the nurses as

Tatum seemed to struggle to even stay conscious.

"Swear you won't stab us and we will tell you everything," one of them begged, her eyes on the knife in Saint's hand.

"Done," he agreed without even glancing toward me and Tatum, his focus on the last remaining threats.

"Her body is struggling because we took a lot of blood from her. She's been exposed to a high level of the Hades Virus to force her to produce plenty of antibodies so that we could harvest them. That's why she has symptoms, she's been pushed beyond what her immunity can cope with all at once," the nurse choked out. The other one seemed to be too terrified to even speak.

"Harvest?" I snarled in disgust, pulling Tatum closer to my chest.

"What treatment does she require?" Saint demanded, ignoring me like he already knew exactly what the nurse meant by that and I bet he fucking did – the fucker had probably become a self-taught virologist in the time we'd spent hunting for her with all of his online courses and bullshit. Not that I was faulting him for it.

"M-mostly just rest, time to recuperate. She needs to replenish her blood levels and fight off the virus. She should make a full recovery though," the nurse said, almost smiling like she thought she was saving her ass by letting us know that Tatum had a good chance of getting better.

"So she has no desperate need of a medically trained nurse?" Saint confirmed and the dumb bitch actually shook her head.

"No. Just rest and lots of nourishing food and-"

Saint shoved the two of them so hard that they fell backwards out of the open door without even seeming to realise what had happened until it was too late. Their screams carried back to us as they fell to their deaths and I couldn't find it in me to feel a single molecule of guilt over them. They'd chosen to take part in this. They'd chosen to hurt our girl. Their morals were clearly beyond questionable and I didn't even care if they'd been telling themselves that they were trying to save the world to justify her sacrifice. Because Tatum Rivers was worth more than the rest of the world in my opinion. Retribution was a bitch.

Saint cast one long look at Tatum as I tightened my hold on her, reaching out to smooth his fingers over her knotted hair as he looked down at her through the visor of his gas mask.

"Don't stop fighting now, siren," he commanded and she shook her head minutely as she held his gaze.

"Never," she swore.

Saint nodded once, giving me a look that said he was trusting me with her then strode into the cockpit, taking a pistol from one of the dead guards as he went and pointing it at the guy's head.

"You can't kill me," the pilot gasped, seeming to realise that he was the only one left, though while we were fuck knew how high up above the city, he couldn't exactly get out of his seat to try and fight us off. "You need me!"

Saint sighed like his patience was being tested beyond measure and I got the terrifying impression that he was about to do something insane as he gave the control panel a considering look.

I sat down quickly, strapping Tatum into the seat beside mine before buckling myself in too and winding a protective arm around her as she leaned her head against my chest.

"I knew you'd come for me," she murmured, seeming to fight for every word she spoke.

"Always," I agreed, holding her as tight as I dared while she was so frail. I was so fucking relieved to have her back, so glad to be touching her, holding her, it made everything else pale into insignificance.

"For so long I thought the only real meaning my life held was in seeking revenge for what Troy Memphis did to my family," I said to her in a low voice, not even certain she could hear me over the roar of the helicopter. "But I was so fucking wrong. So, so wrong, Tatum. Because fearing for your life almost destroyed me. It made me realise that I have so much more to live for than some vendetta. I love you. I love you with everything I am and everything I'll ever be and I'm sorry if I didn't make it clear how strongly I felt that before now, or if you ever felt you ranked below my desire to-"

"I love you too, Nash," she replied, her voice stronger than it had been up until this point and I looked into her blue eyes, wishing I could rip this mask off and just fucking kiss her. "And don't worry. Because we are absolutely going to get that revenge."

Saint fired his pistol before I could reply and the entire helicopter lurched violently, nosediving towards the ground and making me yell out in fright. *He killed the fucking pilot! Holy mother of fuck!*

I wasn't afraid of much in this life or the next, but falling out of the sky and being incinerated in a helicopter crash was a pretty fucking terrifying concept.

"Saint!" I bellowed as my gut plummeted and I twisted my head to see him ripping the pilot's corpse out of his seat behind the controls.

"Calm down," he snapped back, like we weren't moments away from colliding with one of the many towering buildings below us. "I am more than capable of flying a basic model like this."

I just fucking gaped at him as he took the pilot's seat, grabbed hold of the joystick looking thing in front of him and began to battle against the tailspin we'd begun to fall into.

My heart raced and thrashed in my chest as I saw my death flashing before my eyes and Tatum's hand found mine, squeezing tightly for a brief moment before falling slack again.

We lurched to the left then somehow the helicopter righted itself and we were soaring away across the city.

As I tried to catch my breath, I brushed Tatum's hair out of her eyes and found her struggling to look up at me as she seemed on the edge of passing out.

"The vaccine," she breathed, her voice so weak I could hardly make out the words. "In the silver box. It works."

Her gaze flicked to the far side of the helicopter and I followed her line of sight to a silver box which was strapped to the wall there.

"Well, fuck," I breathed as I stared at the most valuable commodity on the planet right now, tugging my girl closer as I bathed in the feeling of her body against mine and Saint flew us towards the crescent moon in the distance.

What the hell were we gonna do now?

CHAPTER TWELVE

"We've got her," Saint's voice came over the comm at last and my heart soared as I took cover behind the elevator bank, pink smoke swirling around us as my shoulder brushed Kyan's.

My chest was heaving and a layer of sweat was making my Kevlar vest feel like a straightjacket, but there was no way I was taking it off. Especially after seeing it save Kyan's life.

"About fucking time," Kyan snarled, his visor peppered with blood splatter and a savage, triumphant grin making his eyes blaze as he looked at me.

A relieved laugh spilled from my lips and if we didn't have armed men hunting us down and trying to kill us, I would have whooped in triumph too.

The sound of the fire trucks and police sirens approaching were growing louder by the second and I peeked out of my hiding place to take a glance towards the stairs, wondering if we should make a run for it.

I ducked back into cover just as a bullet flew towards my head and my heart leapt as bits of the wall sprayed over me as it hit.

"I took control of the heli-" Saint's voice was lost to the roaring sound of an engine and I exchanged a look with Kyan, wondering if I'd just imagined what I thought he'd said. "Plan X," Saint added in a firm voice.

"Plan X?" I questioned, activating my comm and wondering if I'd misheard him.

"I assume you're capable of carrying out that simp-" his words were drowned by more roaring and as the flash of red and blue lights flared through the glass front of the reception, we were left with no more time to confirm what he'd said. But it had been pretty clear. Plan X it was then.

Saint had contingencies for his contingencies, and we'd spent the day in the car watching Jonas's house memorising each of them and his code names for them so I knew exactly what he wanted. But shit, I hadn't in my wildest dreams expected to be implementing Plan X.

"Let's get the fuck out of here," Kyan growled, checking the assault rifle he'd stolen and tossing it aside when he found it was all out of ammo.

"Easy," I agreed with a frown, wondering how the fuck we were supposed to do that.

The emergency exit was on the other side of the room and no doubt surrounded by cops even if we could make it there with the guards still firing on us. I could see the squad cars lining up beyond the glass front of the building through the haze of pink smoke too, the police leaping out and aiming weapons our way.

We were surrounded. And I sure as fuck didn't want them catching us. Not least because then Troy would definitely figure out who had rescued Tatum and we couldn't let him find her again.

Kyan pointed to a sign for the restrooms in the rear corner of the reception area and took off running with no further explanation than that, firing wildly towards any guards who might see him.

I sprinted after him, keeping my head down and conserving the last two bullets in my pistol just in case.

Kyan shoved through the door but just as I darted in behind him, a shot crashed into my spine and I was knocked from my feet onto the tiled bathroom floor.

I groaned as Kyan slammed and locked the door behind us, prizing my cheek off of the tiles and hoping to fuck that they were just damp because they'd been mopped recently. Why the hell did men's restrooms always have such gross floors? I certainly didn't aim that badly.

"Get up, buttercup," Kyan growled, heaving me to my feet despite my curses as the pain of the bullet's impact through the Kevlar made me wince.

Fuck getting shot. Fuck it right up the ass.

Kyan plucked the bullet out of the bullet proof vest and slapped it into my hand, letting me look at my would-be murderer for a beat before we were moving again.

"There aren't any windows in here," I said, trying not to panic, but seriously, we were fucked if we couldn't get out of this building.

"Yeah, so no one will expect us to escape this way," Kyan agreed before moving to the cubicle at the far end of the room and kicking the door open.

I hurried after him and found him standing on the lid of the toilet as he jammed his hunting knife into the edge of the vent there. He ripped the grille from the wall and tossed it aside, quickly followed by the fan before looking at me.

"It's gonna be tight," Kyan warned and I glanced at the hole in the wall with a frown.

Before I could voice my concerns about getting trapped in there, Kyan had already heaved himself halfway up into it. A loud banging sound came a moment later and I moved to brace his legs for him while he worked to break the outer grille too.

The sound of it shattering carried to me and Kyan started heaving himself forward, cursing as he went. I shoved him hard when he seemed to get stuck, my hand smacking his ass as I forced his big body forward and suddenly he fell through to the far side.

The sound of someone trying to break down the bathroom door made adrenaline spike through my limbs and I shoved the cubicle door closed before locking that too. I doubted it would do a whole hell of a lot to save my ass, but maybe it would buy me a few more seconds.

I climbed up to the hole left by the broken vent and forced my way into it, wondering how the fuck Kyan had made it through as I got jammed inside it almost instantly.

I cursed and Kyan's hands found mine from outside, tugging me roughly and damn near ripping my arms from their sockets, but it worked.

I fell out of the hole in the wall and scrambled to my feet behind some bushes. Kyan pressed a finger against the ventilator on his mask as he warned me to be quiet.

I nodded my agreement and he pointed towards the building on the far side of this little area of green, giving me all of half a second's warning before taking off towards it.

I stayed low like Kyan, ignoring the flash of red and blue which showed around the side of the building and thanking our luck that the police didn't seem to have the place entirely surrounded yet.

My heart was racing as I sprinted after Kyan, over to the next building then down an alley which ran along the back of it. We vaulted a wall then ducked down another alley and somehow, we made it to Saint's mom-mobile where he'd parked it up in the shadows.

Plan X was one of Saint's contingencies for this all going to shit, and he'd made certain that each of us had a key to the mom-mobile on us in case we got split up. I yanked mine from my back pocket, unlocking the car as we closed in on it.

Kyan went for the driver's seat, but I was faster, laughing as I knocked him aside and leapt in. Kyan grumbled as he slid over the hood and got in on the passenger side. I locked the doors because I couldn't actually allow myself to believe that we'd escaped yet then started the engine.

My heart was still racing, but as I turned us around to exit onto the street furthest from the cops, I couldn't help but let out a whoop of laughter and Kyan started chuckling too. Against the odds, we'd somehow made it out and I couldn't believe our damn luck.

I had to force myself not to drive too fast as we sped away from the lab and left our problems in the dust. But by the time we hit the highway, I slammed my foot down on the gas and really made the mom-mobile work. To be fair to Saint, he had clearly bought the best soccer mom wagon money could buy and the thing was a beast, but I'd never admit to him that it actually drove pretty damn nicely.

"Are you there yet?" Saint's voice came over the comm just as I turned us off of the highway towards the empty farmland we'd chosen at random for our rendezvous point in case things went to shit. I only remembered where it was because Saint had fucking drilled the coordinates into my mind a million times, and I'd used the sat nav to get us here. *Meticulous asshole.*

"Coming up on it," I confirmed.

"Good. We'll have no time to waste once we land." He cut the communication off and I glanced at Kyan.

"He seriously stole their chopper, didn't he?" I said, my eyebrows arching.

"Only Saint Memphis," Kyan replied, shaking his head as we came to a stop.

No sooner had we stepped out of the car into the cool air, did we hear the unmistakable sound of a helicopter drawing close and I watched as the chopper lowered down onto the field beside the road.

"Blow this thing up, Kyan," Saint barked as he hopped down, carrying a silver box in his arms and striding towards us. "With a bit of luck they'll think it crashed and all the dead bodies we scattered over the city were people who either jumped or fell from the aircraft before it hit the ground."

Kyan gave him a sarcastic salute as he stalked forward to carry out Saint's command, but my eyes were fixed on Monroe as he leapt down, cradling an unconscious girl in his arms.

I ran to open the back door of the car for him before retrieving the blankets Saint had stashed in the trunk. The moment he climbed in with Tatum, I wrapped them around her and climbed in behind him.

"Is she alright?" I asked, trying not to freak the fuck out at the sight of her lying there looking so damn frail.

"Don't worry about me, golden boy," Tatum murmured without opening her eyes, her hand reaching out in my direction.

I ripped my bloody, dirty gloves off and took her fingers in mine, wrapping them up tight and lending her my warmth as a smile touched the corners of her lips.

Saint climbed into the driver's seat and he glanced back at us, nodding once as he determined that we were all breathing. He shoved the silver box into the gap between the chairs and I eyed it curiously for a moment before turning my attention back to Tatum.

Kyan ran to leap back into the passenger seat and Saint tore away from the helicopter a moment before it went up in flames with an enormous boom that made the entire car vibrate.

"Are you okay, Cinders?" I breathed, my eyes still on my girl.

"I am now," she replied softly. "I'm back where I belong. With my Night Keepers."

Kyan twisted in his seat, staring at Tatum for the longest time as she passed out and the miles slipped away before some of the tension eventually seemed to ease from his posture.

"What's in the box then?" Kyan growled as the silence grew thick between us and Tatum slept on.

"That would be the vaccine the world has been aching for," Saint growled. "And as soon as we get home, the four of us will be getting a dose."

My brows rose with hope at the idea of that and I sucked in a deep breath. "What about my dad?" I asked, unable to help myself. But I didn't care what he had to say about that unless it was an agreement. I couldn't lose the only parent I had left.

Saint was silent for a long while and I ground my teeth, wondering if I was going to have to beat the shit out of him to make sure my dad got one of those vaccines.

"Yes," he said eventually. "We will figure out a way to get him one too. I suppose we'll need to decide who gets the rest of the doses, but for now we need to focus on the most important tasks at hand."

"Which are?" Monroe asked.

"My father's demise. Royaume D'élite. Kyan's family. The Justice Ninja. Our futures."

"Oh, just that," I muttered, shaking my head at his bland tone.

"Just that," he agreed and though I couldn't see it with the ski mask and ventilator still in place over his features, I could have sworn the bastard was smirking at the challenge those issues presented.

CHAPTER THIRTEEN

I woke in a warm bed held against a bare, muscular chest and I was certain I was dreaming.

I ran my fingers down his body, knowing him by touch and scent alone. Leather and smoke and danger. My husband.

"Are you awake, baby?" his voice was deep yet velvet soft, his breath fluttering the hair against my forehead. How many times had I imagined waking up in each of their arms? And how many times had my heart sunk when I realised they weren't truly here? It made me afraid to open my eyes, afraid my beautiful, tattooed beast of a husband would vanish and I'd be alone once more, pining for him and every one of them.

"Mmm," I hummed.

"Is that a yes?" he asked, gruffer this time and the way his voice vibrated through me and his arms tightened around my body told me he really was here. And slowly, reality came rushing back to me.

I'd passed out at some point in the helicopter. I must have exerted myself too much and now I was confused, dazed.

"I think so," I croaked. "Where am I?"

"Home. Safe," he swore, holding me tighter and I had never felt so secure about those two things in all my life.

But I wasn't content yet. I needed the others close. My mind was foggy and things were slotting together all too slowly. I jerked away as I remembered the virus that plagued my body and panic tore through me. I'd nearly lost Kyan to this monster once before, I couldn't see that happen again.

"It's alright," he growled, catching my hand and not letting me put one more centimetre between us. "I had it before. I have protection. And I'm not leaving your side, Tatum. You didn't leave mine when I was on my knees. I *will* repay the favour to my wife whether you agree to it or not."

I took in the bandage on his arm and the nicks and bruises lining his flesh, including a huge, blossoming red and blue mark across the centre of his chest. "Kyan," I gasped and he dragged me closer again as I lay my mouth on the blazing flesh. "What the hell happened to you?"

"I took a bullet or two for you," he said like that was nothing. "Small price to pay, beautiful."

The fear of knowing those bullets could have killed him made me seize up and he released a growl in his throat as he noticed my concern. He captured my chin, tilting it up until my lips found his, soothing my worries. I knew it was dangerous, but we were already sharing air and he was right, he should be protected from the virus for a few months at least. That was what they'd reported on the news. Though nothing was certain.

His tongue met mine with a fervent, desperate kind of hunger that made my body tremble and a moan of need chafed my sore throat. I tried to pull him even closer, but found my muscles still weak and the longer I kissed him without coming up for air, the more my lungs laboured and burned. A murmur of pain escaped me and he broke the kiss, his dark eyes stormy and furious as I sagged against him.

"Take these. Saint's got every vitamin and painkiller you'll need to get through this." He grabbed a glass of orange juice and a bunch of tablets beside it on the nightstand.

"Will they make me sleep?" I asked in fear and he shook his head. "Promise?" I breathed. "I don't want to sleep. I want to be wide awake here with you."

He cupped my cheek, pain glittering in his eyes as he sensed my distress. "They won't make you sleep. You're not going anywhere you don't wanna go, baby."

I took the glass and washed down the tablets, my throat scraped raw from screaming and coughing.

When I'd drained every drop, he placed it back down and pulled me against him, his arms winding tight around my waist. He explained how they'd driven us back here in Saint's car, sneaking me into The Temple then given themselves all vaccines – a fact which made me seriously happy. I may have been through hell at the hands of Troy Memphis, but if it meant my boys were going to be safe from the Hades Virus, then going through that pain had been worth it in one way.

I'd have to remain hidden here now. No one could know I was at Everlake. If word got back to Saint's dad, I was fucked. They all were too. I wasn't sure what the future held or how we were going to get away with what we'd done but for now, I was too exhausted to feel anything but relief over being here.

"Thank you for coming for me," I said, tears of gratitude pricking my eyes.

"Always," he swore, his lips brushing my temple. "Tell me what you need. I'll give you whatever you want."

"I want to see the others."

He nodded and my heart beat harder at the thought of them all being close again. I knew they couldn't come into this room, that I'd have to isolate until I was better. But I *would* get better. No force on earth could take me from my men again now I was returned to them.

Kyan took his phone from the nightstand, sending a message to the group chat then wound his fingers around mine. I felt his eyes on me and I lifted my chin to meet his gaze, soaking in his presence as peace washed through me.

"Tatum," he sighed. "I'm so fucking sorry."

"For what?" I gasped, a chill running through me as I curled against him.

He tugged the covers up around us and the warmth of his body surrounded me.

"For them taking you. For not finding you sooner. For…fuck, baby, everything they did because I couldn't get to you in time to stop them." His brow creased and guilt marred his beautiful face, making my chest constrict.

"This isn't your fault, Kyan Roscoe," I said seriously, speaking directly to his dark soul.

He growled like a beast, his hands gripping my waist, knotting in the material of the t-shirt I was wearing and making me realise they'd changed me out of the awful hospital clothes. I was coated in the scent of Kyan and swamped in material far too big for my frame and I'd never loved that feeling so much in all my life.

"You found me, you all did," I said firmly. "An army couldn't have done what you did for me. You're my saviours."

The crease on his forehead eased and he stroked his calloused fingers along the line of my jaw. "Don't go getting any ideas about me being a hero, baby."

I smirked, his touch sending tremors deep into the centre of my being. "I know exactly what you are, husband."

"And what's that, wife?" His eyes glittered and he reached for my hand, running his thumb over the skull on the ring that branded me as his. I couldn't even count the number of times I'd done that very thing myself while I was trapped in that lab, taking strength from the knowledge of how much he and the others loved me, how they were surely fighting for me. I'd never doubted that for a single second.

I sought out the tattooed ring on his own hand and brought it to my lips to kiss it. "You're mine."

A hungry noise rumbled through his chest as he drew me closer and despite how exhausted I felt, desire still coursed through me like wildfire. He paused before claiming a kiss from me, the tip of his nose grazing mine. "I won't be touching you while we're locked up in here, baby. You need to rest. But when I do lay my hands on you, I'll drain every drop of your strength all over again. So you need to focus on building it back up."

"Thanks for the incentive," I teased then a loud knock sounded at the window.

I tried to jump up, excitement warring through my body, but my legs gave out and my knees hit the floor, blackness washing over my vision. Kyan cursed, his arms looping around my waist as he pulled me upright and I leant against him for support.

"I'm okay," I panted as he pushed my hair away from my face.

"I know I'm not the best one to look after you, baby, but Saint knows what to do. He's been ordering up all kinds of health foods and shakes and shit. I'll get you better if it kills me, I fucking swear it."

I gripped his bicep as my vision cleared and I caught my breath, gazing up at this dark sinner who vowed to save me. "I know you will," I said. "I trust you. All of you."

"Fancy that, huh?" He grinned and the knocking grew louder, more impatient.

He was right of course, how could I ever have predicted a future like this with all of them where I loved and trusted them so implicitly after the way things had begun between us? But I wouldn't change a second of it now. Not a single, bloody, brutal one. Because if this was where it brought me, then it was more than worth all of the heartache and every single tear.

I let Kyan guide me over to the window and he pulled the curtain back, making my heart swell as my gaze fell on the final pieces of my puzzle. I rested my hand against the pane and Blake, Monroe and Saint all stared in at me with a deep longing in their expressions that was mirrored in my own heart. Dawn coloured the sky gold behind them, making their skin seem dipped in molten metal.

"I can't thank you all enough for what you did," I choked, emotion flooding me as I stared at my beautiful warriors, wishing I could draw them all close. I needed them together, surrounding me, flesh against flesh. As much as I adored Kyan being this near, I needed Saint's possessive touches, Blake's firm caresses and Monroe's strong arms to hold me too. To anyone outside of us, I was sure it would have seemed strange. But I desired all of these men equally. I craved them like they were four ingredients to my own brand of heroin, catered perfectly to my needs.

"There's no need to thank us," Saint said, his jaw tight as he gazed in at me. There was a shadow in his eyes that spoke of how little he'd slept and my heart squeezed for him.

Blake placed his hand to the glass where mine was, moving forward as his brows lowered and an urgent need filled his deep green eyes. "You need to get better," he croaked, fear flickering across his face at the thought of losing me. My poor golden boy had lost far too much in this world and I wasn't going to be another scar on his heart.

"I'll be okay," I promised. "One of the doctors gave me some cutting edge drugs yesterday and I've felt so much better since. I'm just…" I bit my lip.

"What, princess?" Monroe growled, his shoulder pressing to Blake's but not in a way designed to push him aside. I could see the bond between them had grown since I'd been gone. He fit among them all better than ever, had slid so perfectly into their ranks it was like he'd never been missing from their tribe at all.

"I'm just weak," I admitted. "I've got no energy. It feels like the life's been sucked out of me."

"Then we shall put it back," Saint said, matter of fact. His features were neutral, but the intensity in his eyes hinted at the desperate creature who lived beneath his hard exterior. He was aching for the need to control this situation, to take charge and stand in Kyan's place beside me. But the trust he had in his brother was iron clad. And I knew he could manage to restrain himself. It was what he did best. I just hoped it didn't take too much of a toll on him.

"Rest," Monroe demanded and Saint nodded his agreement, directing the others away from the window, his eyes lingering on me the longest before they walked away.

Blake clapped his hand to Monroe's shoulder and even Saint was closer to them than he'd usually be, his arm brushing theirs like wolves taking comfort in their pack mates.

Kyan drew me away from the window and I turned around in his hold, my fingers moving intimately along his arms and chest, still trying to convince myself I was really out of that hell hole and back where I belonged.

"What do you need?" he asked, his voice a deep baritone that set my pulse racing. If there was one way to inject life into me, it was being this close to any of my Night Keepers. They set my soul alight and made it burn brighter and hotter than any star in the universe.

"I need…" I thought on it, then noticed the way my hair was hanging lank around my shoulders and a hopeful smile pulled at my lips. "A bath."

Kyan didn't make any suggestive remarks as he picked me up and carried me straight into the bathroom and started filling the huge clawfoot tub. I glared at the plain white clothes I'd been given by the nurses where they lay discarded in a corner, never wanting to lay eyes on them again.

Kyan's gaze lifted as he knelt beside the bath, his hand cutting through the water as he stirred some honey blossom body wash into it. His throat bobbed as he took in my naked skin, but there was no desire in his eyes. There was an arctic, serial killer rage that chilled my bones. His gaze was skimming over the bruises where needles had punctured my arms countless times, the marks no doubt left on my neck by Jonas and finally to my waist which was slimmer than it had ever been, showing off my hip bones far too much. The virus had taken a bite out of me and it was clear to see.

"I'm a survivor," I told Kyan, needing to say it out loud because I didn't want a scrap of his pity. "I may have scars, but they don't define me. Don't look at me like I'm some wounded animal you want to avenge, Kyan."

He stood up, his shadow falling over me as he stalked forward and leaned down to rest his forehead to mine. His thumb tracked the length of my spine, making a deep tremor resound through my bones. "I don't pity you, Tatum, I fucking worship you. Your pain makes me want to sin, but your strength makes me want to repent. I'm a demon trying to grow wings by standing in the blinding light of you."

"I don't want wings from you." I wrapped my hands around him, scoring my thumbs over his shoulder blades. "I love you just as you are. Every sharp claw, every dark shadow on your heart, and all the sweetness in between that you can't even see."

"Why do you love me?" he asked in a boyish voice that made my heart shatter. I looked him dead in the eyes, needing him to know. How could he not already know?

"Because your soul is made to fit mine. I love you with all I am and all I will ever be, Kyan. And I'll spend every day at your side making you see why you're worthy of everything the world has to give."

"Even you?" he asked, pulling me closer by the waist. "Am I worthy of you, baby?" There was a desperate plea to his voice like he needed to know this above anything else and it hurt me that he could doubt it. But I understood him. The life he'd led had moulded him this way. So I would make it my mission to ensure he felt worthy of the whole universe and every atom in it.

"Especially me," I growled and he closed his eyes as he soaked in those words, his hands tightening on me to the point of pain.

He hoisted me up, carrying me to the bath and laying me in the water. The bubbles foamed up around me and I tipped my head under the surface to wash away the feel of that horrid place on my flesh. And when I arose from the water, I felt like a phoenix rising from the ashes. I had two pieces of myself back. And in a couple of weeks, I would reunite with the final three pieces of my soul and be whole once more.

Saint

CHAPTER FOURTEEN

Despite my best intentions, I couldn't sleep. Midnight had come and gone and that fucking clock just kept tick, tick, ticking until it threatened to burn the sanity from my mind and leave me as nothing but a monstrous wreck of a man.

I pushed myself upright, hating the disruption to my routine and yet knowing that I wouldn't be able to claim sleep now. It was a difficult beast for me to wrangle at the best of times and tonight there was no chance.

It had been two weeks. Two weeks precisely since we'd made our way into my father's secret lab and stolen his most precious commodity and ours in one fell swoop. The vaccination I'd taken would be in full effect now and Tatum's period of isolation would end at four minutes past one. The exact time it happened to be now as I stood from my bed and stalked towards the edge of the balcony to look out over the sleeping Temple below.

There was an ache in my chest. A desperate, selfish need to go to her, to rouse her from sleep, pull her into my arms and reassure myself that she was here, wholly and fully herself once more. Recovered after her time of rest and the rigorous recovery schedule I'd set for her. Replenished and vibrant and once again ready to take her place as master of my soul.

My obsession with her was dangerous. My need for her unfathomable.

And in all the time we'd spent apart, all I'd been able to think of was the sweetness of her kisses and the unavoidable fact that I wasn't worthy of them. But I was her creature now. And I wasn't certain I could continue to avoid the call of her.

The distant click of a door opening reached me in the silence and my breath caught in my chest as she emerged. Tatum walked out into the open space below in a white tee that must have been Kyan's with her bare feet padding across the flagstones.

I glanced at Monroe where he lay sleeping on the couch as had become his routine, but he didn't stir and I gave my focus back to her.

My heart ceased to beat as I watched her, waiting for permission to go on as I just stared down at this siren who had thoroughly enthralled me.

Her gaze lifted suddenly to meet mine and my heart catapulted into motion once more, blood pounding through my veins at a furious pace as the need to go to her overwhelmed me to the point of immobilisation.

My grip on the railing before me tightened until I was certain my fingernails were gouging crescents into the wood. Neither of us moved. We just stood staring at one another while a storm built between us and my skin prickled with the energy that was entirely her.

If I moved so much as an inch, I was going to break. My control would snap. I'd take her, possess her, consume her and devour her in every way possible until there was nothing at all left of either of us.

She broke the stillness between us first, holding my gaze as she began to walk. My jaw clenched with tension as I held myself immobile, watching, waiting, trying to figure out this enigma even though I knew I'd never get an answer to her.

She was an impossibility. An answer to all the things I'd been missing. An itch I'd been needing to scratch for longer than I could recall. A piece to a puzzle which I'd assumed would always remain incomplete.

She took the stairs slowly, pacing up them one at a time, my heart thumping with every step she took, my limbs trembling from how tightly I held them contained. If I broke now there would be no coming back from it.

My head turned slowly as she climbed the stairs, keeping her locked in my gaze until she made it to the top of them and moved towards me at that same, measured pace.

There was an orchestra starting up in my head, playing a piece I'd never heard before but was desperate to compose. Because it was the music of her. It was every beautiful, intricate, complicated note of her perfection, it was a symphony in the making, a story with unbound potential. It was dark and brutal and light and powerful, pure and tainted. Her. The girl who tamed monsters. The one who owned me.

My dick swelled with an ache that I felt right through to every single bone in my body and for each step she took towards me, the throbbing need in my entire being only grew.

Tatum fell still at my side, her blue eyes flaring with so much heat that it burned me as she met my gaze. Her skin had regained its healthy glow, her lips like two red rose petals and her eyes the most stunning shade of sapphire I'd ever encountered. Her nipples were hard and pressing against the fabric of the white shirt she wore, visible through it even in the patchy moonlight that spilled through the stained-glass window. It gilded her in a rosy silver colour which only made her seem more ethereal than ever.

I wasn't even sure how long we stood staring at each other, my normal grasp on every precise minute of time slipping away like it didn't matter at all as I looked upon the face of my deity.

Her tongue swept across her bottom lip, making a growl of desire rumble in my chest as her eyes dragged down my bare torso to the less than subtle outline of my cock which bulged through my boxers for her.

Tatum shifted, her knees bending as she began to sink towards the floor, but my hand snapped out and I caught her wrist before she could kneel, shaking my head as confusion grew in her eyes.

"You don't kneel for anyone tonight," I said, my voice raw as I fought to contain the worst of me, desperately clinging to the chains that bound the demon in me as they began to slip through my grasp.

Her lips parted on what I was certain was a complaint, but before she could utter so much as a sound, I turned fully to face her and dropped to my knees instead.

Tatum sucked in a sharp gasp and my resolve began to shatter, my fingers brushing against the tips of her toes as I gave one final bit of energy into trying to resist her before realising I was fighting a battle I'd already lost.

I slid my hands forward, my fingers slowly carving lines across the tops of her bare feet before encircling her ankles. I dragged my hands up her calves as her breaths came deeper, my chin tipping back as I looked up into her eyes. I continued the path of my fingers up her legs, caressing the soft skin at the backs of her knees before venturing higher up her thighs, only stopping when the fullness of her round ass was clasped tightly in my grip.

I groaned as I realised she didn't have any panties on, my fingers digging into her warm flesh as I tried to find the strength to restrain myself.

"If you don't want me like this, tell me now," I commanded, holding her gaze as her pupils dilated. "Because I'm teetering on the edge of a knifepoint here and I need you to make it clear to me. What do you want, siren?"

A beat of silence hung between us with no words puncturing it, then Tatum took hold of the hem of the t-shirt she was wearing before peeling it off of her body to reveal her nakedness beneath.

Her chest rose and fell heavily as she tossed the shirt aside and I didn't even give a fuck that it must have landed in some reckless heap on the floor as I just stared at her, golden hair cascading down around her face as she looked right back at me.

"All hail the queen," I breathed, just loud enough for her to hear and her breath hitched as I tugged her forward a step and my mouth landed on the heat of her bare pussy.

Tatum's hands moved down to grasp my tightly curling hair and she drew me closer, taking as much as she could from me as a breathy moan escaped her lips.

The symphony in my head was building in pace now as I caressed her with my tongue, basking in the shivers of pleasure I drew from her as I circled her clit, my hand shifting between her legs until I was driving two fingers into her drenched pussy.

She cried out as I pumped them in and out in perfect synchronicity with the movement of my tongue on her clit, playing out the music I was hearing on her body as my thumb teased over her ass. She gasped as I exerted a little pressure, her grip in my hair tightening as my name slid from her lips and my cock throbbed with an ache I was desperate to satisfy, precum making it slide against the fabric of my boxers. It was the tiniest bit of friction but combined with the taste of her in my mouth and the feel of her pussy tight around my fingers, it was enough to make me groan.

I pumped my hand faster, my thumb pressing down on her ass a little harder with each thrust until I finally drove it into her too and she came with a cry loud enough to make Monroe say something in his sleep down on the couch.

The sound of her coming for me was enough to fracture the last fragments of restraint I was clinging to and I lurched to my feet, lifting her into my arms and winding her trembling legs around me as I kissed her hard and hungrily.

I slammed her back against the bathroom door, grinding my cock between her thighs and making her whimper as I drove my tongue into her mouth and tasted the perfect mixture of her desire dancing between us.

Tatum's hands were still in my hair, gripping almost tight enough to yank it from the roots and I growled as I thrust against her harder, the barrier of my boxers the only thing dividing us as her wetness soaked them.

Monroe murmured something again and I growled as I took a hand from her ass, reaching for the door handle and spilling us into the bathroom. I wasn't sharing her. Not now. Not this first time. This was going to be me and her and I wasn't going to stop until the two of us couldn't even remember our names, let alone our problems. They'd had their chances to claim her like this and now it was mine.

I kicked the door shut and locked it for good measure as Tatum took her legs from around my waist, landing on her feet and scraping her fingernails down my chest as she went for my waistband.

I tangled my fingers in her hair, kissing her bruisingly as she shoved my boxers down and my cock sprung free, hard and aching and desperate.

It was pitch black in here with the door closed but our bodies were so in sync with each other that it didn't make a bit of difference.

I caught her hips and turned her around, bending her over the sink and driving my cock into her with a savage thrust that made her scream as my balls struck against her clit.

She was so fucking tight, her pussy gripping me and making my dick throb with more need than I'd ever felt in my life.

My fingers curled around her hips and I started fucking her as hard as I could, a wild beast unfettered and unable to stop as she cried out and gasped and cursed my name at least as often as she praised it.

The products on the shelf above the sink started rattling with the force of my thrusts and I didn't even give a shit as they all began to tumble down onto the floor.

Let chaos fucking reign for my goddess.

The darkness made the music in my head seem louder, her voice pitched in pleasure the perfect melody to the crescendo I could feel coming. But I wanted to see her. Needed to watch her come apart for me and shatter and fall into my grasp, never to let her go again.

I released my hold on one of her hips as I reached for the light above the mirror, my fingers slipping over cool glass as I cursed and panted and she moaned for me even louder.

I finally managed to find it, yanking the string then slapping my hand down hard against her ass just as I lost control of my body and Tatum called my name as the light flickered on. Her blue eyes met mine in the mirror as we both came hard, crying out in pleasure, her pussy milking my cock for all I had. I didn't think I'd ever come as powerfully as that in all my life and as I drew back, panting and aching in all the best ways, I turned her around to kiss her softly.

"Saint," she murmured, her arms coiling around my neck and I found I really liked her touching me like that. Even if it was unexpected or out of control, I wanted more of it. Every last drop of it.

"I love you, Tatum Rivers," I growled, painting my fingers down her chest, stroking the full rise of her breast and teasing her hard nipple. "I didn't think I could even feel something like the things I feel for you. I didn't think there was enough good in me for it. And my love isn't something light and freeing, its obsessive and toxic, controlling and insatiable. But I feel it all for you."

"I love you too, Saint," she breathed. "You may be the worst person I've ever gone up against but you're also one of the best. I feel alive when I'm with you in the most incredible of ways and I just want it to go on and on and never end."

"Never end, huh?" My lips turned up at the corners as my hand moved between her thighs, tracing through the mess of my cum which marked her, stained her, proved that I really had claimed her.

Her hands caressed my chest, running back and forth across the words of my tattoo and I liked that a whole hell of a lot. I liked her having control almost as much as I liked taking control of her.

"Tell me what you want," I growled, walking her back until we were inside the shower and I flicked the water on.

"To own you," she breathed, her eyes full of honesty. "Just like you own me."

"Just me?" I asked as I reached up to remove the shower head from the holder to spray it between her thighs and wash away the mess we'd made there.

"No," she panted as I used my fingers to help wash her off then moved the shower head closer to her clit. "I want to own all four of you."

That should have pissed me off. That would have been the normal reaction, wouldn't it? But instead of that, my cock was hardening again and I was thinking of all the ways we could make that dream come true.

"Good," I breathed, kissing her as I slid the shower head over her clit and devouring the moan that fell from her lips.

The water pressure was fucking heavenly here. I'd made certain it was when the Temple had been converted for us and I kept kissing her as I shifted the spray back and forth between her thighs.

Tatum moaned as I toyed with her nipple and every unexpected touch of her hands on my flesh just made my pulse race faster as I continued to play with her.

My dick was aching for her again already and I knew I was never going to fully satiate this need in my body for her. My addiction was only growing, my dependence deepening and I intended to take as many highs from it as I could before exhaustion forced us to stop. Because I could see no end to it aside from that.

Tatum gasped as she got close to her orgasm, her hand grabbing my bicep to direct the shower head to the exact spot where she wanted to feel the pressure of that water.

I released my hold on her breast and shifted the dial on the shower, changing the temperature to bitingly cold just as she came, the combination of pleasure and shock driving her body to new heights.

Her scream was beyond the confines of this bathroom and I was certain she must have woken the others by now, but I didn't care. Tonight she was mine. Tomorrow we'd figure the rest out.

I flicked the shower back around to hot and placed it above us again as I lifted her up and pinned her to the wall. My solid cock pressed against her heat and I looked into her eyes as I hesitated there with water crashing down over us.

"My whole life I've fought with all I have to maintain control in everything," I said to her as she looked down at me, her hands resting on my shoulders, wet hair sticking to her skin. "And then you came along and brought more chaos to my life than I ever would have believed I could handle. I tried to break you. But you were the one who broke me. You forced me out of my comfort zone again and again until I no longer knew what comfortable felt like. You make my skin itch with a need for more. And you are that more. I hope you realise I'm never going to let you go now."

"Do you promise?" she breathed, making my soul burn for her as I pushed forward, my cock sinking into her like it was made for that purpose alone and I groaned at the perfection of that feeling, of her body owning mine.

"I promise, siren."

A smile lit her lips that was so pure and bright that it set my heart racing and as our bodies began to move together once more, I found myself feeling lighter than I had in as long as I could remember.

Tatum Rivers might have been the perfect bait for the monster in me, but she was the balm for it too. She had tamed four broken, wild men and all we could do now was worship her and hope she never wanted to escape us. But either way, I wouldn't be letting her go.

CHAPTER FIFTEEN

I woke in the arms of a different monster for the first time in two weeks. Saint lay behind me, my body curved against his as he held me, not a single layer of clothing parting our heated flesh. His muscles were locked around me, keeping me his captive even in sleep. But it turned out, he was my captive too and I wouldn't ever be releasing him.

My skin buzzed and hummed from what we'd done last night. Saint had claimed me with the punishing ferocity of the Devil. And I wouldn't have had it any other way.

My eyes fluttered open and I took in the time staring back at me from the clock on his nightstand, my confusion giving way to a little knot of panic. *Oh shit.*

It was three minutes past ten and Saint was going to lose his head. *What the hell happened to the alarm?*

He stirred, his mouth brushing my neck and I arched into him automatically, savouring the way his touch sent a rush of electricity through my flesh. His cock was hard and pressing keenly into my ass as I ground my hips back against him, a sigh leaving him that was so un-Saint, it made me grin. He sounded content. And when was the last time the black hearted beast who resided in this church was ever content?

I reached out quickly, knocking the alarm clock so it wasn't facing us before rolling over to look at him. He arched an eyebrow at me. "I am quite aware of the time, Tatum. Who do you think turned the alarm off? A fucking pixie?"

My lips parted in shock. Like, legit shock. "Why?" I balked. "And why aren't you climbing the walls right now?"

He grabbed my waist, tugging me flush to his body and kissing me, his tongue driving into my mouth in controlled movements that seemed to press every button of my desire. He broke the kiss before I was even close to done with it, leaving my lips tingling and hungry for more.

"There is only one time which matters right now. And that is the time I am spending with you," he said, his eyes devouring me as they trailed to my mouth, my throat, my breasts. "Besides, you still need rest. I am not above breaking my routine, for that purpose alone."

"I'm completely fine now and you know it. You don't ever break your routine," I said. "It makes you crazy."

"Well I am hopelessly crazy then, I suppose," he said, sounding entirely sane and sexy as hell. He pushed me over onto my back, moving on top of me in a fluid motion, pressing his weight down as the tip of his hard cock slipped against my slick entrance.

A breath snagged in my throat as I gripped his powerful shoulders, raising my hips as I urged him to take me. But he didn't, he smiled darkly, watching my expression as he held me in suspense, revelling in having me in this position. I still couldn't quite believe he wasn't descending into world war three right now over the damn time. But I certainly wasn't complaining.

"Aren't you craving control over your day?" I asked huskily as he trailed a line of kisses along my jaw, each one considered and deliberate.

"I have *you* at my mercy, how much more control could any man desire in this world or the next?"

My stomach fluttered and I turned my head to seek out his mouth, but he denied me it, forcing my head back the other way with his fingers so he could continue delivering kisses how and where he wanted.

"You're actually a total romantic, do you realise that?" I teased breathlessly, my core so soaked, I was pawing at his hips in an effort to draw him into me. But he'd probably have me fall like the Berlin Wall before he gave me what I wanted.

"Romance is a concept. I simply speak the truth as I perceive it," he reasoned.

"That's what makes it romantic," I continued to taunt him, running my hands down the hard planes of his muscular back. He flexed over me, a growl rumbling through him that reminded me of the animal in him who had claimed me last night. He'd finally relinquished control. Complete and utter control. And it had been for me. Maybe he really didn't need his routine today.

"So are you going to live wildly now? Get up at seven minutes past any hour you like, skip the gym and eat a bowl of Cap'n Crunch for breakfast?" I joked, but he winced, his expression becoming tight.

He tried to draw away, but I gripped his arms, refusing to let him go as guilt washed through me.

His eyes moved somewhere beyond my head as he sighed. "I know that I'm difficult, I know I'm not like other people…"

"I didn't mean to upset you. In fact, I want to understand. Explain it to me," I asked seriously. "Tell me what it's like."

Saint drew in a long breath, regarding me as he brushed a lock of golden hair behind my ear. "There's a deep, burning need in me for everything to be wholly unchangeable. Sometimes, I can find a single moment that lasts a few seconds where I hold my breath and my entire existence seems worthwhile. Everything is still, clean, perfect. Every error in my past is erased, every blip, tarnish, and stain vanishes until all I can see is a pure, white sea of calm. But I can't hold onto it. It slips through my fingers like grains of sand, piece by glorious piece until I'm left trying to pick each one of them up off of the ground. It's…chaos."

"That sounds like a nightmare," I breathed sadly and he nodded, his thumb skimming smoothly across the swell of my throat.

"With each grain of sand that falls, I face each failure in myself once more, until I remember how disgustingly average I really am. Yet every time, I trick myself into thinking I can find that place of perfection again. That the next time I reach it, I'll keep it. Next time, it will be here to stay. I hold myself to brutal, savage standards that cut through flesh and bone and demand me to stand atop a mountain as a god. Every decision I make is analysed, criticised, deconstructed then reconstructed all over again. And to make it all worse, I have held you to those standards too, Tatum. I have demanded you to be perfect, yet it took losing you to realise how vile a demon perfection really is. And it was always my demon to bear, never yours. You are beautifully, astoundingly human. And I no longer fear being human too. Because if I am to hold myself to any standard, my siren, my heart, my fucking everything, then there is no greater standard on earth than you."

"Saint," I gasped, leaning upwards, feeling his breath against my lips.

"I thought for so many years that happiness was a word which belonged to fools and simpletons, to those who had no ambitions of greatness, who would achieve nothing but pointless dreams while living little, irrelevant lives. But now I see it was my life that was small. And that love is not an infantile dream, but the only dream I have ever had that serves a greater purpose than myself. I have fallen for you like those grains of sands that once bound me so completely, slipping one by one, slowly over time, without me ever noticing at all. And somehow, there is no chaos now that the last has fallen, just peace, entire, fucking, *peace*. So I will let them lie, Tatum Rivers. I will let them lie for you."

I captured his lips, my heart expanding, filling up with the beauty of his words and the sacrifice I knew it had taken for him to say them. He held my hips, angling my body for him to claim and my fingers bunched against his shoulders as I anticipated the fullness of him inside me. He reached down to hook my knee under his arm, drawing it up in a slow and deliberate move that made my heart thump unevenly.

"If you're going to fuck each other again can you give me a heads up because I'll find some other couch to sleep on," Monroe called from downstairs, a note of irritation in his tone.

Saint was clearly about to fuck me anyway so I slapped his shoulder and gave him a firm look.

"Don't be a dick," I hissed and he smirked. I pushed him back, my heart aching to be close to my other Night Keepers too and Saint's expression softened like he understood exactly what I wanted.

He drew away from me, suddenly on his feet, yanking his boxers on as he strode to the edge of the balcony. I leapt after him, grabbing a silken dressing gown and pulling it on, tying it in place as I ran to Saint's side. I looked down at Monroe on the couch, the dark tigress tattoo on his broad chest looking somehow more monstrous than usual as it gazed back at me.

"Morning," I called and Monroe smiled at me before tossing a jealous look at Saint.

"Good morning, princess," he said, pushing a hand through his messy blonde hair and my fingers twitched with the urge to do the same. He looked freaking edible in the mornings, all sleepy-eyed and beastly.

Blake was in the kitchen making coffee and he looked up at me with a longing in his eyes that pricked my heart. I was itching to go to him, to Monroe, to Kyan. Hell, I needed all of them surrounding me. I didn't know how to explain it or what they thought of it. The idea that I could be in love with four men was insanity, and yet it was true. But I didn't know how to divide myself between them all. I didn't know if I would always be enough for them this way either. And I wanted them all to choose this just as I wanted to choose it. Because if they thought I could be enough, then I would make it my life's mission to be. I would love them all just as deeply, just as fiercely as each other. And I needed them to know that.

"I don't know what you're both staring at," Saint said curtly. "I claimed our girl just like the rest of you have."

"I'm mostly annoyed that you treated us to the gift of hearing it," Monroe growled, his eyes darkening.

"Well, I'm not going to apologise for your lack of ingenuity, Nash," Saint said coolly. "You could have procured yourself some earplugs from any of my drawers, or you could have moved to sleep in with Blake or Kyan. Or even gone back to the Headmaster's quarters. I'm hardly responsible for where you decide to be while I'm fucking-"

"Stop it." I jammed my elbow into Saint's side and he gave me a psycho's smile.

"Just for the record, I heard you too," Blake added and heat flushed up my cheeks. Holy shit, was I that loud?

Saint shrugged, his expression faintly smug. "Again, not my issue."

Kyan walked into the room, one hand stuffed down his boxers as he openly rearranged his junk and his eyes only half cracked open as he clung to sleep. His eyes widened fully though as he sought me out up on the balcony and a sideways grin pulled at his lips. "So you two finally fucked?"

"Jesus, Kyan," I growled. "Don't tell me even *you* heard it?"

"Yup," he said, his grin growing ravenous. "Oh, I stabbed a pillow fourteen times when I was woken up by the way, so if you could order a new one of those, brother, that would be swell." He winked at Saint who bristled.

"Tatum will never sleep in your bed again if those words are true," Saint warned and Monroe and Blake looked set to agree. I mean, they had a point. I didn't wanna accidentally wake up Kyan one time and end up gutted by his hunting knife.

Kyan yawned widely, moving to the fridge to grab out the milk and start chugging from the bottle. "Don't worry, the only thing Tatum's in danger of getting skewered by is my cock."

"Hilarious," I deadpanned. "You're officially not allowed to keep knives in the bed."

"I wouldn't stab you, baby," he said seriously. "I can sense when you're close like that kid in that creepy movie who can sense dead people."

"That's not comforting," I said, wrinkling my nose.

Blake slammed the coffee pot down, drawing everyone's attention and my eyes roamed over his golden, muscular body as he gazed directly at me. "No more arguing. Get down here, Cinders, I need to fucking touch you. I've been starved of you for too long."

"I want her first." Monroe stood from the couch and I sank my teeth into my lower lip as Kyan looked ready to go to battle for me too, even though he'd had me for two whole weeks. But he hadn't had me like *that*. He'd actually kept his word about that, insisting I needed to recover and not so much as using his hands on me this whole freaking time. Honestly, it had been almost as torturous as being locked up in that damn lab. Having him so close and yet refusing to touch me the way I yearned for him to had been a special kind of hell.

Saint's fingers brushed up my arm possessively like he was considering whether he was going to allow me to leave his side or not. But it definitely wasn't up to him.

"I'm going to take a shower," I announced. "Then I want to talk to you all together."

Blake's brows lowered, looking like he was tempted to come up here and grab me. Part of me wanted him to. But I had things I needed to get clear before I fell into my desires again. Even though my body was already humming with the idea of getting Blake's hands on me. All of their hands on me…

Oh my god, what would it be like to have them all at once? I nearly moaned with the thought of it alone, then pulled away from Saint and marched pointedly into his bathroom, locking the door behind me and releasing a steadying breath.

We'd made a fucking mess of this room last night and my eyebrows rose as I found all of the bottles that had been on the shelf above the sink still scattered across the floor. The used towels were strewn haphazardly over the space too and I bit my lip as I remembered the way Saint had dragged me out of the water after he'd finished ruining me against the shower wall, only to pin me to his bed and start devouring me all over again. I'd actually lost track of the amount of times he'd destroyed me last night, but as I caught sight of my ass in the mirror I smirked at the pinkness of my butt cheek and the faint outline of his handprint on my skin.

I showered quickly, my fingers gliding over my hardened nipples as I couldn't draw my attention from the thought of my Night Keepers all pressed close to me at once, their skin against mine, their mouths roaming my body.

I dried quickly, my hair damp around my shoulders as I stepped outside, finding the room empty and the boys talking downstairs. I headed into the closet, dropping my towel and opening one of the drawers, eyeing all of the beautiful underwear Saint had bought for me.

An idea entered my mind as my finger snagged on a silky white corset. I slipped it from the drawer, putting it on and pairing it with some matching panties before rolling on some sheer tan stockings and using the suspenders on the corset to hook them into place.

I dried my hair and put my makeup on, taking my sweet time as I preened myself to perfection, wanting to feel like royalty after feeling like hell for so many weeks. I painted on a dark, rose coloured lipstick and pushed my feet into the same shade of pink high heels with black soles, smiling at myself in the mirror as I styled my hair. My gaze hooked on the crown I'd worn when Monroe had been made a Night Keeper and I paused, a breath of amusement escaping me. *Would it be totally ridiculous if I put it on..?*

I hooked it onto my finger, placing it on my head just for myself and taking in the effect in the mirror. *Well shit, why can't I wear a crown every day of the week? Social norms are so dull.*

I glanced over my shoulder at the door and figured screw it, exiting and walking to the edge of the balcony. I peered over the edge and found all of them still in their boxers, looking wholly delicious.

Blake and Kyan were wrestling over the TV remote while Saint and Monroe egged them on, all of that muscular flesh making my thighs clench together with need. I watched them for a while longer before heading downstairs, figuring it would be fun to surprise them. I sat on the dining table, crossing my legs and grinning as Blake snatched the remote and jumped up, howling his victory. But his howl died in his throat as his gaze landed on me and the remote fell from his hand, hitting the coffee table with a clatter, the batteries bursting out of it.

"Mine," he snarled like a beast then shoved through Saint and Monroe on the couch, vaulting over it and running towards me. The others twisted around as Kyan jumped up and I swear their jaws actually dropped.

Blake made it to me, slowing his pace as he dipped his head and his eyes swirled with sinful ideas as he drank in my outfit. He reached out, but I spoke up before he could place his hand on me.

"No touching. Not yet."

He swallowed hard, dropping his hand in disappointment as the others moved to stand either side of him, the four of them gazing at me like stray mutts hungering for scraps.

"You look incredible," Nash rasped.

"Beautiful," Blake added.

"Sensational," Saint clipped.

"Fucking edible." Kyan smirked and my toes curled up in my shoes as they all stared and it felt like they were looking directly beneath my flesh.

I smiled seductively back at them, though my heart was pounding fiercely as I considered what I wanted from them. I swallowed the rising ball in my throat and took a measured breath, a flicker of anxiety running through me at the truth I was about to draw from them all.

"I need to ask you all something, and I need an honest answer," I said and they nodded, waiting expectantly. "I know this situation isn't exactly… normal. The four of you and me, it's pretty crazy. But the thing is, it doesn't feel crazy anymore somehow. Being in that lab alone made me miss you all more than I ever could have imagined I'd miss anyone or anything. Not a single one of you means less to me than the other. I need you all. Being without any one of you would break me. But I also understand that, well, I know it's a lot to ask of you to share me. Only me. When I'm asking to have all of you in return." My words hung in the air for what felt like an eternity and the four of them exchanged intense looks that made my heart race. But when they turned back to me, there was certainty in their eyes, not a single shadow of doubt.

"You bound yourself to all of us, baby," Kyan said darkly. "I understood that from day one. I will share you with my brothers, but no other man or creature on this earth will touch you aside from them and me. And I will never want another woman but you."

My heart pounded unevenly, but I didn't have time to respond as Blake spoke next.

"I'm yours. You're mine. And theirs. We're one unit. Bound by blood and pain and love. There is no other way that makes sense to me, Cinders."

"Yes," Saint agreed, nodding firmly. "Our claims will always be equal. Our souls are irrevocably linked. This is the only path for us. And the only one I want."

I looked to Monroe, doubt making my heart crush as I waited for his answer, needing to know he could commit to this too. He hadn't been bonded to the others for as long, he'd wanted me to himself before now. But if he said he couldn't do this, I didn't know what I'd do. It would break me. Without one of them, it couldn't work. Somehow, this impossibly powerful bond holding us together could only function if the five of us maintained it. If one link was broken, it would break us all.

"Nash?" I breathed, hope and fear wrapped up in my voice.

He stepped forward, his knuckles brushing my thigh, running up to my hip and leaving tingles in his wake. He continued to drag them up my body, over my stomach, following the curve of my breasts, along the length of my throat until he propped my chin up on his thumb and tilted my head so I looked him directly in the eyes. His gaze was a well of endless desire and want and adoration, the sight making my heart thrash and kick against my ribs.

"I have found a home here with these men, and with you. I've never felt so seen as I am here. I can be the untamed beast I was born to be without fear of judgement. You make me feel like I have a place in this world. So I want to stand in it and make every single day you have on this Earth the happiest it can be. And if it takes these three men to ensure that too, then there is no doubt in my heart that this is where they should be as well. I won't lose you again, princess. We're yours. So do what you want with us."

A shaky breath made it through my lips as I savoured the weight of all of their pledges to me. There was no way to solidify this bond with words. It had to be done with flesh. And I was no longer afraid to have them all possess me at once, instead I anticipated it with the thirst of a desert for rain.

I took hold of Monroe's hand under my chin and lowered it to my breasts, reaching out to curl my other hand around the back of his neck. He released a deep, carnal noise, his hand sliding beneath my corset and scoring his thumb across my nipple as his mouth clashed with mine in a hungry, fervent kiss that made my head spin.

He stepped between my thighs and I arched into him, running my hands over his firm shoulders as my core squeezed tightly in expectation of what I wanted.

He broke our kiss, his mouth falling to my throat and I tilted my head to give him more access, gazing over his shoulder at my other boys who looked desperate to come closer.

I reached for them, a demand on my lips which was drowned out by a moan as Monroe's mouth slid down to suck on my nipple instead of using his thumb. Blake and Kyan strode forward while Saint watched, squeezing the huge bulge in his boxers. Always clinging to control until the final damn second.

Kyan grabbed my hips, yanking me to my feet and muscling in behind me while Blake claimed a fierce kiss from my mouth. I hummed my pleasure at the burning heat of his lips and the way his tongue moved in a furious pattern against mine, making my body quiver from that singular touch, let alone the way Nash's mouth was moving on my flesh too.

Behind me, Kyan grabbed the silk ribbon tying my corset, yanking it free with harsh tugs that nearly pulled me away from the other two. But Monroe held my hips and Blake fisted a hand in my hair, neither of them letting me go as they worked together to destroy me.

When the corset was loose, the three of them shimmied it off of me and I stepped out of it as my hooded gaze met Saint's. He dropped his boxers and fisted his thick cock in his hand, slowly running his hand up and down the length of it in taunting strokes.

"Saint," I beckoned him in a firm order, but he didn't move, his eyes dark as he watched.

"I want to see you come at least once before you're mine again," he said, his words sending an electric shiver down my spine.

Kyan's palm ran the length of my back as Monroe dropped to his knees and Kyan knelt down too, his breath fanning against the backs of my thighs. Kyan ripped my panties off with a sharp pull while Blake kept my head angled toward him as he kissed me, lowering one hand to my breasts, massaging them in firm, possessive squeezes.

Monroe's tongue ran up my centre in one long lick that made me moan into Blake's mouth. His tongue settled against my clit and started circling in soft, filthy movements that made my whole body shake violently.

Kyan squeezed my ass with both hands, then parted my cheeks and ran his tongue over the most intimate part of me and I jerked forward into Blake's hands with a gasp of surprise. Kyan chuckled like a demon, licking me savagely as Monroe's tongue seemed to find the exact same, wicked rhythm against my clit.

"Oh my god," I moaned against Blake's lips.

"Is that good, Cinders?" Blake purred and I nodded, my hips jolting and jerking as Monroe and Kyan seemed to battle for who could make me twitch the most. "It can be even fucking better."

Blake's hand slid from my breast and he dropped his shoulder, reaching under Monroe's chin and slipping his hand into the party. Two thick fingers pushed deep inside me and Blake cursed at how wet he found me, pumping his hand and making me cry out at the unbelievable sensations the three of them were giving me. It was too much. I was falling or flying or fucking combusting. I gasped and moaned, unsure who was even holding me up because it sure as shit wasn't me. Ecstasy tumbled through my body like an earthquake and I cried out, my head falling back as Blake's mouth fell to my throat and licked up the length of it.

I was still moaning as he withdrew his hand and Kyan and Monroe's mouths retreated from my body, giving me relief for my sensitive, quivering flesh. But I only needed a second because I wasn't even close to done with any of them.

"Nash, you have her first," Saint commanded suddenly. "Lie her on the table."

"Fuck no." Blake yanked me toward him and a breathy laugh escaped me.

Kyan caught my hips, tugging me out of his arms, his teeth sinking into the shell of my ear. "I'll fight to get inside you first, baby. I'll lay them all out for you." His hard, throbbing cock pressed against my ass and Monroe growled, shoving his forehead to knock him back and pulling me against his chest with a demonic look that said he was about to do anything to win this fight.

"I want all of you," I insisted as Blake and Kyan's palms fell on me again. I nuzzled into them as the three of them surrounded me, my hand curving around Kyan's neck behind me and my other hand moving from Monroe's chest to knot in Blake's hair as they caressed and pawed at me. My gaze fell on Saint again as the final piece of my jigsaw alluded me.

"Join us," I demanded but he just licked his lips, leaning back against the couch and slowly pumping his beautiful dick.

"I will when I'm done enjoying the view," he said, his eyes two wells of hunger and I guessed I didn't mind putting on a show if that was what he liked.

"Come on, princess, make a choice," Monroe growled urgently, nipping at my jaw and my breaths came too heavily.

"Saint can choose," I decided, knowing he revelled in it. And I kinda did too. If he wasn't going to come over here and put his hands on me then he could at least have this connection to us instead.

Kyan growled his disapproval, looking over at Saint in frustration.

"Nash it is," Saint reiterated smugly and Monroe clearly didn't care to argue with Saint when he was being picked, so he grabbed my waist, lifting me up and carrying me to the table.

He lay me down, spreading me out on it like I was his favourite meal and I grinned at him as I wrapped my legs around his waist, my soul igniting from the way he watched me. My crown fell to the table and I didn't bother to retrieve it as I was captured by the sight before me, my dark angel towering above me, ready to show me the depths of his sins.

"Eyes here," Monroe commanded, pointing to his own blue gaze and I nodded, biting my lip as he tugged his boxers down, freeing his impressive, throbbing length.

His eyes lingered on my lips as he guided himself to my entrance, feeling how soaked I was and he sighed as he circled the head of his dick in my wetness.

He held my jaw so I couldn't look away, not that I wanted to look at anything but him in that moment anyway, then he shoved his hips forward, slamming himself inside me fully and making me cry out. His gaze locked with mine as he pounded in and out of me, his teeth bared as his fingers dug into my chin and his whole body tensed, his abs tight, his muscles gleaming, making me even slicker for him.

"Fuck, you feel so good," he groaned, his other hand moving to caress my swollen clit as my back arched against the hard wood table. "*Yes*."

"Slow down, Nash. I said you could go first, not that you could finish first," Saint said cuttingly, but Monroe ignored him, driving harder into my body as another orgasm built and built in me from his skilful touch.

"Nash," Saint snapped.

"Shut up," Monroe spat, still not letting me look anywhere else but at him.

I moaned as I gave myself to his power, my eyes half rolling back into my head as my thighs clenched around him. Ecstasy was about to crest through me like a wave, but before I could dive into that sea of pleasure, Monroe was yanked away from me and I yelped, half sitting up as I found Saint tugging him aside.

"Hey!" I snarled.

"Kyan, get under her," Saint tossed at him and Kyan didn't hesitate, grabbing me off the table and pulling me down to straddle him on the carpet.

I turned my head to try and see Monroe, but Kyan lifted my hips and slid himself inside me with a powerful thrust that made me fall forward over him. My mouth met his and he bit hard on my lower lip, grabbing my hands and holding them at the base of my spine as he controlled me riding him.

"Motherfucker," I panted and he laughed.

"Blake take her hands for him," Saint commanded and Kyan growled as he drove himself in and out of me.

I dug my knees into the carpet to try and gain some control, but as Blake took hold of my hands for him, Kyan was free to grip my hips, his thumbs slipping beneath the straps of my suspenders and I lost any power I'd had at all as he pumped himself in and out of me, his cock hitting that sweet spot inside me and making me release noises that sounded purely fucking animal.

"Jesus fucking – *Kyan*," I gasped for air as he didn't slow even a little, his ruthless thrusts almost painful, but they were so fucking good too.

He squeezed my ass, slapping hard enough to leave a mark before doing it again and again.

"You're a savage," I growled angrily, loving it almost as much as I wanted to punch him for it.

"I would've thought you'd be used to that by now, baby," he said, smirking as he watched my breasts bounce, looking like he was in heaven.

"Fuck her from behind, Blake," Saint instructed and Blake's hands shifted on my wrists so he held them in one while moving his other to slide into the arousal between my thighs.

"Ah, that's my balls, asshole," Kyan grunted and Blake growled his annoyance while a breathless laugh escaped me.

"You like it really, *baby*," I taunted and Kyan gave me a sadistic grin that spelled trouble.

He pulled out of me, lifting me by the hips and forcing me to turn around so I faced Blake. I steadied myself on Blake's shoulders, having no time to prepare as Kyan eased himself into my ass instead, using the slickness from my body to open me up to him.

"For fuck's sake, Kyan," Saint huffed. "Do as I say."

"Asshole," I snarled at him as he ignored Saint, but the breathy pleasure that filled my voice kinda lessened the sting of my insult.

"Are we naming places I plan on fucking you today? Pussy, mouth, tits," Kyan said casually in my ear, grinding his hips in a slow, teasing movement that told me he wasn't going to be a complete beast about fucking me this way at least.

"One day I'm going to buy a strap on and see how you like it," I panted and he chuckled, biting down on my neck.

"Good luck with that, baby," he purred.

He pulled me back to lie on him, his hand moving to my clit as Blake knelt between both of our legs and snared all of my attention. My golden boy had a playful grin on his face as he stared at my body, clearly not too bothered about the change of plans as he got to look at me fully. He knocked Kyan's hand away from my clit, leaning down to suck it and make me whimper, my eyes falling on Saint and Monroe who stood just beyond him, watching as they stroked themselves, seeming hypnotised by the view. Their eyes on me were enough to push me over the ledge I was already teetering on thanks to Kyan and Blake, and I moaned as pleasure rippled through me once more.

Blake ran his mouth up my body as Kyan slowly rocked his hips, controlling our movements as I gripped Blake's shoulders tighter. I slid one hand down to line up Blake's twitching dick with my core, running my thumb over the bead of precum waiting for me before twisting my hand down his shaft and squeezing it at the base.

He released a low noise of total desire as he thrust his cock forward and I drew him inside me. His body weighed down on mine and Kyan grunted as he was pressed down too and holy shit, there weren't many better places in the world than being crushed between these two Adonises as they brought me to ruin.

Kyan wrapped my hair around his fist to keep it out of his face. It might have been awkward but it was so damn hot. Blake pushed in deep until I was so full of both of them that my moans became garbled noises that were somewhere between whimpers and demands for more. They started moving in and out of me at different times, one of them thrusting while the other pulled back, their pace matching each other's as they built me up and up towards impossible heights.

I wrapped my legs around Blake's waist and Kyan gripped the backs of my thighs, moving me to his demands until I was lost to both of them as they took complete control of my body.

Kyan growled in my ear, cursing and biting and suddenly he was stilling and swelling within me, his breaths hot on my neck.

"God you're fucking perfect," he groaned, slapping my ass hard again before drawing out of me.

Blake laughed victoriously, lifting me off of him and planting my ass on the back of the couch, his mouth meeting mine as he circled his hips and rubbed my insides in a way designed for purest pleasure. I moaned and panted, my nails tearing into his back as his forehead pressed to mine. Sweat beaded on his chiselled body as he finished with one final, earth-shattering thrust that had me coming apart again too.

He pulled out of me, kissing me sweetly and I pushed back on his chest, letting myself flop down onto the cushions of the couch to catch my breath, a heady laugh escaping me as I felt the evidence of two of my men's desire for me seeping between my thighs.

I swung my legs around so they hung off the side of the couch and two dark demons moved into view around it, making my heart rate spike. Monroe held a glass of water in his hand, holding it to my lips and I drank it greedily as my eyes locked with his. Saint watched me with intent and as Monroe placed the glass on the table, I bit my lip with excitement, ready for more.

"You sure you haven't had enough?" Monroe asked with a smirk and I shook my head.

"I need you both. I can handle it just fine," I said, reaching down to fist his hard cock and tease him as I pumped it slowly.

"That's enough, siren," Saint purred. "Get on your knees for us."

I wet my lips, nodding eagerly and moving to obey, a thrill rushing through me from his bossy tone. Saint moved in front of me beyond the arm of the couch, nodding to Monroe who drew my hips back to line up with his cock, angling his tip against my pussy. Saint waited as Monroe thrust into me and I groaned as Monroe showed me no mercy, his fingers biting into my hips as he powered in and out of my body.

I tightened around him, moaning his name and Saint gripped my hair, yanking sharply to make me look up at him.

"Say my name like that," he commanded greedily.

"*Saint*," I moaned as Nash slid his fingers onto my swollen clit and demanded even more pleasure from my body, but I was unsure if I could really come again. There had to be a limit, right?

"Good girl," Saint sighed, stepping closer and bringing his cock to my lips.

I took it into my mouth without needing a single command, slackening my throat and taking him in as far as I could before drawing out again in a deliberately slow move. He swore as I swirled my tongue around his shaft and I sucked the tip in a way that made his whole cock jerk in my mouth.

Monroe's fingers dug harder into my hips and I felt his dick swelling as he came close to finishing. I sucked Saint's shaft, pushing my ass back against Monroe as I swam in the ecstasy of claiming these two men who had once been bitter enemies. Nash's fingers worked miracles between my thighs and I almost bit down on Saint's cock as I found another burning release, pulling my mouth off of him at the last second as I shuddered my way through the pleasure. Nash followed me into oblivion, his hands sliding up my back as he finished deep inside me with one fierce thrust that shook the foundations of my body.

Saint laughed darkly as Nash pulled free of me and fell back into the closest armchair with a sigh of satisfaction.

Saint leaned low to speak in my ear. "Now you're all mine." He took my hand, guiding me over to his wingback chair and dropping into it, tugging me down to straddle his lap. He angled his cock against my opening and drew me down onto him with a groan, his penetrating eyes gazing directly into my soul.

I lay my hands on his shoulders as he held my hips and we started moving, staring at each other in a trance as we rocked in a perfect rhythm with one another. I placed one hand to his chest, pinning this monster in place as I rode his solid length, my lips parted in an O as I felt every inch of his thickness claiming me. His hands grasped my butt cheeks and I cursed as he slid two fingers into my ass, making me ride them along with his cock as he smirked cruelly at me.

"Ever the devil," I panted.

"Always," he promised, his expression tensing as my hips moved faster and all we could do was pant and groan as we wrung pleasure from each other's bodies harder and harder, working ourselves up to a sweaty, wild rhythm that had me struggling for breath.

Saint came with a string of filthy words and I followed him, falling forward so my face rested against the strong column of his neck as all the strength went out of my body.

"Shower!" Blake cried, snatching me off of Saint's lap before I had a moment to recover and throwing me over his shoulder as he ran for his and Kyan's bathroom. A thundering of footfalls came after us and I lifted my head in a daze, seeing Nash and Kyan charging after us. Blake made it into the bathroom, swung the door shut in their faces and locked it before racing to the other side of the room and locking that door too.

"Blake!" Kyan snapped, the sound of a heavy body hitting the wood. "I'm not beyond breaking this door down."

"Can't hear you," Blake sang, switching the shower on as he stepped in and planted me in front of him.

He kissed me and I laughed, wrapping my arms around him as he washed me, soothing the aches away that I was left with after claiming my four Night Keepers together. "I love you, Cinders." He nuzzled my neck and I moaned lightly, pushing my fingers into his wet hair.

"I love you too, golden boy," I breathed and he sighed, closing his eyes as he relished those words. I carved my fingers over his face and into his hair, my soul rising to the surface of my flesh for this boy. "I love every ray of sunshine that's housed in your skin, I love that each one burns into me and makes me feel lighter than air. But I love your darkness too, the shadowy side of you that lurks beneath that sweetly cruel exterior. I want both halves of you, Blake Bowman, because they make you real. They make you a villain and a hero. A god and a devil. The creature in between it all is the most tempting, beautiful man. And he's *mine*."

"Fuck, sweetheart, how am I ever gonna live up to your love? It's too fucking pure," he growled, pulling me closer.

"You already have," I said firmly, drawing him into a passionate kiss.

We didn't leave the bathroom for nearly half an hour as Blake decided to make me come once more with his mouth and hands before he let me go. And when we returned to the living room in sweats, I was feeling thoroughly satisfied and aching all over in the best way. The others were dressed too, clearly having all used Saint's bathroom.

My gaze drifted to the door as I had the urge to go and find Mila, hug her and tell her I was okay. But if I did that, I knew I'd be putting her at risk. Troy Memphis was too dangerous a man to put her in the line of his fire. The knowledge of my whereabouts was best to remain within these walls until we could figure out how to get him off our backs. I just didn't know what we were going to do long-term. I couldn't stay holed up here forever.

"We're going to need to work out some new ground rules. I'm not living this caveman way where our girl is grabbed by whichever neanderthal gets to her first," Saint commanded, his ankle balanced on his knee as he pushed his hand through his tightly curling hair.

"Agreed," Monroe said and they exchanged a look as Blake and Kyan shared one of their own that said they preferred the caveman lifestyle.

"That kinda seems like a you guys issue, so I'm gonna get some food," I said, grinning as I headed to the kitchenette and took out some bread to make a sandwich, my stomach growling loudly. "Anyone want one?"

"Me."

"Me."

"Me."

"I shall have smashed avocado spread on toasted rye," Saint said and I looked over my shoulder at them all with an arched eyebrow.

"Well I'm gonna need a hand for all those, kay? I'm not your servant anymore," I said lightly and Monroe jumped up, seeming more than happy to help as he joined me and grabbed the mayo from the fridge, placing a kiss behind my ear that made my heart flutter.

"Anyone wanna go for a run soon?" Blake asked, stretching his arms above his head.

"Do you ever run out of energy?" Saint inquired and Blake laughed.

"Nope," he said, pushing out of his seat and heading to the closest window which was covered by a blind. "I hope it's not raining anymore…" I heard him open it as I buttered some bread and he swore loudly, making me turn around in surprise.

My heart stalled as I took in what looked like red paint on the window, the word *mine* written in thick letters across the glass. As the sun came out from behind a dark cloud, it cast the Temple in a deep red glow. My gut knotted and my breathing came unevenly. *What the fuck?*

Saint's knuckles were turning white where they were fisted on the arms of his chair, his face fixed in a steely mask. He stood abruptly, marching upstairs without a word and Kyan pushed out of his seat, looking ready to murder the next person who came close to him.

"Is it the Justice Ninja?" I asked what everyone was surely thinking, my heart thrashing in my chest. How could they know I was here? We'd kept all the blinds closed. I hadn't been outside. It wasn't possible. And yet…

Monroe took my hand, his jaw ticking furiously as he caught my attention. "You're safe here, princess."

"I know," I said earnestly, a dark, murderous energy filling me. "I just want to find them and make them pay."

"We will. And we'll throw them in with Bait," Kyan growled and I looked over at him.

"What did you do with him?" I asked curiously and a psychotic look entered Kyan's eyes.

"He's locked up in an unused classroom over in the Pine Auditorium. We toss the odd apple or bag of cooked rice in there occasionally. The stench is pretty rank though." He smiled like that pleased him and it pleased me too.

I was glad he was suffering after everything he'd done. He could have killed me with those bow and arrows, or worse, he could have killed one of my men.

Saint came striding down the stairs looking at his phone. "The CCTV shows the Ninja in their mask outside The Temple not ten minutes ago. They headed down towards the sports hall."

"Well what are we fucking waiting for?" Blake growled, cracking his knuckles as he followed Kyan toward the door.

Saint strode up to me, handing me his phone before walking over to the secret compartment in the floor where his safe was hidden. He tapped in a code, taking out a gun and giving that to me too.

"What are these for?" I frowned.

"You're staying here. You can follow the others' trackers on this app. If my phone locks, the passcode is one-seven-five-two-nine-seven." He tapped the screen to open an app and three dots showed up on it for Kyan, Blake and Nash's phones. "The gun is for any motherfucker who walks in that door who isn't one of your Night Keepers." He kissed my cheek, leaving a burning mark on it and Nash squeezed my fingers before heading after the others.

I knew I couldn't risk being seen around campus, but I still hated not being able to go with them.

"Destroy them," I commanded, my spine straightening as all of my boys nodded at me, their eyes glinting as they hungered to obey that order. "Make them goddamn suffer."

CHAPTER SIXTEEN

Something about the time the other Night Keepers and I had spent working together to return Tatum to us had changed my outlook on this group of black hearted boys. I no longer saw three soulless demons born of entitlement and privilege into a world so bountiful that they had grown to have nothing but disdain for it. I now saw three men forged of different hurts and pains with different damage and different ghosts haunting them, but we had all come together for one, single dream. And that dream was more than just the girl we all so clearly loved, it was the family we had managed to build with one another, it was the determination to combine our strengths and use them to destroy our enemies.

So as I raced across campus, my shoulders rubbing against Saint and Kyan's, instead of feeling like a man wearing a mask and playing pretend, I felt free for the first time in as long as I could remember.

I wasn't lying to anyone anymore. They knew my story, every dark, rotten facet of it. They knew my birth name. They knew my grief. And instead of punishing me for it like I'd once believed would happen if they ever discovered my truth, they'd pulled me up onto their pedestal and crowned me right alongside them. I wasn't lost in memories of a past I couldn't reclaim anymore. And even with the prospect of making Troy Memphis suffer and pay for what he'd done to my family looming on the horizon, I found that I was living for so much more than that now too.

Tatum had bound our wandering souls together and though I'd once wished to claim her for my own, I had grown to see that my relationships with each of the men she'd chosen were precious to me too. Even Saint fucking Memphis.

We weren't four men hunting this Justice Ninja asshole through the trees. We were a single entity. A flock of ravens, a stampede of bison, a wolf pack, a family. Five souls, one unit. And we'd destroy any threat to the sanctity of that union - especially if they were dumb enough to come at our girl.

Blake charged ahead of us while Kyan whooped excitedly, swinging his baseball bat at his side and promising swift punishment to our quarry once we caught them.

The Acacia Sports Hall loomed ahead of us and Blake slowed just enough for the four of us to enter the building as one.

We forced ourselves to walk as we moved down the long corridor which led towards the locker rooms and Kyan nudged me, pointing out the partially open door to the sports hall itself.

Saint frowned as he looked that way too, seemingly unsure before shrugging one shoulder and indicating for us to check it out.

"Come out, come out, wherever you are!" Blake hollered as he pulled the door wide and we stepped into the hall.

With the lights out, the huge space was dim and shadows hung behind the bleachers but there was no sign of anyone being in here.

We stepped further into the space, glancing between ourselves and as we reached the middle of the sports hall, a prickle rose along my spine, making me whirl back around as I felt the presence of eyes on my skin.

My gaze fell on a hooded figure in a bone white mask just as they threw a canister into the room with us, the shiny, silver tube emitting a strong smelling gas at an alarming rate.

I yelled a string of curses as I ran back towards the double doors and a second canister was tossed in a moment before they were slammed shut.

Saint cursed, yanking his shirt up to cover his mouth and nose as he barked orders at us to do the same and I staggered a step as the gas made my head spin.

Kyan roared a challenge as he ran at the doors like a bull, his shoulder slamming into them and making them rattle, but they didn't give as something clearly held them closed from the outside.

I made it to his side and started throwing my shoulder against the wood in time with him, determined to break out of here before that gas took full effect.

Saint and Blake hurled the canisters away, but even in the huge room, the gas was thick and it seemed to stay low to the ground, the effects of it making me stumble as dizziness pushed into my mind.

"What the fuck is this?" I asked, but my words were so slurred that I wasn't sure any of them could understand me.

I slammed into the door again, but my muscles were losing power, and when I tried to move back to do it another time, my knees buckled and I slumped to the floor.

I turned my head and the room spun so violently that it took me several long seconds to realise the thing I was looking at was Blake's unconscious body.

I fought to stay upright on my knees, but I was losing the battle with my own limbs as they slipped out of control and I slumped to the wooden floor with a groan.

Kyan tried to batter the door down one last time before dropping his bat, the sound of it rolling away echoing in my ears. He fell against the doors before sliding down them and falling onto his back beside me. The gas canister blew the drugged substance right into his face and he coughed as he was overwhelmed by it.

He caught my gaze, the same fear reflected in his pupils as I was sure he could see in mine. With the four of us incapacitated, Tatum was vulnerable back at The Temple. Something we'd all sworn would never happen again.

The Justice Ninja had laid out this trap knowing full well that Saint would see them on the cameras. They must have figured out that he was watching. Knowing we'd have to leave her behind when we hunted them here.

And like a bunch of assholes who believed we were invincible, we'd walked right into it.

I couldn't fight the effects of the gas anymore and my eyes fell closed as a groan escaped my lips which was meant to be a name. But my girl was tougher than anyone I knew. And the last feeling that surged through me as unconsciousness tore me away, was hope. Because I had to hope that she could handle this asshole on her own, otherwise I had no idea what would become of us.

CHAPTER SEVENTEEN

My pulse went haywire as I watched the Night Keepers' location on the app on Saint's phone, all of them at the Acacia Sports Hall. They'd been inside for almost ten minutes and hope filled me over the possibility that they'd finally caught the other Justice Ninja and were currently giving them hell. I just wished I could be there with them to dole out a little justice of my own. But showing my face on campus wasn't worth the risk, so I just had to hope one of them was making a recording for me.

The little dot marking Kyan began to move beyond the hall then started whizzing along down one of the paths faster than someone could easily run. I frowned, coming off of the app and finding my way onto Saint's security cameras, tapping through the feeds from the ones he had set up all across campus. I paused on one showing a golf cart accelerating along the path and a breath got lodged in my throat.

Two masked people were on the cart with Kyan perched in the back seat, his head lolling, eyes shut, hands bound. What the hell were they doing with him??

"No," I gasped, panic igniting in my chest as the cart closed in on the outer gate.

There was only one place beyond there. The parking lot. What if they got him in a vehicle? What if they took him somewhere and hurt him?

I ran for the door as I shoved the gun into my waistband, snatching up Blake's keys and kicking my feet into my sneakers. I grabbed my coat as I went, tugging it on as I sprinted outside, pulling the hood up around my face to try and keep my identity hidden as I stuffed the key into my pocket and felt my tactical knife kissing my palm.

I took strength from that. My dad had taught me all I needed to know to survive any situation to the point where I was almost hunting shadows for some unknown threat. He'd seen the inner warrior in me and encouraged it to thrive. I could do anything if I set my mind to it. And I *would* reach Kyan before the Justice Ninjas did anything to him.

I raced along the path, Saint's phone still locked in my grip as I brought up Monroe's number and hit dial. The call rang and rang and I cursed as no one answered, calling Blake instead. I had to keep my panic from clouding my vision and summoned the strength my training had instilled in me as the call continued to ring.

And then it went dead.

What the hell has happened to them? Why aren't they picking up?

Something seriously fucked up was going on here, but I had no time to try and puzzle it out as I just focused on the task at hand. My husband needed me and I wouldn't let him down.

My pulse thrashed wildly as I accepted I was going this alone. I couldn't stop. I had to get to Kyan.

The CCTV feed was empty, but as I made it beyond Aspen Halls, I saw the golf cart disappearing beyond the gate. I pushed myself to my limits, tearing toward the huge iron gate and finding no guards manning it. I didn't have time to wonder why as I shoved it open and turned right just as the cart rounded into the parking lot far ahead. I ran flat out toward the turning that led beyond the tall bushes to my left, my breaths coming heavily as I took the gun from my waistband and prepared to destroy anyone who stood between me and my Night Keeper. They were fools to believe they could take on my kings and get away with it, but it looked like they didn't know their queen was home.

A car engine revved as I made it to the turning and I stumbled back just in time as a huge Land Rover accelerated out of it. The masked driver didn't seem to see me as I hit the ground on my ass. The vehicle banked hard and sped away from me, picking up pace along the road.

I couldn't hesitate, pushing to my feet with a burst of adrenaline and running into the parking lot, realising I didn't even know what car Blake had. I pressed the button on the key fob and a flashy, dark grey sports car's lights blinked. The thing was an inch off of the ground and souped up to the fucking max. Of course he had to have the world's most impractical, ostentatious car. The door opened like something out of Back to the Future and I dropped into the seat, adjusting it so my feet could reach the pedals as I struggled to get the door closed after me.

When I finally managed it, I hit the on button and the whole dash lit up in an array of colourful lights and gadgets that made the interior look like a damn spaceship.

"For fuck's sake, Blake," I snarled as I turned off the handbrake and slammed my foot to the gas.

The whole thing jerked forward and took off at an alarming pace, kicking up gravel so that it pinged off of the paintwork. I gasped, scrambling to click my seatbelt into place as I got control of the sports car and zoomed out of the parking lot, placing my phone in the cupholder as I followed the tracker on Kyan's phone.

My heart thudded manically as I tore furiously after them, my fingers wrapped tightly around the steering wheel as the engine roared.

The roads were winding as they led through the thick forest and I cursed at how far ahead they were already. But I wasn't going to stop until I had my monster back in my arms.

The two assholes who'd taken him had better be prepared for a fight. Because there was a wolf hunting them in the night. And she was coming for her mate.

CHAPTER EIGHTEEN

The first thing to come back to me was a slight sensation in my toes which slowly spread to the rest of my body as the sorely tempting urge to vomit consumed me, but I found myself unable to even retch.

If I'd been the kind to panic then the fact that I couldn't move might have been enough to make me freak the fuck out. But as I was more inclined towards blind violence, my most pressing thought was about how I was going to make the person responsible for this bullshit bleed.

As I tried to figure out how to make so much as a single finger twitch, the echoing sound of a voice reached me and though my eyes were still closed, I focused all of my attention on listening to it.

"Are you sure about this, Ashlynn?" a guy said from somewhere in front of me and it took me a beat to realise that that was Bait's voice. "He's going to wake up. Shit, he's going to wake up and then he'll beast the fuck out and get free and then he'll fucking kill us."

"He won't hurt me," a girl snapped in reply, her voice closer to me than his, somewhere to my left. "Kyan loves me."

Now I had some serious fucking questions because there was only one girl I loved and she did not have that whiney, nasally voice. In fact, I was almost certain I recognised the person speaking, but my brain was so foggy that it was hard to focus on more than just listening to their words.

"I dunno, man, I dunno," Bait said nervously. "You're a chick. He probably won't beat the shit out of you, but I've been on the receiving end of his fists way too often. I think we should just cut our losses while he's still out of it. I dunno why I let you talk me into this insanity in the first place."

"It's not insanity!" the girl shrieked. "And you'd better not forget that I could have just left you to rot in that school. You should be thanking me for breaking you out-"

"You should be thanking *me* for never giving up your name," he spat back.

"You don't even have a car, *Jeremiah,*" the girl snarked and her words made me realise that we were in fact moving, the hum of an engine underlying their conversation. "And you were more than up for getting back at them under my terms when I laid them out. You always knew this was the plan, so don't try to pussy out on me now or you'll be the one left on the side of the road."

"Jesus fucking Christ, we're going to die," Bait muttered, almost to himself.

"I'm gonna tie you up in your grandma's pantyhose and choke you on the crotch of them," I mumbled, not even really meaning to speak but losing control of my tongue as consciousness drew closer.

Bait shrieked in alarm and the car swerved violently, making the girl curse him. My head crashed into the window beside me as I was thrown by the motion, unable to stop myself from going with it and a moment later a weight settled onto my lap as someone straddled me.

"Shh, shh, baby, I'm here," the girl cooed, her fingers tracing down the side of my cheek as her breath washed over my mouth. "We're together now. Finally. Just like we were always meant to be."

"Is he awake?" Bait demanded.

My eyes were still sealed shut and though more sensation was creeping into my limbs, I couldn't move. I realised my wrists were secured at the base of my spine, my arms crushed behind me where they'd placed me in the car and I cursed them internally.

The girl in my lap tugged a seatbelt over me, buckling it up to make sure I wouldn't get thrown around again before stroking my face once more.

"He's still sleeping," she said after a few moments. "Just concentrate on the road. Once we get to my family's summer estate you can take the car and go anyway. Me and Kyan are overdue some alone time."

"Don't worry, I wasn't planning on sticking around once that psycho wakes up," Bait replied and he would be fucking lucky if he really did manage to escape before I could pay him back for this. But even if he did, we'd hunt him down eventually.

The girl didn't seem to care about him though, her hands touching my face again before the stroke of her hair fell against my shoulder and her lips brushed against my ear.

"Have you been waiting for me, big boy?" she asked and for the first time, my heart lurched as the sound of those words on her lips tossed me back into a memory of her speaking them just like that before. On a night when she'd slipped something into my drink and taken me back to her room.

It was like being back there again, helpless, caught in the confines of my own body and unable to move. But that time I'd managed to fight back. This time I couldn't move anything more than my big toe.

The kiss of cold, sharp metal slid across my collarbone a moment before she used the knife to slit my shirt in half straight down the centre and a grunt escaped me as I tried with all I had to fight my way up out of the dark.

"Do you like that, big boy?" Deepthroat purred as she ran her hands down my chest, stroking her clammy fingers across my muscles before running them down the valley between my abs.

"I'll shove a crocodile egg up your ass and let it hatch," I mumbled, my half asleep ramblings about the best that I could force to pass my lips.

Deepthroat froze for a moment before giggling, grinding her crotch down against my more than flaccid cock as she fingered my waistband. Just the idea of her touching my dick was more than enough to make my stomach writhe.

"I can't believe we're actually free of that fucking place," Bait said suddenly, drawing her attention from me as he followed his own train of thought. "You're unbelievable, Ashlynn. I mean, I think I'd given up hope of ever getting out of there and then you manage to pull this off! How did you even get rid of the guards at the gate?"

"I bribed them," she muttered irritably, like she wished he'd shut the fuck up while I was secretly hoping he'd just go on talking forever and ever and keep her hands from venturing any further south on my body.

"Bullshit," Bait protested. "I tried paying them off and they wouldn't fucking have it. They're all in the Night Keepers' pockets."

"Yes, well," Deepthroat hesitated before sighing. "They didn't want payment in dollars."

"You fucked them?" Bait asked in surprise, but nothing would surprise me about this skanky bitch.

"Ew, no. Don't be gross, Jeremiah. I only sucked their dicks." She leaned in closer to me, her rancid, cock-tainted lips brushing my ear again. "I just closed my eyes and pretended they were you, big boy."

I growled something again, my fingers flexing as I tried to fight with all I had for control of my body. I couldn't let her fucking touch me any more than she already was and even what she'd done so far was enough to make me want to vomit more than the aftereffects of the drug.

With a grunt of effort, I managed to peel my eyelids open and Deepthroat sucked in a breath as she peered down at me from within a curtain of what must have been freshly dyed platinum blonde hair. Her lips were painted in a familiar red shade that I only recognised because my girl often wore it.

"You're awake," she gasped excitedly, leaning down to press her lips to mine and I could only clamp my jaw shut against the invasion as she tried to force her tongue into my mouth.

"Oh, holy fuck, we're dead," Bait whined and I was glad that at least one of them was getting it.

Deepthroat pulled back with a satisfied sigh like that one-sided kiss while I death glared at her had been the answer to all of her dreams.

"Sorry about the knockout gas, big boy," she murmured, her hands roaming over my chest again and making me want to punch her plastic face in. "It was the only way to rescue you from those assholes who were keeping us apart."

"What... the fuck?" I choked out, my tongue sluggish and my words thick.

"You must have been so lonely, waiting for me for so long," she breathed. "Did you get my letters? Did they help to keep you warm at night?"

I just frowned at her, not knowing what the fuck she was talking about and she began tugging on the knotted drawstring at the waist of my sweats as she went on. I hoped to fuck I'd knotted it too tightly for her to undo, but then I thought of the knife she'd used to cut my shirt away and shuddered all over again.

"What?" I hissed.

"I told you in my last one that I'd come for you. That I was done waiting for that whore to take her claws out of you. And now that she's gone, I knew it was time."

My brain was still sluggish and it took me a moment to figure out her ramblings. "You're the stalker?" I asked, realising the truth of it. "What do you want with Tatum? Why were you giving her those letters?"

Deepthroat's nails dug into my flesh, cutting crescents into my skin as she snarled at me. "They weren't for *her*. They were for you. I was warning her off, giving her a chance."

"A chance?" I asked, frowning at her newly blonde hair and wondering why the fuck she'd dyed it that colour. Was it something to do with my girl? My gaze caught on a bit of red bra poking out from beneath her shirt and I was almost certain I recognised it. Had she been stealing Tatum's underwear and...wearing it?

Deepthroat eyed me for a long moment then giggled suddenly, slapping my chest and smearing my own blood against my skin from her fingernails. "You didn't seriously think someone was sending *her* all of those love notes, did you? No wonder you never came to me!"

I looked into her psycho eyes then slid my gaze beyond her to where Bait was driving the car, his nervous gaze darting to us repeatedly in the rear view mirror while he drove.

"Roses are red and violets are blue," Deepthroat breathed, reciting the last letter the stalker had given Tatum. "You need to realise who really owns you, I dressed you in flames and I kissed you goodnight. When will you see what's here in the light? I gave you a chance and you took too much time. Now I'll have to show you that you're really *mine*."

She licked her lips and looked into my eyes and it all clicked together then. The stalker had never been Toby or Bait, or some dude obsessed with my girl. It had been Deepthroat all along. The attacks on Tatum had been designed to scare her away from me. The photographs that had been taken had been almost entirely of Tatum, but the one guy who had been in them with her repeatedly was me. Blake had featured in the ones when we were both working together to get her off, but aside from that there hadn't been any individual photos of her with any of the other guys. We'd even wondered why the stalker hadn't ever snapped a photo of her heading into Monroe's house or even managed to catch them together, and now the answer was so fucking obvious.

Because this bitch had been stalking *me*. And she only went after Tatum to get her away from me. When Tatum wasn't with me, Deepthroat hadn't been anywhere near as interested in her. Fuck, why hadn't we figured this out before?

Blake had even warned me that he thought this rapist whore was still obsessed with me and Saint had urged me to let him send her away for good.

But I'd wanted to watch her suffer and had unwittingly put my family in danger because of it.

"I'm going to fucking destroy you," I snarled, my fingers flexing more as I could feel some small measure of strength returning to my muscles.

Deepthroat slapped me hard enough to wheel my head to one side, before catching my throat in her grip and shoving me back against the headrest with a snarl of fury.

Bait was murmuring prayers from the front seat as he sped up, but I was forced to give my attention to the cunt in my lap as she made me look at her.

"If you haven't realised how much you love me yet then that's okay," she breathed. "Because it'll just be me and you when we get to my family's summer house. And then we'll have all the time in the world for you to realise that you belong with me."

I snarled as she forced another kiss on me and tried to tug my hands out of whatever was tying them behind me. But I still didn't have enough strength in them. It didn't matter though. Because it was coming back to me bit by bit and the moment I could, I was going to snap her scrawny neck. But as her hands travelled down to my waistband again, I got the horrifying sense that I needed to hurry the fuck up with that. Because I had to manage it before she did anything worse than she already had or I knew I'd never get over it.

CHAPTER NINETEEN

I followed the Land Rover, using Saint's phone to guide me as I kept my foot to the gas and tried not to freak the fuck out. Where were they taking him? What did they want with him? Was this somehow connected to his family? Or Troy? These terrifying questions just kept circling in my brain and there was nothing I could do but fight off the urge to panic, pushing the car harder.

I'm coming, Kyan.

I hunted the road ahead of me, but they'd gotten too big of a head start and there was no sign of them.

Just as I made it to an intersection, the dot that marked the location of the Land Rover doubled back onto a road through the trees ahead of me. Holy shit, I could cut them off if I could just get through the woods first. I slowed the car as I spotted a dirt track across the road and weighed my options. There was no sign of it on the map, but it might just pass directly through to the other side. And if it did, I'd make it in front of their vehicle. I knew it was my best chance to catch up to them. But if my instincts were off, it could cost me so much time.

My dad's words echoed in my head, sounding so close for a moment that my heart lurched. *"Always trust your gut, kiddo."*

He had always had complete faith in me. And whenever I'd let my instincts guide me in the past, they hadn't led me astray. Dad had known that. He'd trusted me, so I had to trust myself.

Fuck it.

I slammed my foot to the pedal, speeding across the road, but in my haste I didn't look around and a truck came tearing toward me, blaring its horn. I screamed in fright, giving the car more gas and it took off with a roar, the power of the engine zooming me out of harm's way and down onto the muddy track. *Fuck that was close.*

The car bumped along and a metallic crunching noise said it was not happy with this choice. Fancy ass sports cars which sat a few inches from the ground didn't enjoy dirt tracks apparently. *Sorry, Blake.*

My head was still buzzing from the near collision, but I didn't let up as I forced the vehicle to keep going and drew in a shaky breath. I'd just survived a near certain death by the skin of my teeth. The guys would so not be happy with me right now, but I thought of the bruise that had marred Kyan's chest. That bullet could have ended him when he'd come to rescue me and the fact was, risk came with our territory. We fought to be together even when death was close. For whatever reason, the world was making it damn difficult for us to remain as a unit, but we'd been through too much and were bound too deeply to ever let go of one another. Our enemies needed to realise that ripping us apart was akin to a death sentence. And if they wanted to take us on, then they'd better be ready to face the consequences.

The sunlight was blocked out as the dark trees clustered close, their branches arching overhead. The bottom of the car was so low it kept smacking the ground as I drove through ditches without slowing. The car might not have been happy with the choice, but it was a damn beast and the power in the engine meant it ate up the track despite its lack of suitability for potholes.

I was thrown around in my seat, nearly biting my tongue, but I didn't ease up on the accelerator, watching the little dot that marked my Night Keeper on the GPS, sailing along the road in my direction.

I could make it in time. They were still a way off.

The phone started ringing and my heart lifted with relief as I found Blake calling. I hit the speakerphone, losing sight of the map, but it didn't matter now. There was only one path I could take and it was directly through the forest.

"Tatum?" Blake barked anxiously. "Where are you?"

"I'm following the fucking assholes who took Kyan," I growled. "Are you all right?"

"Fuck, where? What happened? What do you mean someone took him?" he demanded, not answering my question as he sounded like he was running.

"I saw them on the CCTV. They put him in a car and took off out of the main gates so I took chase," I said, wondering why the hell these things always seemed to happen to us. Weren't we due a break?

"What's happening?" Saint demanded in the background. "Give me the phone."

"Where are you, sweetheart?" Blake pressed.

"I'm out near the highway, I took your car," I said just as a loud bang and a screech sounded as the bottom of Blake's car dragged over a rock.

"Are you driving it through a meatgrinder?" he balked.

"Something like that," I breathed as I glimpsed a view of the road on the other side of the trees and my heart lifted. "I've gotta go."

"We're coming. Don't do anything stupid," Blake demanded.

"She can handle herself," Monroe growled.

"Wait for us, siren," Saint commanded.

"Kyan's in trouble," I snarled. "I won't be waiting for anything." I killed the call, tossing the phone back in the cupholder as I checked Kyan's location. They were driving down the road at speed, but I still had the advantage. I was going to get ahead.

"Yes," I hissed, forcing Blake's car to go even faster as mud splashed up around me.

I clenched the steering wheel hard, my heart pounding like it was going to burst right out of my chest.

I'm coming, husband.

I was going to drive right into their path and claim him back from them even if I had to tear the world apart to do it. I didn't know why the fuck they'd taken him, but that didn't matter right now. All that mattered was returning him to my arms where he belonged. We'd figure out what the hell was happening after that.

Adrenaline scorched my veins as the trees parted ahead and Blake's car whined in protest as I made it climb a short, steep hill back onto the road.

I bounced in my seat as the bottom of his car scraped over the tarmac and I slammed my foot on the brakes, coming to a halt in the centre of the road.

I grabbed the gun from my seat, shoved the stupid door up into the air, unclipping my belt and diving out.

The Land Rover was only twenty feet away, tearing toward me, not slowing and my heart stalled entirely as I raised the gun and faced down my enemies.

"Stop!" I cried, but they didn't.

I stared at the driver and my upper lip peeled back as I recognised Bait, that fucking asshole who'd stalked me, who'd terrorised me. My finger twitched against the trigger of the gun, my eyes wide open, my aim true. I took the shot, but the car veered right at the same time, tearing down another track opposite the one I'd exited, climbing a hill up into the trees.

I growled in frustration, racing back to Blake's car and jumping into the seat.

I tugged the door down and started the engine which had decided to turn itself off because apparently the car was on eco mode.

"For the love of fucking god." I got it started up again, the engine roaring as I pumped the gas and took off after the Land Rover, my stomach lurching as I skidded down a muddy bank into the woods and was thrown forward in my seat.

What the hell was Bait thinking? Why would he take Kyan? What did he want with him? Was this to do with me or something else?

Questions kept circling in my brain, but it was impossible to figure out the answers to them and I just needed to concentrate on getting Kyan back.

I clipped my belt into place as the ground levelled out and I didn't slow as I raced after the Land Rover which was fast getting ahead of me, tearing up a steep hill which was going to cause Blake's car serious issues. But even if I had to drive through the River Styx and into the depths of Hades, I'd work out a way to do it. Because no one was taking one of my Night Keepers from me.

Kyan

CHAPTER TWENTY

"Holy shit, she shot at us!" Bait yelled as he slammed his foot down on the accelerator and I twisted in my seat, looking back at my girl as she took chase.

We had a head start on her, but in the brief moment I'd laid my gaze on her, I'd seen that fire in her eyes which I loved so fucking much. They weren't going to outrun her. She was a predator hunting for her prey and her fangs were bared. And I was more than happy to be her damsel in distress. I'd even swoon for her when she saved my ass and happily spend the next few hours thanking her in any and every way she wanted.

One holy asshole of a smirk lit my face as I turned back to look at Deepthroat and her eyes widened as she seemed to finally see the danger in me that she should have been fearing all along. I wasn't the kind of beast you caged. I was the kind who stalked villages in the dead of night and left victims in my wake. I didn't know what fantasy she'd imagined up about me, but I could guarantee she had no true concept of the reality or she would have abandoned this pursuit of me a long time ago.

With every moment that passed, I could feel my strength returning to me and with a grunt of effort, I bucked my hips and managed to knock the bitch off of me, sending her half sprawling into the footwell with a cry.

I only realised my ankles were bound when I tried to aim a kick at her and I cursed as she scrambled back up into the chair beside me, angling her knife towards me.

"If you really believed I loved you, you wouldn't need that," I taunted as Deepthroat tried to push the mess of blonde hair back out of her face. I was guessing she was making some attempt to look like Tatum with that cheap dye job, but she looked more like some basic bitch looking to get fucked by a stranger on a night out than my girl. What my girl had wasn't something you could buy in a bottle and this reject cheerleader never would and never could have a scrap on her.

"I know you do," she snarled. "But I also know that bitch has you under her spell. So until I've fully purged her from your mind, I'm going to have to protect us both from her influence."

The car skidded as the dirt track took a sudden turn and the roar of an engine closing in on us from behind made me swivel in my seat once more, a laugh tearing from my throat as I spotted my girl coming up behind us.

Tatum was smiling like a savage as she chased us down and I wished I had my phone so I could take a photo of her in full psycho mode behind the wheel of Blake's beat up car, looking like an avenging goddess who had made a deal to save the Devil. Fuck I loved that girl.

"Maybe we should just let him out?" Bait yelled as I was thrown into my seatbelt and he accelerated up the track even faster.

"Keep your foot on the gas or you'll be the one getting thrown out!" Deepthroat yelled at him and Bait cursed as he did what she said. It was becoming increasingly clear that she'd been the mastermind behind their Justice Ninja crap, and I was pissed at myself for not suspecting her sooner. But as I always made every effort not to pay attention to her unless I was torturing her, I'd clearly missed the signs.

I was thrown left and right as Bait drove faster and faster, using the off-road capabilities of the Land Rover to put distance between us and my girl, but I knew that wouldn't be enough to stop her. She was a hell hound just like me, and she had the scent of blood in the air.

We sped up a steep incline and gravel crunched beneath the tires as Bait screamed something unintelligible and suddenly my gut swooped, and we were flying through the air.

"Fuck!" I roared as the trees broke apart before us and I was gifted a view of the cloudy sky for several achingly long seconds before the nose of the car tipped down and I was looking straight into a ravine below.

My organs flipped over inside my stomach as the car plummeted over the cliff edge, the wheels just touching down on the steep decline as Bait screamed and Deepthroat yelled while the rocks far below beckoned us into their solid embrace with a promise of death.

We bounced and jolted and we suddenly crashed to a halt as the car smashed into a tree that protruded from the bank.

I slammed into my seatbelt, pain spearing through me where it held me in place as the sound of metal grinding and glass shattering surrounded me. For a moment it seemed like I was caught in the centre of an explosion as Bait's screams disappeared and a beat of silence fell in the wake of the carnage.

I sucked in a painful breath as I lifted my head, my eyes widening at the huge hole in the windscreen right before the driver's seat and my gaze fell on Bait's body crushed and broken at the foot of the ravine far below.

"Shit," I groaned, straining my arms against the restraints holding them behind my back and getting nowhere again.

A pained cry drew my attention to Deepthroat in the footwell as she stirred, seeming to be caught somewhere between consciousness and out of it. She moved a little as she seemed close to waking up and the car whined loudly, shifting against the precarious position it was held in by the tree. My heart leapt as the entire thing slid a few inches to the right.

"Don't move!" I barked, my pulse racing as my gaze moved from Deepthroat's slumped position to the fatal fall that awaited us if this thing overbalanced. And it seemed like we were pretty damn close to it doing that if we weren't careful.

She didn't reply and it looked like she'd passed out. *Thank fuck for that.* Not that it helped me. I was still stuck here, tied up and unable to escape this death trap.

I looked around cautiously, trying to figure out if I had the slightest chance in hell of getting out of this alive, but even that small movement had the metal grinding against the rocks as the car shifted again.

My stomach lurched and I swallowed thickly, useless adrenaline coursing through my veins. I was trapped, tied up and well and truly fucked. And for the first time in my eighteen years on this planet, I had every reason not to want my life to end.

"Fuck," I breathed because I could see my death staring me in the face and this time, it didn't seem like the Grim Reaper was inclined to spare me.

CHAPTER TWENTY ONE

"Kyan!" I screamed, throwing the car door open and running for the edge of the cliff with panic flashing through my skin like lightning. Tears burned my eyes as terror clawed up the inside of my chest. *I can't lose him. He can't be dead.*

"Don't give up on me yet, wife!" His voice came sailing up from beyond the ledge as I skidded to a halt before the steep drop and rocks went tumbling down over it.

Oh thank fuck.

I braced my hands on my knees, drawing in a ragged, desperate breath as I saw the Land Rover nose down, the hood crushed against the trunk of a tree growing out from the side of the cliff. But even as I watched, the whole thing slipped a few inches to the right and panic made my thoughts scatter.

"I'm coming! Just hang on!" I promised, turning back and sprinting to Blake's car, forcing my mind to go to that calm place inside me where I could think clearly. Where I could handle any situation. My father had trained me to manage stress in times like this. I could keep a clear head. I had to. Because I was the only one who could get him to safety.

I tugged the tactical knife from my pocket, crawling into the car and drawing the seatbelt toward me, gathering it up in my hands as I pulled it carefully to tug the entire length out. I couldn't move too fast or it would lock but I was so anxious to get to Kyan, it took everything I had to move slower than I wanted to. As I got the last of it out, I used the blade to cut it at both ends and tossed it out of the car behind me.

I dove into the passenger seat, working to pull the other belt free before cutting that one too then moving to the driver's seat and starting the engine. I drove the car right up to the edge of the cliff, turning on the parking brake and rushing outside.

A metallic groan made my stomach knot and I threw a look over the edge in a panic as the Land Rover shifted further to the right, leaning precariously.

"Tatum!" Kyan shouted. "Did I ever tell you I fucking love you?"

My heart rioted at his words, hating why he was saying them. "You're gonna tell me again when I get you out of there!" I called as I tied the two belts together with a fisherman's knot and tethered one end tight around my waist before tying the other to the towing hitch beneath Blake's car.

Then I gazed down the cliff below as I moved to the very edge of it, the Land Rover slipping once more as the tree trunk started to crack and snap. There was a very real, very desperate fear trying to take control of me, but I wouldn't let it shatter my concentration. Because the moment I panicked, this was over. And if I couldn't get Kyan out, then he was going to die. There was no two ways about it. So I either kept my head or lost one of the most important people to me in the whole world.

Breathe, keep moving and remember everything Dad taught you.

Kyan looked back at me through the rear window and his jaw ticked anxiously, looking like he was fighting against something holding him in place.

"I'm coming," I promised, dropping over the edge and letting the belt slip through my hands as I abseiled down to the side of the car.

The damn seatbelts were only just long enough to reach the vehicle and I thanked any and every god in the sky and devil in the underworld as I fell still, hanging beside it.

Kyan looked at me through the window and shook his head. "If you open the door, the car will tip."

"Then the car will tip," I growled. "But I won't let you go with it."

He nodded, his eyes filled with trust as I opened the door, lowering it gently so it didn't rock the whole vehicle. My gut clenched as a groaning, whining noise sounded, but by some miracle, the car didn't slip again.

I released a slow breath as I dug my feet into the steep hill for purchase and spotted a girl laying in the footwell unconscious. It took me a moment to recognise Deepthroat, her hair now a cheap bottle blonde and my heart stuttered. She was the other Justice Ninja? I guess she fit the bill in ways. She was always hanging around Kyan and had a vendetta against the Night Keepers, but I never imagined she'd be capable of this.

"Never thought I'd have to be rescued like a princess in a tower. Are we going to ride off into the sunset on your horse while fingering me under my dress, baby?" Kyan joked even though his eyes gave away his desperation not to die and I gripped his shirt in my fist as I carefully leaned inside to free him from the car.

"That's the plan, princess, just hold still." I sliced the knife through the seatbelt keeping him in place then cut the zip-tie around his ankles. "Brace yourself on the seat with your feet," I instructed, needing to get his hands free. I wasn't strong enough to carry him out of here if the car fell so he was going to need to use his arms. But we seriously needed to hurry up.

"If I move, the car will slip," he said, his voice rough, his brows pulled tightly together.

I glanced towards the front of the car and the terrifying drop beyond the windshield then shook my head and turned away from it, refusing to fall prey to fear.

"Just go slow," I said determinedly.

He nodded, inching forward and pressing his feet to the seat beneath him as I gripped his shirt so hard my knuckles turned white, praying to any deity who was listening to give me the strength to lift him if the car fell.

A loud snap sounded as the trunk started to give way and I screamed as the whole car lurched away from us to the right and Kyan was thrown that way too. I held onto him, falling into the back seat too which was now almost vertical, my hand going to the zip tie on his wrists and slicing through it. *Keep moving, don't stop. If you freeze, it's over.*

The car continued to slide and jolt and the loud snapping in my ears made me certain we only had seconds to get out.

"Hold onto me," I commanded and Kyan twisted around, wrapping one arm around me while using his other to heave us back up toward the open door above.

The whole vehicle shuddered and we gave up on trying to move slow, scrambling faster to get out. We had seconds to make it, I was sure of it. And any we wasted could equal our deaths.

Sharp nails suddenly gripped onto my leg and I looked down with a gasp of fury, finding Deepthroat holding onto both of us, her eyes wild.

"You can't leave me!" she shrieked. "If I fall, he falls with me." She lunged up, hooking onto Kyan's waist with both arms and he snarled, unable to strike at her without letting go of the edge of the door or me.

The vehicle started falling and Kyan lost his grip on the door as she clambered up his body, sinking her teeth into my arm to try and make me let go. I cried out, the belt around my waist going taut as we fell, the bitch trying to take us to the grave. Deepthroat's gaze locked with mine as she tried to hold onto my man and I saw red, anger scolding my veins.

I threw my fist out with a yell of rage for everything she'd done to him, for what she'd tried to take from him, for the scars she'd left on him. My fist connected with her nose which shattered under the impact and she squealed in horror as Kyan's hand came down on her shoulder, the two of us knocking her off into the car just as it plummeted. The shell of the car dropped around us, the whole world seeming to fall as we were forced to place our faith in the rope I'd made.

Kyan held me tight and we clutched each other with all our strength as the Land Rover tumbled away into the canyon. We were left hanging on the side of the cliff, spinning on the belts, miraculously unharmed.

My back hit the dirt and Kyan's weight crushed me to it, driving the breath from my lungs, but I didn't care. I was half laughing, half crying my relief as he held onto me, one hand moving to grip the belt above my head to support his weight.

Deepthroat's screams were cut off as the car hit the bottom of the ravine with a deafening boom that echoed on for miles into the forest. Birds took flight from the trees, arcing across the sky then silence fell and only our breaths and the wind could be heard in the wake of the carnage.

"Good fucking riddance," Kyan muttered and I had to agree.

"Just don't let go," I warned him, painfully aware that if his grip faltered, there was nothing to stop him from tumbling down there after her.

My heart was thrashing wildly with more adrenaline than I knew what to do with and my muscles shook as I started heaving myself back up the steep incline.

Kyan stayed right with me, his grip tight and his jaw set with determination that promised he wasn't going to die today and I tried to take comfort in that as we climbed.

My foot slipped once and I almost lost my grip on the belt, but as Kyan reached back to grab my wrist, I quickly regained my footing and the two of us hauled our way to the peak together.

We were soon rolling over the ledge at the top of the cliff and I fell on top of Kyan, kissing him as he clutched my face in his hands and growled his gratitude into my mouth. I breathed in his scent of leather and sin, bathing in everything that he was.

"You're my hero, wife." He squeezed my ass to hold me close and I laughed breathlessly as he pushed my hair away from my face, desire rushing out to take the place of the fear in my body. Danger was the hottest kind of aphrodisiac and this boy got me high on it way too often. But damn did I fucking love it.

My cheeks were stained with tears of relief and his face fell serious as he leaned up to kiss them away before his mouth met mine once more, his hand locking around the back of my neck. When my head was spinning from the mixture of his touch and the adrenaline flooding my body, he drew away, his heavenly dark eyes holding me prisoner. "I'm never gonna waste a single day on this earth I have with you, baby," he swore, the oath glittering in the depths of his eyes.

"If death comes knocking on any of our doors again, we'll fight it head on together," I vowed in return.

He smirked, clutching me closer still so I felt his heart drumming powerfully against mine. "With you at my side, I have a feeling the five of us just might live forever."

CHAPTER TWENTY TWO

My head was pounding as we made it back to The Temple and I staggered forward, bracing myself against the wall as I started retching uncontrollably from the effects of the gas that had been used to knock us out. If fate had been a bit kinder, I would have taken half an hour to let my head stop spinning and waited until I could feel all of my limbs properly before attempting to do anything, let alone run across campus, but of course, we were once again headed up shit creek without a paddle and I was going to have to just power through.

"If you're going to vomit, do it quickly," Saint growled as he fumbled the key in the lock for the third time, his motor skills clearly not back to functioning properly yet either.

Monroe grew impatient and tried the handle, finding it unlocked anyway after Tatum had clearly left in a rush. He pushed the door open and the two of them disappeared inside while I was forced to take another moment to try and stop myself from puking. My fingers curled tightly around Kyan's baseball bat which I'd brought back with us from the gym and cursed the people responsible for this beneath my breath.

I was going to fucking end whoever the hell had done this. Their life wouldn't be worth living anymore. They'd rue the motherfucking day.

Just as I managed to force myself upright again, movement at the top of the path which led back towards campus drew my attention and I stilled as a sense of danger prickled along my spine. The trees were blocking my view, but I leaned back until I managed to catch sight of shifting shadows through a gap in the foliage.

There were four men moving down the path, dressed in black and grouped closely together. I could only just see them through the trees, my own position here still hidden, but the strangeness of the way they moved had drawn my focus to them. It was almost like...they were walking in formation.

A breath snagged in my lungs and I darted inside quickly, locking the door, throwing the deadbolt over then securing the two additional bolts that Saint had added when the Justice Ninja had made it clear we needed additional security on this place.

"There's men coming this way," I hissed in answer to the questioning looks both Monroe and Saint were shooting me as I caught them clearly on their way back towards the door.

"What men?" Monroe asked as Saint's gaze sharpened and he nudged past me to lift the blind and look out of the window beside the door.

"How many did you see?" Saint asked in a hushed growl.

"Four," I supplied. And if the way they were moving hadn't been enough of a clue that they didn't belong here, the fact that they were within the locked down perimeter of the school clued me in simply enough.

"I doubt that's even the start of them." Saint dropped the corner of the blind and hurried across the room to close the open one where we'd spotted the word *mine* scrawled across the glass earlier.

"What's going on?" Monroe demanded.

"My father has figured out who rescued his meal ticket. We need to go. Now," Saint replied succinctly.

I didn't bother to waste time asking how he could be sure of that. Saint's dad was a mega asshole of mass proportions and only his son knew the full extent of his psychotic reach. If Saint said it was him then I believed him, no question.

Saint was already at the safe hidden beneath the flagstone, opening it up and pulling out a black bag which I knew was full of cash, two handguns and the last few smoke grenades which Niall had given us.

He looked up to find me and Monroe standing there, unsure what to do with ourselves and snarled like a damn beast.

"Blake, grab the box of vaccinations from the fridge. Nash, put a fucking coat on. We're leaving via the crypt and we won't be coming back, so if there's anything else you need-"

"What about clothes and shit?" Monroe asked as he grabbed a coat from the hook by the door and quickly threw it on.

I already had the silver box which held the stolen vaccines out of the fridge and I grabbed a bottle of water too, pausing for half a second to chug almost the entire thing in hopes of banishing the last effects of that gas from my body.

"My car is already packed with clothes and supplies for all of us," Saint snapped like that was obvious just as I made it back to him. "I also took the liberty of securing Tatum's father's ashes and the letters from her sister down in the crypt."

"What about the necklace she asked me to look after?" Monroe asked, taking a step back, like he was willing to go hunting for it even as we heard a knock at the front door.

Saint pressed a finger to his lips before opening a pocket on the side of the bag of cash he held, revealing the necklace alongside the plaque my mom had given me, Nash's little collection of mementos from his previous life and Kyan's sketchbook. Monroe gaped at him in clear confusion as to how Saint had managed to steal his most prized possessions, but considering our situation he couldn't really fault his methods. I caught a glimpse of the pen and lighter Saint had stolen from me and Kyan oh so long ago too before he zipped the pocket shut again and threw the bag over his shoulder.

My heart surged with love for my brother as we hounded him towards the crypt on silent feet. For someone who claimed not to understand love or sentiments, he'd instantly figured out the few things that meant the most to the people he cared about and had secured them in preparation of this happening. Deep down, Saint Memphis was as soft as butter and he was starting to let it show.

Saint quickly grabbed his laptop and charger from the desk and shoved it into the bag before beckoning for us to follow him as he hurried across the room and another, more forceful knock came at the door. Clearly those assholes were hoping to ambush us by tricking us into opening the door, but if they seriously thought that we were just a normal bunch of high school kids, they were about to get a rude awakening.

We made it into the crypt, closing the door behind us and hurrying down the stairs before crossing through the gym towards the gate that led into the catacombs.

"We're going to have to run like the demons of hell are up our asses," Saint growled and the note of concern in his voice was more than enough to let me know that the men his father had sent after our girl meant business. We couldn't risk them catching any of us.

"Shit, we're never coming back here, are we?" I breathed, casting a look over my shoulder towards The Temple where five broken souls had built a home together, a pang of sadness in my chest.

"Never," Saint agreed and the raw edge to his tone made my heart ache for the little boy who had always dreamed of having somewhere like this. A home to call his own, something he could rely upon and depend upon.

"Home is where your family are," Monroe said in a rough voice, reaching out to place a hand on Saint's shoulder and surprising me as he clearly understood how hard this must have been for our brother too. "And as soon as we catch up to Tatum and Kyan, our family will be together again.

All we're leaving behind is bricks and mortar. The memories come with us. The love too."

Saint actually hesitated in his movements as he got the gate unlocked and the three of us shared a look that spoke of our bond.

"Come on then, brothers," he growled. "Let's go hunt down the rest of our tribe before these assholes do."

I nodded firmly, casting one last, wistful look at the mountain of toilet paper we'd stockpiled as we slipped through the gate and Saint locked it again. In years to come, people would look back on this virus as a time when toilet paper became the nation's treasure. It was sought after like the rarest of gems, hoarded more greedily than gold and in the end, when humanity returned to normal, would anyone ever truly forget the thrill of wiping your ass when you knew there were others who couldn't? That was the legacy this virus would really leave behind.

The gate locked with a solid click just as the sound of the men breaking down the front door reached us. Without another word, we dove into the darkness of the tunnels, the cold wrapping tightly around us and making me glad I had my coat. We ran blind until we turned the first few corners and I kept hold of Monroe's arm to help keep him on the right path as this place was less familiar to him.

Once we could be sure that we wouldn't be seen from the entrance to the tunnels, Saint allowed Monroe to illuminate the flashlight on his phone and we really picked up the pace.

About halfway into the tunnels, Saint paused beside a huge sarcophagus and shoved the lid aside, pulling out another bag which I was guessing contained Tatum's letters, her dad's ashes and no doubt a bunch of other shit we couldn't have left here without.

I couldn't help but be reminded of the night the five of us had been bonded in blood down here. All of us coming together to kill a man. It might have been a fucked up way for us to prove our devotion to our girl, but if I was the spiritual type then I'd have to say that making a sacrifice to her in this place of death seemed pretty fitting to me.

We finally reached the second gate, and my mind was a whirl of fear for Tatum and Kyan as I wondered if she'd managed to catch up to him yet, hating the fact that we were being forced to run in the opposite direction to them now while they needed us. But I had faith in her. She was strong and capable and no doubt she was in the middle of saving our brother right now. I had to believe that or I'd go out of my damn mind.

Saint unlocked the second door, and I exchanged a look with Monroe as he clearly had the murder we'd all committed here on his mind too. It felt like a whole lifetime ago that we'd bonded over a corpse's disposal and yet it was only months in reality. Funny how your entire world could flip on the toss of a coin like that sometimes. And I was really fucking glad it had.

As we made it through the gate, the sound of men shouting in the tunnels echoed down to us and my gut plummeted as I realised they'd found the crypt and were taking chase. I didn't know how the fuck we were supposed to get across campus on foot without being spotted by these mercenaries, but I was really fucking thankful to the Justice Ninja for getting my girl safely off campus exactly when she needed to be.

We raced on and I was glad to find that most of the dizziness that had been clinging to me was passing now, leaving my mind clear to focus on the task of getting us the fuck out of here. The box of vaccines was awkward and heavy to carry and I kept having to shift my grip on it as I ran.

The wind blasted over us from an approaching storm as natural light finally made it into the tunnel ahead and I squinted at the brightness as Monroe flicked his flashlight off and we paused at the exit to the caves down on Sycamore Beach.

I had to fight the urge to hold my breath as we looked out over the sand towards the trees, hunting for any sign that the mercenaries had made it down here. But the catacombs and the connecting caves weren't publicised knowledge, so it looked like luck was on our side and they hadn't figured out where we would exit yet.

The only people in sight were Danny and Mila who were cuddled up on a blanket with a picnic laid out around them, the two of them making out so intensely that I was fairly sure we were about to get a view of them fucking if we stood here much longer.

"They have a golf cart," Monroe pointed out and I looked beyond the two of them towards the pathway where it was parked up.

"Perfect." Saint strode out of the cave, jogging across the sand and drawing Danny and Mila's attention to him as he stepped onto their picnic blanket and cleared his throat loudly. "Give me the keys to that cart," he commanded and Danny frowned.

"What?"

"It's an emergency, dude," I explained, nudging Saint to tell him to stop being a dick, but that wasn't really in his nature. "We can't really get into it, but we're kinda being chased and we need a mode of transport. As a bonus, you can take my crown as king of the school once I'm gone."

"You're leaving?" Danny asked with a frown, getting to his feet and pulling Mila up with him.

"We don't have time for this," Saint snarled, stepping forward aggressively. "We are being hunted by men who will not hesitate to do whatever is necessary to locate us, and our girl is relying on our help. Give us the keys."

"Tatum?" Mila gasped and I felt a little guilty for not letting her know that her bestie was safe once we'd rescued her, but it was a pretty big secret and we couldn't just blindly trust people.

"Yeah," I admitted. "She needs us."

Danny took the key from his pocket and went to offer it to us, but Mila placed a hand over it to stop Saint from taking it.

"If you're being hunted then you can't be seen. You three can hide in the back and we'll drive," she insisted.

"I don't think that's a-" I began, but Saint cut over me.

"She's right. You drive us then. We need to get to the front gates and make sure you avoid the fucking Temple. Don't stop for anything or anyone," he commanded before bending down to grab the corner of their picnic blanket and knocking all of their food and shit off of it onto the beach. "We'll use this to conceal ourselves."

    We all started running after Saint towards the cart and I kept a close eye on the trees in case any of those men appeared. Danny and Mila jumped into the front seats while me, Monroe and Saint quickly lay down in the back of it where luggage was usually loaded before throwing the blanket over us. It wasn't perfect, but at a glance no one would notice us hiding here.

    My shoulders butted against both Saint and Monroe's as the cart started up and Danny drove the thing as fast as it would go as he began to journey through campus.

    As I hid beneath that blanket, my heart raced even faster than it had been while we ran. The light was dim and my breath warmed the space around my face as we waited. Every little noise had me on edge and every time the cart jolted against a bump in the path, I imagined some of those men driving us off the road.

    But the moment never came and though my adrenaline surged like crazy, I never once needed to make use of it.

    We pulled to a stop and Nash threw the blanket off of us as we found ourselves out in the parking lot beyond the gates.

    Saint pulled his car key from his pocket and unlocked the mom mobile as he jumped out of the golf cart, striding away to load his bag into it and climbing into the driver's seat.

    "Thanks, man," I said, turning to Danny and pulling him into a hug.

    Monroe grabbed the other bag and the box of vaccines, thanking them as he jogged away to get into the car too.

    "Where's Tatum?" Mila demanded as I released my friend and looked to her, her dark hair flying about her in the breeze.

    "She chased that ninja prick out of here after they kidnapped Kyan. We're going after them now," I told her. "I'll send her your love, but we won't be coming back."

"I want to see her!" she called after me, but I was already jumping into the back of the car as Saint began to pull away.

Saint hit the button to lower his window as he passed the two of them and called out, "I owe each of you a favour in a future I hope we live to see."

They didn't get a chance to reply to that as he hit the gas and we tore away, leaving them behind with their mouths open in protest and the dust from the rear wheels kicking up over them.

"Take a right. I don't recognise their location, but they're not moving anymore," Monroe instructed at the end of the long driveway and I glanced between the seats to see that he had the tracker app open on his phone. After we'd lost Tatum, Saint had insisted on all of us installing it and I was damn glad he had now.

I took my own phone from my pocket and tried to call both Kyan and Tatum, but neither of them picked up and my anxiety levels rose even higher. What if they needed us? What if we'd lost too much time while getting caught up with our escape?

My body was tight with tension as we raced up road after road, heading much further from the school than I'd expected before turning onto a dirt track. The mom mobile handled it like a pro, bouncing along while Saint's eyes sparkled with a hue of smug that made me think of the sounds my car had been making while Tatum had taken this route too. Yeah, yeah, his soccer mom wagon could get the point for being better off road, but he still looked like a middle aged woman driving it.

We pulled out onto another street then crossed over onto a dirt track again before starting up a steep hill.

"They're just up ahead," Monroe said anxiously and my fists bunched as I prepared myself for a fight just in case.

Saint stopped the car abruptly at the top of the hill and I threw myself out of my door as I spotted my beat up looking sports car parked right in front of us.

I took several running steps towards it before falling still beside Saint and Nash, folding my arms at the sight before me.

Tatum and Kyan seemed to be absolutely fucking fine. He had her pinned to the hood of my car, the two of them kissing with a desperate kind of fervour as her hands fisted in his hair and he drove his cock into her with an animalistic brutality. His pants were around his ankles and hers tossed aside while her panties hadn't even made it off of her, the fabric clearly shoved out of the way to allow for this desperate claiming.

I wanted to be angry at them for making us worry like that when they were clearly alright, but as I looked beyond them to the disturbed ground and the rope made out of seatbelts that dropped over the edge of the ravine, my irritation melted.

I took a step closer to the edge, looking down at the wreck below, my eyebrows arching as I spotted a broken body down there too.

Tatum moaned loudly as she came and Kyan cursed, thrusting into her harder and harder until he was coming too, his hand knotting in her hair as he kissed her through it, driving his tongue into her mouth. It was pretty fucking hot actually. And I couldn't help but feel my own cock stirring as I watched them.

They finally broke their kiss, the two of them sweaty and panting as Tatum turned those big blues on us sheepishly, looking the picture of innocence even while she clearly still had Kyan's dick buried inside of her.

"Looking good, princess, I guess you didn't need help from the cavalry after all," Nash commented as she bit her lip.

"Is there a point in the day when the two of you ever feel is suitable to refrain from fucking?" Saint asked, seeming more pissed over the fact that they hadn't bothered to let us know they were alright before giving in to their need to screw each other.

"Nope," Kyan replied with a grin as he slowly withdrew from her, pulling his pants up again. I noticed his shirt was split apart right down the middle and frowned as he tugged the remains of it off. "Especially not when I was just kidnapped by my stalker and molested again."

"*Your* stalker?" I asked in confusion.

"Deepthroat," Tatum supplied with a sneer and I moved closer to her, wanting to check for myself that she really was okay. "It was always her. She was after Kyan. The only reason I was involved was because she wanted me out of the way."

Saint's eyes flared with understanding as he grasped that idea and he turned away suddenly, throwing his fist into a tree as he began cursing himself for not seeing that sooner, the darkness in him rising to the surface at his perceived failure.

Kyan and Monroe followed, reasoning with him as I approached our girl, stroking my fingers through her golden hair and massaging her scalp gently to make up for Kyan's roughness with her.

She sighed as she reached out to trail her fingers along my jaw and my gaze fell to her parted thighs, sticky with Kyan's cum, the sight of it weirdly arousing.

"So, little old you saved the big bad mobster's grandson?" I teased and she smiled.

"Sure did. I'm not the only one who gets rescued in this story."

I kissed her sweetly, wanting so much to deepen it, but I knew there was no time for that, so I just laid my hand against her racing heart, pleased to have her close.

"We need to get out of here," Saint snapped suddenly, clearly deciding that now wasn't the time for him to lose his shit when there were armed men still hunting for us close by. "I have a safe house we can use. Nash, change the plates."

I looked around to find him tossing a set of fake plates and a screwdriver at Monroe before approaching us with a small hand towel which he'd gotten from fuck knew where.

Saint nudged me aside and I reluctantly let him so that he could clean Tatum up, the gentle, adoring way of his movements making me smile.

Fucking softie. I was gonna have to buy him a teddy bear for him to cuddle at night if he kept this shit up.

Monroe explained the situation to Kyan and Tatum while I moved over to take a look at the damage Tatum had done to my baby. My one of a kind, limited edition car was well and truly fucked. There were no two ways about it. She was scratched, dented, a wing mirror was gone. The seatbelts were currently in use as a rope hanging over the cliff and Kyan had fucked Tatum so hard on the hood that he'd managed to dent that too.

"You owe me a new car, asshole," I said to Kyan, heading over to the mom mobile as the others got in and climbing into the back with him and our girl.

She sat between us, taking each of our hands in hers as Saint began to back us up and turn the car around.

"Well, I just called in a cleaner to get rid of it for you - don't want anyone thinking you had anything to do with the crash that killed Bait and Deepthroat, so let's call it even," he suggested with a smirk, though there was something in his eyes that said he'd just been through something pretty fucked up.

"Do you wanna tell us about it?" I asked him and everyone else in the car was silent as we waited for his reply. Tatum's eyes lingered on him, her need to comfort him clear, but that wasn't Kyan's way.

Eventually, Kyan just shook his head. "Naw. The bitch is dead now. But let's just say I've got a whole new level of respect for my uncle Niall and his preference for killing rapists."

"Did she-" Tatum began in horror but Kyan cut her off with a shake of his head.

"You rescued me before she could do any more than paw at me, baby. But I needed to get my dick in my girl the second I could to wipe the feeling of her hands from my skin." He laughed as he leaned down to press a kiss to her neck and though I was certain all of us could tell the light-hearted attitude was forced, we didn't push him on it.

The main thing was that Tatum had made it there in time to rescue him, we'd escaped the men Saint's father had sent after us and we were currently heading somewhere safe. Beyond that, I had no fucking idea what we'd do. But the point was that we were all together. That was what really counted.

CHAPTER TWENTY THREE

I shed my coat as we made it back to the main road so I was just in my matching pale blue sweatpants and top, the heat of Kyan and Blake's bodies either side of me making me extra toastie. I threaded my fingers between Kyan's as I thought about Deepthroat and all she'd done to him. She'd died in fear and that was something. But it would have been nice to have her alone somewhere for a while before handing her over to death.

I would never forgive the scar she'd left on him, and I hoped her end would help him move past the trauma of her attempted rape. He never spoke about it, but sometimes I wished he would. Sometimes I thought I should try harder to draw the depths of his pain out of him too. Because often bleeding was the only way to heal over the past. So I decided once the dust had settled on this day, I'd try again.

"So where's the safe house?" I asked Saint.

"It's – fuck, what now?" Saint snarled, his eyes glaring at something in the rear view mirror.

I wheeled around in my seat to look out the back window and saw a red

Mercedes tearing up behind us, flashing their lights.

"That's Danny's car," Blake said in surprise as he beeped the horn and Saint accelerated harder.

"Saint, pull over," I instructed as I spotted Mila in the seat beside Danny, but Saint kept driving.

"Dude," Blake growled. "It could be important."

"The only important things in the world are in this car," Saint said matter of factly, but as sweet as that was, he still needed to stop.

"*Saint*," I demanded.

"I'm with the boss man, let's not risk it," Kyan said, yawning and leaning back against his seat like he was planning a nap.

"There's no risk, it's our friends," I growled as Danny flashed his lights again and Mila waved anxiously at us. "Stop the car."

"Just pull over, man," Nash insisted and Saint growled in irritation.

I leaned forward between the seats, gripping Saint's bicep and speaking in his ear. "Please."

His jaw pulsed then he indicated off the road and parked up, putting the hazard lights on even though no one was around but us and our friends.

Blake opened the door and I hurried out after him as Danny pulled his car up behind us, excitement rushing through me. Mila spilled out of the vehicle, running toward us and my heart leapt as she wrapped her arms around me.

"I was so worried, girl," she said, holding me tight. "Where the fuck have you been?"

"It's a long story," I said as I hugged her firmly, stepping back as she continued to grip my hands. Hell I'd missed her. And I hated that we had to go. That our world was so messed up and there was no place for normality in it anymore.

"Yeah, and we can't tell it. We don't have long, we've gotta go," Blake said seriously as Danny stepped out of the car and walked toward us with his brow furrowed in concern.

"Are you in trouble?" Mila asked in a whisper, squeezing my hands and I nodded, not wanting to lie to her. But there were so many things I couldn't say for her own safety.

"We're in deep shit," I admitted. "But we're gonna be okay. Saint has a plan."

"Will you come back?" she asked anxiously.

I shared a sad look with Blake then shook my head. "I don't think so," I sighed.

Mila's eyes swam with tears as she gazed at me and I felt my own eyes blurring too. She'd been a good friend to me. The only true girl friend I'd ever really had. And there was at least one thing I could do for her.

"Wait here," I said, turning and jogging back to the car. I popped the trunk and Saint cursed colourfully as I opened the silver box holding the vaccines, taking out a bottle of the precious liquid and a couple of syringes, drawing up the doses they'd need. I locked the box up tight again, shutting the trunk and running back to Mila.

"Here." I pressed them into her palm and she looked down at the syringes in confusion.

"What's this?" she asked as Blake ran a hand through his hair, throwing an anxious glance back at Saint's car.

"It's a vaccine. A working vaccine for the Hades Virus," I whispered, though there wasn't a soul around for miles to hear us. I just knew how valuable this knowledge was.

Mila's large eyes rounded as she looked over at Danny in excitement then back to me. "Are you serious? Where the hell did you get this, girl?"

"Like she said, it's a long story," Blake interjected.

"I can give it to you guys, roll up your sleeves," I said. Dad had trained me to do it years ago and it was pretty simple.

Mila went first, allowing me to inject her with the vaccine and it warmed my heart to know how much she trusted me. When I'd given it to Danny too, Blake slid an arm around my waist and drew me a step back. "This sucks balls, but we've really gotta go. There's some assholes out looking for us."

"No shit," Danny breathed, glancing over his shoulder nervously.

A decision flashed in Mila's eyes and she grabbed my hand as Blake tried to draw me away. "What can we do to help you?"

"I have an idea," Saint's cutting voice filled the air and I nearly jumped out of my skin as he appeared beside me like a damn ghost.

He held out a bunch of phones to Mila. "Take these. Turn them on and make a call on at least one of them. Then drive south for a hundred miles before tossing them."

Mila gaped at him. "Is someone tracking you?" she asked in shock.

"Obviously," Saint said coolly and I elbowed him in the ribs.

"This is some action movie shit, I swear," Danny said, looking kind of excited by that.

"We'll do it," Mila announced.

"Are you sure you don't mind?" I asked, my throat tight with emotion at leaving her, unsure when I'd ever see her again. But hopefully there was a time beyond this when I could. I just didn't know how we'd get there yet.

"Of course not," Mila said firmly and I pulled her into another hug as my heart beat painfully against my ribs.

"Thank you," I breathed.

"Love you, girl. Call me as soon as you can, okay?" she begged and I nodded as I released her, swallowing down the sharp lump in my throat.

I hugged Danny too then Blake embraced them before they got back into their car, waving to us as they turned around and headed in the opposite direction. A heavy breath left me as they disappeared and I really hoped I'd seen them again soon.

"Well, I suppose the stop was worthwhile after all, but we should have discussed giving out that vaccine, Tatum," Saint said sharply, taking my hand and guiding me back to the car at a fierce pace.

"They deserve to have one," I said fiercely. "And I don't have to ask your permission. They're my friends. And the only reason that vaccine was created was because of what I went through in that lab. I at least want some good things to come from me suffering through all of that."

"I will not allow rash decisions to put any of us at risk," Saint said, not backing down one bit despite my more than valid points.

"Well unfortunately for you, you're not a dictator, so it's not up to you all of the time," I said curtly and he wheeled me around, shoving me up against the side of his car and glaring down at me, making my heart judder violently.

"I will protect you at all costs, siren. I will protect *all* of us, and if being a dictator is what it takes to do that, I am more than suitable for the role."

"Come on, bro, chill. We need to get on the road," Blake called from the other side of the car.

Nash stepped out, walking around to us and posturing at Saint. "Watch how you place your hands on her, Memphis."

"I didn't ask for your opinion, Nash." Saint didn't take his eyes from mine, his muscles bulging against his t-shirt as he kept me in his grip.

As much as I appreciated Monroe looking out for me, I didn't need to be saved from Saint. We had our own language, and this was a part of it.

I slid my hand up his chest, resting it against his furiously thumping heart and his throat bobbed. "I make my own decisions, Saint. And my decisions will always be for the good of the people I love. That includes my friends. So you can be pissed at me all you like, but I'm not sorry."

"We don't have time for this," Monroe snarled, reaching out to grip Saint's arm, but he jerked his shoulder to shrug him off.

"Foolishness breeds dangerous situations," Saint breathed. "I'll punish you the next time you don't consult me on a decision like that." He pulled away and I rolled my eyes, grabbing the back door and climbing in over Kyan who was fast asleep.

Everyone else got back into the car and Saint took off down the road, the silence between us ringing in my head.

"I'm gonna butter the inside of your asshole and let a gopher go to town on it," Kyan murmured in his sleep and I broke a laugh as Blake and Nash cracked up too.

Saint glanced at Kyan in the rear view mirror, his eyes glittering with mirth and the tension instantly disbanded between us all.

Blake threaded his fingers through mine and I leaned against him, breathing in his masculine scent as the miles sailed away beneath the tires.

With Mila and Danny laying a false trail, I hoped it meant we were lost to the wind now and no one would be able to track us down. I didn't know where we were going, but it was part of a plan designed by Saint Memphis. So I wasn't worried. Because if anyone could outsmart the man hunting us, it was the one who'd been made in his image.

Blake breathed softly as he slept beside me and Kyan mumbled nonsense in my ear. I loved the closeness of them, but I was craving the touch of my other Night Keepers too. Ever since I'd gotten out of that lab, I swear I'd formed a seriously possessive streak for them all. I just wanted to be touching them at all times to reassure myself they weren't going anywhere. And after coming so close to losing Kyan, I guessed the feeling had intensified.

I unclipped my belt and climbed through the front seats, dropping smoothly onto Nash's lap.

"No," Saint objected. "Back in your seat, it's not safe up here if we crash."

I wound my arms around Monroe's neck and he hugged me against him. "There's literally no one else on the roads because of lockdown, we're not gonna crash," I argued.

"A deer could run out of the forest," Saint growled.

"He's right, princess. It's not safe," Monroe murmured, looking saddened to say it as he held me close. I thought of what had happened to his family with a pang of guilt knotting up my chest. *Shit.*

"Oh Nash, I-" I started.

"I need a piss!" Blake suddenly announced.

"Here." Saint popped the glove compartment, taking out an empty bottle and tossing it at him.

"Nah, I want a wild piss. I'm not going in a bottle," Blake insisted.

"It's the bottle or nothing," Saint said calmly.

"Just pull over for two minutes," Monroe said, his fingers skating up my spine and I shivered.

"I actually need to pee too and I'm definitely not going to try and go in a bottle," I said with a light laugh.

Saint took a Shewee from the glove compartment in answer to that and my jaw dropped as he tossed the bright pink plastic thing onto my lap.

"No!" I laughed, tossing it over my shoulder into the back. "Pull over."

Saint's jaw ticked, but he indicated off of the road, pulling up beside the forest and I jumped out of the car. Nash followed and Blake took off into the trees ahead of us.

"Watch her," Saint ordered Monroe and I rolled my eyes as Nash took my hand, but I didn't pull it free.

"You can watch me pee if you like, but it might be a bit of a weird bonding experience." I threaded my fingers with Monroe's and he chuckled as I led him into the woods.

"I'll take any bonding experience with you after being without you for so damn long," he murmured in my ear and I bit my lip as we picked up the pace.

When we were far enough off the road, I slipped away from him behind a large pine and squatted down to pee. The forest was eerily quiet, but the silence was soon broken by the sound of Blake singing Genie in a Bottle by Christina Aguilera somewhere nearby in the trees, drawing a smile onto my face. Damn, that was old school.

When I was done, I headed around the tree to find Monroe and he grabbed hold of me, pinning me back against the huge trunk. He pressed his finger to his lips and I grinned as he tilted his head down to kiss me. His tongue moved in fierce, claiming strokes against mine as his hands pressed either side of me on the tree. He smelled like the forest, like a feral man who lived off the land, chopped wood naked and built fires-

"Fuck, I've missed you," he said heavily, cutting through my fantasy as I fisted my hand in his shirt to keep him close. "I've missed all of our plotting too." He smirked as I scraped my fingers through his dark blonde hair. I was totally fucking smitten with him. I didn't know if it was the intensity in his eyes or that godly mouth that was getting me so hot right now, but I knew I couldn't allow myself the temptation when we should be running for the hills. So I drew back and put a little space between us to keep my libido from diving into the driver's seat. That bitch had been working overtime since I'd been back with my tribe.

"Well how about we start plotting together again? Let's sneak up on Blake and scare the crap out of him," I said conspiratorially.

He dipped his head, nipping at my neck with a deep laugh that set my pulse racing. "I'm game if you are."

Monroe's eyes glinted as he stepped back and we snuck in the direction Blake's voice was coming from. He was swinging his hips as he peed, his singing getting louder as we closed in behind him, making a quiet approach. Nash stepped on a branch and a loud crack made Blake wheel around and my jaw dropped at the sight of his dick jammed into the pink plastic Shewee.

"Dude, what the fuck?" Monroe burst out laughing and Blake sniggered.

"Thought I'd give it a go. You only live once, right?" He reached down and tugged on it to get it off, but it didn't move. His gaze fell to it as he tugged again and a yelp of pain left him. "Oh fuck."

"Hilarious," Nash deadpanned as I fell apart laughing. "Come on, we need to go."

"It's not a joke, it's fucking stuck." Blake tugged on it again and swallowed another noise of pain when it didn't move.

"Give it here." Monroe strode forward, knocking his hand away and grabbing hold of it, tugging sharply. Blake jerked forward with a panicked gasp, shoving Monroe in the chest.

"Ow, motherfucker!" he barked.

I clutched my side as more laughter ripped through me, unable to stop.

"*Tate*," Blake growled. "Stop laughing. Your laugh is sexy and that's just gonna make me hard which will only make things worse!"

I literally couldn't, especially when Nash grabbed the Shewee again and yanked hard. Blake cursed then tried to punch him in the dick in retaliation, but Monroe was too fast as he danced out of the way.

"Just hold still, I got some kid's dick out of his zipper once, I can totally do this," Monroe insisted, bending forward to get a closer look and Blake stilled as I worked to smother my laughter. Monroe was eye to eye with the pee hole as he examined it and he slid his hand along the base as he tried to loosen its grip on Blake's dick.

"Ah! That's my balls," Blake growled, smacking Monroe around the ear, making his head dip and the Shewee poked him in the eye.

"Argh!" Monroe reared away from him in horror. "That fucking piss hole went in my eye!"

"How's that my fault?" Blake roared.

"Because you stuck a Shewee on your fucking dick!" Monroe shouted back and another laugh tumbled from my chest but I hurried forward to help Blake, gently taking hold of the Shewee and turning it.

"No twisting," Blake gasped in horror, slapping my hands away and taking hold of the plastic as he tried to work it free.

"For the love of all that is holy," Saint's voice made my heart leap and I turned around, finding him standing behind me, shaking his head at Blake. He reached into his pocket, taking out a tube of lube and walking forward to squirt it into the Shewee.

"Why are you walking around with that in your pocket?" Nash asked in confusion and I was pretty damn curious myself.

"I don't need to explain myself to you," Saint said simply as he slid the

Shewee off of Blake's cock then handed it to him. "You will clean this and return it to Tatum."

"I'm like, totally good living my life without that in it actually," I said, but Saint just fixed Blake with a glare for a long moment then turned, tossing a bottle of hand sanitiser at me before walking back toward the car. "Hurry up, no more games."

Blake tucked his dick away as I sanitised my hands then passed the bottle to Monroe who rubbed it everywhere. Including around his eye, making me stifle a snort which he shot me a glare for.

"Well, it could have been worse anyway," Blake commented.

"How could it have been worse? Your dick poked me in the eye," Monroe growled.

"It wasn't my dick, it was the Shewee. Jeez, dramatic much?"

Monroe dove forward and punched him in the ribs then the two of them started wrestling – hopefully not in the puddle of piss.

Blake caught my hand as I tried to make a run for the car to tell Kyan what had happened and I ended up in the middle of them, being tickled and poked until all of us were laughing, the sound carrying up into the trees. The two of them turned on me pretty damn quickly, crushing me between them so my back was to Blake's chest and my front was to Monroe's.

"Hmm, what are we gonna do with this little bird we've got trapped in our cage?" Blake taunted, his mouth brushing my ear and making me want to lean into his touch. But I wasn't going to be easy prey.

"Maybe you should both close your eyes and I'll give you payment to get out of your trap," I suggested huskily and Nash grinned as he shut his eyes.

I glanced over my shoulder to find Blake had done the same then drew Monroe closer to me by the back of his neck, grinding my ass into Blake's crotch, his dick growing solid against me, so I guessed the Shewee hadn't done any permanent damage. If it had, I'd have stomped on the bitch.

"I'm waiting for your mouth on mine," I purred and Monroe leaned forward as I reeled him in then I ducked aside at the last moment and looked up to find his mouth colliding with Blake's.

"Dammit, Cinders," Blake growled, the two of them lurching away from one another and I laughed my victory, sprinting back toward the car as I escaped.

"Oh no you don't!" Nash cried, racing after me just as Saint started blasting the horn impatiently.

I laughed as I tore through the trees, their footfalls crashing along behind me as they tried to catch up. The car came into view and Saint glared at me from the driver's seat with his brows pulling together. He looked like a father whose patience was wearing thin and we were definitely the kids grinding his gears. Maybe he'd like me to call him Daddy the next time he spanked me.

"Open the door!" I called to him as his eyes moved to Nash and Blake chasing behind me.

Saint opened it immediately and I dove into his lap while he slammed it shut and two heavy bodies collided with the car, rocking the whole thing.

"I'm gonna soak these bagels in gasoline, slide 'em onto your dick and light it up like a bonfire," Kyan slurred as I twisted around in Saint's lap, adrenaline bouncing through my limbs.

"Thanks." I grinned at Saint, then went to climb through to the back seat but he held on tighter, refusing to let me go.

"I think I'm owed a better thank you than that." He smirked like the dark god he was as Monroe and Blake fought to get into the back seat of the car.

"Well, what would you like? A gift basket full of torture devices? Or sex toys?" I asked sweetly and he snared my mouth in a fierce kiss, his tongue hot and demanding against mine.

When he released me, I was flushed and grinning.

"You can send the gift basket too," he taunted.

Blake scrambled his way into the back seat with the desperation of a starving dog as he kicked Monroe away, his need to win sparking in his green eyes. Monroe grabbed the back of his waistband, trying to haul him out by it, but Blake held on to Kyan's arm and his sweatpants went flying down his legs to his ankles, baring his ass while Monroe fell down in the mud.

I fell apart laughing as I rolled into the passenger seat and clipped my belt in place. "Shotgun," I sang and Saint smirked at me satisfactorily.

"Goddammit, Blake," Monroe growled as Blake was forced to wiggle into the middle seat while he tugged up his pants and Monroe climbed in beside him, shutting the door hard. Saint started up the engine, taking off down the road, gathering speed by the second.

I frowned at the phone sitting in a holder on the dashboard in confusion. "I thought you gave all the phones to Mila and Danny."

"I have spares for us all," Saint said simply.

"Does it have the same passcode?" I swiped it up, unlocking it with the code he'd given me earlier and his lips twitched like he wanted to reprimand me for that, but couldn't think of a suitable reason to do it.

And I sure as hell wasn't scared of his punishments anymore. I headed onto his music app, finding it stocked with all kinds of classical songs and a bunch of playlists for just white noise. Not exactly a barrel of fun. I started to build a more Tatum friendly playlist as I connected it to the Bluetooth in the car.

"Don't play anything by that Bieber boy," Saint warned. "I will not have my ears assaulted."

"Oh come on, Saint, you could use the culture lesson," I teased.

"I assure you, I do not need any such thing," he said lightly.

I hadn't been planning on playing some Bieber, but now the temptation was just too high to ignore. I chose Anyone and grabbed Saint's hand as he thrust it towards the off button on the dash. I ran my thumb along the centre of his palm and the tension in his shoulders eased as he met my gaze for a moment.

"Love you," I mouthed, meaning it from the depths of my heart - even if I did say it five percent to distract him.

His features softened and he brought my hand to his mouth, stamping his lips to the back of it before resting both of our hands on his thigh.

I actually really liked this song and when Blake started singing along, I joined in, soaking in the sweet feeling of freedom I felt with being on this endless road that stretched away into the distance with the four loves of my life.

It wasn't much longer before Hemlock City came into view on the horizon and we drove through the suburbs which were deathly quiet. I'd heard the lockdown was especially strict in higher populated areas and it made me sad to think of all those people stuck in their homes, fearing what was going to happen. It was uncomfortable knowing we carried a box of vaccines that could protect some of them. But we had to be sensible about what we did with them. We couldn't just hand them all out, we needed to find someone who would know how to make more from this batch. *Humanely*. Without using me as a damn blood farm.

We drove through the city, the high rises casting long shadows across the ground as the sun began to set, the place eerie with how quiet it was. The few people we did see wore masks and were hurrying along like they were desperate to get to their location. It made me miss normality more than ever. And I hoped we found a way back it. Because seeing the effect of the Hades Virus first-hand like this made me worry there wasn't going to be a normal to go back to.

Saint eventually drove around the back of a boarded up old building and came to a stop in front of a set of metal shutters. They rattled as they opened and I frowned in surprise as Saint drove down into an empty underground parking lot, the camera aimed down at us apparently recognising the plates on the car.

"What is this place?" I asked excitedly.

"A safe house," Saint replied simply.

"I know that," I said in exasperation. It was like getting blood out of a stone with him sometimes and I swear he took a sick kind of pleasure in that. "But I expected some fancy ass manor house or something."

"That would be far too obvious," Saint replied, offering me a dark smile before parking and stepping out of the car. *Cunning bastard.* Why did that get me so hot?

I headed out too and Monroe and Blake followed, clustering close to me protectively and I wondered if they even realised that they were doing it. It was cute as shit though and I certainly wasn't complaining.

"So, who's gonna wake the beast?" Blake questioned, tossing a smirk at Kyan who was still fast asleep in the car.

My heart squeezed at how peaceful he looked and I wondered if Deepthroat's death had helped him sleep better. He wasn't even protecting his crotch anymore like he always did. Though I couldn't imagine he'd wake up like Sleeping Beauty even if I gave him true love's kiss.

Saint hammered his fist on the window Kyan was resting his head against and he jerked awake, reaching for a knife that wasn't there before lunging ferally at the glass.

"We're here," Saint announced calmly. "Wipe the drool from the upholstery and grab a bag." He popped the trunk and we all moved forward to grab the arsenal of shit he had stashed there.

"Jesus, Saint," I breathed. "How long have you been planning this?"

"Six to eight weeks," he said simply. "But I have always had a bag packed in this car for any eventuality since long before you came into our lives, siren."

I had to admire his forethought as I shouldered a pack, but Kyan plucked it straight off my back and shouldered it himself.

"Um, I'm not a mouse. I can carry some shit," I said, trying to swipe a bag from Nash but he lifted it above my head so I couldn't.

"No, you're a queen. We live to serve," Saint replied, walking away and the others smirked at me like his words said it all.

It was totally eighteenth century of them but also damn sweet, so I just counted my lucky stars for these guys and headed after them with a blush lining my cheeks. Apparently chivalry wasn't dead, even if the four of them were more than happy to ravish and corrupt me. I guess I got the best of both worlds.

We all followed Saint to a set of stairs that wound up into the building. When we stepped through a door on the first level, the faint scent of popcorn reached my nose and my brows arched as Saint flicked on a light, illuminating the abandoned foyer of a movie theatre with well-worn red carpet on the floor. There were still posters on the walls for movies dating back five years and old movie tickets scattered around the place. Saint kept walking, moving through a door marked for staff only and I shot a grin at Kyan beside me as he blinked groggily at our surroundings.

Upstairs was a large room with a window that overlooked one of the movie theatres, the huge screen layered with dust. The room looked freshly renovated with two double beds and a suite of leather furniture. There was a small kitchenette with a fridge which was humming softly, telling me it was on and as Saint popped it open, I spotted large bottles of water stocking it, as well as a row of vodka bottles and beers. He placed the vaccines inside, nestling them at the back.

"How long have you had this place?" Nash asked, his eyes wide with surprise as he gazed around it, taking in the huge TV on the wall and the brand new Xbox set up beneath it.

"Long enough," Saint said as he took food from one of the bags, carefully arranging it in the fridge.

As he put some things in the cupboards, I noticed they were already stocked with tinned food. It was a freaking cache.

"You're best to assume Saint can produce million dollar bills outta his asshole whenever he likes," Kyan said. "It'll stop your jaw from dropping every time he does something ridiculous."

"Being prepared isn't ridiculous," Saint clipped.

"Being overprepared is," Kyan tossed back. "Not that I'm complaining, brother. You've saved our asses here. And not for the first time."

A smile danced around Saint's lips and I felt one pulling at my own. He really was amazing.

Kyan tugged the fridge open, grabbing a beer and popping the cap off with his teeth.

"I'll take one of those," Blake called and Monroe headed over to grab one too, passing me a bottle before claiming his own.

We all sat down on the couch with a beer in hand as Saint finished putting everything away. None of us bothered to offer him any help because he'd absolutely refuse it. Saint was in his OCD zone, and he needed to put things in whatever order made sense to him. I'd learned that a long time ago.

"To being on the run." Blake held up his beer and we all clinked our bottles to his before taking a sip.

I snuggled back into my seat between Kyan and Monroe and Kyan slung an arm around me. "So what now?" Kyan asked. "Are we gonna have to ride out the apocalypse here?" He sounded kinda hopeful as he eyed his baseball bat which sat among the luggage Saint was unpacking.

"Obviously not," Saint said, but he didn't elaborate beyond that.

"Sooo, what *is* the plan?" I pressed.

Saint paused in his work, looking over at us then sighed, rising to his feet and heading to the fridge. He poured himself a measure of a vodka in a crystal fucking glass then moved to perch on the arm of the chair opposite us. "We have three urgent tasks we need to accomplish. The first, is to ensure Tatum is never found by my father and remains safe within our care at all times." The boys all nodded and my heart filled up with sunlight. "The second task is finding a virologist of good nature to give those vaccines to. Someone who has the skill to produce more of the vaccine in a timely manner whilst maintaining the secrecy of their source. And finally, the third task is eradicating my father and all that he stands for, including the sadistic club which he is connected to and likely involved in the running of. We will expose him and his friends for what they are and ensure they are so thoroughly crushed beneath our heels that they may never rise from the dust again."

"Wait, your Dad is a member of Royaume D'élite?" I gasped, looking to the others. "How long have you known that?"

"I didn't think we did," Blake balked.

"You did not, but I have spent quite some time working over the facts available to us and it seems like a strong assumption to make," Saint said, brushing a speck of lint from his knee. "Of course, there is room for error in that estimation and believe me when I say, I do not like taking gambles on vague assessments without damning proof. But in these circumstances, I have deemed it necessary to make a…" He trailed off, his features contorting.

"Guess?" Nash finished for him with a smirk and Saint winced like the word repulsed him.

"Yes, if you must call it that," Saint muttered in disgust. "I understand if the four of you would like to debate the validity of such a decision and perhaps take a vote on whether this assumption can be given enough credit to assume it is true for the purposes of our actions from here on out."

I shared glances with the others, everyone's face saying the exact same thing, so I voiced it for us all. "We trust you." The guys nodded and Saint glanced between us, satisfaction filling his gaze.

"Good." He pushed to his feet, walking over to the pile of bags. He took out a collection of new phones and tossed us one each then took his own from his pocket. "You will not contact each other through anything other than this app." He showed us his screen, pointing out the red and white icon and I picked up my phone, finding the same one on it.

"It will take you to a secure server where we can speak through an online chatroom. You can make calls through it too, each of your contact information is stored here under animal codenames. Kyan you're Koala, Tatum you're Tigress, Nash is Nighthawk and Blake you're Baboon."

"Baboon?" Blake blurted. "Why do I get Baboon? Why not Bear or Boa Constrictor or something cool?"

"Because you are a baboon," Saint said smoothly and I snorted a laugh.

"Kyan's hardly a koala," Blake complained.

"On the contrary, koalas are quite vicious," Saint reasoned.

"And cuddly," I added, pinching Kyan's cheek and he smiled wickedly.

"So what are you?" Monroe asked Saint curiously.

"He's Squid!" Kyan announced and I laughed wildly, nodding my agreement.

Saint's eyes turned to deadliest nightshade. "I am not Squid. I'm Scorpion."

"You're totally Squid," Blake said, bouncing in his seat. "Especially if I'm Baboon."

"I am not Squid," Saint hissed venomously. "End of discussion." He turned sharply away, heading back to the bags to finish unpacking the food and I caught Kyan's eye as the two of us cracked up.

"Squid's in a mood," Nash muttered and I roared a laugh, making Saint swear furiously.

I settled back into my seat and we all watched some trashy TV for a while. I started to get a little sleepy as I sat there, a yawn pulling at my mouth. It had been a seriously long day, but despite all the changes and the danger we were still in, I felt kinda happy. Just being with my Night Keepers like this was a blessing after so long in that horrid lab. I was free now, back where I'd ached to be for weeks, imagining how good it would feel to be with them again. And it was better than my imagination had even come close to conjuring.

I got out of my seat as I drained the last of my beer, heading over to toss the bottle in the trash. Then I fell down on the nearest bed and pretended to make a snow angel with my arms and legs. "Whose bed is whose?"

Saint stood up, gazing down at me hungrily and my pulse went haywire. "This place was initially created for just me, Blake and Kyan. Clearly, I would have had this bed and they would have shared."

"*Clearly*," Kyan mocked from across the room. "But now shit's changed so I'll be having a marital bed with my wife and you'll all have to share the other bed or fight over the couch."

"If you start that wife shit up again, Kyan Roscoe, I will make you sleep down in the car," Saint warned.

"But she *is* my wife," Kyan said cockily. "No two ways about it."

"That doesn't serve you extra privileges," Saint hissed and Nash and Blake looked ready to go to war to ensure that was true.

I pushed myself up to sit and glared at Kyan. "I belong to every guy in this room equally. Don't be a dick."

Kyan nodded. "I know. I get that. And I'm *allowing* that." He smiled mockingly, tossing me a wink and I knew he was just winding them up, but they really didn't like it so I didn't encourage him.

"You're not allowing anything," Monroe snarled.

"Aren't I?" Kyan teased, knocking an elbow into his ribs.

"No, you're not," Saint growled. "End of discussion. I'm going to take a shower." He finished putting the food away and headed through a door to what I guessed was a bathroom, taking one of the bags with him.

Kyan grabbed one of the Xbox controls, kicking his feet up on the coffee table and started a game. Monroe grabbed a control too, but I was surprised when Blake didn't join in, instead getting up and heading to the fridge. He spent a minute rummaging before taking out a bottle of water and walking over to me, leaning down to press a kiss to my forehead. "I'm gonna go explore. I'll see you in a bit."

"Want an adventure buddy?" I asked, jumping up and he hesitated for a moment, glancing over at Monroe and Kyan with a faint frown.

"Blake?" I breathed, clutching his arm. "What's up?"

He slapped on a bright smile and shook his head. "Nothing, come on then." He took my hand and led me to the exit.

"You look after her," Monroe warned and Blake gave him a serious nod.

"With my life, Nash."

A shiver ran through me at their protective ways. I could sure as shit look after myself, but them going all alpha wolf pack on me was seriously hot sometimes. I'd just needed to remind them that I was an alpha of my own variety too, with teeth and claws as sharp as theirs.

We headed downstairs into the foyer and Blake twirled me toward him, holding my waist with one hand. "Listen, Cinders. I've gotta go do something. Will you cover for me?"

"What?" I frowned. "What do you mean?"

He let go of me, sliding a hand into his pocket and taking out a syringe and a little vial of vaccine. "My dad lives twenty minutes from here. I'll be back before anyone even notices. I have to do this, Tate. I lost my mom to the fucking Hades Virus, I won't lose-"

"I know," I breathed, squeezing his arm. "I understand. I'd have done the same for my family."

He reached out to tuck a lock of hair behind my ear, a heavy breath leaving him. "I know the others would understand too, but Saint…"

"I'm sure he'd get it," I urged, but he frowned like he wasn't certain of that.

"He loves the five of us, but that means he'll do anything to keep us safe here too. To fit into his little plan." He reached into his coat pocket, taking out a car key.

"Did you lift that from him?" I asked in surprise, kinda impressed.

"Nah, I grabbed it when we were leaving Everlake. He made us all spares." He smirked. "So…will you cover for me, sweetheart?"

"No," I said simply and his face fell as I stepped toward him. "Because I'm coming with you. We'll face Saint's wrath together when we get back. But none of us should be alone right now and we can watch each other's asses out there."

Blake hesitated, but a wild spark of excitement entered his eyes. He loved breaking rules, especially when they involved a little thrill.

"I mean, I would love for you to meet Dad," he said, grabbing my hand. "If you want to?"

"Of course I fucking do," I said with a grin. "Let's go."

We started running, stifling our laughter like kids as we headed downstairs into the parking lot and jumped into Saint's car. Blake took off driving and the shutters opened as the camera read our numberplate and let us out. We turned out of the alley and sailed along the streets, winding into the heart of the weirdly quiet, glitzy city.

The moonlight glinted and sparkled on the glass buildings towering up either side of us, making it seem like we were in a fairy tale world that belonged entirely to us. Anyone who had somewhere else to go had run away from the cities months ago, and everyone else was clearly locked up tight inside their apartments, hoping to survive this pandemic.

It wasn't long before we pulled up outside a huge, shiny building which was the tallest one on this street. Blake popped the glove compartment, taking out a handgun and stuffing it into his waistband before dropping his coat to cover it. After everything we'd faced, I wasn't gonna question that decision even a little.

I followed him out of the car and he took my hand as he led me up to the impressive glass doors at the top of a set of grey stone steps. Blake typed in a code on a panel beside the doors and they slid silently open, allowing us into a huge atrium with silver and white tiles on the floor. The reception desk stood empty and my skin prickled at the overbearing silence as we made our way to the elevator. Inside, Blake had to type in another code on the elevator panel and we shot upwards, climbing through the building at speed.

"Is he gonna lose his shit when he sees you?" I asked and Blake shook his head.

"Nah, he's cool. He'll probably just be pissed I'm missing football practise even when I hand him the gold dust in my pocket."

I chuckled and he grinned at me, seeming a little anxious as the elevator rose higher. "I've never brought a girl home before," he muttered, his eyes scouring my face as his expression filled with pride.

My heart began to race. "Well, I hope he likes me."

"Oh," he breathed as he stared at me and I frowned.

"What?" I questioned and he shifted from one foot to the other.

"Nothing," he muttered. "He'll love you. I'll make sure of it." His complete dedication to me made my chest expand, and I hoped I wasn't gonna blow this. I'd never been taken home to meet anyone's parents and I really wanted to make a good impression. After all the craziness in our lives, it was weird to be doing something so normal. It had my stomach fluttering as if we were about to charge into battle. Why was this so freaking scary?

I couldn't help but think of my own dad and how he'd never gotten to meet Blake properly or any of my other boys apart from Monroe. But he'd wanted this for me, even if it didn't look the way he'd probably pictured. He'd hoped for me to find a man who'd dive into a sea of hellfire to protect me. It just turned out that I'd found four of them. Shit, I was lucky. If Dad was out there somewhere, I hoped he knew that.

Blake took his phone from his pocket, tapping out a message on the app Saint had installed on it. "I suppose we better let Squid know we're alright."

"Yeah, I suppose there's not much he can do now anyway until we get back," I agreed and he sent the message direct to Saint before tucking his phone away. "So is this building where you grew up?"

"Nah, it's my dad's apartment. He used to just use it for parties or the odd night when he had to stay in the city because a meeting with some sponsors ran late or whatever, but mostly it just sat empty. He moved in here permanently after we lost Mom. My home is a place in the country. It's real nice, but I guess it reminds him of her too much." He frowned sadly and I frowned back, feeling his pain.

The elevator doors slid open and we stepped into an incredible penthouse apartment which sprawled out in every direction towards floor length windows. The place screamed man cave with no-fuss furnishings that were in a range of neutral tones, broken up by the maroon colours of the Redwood Rattlesnakes memorabilia that was everywhere I looked. There was a wall dividing the lounge from the kitchen and it was covered in photos of Blake with his mom and dad, plus him with the Rattlesnakes team. Surrounding all the photos were little shelves filled with sparkling trophies. It was like a shrine to Blake and all of his achievements and I freaking loved it.

"Hey, Dad!" Blake called and a man leapt out of the kitchen, his eyes wide in surprise.

"Blake?" he gasped. He was as tall and as broad as his son, his hair had a sprinkling of salt and pepper and his eyes were warm and inviting. They were blue instead of green like Blake's, but apart from that he was the image of his son. He wore a Rattlesnakes jersey and some expensive looking sweatpants, the scent of lasagne carrying after him from the kitchen.

"My boy," he breathed in shock, striding forward and wrapping Blake in a fierce hug, clapping him on the back. "What the hell are you doing here? And who's this?" He stepped back, taking me in and I smiled, offering my hand.

"I'm Tatum," I said.

"Tatum…why does that sound familiar?" he chuckled, looking to Blake.

"She's my girl," Blake said, lifting his chin and his father grabbed my hand, pulling me into his chest and hugging me tight.

I stilled in his hold for a moment, overwhelmed by being embraced by a man who wasn't my father yet who felt so paternal to me instantly that it brought tears to my eyes. I drove them back as he released me, his mouth splitting into a wide grin.

"I'm Cooper, nice to meet you Tatum. Shit, I haven't had a hug in too damn long. I think I just broke a lot of fucking rules, but you've been isolating at Everlake, so it's all good right?" He scored his hand down the back of his neck.

"Yeah, it's all good, Dad," Blake promised. "But um, can I chat to you quick in private?" He threw me a furtive glance and I frowned.

Cooper's brows raised in surprise then he nodded, letting Blake lead him out of the kitchen and I stood there like an awkward duck at a chicken party, unsure what to do with myself.

The low din of Blake's voice carried to me but I couldn't catch what he was saying. I had the creeping feeling it was me they were discussing though. Why else leave the damn kitchen?

"Rivers!?" Cooper suddenly roared and I swear the whole apartment shook.

Oh fuck.

Heavy footsteps pounded back this way and Cooper reappeared looking nothing like the friendly-faced Dad he'd just been as his features contorted with fury.

"Dad!" Blake barked as he came running up behind him. "Listen to me, she's not-"

"I'll tell you what she is," Cooper snarled, pointing a finger at me and I took a step away, my heart racing as the tension in the room made my body go into high alert. "She's the daughter of the man who killed your mother."

"Mr Bowman," I gasped in horror. "Please, if I can just explain-"

"Explain?" he spat, taking an aggressive step toward me as Blake caught his arm, yanking him back. "Explain what? That my son just brought a rat into my home?"

Blake threw himself in front of his dad, shoving him back and squaring his shoulders at him. "Don't you talk about her like that!"

"She's the terrorist's kid!" Cooper snapped, his eyes full of grief and pain as they landed on me. To him, I was his enemy. I represented the pain of losing his wife. But he didn't know the truth and we had to explain it.

"He wasn't a terrorist," I snarled, my blood heating at that word. "He was set up. And then he was murdered to hide the truth."

Cooper gaped at me in disbelief then gripped Blake's arm, trying to draw him away from me like I was diseased.

Blake shook him off, stepping back to join my side. "She's telling the truth. I was there when he died, Dad."

"What?" Cooper blurted, his face twisting as he tried to grapple with that information.

"Everything the people on the news are saying about her dad is a lie," Blake said passionately and my heart swelled at hearing him defend my father like that.

"Bullshit," Cooper growled. "What the hell are you doing? I told you to ruin her life, not make a fucking girlfriend out of her, Blake. How could you do this to your own mother?"

"Listen to me!" Blake roared as my mind spun with that information. Blake's dad had asked him to ruin my life? I should have hated him for that. But when I looked at his face, all I saw was a broken man in need of vengeance for his wife's death. He'd needed someone to blame just like Blake had needed someone to blame. They were cut from the same cloth, and how I could hate him for that when I'd forgiven his son for far worse?

"Donovan Rivers was innocent," Blake said fiercely. "I am telling the truth. Do you think I'd say that to you if I had even a scrap of doubt in my mind? I saw him die. I saw the men who set him up. I know the truth and this is it. Tatum's father is not responsible for what happened to Mom." He grabbed hold of Cooper's shoulders, shaking him and his dad's brow furrowed as he finally listened to what his son was saying.

"You're sure?" he rasped, his eyes shining with unshed tears.

"Yes, Dad," Blake promised. "Please don't blame Tatum. She's everything to me. I love her with my whole fucking heart and I can't bear you looking at her like she wronged us. I learned my lesson the hard way. I hurt her, and I'll never forgive myself for it. Please don't hate her just because you need someone to hate."

My chest filled with warmth at his words and I kept my mouth shut as I waited for his dad to respond, figuring me talking right now wouldn't help. I wasn't the one he was going to trust on this.

"Son, this is..." Cooper shook his head, looking overwhelmed. "This is a lot to process."

"But you believe us, right?" Blake demanded. "Because it's real. I wouldn't lie to you. Trust me, being here at all is a risk, but-"

"What have you got yourself wrapped up in?" Cooper asked in concern and a breath left me over the fact that he really seemed to be accepting this.

"Nothing I can't handle," Blake swore. "Just trust me."

Cooper looked to me, his cheeks flushing a little guiltily. "I'm sorry I…"

"It's fine," I said quickly. "Blake told me about his mom and I'm so sorry about what you both of you had to go through. I know that pain." Grief flickered inside me for a moment and I swallowed the ball rising in my throat.

His brows knitted together as he nodded, his eyes full of sadness. "So why are you both here?" he asked, seeming to sense there was something else going on.

Blake slid a hand into his pocket, taking out the vial and the syringe in a little fridge pack he'd put them in. "We're immune."

Cooper looked to the syringe then up at his son and released a nervous laugh. "Yeah and I'm the Queen of England. Look, I feel bad about shouting at your girl, do you want dinner? I just heated up Christina's lasagne. She's the best housekeeper I ever had, still brings me a delivery of meals every week even though I told her she doesn't have to take the risk of going out during this shitshow of a pandemic. I'd be dead without her, son, I swear." He looked to me apologetically and I smiled back, sensing more of the tension falling away between us.

"Dad, you're not listening," Blake said, hurrying after him into the kitchen and I followed too. "This is a vaccine to the Hades Virus."

"Come off it, Blake, it isn't funny," Cooper said seriously and I lunged forward, grabbing his arm.

He turned back to me with a questioning frown and I gave him an intent look, rolling up my sleeve and pointing at the rose-shaped mark on my arm.

"Mr Bowman," I begged.

"Cooper," he corrected. "I feel old when kids call me Mr Bowman. Do me this kindness."

"Cooper then," I said with a smile and he smiled back. "This scar is from the vaccine I received when I was a teenager. My dad was a part of the team who made it. And long story short, it worked and now we have this one and it's for you. It'll protect you."

Cooper stalled, looking at my expression as he hunted for the joke before turning to his son in confusion. "Blake? What's going on?"

"It's like she said, and I'm sorry but we can't say more than that," Blake murmured with a frown that said it hurt him to keep this from his dad. But it was the only way. We couldn't risk telling him anything about Troy Memphis. He probably already knew too much.

"Are you in trouble?" Cooper gave Blake a serious look. "Because if you are, I can help you. I've got money, resources. Whatever you need-"

"I just need you to take this," Blake said, holding the vaccine out to him. "That's it."

Cooper looked anxious, glancing between us then his eyes settled on me.

"I can give it to you, if you like?" I offered. "My dad taught me how."

Cooper's throat bobbed as Blake gave him an intent look that urged him to trust me. And I really wanted him to. He was the father of a man I loved. I wanted him to know his son was with a good person, who would do anything to protect him and his family.

"I...perhaps you'll have dinner with me first?" Cooper asked, glancing over his shoulder at the oven. "It's been a hell of a long time since I've had any company for a meal and we can discuss all of this at length. Figure out your options."

"Dad, this isn't something you can help with," Blake said firmly. "I'm sorry, I know this must seem insane, but I really need you to trust me. Both of us."

Cooper rubbed a hand over his stubble, contemplating his son's words as he examined the vial in his hand. "You show up here with no warning with the daughter of the man being blamed for this entire pandemic. I love you, but as your father it's not in my nature to let you walk away from here without me helping you."

"We're okay," Blake said. "I swear it. We know what we're doing."

"But I don't," Cooper said in exasperation. "You're supposed to be locked down in Everlake Prep where you're safe."

"I am safe," Blake said, his tone rising as he lost his patience. "I'm vaccinated. The Hades Virus can't touch me."

"So you want me to just take this and let you walk out of here?" Cooper asked in desperation and I could see him giving into the idea even as he struggled against accepting it.

"Cooper," I said gently. "Your son is one of the bravest, smartest, most capable men I know. And what we've got to do relies on him walking away from here and you forgetting you ever saw us. No one can know about that vaccine. Not yet. But Blake risked coming here to protect you. So please..." I stepped forward, my heart in my throat. "*Please* let him do that."

Cooper swallowed hard, taking a deep breath then after a moment that seemed to last an eternity, he nodded. "Okay," he rasped. "I will, I'll...I'll do that for you Blake. I'll trust you."

"Thank you," Blake sighed, pressing his hand to his dad's shoulder.

Cooper handed the vaccine to me, his mouth twitching at the corner. "Don't jab me too hard, alright? Never did like needles." He chuckled nervously, still seeming unsure of this situation and I could see the strength it was taking for him to place his faith in us. In me. I guessed the whole world had been destroying the Rivers name for months, so I could hardly be surprised that he was suspicious of me even after Blake had sworn my dad was innocent.

I drew up the vaccine while he rolled his left sleeve back and sat down on a stool in front of a wide, grey marble island. I carefully pushed the needle into the top of his arm and slowly depressed the plunger until the liquid was all gone.

"That's it," I announced, taking the syringe away and tossing it into the trash while Blake placed the vial back in the fridge pack.

"That's it?" he echoed, rubbing his arm. "I'm immune?"

"It takes a couple of weeks to kick in fully," I said. At least that was what Saint had said and seeing as he'd spent the past weeks studying virology day and night, I had to assume he was right. "And we don't know how effective it is, but…all evidence says it's pretty damn good." I thought of how I'd coughed right in Jonas's face and he hadn't gotten sick. If that wasn't a test of its effectiveness, I didn't know what was.

Cooper pulled his sleeve down and Blake hugged him, a sigh of relief leaving him. "Stay for dinner," he insisted and Blake looked to me, seeming unsure.

"Of course we will," I said with a firm nod. Saint would likely shit a brick, but what the hell? Cooper looked starved for company and I wanted to know more about the man who had raised Blake.

We sat down for dinner at a table overlooking the incredible view of the city and ate our way through what was definitely the best vegetable lasagne I'd ever had in my life. The time slipped away and I learned all about how Blake had grown up in some huge manor on the outskirts of the city which Cooper and his wife had bought when they were only in their twenties. He'd become a seriously successful entrepreneur straight out of college, and it looked like money had just snowballed his way ever since. But when he spoke about Blake's mom, all I saw was grief in his eyes and I knew that he'd trade every dime he had to get her back. He and Blake both would have. And after I opened up a little about the loss of my dad and Jess, Cooper announced I was officially part of his family. Admittedly that was after several glasses of wine, but still. It seemed like he finally liked me. And I liked him a helluva lot too.

We headed to the elevator as the hour got late and we couldn't stay any longer.

"We've really gotta go Dad. I'm sorry," Blake sighed. "But hopefully when we do what we've got to do, it won't be long before this vaccine gets out to everyone in the world."

A deep crease formed on Cooper's brow as Blake pulled away and my heart tugged at having to leave him here alone.

"Your mom would be real proud of you," Cooper said, clutching Blake's hand in his as his throat bobbed with emotion.

"Her son is going to help save the world," I added with a grin and Blake ran his fingers through his hair with a low laugh, but I didn't miss the way his eyes darted to his Dad in hopes of approval.

Cooper's gaze swirled with some thought I couldn't read. "Wait here a sec, I've got something for you both." He headed away through a door and Blake gave me a tight smile.

"I hate leaving him here," he muttered. "He's lonely."

"The sooner we get the vaccines to someone who can help create more of them, the sooner he'll be able to get back to his life," I said with a sad look.

"Yeah," Blake said. "I just wish he had Mom."

I wrapped my arms around him and he rested his chin on my head as the weight of our grief washed between us for a moment. We'd both lost parents, we both knew the taste of that pain all too well. And I also knew there was nothing I could say that would ease it. It was what it was. And at least we had each other to lean on in moments like this.

Cooper returned with a little wooden box in his hand, his cheeks a touch red. "When I met Blake's mom, we were juniors in high school," he spoke to me. "I was the captain of the football team, and a complete asshole might I add." He laughed at himself and a smile tugged at my lips. "Anyway, Blake's mom was the quiet type, dedicated to her studies. She wanted to be a lawyer and there was nothing in the world that was gonna stop her. I spent so much time playing football that I basically started failing a bunch of my core studies. So the principal insisted I get a tutor. My dad was gonna hire in some top of the range, Harvard guy and I refused because, well I was an asshole remember?"

"*Dad*," Blake groaned like he'd heard this story a thousand times and was already embarrassed by it.

"I told the principal I wanted Blake's mom to tutor me," he said. "I'd been crushing on her for weeks after she'd done this speech on drunk driving in an assembly. She was so…passionate." His eyes glittered for a moment, but then his pain was masked and he went on. "I'd been looking for a way to get close to her for ages and I finally had a chance to do it. And the principal convinced my dad it was a good idea after showing him the straight As she got in everything. Anyway, I wooed her heart out and the rest is history. But when we went steady together, I bought these as a gesture of my devotion." He opened the box and my gaze fell on two bracelets. One was a delicate silver band with a glittering row of pink sapphires arrange in the shape of half a heart. The other, was a black leather band with a silver crest that had the other half of the heart engraved on it.

"We weren't whole without each other. That's how it felt," Cooper rasped and emotion welled in my chest. "I can see you two feel the same way about each other. I'd recognise that look anywhere. And it would make me so damn happy if you'd take these." He looked to Blake. "Mom asked me to give them to you when you fell in love."

"Dad, I can't," Blake croaked. "They're yours."

"No," Cooper said seriously, moving forward to press the box into his son's hand. "They're yours. It's what she wanted. And your mother always got her way." He smiled sadly and a tear dripped down his cheek. He crushed Blake into another fierce hug and suddenly grabbed my hand, pulling me into it too.

"You look after each other," Cooper growled. "Don't make me regret letting you kids walk out of here."

"We won't," I promised. "Thank you."

He let us go and I was surprised by how much it hurt to say goodbye. We headed back to the elevator and Cooper waved as the doors closed.

"He's great," I told Blake, smiling at him and finding him staring down at the bracelets in the box.

"Yeah," he murmured. "He is." He took the silver one out and offered it to me, making my throat tight at the weight of the offering.

"Are you sure?" I breathed. It was his mom's, and it felt like accepting a piece of his soul by wearing it.

"I've never been more sure of anything or anyone," he told me in a deep tone that brought heat to my cheeks.

I held out my wrist and he clasped it in place then I did the same for him with the other one while he pushed the box into his pocket.

"It's beautiful." I admired the jewellery on my wrist, the sapphires catching the light. I grabbed his shirt in my hand, tugging him close. "I love you, Blake. You're my dark soldier, and I see the depths of your scars. I'll spend forever trying to heal the marks left on your heart."

He lifted me up, crushing me to the back wall of the elevator as his mouth came down on mine. I tasted the weight of his love, his pain, his desire. He was my beautiful, broken, golden boy and I needed to draw the sunlight out from the darkness in him and see it shine from his eyes once more.

I clutched his shoulders and ran my fingers up into his hair, his hands sliding under my shirt at the back, so I felt the burning heat of his flesh against mine. His mouth broke away from my lips and his teeth grazed up my cheek to my ear, leaving a hungry fire in its wake. His cock firmed between my legs and he ground into me so it created friction against my clit and I gasped in pleasure.

"I need to be inside you," he growled and a shiver rolled smoothly down my spine.

"Then get inside me," I half demanded, half laughed as the elevator doors opened on the bottom floor. He carried me through the atrium and out to the car, ripping the door open and laying me down on the back seat. He climbed in on top of me, tugging the door closed and kissing me hard. I kicked my shoes off and lifted my hips so he could pull my sweatpants off with my panties then he tugged his own pants down to free his hard length.

"Are you wet enough for me, sweetheart?" he asked, dropping his hand between my thighs and I gasped and bucked my hips as he circled his knuckles in my soaking heat. "Fuck yes."

He clutched my hips, lining himself up with me and thrusting inside me without mercy, making my whole body arch beneath him.

He smeared his knuckles over my mouth, his eyes lighting up at the sight. "Taste how much you want me, Cinders." I sucked his fingers greedily, my hips rocking to meet his fervent thrusts as he claimed me. I was enraptured by him, getting off on how filthy and good this felt as he tore my shirt up and over my head and smirked villainously at me as he yanked my bra up to gain access to my breasts too.

"God you're fucking perfect," he growled, my body tightening around his as he lowered his mouth and sucked my nipple, dragging his teeth across it in the most amazing way.

I clamped my thighs around his waist as he rolled his hips, rubbing some delicious place inside me and drawing a wild moan from my lips. I was so hot for him that I was coming apart already, especially as he moved his body over mine just right to build up friction against my clit. He slowed his pace a little until every thrust became full of intention to deliver me pleasure and his hands held me down as he worked his magic between my thighs.

"Fuck, *Blake*," I groaned, tipping my head back as he worked my body as well as if it was his own. He knew exactly how to touch me to make me shudder and convulse, and as he circled his hips once more, I came hard, pleasure crashing through me and making my muscles bunch and flex.

Blake cursed. "You're so fucking tight." He groaned like a beast, burying his face in my neck as he found his climax and I felt him filling me up.

We were hot and sweaty and unable to catch our breath as we lay there in a tangled mess which made me impossibly happy. His light was back and so was mine. And it didn't feel like anything in the world could bring us down from this high.

Blake started laughing as he lifted his head to look at me and I laughed too. "Saint's gonna freak when we get back," he said and I gripped his jaw, tilting my head up to steal another kiss which was all bite and passion.

"I'll handle Saint," I purred.

He grinned and I felt him hardening inside me again already. "Well in that case, Cinders, how about round two?"

Saint

CHAPTER TWENTY FOUR

I was staring out of the window in the movie theatre bar as the headlights of my car came into view at the far end of the street and my racing heart finally slowed. I hadn't felt concern like that since we'd rescued Tatum from my father's hold and spending the night experiencing it once more was a perfectly exquisite kind of torture.

My headphones poured O Fortuna by Carl Orff into my ears and I let the intensity of the music permeate my soul, grounding me, reminding me that I was flesh and bone, brutal and breakable and oh so very insignificant when it came down to it. And insignificant was precisely how I felt right now, so it fit me well.

The lack of sleep had me feeling a little edgy, but if I was being totally honest with myself, I knew that these strange surroundings had more than a little to do with my discomfort too. It had been a long time since I'd been thrown into the turmoil and upheaval of a sudden relocation like this and if I was being totally honest with myself, I could admit that it was causing my demons to come out and play.

Between worrying about Tatum and Blake, I'd spent much of the evening tangled in a web of memories I wished I didn't have to face. But I knew from experience that the only way to banish them to the corners of my mind again was to face them, look at them, experience them and relive them. It wasn't pleasant. But I had little choice.

So instead of spending the night surrounded by the family I'd built myself, I spent it reliving my nightmares and facing the worst of my father. Sometimes when I got caught up in memories of him punishing me as a child, I found it hard to breathe. Found it hard to even think straight. And I ended up wondering if I was just deluding myself about being able to take him on and win. Yes, he'd crafted me in his image but he'd weakened me too. And some part of me couldn't help but fear that once all was said and done, I'd find myself alone and at his mercy, locked in the boiler room with no water again, sweat rolling down my spine and hallucinations making me believe I was being cooked alive in an oven just ready for him to devour.

My hands shook the smallest amount as I dragged myself out of that shit show of a memory and I fisted my fingers to make them stop. I refused to be brought to heel by memories of a bully who flexed his power above me to intimidate me. I wasn't a child anymore. And I wouldn't allow him to ever put me in that kind of position again.

I watched the headlights move along the street in silence, my music centring me as I waited while they pulled into the underground parking lot and I allowed myself a moment to just feel relief over their return before the anger in my soul consumed me once more.

I pulled my headphones from my ears and stood slowly, having had no sleep while I worried about Tatum and Blake and I moved out of the bar, glancing at the brief messages they'd sent to reassure me of their location. But it didn't matter. If they'd wished to visit Blake's father, we should have discussed it as a group. The fact that they'd chosen to sneak off instead spoke volumes about their trust in me, and the lack of it didn't sit comfortably with me at all.

I opened and closed the door to the bar, making sure my new phone was set to loud in case the camera in the parking lot detected anyone getting too close to our hideout and the motion sensors sent me an alert. I wouldn't be caught out while punishing them. No one would get the drop on us while I had something to do with it.

The stairs which led back down to the old movie theatre were shrouded in darkness and in my black sweats and hoodie, there was no chance of anyone seeing me in the shadows as I descended them silently. I moved across the foyer like a wraith and headed up to the apartment to lay in wait for them there.

Just as I slipped inside the dark space, Tatum's laughter sent a mixture of rage and relief crashing through my chest as she and Blake came up the stairs a beat behind me. They made it to the door and I watched from my position hidden in the dark as Monroe was roused from his sleep on the couch.

I'd chosen not to inform Nash and Kyan of Blake and Tatum's absence after giving it some consideration. We had no other car here and they'd told me quite plainly where they were when they'd messaged me. I didn't like it. But the others had already fallen asleep, exhausted after such a trying day and with us having no way to be able to chase after them, it seemed pointless to wake them up and worry them.

Nash swiped a hand down his face as he got to his feet and moved towards the door, the dim green light from the emergency exit sign above him illuminating the broad slope of his bare back as he walked.

The door burst open and Blake threw his arms around Monroe's neck, leaping up to wind his legs around him too while hollering, "Honey, I'm home!" at the top of his lungs.

Tatum laughed as Monroe stumbled back a step beneath his weight and Blake placed a dramatic kiss on his forehead before leaping down again and bounding away to where Kyan was sleeping on one of the double beds.

"Where the fuck have you two been?" Nash asked in a voice scratchy from sleep as Tatum stepped close and pressed a kiss to his lips.

"We went and gave my dad a vaccine," Blake announced excitedly, a broad smile on his face as he bounced like a puppy on the edge of Kyan's bed.

"You'd better lube up if you wanna smuggle that eggplant out of here without anyone seeing," Kyan muttered nonsensically, still not waking despite the ruckus.

"You snuck out?" Monroe asked with a frown, looking over his shoulder at Blake. "That could have been dangerous. Why didn't you just tell the rest of us you wanted to go?"

"Saint," Blake replied with a shrug like him not trusting me to understand how important it would be to him to get his father vaccinated was no big deal. And I had to admit that stung.

I didn't move though, still hidden in the shadows while Tatum sighed and reached out to slide a hand inside Monroe's boxers. "It didn't seem worth the drama of an argument with him," she replied. "You know how he gets."

If Monroe had any further protests to that, he didn't voice them, his cock clearly taking control of the decision making for him as he leaned down to kiss her again, his hand slipping inside her shirt to caress her breast as she moaned softly.

I remained where I was, those words of hers echoing around my skull like my head was a pinball machine with no hole for them to drop out of.

Blake was playing a game where he poked Kyan then ducked aside as the big bastard took a swipe at him in his sleep. It would probably end with Blake's nose getting busted, but it was his face to take risks with. Besides, I wasn't inclined to save him from a dose of pain after the worry he'd caused me tonight.

Nash had pushed Tatum back against the wall while she pumped his cock in her fist and I watched as he tugged her sweatpants low on her hips and eased his fingers beneath the waistband.

At another time, the sight might have aroused me, but I was so deep into my anger that I knew I wasn't going to be distracted by sex. I needed her punished. I needed it more than I needed to breathe and the moment I lost this battle with myself and moved out of the shadows, she was going to feel my wrath.

Tatum tipped her head back, moaning in pleasure as Nash fucked her with his hand and I watched enraptured, waiting as he built her up and up and up. When her moaning turned to pleading and I knew she was about to come for him, I stepped out of the shadows and cleared my throat.

"Holy fuck," Nash cursed, flinching and pausing in his movements for a moment as Tatum gritted her teeth at the denial of her release.

"We need to talk," I said in a deadly calm voice as Tatum's panting breaths filled the room.

"We're a touch busy," Monroe grunted and I almost felt bad for denying him too. He wasn't the one who had fucked up after all.

"Yes. I am well aware that our dear Miss Rivers is trying to dig herself out of trouble with you by using her sexuality as a weapon, but do you really think she deserves to come after the stunt she just pulled? I can't be the only one of us who recalls the way she is being hunted. Who remembers what it felt like when she was gone?"

Nash's frown deepened as Kyan muttered, "It's Mrs Roscoe," from his bed, clearly awake at last. One glance his way showed me Blake's busted lip and Kyan's angry scowl. *Good. An accomplice.*

"Perhaps we need to discuss the boundaries of this relationship. And the punishments we can dish out when one of us oversteps?" I suggested.

"I'm down for that," Kyan growled and Blake huffed irritably.

"It was my *dad*, man. I already lost my mom to this shit and even waiting this long to get him a vaccine after we stole them had been killing me. You have to know-"

"I understand perfectly. And I was already concocting a plan for us to deliver a vaccine to him *safely*." I turned my dark gaze to him and he swallowed thickly before nodding.

"You're right. I fucked up. I'm sorry, dude, I should have just trusted you and come to you about it. But you know how crazy I can get about family and I guess I just convinced myself that you might say no or something and I really needed it to be done. I couldn't take another sleepless night worrying about him catching it."

I considered his words for a moment then nodded. His impulsive behaviour was understandable even if it was infuriating. But he was led by emotion and his love for his father. Tatum however, had never met Blake's father. She had no emotional attachment to him beyond just wishing for him to be safe for Blake's sake. She should have known better.

My gaze travelled to Monroe and Tatum as they still stood there, hands within each other's underwear, eyes hot with passion and need.

"Do you think Tatum deserves to come after pulling that stunt, Nash?" I asked him, my gaze fixed on his while Tatum's lips popped open into a little O of shock and frustration.

"I guess not," Monroe agreed, giving our girl an apologetic look as he tugged his hand back out of her sweatpants and she whimpered in disappointment, reluctantly releasing his cock too.

"Saint," she pleaded. "I know you're upset, but we just wanted to get it over and done with. We weren't looking to make you feel like-"

"Like you don't trust me?" I finished for her and Kyan growled something angrily as he stood from his bed, stalking over to stand at my side in solidarity. I loved when he got like this, that anger and rage inside of him pressing out against the confines of his skin as the darkness in him hungered for blood.

"It's not that," Tatum gasped, seeming to realise how deeply she'd cut me with this behaviour as she took a step closer. "It's just-"

"You know how I get?" I supplied coldly, trying not to feel that bite of pain in my chest as I tossed her words back at her.

Tatum's eyes widened and for a moment I was certain that she had realised the cost of her actions to me and I could see how she really hadn't meant to hurt me like this. But it was a little too late for that and we both knew it. There was only one way that the beast in me would be tamed now.

She glanced at the others for a moment then dropped down to her knees in front of me, making my heart lurch as she gave me what I needed so easily. Submitting to my control, offering herself as a sacrifice to the darkness in my soul and giving me this way out, this release which we both knew I needed beyond measure now.

"Look, I know she fucked up in the mind of Saint Memphis," Blake said heatedly as he pushed to his feet and moved to stand between us. "But it was really all on me. So punish me if you have to punish someone. I'm not gonna let her take the rap for my mistake."

"I think we all know that Tatum is a strong, wilful, powerful woman," I hissed. "She was more than capable of making her own choice to go with you, just as she is more than capable of paying for her missteps. But you do make a valid point. You must be punished too."

I flicked a glance at Kyan beside me and he barked a laugh as he lunged for Blake who surprisingly made very little attempt to escape him.

"On the bed," I said casually and Kyan dragged him over to it. "Face down. Ass up," I added.

"You're not seriously going to spank me, are you?" Blake laughed as Kyan shoved him onto the bed and yanked his sweats off.

Tatum lifted her head, her eyes twinkling as she watched, and I retrieved a coil of rope from my bag.

"On your knees," I said casually as I moved towards him and Blake huffed before complying. "Lean forward and grasp your ankles." The moment he did it, I tied his wrists in place tightly then shoved him forwards so that his face hit the pillows and his ass was left in the air.

"Fuck you," Blake said, half laughing as I made him my bitch and the others laughed too.

"Do you like this, siren?" I asked, looking back over at her where she remained on her knees in the middle of the room.

"It has a certain appeal," she admitted, and the hint of a smirk touched the corner of my lips.

"Why don't you count then?" I offered her and she nodded eagerly.

"Does ten strikes seem fair?" I asked my brothers, because this punishment was on their behalf too. I wasn't the only one Blake and Tatum had betrayed tonight.

"That should do it," Nash agreed with a snigger, rolling up a magazine and handing it to me.

"Wait a second," Blake protested. "I thought you were gonna use your hand?"

He tried to struggle as I moved to stand behind the bed, giving Tatum a perfect view and Kyan placed his hands on Blake's shoulders to stop him from wriggling about.

"Take it like a man, naughty boy," he teased and I couldn't help but smirk again as I raised the magazine for the first strike.

"Bare ass, I think is fair," Nash said quickly, yanking Blake's boxers down too and he started cursing.

"Do you want a safe word?" I offered Blake.

"Just get the fuck on with it," he growled, giving up his struggle and I shrugged before clapping the rolled up magazine down on his ass.

Blake swore as I struck him and Tatum dutifully started counting, her blue eyes flaring with excitement as she watched.

The magazine struck his ass repeatedly and his skin pinked from the slap of it against his flesh while Blake called me every name under the sun. For the final strike, I tossed the magazine aside and clapped my bare palm down against his ass as hard as I could.

"You sadistic motherfucker!" he yelled at me, but there was a hint of amusement to his tone which told me well enough that he'd been happy to take this punishment. No doubt he knew he deserved it.

I moved away from him with the beast in me settling just a little. But punishing Blake didn't come close to satisfying my cravings and as my gaze met Tatum's sapphire blues, I could see she knew that too.

I moved to take a wooden chair from the side of the room and placed it down before her then lowered myself into it slowly. The others were all watching us with keen interest, and I knew they were curious about this side of me, wondering if they wanted to share in it or not and I welcomed their hungry eyes on our movements.

I didn't need to say anything. Tatum knew what I needed and she stood slowly, sliding her sweatpants off and stepping out of them before pulling her shirt over her head and tossing that aside too. She was wearing a sheer navy bra which showed her hard nipples through the material but had paired it with a red thong and as her eyes met mine, I knew that the mismatch was intended to rile me. How often had she been wearing unpaired sets, hoping I would get her clothes off and find it, punish her for it?

I ground my jaw to keep from mentioning it and she dutifully moved to lay across my lap as I spread my legs wide to support her better.

She took hold of the chair legs beneath me to brace herself as her golden hair spilled down towards the floor and I ran my fingertips along her spine gently, loving the feeling of her shivering at my touch.

As my hand made it to her ass, I couldn't resist the urge to slide my fingers over her thong, following the material down the valley between her ass cheeks until I found slick, wet material and her swollen pussy. I drew the fabric aside and pushed two fingers inside her, wondering how much of this was for Nash and how much in anticipation of this punishment because I knew she needed this release just as much as I did.

Tatum moaned breathlessly, murmuring my name and making something in my chest settle as she fell to my commands so simply.

"You are our queen. We will worship you and covet you and love you with the might of the monsters we are. But we *are* monsters. And we are a family. Which means that there must be consequences for failing us. Do you agree that you deserve this punishment?" I asked her roughly.

"Yes," she breathed, and it didn't escape my notice that there was a moan in there too.

But I didn't even care if she enjoyed this. If she derived pleasure from her punishments, then all the better. It would just make the message I was delivering to her more memorable.

I dipped my fingers in and out a few more times, listening to her moans before I drew them out suddenly and spanked her hard. The cry that escaped her lips was all pleasure and a groan of longing drew my attention back up to my brothers watching us as she panted, "One," and began to count.

Kyan was unashamedly pumping his cock as he watched the show I was putting on and Nash looked like he was only a moment from doing the same while Blake watched with wild eyes from his position still tied on the bed with his ass in the air. He wouldn't be able to do a thing about it if he wanted to stroke his own dick and I smirked at him as I went back to caressing our girl.

"It isn't really fair that Monroe be denied his release when you're the one at fault," I mused, dipping my fingers back into her heat again.

"It's not," Tatum agreed breathlessly and I jerked my chin to beckon him closer.

He only hesitated for a second as I took a handful of Tatum's hair and lifted her head for him. She opened her mouth obligingly and I watched hungrily as Monroe pushed his pants down so that his solid cock could spring free.

Tatum leaned towards him, licking the tip of it before sliding her lips around it and I spanked her again, hard enough to knock her forward and make her take his cock deep into her mouth in the same movement.

She cried out around his shaft and I paused a moment as he groaned but as she began to bob her head back and forth, I knew she wasn't going to ask me to stop.

My cock was driving into her hips where she lay on me and as Monroe began to thrust into her mouth, the friction of her movements made me growl with desire.

I spanked her again and Kyan took over counting for her now that her mouth was full, his inked hand running up and down his shaft as he just enjoyed the performance we were putting on.

By the count of eight, Tatum's ass was pink and perfect and as she screamed her pleasure around his shaft, Monroe thrust in hard and came with a grunt of satisfaction.

I slid my fingers into her swollen pussy again, pumping them harder, stroking her g-spot and bringing her to the edge once more without letting her fall over it.

Monroe slid his cock from her mouth and she gasped my name, begging me not to stop this time, but I was too angry to allow her to come, needing to finish this ritual before I could let it go.

I pulled my fingers out and spanked her again, loving the sounds she made as I smoothed my fingers over the tender skin, caressing her through the lingering sting of my strike as my dick throbbed almost painfully.

Unsurprisingly, Kyan didn't wait to be offered a place in our party and stepped into Monroe's place, fisting her hair and driving his cock between her lips to finish what he'd been doing with his hand. He thrust in and out hard, fucking her mouth with a groan of pleasure that signalled him coming within moments and proving just how much he'd been enjoying what he was watching.

I spanked her for the final time as he moved back again, a sigh escaping my lips as I finally allowed the turmoil within me to settle and my anger to leave. She was here after all. Safe. Close. As beautiful as ever. It had worked out alright even if I wished they'd gone about it differently.

I ran my fingertips all over her body, unclasping the uncoordinated bra and sliding it from her arms as I drew her up to sit in my lap where I could pull her nipple into my mouth.

She was panting and moaning, her body wound so tight that I knew she was desperate for the release I'd been denying her, and I decided to stop being an asshole and let her have it.

"Touch yourself," I growled, my fingers sliding over her ass and up her spine.

Tatum's hand moved inside her panties without a word and I watched the way she played her body, taking note of just how she liked it as my cock pressed into her thigh with an aching need.

I didn't protest as she pushed my sweats down, freeing me from the confines of them and shoving her panties aside. Her sweet pussy sank down onto me and I groaned loudly as she rode me, still rubbing her clit for me like I'd commanded.

I stared into her defiant eyes as I thrust into her, drinking in the sounds she made as her pupils dilated and she panted, her release drawing closer and closer.

It took her hardly any time to come and as she tightened around me, I took control, my fingers digging into her hips as I slammed my cock up into her as hard as could, making her scream for me until I was coming too and my rage finally fell away. She sagged forward and we merged into a heap of limbs as I found her lips and kissed her softly, the two of us spent and wrung out and relieved to have found one another in the dark again.

We spent several days hiding in our new location. I wouldn't call it a home though and I couldn't deny how much I missed The Temple, but I also understood what Nash had said about family being your true home. I had the only things that truly mattered to me right here and that was what was getting me through the upheaval. Still, I was in the process of designing us a suitable house for after this was over, one which I would have constructed from scratch and built to our perfect specifications once I'd settled on the ideal location for it.

But for now, my focus was entirely on solving some of our problems. The most pressing being the box of stolen vaccinations we now needed to find a new home for. Kyan had plans to give one to Niall and pass on another for his old housekeeper but aside from that, none of us cared about anyone else enough to want them to have one. And the most pressing use for the vaccines was to give them to a virologist who was capable of using them to create the vaccines the world was in need of.

The only problem with that was that it was damn hard to find a candidate who we deemed worthy of the task. They needed to be a leader in their field. They also needed to have a strong moral compass and no ties to anyone connected to my father. The issue was that most pharmaceutical companies were very much run for profit, the owners of them cashing in on medications that desperate people needed while charging exorbitant prices for them. And while I was all in favour of turning a profit, we were in agreement that we wanted someone who couldn't be bought and who would be fair in the distribution of this life saving drug. After all, if the mega rich were the first to claim it and profit from it then we were only making my father's plans come to fruition. And I refused to line the palms of any more greasy businessmen with the profits of this atrocity. Not to mention the fact that Tatum would have had my balls for it if I tried.

"Dr Valerie De La Cost," I announced as I joined the others for breakfast, opening up my laptop and showing them the online profile for the woman in question.

She was a pretty woman in her late fifties, with dark skin and an intelligent glint in her eyes, posed in the cliched white lab coat for the profile picture and yet still not looking like a cardboard cut out of every other doctor in her field.

"She's the one?" Tatum asked with interest.

"Yes. She's a leader in her profession and she has spent her career dedicating her time to the kinds of drugs which make a true difference to the most amount of people, not just the ones guaranteed to turn a profit. She lives modestly, donating more than half of her income to foundations and projects around the globe and has worked to secure deals with many large companies, getting them to sponsor the production of her drugs for distribution in impoverished countries where the population needs them most. I cannot find so much as a hint of a bribe, foul doing or even a suspicious business partner. She looks squeaky clean and no matter how deep I dig, I can't find any dirt. She even refused a large raise in her pay when a competing company tried to poach her, claiming they didn't adhere to her moral code and I believe that was the truth."

"Okay then," Blake said around a mouthful of toast. "So where do we find her?"

"Swallow before you speak, you heathen," I muttered, taking a moment to lament my eggs and avocado as Tatum passed me some toast too. "And she has an office in Cypress City about four hours north of here and her home is close by."

"Alright then. Let's go," Tatum suggested brightly and I gave her a soft smile, enjoying the way she always managed to stay so positive, like she couldn't imagine any way that this might go wrong. I wished I had her faith, but I couldn't help but believe that we were living on borrowed time. That my father was only one step behind us and our temporary peace was just waiting to be destroyed.

"We can eat first," I assured her, forcing myself to lift the toast to my mouth in my hand like some classless cretin and eating it as fast as I could just to get it over with.

Kyan made no attempt to hide his laughter at my expense, passing me an espresso with his wrist positioned to show off that ugly fucking squid tattoo as well. I was pretty sure he'd been trying to goad me into losing my shit ever since the spanking-turned-fuck-fest that had taken place the other day, but I refused to indulge his fantasies by rising to the bait. If he wished for me to take part in some kind of dominant fantasy with him and our girl, he was going to have to ask me nicely.

We finished up our breakfast together without any more talk of the problems we were facing, each of us holding out hope that today might just be the day that we solved at least one of them by ridding ourselves of the box of vaccines we were still carting about. I had to admit that it would be a relief to wash our hands of them.

We loaded ourselves up in my car, packing the trunk with our things and keeping the black bag with our most important possessions in the front just in case. I'd bought this building with cash and funded every single part of the purchase through false names and untraceable accounts, but I wasn't going to underestimate my father now that I knew he was onto us. I only had to have left behind one breadcrumb and I was certain that it would bring him down upon our heads at the drop of a hat. So I wasn't going to relax any time soon.

We pulled out of our hidden location and started down quiet streets, the car thick with tension as Tatum sat in the back with the box of vaccines by her feet. Once we got to Dr De La Cost's place of work, I intended to deliver the vaccines alone. There was no way I was letting any of those people even get a look at Tatum again. She was a ghost now and that was how she was going to stay.

The heavy thunder of a helicopter swooping overhead drew my attention and I craned my head to watch as not one, but two Black Hawks raced overhead, fully loaded with men and women in their army uniforms.

"What's that about?" Kyan muttered from the seat beside me, sensing danger as easily as I did.

"Nothing good," I replied.

We kept driving, more than a little tension filling the car now as more helicopters swooped overhead and I caught sight of a huge military truck up ahead too.

My new phone pinged in the glove compartment and I reached over to pull it out, frowning at the screen as a news bulletin flashed up.

New test and divide measures coming into place in Sequoia State.

Before I could give that much thought, another bulletin appeared.

Tatum Roscoe wanted for question in relation to the release of the Hades Virus.

"Watch out!" Kyan yelled, shoving the wheel as I almost ran us straight up the curb where a little old lady shrieked in horror.

I jerked us away from her, hitting the brakes as I stopped us right in the middle of the road, flipping the old woman off to make sure she kept fucking walking.

"My father has upped his tactics," I growled, flashing the notification towards the others before opening up the story on Tatum.

At the top of the page was a photograph which had been taken of her in her forest green Everlake Prep uniform, posing and smiling for the camera and looking like a typical prom queen type. The image was flat, emotionless and though of course she was breath-taking in it, it didn't capture her soul the way it should have. I looked beneath it and read the article aloud for everyone to hear.

"Tatum Roscoe, Daughter of Donovan Rivers (the man responsible for releasing the Hades Virus into the world) is now wanted in questioning in relation to the events that led up to the virus being set loose. It has come to the attention of the investigating officers that young Mrs Roscoe (formerly Rivers) was likely brain washed by her father and helped him in carrying out the atrocities which have led to the deaths of millions of people worldwide. The young lady in question also married into a well-known crime family mere days after her eighteenth birthday and it is our belief that the O'Briens may be helping to conceal her location from the authorities-"

"Grandpa's gonna love that," Kyan muttered but I just read on.

"We are asking members of the public to stay vigilant and call the number below if she is spotted. However, Mrs Roscoe was well trained in tactical defence by her (possibly unhinged) prepper father and we do not want anyone to attempt to approach her if she is seen. The local and national authorities are on high alert and are hunting for her as we speak. We have every belief that she will be detained in due time."

I stopped reading and looked at Tatum with frustration burning through me, but it was nothing on the venom flaring in her eyes.

"I want everyone who set my father up to take the fall for this to die," she snarled furiously. "Every. Last. Lying. Scheming. One of them."

"Your wish is our command, princess," Nash agreed and the rest of us nodded.

Another Black Hawk helicopter roared overhead and I leaned towards my window, watching its progress across the sky before I lost sight of it beyond the overpass. A chill ran down my spine and I dropped my gaze to my phone again, opening up the other news story with a sense of dread filling me as I read it aloud.

"Sequoia is going to be the first state in the country to implement the much debated 'test and divide' system in hopes that it may just be the answer to stopping the Hades Virus in its tracks. Areas of the state have been emptied out and sectioned off to make way for the division camps where members of the public (particularly those living in highly populated areas such as cities) will be sent after being tested for the Hades Virus. There are to be three camps. One: The Infected. Members of the public found to be infected with the Hades Virus will be relocated to this location where the best of medical care will be on offer and we can isolate the infectious people to protect others. Two: The Uninfected. Members of the public who test negative will be sent to camps where security will be tight to make absolutely certain that the Hades Virus is kept away from you. You will be safe here as we erect an uncrossable boundary to protect you from contamination. Three: The Survivors. In this camp, we will ask any members of the public who have had the Hades Virus and recovered (so currently have antibodies in their blood) to help us in the creation of a vaccine. You will be kept safe and isolated just like the uninfected population, but there will be incentives given to anyone who chooses to help our work by donating blood."

"Fuck that," Kyan growled and I had to agree.

"Let's take a detour," I suggested, not liking the presence of the army here at all.

The article had gone on to make certain those camps sounded amazing, but there was no fucking way I was going to allow some asshole in a uniform to relocate me anywhere if I got a say in it.

I turned the car around and started driving back through the outskirts of the city, taking a path that led uphill towards the suburbs where the edge of the mountain range started. It didn't take long before I was pulling onto a street with a lookout point that I remembered from driving up this way once before and as I drove through the trees toward it, my suspicions were confirmed.

Tatum sucked in a sharp breath as she half climbed between mine and Kyan's seats to get a better look at the view and I frowned as I watched the army erecting barricades in a ring around this part of the city. I could make out more army vehicles and helicopters in the distance too, no doubt cordoning off another section. This test and divide bullshit clearly wasn't going to be implemented on a voluntary basis.

"Shit. How the fuck are we supposed to get out of here now?" Blake hissed as he stuck his head around the side of my chair beside the window.

"We're not," I replied darkly, my gaze scanning back and forth as I took in as much information as I could. The barricades surrounded us in every direction and it was clear no one was being allowed to leave. By bringing us here to hide, I'd inadvertently walked us right into a trap that had been ready to spring. "Not like this anyway."

"So what are we-" Monroe began but I cut him off as I started up the engine again and backed away from the view.

"We'll head back to the safe house," I informed him, locking down the inclination to panic over this and trying to think it through logically. There was a way out here. I just wasn't seeing it yet. But it would come to me. It had to. "And then we will have to try and figure out another plan."

Tatum reached forward and took my hand, squeezing my fingers tightly as I drove and I held onto her, needing her close right now. Because for the first time in a long time, I was struggling to see a way out of this mess. And if this was a problem I couldn't fix, then I had no idea what the fuck we were going to do.

CHAPTER TWENTY FIVE

"Shit. This is bad." I paced back and forth in the little apartment in the movie theatre, determined to figure this out but unsure how. Saint was sat on the end of one of the beds, his fingers steepled together as he worked over a plan. He was as still as a statue, utterly rigid, a single crease formed in his tight brow as I could practically see the cogs turning inside of his brain. If anyone could come up with some kind of miracle escape plan to get us out of here before the army turned up and arrested me, dragged me back to a freaking lab and had me tested on like a lab rat until they killed me, then it was him. But he hadn't offered a single idea yet, and if he was stumped, we were definitely screwed. So, so screwed. I was trying to have faith in him, but fuck, these might have been the worst odds we'd faced yet and as much as we all liked to believe Saint had superpowers, he really was only human and he couldn't fly us out of here like superman even if he wished he could.

"It's really bad isn't it?" I pushed when none of my men replied to my initial outburst. "Like, no way out of it bad-"

"We'll figure it out, princess," Nash snarled like demanding it from the universe would be enough, but we all knew it wasn't.

Saint still said nothing. Did nothing. Just sat there thinking with tension pouring from him so tangibly I could taste it in the air. Blake looked just as concerned as I was and I chewed my lip to stop myself from saying anything else that wouldn't help us, but shit, this was really freaking worrying.

"There's only one option," Kyan said at last, his expression dark and I stopped pacing, staring at him where he was leaning against the wall, realising what he was going to say.

"Kyan, you already owe your family too much. I can't stand to think what they'll make you do if you ask them for more help," I said, shaking my head in refusal. He'd been trying to avoid those people for as long as I'd known him and yet one way or another, he just kept getting tangled up with them again. And it was often my fault. I loved that he was willing to do anything to help me, but I hated him having to pay a price on my behalf.

"They're the only choice we can make. They'll be able to get us out of here," Kyan growled. "And I can face whatever the payment is."

"No," I insisted. "There has to be another way."

Blake and Monroe shared a look, their expressions saying they were unsure about it too. But that wasn't enough. I needed them to stand up and say it outright. We couldn't let Kyan pay the price for this. It was *our* mess. And we needed to figure it out together.

"There isn't," Saint announced, rising from the bed and folding his arms, looking like he hated saying those words while speaking them all the same. "Kyan, call your family. I've weighed the options, there is nothing else we can do."

"Saint," I growled. "I'm not letting Kyan pay for this."

"It's not up to you, baby," Kyan said in a hard voice that sent a tremor of anger through me.

"You don't get to make decisions like that for the whole group. Nash and Blake won't agree." I looked to them, but they seemed even more doubtful now.

"Are you sure it's the only way?" Monroe asked gravely and both Saint and Kyan nodded.

"Then we have to," Blake said in low voice, his eyes on me. "Anything to get Tatum out of the city and that vaccine into the right hands."

"Don't make this about me," I growled, fury pulsing through me.

"It *is* about you," Saint said sharply. "And we have all vowed to protect you. None of us take that lightly. I would bleed in Kyan's place to ensure you are not caught by my father, but I cannot. So this is the way it must be."

I shook my head, refusing this fate, but I could see the decision in all of their eyes. They didn't like this any more than I did, but they were still going to do it. Kyan would once again have to give a piece of himself to the people he'd been desperate to escape for so long and it cut into me like a blade tipped with poison, the initial slice just giving way to more and more agony. I didn't want that for him. I didn't want him to be forced into a life or position that he'd been so adamant he didn't want. I couldn't bear the idea of him sacrificing his dreams and hopes for me. The price was too fucking high. I turned away from them, unable to stand there and just take it as they outvoted me and left me with no fucking say in the matter, marching to the door and heading out. I ran down the staircase, full of raging energy that wouldn't dissipate.

I needed some space. I was so goddamn angry. They couldn't just discount my opinion like it meant nothing. How could they just outvote me like that? They called me their queen, but when it came down to it, my demands meant shit. They put me above all else and dismissed my feelings on the matter because they decided their lives held less value than mine. But fuck that. This relationship wasn't equal and I wasn't going to stand for it. I knew they wanted to protect me, but what about me protecting *them*? I couldn't let Kyan give more than he already had to his family. The more he owed them, the deeper their claws got into his skin. And eventually they might get so far beneath his flesh that he wouldn't ever be able to get free of them. The O'Briens were like a splinter, inching its way deeper and deeper into him and I feared the man he'd be forced to become if that sliver of rot made it to his heart.

I marched across the foyer and through a set of double doors, finding myself in a wide, carpeted stairway and heading up, the urge to punch something rushing through me. At the top of the stairs, I found a little bar with couches and a long window at the far end of it that looked down over the street. I moved to sit beside the pane in a large armchair, gazing down at the road below as my pulse beat fiercely in my ears.

My breaths came heavily as I tried to get my anger under control, but it wouldn't ease. Was this how my life was going to be with them? All four of them ganging up on me every time they made a decision which was 'in my best interest'? It was fucking infuriating. I wasn't going to be the priority in our tribe. Didn't they understand that I wanted to take care of them just as much as they wanted to take care of me? And by taking that decision away from me they were essentially trapping me all over again.

The door opened but I didn't look around to see who had followed me. Whoever it was had made a poor life choice because they were about to get the brunt of my rage if they expected me to come around to agreeing to this.

"Go away," I said icily.

"No," Monroe spoke and goosebumps raised along my arms and neck, but I didn't turn to face him.

"Yes," I demanded.

"I don't want to argue," he said placatingly.

"Well that sucks for you, because I do. So if you're gonna stay then you'd better glove up."

"Funny you should say that." The pink and black boxing gloves he'd gifted me dropped into my lap and I finally turned to look at him, finding him strapping on his own.

"I came for a fight, princess, just not the kind you're looking for." He smirked and the sight angered me further.

"I'm not playing games, Nash," I growled.

"Come and show me how much you're not playing games," he taunted, his words designed to poke at me. And dammit, it was working.

"Fuck you," I snapped.

He moved in front of me, jabbing his boxing glove against my cheek and I bared my teeth.

"Fuck. Off," I snarled and he did it again. "Nash! I'm not in the mood." I aimed my boot at his dick and he jumped backwards with a chuckle. A freaking *chuckle*.

I threw my gloves at him and he just grinned, kicking them back at me. "Fight me."

I stood up, moving to walk past him, but he grabbed me around the waist and threw me back down onto my seat, drawing an honest to shit growl from my throat. "Why are you being such an asshole?"

I got up again, shoving him in the chest to get by but he threw me back down into my seat with more force and my heart thundered up into my throat. *That's it.*

I stood up, ignoring the gloves and throwing a furious fist into his gut. He absorbed the blow with a curse then threw one back into my kidney and another to my chest, forcing me to defend myself as he didn't hold back. I went at him like a savage, throwing hard punches, but my rage was clouding my skill and he managed to uproot my legs with a sweep of his own so I hit the floor on my back.

"Again," he demanded, and I lunged up at him in a rage.

"Stop acting like you're my fucking teacher," I snapped, throwing fists at his sides, his arms, his head. He blocked eighty percent of them then shoved me hard, making me fall down onto the couch again.

He barked a laugh and I went fully feral, diving at him and not bothering with kickboxing customs, using teeth and claws in an effort to make my point. I bit into his right bicep and he snarled, locking me in a choke hold and keeping my head under his arm. I kicked and punched and fought, but he just started applying pressure to my neck until I was struggling for air.

"Ass - hole," I forced out.

"You're better than this, Tatum," he taunted. "Fight me off. Your anger is making you sloppy."

I slammed my booted foot down on top of his and he winced, his grip easing just enough for me to wriggle free and throw two solid punches against his back. He wheeled around and I drove a roundhouse kick into his chest, making him stumble away again. Then I launched myself at him, wrapping my legs around his waist as I used my entire bodyweight to try and knock him to the ground. It didn't work. He threw me off of him onto the couch again and I bounced on the cushions, glaring up at him through a mess of golden hair.

Nash peeled off his gloves, tossing them aside. "Well, if you're gonna fight dirty, then so am I." He was still smirking like a prime dickwad and I really wanted to make him stop.

"Nash, I am *not* in the fucking mood," I snarled, shoving to my feet again.

"You're not? But you seem so approachable right now." He grinned tauntingly and I shrieked, diving at him, aiming a savage kick at his legs.

He staggered back before coming at me with a punch that winded me followed by another shove that made my ass hit the floor. I gave up any pretence of being civilised and went for his legs, sinking my teeth into his calf.

"You little beast," he half laughed, half choked on a groan of pain as he leaned down to get me off of him. But when I didn't let go, he wrapped his hand in my hair and pulled hard, yanking my head back to look up at him. "Bad girl," he growled, those words having a sinful effect on me and as I licked my lips, I was sure he knew it. I wasn't giving into that urge though. Fuck my libido. She was a whore whenever things got tense between my boys. But the way to solve this issue was not to pull my panties down and get my kicks. Even though she was making a decent effort at convincing me it might help me relieve some of this stress. If it was up to her, I'd be straddling Nash's face right now and putting his tongue to better use than taunting me. Which was exactly why she wasn't in the driver's seat right now. The bitch had no shame.

His grip in my hair tightened to the point of pain and I liked that even more. But I was not going to let him distract me. I was, however, going to use it to make him let go.

I ran my hand up his leg, over the hard muscle of his thigh and onto his cock which swelled beneath my palm, growing rigid within his sweatpants as I rubbed him.

His throat bobbed and his fingers loosened in my hair which was a fatal freaking move. I reached up and grabbed his hand, twisting his fingers sharply and he swore as I got out from under him and went for a knee to the balls. He hooked his arm under my knee to stop me, his other hand landing on my back as he leaned down in my face, tilting me backwards. "You're not fighting fair, feral girl."

"You know what's not fair, Nash?" I hissed. "The four of you teaming up on me whenever you think you're making a decision for my benefit. I'm not a pet."

"No? Then why are you acting like an animal?" he asked, letting go of me and I squeaked as I fell and hit the carpet on my back.

The door swung open and I turned my head as Saint stepped in. "We need eyes on the street. I got an update on my phone that says the army are knocking on doors. We need to be ready if they show up in this neighbourhood."

"We'll watch from here," Monroe said, jerking his chin at the window.

"Good." Saint's eyes fell to me on the floor. "Have you calmed down yet?"

"No," I spat.

He nodded and walked out of the room, like he just needed my answer and wasn't interested in the feelings behind it at all. *Fucking ass baguette.*

Monroe offered me his hand to get up and I slapped it away, pushing myself to my feet.

"Truce?" he asked and I rolled my eyes, falling back into my seat to gaze out of the window. He folded his arms, standing in front of me and glaring, but I just pointedly ignored him. "You're asking for trouble."

My pulse raced at his words, but I kept my expression neutral, pretending he wasn't there. He was just a ghost trying to haunt me and I was going to mentally exorcise his ass out of existence.

"One more chance to talk it out or I'm gonna disarm you whatever way I see fit," he warned and I offered him my middle finger without looking at him.

He grabbed my hand and pressed it against his hard cock, rubbing it up and down as I bit my tongue and kept my gaze levelled on the window like I wasn't remotely affected. So he slid my hand inside his pants and wrapped my fist around it instead, keeping my hand in his as he worked my palm up and down his hot, silky shaft. Saliva built up in my mouth and my core clenched at how good he felt, but my face absolutely didn't give that away.

He took hold of my chin and yanked my head around as he shimmied his pants down and made me watch as he forced me to jerk him off. It was fucking hot, but I wasn't going to lose this game. My poker face was supreme. So bring it on.

"Eyes up here," he commanded, but I ignored him, turning to look away again, but he yanked my chin up, forcing me to look him in the eyes. And shit, that made a vat of lava pour into my blood.

I swallowed and he smirked, seeing that small sign of weakness as he pumped my fist harder over his dick. I could have pulled away, but we were in a game of wills and I never backed down from a challenge. Besides, maybe I was one percent into it.

"I'm not gonna talk to you," I said coolly.

"No?" he questioned in a deep tone that sent a quake through my bones. "Then maybe you should put your mouth to good use another way." He brought the head of his dick to my lips and gripped the back of my head in a clear demand.

"You're not gonna-" I started, but he shoved the tip between my lips and pumped the base of his cock with my hand. I tasted his precum on my tongue and I squeezed my thighs together at how fucking good it was. Why the hell was I getting off on this?

"That's better," he taunted as he drew the tip in out of my lips. "Not such a bad girl now, are you?"

I looked up at him and rolled my eyes, giving him as much sass as I could as I casually flipped him off again with my other hand. He cursed under his breath, his dick twitching against my tongue as I swirled it around his head and took the power back from him.

"Tatum," he groaned and I smiled around his cock, wrapping my fingers tighter around him. As if I was going to make him come though.

He slid his hand down to grip my throat as a noise of carnal desire rumbled through his chest. I teased him with slow, lazy strokes of my tongue which brought him closer to release only to let my mouth go slack before he reached climax and make him swear colourfully. His hand tightened on my neck and he pushed me off, tugging his sweatpants up as he knocked my hand away from his dick too.

"Now what are you gonna do?" I arched a brow mockingly and he pursed his lips at my attitude. But I'd gone full bitch and I wasn't coming back for a while. So he needed to deal with it or leave me the hell alone like I'd asked.

"Mouthy today, aren't you?" He leaned down, grabbing my hips and flipping me over, fisting his hand in my hair and pushing my face down into the cushions of the couch.

"Nash!" I snapped, my voice muffled by the upholstery as I fought to get free, but he wasn't letting me go, his other hand yanking my yoga pants down and leaving them wrapped around my knees so I couldn't move. He slid his rigid cock between my legs, angling it to press the smooth length against my pussy then started jerking himself off, rubbing himself back and forth in my wetness as he used it to lubricate his hand.

"Motherfucker," I snarled, pressing my ass back to try and stop him, but he just slapped it and continued to pleasure himself with my body while giving me nothing. I clawed my hands against the cushions, fighting to get up but the pressure of his palm on my back increased as he carried on, groaning and grunting as he used me, punished me. My attitude had clearly brought out the asshole teacher in him again and despite my best intentions, I was so freaking here for that.

He leaned over me so his ragged breaths tickled my ear and sent shivers along my skin. "Are you going to stop being a brat and fuck me like you're aching to?" he asked.

My body quivered and my pussy clenched with the need to feel him inside me, but I didn't say a word, biting my lip hard to keep any noise from coming out. I'm a strong, independent, totally in control wom –

"*Ah*," I moaned as his cock rubbed my clit for the briefest moment. *Goddammit.*

"I can feel you trembling, princess," he laughed. "Are you really gonna be that stubborn?"

He slid his thick shaft along the centre of me again and my back arched involuntarily to give him more access. I felt him shudder with need and the feel of how much he wanted me made my head spin. But I could not give in. I had a damn point to make. I wasn't exactly sure what it was anymore, but I was determined to make it anyway.

"Well? Are you?" he demanded, my pulse daggering as he yanked my hair, pulling my head up so he could hear me speak.

"Yeah, I am," I said and to my credit, the words came out sounding pretty icy. He rocked his hips and his dick rubbed against my clit again, making another heady moan fall from my lips and give the game away entirely.

"Are you sure?" he asked mockingly.

I could hear the damn grin in his voice and it made me more resilient than ever, but as he pressed the head of his cock to my opening, my entire body convulsed. I ground against him, desperate for more, but he clearly wasn't going to give it to me unless I said the words.

He reached under my hips, his fingers sliding through my wetness as he coated them in my arousal before toying with my clit.

"You don't play fucking fair," I snarled, but it came out breathier than

I'd planned, pleasure twisting through my flesh from his touch.

"News flash, gorgeous, I'm not a good man," he growled. "And I'm getting tired of your games. So I'm gonna fuck you for my own enjoyment. Feel free to change your mind before I finish though." He shoved himself inside me and I cried out, bracing myself on the cushions as he started dominating my body, moving furiously to climb towards his own release while giving no care for mine. But screw that.

I slid my hand beneath me, reaching for my clit, but he yanked my arm out before I got close and pinned it to my back. *Assbag.*

"Ask nicely," he demanded and I bit into the cushion to stop myself. He drove himself in harder, his thickness filling every space inside me, his dick jerking as he came close to finishing. I growled like a heathen and his hands moved to grip my hips as he held me at an angle he liked. I threw an elbow back, but it was too late as he groaned, rearing over me as he drove himself up to the hilt inside me and found his release.

"Oh fuck," he groaned, the sound so hot it made a tremor ripple through me.

Anger charged my veins with electricity as he pulled out of me and his grip eased on my hands. I twisted around and kicked off my yoga pants then pulled off my top and flung myself to lie down on the couch. *He wants to play dirty? Then fine, I'll play dirtier.*

"You can go now," I said airily, grabbing my phone up from where it had fallen on the floor and finding my way onto a porn website.

I played it loudly, not looking at Nash as he pulled up his sweats and I dropped a hand between my thighs, holding the screen in front of me and fingering myself just the way I liked. I propped the phone up against my thigh and pushed one hand into my bra, moaning as I watched the two dudes on screen DP a girl, though my mind was wholly on what Monroe had just done to me. Especially because I could feel the evidence of it between my legs.

"Tatum," Nash snapped and I ignored him, moaning louder as I kept my gaze on the screen, pretending it was getting me hotter than he had. But no porn site could come close. He'd claimed me for his own pleasure, fucking defiled me. Why was that so damn sexy?

"This game isn't funny anymore," he growled.

Weird how it wasn't funny now the tables had turned. I bit my lip, putting on my best porn show as I tugged my bra down beneath my breasts and squeezed them for my pleasure, but mostly to taunt my little voyeur.

"What's wrong Nash, can't you hack it when you're the one being left out?" I asked without looking at him.

He leaned down, snatching my phone and throwing it across the goddamn room. It bounced over the carpet out of sight and I gaped at him in surprise. Before I could get a word of anger past my lips, he dropped down on the couch between my thighs, yanking me toward him by the hips and driving his tongue into me. I cried out as he lapped away the wetness between my legs, worshipping me in furious, hungry strokes of his tongue that drove me wild. He ran his tongue in a figure of eight across my clit, looking straight at me as he made my thigh muscles tighten and quiver.

"You don't get yourself off over anyone who isn't a Night Keeper," he ordered then ran his tongue over my clit possessively again. My head fell back against the end of the couch as he sucked and licked and I was lost in a sea of blinding pleasure.

He didn't torment me this time, quickly bringing me towards my orgasm which was so close already that it didn't take long. I trembled and clawed at his hair as his tongue slid over me and suddenly I was shattering, screaming, praising his fucking name and left panting in the wake of his power.

"Forgive me?" he smirked, crawling up my body and laying his weight on me.

I couldn't help but smile, pushing my fingers through his messed up blonde hair. "On one condition."

"Oh yeah, what's that?" His smirk grew.

"Admit that I won," I said and his smirk died a sudden death.

"Damn you," he muttered, holding off for a beat longer, but I could see the defeat in his eyes. "Fine, you won, princess. Happy now?"

"Very." I wrapped my arms around his neck and kissed him again, his heart racing against mine as I bathed in the weight of him holding me down.

"So I actually came here to give you this back. I thought it might cheer you up." He reached into his pocket and took out the necklace he'd been keeping for me. "No need to hide it from the Devil anymore." He slid it around my throat, shifting my hair aside as he put it on me and a smile lit my face at having it back. My little memento of Jess was in its rightful home once more.

"Thank you for keeping it safe for me," I said and he grinned, kissing me sweetly again.

"My pleasure." He stood and I pulled my clothes back on while he flattened his hair, tucking it behind his ears. As I got up, he headed to the window, peering outside and his whole body stiffened.

"Oh fuck," he hissed, turning to me with wide eyes. "The army's here. They're two doors down."

"Shit," I gasped. What the fuck had we done? We were supposed to be keeping watch. Saint was going to shit a brick, spank us both until our asses were red raw then shit another, bigger brick.

We ran from the room, tearing back through the movie theatre and racing up to the apartment. We spilled inside and my three other boys leapt out of their seats on the couch, instantly seeing that something was wrong, tension coursing through their muscles like they were prepared for a fight to the death.

"They're almost here," Monroe blurted.

"Jesus – fuck, why are we just hearing about this now?" Saint demanded, then his eyes skated over us and he cursed. "You had one job, Nash."

"It was my fault too," I said.

"Oh I am well aware of that," Saint said coolly, his fingers twitching like he was hungering for a spanking. But there definitely wasn't time for that right now.

"Well what are we gonna do?" Nash pressed.

"I called Niall. My family's on their way here," Kyan said. "They're gonna breach the barricades somewhere. If we can hold out for an hour or two-"

"We don't have a fucking hour or two," Saint growled.

"Maybe they won't come in here," Blake offered with a shrug. "They're checking houses, right? Why bother hunting through some old boarded up movie theatre?"

"They're clearing every building in the city," Saint hissed. "Of course they're going to check here, that's their damn job. This is the army we're talking about, not a bunch of backwater hillbillies out hunting for a missing alligator. They're looking for people who could be hiding. People like *us*."

CHAPTER TWENTY SIX

A loud bang came from outside and we looked between each other with concern.

"Tatum," Saint hissed, echoing all of our thoughts. It was one thing for us to be found here but after that article had been released implicating Tatum in the Hades Virus scandal, there was no way we could risk her getting caught.

"Over here," Kyan growled, moving to the nearest bed, pulling it out and opening a cupboard behind it. We all followed after him like a flock of sheep being herded, hoping he had some solution for us. "There's enough space in here. You can fit, baby."

"I'm not hiding away in there while the rest of you are left to deal with the army," she hissed, glaring between the four of us as we all pushed her towards the tiny space. I wasn't even totally convinced she'd fit in there and there was no chance for any of us to join her.

"They're hunting for you, siren," Saint replied urgently, dropping the bag filled with our most important possessions onto the countertop and unzipping it. He grabbed an envelope full of fake passports and handed them out. "They won't know who we are. Even if they make us leave with them for this division shit they're implementing, it won't matter. All you have to do is wait here to meet Kyan's family and go with them. We'll meet you at the O'Brien's. You'll be safe with them, won't she?" he asked, turning dark eyes on Kyan.

"I'll message Niall and tell him to look after you personally," he replied with a nod. "You stick by his side until we get back to you and I swear you'll be safe."

"With a man you've told me is fucking insane and kills people for a living?" I asked incredulously. "How the hell is that her being kept safe?"

"Uncle Niall might be a gun for hire, but he's also got a moral code hiding beneath the crazy. We don't exactly have time to get into it now, but long story short, about ten years ago his wife was kidnapped, raped and murdered. He hates men who hurt women and he's loyal to me. You can trust that he would die to protect Tatum and it's not like we have anyone else to ask." Kyan quickly finished typing out the message to his uncle then shoved his phone into his boot to conceal it.

"Not to mention the fact that I can protect myself," Tatum added.

A loud pounding came from the bolted door and we all froze. "This is Sergeant Jeffers with the Sequoia State Hades Defence Squadron," a man called loudly. "We need you to open up and submit to a virus test."

Tatum hesitated, but I gave her a little push towards the crawl space Kyan had found. "Go, princess. We can escape some camp easily enough, but getting you back from Troy Memphis for a second time might be impossible," I whispered, begging her with my eyes to accept that this was the way it had to be. I knew she hated us making sacrifices to protect her, but she had to see that in this instance it was the only way. And frankly, I was gonna end up gagging her and shoving her in there myself in a second. I wasn't going to lose my girl again. No matter how mad she might be at me for making that choice for her.

"Just a second!" Blake called out to the officer, tossing a worried look towards Tatum before she finally nodded and dropped down to crawl into the gap behind the bed. It was clear she didn't like it, but she obviously realised this had to happen.

She shuffled right back into the shadows and Saint passed her the bag of guns, cash and our most valuable possessions before I grabbed the box of vaccines out of the fridge and just about managed to force it in in front of her. The last thing I saw was the fear for us reflected in her blue eyes before Kyan gave her his hunting knife and baseball bat then placed the wooden shelf back in front of her, concealing her from view. He closed the cupboard door and pushed the bed back into place before standing upright again.

I exchanged a worried look with Saint before jogging over to take a seat on my bed and Blake checked we were all spread out around the room looking innocent before he unbolted the door and pulled it wide. They must have broken in downstairs somehow and I guessed that meant they really weren't messing around.

Two big guys in army uniforms complete with full ventilator masks stood in the doorway and as Blake backed up to let them in, another four soldiers followed them into the room.

"What is this about?" Saint asked casually as he moved towards them.

"You may have seen on the news that we have now taken the decision to split the population of our state into different groups in an effort to contain the spread of the Hades Virus to prevent any more people from catching it. As such, we have currently locked down Hemlock City and divided it into quadrants while we go door to door testing everyone and assigning them a group. This is not voluntary. Everyone must submit to a finger prick test and throat swab. Failure to do so will result in you being grouped with the infected members of the population. Do you understand?"

"Yes sir," Kyan replied from his position laying on the bed, sounding anything other than respectful.

"We need to see some ID if you have it on you," a female soldier said, stepping forward and glancing around at the apartment in an old movie theatre like she was wondering what the hell we were doing here.

I pulled my new passport out of my back pocket and got to my feet, my pulse racing as I thought of my girl still hiding in that cupboard. What would happen if they found her? We couldn't take on the fucking army, but I knew we'd fight for her all the same. I eyed the assault rifles the four soldiers carried and swallowed thickly. Shit, I really hoped they didn't find her.

The female officer took my passport as I offered it up and I realised I should have double checked the damn information on it in case she asked me to confirm it.

My heart thundered as I waited for her to flick through the pages and find whatever photograph Saint had used to get this forgery made. She looked at it for a long moment before snorting a laugh which she tried to cover with a cough.

"Is everything alright?" I asked her, my brow furrowing as I wondered if she could tell it was fake. I'd just blindly trusted Saint to have gotten us good forgeries but how the fuck was I supposed to know if it would be good enough?

"Your name is Simone Dipsickle?" she asked, clearly biting her tongue on another laugh as one of the other officers snatched it from her to see, this one laughing shamelessly as he looked from the document to me. "Isn't Simone a woman's name?"

My lips parted as a mixture of confusion and annoyance filled me. *Simone fucking Dipsickle??*

"He insists that it's a male name in Italy," Saint deadpanned but as I looked at him, I caught the edge of an evil smirk at the corners of his lips.

"You don't look Italian," the male officer pointed out. "And Dipsickle sure as shit ain't Italian. Did your momma hate you or something? Why else did she give you a name like that?"

"It's a family name," I ground out, not needing to hide my irritation because if my name really had been Simone Dipsickle, no doubt I would have been fielding this shit my entire life.

"Okay then, Mr Dipsickle, will you submit to a finger prick test?" the female officer asked, handing my passport back.

"It didn't much sound like we had a choice," I replied, holding my hand out to her as she produced the testing kit.

Saint handed his passport to another man and Kyan climbed out of his bed, making a show of hunting around for his in the pile of crap beside his bed. Most of our stuff was still loaded up in the car, so at least we didn't have to worry about them finding some of Tatum's clothes or anything because Saint might have told them my name was Simone, but I wasn't going to pretend I liked wearing lacy thongs too.

The sharp prick to the pad of my finger drew my attention back to the soldier standing in front of me and I watched as she carried out the test, using a pen to add my fake name to it as she set it down to wait for the results.

I obliged her as she took a throat swab too and she directed me to sit down and wait as she started work on Blake.

Saint took a seat beside me when he was done, his thigh pressing up against mine as he kept his eyes dead ahead. None of us had so much as glanced towards the cupboard where Tatum was still hidden behind the bed and the adrenaline surging through my veins was making my fingers tremble a little.

It felt like we should be running. Or fighting. Anything but just sitting here while these armed people sniffed about and drew closer to discovering our girl.

A couple of the soldiers headed off into the rest of the building, searching for other people despite the fact that we'd told them we were alone when they asked.

I noticed Saint's passport poking out of his pocket and reached over to pinch it, needing something to take my mind off of freaking out about Tatum being discovered.

"Rex Power?" I muttered, making sure my voice was too low to carry to anyone else.

Saint didn't reply but that hint of a smirk was back as he took the passport from me and returned it to his pocket.

Asshole.

I snorted a laugh and nudged him with my elbow, hard enough to knock him forward a few inches as I swear he actually laughed too.

Blake and Kyan came to sit with us once their tests had been carried out and we watched as the soldiers moved around the space, opening doors, looking behind the couches lined up against the rear wall. One of them even yanked the bed back to open the door to the cupboard where Tatum was hiding, and my pulse raced as I tried not to look that way.

I shifted in my seat and Saint's hand landed on my thigh, squeezing once tightly before he released me, a clear warning for me not to do anything stupid but my heart was thrashing and my need to protect Tatum was overwhelming me, urging me into action.

Kyan cracked his knuckles in a move that almost looked casual, but let me know he was readying himself for a fight too. Just in case. Because if they found her, we'd do everything and anything it took to stop them from taking her. She wasn't going to end up in some lab again. No matter what it cost to keep her out of it.

But thankfully, he knocked the door shut again with less than a glance, the shelf Kyan had replaced to hide her clearly working.

The female soldier checked her watch before moving over to take a look at our test results, carefully photographing them like she had our passports before typing away on the iPad in her hand.

"So, what's the result?" I asked her when she failed to tell us and she glanced around at me through her visor.

"I assumed you already knew?" she asked, confusing me, but of course Saint didn't skip a beat.

"It would be rather hard to forget the weeks the four of us spent battling through the hell of the Hades Virus," he said in a dry tone. "So I assume we have antibodies now that we've survived, but a confirmation would put our minds at ease about the idea of us contracting it again."

"The four of you all survived?" Sergeant Jeffers asked in surprise. "None of your group died?"

"Thankfully not," Saint clipped. "But it was a closely fought battle."

"Not the kind of thing you forget easily," Kyan added. "I doubt I'll ever be able to cough again without being reminded of the feeling of my lungs shredding apart inside my own body. But apparently, we're a bunch of tough bastards so we made it through."

Sergeant Jeffers nodded like he'd seen enough stories like ours to buy into it, though I could tell the female soldier was surprised to find that we had all survived it without losing anyone in our group. It seemed simpler to stick to that story than it would have been to invent someone for us to be grieving though so I didn't add anything.

"So we have to relocate to somewhere where you're housing other survivors?" Saint asked. "How long do we have to get ourselves there?"

"No need to worry about that, lad," Sergeant Jeffers said patronisingly and if looks could kill, Saint would likely have made his head explode on the spot for that little endearment. "You can grab some basic supplies now and we'll be on our way. There are vehicles ready to transport you to your new location."

"We can get there ourselves," Kyan said, folding his arms. "Just give us an address and-"

"Refusal to cooperate can and will result in arrest under martial law in defence of our country and our citizens," Sergeant Jeffers replied, his hand falling to the gun at his hip in a less than subtle gesture. "Are you going to make this more difficult than it needs to be?"

The four of us exchanged heavy looks, but we'd already figured out that this was coming, so we just had to accept it and trust our girl to get herself out of here. She'd wait for Kyan's uncle and we'd get ourselves away from their camp before the day was out then reunite with her. It was the best hope we had of all of us making it out of here in one piece and no matter how much I detested the idea of parting from her, I wasn't going to risk her life just to keep her within my line of sight.

"Alright," I said, lifting my hands in a placating gesture as I got to my feet. "We'll grab some of our shit and come quietly."

"One bag," Sergeant Jeffers replied. "We don't have room to carry too much crap."

"We don't have much here anyway," Blake replied in the smartass tone he always liked to use on me when I was teaching him and I could tell that pissed our new soldier friend off a bit. He should try teaching a bunch of preppy, entitled little shits day in day out. He might have been used to bossing soldiers around, but elitist little assholes were a whole other kind of beast.

I tossed a few spare clothes and my toothbrush into a bag, focusing on keeping my face blank of emotions as we followed the soldiers out of the abandoned movie theatre and left our girl behind.

I swear it went against every single fibre of my being to do it and I wasn't even sure I could. But as Saint clapped a hand on my shoulder, encouraging me to follow the soldiers out, I made my feet keep moving. One in front of the other. Step after step leading me further and further from Tatum. But I just had to focus on the fact that we were leading the soldiers away from her too. This was what it took to keep her safe and that was all I cared about.

We walked down the street outside with our little group of soldiers and were directed to climb up into the back of a huge, covered army truck where there were already a bunch of people inside waiting for it to leave.

I hesitated a moment before climbing the steps, wondering if I'd ever feel totally comfortable in the company of strangers again or if I'd forever be left with this niggling sense of nervousness when it came to interacting with people I didn't know. Months of lockdown and fearing the Hades Virus had definitely changed my outlook on the world. It had made me more thankful for the things I had, more appreciative for the things I'd once taken for granted and had shown me just how easily the entire world could be thrown into turmoil. Yeah, the virus had changed a whole hell of a lot, but we'd survived it, so I guessed we were doing better than some and I was determined to come out the other side of this crisis stronger for it.

I dropped onto one of the benches and Saint took the seat beside me while Kyan and Blake sat opposite us, all of us sporting the same grim looks as we were forced to leave our girl behind.

"Before you ship out, we need all of you to take a look at this flyer and let us know if you've seen this girl anywhere in the last few weeks," Sergeant Jeffers called out, handing the flyer to Saint and making my damn heart skip a beat as I spotted the photograph of Tatum in her school uniform.

Saint didn't even blink of course, studying the picture for a few seconds before shaking his head and passing it to me. I gave it a long look then muttered a no before passing it to the guy closest to me.

Blake yawned widely as the thing made its way around the truck and I couldn't help but side-eye everyone who looked at it. We'd been damn careful to stay out of sight since arriving here, but you could never be totally sure that we'd gone undetected. What if someone had seen her when she and Blake had run off to go visit his father? Or when we were coming in and out of the building? What were we going to do if those army assholes strode back into that movie theatre and hauled her out here? Was I about to get myself shot down trying to wrestle her from their arms?

I tried not to think about how that might play out, but it was impossible. My life was worth offering in sacrifice for Tatum Rivers. After I'd seen how weak and hurt she was by Troy Memphis's people, there was no way I was letting him get near her again. But I prayed death wouldn't be what it cost me to save her, because I still planned on being there when Troy fell from grace, wetting my hands in his blood and marking his death on my body for Mom and Michael.

The flyer made it back around to Blake and he gave it to Kyan last who released a low whistle.

"Holy hell, if you find her can you give her my number?" he asked with a grin. "She looks like the kind of girl I could have real fun getting naked with."

"She's hot as fuck," Blake agreed and Sergeant Jeffers snatched the flyer back from them.

"She is also a wanted woman who may have had a hand in releasing the Hades Virus into the world, so perhaps you should be choosier about who you want to stick your cock into," he snapped.

"Well I could still hate fuck her pretty good," Kyan reasoned. "But I can't guarantee she'd come quietly - get it?"

Sergeant Jeffers huffed a breath of frustration which momentarily fogged his visor before he hopped out of the truck and thumped the side of it a couple of times to get the driver going and we took off down the street. It was a relief to know they'd bought our bullshit, but the knot of tension in my chest still didn't ease.

"I don't like this," I muttered, my voice so low that only the other Night Keepers would be able to hear me.

"She's a strong and capable woman," Saint replied as if I needed reminding of that fact. "Besides, *Simone*, we need to concentrate on how exactly we are going to be getting ourselves out of this, because as it stands, I think we are the ones in the worse situation."

"Simone?" Blake asked, cracking up at my fake name.

"Simone Dipsickle," Saint confirmed, that smug almost smile on his lips again as I growled irritably at him.

"You're an asshole," I muttered, allowing myself a moment of amusement too.

"I had no say in the names," Saint replied but he was so full of shit I could practically smell it.

"Yeah, sure. I guess the fact that Rex means king has nothing to do with your name, Mr Power."

Kyan laughed loudly and I glanced at the other people in the truck, but they seemed to have noticed the dangerous vibe our group gave off and had all shuffled the fuck away from us. Good thing too because I didn't want some mouth breather getting up in my business even if we were vaccinated now.

"What's yours then?" I asked the others.

"Rodger Cumming," Blake snorted.

"Levi Grinder," Kyan added with a dirty as fuck smirk.

"What the fuck?" I complained. "How come they get to be porn stars while I'm a fucking Dipsickle?"

"Perhaps, you shouldn't have lied to me about your past identity," Saint said in a low voice, shrugging one shoulder. "You do realise I have the power to eradicate your badly fabricated persona of 'Nash Monroe' and make you forever Simone Dipsickle, don't you? Perhaps you should remember that in future if you consider lying to me again."

My lips fell open, but I knew there was no point in me arguing with the Devil especially after it was done, so I just blew out a laugh and embodied my inner Simone. I just hoped she was a badass bitch because as I cast my gaze over the rows of military vehicles lining the streets, I got the feeling she would need to be if we seriously hoped to get out of this.

CHAPTER TWENTY SEVEN

I'd forced myself to wait until the sounds of the army in the streets outside were long gone before I moved. Every muscle in my body was cramping up as I shoved the door to the cupboard open, pushing the bed out of the way as I scrambled back into the room. I took a moment to grab everything that had been stashed in there with me, tossing the full pack on the bed with Kyan's bat before placing the box of vaccines back in the fridge. I took out my phone, switching it back on as my heart beat fiercely in my chest.

My Night Keepers were gone. Taken. And as capable as I knew they were, that didn't make me feel any better about that. So I was going to do everything within my power to get to them.

I tapped on the app I could use to contact them, sending a message as my breaths came a little heavier.

Tigress:
Are you okay??

Koala:
Just fine, baby. They've taken us beyond the barricade out of the city. We'll get away as soon as we get to the camp. Squid has a plan. I've spoken to my uncle Narwhal, he's gonna be with you soon.

Scorpion:
I will not respond to 'Squid.'

Baboon:
You just did!

Nighthawk:
squid emoji
Miss you Tigress, I plan to steal you away from these assholes when I see you next and get real *pretzel emoji* with you.

Baboon:
Oh fuck, can I get in on that *pretzel emoji* action?

Koala:
I'll be too busy *octopus emoji*-ing the fuck out of her for you guys to try that.

Tigress:
Glad you're all taking this situation seriously…you could at least be a little *onion emoji* about it.

Baboon:
Nothing can keep us from you, sweetheart, we'll be back inside you in no time *wink emoji*

Scorpion:
I'm done with this conversation. See you soon, Tigress.

Nighthawk:
*byyyye Squid *waving emoji**

Scorpion:
At least use proper punctuation and grammar, you halfwit.

Baboon:
i TINK we fckd off squid wot u guys fink?

Scorpion:
I will leave you all behind when I escape.

Tigress:
*You can't do that! I need you all to *protractor emoji* in my *wastepaper basket emoji* when I see you next.*

Koala:
*FUCK. YES. Me first. *squid emoji**

Scorpion:
Ha! You gave the game away. The squid is clearly used as a symbol of excitement.

Koala:
*Well now you've got me feeling *squid emoji* about it *crying emoji**

Scorpion:
Fuck, I give up. Cease and desist.

Scorpion has left the chatroom

Tigress:

Love you guys. Stay safe xxxx

I tucked my phone away just as a loud thump came from downstairs and I swiped up Kyan's bat, raising it defensively. Heavy footsteps pounded toward the door and I weighed my options against whoever was on the other side of it. They sounded like a big bastard.

Screw that.

I snatched the gun out of the bag on the bed, trading it out for the bat. I was opting for bullets over brawn. It was definitely the better option right now. I primed it, taking aim, my breaths coming unevenly. *Keep your head, Tatum. If they have a gun, shoot first.*

The door flew open and my heart lurched into my throat as I found a huge man pointing a sledgehammer at me. He was at least as tall as my Night Keepers, though may have had a few inches even on Kyan and his dirty blonde hair was swept away from his face in a casual I-give-zero-fucks way that a lot of men spent hours trying to perfect. I guessed it just came naturally to him because I seriously couldn't imagine him standing before a mirror and preening. Colourful tattoos crawled over his hands and up his neck and the smile on his face was next level psycho.

Niall burst out laughing, slinging the sledgehammer over his shoulder to rest there and the tension ran out of my body as I recognised him. Though I could bet that pretty much anyone else who found this monster of a man darkening their doorway had a very different reaction to spotting him.

"The cavalry's here!" he announced in his Irish accent, his voice as deep and rich as his nephew's. He strode into the room like he owned it, carving his tattooed fingers over his stubbled jaw and taking in the apartment.

"Thanks for coming," I said earnestly.

"That's a weird thing to thank me for, but I'll give your regards to the sock who was a top-notch lover this morning." He strode forward as I snorted a surprised laugh. "It's good to see you, lass."

I glanced over his shoulder, expecting more of Kyan's family to appear, but no one did.

"Is everyone else downstairs?" I asked.

"Nope, it's just me. Unless you're referring to the ghosts of my past, then they're here too, but they're not much good in a fight. Or much fun to hang out with all the damn time if I'm being totally frank. And speaking of fights…"

"You came alone?" I questioned in concern as he looked around the place, taking in the possible exits and looking like he was only half listening to me.

"Yep. I thought about bringing the rest of the family, but I'm feeling kinda stabby today and they all annoy the ever loving fuck outta me, so I decided to just go rogue and do it alone. Don't worry though, I've got a plan."

"What's that?" I asked nervously, hoping it was a damn good one because if Saint and the others had been sure that we'd need an O'Brien army to get me out of here, then I was inclined to trust their judgement on it over Niall's.

"Not sure yet. But it'll come to me. Always does." He flashed me a grin and I balked, wondering if Kyan had seriously misjudged how good his uncle's word was because that sounded a whole hell of a lot like he was going to wing it.

No doubt Saint was having an aneurism over the mere idea of that somewhere as we spoke, sensing on the wind that someone had just uttered the words *not sure yet* about a plan we were already in the middle of.

Shouts sounded downstairs, making my pulse jackhammer and my grip tighten on the gun.

"We gotta go." Niall picked up the bag on the bed, shouldering it and holding the sledgehammer ready to swing.

I ran to the fridge, taking out the box of vaccines and shoving it into a backpack before putting it on. I slid Kyan's bat under the straps over my shoulders to keep it there then nodded to Niall. The guy was missing a few screws, but I didn't have much choice in trusting him now. He'd gotten into the city, so I just hoped he had a way to get us out too.

"Alright, lass, stay close to my side. We're getting out of here." He jogged to the door then took a grenade from his pocket and pulled the pin out with his teeth.

"Niall!" I gasped in fear.

"It won't blow until I'm ready for it to blow," he said calmly and my throat thickened as he started running down the stairs, keeping his thumb on the trigger. But one false move and he'd blow both of us to hell, so I wasn't exactly reassured by his words.

I hurried after him as we made it to the foyer and Niall threw the grenade before I even knew what was happening. Soldiers started shouting and running away as the grenade bounced across the carpet and the timer within it ticked down. Niall dragged me toward an emergency exit just as a bang filled my head and a cloud of pink smoke and glitter burst over us. I glanced back in surprise, the grenade clearly just a decoy as it filled the foyer in a shimmery fog while Niall yanked me out into an alley.

"What now?" I demanded, but Niall didn't answer, shoving the emergency exit door shut and casually hanging a Christmas bauble on the door handle.

"Now you're gonna wanna run for your fucking life, lass." He sprinted out of the alley and I didn't need to be told twice by Mr Psycho, tearing after him and making it around the corner just as a deafening boom came from behind us, making my heart thrash like crazy.

Niall kept running, continually checking that I was behind him as he powered along the street. And I sure as hell was. I wasn't gonna stray a foot from his side because the guy was showering crazy through the city and maybe that was what we needed to get out.

"Hey – stop!" a woman shouted then a rattle of gunfire rang in my ears

294

and I ducked my head with a gasp, pushing myself even faster.

Niall stopped dead in the street, taking a pistol from his hip and returning fire. "Keep going!" he barked at me. "Down that alley." He pointed to the right and I fled into it, pressing my back to the wall at the very edge of it and peering back the way I'd come with my gun lifted. There was a huge armoured vehicle at the end of the street with soldiers pouring out of it while two of them stood firing at Niall. The crazy asshole shot at them out in the open, ducking and weaving left and right like that would give him some protection.

"Niall!" I shouted anxiously as bullets whistled past him. He launched another grenade down the street and shouts for cover came from the soldiers as it pinged along the ground.

Niall ran after me as a deafening boom split the air apart and I gawped at him as he clamped his hands over my ears to protect me from the noise.

"Do you even know what's a bomb and what isn't?" I asked as he dropped his hands.

He shrugged. "Sometimes. Mostly it's a lucky dip what I pluck outta my belt. He patted the tactical belt around his waist then charged ahead of me down the alley, hefting the sledgehammer above his head and slamming it through a wooden door in the far wall. He shoved his hand through the hole, unlocking it and swinging it wide, bowing to me as he gestured for me to go ahead. "My lady."

His methods were next level insanity, but I just had to back them and hope they paid off. I ran inside and he jogged after me, shutting the door and we ran up a dark stairway as more shouts sounded somewhere back on the street. I ran full pelt, the two of us moving faster and faster as sweat beaded on the back of my neck. My desperation to get out the city and reunite with my Night Keepers drove every one of my movements. I wasn't going to let them down. I'd return to them no matter what.

"Get to the roof," Niall insisted just before the roaring of a helicopter sounded overhead. "Alright, don't get to the roof." He pulled me roughly out of the stairway and shouted a battle cry as he charged down a door ahead of us, sending it flying off of its hinges as he fell flat on his face inside someone's apartment.

A woman screamed as I followed him into the place and she dove off of her couch, hiding behind it as Niall rolled and leapt to his feet again.

"No need to be dramatic, love," Niall said, jogging up to the sliding door that led out onto a balcony. He opened it, jerking his head to beckon me after him and I threw an apologetic look at the cowering woman before following.

We were up three floors overlooking a large park that stretched out toward a lake in the distance. There was a stone boathouse beside it and I fisted Niall's shirt in my hand as I wheeled him around to point it out.

"We could head there," I said. "We're not getting out of the city now until they lose our trail." I pointed to the trees that ran nearly all the way up to it through the park. "We can stay under cover."

The helicopter circled somewhere behind us and we quickly pressed back against the wall. The balcony was covered by a plastic roof, but it wasn't worth taking any chances in being seen.

"Alright," Niall conceded. "We'll do your plan with a sprinkling of my idea."

"And what's your idea?" I asked nervously as he shifted his grip on the sledgehammer.

"I'm gonna cause a distraction and you're gonna run to that boathouse like the little piggy who went home," he said gruffly.

"That's a bad idea," I growled.

"Why? You just have to go weeee weeeee weeeee all the way-"

I thumped his arm and his eyes widened in surprise. "No, we're not splitting up. If they see you, you're fucked."

"The army are gonna be crawling all over this place in minutes, lass," Niall reasoned. "There ain't time for grand plans."

I eyed the few people out walking in the park with their faces covered by masks and knew what we had to do.

"Okay, can you tie that woman up and gag her to stop her from giving us away?" I asked and Niall beamed.

"Just call me Christian Grey on speed." He took a zip tie from his belt and strode back inside.

I followed him, focusing on what I had to do as ran into the woman's bedroom and tried not to feel too guilty when she started screaming again. I rifled through her closet, grabbing a couple of large men's coats, a hat and some face masks. I ran back to Niall, finding the woman hogtied on the couch with a potato stuffed in her mouth.

"That's a bloody work of art," he announced, taking his phone out to snap a photo. He reached into her handbag on the floor, taking out her purse and reading the name on her I.D. "Telisha Collins, hmm, don't move now, lass. Let's see how long you can balance this on your noggin for." He placed her I.D. on her head then threw her purse back in her bag.

"Come on," I hissed impatiently, grabbing his arm.

"This is the Sequoia State Hades Defence Squadron, please evacuate this building immediately," a voice sounded through a megaphone somewhere in the apartment block and my breathing quickened. We were running out of time. And I was *not* gonna be caught.

We raced to the balcony and I tossed Niall a black coat and a mask as I pulled on my own. I tucked my hair up into the black beanie and pointed at Niall's sledgehammer. "You have to leave it."

"But *Mary*." He hugged it to his chest just as someone shouted an order back in the building.

"Niall," I hissed. Did he seriously name that thing Mary?? "Dump it."

He kissed the damn hammer, looking like he was leaving a beloved child behind as he placed it down and gave it a salute in goodbye. Then he swung over the side of the balcony, reaching for a drainpipe. "You wanna go on my back, lass?"

"I can manage," I said firmly and he smirked like he was impressed as he started climbing down it. I made my way onto the pipe and followed him, the two of us reaching the ground and darting across the road toward the park without the helicopter making another appearance.

I tugged Niall's sleeve to slow him down as we walked through the gate side by side, his hand suddenly looping through mine like he was a gentleman escorting a lady. Which was about as convincing as a horse escorting a pigeon, but whatever.

The sound of a heavy truck rolling along the road behind me made me turn and my tongue felt leaden as more soldiers spilled out of it, hunting the area. We slipped into the trees, walking along a woodchip track towards the boathouse as my body hummed with adrenaline. This might have been crazy, but I couldn't deny I was thriving on the wildness of it.

"She was a good girl. Ten kills to her name," Niall said, his voice wistful and I realised he was talking about the sledgehammer.

"You can get another one," I breathed, fighting the urge to look back again as more orders were barked by one of the sergeants.

"There won't be another like Mary," he sighed.

"Mary would have wanted you to move on," I whispered, not wanting him to lose it entirely.

Niall O'Brien was seriously volatile and who knew what he might do if he had an emotional meltdown over Mary. I needed to get him to that boathouse because he was my ticket out of this city and back to my men. And more than that, he was important to Kyan. The only member of his family he really loved. So I wasn't going to risk anything happening to him for that reason alone.

"She made such a beautiful sound when she hit a skull, it was music, lass, *music*," he lamented.

"She must have had a few bad points," I tried, my nose wrinkling at the unwanted mental image.

"Well…" he started thoughtfully. "Come to think of it, her head got loose from time to time. Bitch let me down at the crucial moment of death once. She made it a real dirty job that day."

I tried not to picture him smashing skulls in, but it was pretty hard. Niall really was a freaking psycho, but I wasn't gonna complain about that when he'd risked his neck to save me. "See? You can do better."

"You're right," he growled. "I deserve a weapon I can depend upon."

I caught sight of the boathouse through the trees and we quickened our pace a little, my heart pulsing out of beat as the helicopter sounded in the distance. But it was nowhere near here luckily.

We hurried over to the stone building, finding a thin chain and a padlock holding the door shut. Niall took a screwdriver from his belt, jammed it into one of the chain links and twisted it hard, using brute force to break it. He pushed the door open, shoving me inside and following after, bringing the broken chain with him and closing the door. He grabbed a paddle for a canoe and used it to bar the door as I gazed around the interior. The place was cold and full of little pedalos and canoes. A shutter was pulled down which stopped anyone accessing the boats from the jetty that led inside so we were completely isolated in here. And that was perfect.

"We'd better wait here 'til dark," Niall said as he moved to sit in a rowing boat on the concrete beside the water and jerking his head for me to follow.

I stepped in after him, sitting at his side and he wrapped an arm around my shoulders, patting me awkwardly. It was weirdly sweet, especially as I got the feeling the guy didn't do affection often. I couldn't help but think of his wife, the woman he'd lost and avenged all those years ago. Had something cracked in him after losing her? Or had he always been like this? Somehow, I sensed it was a mixture of both, but I wasn't dumb enough to ask him anything about the woman he'd lost. I was guessing he'd find that kind of triggering and he was not the sort of guy I wanted to set off. Hell, he made my Night Keepers look like upstanding pillars of the community. And if he'd been upset about Mary, then mentioning his dead wife seemed like a seriously dangerous idea. It made me sad though, to know he'd experienced such pain and I wondered if he'd ever opened up to Kyan about it. I hoped they were close enough to talk to about the hard things, because if Niall didn't have him, I had the feeling he'd be all alone in the world. And no one deserved that.

"Did I ever tell you about the time I skewered a barber on a pitchfork?" he asked conversationally.

"No," I said with a little laugh. "We've spoken like twice in our lives, so…"

"Well lass, it's quite the story. It all started on a day when I woke up tied to radiator dressed as a Moomin…"

CHAPTER TWENTY EIGHT

We drove east for several hours, bumping along in the back of the army truck with countless other vehicles just like ours all going in the same direction and just as many empty ones heading back to the city as well.

It was cold in the back of the open sided truck, the flimsy canvas overhead offering only the smallest amount of protection from the rain which had been drizzling down on us for the past hour. I guessed the weather was just mirroring how I felt over the distance which was growing between us and our girl.

Niall had messaged to let me know he was with her and was going to get her out of the city, but I hadn't heard anything since and the not knowing was driving me crazy.

The four of us had made the other members of our truck move their asses off of the bench at the back of the bed within the first hour of getting here so that we could sit with our backs to the cab in the best position available, but it was still pretty fucking abysmal. And by 'the four of us' I really meant me. Nash had seemed a little less than impressed when I'd gotten my ass up and told the fuckers who had been sitting here to vacate while Saint had a look on his face which said it was about damn time. I didn't care if I was just proving how much of an asshole I was by doing it either. This was a dog-eat-dog world, and I was a wolf come to devour them all. The sooner they learned it, the faster they'd figure out that it was best to keep the fuck out of my way.

The truck finally pulled to a halt and I blew out a frustrated breath as I stood up, hating how far we'd just come from our girl while running over the best ways for us to get the fuck out of here and back to her as soon as we could. But as Saint had pointed out on plenty of occasions, I wasn't really the brains of this outfit, so most of my plans hinged on me beating the shit out of some soldiers, stealing their guns and shooting our way out of here. No doubt Saint would come up with something a little less suicidal.

"Queue F!" a soldier called out, like that was supposed to mean something to us as he unbolted the back of the truck to let us all off.

I shoved my way through the crowd of people surrounding us as they stood to get off and they quickly cowered back out of the way to let the four of us pass.

My height made it easy enough for me to see over the huge crowds of people to the different queues that had been formed with letters hanging above the entrances to white tents ahead of us.

I hopped down and pointed the way to the queue for Tent F, taking off through the crowd and shoving anyone aside who didn't see me coming fast enough to move.

"I'm not standing around in some fucking queue," Saint growled behind me and I snorted a laugh as I glanced about.

"Of course you're not, Your Highness," I mocked. The thought of Saint Memphis queueing with the norms was damn laughable even if I would have liked to see it.

The soldiers were ringing the crowd in a loose perimeter, each of them armed with assault rifles and looking more than ready to stop anyone who tried to leave.

"I'm guessing our best bet is to head inside before we try to escape," Monroe muttered, echoing my thoughts and I nodded.

"Let's hurry up and get inside then," Saint agreed. "I'm not wasting any more time away from our girl than we have to."

I nodded and took the lead again, carving my way through the crowd towards the front of the queue, ignoring the protests from the people who had been waiting out here for hours already as I set my sights on the head of it. Saint wasn't the only one of us who wasn't going to be forced to stand about out here. I may have been less high maintenance than my elitist friend, but I was still an entitled prick at heart, and in instances like this I gave no shits about that at all.

We made it to the front of the queue, and I stepped in front of the guy there, giving him a hard glare that promised I'd knock his teeth out if he tried to fight me on it. He dropped his gaze to the floor as his cheeks flamed red with unspoken fury and a sense of injustice that would no doubt keep him up at night. Not me though - I'd be sleeping like a baby perfectly comfortable in my dickhead ways and not thinking about the fact that I'd ruined his already shitty day ever again.

A soldier stepped out of the tent to call us forward, pausing as she seemed to realise we weren't the people who had been standing here thirty seconds ago before clearly deciding she didn't give a shit and beckoning me forward.

"We stay together," I said firmly as the other Night Keepers stepped up behind me.

"You can wait for them on the other side," she protested and I shook my head.

"No. We're brothers. We stay together," Saint clipped. No room for negotiation.

The soldier frowned, looking like she'd already had altogether too much shit from people today. And though I couldn't see all that much of her face behind the ventilator mask she was wearing, I could tell she was fairly young and I wondered if a different approach might work better on her.

"Look," I said, softening my tone and stepping a little closer to her like I was all reasonable and shit. "We've been through a lot - lost people, I'm sure you understand. It's rough out there and we made a pact not to split up until this whole thing is over. Would it really be the worst thing for us to just go through this...whatever it is in there together?"

Her gaze roamed over my face and the sincere as shit look I was giving her then she sighed as she glanced at the three men at my back. Blake stepped up and gave her his pretty boy flirtatious grin and I could see her giving in as he placed his hands together in gesture of a prayer.

"Come on then. We allow family groups to be processed together anyway, so seeing as you're brothers..." She cut a doubtful glance over our vastly differing features and skin tones before rolling her eyes like she didn't have it in her to call us out on it. "Just don't cause any shit. If I have to, I'll haul your asses down to the detention block myself."

I gave her my best smile while Blake tossed her a wink and I was pretty sure she swooned just a little bit. She led the way into the tent and I punched Blake's shoulder for flirting with her while he gave me a flat look which made it all too clear he had zero interest in anyone other than Tatum. Which I knew, but as her husband I felt it was my duty to keep her boyfriends in line.

We stepped into the white tent and found another soldier waiting there to search us.

"We need to make sure none of you are carrying any weapons," he said, beckoning for one of us to step forward. I did the honours, holding my arms out and everything as he began to run his hands over me. "And we have to confiscate cell phones for a short time too."

My ears pricked up at that casual announcement, like taking people's phones wasn't fucked up at all.

"Why do you want people's phones?" I asked.

"It comes from higher up. You'd have to ask someone more important than me if you want to know that. Don't worry though, we'll bag it up for you and you'll get it back soon."

"I don't have a phone," I replied casually, hoping he didn't wanna check inside my boots. "Broke it a few weeks back and it hasn't exactly been possible to replace it."

"I'll just have to check you for weapons then," he replied, sounding tired. The others were clearly going to lose their phones, but we only needed mine to make sure that I could contact Niall and check up on Tatum.

"What about if I am a weapon myself?" I asked, deciding to leave it at that. "Are you going to confiscate me?"

The female soldier laughed while the guy searching me just muttered something pissy before running his hands up the inside of my legs. His hand got high enough to arguably call it a cavity search and I was a second from slapping him off of me before he stood back and directed me to the other side of the tent where a nurse was waiting.

"We need to take some blood to confirm you definitely have some active antibodies then we will test for how effective those antibodies are. Can I have your ID?" he asked as I took a seat on the little stool beside him.

"Sure."

I tossed him my fake passport and he quickly took a photograph with the iPad beside him and he got me to sign the bottom of the page which I did with a vague squiggle that might have been my false name or anything at all really. Then he got me to stand on a set of scales, measured my height and checked my blood pressure. When he was done with all that, he listened to my heart and lungs with a stethoscope, made more notes on the iPad and finally prepared a syringe to take my blood.

I glanced at Saint as I rolled my sleeve back, wondering if I should be letting this guy take a sample from me now that I'd had the vaccine, but Saint just gave a faint nod, letting me know we needed to keep playing along. I guessed the main thing was that we didn't draw any attention to ourselves for now and make it harder than it needed to be for us to escape this place.

"Would you be willing to donate more blood in the pursuit of a vaccine if it turns out your sample indicates your suitability?" the nurse asked me and I shrugged.

"What's in it for me?" I asked.

"You'd be helping us bring about an end to this pandemic," he replied, clearly not liking my attitude.

"Right. But I'm talking personally. I mean, I've already survived the Hades Virus, so I don't need a vaccine. I'm assuming you're offering some kind of financial compensation or something if you expect me to donate my blood?"

"Well...no," the nurse said, frowning like he thought I was a total jackass and I smiled broadly at him before standing. "There is talk of a possible future tax break as an incentive but as of yet that hasn't been officially-"

"That'll be a no from me then," I said. "I have no interest in becoming a pin cushion for no reason."

I didn't wait for him to argue with me on that before moving aside so that Saint could take my place. I stood and waited patiently until the others had all been through the same routine as me then the first soldier came to lead us through the back of the tent and outside again.

"You're going to be allocated a sleeping area - for now, everything is fairly basic and we apologise for that, but it's safe, warm, dry and there will be hot meals provided in the mess tents three times a day. Over the next few days we will come around and assign work allocations to everyone which will include building better accommodations and we anticipate being able to move people out of the tents within a month at the longest." She moved over to a printer and hooked two pieces of paper out of it before handing them to us. "This is a map of the camp. The mess tents, shower rooms, bathrooms, toilets and exercise space are all clearly labelled and the four of you have been allocated bunks in tent sixteen-eighty over on the north side of the camp, which is marked with the X. There are bed rolls and basic supplies there for you so that you can go and settle in. If you are in need of anything else, you can come to one of the information points where officers will be able to answer any questions you have." She pointed those out on the map too and I took it with a nod.

"Thanks," I replied, trying not to look at the horror on Saint's face as he gazed out across the maze of dark green tents which filled the valley ahead of us in every single direction for miles on end.

Another soldier appeared with our bags, clearly having given them a thorough search and I slung mine over my shoulder as the others grabbed theirs too.

The soldier left us to go call the next people inside and I clapped a hand on Saint's arm as we started walking.

"If we don't get out of this cesspit within the next hour, I'm going to end up dead from exposure," Saint muttered, not even trying to hide the sneer on his face.

"It's not that cold," Monroe replied, shaking his head at him.

"He doesn't mean exposure to the cold," Blake said with a laugh. "He means exposure to the masses. Saint's snob is showing."

"Thank you for that accurate assessment, Bowman," Saint muttered. "But I have no objections to being called a snob if it means I don't have to mingle with the likes of these...peasants." He pointed out a dude who had a finger jammed up his nose while he rooted around his nostril in hunt of something up there and I laughed.

"That guy is a particularly bad example," Monroe huffed.

"Regardless. We need to escape this farmyard before we catch anything worse than the Hades Virus," Saint hissed.

"Like poverty?" I teased.

"Heaven forbid," he agreed.

Nash rolled his eyes and I laughed as I tried to scope out the best way for us to escape this place, striding down muddy walkways and glancing about before taking my cell phone from my boot.

The others all clustered around me as I sent a message to Niall, but the signal was fucking non-existent and the damn thing wouldn't even send.

"Shit," I cursed, wondering if there were messages I hadn't been able to receive too. But I had faith in Niall and I just had to hold onto that. If I could just trust in him to keep Tatum safe then all I had to do was focus on getting us the hell out of here to meet her.

"Take some footage of this place," Saint said, his lip still curled in disgust. "There's no way they only just opened it today. And the conditions are barely humane. We should leak the images to the press - really fuck with my father's plans by showing everyone the shit show they can look forward to if they go along with this division bullshit."

"Yes sir," I agreed, hiding my phone in my hand and casually filming shots of the place, making sure I showed the mud and the insane queue for the bathroom. If I saw a video like this, I sure as fuck wouldn't wanna leave my cosy house to come stay here.

We walked right out to the edge of the camp where we found a freshly erected metal fence ringing it, manned by armed officers and lit up with huge flood lights.

"How the fuck are we supposed to get out of here?" Monroe asked and I bit my tongue against the curses which begged to spill from my lips.

"We're gonna need a distraction," I said, glancing down at my phone and smiling as I found a bar of signal on it. "Cover me while I make a call."

I turned away from the fence ringing the camp and ducked down like I was going to retie my shoe while calling my uncle instead. Thankfully I had a bar of signal again so it rang as I held it to my ear.

"Hello?" he answered, the sound of a large bang in the background making my heart lurch.

"What the fuck is going on?" I snapped as my heart leapt with fear for my girl.

"Nothing, nothing. I just knocked something over. We're hiding out until nightfall then I'll get your pretty wife out of the city. Besides, you know there's nothing I can't handle," Niall replied excitedly, his Irish accent coupled with the thought of violence raising memories of my childhood to the surface of my mind. "What's up?"

"We're trapped in this camp. Gonna need a distraction to keep the guards' eyes off of us while we escape. Do you think you can help us out?" I asked just as Tatum laughed breathlessly in the background and the vice around my heart loosened a little. She was alright. Having fun too by the sounds of it and I had to admit Niall could be a lot of fun – assuming he didn't flip the fuck out. But I trusted him not to harm her anyway so the worst that would happen in that case was that she might end up witnessing a murder or two which wasn't anything new to her these days.

"I'm on it. I've already got your location and we're practically on route. Just a little issue to finish up with first. Then I'll let you know when I'm ready with that distraction," Niall confirmed.

"What's going-" I began but the line went dead and when I tried to call back, I just got his fucking voicemail.

I cursed as I stood, leaving the phone in my boot once more and the others all looked at me in concern.

"What did he say?" Blake demanded and I shook my head, glancing towards the closest group of soldiers and leading them back into the maze of green tents.

"He's coming. And Tatum's fine," I replied, deciding not to worry them with any more details about my crazy ass uncle. "Maybe we should just get some rest until then."

"I hardly think I'm going to sleep in some heap of canvas," Saint muttered, but he didn't complain as I took the map from my pocket and we headed back into the camp in search of our tent.

I cast one look back over my shoulder at the perimeter the army had erected around us and I just had to hope that whatever Niall came up with as a distraction was enough to get us out of here. Because if it wasn't, then I was beginning to think we might be in more trouble here than we'd expected. And it was looking like we should have run before walking into this place.

But now that we were inside it, we were going to have to break out. Because there wasn't a force on earth that could keep the Night Keepers away from Tatum Roscoe. So even if it came down to a fight with an entire army, we'd do whatever it took.

CHAPTER TWENTY NINE

Darkness had fallen and there were no more shouts coming from the soldiers back on the street or even the sound of the helicopter circling. Niall had told me far more murder stories than I'd ever planned on hearing, but he somehow managed to tell them in a way that made them kinda funny. I didn't know if that made me a sick person for laughing, but maybe it was just that his stories didn't even sound true with how ludicrous they were. Knowing what I did about Niall though, they probably were.

He was examining a map on his phone as he plotted out a route to the barricades surrounding the city. Apparently there were weak spots that weren't manned too heavily and he'd gotten through one of them earlier. I just hoped that would still be the case by the time we got there because we'd certainly caused a stir earlier on. And those soldiers weren't going to stop looking for a guy who'd opened fire on them. The only chance we had was getting out now, and I for one was going to make damn sure we pulled it off.

"Okay, lass, time to go," Niall said, pushing to his feet. The thick coats we'd taken from the woman's apartment had turned out to be a godsend against the cold, but I was still a little numb as I got up.

I flexed my frozen fingers, checking my phone for messages from the guys for the millionth time.

We headed to the door as I put my bag on my back with Kyan's bat. Niall tossed away the oar which had been holding the door shut before slipping outside. I followed him, the night air weirdly still as we slipped quickly back into the trees and followed the path towards the opposite side of the park to where we'd entered. The city was freakishly quiet and goosebumps prickled along the back of my neck as we made it to the exit and Niall opened the gate with a groaning of hinges.

I headed along after him on the dark street beyond it, pressing a bottle of hand sanitiser into his hand. I'd given him the vaccine while we waited in the boathouse and he'd mentioned wanting another two doses for his friends when he went home. I didn't mind. There were still plenty left to be given to Dr De La Cost, but I was kinda curious about who Niall gave enough of a shit about to give a vaccine to. He struck me as more of a loner type. But it was good to know he wasn't totally isolated in the world.

We crept through the silent streets, avoiding any patrols we saw or could hear close by as we continued on toward the edge of the city.

I focused on returning to my Night Keepers, trying not to worry about the camp they were in or how they were going to get out of it. If anyone could do it, it was them. And it wasn't like they were prisoners there. They'd be able to slip out somehow. I just hoped Niall and I could do the same.

We reached the end of a long road and pressed back into the shadows as we gazed down the adjoining street to where a metal barricade had been erected. There was one truck in front of it and a soldier was leaning against it, talking to another guy a few feet away.

"The third one's our problem," Niall said quietly.

"I can only see two," I breathed.

He took hold of my chin, tilting my head up and pointing to the roof of the building in front of us. "There's a little birdie in his nest up there."

"Shit," I cursed. "How'd you get past them the first time?"

"I didn't come in this way," he said. "They'll have put a fuck load of soldiers on guard where I did come in because I caused one hell of a fucking stir." He chuckled, but as curious as I was to hear more, there wasn't time for that story. We needed to move.

"Well how do you know there's someone up there?" I asked as I knocked his hand away from my chin.

"There's always an asshole on a roof." He shrugged.

"But how can you be sure?" I hissed.

"I'll be sure when I'm choking him out and he's begging for his mammy," he said with a smirk. "I'm gonna head up there. When I give you the signal, run for the barricade. There's a gap in it where the truck is parked. Oh, and throw this if things get ugly." He placed a grenade in my hand and my throat tightened.

"Is it smoke or a bomb?" I asked.

"Guess you'll find out if you have to use it." He dropped a car key into my hand too. "My truck's parked on Opal Street. Just in case I don't make it." He winked and darted across the road, leaving me behind before I got a choice in the matter.

"Wait, what's the signal?" I whisper shouted after him, but he ignored me, using his screwdriver to jimmy the door open and slip inside. *Crazy bastard.*

I took a calming breath as I waited, keeping my eyes on the soldiers up ahead as I remained in the shadows of a doorway. I pocketed the key and the grenade, unsettled by the thought of Niall not making it out of this.

The seconds ticked by so slowly, I could almost hear them ticking in my head.

Come on Niall. Hurry up.

He suddenly started yodelling from the top of the roof and my lips popped open at the sound. The two soldiers on the ground looked up at the roof in alarm and ran forward into the front entrance of the building. I guessed that was the freaking signal, so I ran out of my hiding place, tearing up the street toward the truck. I slipped behind it, finding the gap in the barricade and looking behind me up at the roof. Niall was standing there yodelling at the top of his lungs and he suddenly threw himself over the edge.

A strangled scream left me just before a rope I hadn't noticed snapped taught and he started rappelling down the side of the building. *Jesus fucking Christ. He almost gave me a heart attack.*

"Hey!" a soldier appeared on the roof, moving to lean over the edge and point a gun at Niall. "Stop or I'll open fire!"

Niall let go of the rope six feet from the street, grabbing his pistol as he fell and shooting like a mad man as he hit the ground on his back. The soldier was forced to retreat, but Niall only had so many bullets and there was no way he was going to make it to where I was after that gun rang empty.

I cursed, making a decision as I pulled the pin on the grenade and aiming for the side of the building. It was either gonna blow a hole in it or offer Niall some cover. Either way, it might just buy him enough time to run. I threw it with a growl of effort and it hit the wall before exploding in a growing cloud of pink gas and glitter which filled the air fast.

Niall leapt to his feet just as his pistol ran out of bullets and gunfire tore through the air a beat later. But he was already in the growing cloud of smoke, running toward me, just a shadow in the fog. He burst out of it and half knocked me over as he shoved me through the gap, his hand latching around my waist so I didn't fall.

I turned and ran with him down the street beyond the barricade and he let go of me so we could sprint, taking a hard right down another road between a row of houses. We didn't stop running until our lungs burned and we literally couldn't go a step further, my heart thundering against my ribs.

I buckled over as we hid behind a large van, dragging down heavy breaths. "Holy shit," I panted, laughing wildly.

"That was fucking beautiful, Tatum. You really are Kyan's girl," Niall chuckled, clapping me on the shoulder before taking out his phone and opening the map.

"And you sure as hell are his uncle." I grinned and his mouth hooked up with pride.

"We're only two blocks away from my car, come on." He jogged away and I headed after him, ignoring the burning stitch in my side as the desperation to put as much distance between us and those soldiers as possible took over every other instinct in my body.

We finally made it to Niall's car which was parked up in a quiet suburban street and my brows arched at the huge black Jeep Wrangler.

I climbed into the passenger seat as Niall started it up and tossed his phone in the cupholder with directions loaded into the map.

"Kyan shared his location with me." He smirked, pushing his tattooed hand through his blonde hair to shove it out of his face.

I beamed with joy, my heart pounding excitedly. "Let's go swoop in and save their asses."

He grinned like a demon. "That's the fucking spirit."

CHAPTER THIRTY

Our tent was laid out with basic bunks, each with a blanket, pillow and little else. It was big enough to house ten, but Kyan had made quick work of scaring off the other people who had been in here, affording us some level of privacy while we waited for Niall to get here and cause enough of a distraction for us to escape.

I was sitting on my bunk with Nash beside me and Kyan sitting opposite us, his knees brushing mine with how closely packed the beds were. Saint stood ramrod straight between the bunks, arms folded, contempt burning hot in his dark eyes and an aura of 'I shall die before I so much as touch one of those so-called beds' hanging about him.

I mean, he had a point. These things were uncomfortable and beyond basic, but I wasn't really keen on staying on my feet for hours on end rather than just taking a perch. It must have been damn hard work being inside that dude's head all the time.

"Have you heard anything since you shared your location?" Monroe asked and Kyan took his phone from his boot, checking it and shrugging.

"Nope. But the service here is next to fucking nothing so for all I know they can't get a message out to me or I can't get one to come in. Either way this thing is starting to run seriously low on juice and at this rate the battery will die without us even knowing what's happening out there."

"You will substantially lessen the amount of time the battery will last if you keep on illuminating the screen," Saint growled, reaching out to take the phone from Kyan who gave it up easily. "I'll close down any apps which don't need to be running and put it on low power mode, then for the love of all that's holy to you, stop looking at the fucking thing until it goes off."

"Sure thing," Kyan agreed, not even bothering to argue as he took it back and slid it into his boot once more.

Saint wasn't the only one of us on edge, but we weren't about to turn on each other. We might have bickered and fought when we were on our own time, but when shit mattered, we were a unit. The Night Keepers. All in and no turning back.

We'd already discussed as many plans as possible for how we were going to get ourselves out of here but when it came down to it, it was simple. There was a fence surrounding this place and we needed to get the fuck over it. Or under it. Through it. Whatever way, beyond the fence was where we needed to be at.

Our brief amount of planning with Niall had drawn us all to the decision that he needed to be in position to the north of the camp to be in with the best chance of avoiding the notice of the armed forces who were all coming and going from the south. But even that was a bit of a shot in the dark, the military weren't idiots. They'd have eyes watching in every direction surrounding this place. We were just counting on being able to lose them in the forest and then figuring out the rest from there.

"Which one is it?" a female voice came from somewhere beyond the tent.

"Sixteen-eighty," a man replied. "All four of them came in together - said they were brothers but that sure as fuck ain't true by the looks of their faces and the names on their documentation."

"Maybe they went through the foster system together?" the woman replied.

"Who knows? All we know for certain is that their blood samples have raised the interest of the people at the top. Something about their levels of immunity being off the charts in comparison to everyone else. So let's just concentrate on securing them and hope that this could be a good thing for all of us."

"Fuck," I breathed, looking around as the voices drew closer to the entrance to the dark, green tent but when my eyes fell on the space where Saint had just been, I found him already half way outside beneath the bottom of the canvas.

Kyan grabbed my arm and gave me a shove to make me follow and I did so instantly, dropping down onto my belly and army crawling out beneath the tightly pegged canvas.

Saint caught my hand and hauled me upright, pressing a finger to his lips as we crouched in the narrow gap between our tent and the one beside it. The front of his clothes were smothered in mud and I glanced down to find myself in the same condition.

The moon hung low beneath a fine haze of clouds above us and my breath fogged in the cold air as I looked up at the dark sky, thankful for the cover it offered as my pulse raced with the thought of getting caught.

Monroe was right on my heels and I heaved him up beside me before Kyan scrambled out.

We'd had to abandon our bags, but there wasn't anything in them aside from a few clothes and toiletries anyway, so who gave a fuck?

We didn't dare move, nothing passing between us but ragged breaths and silence as we hid in the shadows and waited for the soldiers to draw closer.

"Dammit, they're not here," the man huffed from inside the canvas.

"Of course they're not. Nothing is ever that simple, is it?" the woman sighed. "I'll put an alert out, send their photos around the rest of the unit and make sure someone rounds them up."

"Go and ask around the neighbouring tents to see if anyone knows where they went," the man snapped and there was a chorus of 'yes sirs' that made it clear a whole squad had just come looking for us. Shit, this was bad.

"I'm not gonna end up as a guinea pig in some lab," Kyan growled in a low voice as his hands curled into fists and I agreed with him wholeheartedly on that.

"Niall or not, we need to get the fuck out of here," I hissed and the others all nodded as a group of soldiers hurried past the gap we were hiding in, splitting off to ask the people in the surrounding tents about us.

We looked between each other as we tried to decide whether to stay hidden here until they left or take this chance to run and Saint jerked his head towards the rear of the tent.

I nodded my agreement, wanting to run rather than wait here like sitting ducks and we all started creeping along after him.

Saint hesitated when he reached the end of the line of tents then leapt out of the gap and darted across a muddy walkway before slipping into a gap between the next row of tents.

I raced after him with Kyan and Nash right behind me and we hurried down another narrow gap, my back brushing one of the tents as I was forced to move along sideways to fit through.

The sounds of more soldiers calling out to each other and jogging in formation kept reaching us. I couldn't decide if there were more of them about than earlier or if it just seemed that way to me because I knew we were being hunted.

As we made it to another pathway, a huge floodlight suddenly came on from a watchtower to our right and my pulse thundered as I ducked down quickly, taking cover from its penetrating gaze behind one of the tents as I looked between my brothers in fear.

"How the fuck are we supposed to get out of here?" Nash hissed, his blue eyes wide with concern.

"We focus on what matters to us," Saint growled. "What matters more than anything else. The one thing we have to get back to. You put her to the front of your mind, and you don't fucking stop until she's in your arms again. Got it?"

"Hell yes," Kyan agreed, the crazy motherfucker actually grinning like this was some great game we were playing.

"Alright then. I think we need to run like hell," Saint said. "The next time that searchlight sweeps away from us, we go and we don't stop until we're at the northern fence."

"We don't stop," I agreed.

"If we have to go through those soldiers to get out of here, so be it," Kyan added, a hungry glint to his eyes that said he was almost hoping for that.

"Let's get the fuck out of here then," Nash agreed.

My blood was pumping like it did before a competition and I let a smile bite into my cheeks as I zeroed in on that feeling. I always performed best under pressure. It was where I shone.

"First one to the fence gets a night alone with Tatum," I challenged.

"Prepare to lose in that case, Bowman," Nash teased.

"Don't be dumb. And don't fucking stop," Saint growled.

The light swept by and we dove out onto the path. Instead of heading for another narrow gap, Saint turned left and started running. In all honesty, I had no fucking idea which direction north was, but Saint probably had built in GPS in his goddamn head so if he'd chosen that direction then I was all for it.

We charged down the muddy pathway as fast as we could, leaving the watchtower and the spotlight behind us, powering on in hopes of outrunning it before it was turned this way again.

My lungs expanded and contracted as my muscles laboured to power me along as fast as I could go and when the path hit a fork, I was the first one there.

"Right," Saint barked from just behind me and I turned that way, my heart leaping as I spotted a group of soldiers at the far end of the path.

Luckily for me, they were passing by, not looking our way and I managed to leap into a gap between two tents again to avoid them.

The others followed as I moved as fast as I could, adrenaline singing in my veins as I shimmied along the tight space.

There were shouts from within one of the tents as someone in there noticed us forcing our way by. Then all of a sudden, soldiers were barking orders and as I spilled out onto another path, I spotted a squadron of them turning our way.

"Oh, fuck," I gasped as they yelled instructions for us to stop where we were and the others all scrambled out of the gap to join me too.

"Run!" Monroe barked and I didn't need telling twice.

I took off away from the soldiers, unable to focus on where north was and just keeping my gaze fixed on the path ahead as I led my brothers away from the danger behind us.

We ran like our lives depended on it and I was pretty fucking certain they did. Saint's dad would hear about these kids with the super immunity, he'd see the photos and the fake passports. He'd know exactly who the fuck we were and precisely why we had such amazing antibodies. We couldn't get caught. No fucking way.

The shouts of the soldiers behind us were loud and demanding, but none of us slowed for so much as a beat.

We ducked and dived between the maze of tents then found ourselves outside the mess tent where they'd been offering dinner hours ago. It was quiet now and the open space surrounding it gave us the chance to really sprint, putting some distance between us and the soldiers following.

We rounded the side of the huge tent then ducked behind a toilet block and managed to wedge ourselves into a gap behind it where nothing but shadows lingered.

I held my breath as the sounds of the chasing soldiers reached us and they started shouting orders to split up and search the place high and low.

"How far to the fence?" Monroe breathed when we were sure none of them were close enough to overhear us.

Saint's brow furrowed and I knew he didn't like the answer he was about to give. "We've gone west," he breathed. "So it's far enough."

"Shit," Kyan murmured, and I thought it was in response to our situation, but he ducked down and pulled the phone from his boot instead, showing us the message on the screen from Tatum.

Tigress:
Twenty minutes and counting *squid emoji*

My eyes widened at that, especially as Kyan pointed out that the thing had been sent ten minutes ago even though it had only just been delivered.

"Tatum's with Niall," I breathed, worried about her now that I knew he hadn't taken her back to Kyan's grandpa's place. But I wasn't sure what else I'd expected; that girl wasn't the type to wait somewhere just so that we would feel better about her being safe away from here. Though I seriously would have been happier if she had.

"It's going to take us more than ten minutes to make it to the north fence," Saint said in a low voice. "And that's assuming we're able to stop hiding like this any time soon."

"You don't think we can make it?" I asked.

"I can't get a message to send back to them," Kyan growled. "So it's either now or never. Niall won't hold back on the plan unless he is specifically called off."

"And when he goes through with it, all eyes will be drawn in that direction - towards our girl," Nash pointed out, his eyes flaring with determination to make it there before that happened.

"Then let's make sure we get there in time," Saint commanded, like he could make it happen through will alone. And this was Saint Memphis, so he probably could. "And once we are safely out of here, one of you is going to explain the fucking squid emoji to me."

CHAPTER THIRTY ONE

Niall drove like a fucking maniac and I had to press one hand to the door to brace myself as he took turnings at speed. I'd been kinda relieved when he pulled onto the highway so I wasn't jerked around in my seat anymore. But then he started driving at nearly a hundred miles an hour and I wasn't sure it was an improvement at all.

"Um, Niall, I know we're in a rush, but is there any chance you could drive at a speed we won't fucking die at?" I demanded.

"We won't die, lass," he laughed. "The Grim Reaper's not after me today."

"That's not a comforting answer."

"He's had more than enough chances to take me," he assured me. "But he prefers to keep me doing his job for him instead. I haven't yet decided if it's because he likes me or if he just enjoys making my suffering go on and on in payment for my failures."

My lips parted at his words but his smile didn't falter and he laughed harder as we sped along, eating up the road as we closed in on the location of the camp. My heart beat wildly when Niall finally exited the highway and tore along a winding road surrounded by woodland, hardly slowing for the bends as he raced on, singing Godzilla by Eminem feat. Juice WRLD and knowing every damn word. He was a freaking good rapper too.

"Ah, here we go." He turned off the road and I yelled in alarm as we practically nose dived down into the trees and the wheels slammed into the mud. He pumped the gas and carved a path through the woods while I winced every time he narrowly missed a tree trunk.

"I'm not gonna crash," he insisted as he caught sight of my expression. "Do you think I'd let Kyan's girl get crushed up in this vehicle like a tin can?"

"Watch where you're going!" I screamed as the car sailed toward a huge oak and he cursed, twisting the wheel hard so we went careening past it and my heart rate went through the roof.

"See?" he laughed. "I could do this with my hands tied behind my back and my eyes shut." He shut his eyes to make that point and I lunged at him, forcing them open with a snarl.

"You either drive properly or I'm taking over," I growled.

"Be my guest." He let go of the wheel and I gasped, unclipping my seatbelt and diving into his lap as I regained control of the vehicle. He slid his feet off of the pedals and I put mine in their place as I slowed the car to a reasonable speed and glanced at the map on Niall's phone.

When we'd driven nearly a mile through the forest, I switched the headlights off and drove us up as near as I could get to the camp. My boys were close, I could practically sense them here and I wouldn't be leaving without them.

I glimpsed floodlights beyond the trees, illuminating a fence ringing the camp and the tents filling the whole place. It looked like something from an apocalypse movie and I didn't like it one bit.

I stopped the car and Niall laughed, slapping my arm. "That was fun. For a second there I thought you weren't gonna take the wheel and we'd both die."

"That would not have been my fault," I said in disbelief, opening his door and sliding out onto the ground, my legs still shaking with adrenaline. Fuck him for driving like he had a death wish, but I couldn't deny I was feeling as high as a kite right now.

"Liar," he scoffed. "I wouldn't let my nephew's girl die. What kind of person do you think I am?" He opened the glove compartment, taking out a machete, a Zippo lighter with the words *If you can't fix it, burn it* engraved on the side and a pair of night vision goggles.

"I'm not going to dignify that question with an answer," I said as I gave those items a pointed look and he smirked, walking around to the back of the car and opening the hatch to the trunk. He casually took out a box of fireworks and a gallon of gasoline then tossed me the goggles.

"Here, you can watch our backs while I set up a decoy," he said as he took out a green T-Rex mask and pulled it over his head.

I took the gun from where it was wedged in my waistband and let him do his crazy thing as I followed him through the trees, putting the night vision goggles on so I could see the way forward.

We made it close to the edge of the woods and Niall set about placing fireworks in a long row through the trees. He doused the whole lot in gasoline as I kept my gaze on the perimeter of the camp and the single watchtower in the distance. The soldiers wouldn't be able to see us unless they managed to cast some light this way or were watching with goggles of their own, but we needed to be quiet all the same and I continually told Niall to *shh* as he broke into song, started whistling or cracking jokes. Thankfully, he listened and he soon had his decoy set up and ready to blow. He tugged his mask up, lighting a cigarette as he smiled at his work.

I took out my phone, finding a reply from Kyan and my heart swelled.

Koala:
On our way, baby. See you soon for a *squid emoji* reunion.
P.S. we might be running late

Tigress:

Looking forward to it.

*We're on the north side of camp ready and waiting *octopus emoji**

I sniggered and looked to Niall as he dragged on his cigarette, seeming lost to some daydream as sadness crossed his eyes. For a moment I found myself captured by that look on his face, like I was getting a glimpse beneath the mask he wore to the man who had lost his wife in such a horrifying way all those years ago. It sent a chill down my spine as I imagined living with grief like that and I was struck with the urge to hug him, but I held off on account of him being a beast of a man and a psychopath.

"They're coming," I said and he nodded, his face immediately lighting up again.

"Alright, I got a quick favour to ask though," he said, holding out his hand. "This is the address to my house. If I die, can you make sure the girl in my basement is let out. You can leave the guy there to rot if you like, but the girl..." He pressed the folded piece of paper into my palm. "Don't let that one die."

My lips opened and closed at his words, shock racing through me. "Is it that girl from Royaume D'élite?" I blurted. I'd thought of her a bunch of times since Niall had bought her and had often wondered what had become of her. Ending up as someone else's prisoner didn't seem like a much improved fate, but surely Niall wasn't harming her, was he?

"Maybe." He shrugged. "What's it to you?"

"People don't deserve to be kept in cages, Niall," I growled, wondering if I'd gotten the guy all wrong. Sure, he was as nutty as a pistachio and was clearly used to killing people, but...

I didn't really know where I was going with that argument. It didn't seem like it was gonna redeem Niall O'Brien.

"It's a nicer cage," he said with a shrug like that made it okay. "Besides, she owes me. Can't let her go without that debt being cleared now, can I?"

He sounded so damn reasonable that it was hard to remember that we were discussing the fact that he was keeping prisoners in his damn basement.

"A cage is a cage," I replied firmly and he pursed his lips as he considered that then shrugged lightly.

"Well, you'd best pray I die then so you can go set her free. Oh and if I survive, don't look at that address and be sure to destroy it. No one gets to know where my home is and live to tell tales about it." He winked and pulled his T-Rex mask down, leaving me to wonder if that last bit was a joke or not as he turned away, flicking his cigarette towards the fireworks. They went up with a whoosh as the gasoline caught light and my heart hammered as the fireworks started going off with loud bangs and colourful plumes of light.

I tore the night vision goggles off as the whole world lit up in a giant bonfire before me and as fireworks started flying in every direction, I turned and ran the fuck away. *I am not gonna die from a Big Banger to the face.*

I made it back to the Jeep, getting in and starting the engine, realising Niall hadn't followed.

He was still in front of the fire, shooting rounds off into the sky from his freshly reloaded pistol to cause as much noise as humanly possible.

"Fucking idiot," I hissed as bullets were fired in return from the watchtower.

I pressed my foot to the gas, tearing toward him as he darted behind the fire like it was a shield that would protect him from a bullet, but it sure as shit wasn't. The mud exploded at his feet where bullets hit the ground and I ducked my head lower as more bullets peppered the front of the car, my pulse pounding in my skull.

I turned the wheel hard, pulling up beside Niall and shoving the door open, trying to call him inside. He let out a curse as a bullet hit him and he fell down in the mud as I gasped in horror.

I dove out to help him up, frantic as my hand slid through hot blood on the top of his arm and more cursing came from within his T-Rex mask.

"It's just a scratch, lass," he chuckled, letting me help him to his feet and he picked me up with his good arm, tossing me into the driver's seat before climbing over me into the passenger side, nearly kicking me in the face with his dirty boot and crushing me beneath his huge body.

I pressed my foot to the accelerator before I got the door closed, needing to get out of the light of the fire as I tore away, keeping parallel with the camp as I hunted for my boys in the dark.

"Put pressure on it," I commanded Niall as he tore his freaking dinosaur mask off and popped the glove compartment.

"Yeah, yeah, I know what I'm doing. I know how to hack off every limb and keep a guy alive for days after, so I can get myself through this." He tore off his shirt, revealing a fiercely muscular body painted in countless tattoos before taking out a bottle of white rum and pouring it over the wound. He followed that up by drinking a healthy shot of it then he wrapped his shirt around the wound, tying it off and kicking the glove compartment shut.

"Where are they?" I said through my teeth, hunting for signs of my Night Keepers in the direction of the camp. Soldiers were going to be swarming the woods any minute and we didn't have time to spare.

Come on, come on.

I gripped the steering wheel anxiously, determination coating my heart in steel. I was going to leave here with my Night Keepers. There was no alternative. Not one I would ever submit to. I was their ride or die, so they needed to get here and fucking ride.

CHAPTER THIRTY TWO

My chest was heaving with the effort of running and hiding and being chased all over this fucking rabbit's warren of a camp and with every step I took, I was terrified that we were about to get caught, dragged away, taken to some lab and used the way Tatum had been. I knew if that happened it would be the end of it. There wouldn't be anyone to come charging in to rescue us. We'd be buried. Locked away in some secret facility that no one would ever find even if they tried and if Tatum attempted to come for us, she'd end up caught too.

Troy Memphis would get away with everything. Killing my family. Unleashing this virus. Running that sick club. Abusing his son. All of it and no doubt countless more atrocities too. The man was a fucking plague on our state, our country - hell, the entire world. We had him to thank for the mess we were all in with the Hades Virus and I was going to take him down if it was the last fucking thing I did.

I looked between the others as I pressed my back to a huge metal storage unit and we waited while the searchlights swept past. The entire camp was abuzz now, soldiers darting left and right, flashing our photographs at people and hunting for us. They knew we were running from them and no doubt the security around the fences would be insane, but we had no choice. We had to take our chance and hope for the best.

The scent of smoke blew over us on the wind and I strained my ears to listen as the shouts of the soldiers turned harsher, the chain of command snapping into place as orders were barked and uniformed men and women ran past us, all of them heading in the same direction.

Something new was happening.

I chanced a look out of our hiding place as a unit ran by, my eyebrows rising as I spotted an orange glow lighting up the sky in the distance.

"Do you think your uncle might have anything to do with that?" I murmured, ducking back out of sight and looking at Kyan.

"He does enjoy a bonfire," he agreed just as a high-pitched whistle cut through the air and I tipped my head back in time to see a huge red firework explode across the sky.

"What the hell?" Blake murmured but Kyan just laughed.

"Yeah - that's Niall alright. Time we got the fuck out of here."

"Come on then," Saint barked, pushing past me as he peeked out of our hiding place then took off down the pathway outside it.

I sprang into motion, chasing after him with the others right beside me as more and more fireworks lit the sky overhead.

There was so much noise coming from the soldiers as they tried to get the situation under control that I didn't even notice the sound of footsteps ahead of us until we rounded the corner right before the fence.

We skidded to a halt in the mud as we came face to face with the three soldiers who stared at us in surprise for a beat before seeming to recognise us as the guys they'd been searching for.

The one in the centre of the group opened his mouth to say something but Kyan roared as he charged forward, tackling him into the mud without so much as missing a beat.

The briefest thought of how fucking insane this was crashed through my mind, but as the soldier closest to me went for his sidearm, I slammed my fist into his elbow to stop him, my shoulder connecting with his abdomen a moment later as I took him to the ground too.

Saint and Blake dove on the third soldier and I was lost in a tangle of flying fists, freezing mud and desperation as we fought with all we had to overpower them.

This wasn't like fighting some random dude in a street brawl, these men had training and they knew how to fight. But they had also been taken unawares and were encumbered by their bulky uniforms while we had the advantage of fighting for our damn lives. Desperation was a powerful tool when it was put to good use and there was no greater motivation than the need in us to escape this place and get back to our girl.

My ribs flared with pain as the guy beneath me punched and kicked, his blows heavy and meant to wound, but I was a big motherfucker who had spent years training to fight. I had the edge on him and we both realised it in the same moment.

I punched him hard then managed to hook an arm around his neck, flipping him onto his front and exerting pressure as I drove my knee into his spine.

A glance to my right revealed one of the other soldiers lying unconscious in the mud and a beat later, Saint had a gun pressed to the head of the guy beneath me.

He stopped struggling instantly and I pulled back, relieving him of his weapon as I got to my feet, finding Kyan holding onto the other soldier with a pistol pointed at his head too.

"You're going to make sure we walk out of here," Saint snarled, indicating for me to take hold of the soldier pinned beneath me and I jerked his arms behind him, holding them tightly as the taste of blood coated my tongue from my busted lip.

"You can't seriously believe you'll escape this place?" the soldier coughed out.

"I can and we will," Saint assured him. "You're the ones who are delusional if you honestly believe that we would just allow you to lock us up in some lab to experiment on."

"I'm sure it isn't like that," said the soldier Kyan was restraining. "They just want to question you about your antibodies."

"Thanks, but no thanks," Blake said, stooping down to take the unconscious soldier's weapons.

"Let's go," Saint added, ending this pointless discussion.

I couldn't help but glance over at the closest watchtower as we stepped out into the open space before the fence and we all clustered together, forcing the soldiers to walk between us and it. If anyone up there spotted us, they'd have to shoot their own men to stop us and I knew there was no chance of them doing that.

We jogged across the muddy ground to the fence, the soldiers giving in to the inevitable as we made them run with us and my heart was thundering by the time we reached the metal wire panels which penned us in.

Fireworks continued to explode overhead and as I turned to look to our left, I spotted them shooting out of an enormous fire that was blazing in the trees just outside the fence at the edge of the trees.

The blast of a car horn beeping twice drew my attention back to the thick trees ahead of us and my heart soared as I spotted two people sitting in a huge black Jeep Wrangler, waiting for us. Tatum's long, golden hair was unmistakable even from this distance and a mixture of excitement and fear filled me at the sight of her here. I just wanted to bundle her up and get her the hell away from this place, which meant we needed to hurry the hell up.

Blake managed to shove the metal fence hard enough to create a gap in it between two of the metal panels just as the blaring spotlight from the watchtower swung around to us. I ducked down behind the soldier I still held, making sure there was no chance of them getting a clear shot at me.

"Stop!" a voice roared from the tower, but there was no fucking chance of that.

"Like fuck we will!" Kyan yelled back as he ducked through the gap in the fence, dragging his human shield with him to protect him and Blake.

The soldier I was holding tried to jerk free of my grip, but Saint took hold of him too, forcing him to follow us as we awkwardly shifted through the gap in the fence.

One of the guards in the tower fired a shot into the ground a few meters from us in warning as he continued to yell at us to stop and my heart leapt for a moment before we started running.

More shots were fired and lumps of grass sprayed into the air, but I ignored them, keeping the soldier between us and his friends as we raced into the safety of the trees and none of them came anywhere close to hitting us.

Tatum scrambled over her seat and flung the back door of the car open as we raced for it, a man's wild laughter sailing to us over the sounds of gunshots and fireworks and Blake dove into the car while Kyan kept hold of his soldier.

Niall climbed into the driver's seat and Tatum clambered into the front passenger seat to make room for us as Blake scooted right over in the back.

I stopped beside Kyan, letting Saint jump in before we shoved the soldiers away and leapt in too.

The wheels spun in the dirt as Niall hit the gas and I half fell into the footwell as Kyan sprawled on top of Blake and Saint.

We bounced over the rough ground and I smacked my head on the side of the door before managing to scramble upright and look out at the dark forest speeding by outside.

"Hold onto your asses boys!" Niall yelled. "We're going off road."

I managed to force my way onto a seat, half sitting in Blake's lap as I reached around the chair in front of me to grasp Tatum's hand.

She looked back at me with a wide smile, her eyes sweeping over all of us like she was making absolutely certain we were all okay and I found myself laughing as I realised we were.

"You almost gave me a damn heart attack making me wait like that," she said, trying for a pout but unable to keep the grin away for long.

"Sorry about that," I replied.

"They'll be chasing us," Saint said, his voice stern like he was warning all of us not to get over excited about our escape.

"Good point, lad," Niall said, flicking the headlights off and plunging us into darkness.

My gut plummeted as he continued to accelerate, driving deeper into the forest with hardly any light to show him if there was a tree coming up ahead of us.

"Are you insane?" I asked him, gripping hold of the headrest in front of me as I took in Kyan's uncle. Niall was grinning as he drove, his dirty blonde hair pushed back out of his eyes and a collection of tattoos crawling over his bare chest and up the side of his neck. He had tattoos coating his hands where they clasped the wheel too and he flexed his fingers like he was brimming with energy that was desperate for an outlet.

"Some people say I am," he replied with a nonchalant shrug which said he didn't care. Or maybe that he wasn't sure.

I turned around to look out the back of the car, finding nothing but darkness and trees all around us as we drove further and further into the forest.

"Where are we heading?" Saint demanded.

"Don't know," Niall announced with a smile. "No one can predict yer movements if you don't have a plan to follow."

"You have no plan?" Saint blanched, looking like someone had just taken a shit on his pet cat and styled its fur into a poohawk.

"It's the best way to be," Niall said and Tatum breathed a laugh as Saint looked like he was about to start up a tirade.

Kyan punched him in the arm before he could start that though and he gave us a pointed look as Saint shot him a glare.

"I told you assholes that Tate is safe with Niall. The rest of you though? I don't like your chances if you piss him off," Kyan explained.

Niall laughed loudly as the car hit a bank and my stomach dropped as it felt like we were only driving on two wheels for a couple of endless seconds before it banged back down onto solid ground.

"Does someone wanna take the wheel?" Niall called. "My arm is hurting like an arse that just got fucked with no lube."

He didn't actually wait for anyone to respond before slamming on the brakes and jumping out of the car and as he opened his door, I noticed the bloodstains on his seat.

"What the fuck happened to you, old man?" Kyan asked as he opened his door too and stepped out. I followed right behind him, looking at the blood that was dripping from Niall's left arm down to the floor.

"I got shot a little." Niall ripped a makeshift bandage off of his arm which looked like it had once been his shirt. His heavily inked and scarred muscular torso was flecked with red and I sucked in a breath as the blood pissing down his arm began to drip from his fingertips.

"I told him to do something about that," Tatum insisted as she got out of the car too and Saint took her phone from the cupholder, clearly deciding that he'd be the best one to make the plan if Niall wouldn't.

"It's nothing, lass," Niall said, waving her off as she tried to get a better look and he unbuckled his belt before slipping it around his arm and cinching it tight above the bullet wound.

He strolled around to the back of the Jeep and opened it before grabbing a roll of duct tape and I took Tatum's hand as we followed after him, my eyes falling on the weird array of items he kept in his car.

"What the hell is all of this shit?" I asked as I looked over the assortment of tools from axes to hammers to a nail gun, the four rolls of duct tape, thick coil of rope, box of fireworks, bolt cutters and what looked like a blindfold tossed on top.

"Hitman," Niall said, pointing at himself before winding the duct tape around the bleeding wound on his bicep a few times and ripping it off with his teeth. "But if the cops pull me over I just say I'm a handyman."

"How do you explain the blindfold?" Tatum asked curiously.

"I tell them I'm a submissive and that if my mistress calls me I've gotta be ready for her to come choke me no matter what time of the day or night it is. Folk don't tend to question that shit."

Tatum snorted a laugh while I held back on saying half the things that were running though my head. I'd already known he was a gun for hire from what Kyan had told us, but standing here looking at his killing gear kinda made it more real.

"It looks like you've got a good set up here," I said, wondering if complimenting his murder weapons was the thing to do in this situation. All I knew for certain was that this was fucking weird.

"Why? You need someone dead?" Niall asked casually like he was offering me a soda. "I don't have any openings this week because I really need to get back home and feed my pets. The feisty one doesn't like it if I leave her waiting too long between meals. She gets real mouthy. The other one gets pissy too, but I don't give a fuck about him so I'm not so bothered on that issue. Still, I wouldn't want him dying on me before I'm good and ready."

Kyan gave me a look that said don't ask, but I was really fucking curious now.

"Is that sanitary?" Tatum asked, pointing at his duct tape bandage and Niall barked a laugh before tossing the trunk closed and rounding the car to get in the front passenger seat.

"Niall doesn't much care about his own mortality," Kyan supplied with a shrug as he ushered us around the car to get back in.

Blake had taken the driver's seat and Saint was looking at a map on Tatum's phone as he muttered about the best route for us to take to avoid the camp as we headed back south towards Kyan's family's home.

I got into the middle seat and Kyan climbed in beside me, drawing Tatum onto his lap before pulling the door closed.

"Follow this route to the best of your ability," Saint said, handing Tatum's phone to Blake who sat it in a cradle on the dash with the satnav highlighting a route Saint had clearly drawn out himself.

"On it," Blake agreed, pulling into the trees once more and we headed away from the camp as fast as we could.

"We need to send that footage of the camp to the press," Saint said, holding his hand out for Kyan's phone and I frowned at him as I realised he hadn't even really greeted Tatum yet.

"You need to chill, brother," Kyan teased, tossing him the phone all the same.

"I will just as soon as we are away from here and the threat has passed," he snipped back before focusing on the phone and ignoring the rest of us.

Niall kicked his boots up onto the dash and found a baseball cap in the glove box, putting it on and tugging it down over his eyes as he seemed to go to sleep.

"Are you okay?" I murmured to Tatum as I took her hand in mine, turning it over to inspect it for any signs of injuries.

"I'm fine. Niall was a fierce protector, don't worry."

"I think you need a full physical check-up to be sure, baby," Kyan murmured against her neck while running his hand along her thigh.

Tatum sighed contentedly, turning her head to place a kiss against his lips before leaning over to me next. There was something about that which seemed so simple, so easy, her just turning from one of us to another. I didn't even know when I'd fallen into this rhythm with it, but at least in these kinds of situations, it seemed to make so much sense.

Saint was typing away furiously, sending email after email to as many different news outlets as he could and by the time we bumped back out of the forest and onto a road again, he was done. He wordlessly took the SIM card from the phone, broke it into pieces then lowered his window to toss it out.

As soon as the window was closed again, he reached for Tatum, drawing her over to kiss him deeply. When they pulled apart, she moved to lay across the three of us, placing her head in Saint's lap while twisting her fingers through mine and leaving her legs on Kyan.

It made me uncomfortable to know she wasn't strapped in but Niall's car didn't seem to have any seatbelts back here at all, so we didn't get much choice in that and I tried not to think about it too much.

I relaxed back into my seat as the miles slipped by and Blake drove us in a looping circle away from the camp and back to Kyan's family home. It was still pretty hard to envision an end to all of this, but at least in that moment, we were together and safe and I could focus on that much.

I must have dozed off somewhere before we made it to Kyan's grandfather's house because I woke up sharply as we pulled up outside it.

The place was insanely big, looking more like some kind of resort than a home for a single man, but Kyan didn't say anything to explain it as he got out of the car and moved aside to speak to Niall.

"Is it really a good idea for us to stay here?" I asked dubiously, looking up at the imposing building as I followed the others out of the car.

"Liam has been angling to get Kyan back here for a while now," Saint explained. "He's helped us out a few too many times recently and he won't continue to accept an IOU from Kyan as payment."

"What is he going to make him do?" Tatum asked in a low voice just as the huge front door at the top of the stairs was pulled open.

It was still dark as it was only three in the morning, but apparently nothing took the staff here by surprise as a woman dressed in a servant's uniform waited for us to greet her.

"Don't worry about it," Saint said softly, stepping close to Tatum and pressing a kiss to her forehead. "We need a place to stay and Liam O'Brien's house is locked up tighter than a gnat's asshole. For now, we will allow him to believe that Kyan is falling into line. It will buy me some time to get the vaccinations to Dr De La Cost and for me to hunt down my father and figure out exactly how we wish to finish this. Once we no longer have need of Liam O'Brien's house and protection, I will find a way to free Kyan from his obligations to him."

"If the dude is as bad as Kyan says he is then I don't see him just being reasonable about anything you might come up with," I pointed out.

"If the only way out is bloodshed then I'll be happy enough to wet my hands," Saint said with a shrug. "I'll let you know once I've decided if it's necessary or not."

He turned away from us and I sighed as I fell into step behind him with Tatum between me and Blake. I still hated it when Saint tried to pull rank like that, but I could admit that when it came down to all of this plotting and scheming, I was out of my depth. So I'd let him think he was in charge for now if that was what it took to keep the peace.

Kyan moved to stand between us and the house before we could go any further while Niall hung back and lit up a cigarette as he leaned against the hood of his car.

"Niall has asked for a favour," Kyan said, rubbing a hand over his jaw. "He said Tatum already gave him a vaccination when he first showed up to help get her out of the city-"

"I did," she agreed. "It made sense. Plus it felt like the least I could do."

"You should have run that past the group," Saint ground out.

"It would have been pretty difficult to explain my attachment to that cooler box if I hadn't told him what was in it," she shot back, tilting her chin in that way which told us all she was up for a fight if he kept questioning her on it. "And once he knew, it would have been kinda rude for me not to offer him one, don't you think? Considering he saved my ass. Followed by all of your asses, might I add."

"Fine," Saint sighed. "So what else does he want?"

"Two more doses," Kyan said, glancing over at his uncle who grinned at us as he took a drag on his cigarette.

"Who for?" Blake asked.

"For...the people he has locked in his basement." Kyan shrugged like that wasn't weird as fuck. "I mean, he says he mostly wants one for the girl - that one he purchased from Royaume D'élite - but he says the other one 'would be handy.'"

Saint pinched the bridge of his nose and sighed heavily. "Fine. It's a small price to pay for him keeping Tatum safe," he said, though it still sounded like he was kinda pissed.

"Let's just keep the serial killer happy," I agreed. "There are enough people trying to kill us without us adding another one to the list."

Kyan laughed like I'd been joking and took the box from Tatum, removing a couple of doses for him and giving them to his uncle.

"Do you want me to explain how you give them?" Tatum began but he just waved her off.

"I'll stab 'em in the arse with them and hope for the best, thanks all the same. I'll be seeing ya then," Niall called cheerily, blood running out from beneath the duct tape bandage on his arm.

"Maybe you should get that checked out?" I suggested as he started to turn away and he glanced down at the blood like he hadn't noticed it before.

"Shit," Niall gasped and I raised my eyebrows as he pointed at me. "I just realised who you remind me of. It's been bugging me all fucking night."

"What's that got to do with the-"

"He's the fella from that show with the bikes and the guns and that shit," he went on, making a gun with his fingers and pointing them at me.

"That could literally be any one of so many shows," I pointed out.

"Yeah, but you know the one I mean. The one with the fella who looks like you." He fired his finger gun at me then turned away and grabbed Tatum in a big bear hug, squeezing her tight and spinning her around as she laughed in surprise.

He set her down, tussling her hair like she was a little kid before embracing Kyan too and taking off in his car again without another word.

"Take care of yourself," Kyan called after him and Niall's laughter carried back to us on the wind as he flicked his cigarette out of the car window.

"I'm like a cockroach, lad. You can try to kill me all you like but I just keep fucking kicking."

"Your uncle is fucking crazy," Blake muttered as he waved him off and Kyan chuckled as he led the way up the steps.

"Yeah, well, when you come from a family like this, I think it might just be the best way to survive. Besides, he's lived through shit you don't even wanna imagine. I doubt any of us would be doing any better in his circumstances."

"I doubt I'd ever turn into a raving clown," Saint tsked.

"He's not a clown," Tatum muttered, looking back over her shoulder and frowning after Niall's car. "I think he's lonely. And desperately sad."

Kyan sighed heavily, nodding and taking her hand before lifting it to his lips and pressing a kiss against her knuckles. "You always see the truth of people, don't you baby?"

"It's a good thing I do," she replied, looking between the four of us. "Or I never would have given any of you a shot. You were all such assholes when we met."

"Ugh, why do I feel like you're gonna use that against us for the rest of our lives?" Blake joked and Tatum rolled her eyes as we started walking again.

"Maybe I will. I'll use it to make you guys do whatever I want whenever I want," she said.

"We already do that," I teased and she smirked.

"Good evening, Coco," the housekeeper cooed as we moved up the steps. "Your grandpa has already retired to bed for the night, but he requested that you all take a Hades Virus test before you come into the house." She pointed to a tray which she'd placed on the top step and Kyan made small talk with her as we all quickly carried them out.

We had to wait three minutes for the results to show up, but once they proved us to be negative, she let us inside and told Kyan that we'd have the run of the west wing during our stay. That's right - an entire fucking *wing*.

Who had houses with wings?

I didn't really have anything to say to that fucking insanity, so I just kept my mouth shut and tried not to gawp like the only pauper in the room as I followed Kyan and the others to this fancy ass *wing* we were being gifted the use of.

Kyan sent the housekeeper off to bed, assuring her we were capable of sorting ourselves out but when he led us into a huge suite, we found a table laid out with sandwiches and drinks as if she'd somehow magically known we'd be wanting them.

"Martha is worth her weight in gold," Kyan groaned as he grabbed a sandwich and started chewing before he'd even finished his sentence.

"We will need somewhere to refrigerate the vaccines," Saint said, barely even looking at the lavish bedroom with the four poster super-king bed and vaulted ceilings.

In fact, Blake didn't either. Like this kind of lavish opulence was so ordinary to them that they didn't even notice it. I swear I'd never felt more out of place in their group than I did in that moment.

"Mini fridge is over there," Kyan said dismissively, pointing at a panel in the wall which did in fact open up to a mini fridge with chilled bottles of water stacked inside it when Saint opened it up to place the silver box inside. Because that was totally normal apparently.

A warm hand slipped into mine as I just kinda stood in the middle of the room and Tatum gave me a knowing smile as she tiptoed up to speak in my ear.

"Give me a cosy little B&B and a takeout pizza any day," she teased. "This place is fucking ridiculous."

I broke a smile for her, relieved to find I wasn't the only one thinking that as she started tugging me across the room.

"Where are you taking me, princess?" I asked as I let her lead me along.

"Right now, all I want is to wash this day off of me, crawl into that big bed with all four of you and sleep it away," she explained as we made it into a massive bathroom which I refused to believe was just the en-suite. No one had gold fucking taps and a freestanding bath in an en-suite.

"Wish granted then," I promised her, following her lead as I dragged my muddy, torn clothes off and hounded her into the giant shower which stood against the far wall. There wasn't even a screen partitioning it from the rest of the room, just a massive waterfall shower standing over a drain set into the navy tiles.

Tatum set the shower running and I stepped beneath it with her, my eyes drinking in the sight of the water flowing down her naked flesh for so long that I didn't even notice the others following us in until we were all wet and brushing against each other while we washed.

We were too exhausted to turn it into anything more than what it was, though somehow all four of us ended up washing Tatum, our hands touching and caressing her as bubbles slid over her silky skin. My hand may have dipped between her thighs briefly, teasing her clit with a gentle caress while the others toyed with her hardened nipples and tight ass until she was gasping and clinging to my arm, her fingernails cutting into me as I drew her into bliss.

We dried off quickly and piled into the super-king together after that. I found I didn't even give a shit that there were three other naked guys in my bed as we all drifted off. Because we were together and we were safe and that was more than could have been said just a few short hours ago. So I was going to count my blessings, hold our girl tight and pray that I'd never have to let go again.

I woke to the feeling of gentle fingertips trailing across my arm and my cock hardened as I reached for the girl I'd fallen asleep beside. The scent of her clung to the pillows as I searched for her in the sheets and I felt the warmth of her body just out of reach.

The thought of her naked skin so close had me aching to claim her and though I knew she probably needed more sleep, I couldn't resist the idea of waking her up and seeing if she might wanna take me up on that idea. I'd do it nicely though, with my head between her thighs, waking her up as I ate her out like my favourite breakfast and made her beg for the rest of me.

I shifted closer to her, my hand reaching for her thigh, but instead of finding it, my fingers landed on a solid cock instead.

"Gah!" I jerked my hand back and opened my eyes, finding myself in the bed alone with a naked Blake Bowman and no one else. Not exactly how I'd been hoping to start my day.

"Good morning, beautiful," Blake murmured sleepily as I found my hard on sinking fast.

"Goddammit. Where's Tatum?" I grunted, scrubbing a hand down my face as Blake shrugged and closed his eyes again, clearly deciding on more sleep.

I pushed myself up with a frown and found Saint sitting at a small table, drinking coffee while typing away on his laptop. The amused smirk on his lips said he'd just enjoyed that little show though. *Asshole.*

"Morning," I mumbled, looking around for Kyan and Tatum and coming up blank.

"It is nine twenty-three," Saint said without looking up from his work. "Hardly what I would refer to as morning."

"What do you want me to say then?" I asked, getting out of bed and stretching as I tried to work a kink out of my neck.

"Kyan brought some clothes for us," Saint said, glancing at me with the hint of a sneer and I rolled my eyes as I headed over to the neatly folded clothes on the chair that he was pointing at.

"What's the matter? The sight of my dick offends you unless you're watching me stick it into your girlfriend?" I teased and Saint shrugged.

"A flaccid penis dangling about for no reason is just a distraction to the eye," he said casually, turning back to his work. "A solid one making Tatum

Rivers come so hard she can't help but scream holds a lot more appeal."

I barked a surprised laugh as I picked up a pair of grey sweats and Saint actually smirked, making me realise he'd been fucking with me. Who'd have thought the devil would have a sense of humour?

I yanked a t-shirt on too, then moved over to the table to snag myself some toast and a cup of coffee from the spread that had been freshly laid out for us. I must have been really out of it to have missed Martha or whoever delivered this, but I knew Kyan had said she'd be leaving a breakfast cart out overnight so I was guessing Saint had wheeled it in. I wasn't complaining but it was fucking weird to have that kind of service in your damn house. Food that magically showed up when I wanted it was one rich person perk I could get used to.

"Where are Kyan and Tatum?" I asked and Saint shrugged.

"They left to find the food, but the food arrived and they didn't return with it. My guess is that they've either been waylaid by Kyan's grandfather or he's fucking her somewhere as we speak."

I clucked my tongue, glancing towards the door as I made swift work of my toast and Saint continued typing. He didn't seem to mind me talking to him, but he was clearly in the middle of something and I was hungry to get more of a look at this crazy mansion anyway.

"I might go find them," I announced as I got up, draining the last of my coffee.

"Be sure to be mindful of your tongue if you run into an O'Brien," Saint said. "They really are a brutal bunch of thugs and you, my dear Nash, are easy to dispose of. Don't give them a reason to make you into a corpse."

"Aww, I didn't know you cared so much, sweetheart," I teased as I pulled the door wide and just before I could close it again, his reply reached me.

"Yes you did."

I grinned before I could stop myself then headed off down the corridor, trying to remember which way we'd come to get here last night.

I walked down long hallways and short ones, took stairs up and down and opened a few doors, finding things from a games room to a library, but I didn't come across another living soul.

This house was so fucking big that I swear I'd gotten lost more times than I ever had while figuring out my way around Everlake Prep, and after a while the thrill of exploring it wore off, making me want to head back to our room.

I turned around, intending to do just that - assuming I actually *could* find my way back to it when a muffled noise drew my attention to a room at the end of the hall. I strode towards it, thinking I heard the low rumble of Kyan's voice. I was so turned around in these grandly decorated hallways that when I pushed the door open and found myself in another bedroom I was actually surprised. I'd thought this part of the house was all entertaining rooms, but I was clearly wrong about that.

Tatum gasped as I threw the door wide and for a moment anger and jealously pulsed through me as I took in the sight of her pinned beneath her tattooed husband on the bed, her hands bound at the base of her spine and her ass in the air. Kyan was standing directly behind her, fingers digging into her hips as he fucked her hard and fast. He didn't even seem to notice me as he reached out and caught Tatum by the throat, drawing her upright so that her back was pressed to his chest. But as he lifted his gaze from biting her earlobe to look me right in the eye and smirk, I knew he'd been well aware of my arrival.

"Are you looking to join us, brother?" he asked, grinding his hips slowly while reaching down to caress Tatum's clit, making her moan as her hooded gaze fell on me.

I frowned as he tightened his hand around her throat, the urge to drag him off of her consuming me for a moment before I stepped inside and knocked the door closed behind me. She'd made it more than clear that she enjoyed how rough Kyan was with her, but I couldn't deny that I was still struggling to fully understand why she'd allow him to half choke her like that.

"Is he hurting you princess?" I asked, unable to help myself.

Kyan chuckled as he relaxed his hold on her throat and she licked her swollen lips. "Only in the way I like," she panted.

"Why don't you come and give it a try?" Kyan offered, jerking his hips back so that he pulled his dick out of her and Tatum gasped a frustrated sound as she was left wanting.

"The idea of doing that to her doesn't really appeal to me," I said with a shrug, though her hands being bound at the base of her spine like that did thrust her tits out in the most delicious way. So maybe I wasn't totally against all of it.

"You're so vanilla," Kyan joked and Tatum tried to bite him in a half-hearted attempt to tell him off.

"I'm not," I disagreed. "I just struggle to understand what Tatum gets from being trussed up like that and used for your pleasure."

"I don't just use her for my pleasure," Kyan scoffed. "When I fuck her, she comes a lot more times than I do."

Tatum bit her lip, her eyes flaming with an idea as she looked at me. "Why don't you give it a try, Nash?" she asked.

"You want me to try fucking you while you're tied up?" I asked and in all fairness my cock was rock hard and I was more than willing to step into Kyan's place. I just doubted I'd start choking her.

"Or you could find out what being tied up is like?" she suggested, that hungry look in her eyes flaring with excitement at that idea.

"Fuck yes," Kyan agreed enthusiastically. "Then I'll top you both."

"The day I let you top me would be a cold day in hell," I pointed out with a scoff.

"Fine," he conceded. "Strip down and let me tie you up then. Tatum can be the one topping you and I'll just enjoy the show."

I wanted to protest that I had no desire to be tied up, but that vanilla comment was pissing me off and I had to admit that I preferred the idea of that to the idea of choking my girl while I fucked her. No matter how much she seemed to enjoy Kyan doing it.

"Unless you're chicken shit?" he taunted.

Tatum bit her lip, but I could see she wanted me to agree so I yanked my shirt over my head and tossed it aside before crawling onto the bed in front of her and stealing a kiss.

She moaned into my mouth as I palmed her breasts, tugging and caressing them so she was panting then moving my mouth down to take her nipple into it and sucking hard until she drew in a sharp breath.

I grabbed hold of her ass and lifted her onto my lap as I lay back on the bed, groaning as she ground her wetness against my cock where it strained through my grey sweats.

Kyan caught my wrist and tugged it off of her ass, tying it with a black rope and securing it to the bed frame. My heart rate picked up as he caught my other hand next and I didn't miss his amused smirk as he spread that arm wide and tied it in place too.

Tatum looked down at me hungrily as she continued to grind against me and I yanked on my wrists as I realised I couldn't do anything to get rid of my pants. And with Tatum's hands still bound behind her back, she couldn't either.

"Untie her," I said, my cock aching as she kept up that torturous grinding.

"Naw," Kyan replied with a chuckle. "I think you'll have to invite me to play after all if you want help getting those bad boys off."

I swore at him, yanking on the ropes as hard as I could and making the metal bed frame rattle, but they wouldn't fucking break. The bastard had tied me too well. And I'd fallen right into his damn trap.

Tatum released a breathy laugh at my frustration, panting as she ground her clit down on me, getting herself off and making my dick throb. I was going to come in my pants if this went on much longer, but that wasn't what I wanted. I wanted to be deep inside my girl, making her scream as I pounded into her, not coming inside my fucking boxers.

"You just have to say the word," Kyan purred, leaning in and blowing softly over Tatum's hard nipple, making her moan with the desire for him to close that distance. But I knew he wouldn't. Not unless I invited him. And it was clear how much she wanted him too.

My eyes fell on the way her tits were bouncing and I groaned as I nodded my head, needing more than I was getting right now and giving in to fucking Kyan and his stupid game. I'd get him back for this at some point, but right now I was willing to concede defeat in the name of getting my dick inside my girl.

With a filthy laugh, Kyan moved around behind Tatum and encouraged her to lift herself up so that she was kneeling over me, but not touching me anymore. He reached between her thighs and hooked his fingers around my waistband, grinning like an asshole before tugging my pants down and off of me.

He tossed them aside, leaving me naked, but caught hold of Tatum's hair, stopping her from lowering onto me again as he kneeled over my legs behind her and dropped his free hand between her thighs.

I let out a groan of frustration as I was forced to watch him toying with her, his fingers dipping inside her as he pressed his thumb down on her clit and yanked her hair back so that she exposed her throat for him to suck and mark.

Precum was beading the tip of my cock as I was left to watch the show and Tatum was held hostage before me, fucking his hand and moaning so loudly that not being able to join in was akin to fucking torture.

By the time she came for him, she was screaming and my cock was so hard that I was almost certain I was going to come just from watching the perfect performance she was putting on for me.

Kyan didn't even give her time to recover as he pushed her down onto me, gripping the base of my cock in his tattooed hand and guiding it inside her with a sharp push.

"Jesus," I cursed, but I couldn't exactly stay mad at him for overstepping, because he'd moved his hands to her ass and was rocking her on my cock in a way that made my balls ache as he controlled her movements.

I growled her name as I drove my hips up and thrust into her, making her moan with every hard thrust while Kyan shifted a hand up to toy with her nipple.

Tatum's blue eyes met mine as she rode me, her hands still tied behind her while mine remained attached to the bed, leaving nothing but that one, vital point of contact between us as she rode me harder and faster, chasing another orgasm like she was desperate for it.

Kyan stopped rocking her hips, stepping back and watching us as he took a bottle of lube from the pocket of his sweatpants which were lying on the floor near mine.

"Do you just keep lube in your granddad's house?" I grunted as he slicked some over the length of his solid cock and he smirked at me as he shook his head.

"Didn't you take a peek into that black bag Saint's been clinging to since we left The Temple? The dirty fucker brought almost as many sex toys as rolls of cash."

I forgot about asking him questions as Tatum leaned back and started moaning louder, my cock clearly finding that perfect spot deep inside her and I focused on driving it up and into it as hard and as fast as I could.

"Fuck, Nash, don't stop," she commanded breathlessly and I did as I was told, fucking her hard and deep until her pussy clamped tight around me and she was screaming my name, making my balls tighten with the need for release.

"Don't you fucking dare come, Nash," Kyan warned me as he moved back onto the bed and by some fucking miracle I managed not to, gritting my teeth and slowing my pace as Tatum slumped down on my chest.

Her pussy kept pulsing around me as she let her weight fall limp on top of me and I pressed kisses to the side of her head until she lifted her mouth to meet mine.

The bed shifted beneath us as Kyan moved up behind her, and I knew what he was planning even before I felt the cool drip of the lube against my inner thighs as he spread some over her ass.

Tatum's teeth sank into my bottom lip as he pushed himself into her and I groaned as I felt him sliding in too, the thin wall of flesh dividing our cocks feeling like next to nothing as she grew impossibly tighter around me.

Kyan slid in and out of her a few times slowly, making her gasp and moan until I began to move again too, finding my rhythm with him and groaning at the added friction of his cock within her body at the same time as mine.

As we began to move faster, Kyan wrapped a hand around Tatum's throat and drew her upright, squeezing just a little as she moaned even louder.

I didn't want to like it, but as I watched the pleasure dancing in her eyes as he held her entirely at his mercy, I couldn't help but agree that she was clearly getting off on it. I could feel it in the shivers of her flesh and the way her body convulsed around mine.

"Okay," I muttered. "I get it now."

"Do you think he does, baby?" Kyan breathed in Tatum's ear, using his grip on her throat to angle her head towards me as he continued to fuck her ass in time with me driving into her tight pussy.

Tatum just moaned in reply, too lost to the feeling of the two of us possessing her to give a coherent answer, but as Kyan looked down at me over her shoulder, I could tell he wasn't done pushing me.

He reared over Tatum, making her lean over me more as he reached out with his free hand and lightly placed it around my throat. I stilled for a beat, frowning as I realised what he wanted to do, and I was about to refuse until my gaze flicked back to meet Tatum's.

I could see the excitement there, even if I knew she wouldn't say it. This was my choice, but she wanted me to feel the rush she got from this too.

"Fine," I grunted, my cock thick and desperate for release inside her and my mind clouded by my hunger for her. "Do it."

Kyan grinned broadly as he instantly complied, his fingers flexing around my throat as he squeezed just tight enough to restrict my breath, though not enough to cut it off entirely. My instinct was to fight him off, but as I tried to yank on my arms, the ropes just pulled tight and I groaned in frustration, giving in instead and upping my pace once more.

Tatum cried out as I thrust up into her harder and Kyan met my pace, his grip flexing on both of our throats as he drove into her with a growl of desire and the restriction to my oxygen began to make me feel lightheaded.

A part of me ached to be fighting him off while a small piece of me relished the opportunity to relinquish this control to him. I didn't know why, but it felt freeing, like the shackles of all the bad things that usually weighed me down were stripped away and I was able to let go of more than just my control of my body, but it was liberating my emotions too. And as I looked into Tatum's blue eyes as she gave in to that same freedom, it felt like we were freefalling over a cliff together, all of us diving into some unknown depths of our bonds and coming together in the purest way I'd ever experienced.

The feelings in my flesh zeroed in to those few most important points of contact and I thrust up harder, deeper, Kyan's cock meeting mine in pace and depth until Tatum was screaming. Her pussy tightened and gripped my cock so firmly that before I knew it, I was coming so hard that I almost blacked out.

I cursed and panted as Kyan released his hold on me, slamming his cock into her a few more times before he came too with a deep groan of release.

Both of them fell forward on top of me, their combined weight crushing me down into the bed in the most deliciously satisfying way.

We stayed like that for several achingly long minutes before Kyan rolled off, untying Tatum's hands so that she could drop down into the space between us on the bed.

"I love you," she said breathlessly, her words so clearly for both of us that I couldn't help but smile.

"I love you too," I said in return and the funny thing was that I included Kyan in that statement. Not in the exact same way, but I did love him. He was my family now. Just like the other two. And there was a time when I hadn't ever thought I'd have a family again so that meant a whole damn lot to me.

He chuckled as he untied me and the three of us just stayed there on the bed, our hands caressing our girl and him gloating over topping me while I gave absolutely no shits about it. Because anything that made my girl come like that was more than worth it for me and I wouldn't try to deny that I'd more than enjoyed it myself too.

I couldn't say it was exactly going to become a regular thing, but with this unusual relationship the five of us had going, I was pretty sure that being open minded about everything in the bedroom was the way forward. And I was here for that. For this. For her. Hell, I was here for *us*. And I wasn't going to apologise or make excuses for it, because for the first time in a long damn time, I was happy. So I had zero intentions of sabotaging that.

CHAPTER THIRTY THREE

We got an invite which was slipped under the door of our room in a fancy little envelope, telling us to join Liam for dinner. It was a totally weird thing for a Grandpa to do, but Liam wasn't exactly the cuddly kind. He was the kind who gave people sleepless nights and made them jump at their own shadow. Kyan said the dinner was non-negotiable and that Liam would expect us to dress up, so we were soon heading downstairs in some fine clothes. The suits were Kyan's but a dress had been brought to the room for me by a maid.

The gown was a deep blood red and hugged my figure with a plunging neckline that almost reached my belly button. It was seriously overkill for a family dinner, but I'd had dinner with this family before and knew it was no normal affair. I couldn't imagine what it must have been like for Kyan growing up around these psychopaths. And it was odd to think that the one of them who cared for him most was possibly the most bloodthirsty of them all. It was clear to me Niall would go to the ends of the earth for his nephew, so that made him a friendly psycho I guessed.

Kyan walked on my left with Blake beyond him and Saint and Monroe flanked my right. They were dressed in expensive black suits that matched, all of them looking good enough to eat. And I got the feeling they felt the same way about me as their eyes kept raking over my body.

I drew on the power of their company, feeling like an empress among emperors. The five of us could face any fate together. We'd defied death itself, looked it in the eye and made it bow to us. And we were fully capable of making life follow suit.

Saint slid his phone out of his pocket beside me, a notification lighting up on the screen for a news report.

He smiled smugly as he clicked on it and he was taken to a website showing the video Kyan had made of the inside of the camp they'd been taken to.

"Troy Memphis refuses to comment on the footage leaked from inside what are being termed Hades Camps," Saint read the article aloud, his voice filled with victory. "The Governor of State is being asked to answer for the terrible conditions seen in the footage received by an anonymous source and offer an explanation as to the need for such camps when the public could simply continue to isolate at home. The video has sparked more fear among an already fearful nation and protestors have been swarming the streets in Hemlock City to fight the quarantine rules they have been put under. Troy Memphis's wife has publicly announced their separation this morning in response to the news. She was quoted saying that he had 'lost his way' and she asked him to 'give the people an answer to the questions being asked of him.' She states she was unaware of any such camps and that she and Mr Memphis have been separated discretely for the past year."

"Is that true?" I asked in surprise and Saint nodded.

"There's been no love lost between them for a long time. His usefulness to her has run its course. She's separating herself from a man she barely knows, let alone desires. She would occasionally ask me to meet up with her in the past, but I've been spared that chore since lockdown. Honestly, the woman is mostly harmless, but she also just stood by and allowed that man to raise me with whatever methods he deemed fit. So I feel no great affection for her," Saint said, no emotion in his voice and I could see in his eyes that he really didn't care. He smiled wickedly, tucking his phone away. "The fox is on the run," he said with a grin. "And the hounds of the Devil are coming for him."

"We'll catch him," Kyan growled and the rest of us nodded. "And we'll end this."

We made it to the huge dining room where the table was set for six at the far end. Kyan took a seat to the right of the head of the table, pulling me down beside him.

"The rest of you had better sit on the other side," Kyan instructed, taking my hand and clasping it tight.

They all shared annoyed looks as Kyan leaned back in his seat and rested my hand on his knee.

"She's my wife and belongs to no one else as far as my grandpa knows," Kyan said seriously and Saint pushed Blake and Monroe towards the seats beside him as he dropped into the one beside the head of the table.

"We will play along for now," Saint said, smoothing down his shirt as he undid his blazer button at his waist.

"For now," Monroe growled, and Blake nodded stiffly.

"Only for Liam," I said.

"Come on, it's not just for my grandpa. We all know I'm your favourite, baby," Kyan purred and I opened my mouth to rebuke him as the others did the same, but then the doors opened and Liam strode in followed by a butler with a tray of drinks.

Liam's imposing aura filled the room as he moved to the end of the table, ignoring us as he dropped into his seat and the butler placed a crystal glass of whiskey in front of him before placing one in front of each of us. He wore a smart grey suit which matched his hair, perfectly put together just as he'd been every other time I'd seen him. He lifted his glass, taking in the aroma of the alcohol as he swirled it under his nose, still acting oblivious to our presence. And I got the feeling he wouldn't like it if any of us broke the silence before he did.

"This is the perfect whiskey to make a toast with," Liam mused in his lilting Irish accent, raising his glass and we all lifted ours in response. "To my nephew, his beautiful wife, and his faithful friends. May loyalty run thick in your veins, lest your blood be spilled like a river through this very house." He sipped his whiskey and my skin prickled as I mimicked him, his warning clear and ringing in the air.

"Hm...notes of mango, apricots, a touch of honey and...a finish of woody spices," Saint said, his eyes closed like a prime pretentious douchebag and I almost snorted at how intrigued Liam looked by the comment. "Is it Bushmills twenty one year single malt?"

"It is," Liam said in surprise, glancing at Kyan. "I didn't realise your friend had such good taste."

"He has the finest taste," I said a little teasingly and Liam's eyes cut to me.

"That so?" he asked as Saint smiled smugly.

"Yeah, well he thinks he does anyway," I replied.

"The kings of the world know they are royal before they are crowned," Saint said. "If you assume the life you wish to lead before you have it, the world must one day offer it up. It is inevitable."

A beat of tense silence passed then Liam laughed, clapping a hand to Saint's shoulder and shaking him. "I like you, lad."

Servants arrived with our first course, laying out little plates of bruschetta for everyone and we all silently tucked into our food.

By the time our main course arrived, the silence was making my ears ache and I glanced over the table, catching Blake's eye as he offered me a cheeky wink when no one was looking. It was super risky and made my heart race, but I couldn't help but slide my foot further under the table to brush my leg against his.

"So." Liam dabbed at his mouth with his napkin as he finished his meal, tossing it down and taking a sip of water as his eyes fell on Kyan. "We have received an invitation to the annual Moguls' Banquet at Royaume D'élite," he announced, letting that axe fall and my stomach knotted as I glanced nervously at the others. "We will head there together next week."

"No," Kyan's hard voice rang through the room.

"Excuse me, lad?" Liam asked dangerously, his fingers brushing the knife beside his plate.

I took Kyan's hand, sitting upright in my chair as I readied to go to bat for my husband if he needed me. Because there was no way he could go there again. Not when Troy would have seen the passport photos from the camp they'd been sent to. He'd have put the puzzle together and realised their antibody levels were so high because they'd taken a vaccine, figured out that my boys were the ones who'd saved me from his fucking lab. And we couldn't go anywhere near that man unless we were in a position to destroy him.

"I can't go," Kyan said, staring his grandfather down while Saint observed the situation critically.

"And why not?" Liam growled, his eyes glinting with darkness.

Kyan looked to me then the others, his lips pressed tight together. "I just can't."

Liam opened his mouth, but Saint got there first, speaking calmly yet capturing all of our attention with the power behind his words. "Unfortunately, Mr O'Brien, your grandson - along with the rest of us - have made a few powerful enemies recently. Enemies who include my father." My heart pounded harder, unsure if this information should be handed over to Liam so easily, but I trusted Saint's judgement. And if he thought this was what needed to be done, then I had to let him do it.

Liam's eyes narrowed as he regarded Saint. "Oh?" He rounded on Kyan. "What've you gotten yourself into, lad?" His voice was cutting, and I could see the murderous man he was on full display, his shiny exterior cracking to show the monster within.

Saint continued as if Liam had addressed him. "We stole vaccines from my father's laboratory and took them. All of our blood now contains valuable antibodies and he's on a war path to destroy us for the mess we left of his facility. I have had my suspicions for some time that he is an important member of Royaume D'élite, so Kyan cannot risk going there or he will be captured the moment he arrives."

Liam drummed his fingers on the table and I noticed a large gold signet ring with a shamrock engraved in it on his middle finger. "Vaccines, you say?"

"Yes, they were in the trial stages, but by all accounts are entirely effective," Saint said.

"Hmm." Liam grazed his hand over his smooth jaw as he looked from Saint to his grandson, his expression giving nothing away about his feelings on the mention of a vaccine. "Well, it seems you've got yourself into quite the mess, Kyan," he said coolly. "I will give you until the end of the month to fix it. Troy Memphis is a powerful man. If you can handle him, I'd say you may just be able to handle the family business. But you will do this by your own hand, don't go calling on your uncle Niall or I'll step in and deal with this situation myself." He smiled conspiratorially as he pushed out his seat. "Consider it a test of your capabilities." He strode past Kyan then laid a hand on my shoulder, his skin hot against mine as he dug his fingers into collar bone. "And if you fail, I'll be forced to offer up retribution to Mr Memphis somehow. There are three people sitting at this table who would go a long way to pacifying him. Remember that, my boy." He strode from the room and a chill swept down my spine from his threat.

"Let's adjourn to our room," Saint said, standing from his seat, not seeming at all rattled by the threat, but I sure as shit was. "Our next conversation is best had in private."

"*Adjourn*," Blake sniggered and Saint smacked him around the head as he led the way out.

Monroe followed them but as I got up, Kyan tugged on my fingers to keep me there, giving me an intent look. "I'll fix this," he said in a whisper, his words laced with a promise.

I reached up to cup his jaw, the pads of my fingers grazing over his stubble. "No, Kyan, *we* will fix this."

I turned and he hounded after me, his hand on my waist as we exited the dining room. Some of Liam's staff were walking toward us with little glasses of chocolate and vanilla ice cream, seeming surprised we were leaving already. Blake grabbed one, dunking his fingers into a glass and sucking the sugary gloop off of them with a grin. "I'll take them all." He gathered them up in his arms as Saint tsked at him and kept walking while a smile pulled at my lips. I jogged forward, snatching one from Blake and hooking a spoon off a tray before dunking it into the ice cream. It tasted like a dream and I moaned as I swallowed, earning myself hungry looks from all of my guys.

Saint arched an eyebrow at me over his shoulder and I smirked.

"What? Are you gonna try and force me back onto the lettuce and carrot diet you had me on before?" I asked, my voice sharp enough to tell him I wasn't fond of that memory. "Because I will fight you."

"No," he said simply and I frowned, jogging to his side and swallowing another mouthful of ice cream.

"Because you know I won't listen or…" I trailed off, leaving it open for him to answer.

"Because I have witnessed your waist too thin and your ribs too prominent at the hands of my father. I will never control a single thing that enters your body again, siren. I will not be like the man who tried to own your body and use it as he saw fit."

My heart stuttered and I leaned my head against his shoulder, grateful for his words as he wound an arm around my waist.

"You're not like him," I whispered.

"I am. But I would like to be better than him too," he said.

"You are," I swore and his fingers ran in soft circles against my side, the tension in his brow easing.

We made it back to our room and headed inside, the sound of the door locking making the tension run out of my shoulders. I placed my empty ice cream glass down on the side with the spoon, still a bit hungry for more.

"Will you undo my zip? This dress is digging in everywhere," I asked Saint and he moved behind me, his fingers skating down my spine as he freed me from it.

I let it drop to my ankles, stepping out of it with a sigh of relief and throwing myself down on the bed in nothing but my silky green panties with my black high heels still on. The dress hadn't allowed for a bra.

"Get dressed," Saint clipped. "We need to have an important conversation and I cannot lay out my thoughts clearly with you looking like that and while the others are staring at you like hungry dogs."

I lifted my head up, finding Blake, Kyan and Nash all shoulder to shoulder at the end of the bed, their eyes darkened by sinful thoughts. *Ooh.* Blake was still eating a pot of ice cream and it looked like he was having ideas about where he wanted to put it next. I had some ideas myself…

I bit my lip, fluttering my lashes as I soaked in their attention for a moment, but I knew Saint wasn't going to let us have our fun.

"Come on, I'll help you find something comfortable." Monroe scooped me up, throwing me over his shoulder and I laughed as he strode into the walk-in closet and kicked the door shut. He set me down and kissed me roughly, his desire for me making me ache. But Saint had a point. We needed to discuss this. So it was with a lot of effort that I slipped away from Nash and grabbed a white cami, pulling it on.

Monroe rested his shoulder on the wall beside me, watching me with an intensity that could have burned the world to ash.

"You make being a good girl very hard, Nash Monroe," I teased as he slid his thumb across his lower lip.

"You make being a bad man so very fucking easy, Tatum Rivers," he purred.

"Roscoe," Kyan corrected as he shoved through the door, folding his thick arms with a cocky smirk.

Nash grimaced. "I think we need to change that."

"Seconded," I sang, pulling on a pair of light pink sweatpants before grabbing some comfy socks and jogging between them to exit the closet. Kyan slapped my ass as I went and I tossed him the finger in response, a grin tugging at my mouth.

Blake was on the bed, polishing off the last of the ice creams and I jumped on the mattress to lie beside him, swiping one from his grip and swirling my finger inside the glass. He smirked at me as he swallowed a mouthful, his dark hair falling forward into his eyes. He'd shed his blazer and rolled up his shirt sleeves to reveal his muscular forearms and I eye-fucked him shamelessly as I rested back against the pillows.

"Looking good, golden boy," I purred.

"I taste good too. C'mere and have a lick." He wiggled his eyebrows, leaning toward me and Saint clapped his hands.

"Enough," he said sharply from across the room, looking from us on the bed to Kyan and Nash as they slumped down in chairs beside a roaring fire. "We must talk before this descends into another orgy. Christ, I cannot get a word in edgeways without someone whipping their cock out these days."

I snorted a laugh as Kyan tugged his tie loose from his throat, tossing it on the floor before throwing his blazer away too and starting to unbutton his shirt. He left it hanging open when he was done and I eyed the tattoos peeking out from beneath the white material with my fingers itching, the urge to explore them rising in me.

"Must we all act like hellions?" Saint clipped, clasping his hands behind his back. "I was quite enjoying the attire. Nash is the only one of you who has any decorum."

"Sorry, bro. Dressing smart ain't my bag." Blake shrugged.

"And I'd hardly say I have decorum," Nash snorted.

Kyan sniggered beside him. "You definitely don't, brother. Not after you bent Tatum over the other day and-"

"I said *enough*," Saint hissed and everyone fell quiet as his eyes swung between us. "Now, we have to discuss the matter of Royaume D'élite. We don't yet have ample information to connect my father to it."

"But you made a guess so we can be pretty sure, right?" Blake asked and Saint shuddered at the word 'guess.'

"No, we cannot be sure," Saint growled. "And even if we were, my father is already in hiding. He could disappear altogether if we are not careful. What I need is cold, hard evidence so I can drag my father's name through every media outlet in the country when I expose him, hunt him down and make sure he pays for every crime he has committed. When I am through, there won't be an American citizen alive who doesn't know his name and what a loathsome cockroach he is."

"So how are we going to get that evidence?" I asked, sitting up and folding my legs, willing to do whatever it took. "And how are we going to destroy that disgusting club while we're at it?" My upper lip peeled back and Kyan smirked at me across the room, his eyes glittering darkly.

Saint straightened his tie. "We are going to go to Royaume D'élite and find it, siren. I have weighed the options, the risks and have deduced that the club is the only place which will hold such evidence. There must be a file either on a computer or in hard copy form within the building itself listing the founders and the members of the club. It is the only way they could conduct business between one another, the only way a number could be assigned to new members. Therefore-"

"We're going on an adventure?" Blake finished, bouncing on the bed beside me and I laughed.

"Not my words, but yes," Saint said, a vicious smile pulling at his lips. "Of course, I would like to propose the four of us go and Tatum stays behind, but-"

"No," I growled instantly, and he nodded firmly.

I wasn't going to let my Night Keepers risk their necks while I just sat at home waiting for them to come back like some nineteen fifties housewife. I'd be right there at their sides, ensuring that they got out of there and that that vile place was brought to its knees.

"*But*, I am well aware you will refuse regardless and I believe your capabilities in such an operation outweigh the risks of taking you there anyway," Saint continued.

"I want to burn it down," I announced, setting my jaw. "I want it turned to ash so no one else can be hurt there."

"Fuck yes," Kyan said excitedly and Nash cracked his knuckles, nodding his agreement.

"I'm down," Blake growled, sucking the last of the ice cream off of his thumb.

Saint considered that for a long moment and I could almost see the pie charts and bar graphs being mapped out in his mind before he nodded. "Yes, that should be possible."

"But we'll have to get the prostitutes and any other captives out of there first," I said decisively. I wasn't going to hurt innocent people, but if the assholes who ran that place were stuck inside when the flames started devouring it, then all the better. It was the least they deserved.

"We can do that," Kyan announced as Saint fell into thoughtful silence again. "The annual Moguls' Banquet is this boring ass members only thing. There won't be whores at it until the afterparty which normally kicks off around ten."

"And where will they be kept before then?" Saint asked curiously.

"Locked up," Kyan said with a sneer. "There's holding cells in the basement. When I was in their…game, they put me there with the other contestants for a while." His eyes darkened with some awful memory and my heart squeezed. That decided it. I was going to make sure the fuckers burned. All of them.

Monroe knocked his arm against Kyan's in a gesture of comfort and I felt their bond humming between them like it was made of iron.

"Well, I think we have ourselves a plan," Nash growled and Saint nodded.

"I shall work out the details," Saint said then a knock came at the door and we all looked to it in surprise. He walked over, unlocking it and pulling it open. "What the fuck?" he breathed, his shoulders bunching and shock dripping through his posture. I didn't even have to see his face to read that emotion from him; I didn't think I'd ever seen Saint Memphis taken by surprise by anything.

"Who is it?" Kyan popped out of his seat and I jumped up too.

Saint stepped aside and let in a woman with dark skin, full lips and a short afro. She looked like she was in her thirties and her gaze was pinned on Saint as she smiled smugly.

"Aunt Jada?" Kyan questioned in confusion. "What are you doing here?"

"Hang on..." Blake balked as recognition filled his eyes.

"Oh," Saint breathed, starting to laugh and I frowned, confused by what the hell was going on as he threw his head back and began clapping.

"Hey, Kyan," Jada said with a grin. "I just came here to say hello to Saint. And rub a little salt in the wound I just gave him."

"Of *course*," Saint laughed then composed himself, extending his hand to Jada. "Bravo. Truly, I had no idea." Jada took Saint's hand, shaking it firmly as she grinned victoriously at him.

"No idea of what?" I pushed, sharing a look with Nash who looked equally stumped.

"I'm so fucking confused, man," Kyan muttered, running a hand over his head. "You know Saint?"

"Of course she does," Saint said, his eyes full of light. "This is my maid, Rebecca."

My lips popped open and I looked to the woman in surprise.

"What?" Kyan frowned, at a loss. "But-"

"Clearly she was your father's spy," Saint announced. "She was planted at Everlake Preparatory to keep an eye on you."

"Yep," Jada said with a shrug like it was nothing, but clearly it wasn't. "And it took a lot of planning, let me tell you."

"I had background checks done on your fucking background checks," Saint said, shaking his head in disbelief. "How did you manage it?"

"I've got an army of O'Brien gangsters at my back, Saint. Including my husband, Finn, who does the fake papers for our whole family. Rebecca's persona has been set up for years. She was the perfect fit when Kyan came home from school one time complaining about you firing another maid and humiliating her in front of half the school."

"That was cold blooded," Blake said as he remembered it.

"She left my hand-stitched loafers outside in a snowstorm, Bowman," Saint said icily. "They were one of a kind."

"Jesus," I breathed, my head still spinning. "So you've been spying on Kyan?" I stepped toward the woman, not liking the idea that there'd been someone watching him and not even Saint had worked out it was her. What did she know? She'd never been at The Temple unless we weren't there, but what if she'd set up cameras or – no…she couldn't have. Saint would have known. And if she had, Liam would know about everything. That I wasn't just with Kyan but all of my boys. And Liam wouldn't have let that lie.

"Just watching out for him," Jada said with a shrug as Kyan folded his arms.

"You wanna elaborate there, Jada?" Kyan pushed and she rolled her eyes.

"I was tricking the Lord of OCD," she said. "How close do you think I could ever get to you? I was just put on campus as a set of eyes on Liam's favourite boy."

"Yes," Saint said thoughtfully. "You must have had to be very careful indeed not to step a toe too far in Kyan's direction or I would have caught you."

"Yeah, and you didn't," she said smugly. "Anyway, seeing as you're all hiding here for the foreseeable, I figured the game was up and I just needed a moment to gloat."

"Well deserved," Saint commented and I was kind of surprised at how well he was taking this. But I supposed it did make sense that he'd appreciate anyone who could outwit him. I guessed it was a pretty rare occurrence. "And if you want a position as a maid in future, do let me know. You were impeccable."

"With my help," Blake coughed and Jada snorted a laugh.

"Nah, I'm good thanks. Though the perks were fucking excellent, I wouldn't mind you being my boss again, just not for cleaning toilets." She winked, waved and headed out the door just like that.

Saint tossed the door closed then scowled at Blake. "What was that about your help?"

"Humans make mistakes," Blake said with an eyeroll. "After the last maid you fired, I decided to give this one a helping hand."

"No one's perfect," I said, remembering what Blake had told me about Rebecca accidentally staining Saint's whites pink in the wash once.

Saint sighed, his shoulders dropping. "How disappointing." He walked toward me, gripping the back of my neck and pulling me in for a delicious kiss.

"What was that for?" I asked as he released me, heat rising in my cheeks from his touch.

"It's a goodbye. You will have to stay in here alone with Kyan tonight. While Rebec- Jada is here, it clearly isn't safe to take the risk of us staying together in case she comes snooping on us."

"Oh man," Blake complained.

"I'm tired of you getting privileges because of your fake wedding," Monroe growled, getting to his feet.

"It wasn't fake," I reasoned. "But that doesn't mean I want him more than any of you."

Kyan yawned broadly, walking over and slinging an arm around my shoulders. "That's it, wife, feed them the bullshit so you can spend some time with your favourite."

I dropped my hand and grabbed his balls, squeezing tight enough to make him release a very un-Kyan noise.

"I don't have a favourite," I growled and he gripped my wrist, pressing down on pressure points to try and make me let go of his junk. But my fingers were locked tight.

"Alright," he rasped and I released him while the others chuckled.

Nash and Blake came to kiss me goodnight, grabbing some of their stuff before they left with Saint and my heart ached to be parted from them.

Kyan caught my waist, pulling me onto the bed on top of him with a grin then winced a little as I pressed my weight down on his thigh.

"Are you hurt?" I asked in alarm, kneeling up between his legs.

"Naw. Well, it's nothing a good cock sucking won't heal, baby," he said, placing his hands behind his head.

I punched him in the stomach and he wheezed a breath as I smirked at him then started unbuckling his pants. He chuckled as he lifted his hips, kicking his shoes off as I pulled them down and found a dressing on his thigh.

My lips parted. "Did you get a new tattoo?"

He sat up, picking at the tape on his skin. "I couldn't sleep last night so I started one."

"Let me see," I asked excitedly and he peeled it off, showing me the beautiful outline of a compass. It was big, covering most of his upper thigh and done in black and grey. The centre of it was filled with a portrait of a woman with flowers in her hair and makeup on her face that made it look like stitches ran from either side of her lips up her cheeks. There was face paint around her eyes and nose too. It reminded me of one of those beautiful Day of the Dead costumes. The compass surrounding her held letters at its points but instead of N E S and W, they were S K N and B. "It's beautiful."

"I was going for badass, but I'll take it."

"Wait a second," I said as I continued to look at it. I bit my lip as I drank in the details and suddenly recognised myself in the face of the girl. "Is that… me?" My cheeks flushed at the idea of him branding his skin like that for me and my heart began to pound.

"Of course it is." He grinned, capturing my wrists and pulling me against his chest, his trousers still halfway down his legs. "Now how about that blowjob, wife? I'll eat you out for an hour after."

I laughed, kissing the corner of his mouth, an idea circling in my head. "There's something I want first."

His brows arched. "Oh yeah?"

"Yeah…" I ran my fingers down his chest, pushing the open shirt aside to caress the ink over his pecs. "I want a tattoo."

His eyes lit up like a little kid's. "You wanna write 'property of Kyan Roscoe' above your pussy?"

I smacked his shoulder with a laugh. *"No."*

"What then?" he asked teasingly.

"I want…something that represents all of you." I chewed my lip, running my hand over his shoulder to brush around the back of his neck. "I want an arrow. No, I want five arrows. One for each of us."

His expression became thoughtful and he suddenly scooped me off of his lap, dumping me on the bed and pulling up his pants as he jogged into the closet. He reappeared with his sketchbook and placed it on the desk, taking a seat on the cushy chair and flipping it open. He started drawing, his eyes intense as he focused, a small crease forming between his eyes. He looked fucking beautiful, like a Roman statue poised for someone to sculpt.

I stood up and moved toward him, curious as I eyed the page over his shoulder as his pencil moved back and forth across it. I cocked my head to get a better look, but he ripped the paper out, screwed it up and tossed it across the room.

"Not good enough," he muttered, starting again.

"Can I do anything to help?" I asked and he looked over his shoulder at me, wetting his lips.

"Yeah. Fetch a bottle of Jack Daniels from my bag," he asked and I nodded, heading to the closet to where I knew he'd stashed some last night. I grabbed the whiskey then eyed myself in the mirror and smirked as I made a decision. I stripped out of my clothes, walking back into the room buck ass naked. He couldn't see me from where he was hunched over the desk, sketching in furious lines then tearing the page out and screwing it up again.

I took a glass from beside a bottle of water on the nightstand and poured out a measure before filling another one for myself. I took a sip then walked over behind Kyan, placing his whiskey down on the desk.

He caught my hand before I could pull away, kissing the inside of my wrist and leaving charcoal fingerprints on my skin then starting to draw once more, making my heart beat harder.

I moved to the bed, lying down on my back and swallowing the measure of whiskey in my glass, the burn of it rolling all the way to my gut.

"Fuck," he hissed before draining his own glass. "Just gimme the bottle."

I swiped it off of the nightstand, bringing it to my lips and taking a swig. "You'll have to come and get it."

Kyan looked over and his eyes widened as he found me lying there naked with his favourite drink in my hand. I smiled seductively as my heart stammered from his penetrative gaze and he rose from his seat, striding toward me at a slow pace. He drank me in like I was the whiskey he wanted, and goosebumps prickled across my flesh.

He leaned down as he reached the bed, taking the bottle from my hand and drinking a long measure. His chest heaved and fell as his eyes raked over me and he reached out to touch me.

I knocked his hand away, snatching the Jack Daniels from him. "Uh, uh. You can't touch me until you're ready to brand that tattoo on me."

His eyes flared and he wet his lips. "Well talk about fucking motivation, baby." He shoved a hand down his pants, rearranging his hard dick before dragging his eyes away from me and moving to sit back at his desk.

He started working on the image again, his brow pinched in concentration and the tension ran entirely out of his body as he fell into the art. I rolled onto my side to watch him, propping my head up on my hand as I studied his handsome face and every hard line of his features. His eyes held a sea of dark and light in them, twisting together in an endless tunnel as he poured his whole soul into the work.

I'd forgotten all about the deal I'd made with him by the time he looked up, tilting his head to one side as he regarded his work.

"This is the one," he said gruffly, turning to look at me. "It should go on the back of your neck, like ours."

I nodded, my throat tightening as he got up, walking to the bed and placing the sketch down beside me. His eyes fed on me as he headed away to the closet and I picked up the paper, my breath hitching at the incredible, intricate image on it. The four arrows of the Night Keepers crossed each other and the fifth stood at the heart of them, pointing upwards, the feathers on the end of it softer than those on the boys and decorated with little flowers.

Kyan knelt on the bed as he returned and I looked up at him with my heart in my throat. "I love it," I said seriously and his face softened with pride.

"I've wanted to mark you with ink from the moment I first saw your body, baby. All that pure, golden flesh has been begging for my tattoo gun for the longest time. I've ached to brand you as mine. And all jokes a-fucking-side, I'm happy I can brand you for the other Night Keepers too. It just feels… right."

I reached for his hand and drew him toward me. "It feels right to me too."

He took hold of my waist and flipped me over, his hand clapping hard against the back of my thigh. "Now stay down or I'll end up fucking you before I even start," he growled and I laughed into the pillow.

He set up the tattoo gun then straddled my back and pushed my hair away from my neck, his calloused fingers dragging over my skin in the most enticing way. He ran a cold alcohol swab over the flesh he was about to mark and a shiver ran through me, making him curse as his hard cock pressed firmly into my spine.

"Stop being so fucking tempting, will you?" He pulled the pillow out from beneath my head and I rested my cheek on the mattress as he turned the tattoo gun on and a buzzing filled the air. "It's gonna hurt a bit."

"I want it to," I breathed and he released a deep noise in his throat that said he liked that response.

When the needle pressed to my skin, the sting of pain made me bite down on my lip, but there was something addictive about it too.

He was silent as he worked, the teasing and joking falling away as he concentrated and I couldn't help but love being the sole focus of his attention like that.

It took almost two hours for him to finish it and he gently wiped away the blood, his breath warm as it fluttered over the mark.

"Ours," he growled, placing a kiss to the sore skin and making a moan pass my lips.

"In every way," I agreed.

He started trailing kisses and bites down my spine and my breaths turned to pants as he made it clear he was going to mark me as his with a carnal act too and I was more than happy to go along with that. But as he pulled my hands behind my back and locked them at the base of my spine, I frowned.

"Kyan?" I tugged at my hands and he held onto them for a moment before his grip loosened.

"You okay, baby?" he asked and I pulled my wrists away from him, rolling onto my side. He dropped down beside me, pushing my hair behind my ear with a gentle stroke that made me feel loved so fully, my heart swelled. I snuggled up closer to him, laying a soft kiss on his lips and he watched me, seeming a little out of his depth. Things with Kyan were always passionate, rough and raw. And I loved that about him. But I wanted him to know it didn't have to be that way all the time. I wanted him to feel comfortable enough to be vulnerable with me. That he didn't always have to be the big bad wolf.

"What if I said I didn't wanna be restrained tonight?" I asked, biting my lip as I gauged his reaction. A shadow slid over his eyes and his adam's apple rose and fell.

"Don't you like it?" he asked gruffly, his brow furrowing.

"Of course I do," I said, laying my hand on the curve between his neck and shoulder. "But we don't always have to do it that way. Sometimes, I really wanna touch you…" I ran my fingers down his chest and I could see him fighting some fervent urge in him. It made my heart hurt to know this was causing him discomfort. But I wanted to break this barrier down between us. I knew we could do it if we worked together.

"Is it because of Deepthroat?" I whispered and he cringed at that name, his eyes moving somewhere over my head so he didn't have to look at me when he answered.

"Nothing about what happened with her is relevant to you," he gritted out, but I didn't believe that.

"It's alright," I said, sliding my hand up to cup his jaw as I tried to get him to look at me. And he did, but his eyes were filled with endless pain and regret. It hurt me to see that chasm of suffering in him and I wished I could crawl into him and heal it.

"I don't want you to feel like I only want you one way," he said in a growl. "Or that restraining you means I love you any less. It's just…" He leaned toward me, kissing my neck as he pushed my hair away from it. "Something I need to do."

"Kyan," I sighed in protest as he pushed me onto my back and knelt over my hips, kissing up my throat to my ear and teasing it in the perfect fucking way with soft nips of his teeth. "*Kyan.*"

"I don't have to be rough all the time," he said, his deep voice sending a quake through my body. *God damn him.*

He started kissing his way down my body, worshipping every piece of my flesh he found as his hands skimmed along my sides. I started panting, unable to think straight as he moved between my thighs and showed me how slowly, softly and catastrophically he could touch me with nothing but his mouth.

I parted my lips on protests that wouldn't come out as he brought me to an earth shattering crescendo that made my whole body tremble. Then he laid his weight on me and pulled my arms above my head, holding my wrists with one hand in a hold that was firm but not tight.

"Kyan we should really ta-" I started but he pushed inside my body in one slow and fluid movement and my back arched as I gasped. He started claiming me with controlled thrusts of his hips, kissing me like he was born to love me, to die for me. It was too perfect to stop and I fell into the dark sea of his eyes as I kissed him back, letting him know I loved him with everything I was, and when he was ready to deal with this, I'd be here. I hoped we could find a way to overcome it together, because the thought of my inked god forever being haunted by his demons broke my heart. I just wished I could fight them for him.

CHAPTER THIRTY FOUR

Waiting a week to head to Royaume D'élite was its own special kind of torture as we were stuck in the purgatory of knowing that we were so close to ending this while feeling so distant from it all the same. It was like that feeling you got while reading a book, glancing at the pages left or the percentage remaining and seeing that you were coming towards the end. In a way it was exciting because you were about to get all of the answers you'd been waiting for, about to find out who survived and who had to pay the ultimate price. But it was terrifying too, because you knew that this right here was when the pace was about to pick up, all the shit was going to hit the fan, and everything was about to collide in an explosion of words and pain and adrenaline that just might leave you a deranged mess on the floor once you were finished with it. And even then, there was the very real possibility that it would haunt you afterwards, the characters lingering in your mind like old friends instead of constructs of your imagination. I just hoped I made it to the epilogue of our fucked up little story - the one where Goldilocks met the three bears and rather than running for the hills, she called the wood cutter in to join them and crowned herself their queen. That was the kind of fairy tale I wanted to live in forever.

Niall had been banned from joining us by Kyan's asshole grandfather. But the crazy bastard had apparently taken enough of a liking to us to help us out by arming us and lending us his car, so we were currently on route to the club of horrors in Niall's Jeep Wrangler with Saint behind the wheel.

I sat in the front passenger seat, listening to the exquisite combination of Saint's classical music while 21 Hungarian Dances No. 5 By Brahms played through the speakers and Tatum moaned loudly in the back seat. I pulled the visor down in front of me, flicking the mirror open to watch as Kyan kissed her passionately while his hand moved beneath the waistband of her black yoga pants. Her hand was on Monroe's thigh as she leaned against him to give Kyan room, her fingernails biting into his flesh, but he clearly had no objections to that as he watched them and kissed her neck.

I licked my lips as her moans turned into the sound of her coming and Kyan chuckled like a self-satisfied asshole as he drew back to let her catch her breath. I was pretty sure every one of us was hard as stone after that little performance, but as much as we'd enjoyed it and would no doubt enjoy it even more if we pulled over for an hour or so, we needed to focus on what we had to do now.

I glanced at Saint, wondering if he was going to have anything to say about it, but he just rolled his eyes, a smirk dancing around the corner of his lips as the track playing shifted to 3 Gymnopédies by Frank Glazer, a quieter piece which seemed to bring a sense of calm over us.

"You all know what you need to do?" Saint confirmed as we pulled down a little dirt track in the middle of fucking nowhere.

Thank fuck Saint had managed to get a lock on this location when Kyan and Tatum had last come here, or I got the feeling we never would have been able to find the place.

"We've been over the plan about a hundred times," I reminded him and he nodded.

"Good." He pulled the night vision goggles Niall had leant us down over his face then switched the headlights off, plunging us into darkness.

Tension built in the car as Saint took the Jeep off road and I held onto the door as we bounced through ditches and over bumpy terrain through the pine forest that surrounded Royaume D'élite.

This was going to be one hell of an accomplishment if we really did manage to pull it off, but I was seriously looking forward to getting my hands dirty. For too long I'd had to see the look in Kyan's eyes that had been present since he'd been forced to enrol in this club for rich assholes. I hated that they'd made him do the things he'd done, and I hated that he'd felt he had to lie to us about it afterwards. But now that I had a monster to blame for the darkness that had been haunting him, I was ready to drive a dagger into its heart and see every last member of this society of motherfuckers burn for their crimes.

Saint stopped the car and a deep silence fell as he cut the engine. We all got out without a word, our black outfits covering us and blanketing us in shadow.

I caught Tatum's hand, tugging her close and kissing her deeply as my fingers ran up the back of her neck, caressing the Night Bound tattoo Kyan had given her and smirking to myself. I couldn't get over how much I fucking loved it. I'd gotten her to tie her hair up and let me fuck her from behind at least four times since she'd gotten it just so that I could feel the perfection of her body wrapped tight around me while looking at that permanent brand on her flesh which said she'd claimed us too. Ours. Forever.

Saint had been caught between being thrilled and pissed over it of course. He'd punished her for marking her body without consulting all of us by spanking her with some crazy leather paddle thing he'd bought and then getting her to suck us all off without letting her come. All of us aside from Kyan who he'd put on a sex ban for the week as his punishment. But I knew for a fact that he'd been screwing our girl in the laundry closet last night and I was pretty certain he'd taken her out to Liam's car a few days ago too. But I hadn't called him out on it because I personally didn't think he'd done anything wrong by marking her for us.

I reluctantly broke our kiss as we all covered our faces with the ski masks and made sure we had knives and guns stowed on our belts. Niall had really come through on the weapons he'd supplied us with and we each had a shiny new nine millimetre fully equipped with silencers, knives and plenty of ammo. Though we were hoping we wouldn't have to use them. Me and Kyan were carrying a couple of gallons of gasoline too for the finale of our plan.

Once we were ready to go, Saint locked the Jeep and turned to look at the rest of us with a deep frown which I could hardly even see in the darkness beneath the trees. It was a cloudy night, the threat of rain hanging in the air and next to no moonlight making it through. But that was a good thing because it meant no one would be able to see us coming either.

"The five people standing here are the most important people in the world," Saint said heavily, looking between all of us to make certain we were listening. "Everything that we are doing here tonight pales in comparison to keeping us alive. Nothing is more important than that. Swear it."

"We won't take any unnecessary risks," I promised, knowing he didn't like that we were going to have to split up once we were in there.

"In and out," Kyan agreed. "Just the way Tatum likes it."

She slapped his chest to tell him off as I laughed.

"Let's just get in there and do what we have to," Nash said. "The sooner it's done and our girl is safely away from here the better."

"Oh *please*," Tatum said. "I bet I'll be the one keeping you assholes safe. I'm not the one who has issues with impulse control."

Saint stepped forward and placed one arm around my shoulders and another around Monroe's. Kyan completed the circle with Tatum standing in the centre of us as we all leaned forward and pressed our heads together.

"I am the dark in the dead of the night," Saint said in a low voice and we all growled the response instead of yelling it for once.

"Here me roar."

We broke apart and started moving through the trees at a fast pace, the lights of the huge manor house up ahead piercing the darkness before long.

When we reached the edge of the trees, we took cover and looked out over the manicured lawn at the back of the imposing gothic building. There was no one in sight on this side of the property, but a car drove up the gravel driveway to our left as we stayed out of sight and we waited as it pulled up before the building to let out the member who had just arrived.

"Ready?" Saint breathed and I nodded along with the others as we darted out of the trees and started running across the lawn.

It was so dark that we were little more than shadows in the night and thankfully, every window at Royaume D'élite was carefully shuttered - no doubt to make sure no photographs could be taken from outside to document the fucked up things that went on within that place. But it served us too, because it meant that no one was looking out either.

Kyan took the lead as we made it to the wall of the imposing building, creeping along the side of it until he reached a narrow sash window where he quickly took a thin wire from his pocket and slid it beneath the gap at the bottom of the pane.

My heart pounded as he cursed beneath his breath a couple of times before he managed to hook the catch and force it open. He slid the window up as quietly as possible, but my teeth still ached at the sound it made and we all held our breath as he leaned forward to peer through a gap in the wooden shutters which blocked the way on.

"The Moguls' Banquet is to the right and up the stairs," he murmured. "The whores and fighters are kept to the left of the building downstairs. Just make sure you keep the fuck away from that meeting. If they catch any of us here, they'll strap us to a table and carve us into pieces while the whole club watches and laughs. So no fuck ups."

"Noted," I replied, moving closer to him and drawing my gun as he prepared to open the shutter next. "I'm too pretty to get carved up."

"Just remember, anyone wearing a mask is an enemy," Saint hissed. "If they get in your way, kill first and ask questions later."

"Simple," Nash replied dryly as Kyan took his hunting knife from his belt and slipped the blade between the thin gap in the shutters. He used it to flick the catch securing them and in the next breath, he'd hopped inside. I gazed in after him, making sure there was no one lurking in the shadows before holstering my gun again.

I paused to give Tatum a boost and she smiled as she let me. "Thank you, Prince Charming," she teased and I followed her inside with the gasoline the moment she was through the window.

I wasn't sure Prince Charming was anywhere near as depraved as me, but I'd play the role if she enjoyed it in her fantasies.

Saint and Monroe were right behind us as we found ourselves in a narrow corridor. A prickle of adrenaline ran through me as Saint quickly closed the window and shutters behind us to cover our entrance.

I took the lead with Kyan as we crept through the huge building where far-off music was playing, nothing but a dull beat reaching us that seemed to make the walls vibrate with the power of it. There was a faint smell of cigars and sex hanging about the place and I wrinkled my nose, thinking of all these old men buying girls to use and discard just because they could. Sometimes I fucking hated people. They were the goddamn worst.

The floorboards creaked around a corner ahead of us and we all froze, my heart racing as the sound of footsteps thankfully moved away from us.

Kyan led us down a flight of stairs next, before pointing out the door to the room where they stored the capes and masks of the members who couldn't attend the party. Relief spilled through me at the sight of it and I took the lead as we crossed a wide hallway with deep red carpet. Once we were wearing their bullshit regalia, we would be able to move around more freely, hiding in plain sight and the chances of being caught would lessen substantially.

I pushed the door open, but just as I did, it was practically yanked from my grasp as someone inside pulled on the handle too.

My heart leapt as I came face to face with a man dressed in a cape and black mask and as he spotted me, he yelled out.

I dove on him, my hands latching around his throat as I squeezed hard, cutting off that sound and stumbling back into the room with him. We slammed into a wall and he kicked and flailed as my hands stayed locked tight around his throat and I fought desperately to keep him silent.

The door closed behind me as the others chased us inside and we were plunged into total darkness as the man I was choking punched my ribs with savage blows. But I just took the fucking pain of them because I knew the moment my hold failed, he'd scream bloody murder and bring this whole place down on our heads.

I grunted as he hit me again then he began clawing at my gloved hands, trying to prise my grip from his throat. But I couldn't let go. I wouldn't. And as the lights suddenly flicked on and I met his grey eyes through the holes in his expressionless mask I saw true panic and desperation there.

I gritted my teeth and held on tight as I squeezed and fucking squeezed and when he finally stopped struggling and fell still, I dropped him with a curse.

"Do you think anyone heard that?" I hissed, turning to find the others watching me.

"I think they'd be here by now if they had," Saint replied after a beat and we all agreed with that.

Nash started grabbing cloaks and tossing them to us to put on over our black outfits and my hands shook a little from the adrenaline of the fight as I fastened mine around my neck.

A gold and black skull mask was pressed into my hands and I looked up to find Tatum standing before me, her eyes wide and full of fire.

"You saved our asses there, golden boy," she teased, tiptoeing up to press a brief kiss to my lips before stepping back and pulling her own mask down over her face.

"All in a day's work, sweetheart," I replied, glancing at the body I'd left slumped on the floor before fixing my own mask over my features and drawing my hood up. There was a time that I would have freaked the fuck out over what I'd just done, but not anymore. I'd learned the hard way what it took to survive in this world and I was ready to do whatever it took to make sure we did.

"Take note of each other's numbers," Saint commanded and I looked at the golden number 327 stitched onto the breast of his cape. "We don't want to accidentally shoot each other."

Monroe laughed like that was a joke, but as I looked between the other Night Keepers and our queen, I had to admit that it was pretty hard to recognise who was who beneath the masks and capes. But I was so in tune with all of them that I very much doubted I'd get them confused with anyone else even so.

Kyan grabbed the dead guy and shoved him beneath the rack of cloaks, kicking his feet out of sight so that it was impossible to see him beneath the hanging black material and we quickly flicked the lights back off and headed out into the building again.

"This way," Kyan said, striding off down the dim corridor like he owned the place and we followed on after him past oil paintings and closed doors, through several twists and turns and up a flight of stairs.

"Gentlemen!" a voice called out from behind us and we stilled as we turned to look back at the man in a black mask who had paused at the foot of the stairs to call out to us. "Oh, and lady too," he added, noticing Tatum amongst us. "The meeting is already underway and the Grand Master-"

"We are well aware," Saint barked in his most entitled dickhead voice. "Is it your job to question us, or are you here to serve?"

"No, Master," the man replied hastily, cutting a bow to us like we were lords or some shit from Bridgerton. "I just wanted to be sure you knew."

"Well now you're sure, you can fuck off," Kyan growled and the guy promptly did just that, scurrying away like a rat down a hole.

"Jesus," Monroe muttered and I got the feeling he was both relieved that had worked and kinda disgusted at this privileged world we'd grown up in. But at least we weren't here to join up. We might have been a group of entitled rich boys, but we were here to fuck up the establishment just like him.

"That's the office we found before," Tatum said as we drew close to one of the nondescript wooden doors and we waited while she dropped down to pick the lock.

My heart was ticking to a heady rhythm as we waited for her to do it and the sound of laughter reached us from somewhere around the corner at the end of the corridor.

Before I could even think about drawing my gun, the door clicked open and Tatum hurried inside with us all right behind her.

I closed the door and she moved across the space, opening the secret door they'd found behind the bookshelf and letting Saint and Monroe head into the office that was hidden there. Saint's eyes lit up behind his mask as he looked around at the opulent space. It wasn't huge, but everything in here was expensive and clearly owned by a rich douchebag.

"You know what you have to do?" Saint asked, looking between me, Kyan and Tatum.

"Avoid the secret society assholes, free the sex slaves then get ready to run like hell?" I asked with a smile that no one could see behind my mask.

"Be careful," Nash growled, his eyes on Tatum and I knew he hated us splitting up like this, but we'd all agreed it was the only way.

Saint needed time to find whatever he could in this office but we also couldn't hang around, so we needed to get to work on our part of the plan while he did his.

"I always am," Kyan replied with a chuckle that said he was excited about fucking things up.

"So help me, you neanderthal-" Saint began, but I cut him off.

"Me and Tate will make sure he doesn't go over the top, won't we?" I asked and she nodded.

"We have a job to do," she agreed. "So let's hurry up and do it."

She led the way back out of the office and me and Kyan fell into step behind her like a pair of attack dogs, our arms brushing against each other.

"Into war we go," I murmured and Kyan chuckled.

"To the death, brother."

"To the death," I agreed. I just hoped it wouldn't come to that.

CHAPTER THIRTY FIVE

Kyan led the way through the club, the hallways so quiet it made my adrenaline spike every time I heard a faraway noise. There didn't seem to be anyone in this part of the huge building, but we had to be cautious. We were in a snake pit and we couldn't disturb the serpents until we'd laid our trap and were ready to cut their heads off.

We stashed the gasoline in a cupboard then had to take a detour away from two huge doors that led into the wing of the house we wanted to enter. It had been guarded and too many staff had been around to do anything about it. But Kyan had said he knew another way, so we'd headed upstairs and prowled through the corridors like predators on a hunt.

We moved along a landing with dark green carpet and glanced over the balcony railing to the floor below. Empty.

Blake walked close behind me as we reached the top of the stairs and Kyan glanced back at us through his mask.

"This is the only way on, but there might be guards down there and they're not gonna be polite even if we do look like members. This area is restricted even during parties," he whispered, taking the knife from his hip.

I took out my own, gripping the hilt tightly and taking a steadying breath. We had to be covert. No guns unless it was absolutely necessary. Even a silencer wouldn't cancel the noise of a gunshot completely. But I knew hand to hand combat. And Nash had improved on the base my father had laid for me, bolstering my confidence and preparing me for anything. I wasn't going to hesitate, lose my head, or fail. If it came to a fight, I'd win. For me and my boys.

Kyan moved down the stairs, placing his feet carefully, testing each step to make sure they didn't creak. I followed steadily and Blake placed his boots wherever I placed mine.

We were almost at the bottom when voices sounded from somewhere nearby.

"Hey, they're all in the hall so I'm gonna go and have a little fun," a man said. "Cover for me, will ya?"

"Alright, but fifteen minutes max. And when you're back, you can cover for me," another man replied.

"Deal," the first man chuckled then a beep sounded and a door opened and shut.

Kyan made it off of the final step and a loud creak came from the floorboard beneath him. We all froze and my pulse thundered on the inside of my skull as I held my breath.

Shit, shit, shit.

Footsteps started stomping this way, the crackle of a radio reaching my ears.

Kyan moved flush against the wall and me and Blake pressed against it too.

The guard moved closer and closer and my muscles coiled like a spring, a fierce energy within me waiting to be let loose.

The guard stepped past us and Kyan lunged, slamming a hand over his mouth, but as he brought his knife up, the guard jabbed his hand back and Kyan was thrown off of him as a taser took him to the ground. I launched myself at the guard without a thought, my knife sinking into the flesh of his throat as he flung around, his fist crashing into my gut and sending me stumbling back into Blake. But my golden boy didn't slow as the guard snatched his radio, clutching the bloody wound at his throat, his lips parting to call for help. Blake's fist smashed into the radio, sending it to the floor in pieces and Blake's knife sank deep between his ribs before he could get out a scream.

Blake held onto the guard as he died, not letting him hit the floor as I dropped down beside Kyan, ripping the taser off of him and pulling his mask away to see he was okay.

"You worried about me, baby?" he wheezed, his expression cocky but the tightness of his voice told me that had hurt like a bitch.

"That's not the first time you've been tasered, is it?" I teased in a whisper and he shook his head as I helped him up.

"Saint tasered my ass once for being 'an obnoxious caveman.'"

"Sounds like you deserved it." I smirked.

"Come on, we need to move," Blake hissed as he stuffed the guard into a small closet full of cleaning supplies, hiding him among them before shutting the door.

A bang said the guy had just slipped forward and hit the door and it flew open again as the asshole rolled out onto the floor.

"Goddammit," Blake growled, hoisting him up by the shoulders. Blood was dripping onto the wooden floor and it was definitely not fucking covert.

"*Blake*," I hissed as we jogged over to help him and he and Kyan squeezed the guy into the tight space. I grabbed a mop and cleaned up the blood before tossing it in after him.

Kyan closed the door but it hit something and I looked, finding the toe of the man's boot was poking out.

"For fuck's sake." I moved forward, shoving the foot further inside and shutting the door with a click.

We shared an awkward glance then Kyan fixed his mask back into place and looked to the door under the stairs across the hall. "Oh."

"Oh what?" Blake breathed.

"We need a security pass," he said, turning to the closet again.

I groaned, glancing around us and listening to make sure no one was heading this way. "Come on then, we need to hurry."

Kyan popped the door open once more and the guy spilled out on a tide of cleaning supplies.

"Oh for the love of-" Blake started then a loud voice sounded further off in the building, heading this way.

"Hey two-oh-two, you can take your break now." He strode into the hallway, his eyes falling on us and the dead guy at our feet.

My heart lurched as Kyan charged at him, taking him down in a football tackle that made the floor shudder as they hit the ground. He drove a knife into the guy's chest before he had a chance to do anything but die and more blood pooled out across the floor.

"Fuck," Blake growled as more footsteps sounded this way.

"What was that noise?" a woman called and we all moved faster than lightning. Kyan carried the guy he'd just killed to the closet and we furiously stuffed both of the assholes inside in a tangle of limbs. Kyan snatched a security card from one of them before wedging the door shut.

I grabbed a rug from further down the hall, laying it over the small puddle of blood the last guard's death had caused and Kyan grabbed my hand as he towed me to the door across the hall.

He slapped a security card against a keypad and it beeped as it opened, the sound making my adrenaline spike. We rushed inside as the woman's footsteps sounded seriously close by and pressed the door shut behind us, leaning against it. I was squashed between my two men in the dark as we listened and the guard strode through the hall without stopping.

I released a slow breath and stepped away from Blake and Kyan, moving down another set of stairs.

"Leave the light off," I breathed. We couldn't risk alerting anyone to our presence before we made it down to the basement.

A scream carried up from the depths of the darkness and we started moving faster into the gloom, my gut clenching at the noise.

We tip-toed on until we reached the bottom where a slit of light spilled under a door. I took hold of the handle, cracking it open silently and peering into the room that awaited us beyond, holding my breath.

Rows and rows of large cages were stacked up two high, full of people who wore varying amounts of clothes. Sickness made my upper lip peel back at the sight, especially when my gaze fell on the guard who was struggling to pin a half-naked man down over a bench at the centre of the room.

"Dibs," I breathed to the others, hatred licking the inside of my flesh.

"Make it hurt, baby," Kyan purred and I pushed the door open, stalking my prey like a tiger in the long grass.

I felt the eyes of the captives on me, but they seemed to sense what I was here for as I held my blade ready and crept up toward the man trying to rape the guy on the bench.

As I got close behind him, the scent of body odour reached me, making me grimace. I aimed my blade just right then stuck him in the liver with one sharp stab. There was no way he'd be heard down here so I wasn't gonna be gentle. He screamed in surprise and agony, wheeling around as I yanked the blade out and ducked down to slash at his legs. He screamed louder, hitting the concrete floor and the captives in their cages cried out excitedly, banging their fists against the bars.

The man he'd been harassing stood straight, tugging up his boxers, his hands shaking. His gaze met mine and I took in his handsome face, his eyes hard and full of unspeakable tortures. I tore my mask from my face, wanting him to see I was on his side. That I was here to help. Then I held out the knife for him and he took it with a determined nod, leaning down to finish his enemy. The bastard's strangled screams followed me as I turned, running to help Kyan and Blake as they used the key card to unlock the cages.

The freed men and women soon gathered around us, seeming unsure what to do as they hugged their bodies and shared frightened looks with one another.

"What's happening?"

"Where do we go?"

"How do we get out?"

"There's a way out upstairs," Kyan announced.

"We're going to get you out of the manor then the police will come and pick you up," I promised. "We're going to burn this place to the fucking ground and destroy the people who hurt you."

Sobs of relief came from the crowd mixed with cheers and murmurs of doubt.

"Follow our queen!" Blake cried dramatically and I released a breath of amusement, only to find every pair of eyes in the room set on me. So I sure as hell wasn't going to let them down.

Kyan moved to my side and we headed back to the stairs as he murmured in my ear. "There's an exit which is a straight shot across the hall upstairs. But we might need to force it open."

"Okay, let's get them out of here. Then we can finish this," I said.

"I love burning the world down with you at my side," Kyan said in a low voice.

"It's not burning yet," I tossed back with a grin before placing my mask back on as we made it to the top of the stairs.

I glanced back, finding Blake helping a woman walk who looked heartbreakingly weak. I frowned at my golden boy, his eyes full of hate and injustice over what had happened to these people. But we weren't letting it lie. We were going to make the monsters of this place pay.

"I'll get the door open," Kyan said, slipping out into the hall and heading across it as we waited in the dark. After a minute, I poked my head out, finding him pushing it wide and pocketing a pick, the spring night air blowing inside.

My adrenaline spiked as I led the way across the hall and the captives raced towards freedom, tearing out into the dark. Relief rushed through me at the sight and I knew the risk of coming here had been worth it for this alone. It had haunted me knowing what was happening to people at this club and nothing could rival the feeling of being able to do something about it at last.

I pulled the long cape from Blake's shoulders, wrapping it around the woman he was helping and a tall man came to her side to take her from him. She caught Blake's hand before they parted, her hooded eyes finding his. "Make them scream."

"We will," Blake swore, the darkness in him swimming in his gaze, full of the retribution he was going to bestow on every twisted motherfucker in this place.

Kyan offered his cape to another woman as the last of them ran outside, then he swung the door shut and looked to us with hunger in his eyes. "Let's go kill some rats."

CHAPTER THIRTY SIX

I rifled through drawers with Nash at my side, looking for anything at all that could give us some of the answers we needed. There were files on countless companies, evidence of insider trading and illicit deals which would be more than enough to send all of the people complicit in them to prison. Or at least it would be if their names were on the documents. Which of course they weren't.

Every single deal only ever referred to the people who had taken part in them by the number they'd been given in relation to their membership here. So while I took countless photographs of every single piece of evidence I could lay my hands on, I knew that it would be damn hard for any convictions to be made unless I found the key to those numbers and linked the right names to them.

It had to be here somewhere. There had to be a record of who the members were and which numbers they'd been assigned or there was no way this place could work. When Kyan had come here before, the car that had collected him had shown up with his robes waiting inside it and the number clearly marked on them.

That meant that whoever he had contacted about coming to the club had been able to link him to the correct number. There had to be a system in place for that. It may have been the case that only the people in charge of running this place had access to it, but it had to be here.

"For the love of all that's holy," I growled in frustration, slamming the drawer I'd finished looking through and moving over to the desk where the computer stood.

It wasn't connected to the internet so it would be impossible to hack into it from the outside, but it was possible that I could do it in person now. I knew that it was where I was most likely to find the evidence I really needed to take this place down, but I also knew that with the very limited time scale we were working on here that it was unlikely.

"Perhaps we should just take the entire computer with us and leave," I suggested. "Or better yet, I'll just break it and take the hard drive out."

"I'd guess that makes the most sense," Nash agreed. "Hand it over to the authorities and let them handle it."

My jaw clenched as I took a seat in the leather chair behind the desk, the idea of that rankling me. Yes, it would make sense. But it would also haunt me for the rest of time. This was *my* fight. *Our* fight. I wanted to see the evidence here for myself and wield it how I saw fit, not hand the fight over to some federal bureaucrat in a suit.

"Ah shit," Monroe said, turning to look at me with a file held loosely in his hand. "This is the moment isn't it?"

"What moment?" I asked dryly.

"The moment when the great Saint Memphis realises that he isn't actually a superhero. When you have to admit that you can't actually do this alone. That you need help." He looked far too pleased at that guess and I huffed out a breath as I stacked my gloved hands together on the desk. We'd taken our masks off when we began our search so I could see his expression plainly enough and quite frankly, I was tempted to smack the look off of his face.

"I have never claimed to be able to do everything alone," I said in a low voice. "The four of you have proved yourselves more than valuable to me in countless ways. I appreciate that I am not well suited to every task, nor capable of doing everything myself. But there are certain things which I excel at-"

"Name one thing you don't excel at," he challenged, his tone teasing like he believed there wasn't anything, but if he truly thought that I was so deluded then he was very wrong indeed.

"I am not a person who is easily liked, let alone loved," I replied matter of factly. "I don't perform well in most social situations and I don't make friends easily. I don't even like very many people to wish for them to be my friend anyway - but that in itself is likely a flaw."

"I didn't realise you'd admit that was a flaw. I just assumed you enjoyed being an overbearing asshole who terrifies almost everyone you meet," he said, seeming intrigued by my candid response.

"I don't hate it," I admitted. "But sometimes..." I sighed, knowing this wasn't the time for this conversation and yet needing the momentary reprieve from my task to allow my brain some space to think. "Sometimes, I watch the way the four of you are and I can see that I...don't fit. Not in the same way."

Nash blew out a breath and shrugged. "*You* feel like the outsider? Try being the guy who joined up last. Who used to be your teacher. Who comes from a poor family and the foster system while all of you just shit dollar bills and flush them away like they're meaningless. If any of us doesn't fit, it's me."

A smile tugged at the corner of my lips. "And yet you do," I pointed out. "Besides, you had something growing up which I can never lay claim to."

"You have love now," he objected, knowing exactly what I meant. "We all have love now. Tatum gave us that."

"Yes. Our family is the one truest light in an otherwise very dark world. I'm proud to call you my brother, Nash," I said honestly.

"Well, I suppose brothers are meant to drive you mad half the time, so that label fits my feelings for you rather well," he admitted, looking a little surprised by the fact. "Though I'm glad there's no blood that binds us because I've witnessed way too much of you having sex for that."

"Come now," I said with a knowing smirk. "You don't just witness these things. I think we both know you and Kyan passed the point of merely sharing Tatum last week. I saw the marks on your neck. Clearly you've moved into the territory of touching each other during it rather than just watching."

Nash barked a laugh and tossed the file he'd been holding down onto the desk as he turned back to continue looking through the cabinets. "I might have let him choke me a bit, but don't go getting caught up in any fantasies of me actually fucking him."

"No, you're far too linear for that," I agreed, my gaze skimming over the computer as I switched it on and waited for it to load up. "Though I have to admit that if a few of us experimented with a little interaction between each other it would give poor Tatum a break from having so many of us vying for her attention all at once."

"I think Tatum likes having the four of us vying for her attention just fine," Nash replied. "That girl was practically made for us. All of us. But if you think Blake and Kyan might like to start hooking up with each other, then feel free to encourage them all you like."

I laughed, knowing as well as he did that there wasn't any chance of any of us turning our attention from our girl for that.

"I am not surprised you enjoyed him choking you," I said casually as the monitor lit up, asking me for a password I couldn't guess.

"And why is that?" Monroe asked, not denying it.

"Men like us are obsessed with control - or the lack of it that we have in our lives. You have spent the better part of your life hungering to reclaim the control you lost the night your family was killed by my father. You strive to dominate in a world that has kicked you so many times you've lost count. But that fight is tiring and never ending. You will never be able to reclaim what you lost. And that means you will never be fully satisfied no matter what vengeance we exact upon the man responsible for your losses. So, you will likely continue to strive for control, you will enjoy claiming it, dominating, possessing and proving your worth. But on occasion, when the weight of fighting so much and so often to possess all the things you desire gets too much, you will find yourself aching to break that cycle. There is a very real relief in relinquishing control of yourself to someone else. And using it for sexual gratification seems perfectly acceptable to me. Sometimes my need for control consumes me and Tatum gives in, she offers me her body and allows me to own it, if only for a brief time. But she is also the creature most likely and able to make me lose control too. And when she destroys me like that there is nothing that compares to it. It may be a little terrifying, but isn't that why it's so thrilling?"

Nash turned to look at me in surprise then grinned. "Maybe you should let Kyan choke you then?" he suggested. "Or better yet, let me do it."

"Unlikely," I replied, rolling my eyes and my gaze fell on a little note stuck to the file he'd dropped onto my desk.

It was nothing really. Just four words. *File with Farringbridge Group*. It didn't even bear any relevance, except that I recognised that handwriting. Perhaps I'd been a fool in underestimating my father. What if he wasn't *involved* in running this place? What if he *was* this place?

I turned back to the computer and my fingers flew over the keyboard as I tried one of his favourite and most complicated passwords. They were random assortments of letters and numbers, but I'd long since figured out all of the ones he used.

The first attempt failed so I tried another combination. That failed too and I took in a long breath as I typed out the third.

The monitor flashed as it was accepted and within a moment, I was staring at the home screen.

"I'm in," I breathed.

Nash dropped the file he'd been photographing and hurried over to stand beside me as I looked up at him with a dark smile.

"How?" he demanded and I only hesitated a moment before giving him the answer he craved. I trusted him to know I wasn't my father's son by now. He knew I hungered for that man's demise just as much if not more than he did. This wouldn't affect his opinion of me.

"I just confirmed our suspicions about the man who gave me life," I said, turning back to the screen as I started typing. "Troy Memphis is the Grand Master of this place. He's the man we have been hunting. And now we have his scent, I'm certain that we'll find him."

"Then he has to be here," Monroe growled excitedly. "The members of this club aren't just helping him hide. He's presiding over it and they're down there right now having that meeting."

I followed his train of thought easily enough but then sighed as I dismissed it. "We can't assassinate him here. There is no way that we could be certain of our escape if we head into that snake pit so outnumbered. I won't risk Tatum like that. I won't risk any of you like that. The fire might kill him of course, but I seriously doubt he will be that easy to dispatch. It would be a rather anticlimactic and simple ending, wouldn't it?"

"Nothing wrong with simple. Seems like that could be pretty damn satisfying to me. We charge in there, kill him. Then live happily ever after."

"I don't foresee this ending that easily at all," I replied firmly. "It will take blood and guts and tears and even then, who knows if we'll all make it through in one piece? But if we want to do that, we need to be smart. Brains over brawn."

Nash looked ready to stride right on out of the room and hunt my father down himself, but I caught his wrist and made him look at me.

"Today is not the day," I insisted. "But it draws near."

He nodded with a grunt of frustration then stayed by my side as I began my work dissecting the files on the computer.

Within minutes, the membership list flashed up on the screen and I sucked in a breath as the names of more wealthy people than I could easily count flashed before my eyes. There were plenty of names I recognised from members of the government to judges, police, lawyers and all kinds of businessmen and women. This was a powerhouse of immeasurable worth. And I had it right here in my hands.

I scanned through the list of names and hurriedly found Kyan's and deleted it, working to remove it entirely from the list so that no matter how hard someone searched, they'd never find any evidence to support him having been a member here. My gaze fell on his uncle's name and I decided to offer him the same gift too, removing Niall from everything as permanently as I could. The rest of the O'Briens could rot for all I cared, but after a few moments of consideration, I decided that it was best to remove them too. I needed them fully beneath my thumb if I wished to cut all of Kyan's ties to them and it was best that they didn't get dragged down with this place.

I took an external hard drive from my pocket and quickly began downloading everything that I could from the computer as I hunted down the information about Serenity Pharmaceuticals. There were details on all of the dodgy shareholders as well as information on the Hades Virus, hopefully with evidence of how they'd unleashed it into the world in hopes of making a profit off of their vaccination. But I'd need a lot longer to look through it if I wanted to be certain of that. Time I didn't have.

There were a lot of files which were encrypted, hiding fuck knew what and were impossible for me to break into right now, but I downloaded them all so that I could do it later. I just needed to get everything away from here and take my time dissecting it. I had no doubt that I'd be able to figure out exactly where my father was hiding plus uncover any more secrets he might have been concealing from me if I just had more time.

My heart was racing as I downloaded everything I could get my hands on. File after file, details of so many crimes and so much corruption that I couldn't even take it all in at once. But there was enough here to destroy each and every member of this fucking place and see them rot in jail for the rest of their miserable lives too. I was going to crack the computer open and take the hard drive with me when we left as well. I didn't want any of this information falling into the wrong hands. I'd take it, analyse it, use it then make sure it ended up in the hands of the right authorities – agents I'd hand select to handle the case once I was certain I'd done all I could with it.

"We've done it," I breathed as my fingers flew over the keyboard and Nash gripped my shoulder as he watched me work with a savage smile on his face. "We've destroyed this place already and they have no idea."

CHAPTER THIRTY SEVEN

We ran through the halls, pouring gasoline everywhere, splashing it up curtains, over expensive carpets and wallpaper. My heart pounded with exhilaration as we moved from room to room, priming this entire place to go up in flames.

We had to be wary of guards as we worked, moving methodically through the quieter wings first in the direction of where the annual banquet was being held. The closer we got to it, the more guards we found. And the more guards who fell at our hands.

Saint had messaged to say they had what they needed, so all we had to do now was wait for them to get to us then light a few matches and get the hell out of here.

When we reached the entrance hall, we slipped into a servant's staircase and waited, stashing the gasoline cans out of sight in the shadows. Kyan had given Saint directions to where we waited and I had complete faith that he and Nash were gonna make it.

I just didn't know how much longer we had before we were found out.

It was almost inevitable someone was going to realise guards were missing, or a body would be discovered, or the gasoline noticed. We were down to our final minutes and every second that passed felt like an hour.

"Where are they?" Blake growled impatiently.

"They'll be here," I insisted, though anxiety was starting to grip me as I feared something had happened to hold them up.

I shot another message to the group chat, but no reply came.

Something was wrong. I suddenly knew it in my gut. Saint wouldn't be late. Not even under these circumstances.

"We have to look for them," I said decisively.

"If we move and they show up then we'll only end up running around this house in circles," Kyan said in a growl.

"Then someone has to stay here," I said. "I can go alone."

"Like hell you will," Blake hissed, his hand curling around my arm.

"I am the dark in the dead of night!" Saint's voice suddenly boomed from the next level up and my heart lurched into my throat.

"Hear me fucking roar," Kyan snarled, lurching toward the stairs and we ran after him, tearing along as fear crashed through my limbs.

Saint was in trouble. He wouldn't have risked shouting unless he was desperate. He needed us. And we wouldn't let him down.

Kyan burst through the door at the top of the stairs and I saw the gun wheeling toward him a heartbeat before I acted. I shoved him aside and a hole was blown in the door frame an inch to my left as Blake returned fire, making my head echo with the noise.

Saint and Monroe had four guards holding them, their arms secured behind their backs, their expressions fierce. I refused to let panic claim me. I had to focus to get them out of this alive.

I whipped my own gun from my hip as bullets whistled past me, too fucking close for comfort. Blake charged toward us and the weight of him flattened me as he threw us behind the cover of a wall into an adjacent corridor. Bullets ripped chunks out of the corner of the wall and my heart crushed in my chest. *Saint, Nash, I have to save them.*

Blake rolled off of me and Kyan pushed to his feet, reloading his gun as he pressed his back to the wall and edged up to the corner. He threw a look around it and lurched back as a spray of gunfire blasted at him. *Holy fuck.*

It fell deathly quiet once more and I moved to crouch by Kyan's legs as I gripped my gun. We couldn't let this go on much longer. The men in that meeting might have heard this and if we didn't get away from here before they came looking for us then we were fucked.

"Hold your fire," a booming voice said. "Or your friends are dead."

"Fuck you," Monroe spat then let out a curse as a blow was struck, making me clench my teeth in fury.

"Let them go and we'll think about sparing your lives," I called, and the four pieces of shit laughed darkly.

"Toss your weapons or this cunt gets it," the deep voice said and ice froze my veins solid. Dead, he was dead. They were all fucking *dead.*

"Watch your mouth you uncouth fucking hillbilly," Saint snarled then cursed as someone hit him too.

My heart hit a wild beat and I looked up at Kyan, my jaw set. He took another gun from his hip and tossed it out into the hallway, nodding to me. I threw my knife and gun away while looking around for Blake. But he wasn't there. What the fuck?

"Right, now I'm gonna count to three and you're gonna come out here or we're all gonna find out what the inside of this one's head looks like," the man growled.

Acid burned the inside of my veins as I marked this scum, branded his death on my soul and swore to fulfil it.

"One," he said calmly.

"Don't come out here," Saint demanded.

"Stay where you are, princess," Nash begged.

"Two."

"Kyan, you will look after her above all else, you fucking swore it,"

Saint growled.

Kyan looked at me and I glared at him, daring him to try a single thing. I told him with my eyes I was going out there and I would never forgive him if he stopped me. And he inclined his head in agreement as he pushed his gun into the back of his pants.

"Three."

We stepped out as one and I didn't have time to think what would happen without Blake appearing too.

"Where's the other-" the leader started then a bullet ripped through the centre of his eyes. He fell down in a heap, knocking Saint over who was on his knees. Blake stood in the asshole's place, twisting around fast and firing off three shots. The noise was muffled by the silencer but the shots still made a pap. I stared at my golden boy surrounded by four guards' bodies, his chest heaving, his teeth bared. He looked like a beast sent from the depths of hell to reap souls, our dark saviour.

I snatched my knife from the floor and ran forward to cut the tie on Saint's hands while Kyan freed Monroe. I turned to the piece of shit who'd threatened to kill Saint and spat on his corpse. Saint caught my cheek, pulling me around to face him as my heart beat like crazy.

"Spitting is so very animal of you," he remarked, his eyes drinking me in as if he liked that.

He drew me to my feet and I turned to hug Nash, pulling all of them close for a moment as I savoured the knowledge that we were all still okay. Still walking, still breathing, still primed to ruin this entire empire.

"That was badass, brother," Kyan said to Blake as he moved to pick up his weapons. He tossed me mine and we moved swiftly into the stairwell.

"I knew I could do it, I can't be beat," Blake said with a smirk and I dropped back to squeeze his fingers in gratitude.

He was never going to let us forget this victory and I didn't give one shit about that. He'd just saved all of our asses. And I'd be repaying him for it in any way I could the second we got out of here.

We ran downstairs and crept back into the main hall, passing the gasoline cans we'd hidden in the stairwell. The laughter of a crowd came from somewhere close by and we stilled. I couldn't quite believe that they hadn't overheard our fight upstairs, but I guessed they were making more than enough of their own noise to cover the sounds.

"I say we check it out," Kyan growled. "See if we can't ensure those hall doors are locked when we set the fire."

"Agreed," Saint said coldly, surprising me. "I don't truly believe my father will be so easily defeated, but I'm happy to take a chance on it. We will assess the situation."

We clustered close together as we closed in on the hall where the banquet was taking place and as we made it to a corner, I glanced out to see two guards manning the doors.

"We can manage this," Saint whispered.

"We need a distraction to get close," Kyan breathed and we fell into thoughtful silence for a moment.

We couldn't tip off these guards or every asshole in that hall would know we were here. No, we needed to barricade them in there and make sure as many of them died as fucking possible when we set the place on fire.

Saint leaned close to my ear, whispering softly. "I don't like it and neither will the others, but perhaps you can pretend to be a girl sent for entertainment."

I nodded to him quickly, jumping on the plan. "Escort me," I insisted, pulling my mask off and stripping out of my clothes.

"What the fuck?" Nash mouthed as Kyan barred my way forward.

Saint gave them all a stare that told them to back down then straightened his spine, swapping out his mask for a black one. I guessed he'd stolen it off of one of the guys Blake had just killed. He really did plan for every occasion. I stepped forward in nothing but my underwear and he dragged me firmly down the hall. He held me close, slightly in front of him with a knife grazing my back as he prepared to kill these motherfuckers.

I struggled against his hold, releasing a whimper of fear and the guards looked around in surprise.

"What are you doing down here?" one of them asked.

"I got a message to bring up a pretty one. I guess the celebrations are starting early," Saint said smoothly, his acting skills fucking top notch. But of course they were.

The guards' gazes moved down my body and they sniggered, turning towards the door to open it. Saint pressed the hilt of a knife into my hand, releasing me as we came up behind them.

I stabbed hard and true before they could open the door as I slapped my hand across his mask to stifle his cry.

Saint struck at the same time, slashing the other man's throat with a vicious swipe of his blade. The two of them fell at our feet and my breaths came unevenly as I gazed at Saint with no regret in my heart. Kyan, Blake and Nash ran toward us, picking up a huge dresser between them while Saint and I dragged the bodies away. They placed it in front of the doors to bar the exit and my heart pounded with exhilaration.

We shared a satisfied look then turned and started running. Blake held my clothes in his grip and tossed them to me as we went. As we reached the main hall, I pulled them on and Saint took out five zippo lighters from his pocket, handing them out to us.

"Together," he announced like there was no other way to do this. And he was right. We were a team, an unstoppable force.

The pond scum in this place were about to find out what happened when they came up against us. We moved to the end of the hall then lowered down, each of us sparking our lighters and holding them to the huge rug. It went up in a whoosh and we turned tail and ran, holding up our flames to curtains and drapes and gasoline-soaked wallpaper as we ran from the fire tearing out behind us, the heat flaring ferociously against my back already.

My boys ran on either side of me and all of them were smiling as we raced for the end of the corridor where a window would let us out. A savage grin pulled at my lips as I felt like I was running with a pack of wolves, the five of us joined by spirit and promises and love.

We made it to the window and Monroe wrenched the shutters wide before sliding it up. He grabbed my waist and helped me up onto the sill. I dropped outside onto the grass and turned back as they all dove after me, loving them so fiercely in that second it burned a mark on my heart. Kyan slammed the window shut and we ran into the night towards our car.

We'd call the police, they'd come for the people we'd freed, and in time they'd discover the truth lying in the ruins of this place, especially when we released every scrap of information we had on Royaume D'élite and their entire organisation. Then the world would know a den of monsters had been destroyed.

CHAPTER THIRTY EIGHT

I leaned back in my chair and kicked my feet up onto the table as we sat around the dining table in my grandpa's house, the roaring fire warming my skin as I linked my fingers together and cupped them behind my head.

Saint sat across from me, typing away furiously, scowling at his laptop and muttering the occasional curse as he worked to crack into the encrypted files he'd downloaded from the computer at Royaume D'élite.

He'd pretty much been doing that since we'd gotten back here that night and though he'd managed to break into a few of them, he hadn't found what he was searching for. We still didn't know where his father was hiding out which meant we hadn't been able to use any of this evidence yet or pass it on to the FBI either. I personally held out hope that Troy had been burned alive in that horror show of a club, but Saint refused to believe that and I eventually had to agree. It would have been rather poetic, but that bastard just wouldn't die that easily. Saint was clearly both relishing the challenge presented to him and frustrated as hell by the idea of not being able to outwit his father more easily.

We had the room to ourselves, Liam preferring to eat breakfast alone while he smoked and read a freaking newspaper in his parlour which he still got delivered daily somehow despite the lockdown. He was nothing if not old school, the ultimate sophisticated mob boss, destined to keep to his rituals until his dying day.

Luckily for me, he had some business to attend to this morning with the Russians and didn't want me in attendance, so I was escaping at least a few hours of his lecturing and so called 'preparations for my future role.' The thing was, he was definitely training me up to take over from my dad after graduation, wanting me to spend time learning the ropes of his job so that I would be ready to front the legal side of the family business, but he was teaching me a lot of shit that had nothing to do with that too.

Like last night, when he'd sat me down with a goddamn family tree and talked me through the way each and every one of his brothers, kids, cousins and the rest of the family were strong and how they were weak too. I now knew my uncle Dougal was both lethal, hard-nosed and a perfect enforcer, but that he also had a taste for coke and hookers after celebrating a job, which made him loose lipped from time to time. He'd never given up anything incriminating enough to warrant his death, but I could tell that he was treading a fine line. Betray the family and you weren't family anymore. Every single O'Brien knew that. And if you weren't family, then you were dead. No two ways about it. Once you were in through blood or marriage, you were in.

It made me more than a little uncomfortable to know that Tatum was enveloped under that mantra now too. But I also knew she'd never betray the O'Briens because she'd never get caught up with them beyond her link to me. I wouldn't allow it. No matter the cost to myself.

Most of the secrets I'd learned about my family weren't all that hard to have figured out myself, though my grandpa's clear disdain for most of them was a little surprising. For someone who was so caught up on the ideals of this family shit he spouted all the damn time, he certainly didn't think much of his relatives. The only one he'd spoken about with pride so far as I could tell was Niall. Though he didn't fail to list all of his weaknesses too. He'd said,

"Niall is a good soldier. Ruthless, merciless and thorough. If I give him a job he gets it done no matter what. But losing his wife cracked something loose inside his skull that was already a little fractured to begin with. He's callous, reckless and fearless which are all skills to be admired. But he doesn't plan for anything and he takes unacceptable risks. He's no threat to the family because he lives and breathes this life. But he's a threat to himself every damn day. He has a reputation for being the most terrifying O'Brien and I'd say that's well earned. But it's also well-known he's unhinged. Something broke in him the day those bastards killed Ava and without it he'll never be a good candidate for leadership. He just isn't capable of owning that much responsibility. He doesn't care about his life or anyone else's enough to own it."

Liam had sighed like that disappointed him but mostly it just made me feel sad for my uncle. He deserved more than that from life. He deserved better than to live each day just waiting to die. But I wasn't capable of changing his fate. I just hoped one day he met someone who was.

So over all I was spending the days 'preparing for my role' while getting the impression that that role might be a little different than the job description and the more the idea niggled at me, the more I began to believe it was the truth. But that left me with one rather uncomfortable notion which I needed to discuss with the others sooner or later. Because I was getting the impression that Liam was considering me for leadership. For his role after he died. And if that was the case then in the years between now and his death, I was certain that I'd be tangled up in the web of this family so tightly that there wouldn't even be a way out for me by the time the old bastard croaked. And I had no desire to head up a family of Irish gangsters.

Nash and Blake were bickering over the merits of training for long distance runs, debating the use of weights and sprints and getting all macho bullshit competitive over it. I mean sure, I was all for some macho bullshit, but give me a fight to win and an ass to kick if you wanted to get me riled up about something. Running though? Naw, I wasn't gonna get my panties in a twist about that.

Tatum was sitting opposite me, finishing up her food while I watched her, wondering if I'd ever get bored of just looking at her like that. She caught me of course, arching a brow which was a challenge in itself and I jerked my chin at her, telling her to get her ass over here.

She smiled seductively, lifting a spoonful of yogurt to her lips and licking it slowly before swallowing it down. She held my eyes while she did it, knowing exactly what she was doing to me and my dick got hard for her with no trouble at all.

I held my ground, watching the show and waiting her out as she made a meal of that freaking yogurt, making me wish that I was it.

"I'll prove it to you then," Blake challenged, jumping up with an excited grin.

"You're on. But don't start crying when I beat your ass and you realise that your techniques are inferior," Monroe replied cockily as he got up too. "Does anyone else wanna join us for a race?" he added, glancing around while Blake practically bounced up and down on the balls of his feet.

"What distance are you running?" Saint enquired casually without looking away from his laptop.

"Ten K," Monroe replied.

"Fifteen," Blake countered. "Unless you can't hack it?"

"Make it twenty then," Nash upped and I chuckled at their bullshit.

"Perhaps you'd better get going then," Saint suggested before Blake could raise the stakes again. "Winner gets this." He pointed at a folded napkin before him as he finished writing #1 on it and Blake beamed.

"That winner's napkin is mine, old man."

"When I win it, I'm gonna use it to wipe my ass then flush it away," Nash replied as the two of them offered Tatum brief kisses then hurried out of the room, shoving each other and bickering.

The sounds of their voices carried away from us and Tatum finally set her spoon down.

I took my hands from behind my head and patted my knee as I met her gaze, summoning her to me again and she smiled as she slowly rose to her feet.

"I'm so hot," she purred in a voice that drew Saint's attention from his laptop as she slid her cardigan off of her shoulders.

"I can help you out with that, baby," I promised her, and she gave me a lingering look before shrugging.

"Thanks for the offer, *baby*, but I think I'm just gonna go for a swim instead. I'll catch you later." She winked at me then turned and strode out of the room as I battled with the desire to chase after her like a whipped bitch or keep my composure and suffer the blue balls.

"Dammit," I muttered, taking my boots from the table and letting the legs of my chair slam back down onto the hardwood floor.

"If you think *you're* frustrated, you should try sifting through all of this," Saint said, pointing at his laptop and looking like he was tempted to smash the damn thing.

"Why don't you just go public with what you've got?" I suggested. "Let the world know exactly what kind of a scumbag Governor Memphis really is."

"Because," Saint hissed through clenched teeth. "Then he really will run. I may be having trouble determining his exact location at the moment, but I do know that he won't be far away. He won't leave his precious state and the power he has accrued here that easily. If we give the FBI or the press the information we have on his involvement in Royaume D'élite and the deals they were making in that place, then he will be on a private jet and out of the country before the first news report is even over. And then we will never find him again. Even the financial ruin I have primed for him won't be enough to stop that. There are accounts that I won't be able to shut down quickly enough, friends I haven't quite got enough dirt on or even just low lives willing to take a bribe to help him."

"Can I do something to help?" I asked, because it looked like my ideal plans for the morning had just gone swimming in the indoor pool. Though I wasn't totally sure I cared enough about my ego to stop myself from following her. I would give it a beat though - no need for her to know I was utterly whipped. She probably already did though so did I even have a point to prove here?

"No," he sighed. "It's something I have to figure out myself. Why don't you tell me what Liam is saying to you in those little meetings of yours that has you so out of sorts?" he suggested.

I ran a palm over my jaw and across the stubble lining it as I sighed. "I'm not entirely sure. But I'm getting the feeling he's trying to prime me to take over from him when he dies."

"Oh, is that all?" Saint asked dismissively and I frowned at him.

"You don't think that's a big deal?" I asked. "Because it seems to me like if he's got that in mind for me, I'm never going to be allowed to leave this fucking house. I'm going to be forced into a role as his second and given more and more work for the family and I won't have a choice about carrying it out. I'll be an O'Brien from head to toe – exactly like they always planned for me to be and exactly like I never wanted to be."

"Do you trust me?" Saint asked frankly and I knew it wasn't a bullshit question.

"With my life," I agreed fiercely.

"Then trust me when I tell you that your time as an O'Brien is running short. I will have you out of this organisation before long and the only family you will ever have to concern yourself with again will be ours. Of course, I cannot promise you that we'll be law abiding citizens, but I get the feeling we might just be happy. So let's aim for that."

A thousand protests danced on my tongue, but I swallowed them back and nodded. If there was a man on this planet who could wrestle me from the clutches of Liam O'Brien, then it was Saint Memphis.

"Okay," I agreed and he smiled.

Saint looked between me and the laptop for a long moment then slammed it shut with a growl of frustration.

"I can feel the answer to this encryption on the tip of my brain, but

I can't quite coax it out. I just need to take a moment to turn my mind to something else, a different problem that needs fixing." His icy gaze fell on me like I was that problem and I frowned as I took a cigarette from a pack that had been left on the table as a part of the breakfast spread.

"Like what?" I asked, placing the smoke between my lips for a moment before drawing it out and looking down at it like I wasn't even sure how it had gotten there. This damn house and this damn family were getting under my skin. The longer I was here, the worse it was going to get.

I flicked the unlit cigarette into the fire with a sigh and swiped a hand down my face.

"You haven't spoken about Deepthroat since the day she died," Saint said calmly as he slid his laptop aside.

"What the fuck makes you think I'd want to talk about that stalking whore?" I snapped, wishing I hadn't tossed the damn smoke.

Saint gave me an assessing look before pouring the two of us fresh coffees and passing me mine.

"The night that Ashlynn slipped you a pill and escorted you back to her dorm-"

"So we're just going to have this conversation then, are we?" I asked, tensing as I prepared to get to my feet, my skin going all hot and prickly. I'd been blocking out thoughts about this shit for a good goddamn reason. "Regardless of my opinion on it?"

"I believe that you haven't dealt with what she did to you," Saint said, not reacting at all even though it must have been clear that I was damn tempted to rip his head off if he didn't shut the fuck up. Tatum had tried to have this conversation with me too and I'd tried to show her how fucking little that whore meant to me in place of discussing it. But in the back of my mind, I knew it wasn't all that my wife deserved on the matter. And that killed me. It was just so fucking hard to face the issues I had surrounding Deepthroat. But I'd found ways to work around them.

"*Tried* to do," I snarled. "The bitch failed to...do whatever the fuck it was that she was trying to do and-"

"Rape," Saint said, the word cutting through the air. "Let's not dance around it, Kyan. The girl was attempting to rape you."

"She was half my fucking size," I snapped. "And there was no fucking way I would have gotten hard for her, so I think you're getting yourself mixed up. Besides, I'm a-"

"Man? What does that have to do with it? You think because you have a penis it is impossible for someone to force a sexual interaction upon you against your wishes?" His calm tone was getting my blood hot and my hand curled into a fist as I glanced towards the door that Tatum had closed after her. I didn't want any of my family getting wind of this shit. I didn't need the headache of that kind of rumour circulating about me.

"Of course I don't think that," I snapped. "I was the one who had her pawing at me. Who woke up with my pants half off and her fucking hand on my dick while she tried to get her mouth on it too. Do you have any fucking idea what that feels like?"

"No," Saint replied calmly. "I cannot begin to fathom how it must have felt for you to wake up like that, your mind clouded by the drug she'd given you and your power stolen from you. But I have had control taken from me on many occasions and I have been forced into a lot of situations I wished I could escape from. I don't understand what it would feel like to be touched like that against my will, but I do know that the effect that night had on you lingered on afterwards. And I know that since she kidnapped you for a second time and you found out that it had in fact been her stalking you rather than some pervert chasing after our girl, you haven't dealt with the knowledge at all."

I stood up suddenly, knocking my chair over behind me in my haste as my heart thundered in my chest and the need to destroy something consumed me.

Saint got in my face as I tried to circle the table and I shoved him hard enough to knock him back a step.

"Get out of my fucking way about this, Saint," I warned him.

"No," he snapped. "You have had time to process it. I've waited for you to either find your own way to deal with it or to come to one of us for help, but I see now that you won't do that. You want to bury it. You want to pretend it never happened and forget she ever existed. But as much as I'm sure you're trying to convince yourself that her death was the end of it, I assure you it wasn't."

I punched him so hard his head snapped back and the fury in me almost boiled over as I waited for him to strike me in retaliation. But he didn't. He just pushed his tongue into his cheek and moved to stand right in front of me again.

"Tell me when you started tying girls up to fuck them?" he asked in low voice and I sneered at him.

"Who gives a shit?"

"I do," he replied firmly. "Not when you were doing it to the girls you were fucking casually, but now that you're doing it to our girl too. I care."

I flinched away from that accusation, shaking my head in a denial that wouldn't pass my lips. "That's not the same," I said eventually. "Tatum likes it. I'm not doing anything with her that she doesn't want me-"

"Of course you're not. Do you think you'd still be breathing if I thought you'd hurt her like that?"

Silence fell between us then because I knew I wouldn't be, and I knew I wouldn't want to be either. We had a bond so unbreakable it might as well have been forged in iron. But there was one thing in this world that would make us turn on each other as quick as blinking and hurting that girl was it. Fuck knew how we'd made it to this place after the way things had started between us and her, but there was no going back for any of us now.

"What do you want from me?" I asked him when it didn't seem like he was going to spell it out without prompting.

"I want you to deal with it and move on. I want that stalking, rapist bitch to be buried once and for all. I don't like to see her haunting you, brother, and I think you need a push to move on from this."

"It's not like I can just scrub what she did from my mind," I pointed out angrily.

"No, you can't. I'm not talking about some magical eraser to make you all better again. This will leave a scar on you that isn't going to just go away, but it will fade. Believe me, I've spent a lifetime trying to cope with enough of my own traumas to have made a hobby out of attempting to deal with them."

"So, what? You want me to start obsessing over the time and freaking out over schedules?" I asked and he scoffed lightly.

"No. Those may be manifestations of my damage, but they're by no means a fix for them. I have only found one fix which works for me in any lasting way. And it doesn't just undo what I've been through anymore than it will erase what Ashlynn did to you. But you need to work on the way that you're allowing your experience with that girl to affect your relationship with Tatum," Saint said simply, like there was anything simple about that.

"I like tying her up," I protested, unsure if I was really up for what he was suggesting or not. "Not just because it stops her from pawing at me. I just like it."

"I know you do. And I'm not kink shaming you or expecting you never to tie her up again. I just think that you're so caught up on what Deepthroat did to you that you can't even bare to let the woman you love have any control during sex. You don't let her touch you or make any choices about what happens with your body. And I think you should work on that."

"How exactly?" I asked, folding my arms as I looked at him and his mouth lifted into a smirk.

"I'm willing to help you on that."

"Pfft, what are you gonna do, tie me up and boss me around?" I teased and his smile only grew.

"Yeah that sounds good to me," he agreed and I laughed.

"I bet it fucking does."

"So what do you say? Shall we track down Tatum? Then I can take control for you and show you how good it feels to face off against your demons."

"While yours get a nice little kick out of the power you'll get by doing so," I pointed out and he shrugged.

"I said I was willing to help you, I never promised I wouldn't be getting anything out of it. So, what's it to be?" Saint asked.

I licked my lips, my mind on Tatum and I realised that if I didn't do this then I wasn't just holding myself back, I was punishing her too. I wasn't allowing her any say in the way we came together, and I'd never even asked her if she would like to have more control sometimes. I definitely couldn't say I'd become submissive or any shit like that, but I could give this a go and see if it helped me get over some of my baggage.

"Come on then," I said, rolling my eyes like this would be some chore and in some part, I knew it would be with Saint in charge, but I was game if he was.

I'd promised to love Tatum with all I was and give her all I had to give, so I was going to stick to those vows.

"Let's go get changed for a swim then," Saint suggested and I followed him as he grabbed his laptop and led the way out of the room, back through the house to the bedroom we'd been staying in.

There were plenty of rooms here for all of us to have one each, but since that first night, we'd just kept sleeping in the one bed. I'd gotten Tatum for one night when Aunt Jada was here – who I was still mind fucked over being Rebecca – but they'd all moved straight back in when we'd heard she'd gone home. The bed was almost big enough and I guessed that while so much shit was going on, we preferred to stick together like that. But I had to wonder if we'd go back to sleeping in our own beds with Tatum rotating between them or not long term. I guessed for now we just needed to get through this shit though, so it wasn't worth questioning.

We grabbed some swimming trunks from the clothes in my room and Saint didn't even complain about borrowing my shit. Officially, this was where I lived so I had a lot of clothes here. Liam had insisted I move in with him after I enrolled at Everlake Prep, but between boarding at the school and spending the summers with my friends, I'd managed to avoid spending more than the odd week here since then.

We got changed and Saint shoved his laptop into the black bag he liked to haul around before we headed down through the house. We had to walk down a little glass corridor to reach the pool house. When we stepped into the wooden building with bi-folding glass doors which ran along the right side of the room, the steam from the warm water enveloped us.

I looked out over the blue tiled pool and frowned as I failed to spot Tatum, but Saint just started walking straight towards the sauna at the left of the space.

We stepped inside and found Tatum there, laying on one of the high wooden benches with her eyes closed but a smile touched her lips at the sound of the door, and she blinked them open again as she looked to us. The dry heat of the sauna wrapped itself around me and I sighed as I breathed in the woody scent of the room, feeling some tension run out of my body just because I was here with her.

"To what do I owe this surprise?" she asked, biting her lip as her gaze ran over our half-dressed bodies.

Tatum was wearing a figure hugging sapphire blue one-piece and the colour made her eyes sparkle even more than usual.

"I brought you a gift, siren," Saint said before I could try to explain our plan to her. "But I didn't put a bow on him because I didn't think he could pull it off."

Tatum sat up and turned so that her feet were on the bench beneath the one she sat on and I was glad to see she seemed more than interested in playing along with us.

"Saint thinks I need to work through my dominance issues a bit. He claims I need to deal with all the Deepthroat stuff more," I supplied, my throat thickening a little as I tried to sound casual about that. "He thinks I should try letting you be in charge."

"I'm pretty sure *I'll* be the one in charge," Saint supplied, placing the black bag down and unzipping it before pulling out a coil of smooth rope.

My mind instantly filled with images of all the ways I'd like to tie Tatum up with it and I huffed out a breath as he looked at me, realising it wasn't meant for her at all.

Tatum bit her lip, a frown pulling at her brow as she looked at me. "Are you sure you're ready?" she asked, like she'd known all along that I needed this. Fuck, had I really been so blind to my own issues?

"Yeah, I'm ready, baby," I growled, wanting to do this for her as much as myself.

"On second thought," Saint said, dropping the rope back into the bag. "It would be a better test if you were just forced to control yourself rather than using the rope as a crutch."

Tatum laughed, standing up and hopping off of the benches as she approached us. "Kyan controlling himself? I'd like to see that."

"You don't think I can do it?" I asked, the challenge in her eyes making me even more determined to prove her wrong.

"I'd like to see you try," she replied, amusement still clear on her expression as she turned and looked up at Saint.

He took her chin in his grasp before cutting his eyes to me. "Watch. Don't touch," he commanded making me instantly want to do the very opposite of what he'd just said as he leaned forward and closed the distance between his and Tatum's mouths.

She moaned into his kiss as he deepened it, his hand keeping her face still while the other slid down her body, caressing her breast through her swimsuit where her hard nipples pressed through it.

Tatum's hands slid up his chest in return and my mouth dried out as I watched the way she touched him, knowing that whenever she did that to me, I usually put an end to it pretty quickly. But why did I do that? Just because some bitch had tried to take my body without my consent? Tatum wasn't her. She wasn't looking for anything from me other than what I was more than willing to give.

Saint took something from the pocket of his trunks and a faint buzzing filled the air as he moved his hand between Tatum's thighs, making her suck in a sharp breath.

My dick was hard in my trunks, throbbing with the need to touch her too and I licked my lips as I watched Saint slip the strap of her swimsuit off of her shoulder, dropping down to take her hard nipple into his mouth as he continued to move the little vibrating toy between her thighs.

Tatum's eyes opened and she looked at me as she panted for him, breathy moans escaping her as he pushed her towards the brink.

But this being Saint, he didn't just let her come that easily and he stood upright smoothly, taking the toy back and switching it off before placing it in her hand and closing her fist around it. I still hadn't gotten a good look at the thing and I knew that wasn't an accident.

Saint slid Tatum's strap back over her shoulder and leaned close to speak in her ear, though he didn't bother to lower his voice as he spoke.

"Show him you own him, siren," he instructed. "Remind him that he serves for your pleasure."

Tatum's lips pulled up into a grin as Saint stepped aside to let her approach me and I cocked my head at her with a taunting look.

"You think you can bring me to my knees for you, baby?" I teased.

"Close your eyes," she murmured. "And keep your hands to yourself."

My heart lurched at the thought of that and a refusal blossomed on my tongue. I wanted to see what was happening. I wanted to know what was going on. But as I met her blazing blue gaze, I knew what she was really asking was that I prove I trusted her.

The sound of a lock turning drew my gaze over her head to Saint as he locked us into the room before pouring a ladle of water over the rocks beside the door so steam billowed up from them.

"It's just the three of us in here," he said lightly. "And I have no desire to start touching you, so you can rest assured that everything you feel is from the girl you love."

"You can trust me," she added in a whisper, tiptoeing up to kiss me and I let my eyes fall closed as I tasted her lips, keeping them shut even when she moved her mouth along my jaw and down my neck.

My fingers flexed with the desire to grab her and I grunted in frustration as I curled them into fists at my sides and held myself there, my muscles rigid with tension.

Tatum took her time on my chest, kissing and caressing me, tracing my tattoos with her fingertips and making my skin buzz. I wanted to take hold of her, direct her movements or even stop them all together but I forced myself not to do that, concentrating on how it felt to be touched by her like that. And I didn't hate it. When I focused on her touch, only pleasure came from the points of contact between her flesh and mine. The issues were all in my head. It *was* about trust like she'd said, and I *did* trust her. So I blew out a breath and tried to focus on nothing other than enjoying the attention she was laying on me.

But as I felt her drop to her knees in front of me, keeping my eyes closed became a pure battle of will and my hand jerked forward an inch as the desire to grab hold of her filled me. I didn't want her to stop, but the feeling of her fingers slipping into my waistband made my heart race. For a moment I thought about that fucking asshole trying to get me hard so that she could put her mouth on my body.

My fingers brushed against Tatum's hair and Saint's voice filled the heated room.

"No touching."

"I've got you, baby," Tatum promised as she caught my hand and turned it, placing a kiss in the centre of my palm as my fingers skimmed along her jaw.

"I know," I replied, releasing a heavy breath and pushing those dumb thoughts from my mind.

Tatum had nothing to do with what Deepthroat had tried to pull on me and my cock was hard and aching for my girl. I wasn't gonna let memories of something some dead girl had done ruin that.

I withdrew my hand and Tatum slid my trunks down my legs, making my hard cock spring free before I stepped out of them for her.

"Jesus, you're so big," she muttered and I snorted a laugh, feeling the tension ease from my body.

"You've more than proved you can handle it, baby," I reminded her.

"You've more than proved you can handle a lot more than that," Saint added from somewhere behind her and Tatum breathed a laugh as she ran her hand up my thigh.

Her thumb came to rest against the compass tattoo I'd inked there and she pressed down on it firmly, reminding me of what it meant and what I had, before her full lips slid around my cock and I groaned in pure bliss.

She took me in deep, moaning like she was enjoying this just as much as I was, and I managed to keep my hands out of her hair through some miracle of self-control.

Tatum drew me in and out, her tongue swirling, lips tightening and soft hums escaping her which sent tremors right down to the base of my shaft.

When she had me panting for her, on the verge of coming, Saint said a single word which made me want to throttle him.

"Stop."

Tatum pulled back and I couldn't help but open my eyes to look down at her on her knees for me, licking her swollen lips as she gazed back at me with promises in her eyes.

"Give him his gift, siren," Saint prompted and I glanced up at him as he drew closer to us, handing her a bottle of lube.

Tatum smirked at me as she squirted the cold liquid onto my cock and I hissed between my teeth before she slid her hand around my shaft, coating every inch of me including my damn balls.

I wanted to ask what the hell the two of them were playing at, but I got my answer before I did as Tatum opened her fist to reveal a double cock ring with a little vibrating bullet on the top of it.

Toys were really more Saint's thing than mine unless you included restraints, but I didn't complain as Tatum slid the inner ring down my shaft before hooking the outer one over my balls.

It was tight and I grunted a little in discomfort, but the look of excitement in her eyes halted any complaints I might have had.

"Sit down," Saint commanded and I did, moving onto the higher of the two hot, wooden benches and curling my hands around the edges of it either side of me so that I would have something to hold on to.

Tatum took a step to follow me, but Saint moved up behind her, kissing her neck and curling his fingers around the straps of her swimsuit before slipping it off of her shoulders and rolling it down her body.

I groaned as her breasts were freed, her nipples hard and practically begging for my mouth on them. Saint kept rolling the material down until it fell off of her, leaving her naked and panting, looking more than edible and like the most tempting thing I'd ever seen.

Saint's hand moved between her thighs as he continued to kiss her neck and I watched hungrily as his fingers slipped inside her and she gasped his name. The heat in the room was making her sweat and a bead of moisture carved a line between the valley of her breasts as Saint worked her into a frenzy, rolling all the way down to meet his hand.

Tatum's gaze met mine as he fucked her with his fingers and she moaned encouragement until I was watching her come for him, her back arching, hips bucking against his hand as he kept grinding the heel of his palm against her clit to prolong the pleasure.

"Good girl," Saint growled, biting down on her earlobe before removing his hand from her pussy and nudging her towards me. "Brace yourself on his knees, don't touch him any more than that."

Tatum did as he wanted, gripping my knees and looking up at me through a waterfall of blonde hair as my cock ached with need and the torture of having to wait for her.

Saint took the lube from where Tatum had left it on the bench beside him before removing a butt plug from his pocket and coating it.

He stepped up behind her, massaging her ass cheek as he moved the plug into position and Tatum gasped as he eased it into her, her fingernails biting into my thighs where she held herself up on me.

"Are you good, siren?" he asked and Tatum nodded, biting her lip.

"I want you," she begged and Saint smirked as he dropped his pants and lined his cock up to claim her.

"Don't do anything to Kyan until you come again," he commanded and before either of us had a chance to protest that, he was pushing into her and making her cry out for him.

Precum beaded on the tip of my dick as she held onto me, her mouth bobbing so close to it that it was taking everything I had not to fist her hair in my hand and drive her mouth down onto me.

Saint wasn't gentle as he fucked her and the heat of the sauna had us all panting and sweating as she clung onto me and I just watched the show, desperate to take my turn in claiming her while forcing myself to hold back.

When Tatum finally came again, Saint's hand clapped against her ass and she took my cock back into her mouth so suddenly that I bucked my hips in surprise, forcing her to take me deep as Saint slowed his pace a little, letting her adjust.

The cock ring was tight enough to hold my release back otherwise I was certain I would have come in her mouth already. But as Saint began to move faster again, I tipped my head back, enjoying the ride as she sucked and licked me, controlling the motions and making me murmur her name beneath my breath.

Saint seemed to have lost control of the devil inside of him as he moved faster and faster, fucking her so hard that I knew she'd still be feeling it tomorrow as his fingers dug into her hips and she moaned around my cock.

He finally came with a feral snarl, spanking her again and forcing her to follow as he fisted a hand in her hair and yanked her off of me.

I reached out to catch her before I could stop myself and he smacked my hand aside before I could touch her, holding her up as she trembled in his arms.

"Do you want more, siren?" Saint asked breathlessly and she nodded, eyeing me hungrily and showing us the monster in her too. "Then show him who owns him."

Tatum climbed up onto the bench beneath mine and this time when I reached for her, Saint didn't stop me as I took her hands and helped her climb up to straddle me.

"You can pin my hands behind my back if you need to," she breathed against my lips before kissing me and my fingers closed around her wrists as our tongues met and I tasted the whole world in that kiss.

My grip tightened, but I didn't shift her hands behind her back, I laid them on my chest instead, pressing down on the backs of her hands so that I could feel the firm press of her skin on mine.

"I'm all yours, baby," I swore to her. "And I don't want to cage you."

"Maybe I like it in your cage," she teased, one hand running down my chest until she found the little bullet on the top of the cock ring and switched it on.

I kissed her harder as the vibrations trembled through my dick and she lowered herself down onto me slowly, moaning like that was the best damn feeling in the world and I had to agree with her.

Her pussy felt even tighter than usual with the plug in her ass and the cock ring making my dick so hard that it ached. I rolled my hips as I gave her a moment to adjust to so many sensations at once. The vibrating rabbit ground against her clit and she gasped before we began to move together.

I ran my hands down her spine until I was gripping her ass and our movements grew faster, more frenzied as she rode me hard, her hands moving all over my body and I thrust up into her, making her scream between our kisses.

My dick ached as the cock ring held off my release and I pumped my hips harder until she was coming for me, her pussy tightening impossibly more and I was exploding inside her, coming so hard that I swore and she bit my lip sharply enough to draw blood.

"Perfection," Saint murmured as I reached down to stop the cock ring from vibrating and Tatum fell slack in my arms.

I lifted my gaze to look over her shoulder at him where he was smirking at us from the bench he'd chosen as his viewing point, and I knew he was right. This here, us and the others too was all I needed. And I refused to allow anything to ever take it away.

CHAPTER THIRTY NINE

"Time to go, siren." Saint's fingers brushed some hair away from my forehead and my eyes flickered open, finding him standing before me in a smart black coat.

"What do you mean?" I asked, shutting my eyes again as I clung to sleep. The bed was cool behind me, no press of a warm body to be found. "Where is everyone?"

"Saint's been planning a secret mission," Blake said from somewhere across the room as Saint gently pulled the covers off of me and I cracked my eyes open again.

"*Saint*," I complained, the darkness beyond the window telling me it was very much the middle of the night. Maybe I was just having a weird ass dream. But even I couldn't convince myself of that as I shut my eyes tightly once more.

"Nash, help me," Saint commanded then two sets of warm hands started pulling off my nightdress.

I smiled giddily, caressing their arms as I tried to draw them into the bed with me, but then someone yanked a sports bra over my head. "What the hell?" I woke fully, feeling grumpy and sleepy and I was pretty sure one of the Seven Dwarves' cousins was gonna arrive soon too. Punchy.

Saint yanked a soft grey sweater over my head while Nash lifted my hips and dragged a pair of jeans up my legs and over my ass. He'd left me without panties though and that filthy smirk of his said it was intentional.

"Alright, enough. I can do it." I tried to shove them off, but I was pretty sure they were enjoying it as Saint pushed my arms into a coat and Nash tugged some cosy socks onto my feet before kneeling down to lace on my boots. "*Guys,*" I half growled, half laughed. "This is ridiculous."

Saint started brushing my hair next and I swiped the brush from his hand with a pout. "Too far."

Saint smirked, running his thumb over my cheek and leaning down to peck my lips. "Go brush your teeth, siren, or I'll lay you over my knees and do it for you."

"One day I'm going to tie you up in your sleep and spank your ass raw, Memphis," I warned. I got to my feet, finding Blake and Kyan smirking at me by the door and I tossed them the finger as I slipped into the bathroom. I washed my face, brushed my teeth and hair, apparently taking too much time because Saint started knocking on the door.

"My patience is wearing thin, Tatum," he said darkly. "Are you going to start this day with a punishment?"

I grinned as I opened the door, arching a brow at him. "You're not the boss of me anymore, devil boy."

His eyes glinted like he didn't entirely agree. "I may worship at your altar daily, but I assure you I am more than capable of putting a goddess in her place when the occasion calls."

"Stop flirting," Kyan called. "Let's go."

"Is breakfast planned on this mystery trip? I'm starved," Blake said and I realised none of them had a clue where we were going either. I guessed they were used to Saint doing random shit like this, but even Monroe seemed to be going along with it without complaint.

"I want a croissant," I agreed, thinking of Martha's freshly baked ones she brought to us every morning. Damn, they were beautiful. Flaky, sweet, buttery...*mmm.*

Saint opened a travel bag at the foot of the bed, taking out a paper bag and promptly placing a croissant in my hand before putting them back and snapping the bag shut.

"Hey! Where's mine?" Blake complained.

"You can have one on the journey," Saint said simply, gesturing for Kyan to carry the bag and he moved to obey without a word of refusal.

Saint led the way out the door and I jogged over to walk beside Blake, offering him up a piece of my croissant when our hot as shit dictator wasn't looking. He tore a bite off with his teeth then grinned at me around a mouthful of pastry. "You're a life saver, Cinders."

We followed Saint through the huge house, the place deathly quiet as we walked down the dark corridors.

"Where are we going?" I hissed when I'd finished my food and officially woken up.

Saint didn't reply as he led us down a hallway with paintings of Irish landscapes on the walls, apparently knowing his way through this house as well as Kyan did. Maybe better.

"We have a bet on," Blake murmured in my ear as he wrapped an arm around my shoulders. "I guessed he's taking us to sacrifice a goat to Satan and open up a doorway to hell."

Kyan stepped to my side. "Naw, my bet is we're going to some underground African ceremony where Saint can make sure you're married to all of us. Which I will totally fight by the way, baby."

"It's obvious where we're going," Nash said from behind me and I looked around with a question in my eyes. "To see Doctor-"

"Utter that name within these hallways and I shall castrate you and feed your balls to the O'Brien guard dogs," Saint said cuttingly, but I got the message.

We were taking the vaccines to Dr De La Cost. We were finally going to make a difference to this fucking plague sweeping across the Earth. My heart filled with warmth at knowing that. I hated knowing we had access to those vaccines yet couldn't do anything to save the thousands of people dying every day. But we would now.

We arrived in a large conservatory that extended from the back of the house and Kyan moved forward to unlock the double doors that led outside. The night air made me shiver as we exited onto the immaculate lawn and Blake hugged me to him tighter, acting as a barrier to the cold.

Saint marched purposefully across the grass into the thickening darkness and I frowned as we followed. "Is there a way out onto the road from here?" I asked. "Or a garage?"

Saint said nothing, but eventually stopped about a hundred yards away from the house and took his phone from his pocket. "Two minutes," he announced.

"Before what? An alien spaceship beams us up into the sky?" Monroe asked with a snort.

"To be fair, I think Saint could organise that," I said, slipping away from Blake to cuddle with Nash. He hugged me to his chest and I breathed in his pine scent with a smile. I swear my guys were all starting to smell more similar though. There was an apple undercurrent on him too and I guessed that was Saint's doing as he'd packed the shower gel.

The sound of propellors came from somewhere off in the sky and I looked up in surprise as the lights of a helicopter approached.

"What the fuck?" Monroe breathed, the air whipping wildly around us as the helicopter came down to land.

"We will need to board quickly," Saint called to us. "The noise will wake the household."

The skids hit the grass and Saint beckoned us forward, pulling the door open and climbing inside with Kyan. Monroe helped me up and Kyan snatched me away, tugging me down into a seat beside him.

Blake pulled the door shut as lights turned on in the house and my heart rate ratcheted up. Saint poked his head into the cockpit, pulling on a headset so he could speak to the pilot.

Kyan placed a headset in my hand and I put it on as Blake and Monroe moved to sit in the seats behind us.

Saint turned and took hold of the strap at my waist as I finished securing the belt, tugging it sharply to tighten it further before dropping into the seat beside mine. The helicopter took off as he strapped himself in and Kyan spoke over the headset.

"Grandpa's gonna shit a lung," he said with a bark of laughter.

"Don't worry about him," Saint said. "I will explain this when we return."

"Good luck with that, brother," Kyan said, placing a hand on my knee and squeezing.

We flew up and away from the property and the few lights on in the nearest town glittered as we sailed towards it. The moon wasn't out tonight, and I had the feeling that was no coincidence. Saint had planned this down to every detail and the cover of darkness was a part of it.

It wasn't long before the pilot flew us down to land in a wide farmer's field and Saint unclipped his belt. "Stay in your seats," he growled at us before opening the door and jumping outside.

The pilot exited too and they shared a few words then Saint nodded to him before climbing back inside, shutting the door and moving to take the pilot's seat.

He tapped some buttons on the control panel then flicked some switches on the roof above him and suddenly we were taking off again with my beautiful sinner in the pilot's seat.

"Fucking hell, Saint, this is like some Mission Impossible shit," Blake crowed excitedly, and I shared a smirk with Kyan as his hand slid further up my leg, sending a buzz of adrenaline into my veins.

"Calm down, Double-0 Bowman," Saint said, and there was a grin in his voice. "We can't risk bringing anyone to Dr De La Cost's home. I trust no one but the five of us. There's not gonna be any shoot outs or evil masterminds."

"Is that because you're already the evil mastermind?" Blake asked and I snorted a laugh.

"Obviously," Saint agreed.

"Well, we're gonna have to trust that doctor too," I pointed out.

"Hardly," Saint scoffed. "I will blackmail her of course."

"But you said she was squeaky clean," I said in confusion.

"Yes, she is," Saint said with a dark chuckle, but didn't elaborate more than that. "I also just admitted I'm the evil mastermind. Keep up, siren."

We flew for over an hour north and I rested my head against Kyan's shoulder as I gazed out of the window beside him. The further north we went, the darker the world became as we left the towns behind. At one point I thought I caught sight of army trucks moving along the roads below and I guessed that had been Saint's motivation to fly. Army checkpoints were popping up all over the country and though we'd exposed the inside of one of their little Hades Camps, I had the feeling that wasn't going to stop more of them being erected. The situation in the world was getting too dire. And now things had gotten bad, extreme action was being taken by the government in every damn state. By fucking Troy. But splitting people up from their loved ones and dragging them out of their homes seemed barbaric to me. Our country had already lost enough. And it frightened me how quickly the authorities could take over. Sometimes fighting back felt impossible, but we were doing it. We weren't going to lay down and let people like Troy Memphis and his shady friends from Royaume D'élite get away with what they'd done. They had to be stopped. And more than that, they had to be punished.

"Coming in to land," Saint said, and we started descending towards the lawn of a lone house below surrounded by trees on either side of it, the lights beneath the helicopter illuminating the property.

We landed and Saint killed the engine, the propellers starting to slow as he flicked the lights off too and got out. We unbuckled our belts and exited the aircraft while Kyan pressed a gun into my palm. I slid it into the back of my jeans, figuring some doctor in the middle of nowhere wasn't going to be much of a threat against five armed people who'd just landed a helicopter in her back yard. Lights were on in the house and a window flew open on the top floor, a shotgun wheeling out of it. Apparently I was wrong.

"Who are you?!" a woman cried, her voice laced with fear.

Saint raised his palms in innocence. "We have a proposition for you," he called back, totally fucking calm. If I'd known this was his plan, I would have suggested we land the damn helicopter a mile away and walk here instead of freaking the woman out.

"Get off of my property!" she yelled. "I'll call the police!"

"You know as well as I do, the police are too busy corralling the population into Hades Camps alongside the army," Saint said as Kyan moved up behind him, using Saint's body to conceal the gun in his hand. "And if they did happen to come, perhaps you would need to explain the fact that you have no license to bear that weapon." His jaw ground, telling me he'd checked out that information thoroughly and hadn't expected this.

This was seriously not the way to calm someone down who was holding a goddamn shotgun though. I stepped in front of my boys, taking the travel bag from Kyan and holding it up.

"Dr De La Cost," I called up to her. "We need your help. I was given a vaccine to the Hades Virus by my father long before it was released into the world. We have vials of that vaccine right here."

"What are you talking about?" she demanded.

"I was taken by government officials and a new vaccine was produced from my blood," I explained, knowing it sounded crazy, but we didn't have much choice. "When these men helped me escape the facility, we took it with us. And we need someone who can make more of the vaccine to help…well, the whole world really. Someone like you."

She fell quiet and I imagined she was trying to figure out if we'd lost our minds or if there was a shred of truth to my words.

I laid the travel bag at my feet. "I can show you…if you want? The vaccine is in here."

She hesitated then finally gave an answer. "Open it. Slowly."

I crouched down, unzipping the bag and taking out the refrigerated box. I popped it open, turning it around to show her the contents.

Silence stretched out and she finally tugged her shotgun back inside. "Bring it to the porch. Just the girl."

She shut the window, moving back into the shadows of her room and I took my gun from my waistband, passing it back to Kyan.

"Take it," he insisted, shoving it back at me.

"She's a doctor. And she's not going to trust us if we don't show her the same courtesy," I said firmly and the boys shared anxious looks.

I walked away from them, picking up the box of vaccines and walking up the wooden porch steps, knocking gently on the door then stepping back to put six feet between us. It cracked open and the shotgun barrel peered out at me again, making my heart clench. But I'd be frightened too if the tables were turned. So I had to show her she had no reason to be.

"Tatum," Blake called, worry in his tone.

"It's fine. Stay back there," I insisted as two wide brown eyes gazed out at me from the other end of the gun. "I know this is a shock," I said gently. "But we had to come at night, we had to avoid the army and the roadblocks. We've been looking after these vaccines and my boyfriend spent a lot of time researching doctors we could trust. He is a very meticulous man, and he narrowed it down to one person in the entire state. You."

Her eyes darted back and forth between mine then she finally lowered her gun, revealing her soft features and cherub like cheeks. She was in her forties, with dark skin and had straight hair down to her shoulders.

"Come in. Just you," she said sharply, knocking the door wider.

"Aren't you afraid of catching the virus?" I asked and she shook her head.

"I had it three weeks ago. Survived it luckily," she said gravely. "I still have antibodies. So unless you are concerned then-"

"Like I said, I've been vaccinated," I replied then stepped into the house as she nodded, frowning suspiciously.

"Tatum!" Nash barked, but I ignored him, pressing the door shut behind me.

Dr De La Cost switched a light on, illuminating a small hallway with a few potted plants around the place. There was photograph on the wall of what looked like her parents and a few pictures of a white cat around it.

I offered her the box of vaccines and she contemplated her next move before placing the gun down on a table behind her. She took the box, examining the contents with her brows pulling together.

"Serenity Pharmaceuticals," she murmured as she read the name off of a label on one of the vials. "I've not heard of them."

"They're funded by Troy Memphis," I told her, and her eyes snapped up to look at me.

"The Governor?" she asked in surprise and I nodded.

"He was the one who had me kidnapped to their facility," I said, figuring honesty was the best plan here.

"Kidnapped?" she echoed, a flicker of disbelief in her eyes.

"I know this sounds crazy. And you don't need to believe a word that comes out of my mouth except these next ones. That box contains the only working vaccines in the country. Probably in the entire world. So we need someone who can make more. And who will do it subtly, who will make sure they're distributed fairly and efficiently to every man, woman and child on Earth."

Her mouth opened and closed as shock rippled through her features. "Why me?" she rasped eventually.

"Like I said, my boyfriend chose you. And he would have only chosen someone who we could trust to do this, who won't take the vaccine and sell it to the highest bidder instead of offering it to the people who need it most."

Her throat bobbed as she closed the lid of the box. "How can I be sure this isn't some trick?"

I sighed. "You can't. But if you let me bring Saint Memphis inside, he'll explain it to you."

"Memphis?" she gasped.

"He's Troy's son. And he's working to help expose his father for everything he's done. He wants to help. But we need you on our side to do it," I said earnestly.

She wet her lips, glancing from the box to me as she considered it. "Bring him inside. Just him. I need to refrigerate these."

She moved to walk away and I caught her arm as my pulse thundered in my ears. "They're the most valuable thing in the world right now. I don't give them to you lightly, do you understand? You *will* protect them."

Her eyes widened and she nodded, seeming to grasp the seriousness of this situation at last. "I will. I promise." She went to walk away again but I didn't let her go.

"I'm going to need you to give me your phone," I said softly, but there was an undercurrent of threat to my voice. "We need to trust you too."

She hesitated, eyeing my hand on her arm before nodding and taking it from her dressing gown pocket. I took the phone and let her go, turning back to the door and opening it.

"Saint, come in here," I called, and he stepped away from the group who all stiffened sharply.

"What's going on?" Kyan growled.

"She wants to hear the truth," I said. "And you're all pretty fucking scary so you can't all come in."

Kyan shifted his weight from one foot to the other, looking uneasy as he glanced at Blake and Monroe. Saint muttered something to them then picked up the travel bag and walked across the lawn, moving to the door where I let him inside.

He gazed around the small hallway with a wrinkle of distaste in his nose. He was such a freaking snob sometimes. Scrap that - *all* times. I elbowed him in the gut just as the doctor returned and she moved closer to the shotgun on the table, but thankfully didn't pick it up again. I was almost certain Saint had a gun stashed under his coat, but I hoped she wasn't going to make him use it.

"You're the Governor's son?" she asked, her eyes roaming over his features.

"I am," he replied then opened the travel bag and took out a folder of documents. "And I am going to need you to sign an NDA before we have our next conversation, Martina. Is there somewhere more formal we could talk?" He gazed around in disdain at her small home and I pursed my lips at his expression.

"Yes, come through to the lounge." She turned her back on us cautiously and led us into a cosy lounge with furry throws on the couch and mismatching rugs and curtains. She offered us a seat at the small dining table by the window and cleared her throat. "Would you like a drink, a coffee perhaps?" she asked.

"No, thank you," Saint said curtly.

"I'm fine, thanks," I said, and Martina sat down opposite us.

Saint opened his folder, placing various documents neatly beside it before pushing an NDA across the surface towards her with a pen. She read through it before signing her name at the bottom and gazing questioningly at Saint as she waited for him to go on. He explained how his father had held me captive and how the newly procured vaccine had ended up in our hands, leaving out the trail of blood my boys had left in their wake. Then he went into detail about the vaccine itself and I got lost in a sea of science talk which I only managed to follow thanks to my dad's job.

When he was done, he placed another contract under Martina's nose. "You will become my employee effective as of the moment you sign this contract. You will be well compensated for your role in creating the vaccine and your laboratory will have any and every item of equipment you need, including the expansion of your facilities when necessary. Rivers Laboratories will be the most famous pharmaceutical company in the world once the job is done-"

"Rivers?" I blurted.

"Like the terrorist who started all of this?" Martina gasped and I bristled. We'd left out that piece of information in what we'd told her because it was pretty hard to convince people of his innocence when we hadn't yet exposed the truth to the world.

"He was framed," Saint said simply. "And that will become clear in time. But for now, you must go on our word."

Martina nodded slowly, seeming shocked by all this information and I guessed it was a serious headfuck at four in the morning. "Okay," she breathed. "Is there anything else I need to know?"

"Yes." Saint straightened in his seat. "Just yesterday, I selected which of your staff will remain working for you and which will not after completing background checks on each of them. As of this morning, those who had any discrepancies will be notified of their employment termination. I have also recruited several competent and trustworthy staff to your laboratory too, including a security team who will be stationed there twenty-four hours a day. Once you have replicated the vaccine and have enough ready for distribution, they will be rolled out at a capped, low cost to hospital staff and we will start vaccinating children and healthcare staff first. I will take charge of the details, simply contact me when you are ready with the first batch."

She nodded, her face a little pale as the weight of this task rested on her shoulders, but she definitely seemed up to it. "Okay, I can do that."

"You can contact me through the number at the top of the contract." He pointed it out. "And you will refer to me as Mr Sequoia whenever we speak."

"Alright," she agreed.

"And finally," Saint's voice dropped an octave, raising the hairs along the back of my neck. "If you break the terms laid out in this contract, including revealing any knowledge of the vaccine without my say so, or attempt to sell on the information or the vaccine itself, I will ruin you." He brought something up on his phone and passed it to her with some photo on it I didn't get a chance to look at properly.

"This isn't me!" she gasped, her eyes wide with horror. "I'd never touch a child!"

Holy shit.

"I am well aware you would never do this," Saint said calmly, casually tucking his phone away again. "But these images have been put together by one of the best photograph manipulators in the state. And I have far more evidence than this. I have mothers willing to come forward and testify if necessary."

"You can't, I wouldn't. No one would believe this!" Martina said in horror, clearly on the verge of tears with how much the mere thought of doing such a thing horrified her. A pang of guilt filled me, but I knew this was Saint's way of ensuring this information never got out.

"Oh, I assure you they would. I will pay the finest lawyers in the country to ensure it," he said simply, and Martina gaped at him.

"You don't need to threaten me," she said, her lower lip quivering. "I already agreed."

"Yes, but the threat is there just in case you ever decide to dance with the Devil." Saint smirked and she nodded, seeming to accept that though she was obviously shaken.

"Mr Memphis, I do not appreciate you coming into my home and coercing me like this. However, I do understand the magnitude of what you're laying at my door. If you think I would sell the vaccine for profit, then you have greatly misjudged my character."

"I don't think you would," Saint said with a shrug. "But if my father taught me anything of value, it was to cover my back even when it appears to be shielded by ten inches of iron. So…" He tapped the contract in front of Martina while I gazed at him, soaking in his power with a little flutter in my stomach. Shit, he was so hot right now.

"Do we have a deal?" he asked and Martina gazed down at the contract, her eyes widening again. I was surprised they hadn't popped right out of her head already with how many bombshells we'd set off in her face tonight.

"You're going to pay me five million a year?" she gasped. "This is too much."

"You are officially the most important scientist in the country, Martina," Saint said calmly, steepling his fingers together on the table while I blushed over my tyrannical madman. "You are worth every penny and more. There will be perks too and your staff will be well compensated. Pick any house within a five mile radius of your lab and it's yours."

"But I like my home," Martina said, glancing around the place and Saint frowned at the higgle-piggle of white cat ornaments on her mantlepiece.

"Why?" he muttered, and I jabbed him in the ribs with my finger.

"I like this place too," I said with a smile.

Saint looked confused while Martina quirked a grin at me.

A white cat suddenly jumped onto Saint's lap and I expected him to flip the fuck out, but instead his features softened and he stroked its head, making it purr loudly.

"Of course you're a cat person," I said in realisation.

"Cats know their own minds and have no toleration for ninety nine percent of the human population. Of course I feel a kinship to them," he said then looked to Martina who was reading through the contract. "What's his name?"

"Artemis," she replied. "Arty for short."

"Hello Arty." I tickled his chin and he nuzzled into my hand.

"I despise a nickname," Saint muttered then stroked his hand down the length of the cat's back. "You don't want to be nicknamed, do you Artemis?" His voice softened a little and my smile grew.

"Oh my god, was that Saint Memphis's baby talk?"

"I do not do baby talk," he said stiffly as the cat jumped down.

"You just did," I whispered excitedly, and he casually took a pocket-sized lint roller from his coat and ran it over the white hairs left on his clothes.

"You did not just do that," I laughed as he tucked the roller away with a shrug.

"Okay, this all seems very generous," Martina said then signed her name on the contract and passed it back to Saint with hope and fear dancing in her eyes.

"Thank you for this," I told her, reaching out to squeeze her hand. "It means everything."

She smiled, still seeming a little cautious but her eyes said she really did believe all we'd told her. And I felt in my heart that she was going to be the one to save the world.

I crashed out with Blake and Nash back at the house while Saint and Kyan went off to explain where we'd been to Liam. I had no idea what they were gonna say, but I was sure Saint had planned out some whole bullshit story which was infallible. Curiosity got the better of me though so I shot them a message through the private chatroom.

Tigress:
Good morning *kiss emoji*. How did you explain away last night, Squid?

Scorpion:
Good morning, Tigress. I see you're hankering for a punishment already today.

Tigress:
I don't know what you mean *angel emoji*

Koala:
He prefers when we use his full title, baby. Lord Squidington.

I snorted a laugh, typing out my reply, able to picture Saint's furious expression perfectly.

Tigress:
Ah yes, Lord Tentaculus Squidington. Forgive me, my Lord.

Scorpion:
We are quite amusing this morning, aren't we?

Koala:
Holy fuck did you just use the royal 'we'? That's got me feeling all kinds of *octopus emoji*

Tigress:
We shall be most unamused when our fine Lord Squidington takes payment out of our rations.

Squid:
Oh, it shall not come out of your rations, it shall come out of your flesh.

Koala:
Check yo user name bro *squid emoji*

Squid has left the chatroom

Tigress:
Hahahaha how did you do that??

Koala:
In the account settings. LOL. He'll never be Scorpion again.

Tigress:

You played him diiiiirty.

Koala:

That's the only way I play and you know it *wink emoji*

Tigress:

Hm, I don't think I know it well enough. Come and prove it once you're done talking to your grandpa.

Koala:

I cannnnnnn't *angry face emoji*. He wants to take me up to pride rock and show me the lay of the land like Mufasa did to Simba. If I don't blow my brains out from boredom, I'll come eat you out later.

Tigress:

This message is to confirm your dinner reservations at Pussy de la Wife. Please don't arrive late or your table may be given to one of the three hot guys on the waiting list.

Koala:

God I fucking love you. And I won't be late, I'll be there to eat you out of house and home. But be warned, I won't be tipping the waitress Baboon because she stuck a finger in my cherry pie last time without asking. Filthy bitch.

Tigress:

Hahaha. Maybe I like watching when she diddles your pie though. Love you too, hubs. What did Squid say to explain away last night?

Koala:

He said something about a sick relative, I kinda tuned out while he went overkill on the acting. Squid's gonna head back to you guys in a sec so watch out if you don't want your ass spanked red. I'm waiting for G-pa while he washes his balls in liquified diamonds or whatever the fuck it is he does to prepare for mentoring me.
Side note: the only one I want diddling my *pie emoji* is you.

Tigress:

Okay, I'll diddle you later. Miss you. Xxxx (give two of these kisses to Squid)

Koala:

I did. He punched me in the nuts. Xxxxxxxxxxxxxxxxx (don't give any of these away, they're all for you) *squid emoji*

    I grinned stupidly as I put my phone on the nightstand and slipped out of bed, kicking my feet into some slippers and disturbing Blake. He crawled out after me like a hungry animal, nipping at the flesh of my neck as he followed me to the door. He was forever kissing my tattoo and licking it, running his hands over it while he pinned me down and had his way with me. I swear he loved it even more than I did. His skin was hot against my back through his shirt which he'd given me to sleep in and the bulge in his boxers pressed to my ass as his mouth worked up to my ear.

    "I never get you to myself anymore," he growled.

    "Shh," I giggled softly as Monroe rolled over in the bed.

    I captured Blake's hand, tugging him out the door into the brightly lit hallway.

    "Let's go somewhere no one will find us, Cinders," he purred, pushing me back against the wall and pinning my hands to my sides. A gasp escaped me as he raked his teeth down to my collar bone and crushed his huge body to mine.

"Why are you keeping me here if you wanna go somewhere else?" I teased breathily.

"Because I couldn't live another second without getting my mouth on you again," he said, his tone making my heart thrash.

"I've got a game for you, golden boy," I purred, twisting my fingers into his ebony hair and yanking his head back to make him look at me. "I know how much you like to win."

"What's the game?" he growled, his eyes sparking with excitement as he grew harder against my thigh.

"You have to count to one hundred and I'm going to hide somewhere in this big house. If you find me, I'll let you do anything you want with me."

"How long do I have to find you?" he asked, his voice tight and full of desire.

"Hmm, does twenty minutes seem fair?" I asked and he nodded, letting me go a little reluctantly, but his hunger for the win was clear. "Oh and, Bowman?" I said lightly as I backed away up the hall.

"Yeah, sweetheart?"

"If you don't find me in time, you have to watch me get off without you." I turned and ran away down the corridor with a laugh as he started counting out loud.

I took a stairway down to the ground floor and sprinted through the empty corridors. I probably should've put some pants on, but it was too late now and Blake's t-shirt was like a dress on me anyway.

I turned a corner and ran right into someone, stumbling back as I hit their hard body. Saint's hand snapped out to capture my wrist and his eyebrows arched.

"Is something wrong?" he demanded and I bit my lip.

"No…" I glanced over my shoulder. "I've gotta go. I'm playing a game with Blake."

"What kind of game?" he asked curiously, reeling me closer.

"A sexy game," I said with a laugh. "If he finds me, he wins me," I whispered in case anyone was close by.

Saint wet his lips, deliberating something. "You've been a bad girl this morning."

"And?" I grinned.

"And…" he growled quietly, his grip tightening on my arm as he pulled me even closer. "That deserves a punishment. But perhaps I'll let you off if you tell me what the squid emoji means."

"I can't do that, Lord Squidington. I'll die first," I said with a smirk and his eyes glinted sinisterly.

"Then you shall pay the price."

My breath snagged in my throat and I glanced back over my shoulder again as adrenaline beat a path through my limbs. "But I need to hide."

He nodded stiffly. "How long do you have?"

"He has to find me within twenty minutes, or he loses," I said.

"Well then, let's make the King of Competition work hard for his victory." He towed me along, walking back the way he'd come at a brisk pace.

"I was thinking of going to that big drawing room we found the other day," I said.

"No," Saint said. "We will go somewhere unpredictable."

"I mean, I'm not totally against him finding me," I said with a low laugh and Saint tossed me a dark smirk.

"Unfortunately for Blake, I just entered the game. And I will be the one to hide you, keep you, and punish you until he arrives." He dragged me along and my heart beat wildly, but I wasn't going to have my game hijacked.

I twisted my arm free and leapt away from Saint. "If you want me, you'll have to catch me too." I sprinted away, hearing his heavy footfalls following as I darted down another corridor, turning left and right as quickly as I could.

"The Devil's coming for you, Tatum!" he called somewhere behind me. "Beware his wrath when he catches you."

A grin pulled at my lips as I made it to an external door, pushing it open and slipping outside, gently closing it behind me. The air was warmer than it had been the last few days and the sun washed down on me as I raced into a group of trees and darted along a stone path.

At the end of it was a large tool shed and I cracked the door open, peering inside. There was a long work bench to one side of the space and tools hanging neatly across the back wall. Beyond it was a little mancave with a couch, a flatscreen TV and a minifridge beneath it. I guessed it might be for the house staff as it didn't seem like the kind of place Liam O'Brien would hang out.

"Hell yes," I hissed, slipping in and shutting the door behind me before padding over to sit on the couch. This was freaking genius. I mean, okay, maybe I wanted to be found, spanked and ravished. But I also loved winning. And if I got one up on the reigning champion Blake Bowman and Lord OCD, I was not gonna pass it up.

I grabbed a soda out of the minifridge, set myself up on the couch and put on You on Netflix. Nothing like a hot stalker who'd do anything and everything to make you theirs. Of course, I probably wasn't supposed to find Joe Goldberg hot, I wasn't *supposed* to get all flushed over him being a psycho. Were the rest of the female population watching this show thinking the same thing as me? Well, the unhinged ones were. And they were my kinda girls.

I sighed, leaning my head back, missing Mila. She would have loved Joe. She'd have said she wished Danny would murder a few of her exes to keep things interesting. I adored being with my Night Keepers, but I needed my own thing too. And I missed having her around. I really hoped I'd be able to meet up with her again soon. We just needed to dig ourselves out of this pit we were in and find a way to return to normality first.

A whole episode of You later and I was feeling seriously cocky. I got up, about to head back to the house to gloat when the door swung open and two dark shadows stood there, framed by the daylight. My heart rate went from zero to ten thousand and I froze like a rabbit in the headlights.

Oh shit. I've got a couple of stalkers of my own. And they're the hot psycho kind too.

Blake stepped inside first, closely followed by the demonic silhouette of Saint in his wake.

"I win," I sang.

"The game was meant to be played in the house," Blake said in a growl.

"Er, I think you'll find I never said that," I replied, except I definitely had.

"Once Blake caught up to me, he assured me you would be in the house," Saint said, casually rolling up his sleeves like he was about to do some dirty work. And I got the feeling that work was me.

"The game's been up for a long time," Blake said. "You should have come out of hiding so we didn't worry."

I laughed. They did not, still approaching me like wraiths in the night.

"So, what are we gonna do to her, Blake?" Saint asked Blake like I wasn't there and I suddenly remembered what it was like to be at their utter mercy, the memories sending a tremor through me that I didn't entirely hate. Not because I thought back on those times with any kind of fondness, but because the danger these men could spark in me nowadays was kind of exhilarating. And it wasn't the sort of danger I couldn't handle.

"Teach her a lesson," Blake said, his voice hollow and unnerving. Fuck, I liked it. I liked how their power filled the air and hummed through my body. But I needed to get the upper hand back fast.

"How about a rematch?" I offered nonchalantly as they kept approaching.

"It's too late for that," Blake said.

"Hold her down," Saint muttered and Blake ran at me.

I leapt up onto the sofa to escape him, trying to climb over the back of it, but he caught me around the waist. He dropped down to sit on the couch with me on his lap, clamping me tight to him. And okay, I didn't struggle all that hard. When Saint punished me, I usually ended up moaning and panting in pleasure. And with Blake here too, I was probably in for the time of my life.

Saint regarded me, stroking his chin before walking away to the tools lining the walls. He moved out of sight behind us and I ground my ass against

Blake's crotch, making him curse in my ear.

He bit my earlobe in warning, holding my hands in one of his while his arm locked around my waist.

"Run away with me Blake," I breathed temptingly. "Rescue me and I'll give you the best blowjob of your life."

"I heard that," Saint called, and Blake laughed villainously.

"Sorry, Cinders. I'm not going anywhere. Not until you've made up for being a bad girl." His breath against my neck was enough to send me spiralling, and I dropped my head back, offering my mouth up for a kiss. He leaned into it and the second he was close, I sank my teeth into his lower lip.

He growled but my little attack did nothing except spur him on. He yanked his lip free of my bite before plunging his tongue into my mouth with possessive strokes, taking what he wanted then pulling away again.

"Asshole," I panted and he smirked at the breathiness of my voice.

Saint suddenly caught hold of my wrists from behind, pulling them up above my head and linking them around the back of Blake's neck, tying them with a length of rope to immobilise me. Blake's hands roamed down my body, slipping under my shirt and dragging it up to expose my bare breasts. I writhed in his lap as he started squeezing them roughly, clearly doing it for his enjoyment over mine.

"Saint," I growled. "I won that game fair and square. You're all about rules and I'm the one who made them."

"You're a dirty little liar," Blake growled in my ear and I shivered.

Saint stepped in front of me, twisting a large screwdriver between his fingers, his soulless expression making him look like some sort of heartless torturer. "I know when Blake lies, siren. So either he believes his own truth or *you* are lying. And I think you know what I believe."

I bit my lip, feeling guilty as shit. But I wasn't going to admit to anything. This was far too much fun.

"I'm innocent," I insisted, batting my lashes and Blake's hand slid down the centre of my body to my white cotton panties, pushing inside and feeling my wetness.

"You're hardly that," he chuckled and Saint smirked, stepping closer as Blake moved his hand back up to my breast and wet my nipple with my own arousal.

A moan left me and I tugged on my binds as he placed his other hand on my stomach to hold me still.

Saint placed the screwdriver between his teeth and leaned forward, taking hold of the sides of my panties and dragging them down my legs. He knelt on the floor, tugging them off and tossing them aside before taking the screwdriver from his mouth. I wasn't sure if he was just trying to scare me with it or if he had greater plans than that. Both ideas got me hot.

"Hold her legs wide," Saint instructed and Blake pushed his knees up between mine, forcing them open and exposing me to his friend.

My breaths came quicker and I relished the way Blake's mouth felt against my neck and Saint gazed at me like I held the real power in the room. And I knew I did. I could tell them to stop and they'd do it instantly. But I loved when they pushed my boundaries. I was willing to go as far as they could take me and beyond.

"Every time you lie, you'll be punished," Saint warned. "Blake will spank your thigh."

"He wouldn't span-" I started, but Blake's hand clapped down on my inner thigh and my back arched, pain and pleasure rushing through me from his firm touch.

"Yes, he will," Saint said, sharing a dark look with Blake over my shoulder and I could tell their monsters really had come out to play.

Saint dropped his head between my thighs without warning, running his tongue up the middle of me and making me gasp. He took a deliberately slow path to my clit then sucked and bit without mercy. I bucked my hips but Blake flattened me to him to hold me still as Saint dragged his teeth over me in a way that both hurt and sent a shiver of pleasure through my core.

"Oh god," I panted as he devoured me, biting and teasing, sucking hard enough to make me squeak then lapping softly and deliciously to soothe away the ache. "*Saint.*"

I climbed towards my peak, pleasure building and building against a dam in my body which I was sure was about to break. My muscles tensed and I almost went tumbling over the edge of bliss when Saint drew away from me and wiped his mouth with the back of his hand, giving me an icy look.

"So…did you lie about the rules of the game?" he asked as I squirmed with need, frustration making me growl. But I wasn't going to let them defeat me that easily.

"No," I snapped. "Blake got it wrong."

Blake's hand slapped against the inside of my thigh hard enough to leave a red print there and I hissed between my teeth, but the sound was followed by a wanton moan.

"Liar," Saint accused, dropping his head back between my thighs and continuing his torture. He was harsher this time, biting and sucking my flesh, avoiding my clit as he worked my body into a frenzy.

"Saint!" I cursed as he bit the inside of my thigh then ran the pad of his tongue over the skin. He continued doing that along the insides of my legs, making my whole body shake and my skin tingle and burn.

He finally returned his attention to my clit, licking in soft strokes that made me sigh and Blake started toying with my nipples in the exact same rhythm. I moaned both of their names, delighting in their combined touch as I moved closer and closer to the wave of pleasure they were building in me.

"Don't stop," I begged and as if I'd said the opposite, they both stopped. "*Fuck.*"

Saint sucked his lips, his eyes holding nothing but shadow. "Did you lie about the rules of the game?"

I resisted answering for a moment, trying to fight my way free of the rope binding my wrists behind Blake's neck, but it was no use. I growled in anger, fighting a leg out of Blake's grip and kicking at Saint's chest.

He caught my foot, placing it promptly back behind Blake's leg and

Blake widened his knees to hold me there.

"I'm going to need an answer, siren," Saint pushed. "You can have everything you want so long as you tell the truth."

I considered it, seriously tempted to just give in. But I was too damn stubborn for that. "I didn't lie."

Blake spanked my thigh again and Saint cocked his head, amusement flickering across his handsome features.

Saint reached between my legs, pushing two fingers into my soaking heat with a satisfied growl. He reached into his pocket, taking a sanitising wipe from a little packet and I frowned in confusion before he wiped the screwdriver with it.

"What are you-" I started but he brought the handle end of the screwdriver to my entrance and I fell quiet. *Holy fuck.*

My eyes widened as I gazed at him, a question in his eyes. And I stared right back, daring him to do it. He eased it inside me and a lustful moan fell from my lips as he filled me with it.

Then his mouth dropped to my clit and he teased me once more, pumping the screwdriver in and out in time with the movements of his tongue.

Blake's fingers tugged at my nipples and he nibbled my ear in the most perfect way, the feel of so many sensations at once bringing me towards climax faster than I could take. It was a sweet kind of pain and the sounds leaving my mouth were purely animal.

"Saint. Blake," I praised their names while I was sure I should have been cursing them. Because they were going to stop. I was sure they were going to stop. And I couldn't take it this time. I couldn't fucking take it. "I lied!" I practically screamed and Blake laughed in my ear, the sound vibrating through my entire body.

"Good girl." Saint started pumping the screwdriver faster, his tongue rolling over my clit in endless waves and Blake turned my head to claim a hungry kiss from my mouth. I came with my whole body, tensing up and I cried out, a shudder rolling down the length of my spine. Pleasure tingled through my flesh everywhere they'd touched me and made me see fucking stars.

Saint eased the screwdriver out of me, tossing it on the floor as he got to his feet and unzipped his fly. He reached forward, unbinding my wrists behind Blake's neck and my arms flopped to my sides, my strength failing me.

Saint leaned down to kiss me firmly and I fisted my hand in his shirt to pull him closer as I tasted myself on his lips.

But just as I began to imagine what way the two of them were going to destroy me, Saint was suddenly ripped away from me and flung to the floor with an enormous crash. The huge shadow of Niall O'Brien took his place, a crowbar wielded above his head as he swung it around to cave Saint's skull in.

"Stop!" I screamed in fear, jumping up but Niall knocked me aside easily, swinging for Saint with a furious blow and a yell of fury.

Saint rolled aside, kicking Niall's shin hard enough to make him stumble back.

Blake grabbed me, pushing me behind him as the t-shirt I wore dropped down to cover my body once more.

"Yer think you can come into my family's home and fuck my nephew's bride then live to tell the tale, do ya?" Niall roared as he swung the bar at Saint again and Blake leapt onto his back, locking his neck in a chokehold as he pulled him away.

"Call Kyan!" Saint barked, throwing his phone at me as he leapt to his feet.

I caught it with shaking hands as Saint grabbed a plank of wood from a stack by the workbench.

Niall threw himself backwards onto the floor, crushing Blake beneath him and forcing him to let go of his neck before rolling over, tossing the crowbar aside and grabbing Blake's throat instead, squeezing hard.

"When I'm done wringing yer scrawny neck, I'll cut your balls off and make a necklace of them for Kyan to wear," he snarled, his eyes flashing with fury as I finally saw exactly what Kyan had warned me about in his uncle. He was a madman, unhinged, psychotic, unstoppable and fucking terrifying and I had no doubt that he had every intention of killing both Blake and Saint and maybe even me as well.

"Stop!" I screamed, dialling Kyan's number before kicking Niall in the side to try and get him off of Blake.

Saint yelled out, smashing the plank of wood down on Niall's head and it split in two, making Niall roar in anger, but he didn't let go. Blake punched his sides furiously and I clawed at Niall's back while Saint snatched up the crowbar Niall had dropped.

Saint lifted it, readying to hit him in the back of the skull and fear rushed through me. Before he swung it, Kyan appeared, football tackling Saint to the ground and the iron bar went clanging across the floor.

"Kyan!" I screamed as Blake started turning blue, his punches growing weaker as Niall's muscles locked and a cold, dead killer stared out of his eyes.

Kyan pushed me away from Niall as I clawed at him and punched his uncle in the side of the head, making him jolt out of the psychotic rage he'd fallen into.

"Let him go!" Kyan barked, punching him again and Niall released Blake's throat, leaving bright red finger marks on his flesh.

"Get away from him!" I screamed, shoving and pushing Niall as Kyan tugged him away.

I dropped down over Blake, trembling with fear as I checked him over and he blinked up at me with a cough as he sucked in air.

"They're fucking your wife, lad," Niall hissed at Kyan. "We can kill 'em together if you prefer? I'll tie 'em down and we can take turns to cut off limbs. We can even start with their coc-"

"Tell him," I demanded of Kyan and Niall looked to his nephew in confusion.

Kyan's jaw ticked furiously as Saint moved to kneel on Blake's other side, checking the bruises on his neck.

"She's with them too," Kyan bit out, looking over at Niall with a hard stare. "And Nash. All four of us. We're hers and she's ours."

Niall frowned, seeming like he was trying to piece those words together and make sense of them. "But she's your wife."

"I know, but she's theirs too. Not by law. But by… agreement. I dunno what else to call it. They love her and she loves them. It's all of us, that's just the way it is," Kyan snarled, his shoulders tensing like he was struggling to control his anger over what had happened.

Niall stared between all of us as those words sank in, and I swear something in his eyes actually changed. Almost like the green in them turned from a deep forest colour to a brighter, sweeter hue and my racing pulse stilled a little as some of the danger faded from the room. Not that I'd be letting my guard down around Kyan's impulsive uncle any time soon.

"And you're okay with that arrangement. Multi-dicks and all, lad?" Niall asked, seeming genuinely curious and not at all aware of the tension in the room.

"Yes," Kyan said firmly.

"And you're okay with it too, lass?" Niall looked over to me, seeming oblivious to the rage being pointed his way by everyone. It was like a flip had switched inside him and he was just back to his usual, casual self, no mention of the fact that he'd just tried to kill my boys. He really was insane.

Blake pushed himself up to sit, rubbing his neck as he glared at Niall like he was considering another fight. Saint placed a hand on his shoulder in warning and he didn't move again.

"Yes," I said firmly. "I love them equally. And I know you were trying to protect Kyan, but fuck you Niall."

"So it's like a pick and mix for you? If one of your boys is pissing you off, you can just go find another?" he asked me.

"It's not like that, I lov-"

"That actually makes a lot of sense. I always did feel sorry for my wife having to weather my brand of insanity alone. If she'd had a boyfriend too maybe he could have given her some reprieve from my company. Of course,

I'm not certain I could stand another man sticking his cock in my woman..." He rubbed his chin in contemplation, acting as if he hadn't just come damn close to killing Blake or getting his head caved in by Saint. Was this seriously not an unusual day for him? "My Ava wasn't likely to have wanted that though. And my bed has been emptier than a nun's vagina since she was taken from me, so I'm not likely to ever find out if I'd be able to allow it without castrating the other fella-"

"It's a family," Kyan snapped. "I wouldn't just let any man fuck my woman. But I love the three of them too. It's the only way that it ever could have worked for us."

"So you fuck them as well?" Niall asked him, pointing between Saint and Blake and tilting his head like he was picturing it. I mean, it wasn't a terrible picture, so I gave it a little imagining myself for the hell of it.

"No," Kyan grunted, his lips lifting with a hint of amusement. "They couldn't handle me."

"Well, I can't say my horizons are broadened every day, but you've definitely given me food for thought," Niall said, sounding like this really was giving him a lot to think about as he smiled widely at us.

He chuckled, looking to Blake. "Sorry about that then, lad. Look at it this way though, now you can say you survived the wrath of the best hitman in the state – which I don't think anyone else has ever done. Ever. Not once. I don't leave bodies kicking. Or twitching. So everybody wins." He stepped closer to Kyan, lowering his voice. "So tell me more about this arrangement? Do you have a schedule? Or do you all just whip your dicks out and -" He waved his hand between us all. "Act like animals whenever the feelin' takes ya?"

"I'll tell you about it another time," Kyan muttered, helping me to my feet. He checked me over closely then kissed the corner of my mouth when he was satisfied I was okay.

Niall gazed at us all with some dawning thought shining in his eyes. "Well," he said, moving to pick up the crowbar then heading over to the tools on the wall. "I just came here to grab a few new friends." He piled a couple of saws in his arms along with a hammer and a pair of pliers. "I have places to be, skulls to batter, eyeballs to pluck out. I'll be wanting that chat though, Kyan. And I'll keep my mouth shut too – Pa won't like you letting yer friends touch your girl no matter what way you wanna paint it to him. See ya around." He headed out of the door whistling casually and my shoulders dropped.

Blake and Saint moved up close behind me and we all pressed together in an embrace, though it wasn't quite enough. I missed Nash's presence like a lost limb.

"Your uncle is a lunatic," Blake muttered.

"He was looking out for family though," Saint reasoned and I knew he had a point, but I was still pissed at him.

"Violence is Niall's answer to everything," Kyan said.

I sighed. "Let's just never piss off the Grim Reaper again."

CHAPTER FORTY

Tuning a piano was not something I had ever really wished to spend my time doing, but in the years I'd spent playing on the grand piano back at Everlake, I'd found that I was much better off doing it myself. Once, the school had hired a man to come and tune it and I could only assume he'd had some sort of brain haemorrhage while working on my instrument because after he was done the poor thing sounded like a cat being drawn backwards through an alleyway by a pitbull with the shits.

Suffice to say, I had the man fired, his business destroyed, reputation torn apart and I was almost certain he'd been evicted from his home too. It probably wasn't enough of a punishment for the torture he'd inflicted upon my piano, but at the time I'd had exams to focus on, so I hadn't been able to exact sufficient revenge. The knowledge that he got off so lightly still haunted me whenever I heard the dulcet sound of a badly tuned instrument, so he was on my mind as I worked on the piano in Liam O'Brien's drawing room. Would it be worth me checking up on that buffoon? Seeing if he had anything else I could take from him in payment for his failure?

I sighed as I decided to have mercy on him. It wasn't that I felt he'd been sufficiently punished, but I could admit I had bigger fish to fry at the current moment and the diversion of my attention was unnecessary.

Liam's grand piano was much neglected, tucked away here in the rear corner of the room. But I'd found myself in need of the instrument to alleviate some of my tension so had decided to take on the task of giving it life again.

As I finally finished up, I packed away the tuning tools that one of the household staff had acquired for me and closed the cover with a soft exhale.

My blood was tingling tonight, my fingers itching for the keys and as I glanced out of the window at the dark grounds beyond, I took my seat before the instrument and laid my fingers down lightly.

The song I started with was slow, heady, full of dark promises and sweet truths. As my fingers danced across the keys, I could feel the tension slipping from my body as my heart rate slowed and I closed my eyes as I sank into the simplicity of the piece, letting it wrap around me and take me to a better place.

Music poured from the poor, neglected piano and I smiled a little as I felt it coming to life after fuck knew how many years of sitting here forgotten. Instruments needed life to be breathed into them by the masters of their creation. They had a soul that ached to create beauty and wonder, and it was damn near criminal to let such a beautiful piano lay dormant and ignored.

The door opened behind me as I transitioned into my fourth piece, the music growing more complicated as I went, my fingers moving faster, the sound burrowing deeper into my core.

Tatum dropped onto the stool beside me, the sweet honey blossom and vanilla scent of her rising up to me and making me sigh as I continued to play, the song quickening in pace, building and building until it came crashing down.

I turned to look at her as the last note hung in the air, slowing my pace as I split my attention to give her some of it, playing Killing Me Softly by the Fugees. A smile lifted Tatum's lips and she reached out to lay her right hand on top of mine, aligning our fingers so that she could feel the movements of the music as I created it.

"Does my pain call to you? Or am I just lucky that you always appear whenever I'm most in need of your company?" I asked her and she leaned in a little closer, placing a kiss against the side of my neck which made the hairs rise along my spine.

"*You* call to me, Saint," she replied, shifting her hand from my fingers, up my arm and over the sleeve of the black suit jacket I was wearing. She was still dressed up for dinner too, the silky black evening gown dipping low to reveal the full curves of her breasts while her stocking clad thigh pressed against my trousers.

"Mmm," I turned my gaze back to the keys as I continued to play, moving the song on to Halo by Beyoncé.

"I think you may just communicate better with music than you do with words," Tatum teased and I shrugged.

"It's more eloquent," I supplied. "I think the world would be a better place if we all just communicated via music."

Tatum breathed a laugh. "How do you even know all of these songs by heart? I swear you don't even listen to pop music and yet I feel like I could name practically any song and you'd start playing it with no problem."

"How many songs do you know the words to?" I asked her.

"I dunno. Hundreds...thousands maybe. Once they start playing the words just pop into my head."

"It's the same for me, but I just memorise the music as well," I said. "And I don't have anything against pop music, or any kind of music. I only ask that what I listen to emotes and captures true emotion. Music should hurt, bring joy, resonate with memories or just make you *feel*. If it does that, it has value beyond all the money in the world as far as I'm concerned."

"You're just a big old romantic at heart, aren't you?" Tatum asked and I scoffed.

"If you say so, siren."

"Can I put you to the test then?" she asked as the song came towards the end.

"Are you hoping to trip me up?" I asked her, playing Wrecking Ball by Miley Cyrus next and smirking at her. I wasn't certain if she was the one who had come crashing into my life or if it was the other way around, but it seemed fitting for us.

"Maybe."

"Only if you indulge in a fantasy for me then," I said, bobbing my chin towards the top of the piano. "Lay up on there while I play."

"Are you going to ravish me on top of a piano, Mr Memphis?" Tatum gasped mockingly.

"In a room where your husband's psychotic grandfather may walk in at any moment? That sounds like a rather foolish suggestion. I learned my lesson the last time with Niall. I quite like my head being attached to my body."

"It is such a clever head," she agreed as she got to her feet and climbed up on top of the piano for me.

I smiled at her as she draped herself across it, her grin saying she thought this was ridiculous even as she embodied the perfection of the fantasy I wished for. Her long legs lay across the piano and her dress rode up to expose the lacy tops of her stockings, making me groan with longing.

I drank in the sight of her as I continued playing and she started throwing random song titles at me, trying to catch me out with different genres and ages of music. But I managed to capture each choice she selected, replicating the music on the piano for her until she was laughing and reaching out to stroke a burning path along my jaw with her fingertips.

"What's got you feeling so down?" she asked in a soft voice, those blue eyes of hers looking right into my soul.

"Down?" I asked as I continued to let my fingers drift over the keys, flowing back into the familiar patterns of Mozart as the music wound its way around my soul.

"The music you were playing before I came in here was all so...sad," she said, looking down at my fingers as I realised I'd slipped into a rather melancholy choice now too.

"Hmm." I kept playing and Tatum didn't push me as I considered whether there was much merit to her observation. I hadn't been sitting here feeling sorry for myself per se, but I supposed I had been lost to my thoughts and memories, aching for this outlet.

"When I was a boy," I said eventually, keeping my eyes on the keys. "Ten years old, to be precise. My father went away on a business trip. So I decided to take it upon myself to figure out one of his secrets."

"What secrets?" Tatum breathed and I shrugged.

"I have never been allowed to know too much of anything the man is up to. He is something of an enigma - or at least that is what he attempts to be. But I'd been observing him closely, studying my enemy if you will, and I believed that I had figured out the combination to the lock on his filing cabinet. I'd been summoned to his office earlier that week for a lecture on the importance of hierarchy within an empire and I suppose I was a fool for not realising that had been a warning, but-"

"But you were just a kid," she supplied, and I nodded once in acknowledgment of that even if it still irritated me.

"Anyway, I waited until the dead of night when all of the house staff would be asleep and my mother would be half comatose after taking her nightly sleeping pills, and I crept from my bed. I slipped along the dark corridors and made my way to his office. The door was unlocked, which again should have clued me in, but I foolishly believed I was just lucky." I scoffed lightly at how naive I'd been. "I headed into his office with a little flashlight I'd taken from the kitchen drawer that morning and I flicked it on. I crept across the carpet in my flannel pyjamas and bare feet then I made it to the filing cabinet."

I breathed out slowly and continued to play, lost in the way a chill had caressed my skin as I stood there looking at that drawer, how cold the metal handle had felt against my fingers and the way my heart had raced with the idea of finally getting one up on him.

"What was in the drawer?" Tatum asked when she couldn't take it anymore and I offered her a smile which I knew didn't reach my eyes as I shrugged a shoulder.

"A letter. I can still see the words of it as if I took a damn photograph and plastered it to the backs of my eyelids. *'What did I tell you about respecting my privacy, boy?'"*

"He set a trap?" she gasped, and I nodded again.

"There was a camera recording the office. I suppose it had a motion sensor and a delayed timer on it because as I threw the drawer closed in alarm, his computer monitor flashed to life and showed me the feed from it. I could see myself standing in the centre of his office, the camera angled down to record the entire room. I turned and fled, fear consuming me as I raced all the way back to my bedroom, flung the door closed behind me and dove beneath the sheets."

"What did he do to punish you?"

"He didn't return from his trip for three more days and I am still unsure whether those seventy-two torturous hours were worse than his actual return. I was beyond afraid of what retribution he'd demand of me and the fear made me throw up every time I tried to eat." I shuddered at the memory of the bile coating my tongue and my stomach rumbling pitifully as I failed to keep anything down. "When he finally returned, he didn't speak a word to me. He removed his gloves and coat then strode to the dining room silently, not even casting a glance my way as I was forced to hound after him. He sat down with my mother at his side and ate his dinner, ignoring me while yet again, I failed to eat mine. I just...waited."

"Saint," Tatum murmured, reaching out to stroke my face again and I leaned into her touch as I continued to play.

"He laid his knife and fork down carefully, pressed his napkin to his lips then looked right over my head as he said in a firm voice, *'I do not wish to have a son who does not respect me or my privacy. Therefore, until further notice, I want it known that I have no son. No one in this household can see or hear him, much less speak to or feed him. Perhaps, in time he will learn to show enough respect that he may earn his way back into this family. But until then, Saint Memphis does not exist.'"*

"He...I don't understand," Tatum breathed but there were tears in her blue eyes which said she did.

I stopped playing to wipe one away as it fell and she caught my hand, holding it to her cheek as I was captured in her gaze.

"For two months and thirteen days, not one person I saw acknowledged me in any way. I wasn't allowed out. I had no access to the internet or a phone and no one even spoke in my presence. I existed as a ghost in my father's home, scavenging food from the kitchen at night once I managed to stomach it at all. It was...perhaps the worst punishment I have ever suffered at his hands. You cannot fully comprehend the loneliness of a little boy trapped and-"

Tatum leaned forward and pressed her lips to mine, tears streaming down her face so that the salty taste of them bled between our lips as my heart thumped harder from the memories and my breath caught tight in my chest.

Her fingers slid into my hair as I kissed her slowly, devouring the taste of her pain and mine, wanting to pull back and tell her it was alright while not quite finding the strength in me to do it just yet.

Her tears fell against my cheeks and it was so close to feeling something real that my heart began to race and the tightness in my muscles seemed to grow then relax like the push and pull of the tide.

I drew back and kissed her cheeks, one after another, tasting her tears and willing them away.

"Don't hurt for me, siren," I breathed. "I'm not that little boy anymore. I'm-"

"I'll never let you feel like that again," she promised. "Not once. Not ever. You'll never be alone again, and you'll never feel unwanted. That man was no father to you. He's not your family. But we're here now and you'll never be on the outside of anything ever again."

I inhaled those words, soaking them in and letting them wind their way around my heart until they were beating through my veins and permeating every piece of me.

My throat was thick at the weight of what I felt for this girl. This creature born to ruin me and recast me anew.

"I'm sorry for the pain I have caused you," I murmured, sliding my fingers through her long hair and twisting it around them gently. "I'm sorry I didn't accept what you are sooner."

"And what's that?" she whispered, her lips brushing against my cheek like the wings of a butterfly.

"Everything," I replied simply, unable to put it into words more eloquently than that because there was no language on earth that could encompass the depths of what I felt for her. My obsession with her had gone too far, my infatuation unstoppable now and never ending. She would never be rid of me. There was no place in this world or the next where I wouldn't find her, follow her, worship her. She was my light when all I'd ever known was dark and now that I could see, I refused to be blinded ever again. Because it would destroy me if I was.

There were no words that could convey all of that, but perhaps there *was* music. This melody had been writhing through my body and soul for so long that I knew it was desperate to escape. And I found myself needing to share it with her so that she might have a chance of understanding what she was to me.

I took my hand from her hair and leaned back, looking into her blue eyes which still shimmered with tears as I licked my lips and tasted her sorrow on them.

Who was this creature who saw so much and offered me more than I ever could have presumed to take? How was it she seemed to see so much in me when I wasn't even sure there had been anything here to find? She brought out a side of me I hadn't known existed but had clearly been starving in wait of her. And now it was going to gorge itself on everything she had to offer, and I had no desire to even try and stop it.

"I wrote this for you," I said, laying my hands back down on the piano.

"You wrote me a song?" she asked, biting her lip to try and hide a shy smile and the thought of this pleasing her so much loosened a knot in my chest.

"I don't sing, siren," I replied with a faint snort of amusement. "But I do play. So I wrote you a symphony - though I only have a piano to hand and am lacking the orchestra which would be necessary to bring it to life, so it's just this simple piece."

"Simple?" she teased like she knew it would be anything but and I allowed myself a smile.

"As simple as I am able," I conceded.

She shifted back to watch me from the top of the piano and I drank in the sight of her as my fingers moved into position over the keys. I exhaled slowly, finding peace in the music even before it had begun to pour from my soul then I began.

The song started slowly, the first notes piercing the silence of the room like raindrops falling in the night, striking without notice and falling unseen, yet leaving a mark all the same. As the lower notes came in to play, the music got darker like thunder rolling over a deep ocean while the rain continued to fall, so small in the face of all that water and yet changing it irrevocably with every drop that fell.

I lost myself in the music as the rain built into a storm in my mind, an unstoppable tempest that crashed and pounded against the ocean and the land, making itself known, bringing life and passion to a barren expanse of nothing and waking monsters from their slumber.

My hands moved faster and faster, never missing a single key because each and every one was important, necessary, the darkest, deepest notes just as crucial as the lightest, highest ones. And somehow it all just came together, the music fighting to be one just like the rain soaked into the ground and filled the ocean with stories of places it could never see for itself, but changed its outlook on everything.

The music became more complex, making my heart race and I fought to keep the pace just right as it reached the crescendo, an explosion of everything coming together, the battle for power forgotten and peace laying claim to the world as the storm blew itself out.

As I fell into the final notes, my heart ached with the sweetness of them, of how similar and yet how different they were to the notes that had started the piece. That was how I felt for her, like a man reborn, the same and yet altogether different at once. There was no more fighting for control, but a peace built of heat and flames that burned through everything and set it all alight.

As I played the final note, I sat back with an exhale and slowly lifted my gaze to meet hers.

Tatum's pink lips were parted as she stared at me, her chest rising and falling heavily as her pupils dilated and I swallowed thickly as I felt more than a little vulnerable before her. I'd just cut my heart from my chest and laid it bloody and beating at her altar. It was all I had to offer. Just a broken boy in the body of a man. I had so much baggage that sometimes the weight of it crippled me and I was never going to be easy to love. And yet that look in her eyes made me think she really did love me anyway. Despite it all. Never minding the fact that I wasn't deserving of any such thing from her. She was mine as much as I was hers.

The heat between us crackled and my limbs grew rigid as I looked at her up there on top of the piano, her long legs begging me to tear those stockings from them and bury myself between them. I held myself still through pure force of will as the idea of claiming her now overwhelmed me. I wanted her in the way a beast needed its mate. I wanted her clawing at my clothes, her nails biting into my flesh and her ass crashing down against the keys of that piano as I drove my cock inside her and made her scream my name.

And the look in her eyes said she wanted the same damn thing.

The distant ring of a house phone was the only sound to break the silence and I knew it was coming down to a battle of wills between us as we waited to find out who would break first. But my control hung poised on the tip of a knife and I knew I was about to break for her. I'd break and she'd fall with me until somehow, we found a way to rebuild ourselves in each other.

I stood suddenly just as she reached out and grasped my tie, yanking me towards her as she said my name and commanded me to come for her.

I reared over her, my cock hard and aching as I leaned forward, tasting her on the air as I gripped the top of the piano either side of her hips and prepared to claim what was mine.

The sound of footsteps barely permeated the air, but I managed to snap myself out of this spell Tatum had cast on me and I jerked away suddenly, whirling towards the door as she gasped in alarm.

My heart thundered as I realised what I'd almost just done. If anyone in this household had seen us together, they wouldn't have waited around to ask questions. Tatum was Kyan's wife and death would be an easy price for us to pay if any of them thought I had stolen what was his. Niall knowing was one thing, but Kyan had assured me he would take that secret to the grave. There was no one else so trustworthy in this family and I couldn't risk us being discovered together a second time.

The door pushed open and I schooled my features into an emotionless mask as the housekeeper, Martha stepped into the room.

"Good evening, Mr Memphis," she said cheerfully as she held a cordless phone out for me. "You have someone calling to speak with you."

I couldn't even force my tongue to bend around the thanks I should have given her as I wordlessly took the phone from her grasp, nodding stiffly as the feel of it overwhelmed me like it was burning.

Martha bobbed her head, giving Tatum a warm smile over my shoulder then turned and headed out of the room, the door slowly closing behind her.

My throat was thick as I turned to look back at Tatum, her eyes wide where she now sat on the very edge of the piano, her legs crossed and dress straightened out with her hair hanging perfectly. I doubted the housekeeper would have suspected a thing. But that was the least of my concerns right now.

I turned the phone over in my hand as I took a step back towards the girl who had changed everything, finding the handset on hold.

I expelled a breath and placed a finger to my lips, warning Tatum to remain silent as my heart raced in my chest. Not that I was letting it show. My features were a mask once more, nothing slipping through the cracks of my defences, least of all fear.

"Father," I said curtly as I connected the call and placed it on speakerphone so that Tatum could listen in too. I knew it would be him. No one knew I was here and no one else would care to call even if they figured it out.

"Son," he replied in that clipped tone of his that told me right away I should expect the worst. "It appears you have been rather busy."

"I could say the same about you," I replied evenly.

"I have a problem which I am certain you can help me with," he said, not acknowledging my words and I fought against the flicker of unease that sent through me. I never had gotten over being ignored after those months of disregard.

"Oh?" I asked innocently, not a shred of guilt colouring my words, but he wouldn't just be calling unless he was certain I knew what he wanted.

"Recently, some masked assailants broke into an exclusive club which I run and they stole from me. They took countless assets, ransacked my office then set the place ablaze," he said and my heart leapt at the barest hint of rage to his tone. He was about as close to losing his shit as I think I'd ever heard him to be and knowing that me and my family were responsible for rocking the foundations of his hardwired asshole behaviour like that made me want to smirk in triumph. But I knew he wouldn't be calling to let me know I'd won anything, so I held off on any premature celebrations.

"I didn't know you ran an exclusive club," I commented lightly, like the rest of his words meant nothing to me.

"You can drop the mask now, son. Or should I say *Rex*? Because I have just seen a rather confusing photocopy of a passport which seems to imply that you and your friends have taken on new identities. Unless you wish to try and claim there are four doppelgängers roaming around Sequoia with the vaccination to the Hades Virus pumping through their veins?"

Tatum sucked in a gasp, pressing a hand to her mouth and I lifted my gaze to hers, trying to convey an apology to her without words. Because I should have known that this would happen. The apple may not have fallen far from the tree with me and my father, but he'd had many more years to establish his roots. And I was pretty certain that he was about to prove to me that his foundations were solid despite all of my plans.

"Is she there now?" he asked conversationally. "Her lips wrapped tight around your cock in thanks for you saving her from my lab?"

I faltered at his crass words, my gaze on Tatum as the urge to grab her and run as far and as fast from here as possible almost overwhelmed me. He knew. Not just about us rescuing her, but he knew why. He'd always been able to see to the heart of things and despite how often he'd drummed into me the fact that I should never need nor want anyone in my life beyond myself, he had realised what she was to me. And that made him more dangerous than ever before.

"Not presently," I replied calmly though inside I felt anything but. "She's rather exhausted at the moment from me fucking her on my piano."

My father tutted at the mention of the instrument and I knew that if he could, he'd destroy every piano in existence just to stop me from wasting my time on something he saw as so pointless.

"Here's where we stand, son," he said firmly. "You will return all of the shares you have bought up in my companies to me. You will relinquish control of all of the assets you have stolen and sign it all back over to me." The faintest touch of inflection to his voice let me know how fucking angry he was to have realised that I'd done all of that. Me. His beat down little heir who was supposed to toe the line and wait for my time to rise in his shadow had set him up to fall from grace and he hadn't even seen it coming until it was too damn late.

"Unfortunately, I don't think I'll be able to do that," I replied slowly, soaking in the feeling of my victory over him. "You see, I did what you taught me. I set my enemy in my sights and got all of my ducks in a row. I did my research, I played him at his own game, and I walked him right into my trap. Now all I need to do is pull the trigger. So why would I lay down my weapon at the final moment?"

"I will admit I was rather impressed," he replied slowly and the cocky edge to his voice set my hackles rising. I doubted anyone else in the world would even notice it, but I did. And it meant danger was coming. He had some plan beyond his words, and I was the one walking into it. "You've outdone yourself with this. You were thorough, subtle, methodical and really quite brilliant."

"But?" I prompted, ignoring the prickle of pride that tried to work its way down my spine. Why was it that despite my hatred for this man, despite my desire to see him destroyed and broken and dead at my feet, a small part of me still hungered for his approval? All he had ever afforded me was fear, suffering and contempt. But there it was, deep inside of me a forgotten boy who just craved his father's love and affection. I stamped those feelings back down hard though, refusing to give in to them. This man had no love in his heart for me or anything aside from money and power. It was just the way he was and no good would ever come from me lamenting the loss of a man he'd never been.

"*But*," he agreed coolly. "You had to go and fall for the trap of *love*, didn't you?" he said, his voice thick with disappointment.

I glanced up at Tatum and she reached out to take my free hand, the very real feeling of her fingers in mine confirming to me that he didn't have her and making my brows pinch, because if he wasn't referring to her, then who-

"The O'Brien heir I can understand," Father said thoughtfully. "To some degree at least. He has power, connections, and they are a breed of brutality which would hold a certain appeal to your baser nature. A red-blooded man such as yourself needs a little violence in his life. And the girl...well, I never did allow a tight pussy to corrupt my mind and blind me from my interests, but it's well-known that a lot of men are easily beguiled by such things. I had expected better from you, but you're young, no doubt she's eager and fucks well enough to distract you from-"

"You won't speak about her like that," I snarled, a very real warning in my voice. "I won't warn you again, old man. But if you talk about her like she's some disposable whore one more time, I'll come for you with the full force of all that I am and I won't stop until you're nothing but a corpse crushed beneath my heel."

Silence followed my outburst and I knew I should have held my tongue, but I didn't see the point in that. He knew. He knew all too fucking well. She had my heart, and my life was in her hands. He'd already figured out that she was my weakness, so he may as well realise she was my strength too.

"The footballer is in bad taste," he said after a beat. "New money. No connections beyond the flashy world of sports and media - I will admit I encouraged you to make an ally of him for those very reasons, but such people are disposable, interchangeable and have no long-term use. Besides, it doesn't even look like the boy will go pro, so I fail to see the appeal. Still, I suppose he has been in your life a long time and you always did show a weakness for sentiment. But then there's the teacher," he said slowly, like he was waiting to see if I might elaborate on that for him but I stayed silent, so he went on. "Nash Monroe...or is it *Jase Harrington?*"

Tatum's grip on my fingers tightened painfully as my father revealed his knowledge of my brother, but I wasn't even surprised. Once he saw those passports we'd used in the camp, he would have seen that Nash was still keeping company with me. Of course he took a closer look at the working man who had somehow slipped into our ranks, and once he'd started digging it wouldn't have been at all hard for him to uncover the truth of his identity. It wasn't like Nash had been able to pay for the kinds of forgeries that I could, and a change of name was a pretty simple blockade to bypass.

"Of course, you already knew that," Father went on, barely pausing long enough for me to confirm or deny it and taking my silence as his answer. "I will admit, even when his true name was presented to me, I didn't remember him. But my people pulled up all the information I required to jog my memory of his halfwit mother pulling her car out in front of me all those years ago and sealing her family's fate. Honestly, son, I would have expected you to keep a higher class of-"

"She didn't just pull out in front of you, you fucking sicko," Tatum snarled, losing her cool at his casual dismissal of Nash's entire world. "You were drunk, and you killed them! You covered up your own fucking failure with money and lies and one day soon, we're going to hunt you down and put a fucking knife in your throat for it."

"Really, Saint," Father replied, a sneer in his tone. "You should put your woman in her place before she continues to embarrass herself and you-"

"Tatum *is* in her place," I growled. "And that's firmly at my side. She has a mind of her own and will speak it if she chooses. Get to the point of your tirade before I grow tired of it and end this call."

"Fine. Although you have played a very good hand indeed, and I will admit that I would have been hard pressed to resolve the issues you have caused me with my finances and companies in any other situation, I find myself with the trump card up my sleeve. Despite my best efforts, you have chosen to show weakness in aligning yourself with these people and giving in to the illusion of love. So, let's find out how firmly you hold to the notion. I have in my possession the father of your dear Mr Bowman. I would have liked to claim more prizes than that but unfortunately, it seems that the teacher and the girl are all alone in the world and the O'Briens are a nest of snakes I've chosen not to tangle with at this time. But though I believe this threat should mean nothing to you, I want to see how deeply you have fallen into the trap of love. If you wish to see your friend's father again you will return all of my assets to me within the next week."

Silence fell as he let that sink in and my heart raced as I thought about what Blake would say when he found out. I didn't doubt the truth of this threat. My father didn't do things by halves. If he said he had Blake's dad then I was certain he did.

A clock chimed loudly in the background on his end of the line and I sucked in a breath as I listened to the familiar sound.

"And then what?" I asked, because clearly returning his assets to him wouldn't be enough.

"And then we'll talk again. Let's find out who's the better Memphis. Game on, son." He cut the call and for a moment I just stared at the phone as the weight of his words sank in.

Tatum's arms closed around my neck as she threw herself against me and I wound her into my embrace as I pulled her close. My heart was pounding, mind racing and that cold, clinical feeling was sliding through my veins as I detached myself from the world around me to focus on dealing with this. But the warmth of her body against mine was still welcome. And I drew comfort from it as I held her tightly.

"We need to tell the others," she said, untangling herself from me and grabbing my hand as she tugged me from the room.

I followed along mechanically, allowing her to guide me and set the pace as idea after idea ticked through my skull.

We made it back to the huge room that Kyan owned here and found the three of them inside, the Xbox on as they played their asinine games, laughing and joking while swigging on bottles of beer.

But as they turned to look at us, their faces fell and Tatum burst into tears as she released her hold on me and threw herself into Blake's arms.

I closed the door behind me then turned away from them, leaving her to explain as my mind ran over each and every word he'd spoken to me.

I slipped my tie loose and hung it from the back of a chair before dropping my blazer on top of it and heading into the en-suite. I quickly shed the rest of my clothes, my chest tight with barely suppressed panic as my mind just went around and around in circles and tried to find some loophole here.

I turned the shower on, just to give me an excuse to avoid the others and be alone with my thoughts for a while. Because this was on me. My love for them had brought this down on their heads. My father was the one who was causing all of this. Anything that happened to them or the people they cared about at his hands came back down on me. Because I was the one who should have stopped him. I was the one who should have protected them from him. And now I was failing if I couldn't see a way out of it. I'd drown in this feeling of incompetence if I didn't figure out how to make it right.

I stepped beneath the water, barely even noticing that it was cold and not caring enough to change the temperature. I placed my palms against the tiles and let the water crash down on the back of my head so it spilled through my dark curls and washed over my feet, hoping it might give me some clarity.

I lost all sense of the minutes slipping by as I just stood there, but the water suddenly turned warm and I found a hulking figure beside me, his shirt off but pants on as he stepped into the shower and leaned against the wall beside me. Kyan folded his arms and waited for me to look at him and I turned my head his way, knowing he wouldn't back off until I did.

I didn't say anything and he arched an eyebrow at me that said I was being an ass.

"Who the fuck are you?" he demanded.

I ground my jaw, but gave him his answer because I'd played this game with him enough times to know he wouldn't leave until he got it from me.

"Saint Memphis."

"And does Saint-mother-fucking-Memphis fall apart when shit doesn't go to plan?" he asked.

I bit my tongue on the response I wanted to give and straightened as I turned to look him in the eye. "No."

"So tell us how you're going to fix this," Kyan demanded.

My gaze dropped to that hideous squid tattoo on his forearm and my lip peeled back before I raised my chin to hold his eye. The irritation that squid caused reminded me of something important and I perked up a little. I'd been focusing on every word I'd heard during that call, but I'd overlooked one very important detail. That annoying as shit grandfather clock. I hated that fucking thing, not least because it couldn't keep time correctly and was forever falling minutes behind the proper hour.

"I know where he is," I said, a new plan forming in my mind already.

Kyan's face split into a deadly smile as murder flashed in his eyes.

"Good. Put your fucking clothes on and let's go then." Kyan shut off the water and strode out of the shower, his boots leaving wet footprints across the tiles as he went, and I grabbed a towel to dry off.

I hurried back into the room with the towel around my waist and found the others looking to me expectantly. Tatum was under Blake's arm and his eyes flared with anxiety and rage, but he'd gotten it under control so that he could hear me out.

"Clearly, we can't let this stand," I said, more ideas spilling into my mind and I looked between my family, checking to make sure each of them really was ready for what it would take to free us from the monster who had made me. "I'll get my people working on the stocks and shares, they can sell and transfer as much as possible back into his name so that he can see progress is being made on that front."

"You're just going to let him have it back?" Nash asked, his face drawn with fury. "What about making him suffer?"

"I have given it some thought, and it seems fairly simple to me. The money, stocks, shares, all of it is irrelevant. I've seen his will. When he dies it's all mine anyway. So, let him have it back. He can enjoy it until we come and claim it from him in blood."

"I'll cut his fucking throat myself if he's laid a damn hand on my dad," Blake snarled.

"That's what I'm talking about," Kyan said with a dark laugh. "I'll piss on his grave while we claim it too."

"In the meantime, we can't stay here," I said. "I won't have him knowing our location, but on the plus side, I know his. So I say we take this fight to him. I'm done waiting to end this."

"I'm ready, just give me a weapon, any fucking weapon and I'll get it done," Blake growled, his eyes nothing but a monster's. But that rage in him would need to be honed, controlled. We couldn't storm my father's castle without an appropriate plan. But I was already working out the details.

"My grandpa won't just let me leave," Kyan said, not like he had any intention of staying behind, more like he was reminding us that I wasn't the only one with a psychopath in my family who thought he could rule my life.

"Then let's deal with him too. It's time Liam figured out he doesn't own you."

Tatum grinned at that prospect, reaching out to catch Kyan's hand and he leaned in to kiss her, pushing her back against Blake as he did so. Blake held her close and Kyan's hands looped around him too as they comforted him.

"Get changed," I commanded. "Practical clothing. Then pack a bag - wash stuff. Things to sleep in, enough food for tonight. I'll have the rest delivered after that."

No one questioned me and they all began stripping out of the formal wear they'd worn to dinner hours ago.

I pulled on a pair of grey sweatpants and discarded my towel in the hamper before moving deeper into the closet to grab some more clothes to bring. Tatum followed me inside and I turned to find her dressed in sweats and a hoodie too, though hers were pink and made her look far sweeter than she was.

"Jesus, Saint," she muttered, looking me over.

"What?" I asked as I moved to grab clothes for her too.

"Just...you picked grey sweats. You know what that does to a girl, right?"

"No. What?"

"Well... I can basically see your dick outlined through them and considering how big yours is, there's plenty to look at. And that gives me ideas I shouldn't be having when we have to follow through on your master plan."

I glanced down at my pants with a frown and she went on.

"And you're doing that whole, 'I rule the world thing' with the glaring and serial killer eyes. If you're not careful I'll jump you before we even make it out of here," she added in a purr that said she hadn't entirely forgotten where our bodies had been leading us before I got that call.

I cocked my head at her teasing tone as I stalked closer, making her back up against the wall until our chests were touching and we were sharing the same breath.

"You don't want me to break right now," I assured her, and she licked her lips.

"Pretty sure I'd be okay with it," she countered.

Temptation warred beneath my skin and the desire to do just that ran through me, but I knew she didn't really mean it and I couldn't either. We had a job to do and it couldn't wait. But I appreciated her trying to give me something to think about other than this endless abyss of chaos that was opening up around us.

"I promise to give you my worst just as soon as our lives are no longer at risk," I growled, leaning in and kissing her hard, but all too briefly as I jerked away again and stalked from the closet. Another moment in her company and my self-control would snap.

I pulled on a t-shirt and a grey hoodie to match my sweats before tossing the bag I'd packed over my shoulder and leading the way out of the room.

Kyan fell into step by my side and the others flanked Tatum behind us.

"You sure about this?" Kyan asked and I nodded once.

Liam O'Brien was a much simpler monster than my father. I could finish him easily enough. At least I hoped so.

We didn't stop until we made it downstairs and to the smoking parlour that Liam liked to retire to after dinner.

"We'll wait out here," Nash said, holding back with Blake and Tatum as we headed towards the door.

"It won't take long," I replied as Kyan moved ahead of me.

The scent of cigarettes wafted from beneath the door before I even pulled it open and the sound of male voices reached us as we stepped inside.

"I was about to come find you bunch of bastards," Niall said happily as he raised his glass to us before draining the lot.

Liam seemed intrigued by our interruption, his gaze sliding from Kyan to me as he leaned back in his leather chair and stubbed out his cigarette.

"What can I do ya for, lad?" he asked, his question for Kyan as we came to sit at the table with them.

"We're leaving," Kyan said, not beating around the bush and I had to say I liked that about him a lot. "Tonight. Something's come up and Blake's dad is in trouble."

"It doesn't much sound like that's your problem," Liam said, arching a brow at him.

"It is," Kyan disagreed. "Because Blake is my brother, his family is my family."

"You can just pick and choose yer family now, can ya?" Niall asked, rubbing a hand over his chin like that idea intrigued him. "That seems mighty convenient."

"It is what it is," Kyan said simply.

"No," Liam replied, not surprising either of us. "It's clear to me that while this virus is still on the loose you won't be returning to that fancy boarding school of yours, which means it's time for you to return home to us permanently. If your friends need to leave then so be it. But you and I have an empire to run, Kyan."

"I don't agree," I said mildly, reaching down to unzip the bag I'd dropped at my feet and at a look from Liam, Niall drew a revolver and pointed it at my head.

He grinned at me and spun the barrel as I slowed my movements. "I'm not drawing a weapon." I pulled my laptop out to prove my point, but Niall pulled the trigger anyway. There was a dull click and I blinked, realising I would have been dead here and now if that thing had been loaded. This family really were a bunch of insane pricks.

"Christ, yer a cold-hearted motherfucker, aren't ya?" Niall laughed as he failed to get more than that slight flicker of a reaction from me. "I bet I'd have to spend months breaking you if I wanted any of your secrets."

"I'd take them to the grave," I replied earnestly, and his eyes flared like he was wondering if that was true.

"What would I have to do to crack a stubborn fucker like you?" he said conversationally. "Is there any kind of torture that would work, or would you just go to death without ever speaking a word?"

"We're in the middle of a conversation," Liam said, shutting him down and Niall rolled his eyes before leaning back in his chair and flicking the barrel of his gun open, letting a single bullet fall out into his hand.

"Wait," Kyan snarled as his eyes fell on the bullet and he shoved to his feet. "Did you just fire a loaded gun at my brother?"

He lunged towards Niall who laughed as Kyan took a swing at him and he was knocked back out of his chair.

"Enough!" Liam barked, stopping the fight before it could really start.

Niall was already on his feet, his eyes alight with excitement, a feral glint in them which spoke of untold horrors.

"Relax, nephew, I knew the bullet wasn't in the chamber. I just wanted to see if I could make him shit himself," Niall said, pulling a knife from his belt before leaning back against the wall and using it to pick at his fingernails.

Kyan muttered something about him being a crazy bastard before dropping back down into his chair beside me. Niall shot me a wink which I was pretty sure meant he'd been certain of no such thing. I clucked my tongue, unwilling to cause more of a scene over a bullet which hadn't even ended up in my skull as I turned my attention back to Liam.

"You were telling me that you seem to think you're leaving your family to run off and help yer friend's father," Liam said loudly, turning cold eyes on Kyan as I leaned forward to open my laptop.

"I am," Kyan agreed. "I think it's time I made it clear to you that I want to choose my own life, Grandpa. I'm not turning my back on the family, but I don't want to help run your empire - I want to rule my own kingdom. And it's time for me to start charting that course."

"And what makes you think I'd agree to such nonsense?" Liam asked, drawing a fresh cigarette from the pack on the table and lighting it up.

"That would be me," I said, drawing his attention back to me as I opened up the first file on the laptop and pushed it closer to him. "Before we go any further, I'd like you to know that this information will be released to the FBI if anything were to happen to me or my friends and we don't check back in with my associate within the next hour - just in case you get any crazy ideas about having us killed here and now."

"What am I looking at?" Liam asked, but the way his face had paled said he knew well enough.

"That right there is a file on you personally. It documents the way your organisation works, how you launder your money, where it comes from and how it ends up in your pocket. There is more than enough evidence there to send you away for life - which in your case wouldn't be that hard considering your age - and to make it even cleaner cut, I have a video of you personally killing a man called John Cormack which dates back three years. I also had his body relocated from the shallow grave you gave him so it can be exhumed if needs be."

Kyan's eyebrows raised as he looked at the information I was presenting, and the corner of my lips twitched as I took a moment to be proud of the noose I'd just placed around Liam's neck.

"If you're interested in opening any of the other tabs, you will find similar information on each and every relevant member of your family. Aside from Kyan of course."

"What have you got on me?" Niall asked curiously and I lifted my eyes to meet his as he stepped forward eagerly, not like he was worried about what I had, more like he was curious.

"Actually, Kyan requested I bury the evidence against you in light of the help you've offered us," I admitted.

"So, you haven't got anything?" he asked, seeming disappointed.

"I found an awful lot that *could* be linked to you - but I will say you're better at covering your tracks than the rest of your family. So it's possible that you may have been able to avoid incarceration or at least plead insanity. I tend to think it's because you're a deranged madman and your impulses are so random that you're too unpredictable to trace. But perhaps it's just luck." I shrugged and Niall beamed like that was the greatest compliment he'd ever received.

"I'll get Saint to send you a scrap book filled with all the things he found," Kyan suggested with a smirk, seeming to be over the whole issue of me almost getting my brains blown out. And I felt it was beneficial to him to have a good relationship with at least one family member, so I decided to let that slide too.

"Also, as you know, when we took down Royaume D'élite we burned it to the ground, but I haven't been entirely forthcoming about what else I did there. I managed to locate a hard drive which held information on countless highly illegal deals that the members of that club have taken part in as well as the key to the numbers members were given to conceal their identities. In addition to the other information I had already gathered on your organisation, I now have records of all the deals you made with the other members of that club. I know you undertook several high profile assassinations and that you have taken part in insider trading alongside extensive money laundering and other more than questionable activities. All of the information I got on that place and its members will be delivered to the FBI in due course, but as a show of friendship I have taken great care to remove every single scrap of evidence linking anything in there to you and your family. Assuming you accept our deal, it will stay that way."

"What deal are you proposing?" Liam asked, his gaze flying over the information in the file as he found my claims to be entirely true.

"Now, nothing," I replied simply. "Kyan will leave here with us and you will relinquish him from any and every responsibility you had thought to give him within your organisation. We can part as friends, if you like. I understand that your entire reason for joining up to Royaume D'élite was so that you could gain powerful friends and I guarantee you will never make a friend more powerful than me. So you allow Kyan to be his own man and build his own kingdom as he put it. If you have need of me or Kyan in the future I'm sure we could come to an agreement. Similarly, if we have need of your empire, we'll know who to call. We can remain friends, but he will no longer serve beneath you."

"And you want this?" Liam asked, his attention fixed on Kyan. "I had you pegged for top dog, you know that, lad?"

"I do," Kyan agreed, leaning back in his chair. "But I don't want it. I mean, I'm flattered and all that you think I'd be the right fit, but it just isn't me. I want out. I wanna make my own life, Grandpa. That's all."

Liam toked on his cigarette, his eyes narrowed like he was hunting for a way out of this then he exhaled slowly, blowing a cloud of smoke at us.

"Alright," he agreed finally, and my chest deflated as I closed the laptop and slid it back into my bag. "Friends. But don't go thinking I won't make good on that offer. A file or two like this on some of my enemies could be just what the doctor ordered."

"Consider it done," I agreed. "Just as soon as I kill my father."

Niall barked a laugh and Liam clapped his hand into Kyan's in farewell.

"You would have been everything this family needs," Liam said seriously, regret shining in his eyes as he was forced to let him go. But he hadn't grown an empire this powerful without understanding how to pick your battles and he'd clearly seen that this was one he couldn't win. Smart man. I would have liked him if he wasn't such an insufferable prick.

"But that's not what *I* need," Kyan said just as seriously.

Liam nodded and we took our leave, Niall's raucous laughter following us as he shouted encouragement at our backs. *Crazy motherfucker.*

"Is it done?" Tatum asked as we stepped back out into the hall and

Kyan's face broke into a huge grin.

"Clear and free, baby," he announced, sweeping her up into his arms and making her laugh as he stole a kiss from her lips.

"Let's go get my dad back," Blake snarled, the fury in his eyes burning viciously and I knew the demon in him was aching for release.

We turned and headed for the door in a close-knit group and Nash cupped his hands around his mouth, calling back before we stepped out into the cold air of the night. "Byeeee Felicia!"

I snorted a laugh as the door swung closed on one of our problems and I lifted my chin as I looked up at the moon hanging low in the sky. I just wished my father would be so easy to vanquish. But I doubted there was much chance of that.

CHAPTER FORTY ONE

We drove north for several hours and I fiercely anticipated reaching our next destination. Because as soon as we arrived wherever the hell Saint was taking us (he'd been pretty damn cagey so far about the details), I knew it wouldn't be long before we were seeking justice for everything Troy had done and making his screams echo into the night. We'd had to take the back roads to avoid the army blockades and I had the feeling that had made this trip far longer than it would have been if we could have taken the highways. But we were so close to taking down Troy and we couldn't risk being caught now. I knew Saint would have been even more thorough than necessary in that task.

Blake had descended into a dark silence beside me in the back of the car, his hand locked around mine as I offered him any comfort I could. My heart was gilded in pain for the fear that must have been plaguing him. I wouldn't rest until his father was safe, returned to his son's side. But until then, I knew my golden boy would keep hurting, fearing the worst and dwelling in the pain he already felt over losing his mother.

We headed into a valley below the mountains and thick forest swept out around us like artist's strokes through the roiling landscape, lit up by the frosty moonlight.

Saint turned off the road and took a winding track through sprawling farmland and we eventually pulled up outside a beautiful old farmhouse with a long wooden porch, the lights in the windows giving it a cosy aura.

"Stay here." Saint got out, heading up to the house and knocking on the door.

A woman exited with a carpet bag under her arm, nodding to Saint as they shared a few words before placing a key in his hand. She walked over to a blue truck, got in and drove off down the track we'd just come from.

Saint beckoned us out of the car, and I exited after Blake with a sigh of relief, desperate to stretch my legs. I gazed up at the sky as the first stars came out to wink at me and my breath fogged up in a plume above me. The air was much colder here, and I guessed there would be a frost tonight judging by the glittering icy droplets already forming on the grass.

"What is this place?" Blake grunted.

"A stop over," Saint announced.

Blake wheeled around to face him with his teeth bared. "I'm not waiting another night to go after my dad." He squared up to Saint who didn't seem phased by his display of aggression and my heart tugged for my golden boy.

"It isn't up to you. We cannot make it to where he is today," Saint said, moving forward to press his forehead to Blake's. "Do you trust me, brother?"

Blake fell silent, his lips twitching angrily then he nodded stiffly.

"Then contain your rage, keep that fire for when it is time to aim it at my father," Saint said. "But it will not be tonight."

"When then?" Blake hissed.

"I'll explain that indoors," Saint replied, stepping away from him. "I will not have this conversation while Tatum is out here in the cold."

"I can handle a little frost, devil boy," I said, folding my arms and he walked straight past me to the car.

"I'm well aware of that, siren. But for my own peace of mind, I still insist that we move inside."

Saint really did have a mini Voldemort living in his heart, but there was definitely a cute little Weasley nestled in there too.

The boys grabbed everything from the car, not letting me take a single thing as we headed into the farmhouse and the heat of a fire washed over me.

We walked into a large lounge and me, Blake, Kyan and Nash piled onto the couch together as we warmed ourselves in front of the fire.

Saint moved to stand in front of it, clasping his hands behind his back like he was some royal prince about to make a speech. "This house is a three day trek from where my father is hiding." We all fell still as the weight of the task we had ahead of us hung in the air. "So Tatum, we need your mountaineering expertise. Please make a list of all the equipment we'll need to cross a mountain pass in sub-freezing temperatures. I have a man who will be able to get the supplies to us by morning."

"That's your plan?" I asked in surprise as the guys shared looks.

"Yes. I have studied satellite images and the only way in to the property that will likely be left unguarded is the area that backs onto the mountain. My father would never expect an attack from that direction, especially from someone like me."

"You're telling me you're not a mountain man who likes rolling in the mud and wearing flannel shirts?" Nash taunted and we all laughed while Saint rolled his eyes.

"The day I wear flannel will be a cold day in hell," Saint said and I swear he actually shuddered.

I'd read a book about a mountain man once though. He was a mafia prince who'd gone into hiding because of the things he'd found out about himself and he'd sure made being a mountain man sound hot. He'd found a girl up there on that mountain and had torn down heaven and earth to get revenge against the people who had hurt her. The sex had been pretty damn hot too. So maybe Saint could pull off the mountain man thing with the right bit of encouragement. If Nicoli could do it in Beautiful Savage, then why not my OCD criminal mastermind too?

Saint took out a notepad and pen from his jacket pocket and handed it to me. I started writing down what we'd need, my heart pounding at the prospect of going mountaineering. I hadn't been since my dad had taken me a week before I was enrolled at Everlake and I'd missed it fiercely. Just the thought of it made me feel closer to him for a moment and my heart squeezed with a tight ache at how much I missed him. There was no way I'd be letting anything happen to Blake's dad like it had to mine.

"So what happens when we get across the mountains and sneak in your dad's back door?" Kyan asked. "Are we going in guns a-blazin' or what?"

"No," Saint tsked. "It will be covert. We will locate Mr Bowman and extract him safely before we go after my father. Assuring he is alive and well is our priority."

Blake shifted in his seat. "If he's laid a hand on my dad, I'll make him fucking suffer. I'll peel him apart piece by piece," he snarled and I rested my hand on his thigh, squeezing reassuringly.

"Yes, well even if he is alive and well, we will ensure my father suffers regardless," Saint said without emotion.

Blake pushed out of his seat suddenly and marched out of the room, the door slamming shut behind him.

"*Saint*," Nash hissed. "Don't you have any fucking tact?"

"What did I say?" Saint asked with a frown and I got up, pouting at him before I followed Blake out of the room, leaving the others to explain it to him. He really was clueless sometimes.

"Blake?" I called as I moved through the entrance hall, but no answer came from anywhere in the house.

A repetitive thump, thump, thump carried from outside and I pushed the front door open, stepping onto the porch. The thumping continued along with angry grunts and I spotted him punching the side of the barn. My heart lurched and I ran down the steps, sprinting across the yard to my golden boy.

I came up behind him, wrapping my arms around his waist, trying to pull him back to make him stop.

"*Tatum*," he growled. "I don't need a fucking hug."

"Yes you do," I whispered, clutching onto him as he tried to push my hands off of his waist.

"I just need an outlet," he snapped. "Fuck Troy Memphis. Fuck him and his fucking empire. I'll have him at my feet in a pool of blood. I'll kill him for this," he swore, his voice full of vengeance and hate.

"We'll do it together," I promised and his shoulders sagged, his head hanging forward. "Just don't hurt yourself because of him. Please." I knew he had a destructive streak in him. This was how he coped with pain, by causing it to himself, to others. But I couldn't watch as he punished himself anymore.

"I can't lose, Dad," he rasped. "Not after Mom. I can't, Tatum, I just-"

"You won't," I swore, meaning it from the depths of my soul. I would bend the entire universe to ensure Blake's father was returned to his side. I wouldn't let him lose him like I'd lost mine. I would not see that fate come to reality.

The cold air made me shiver as I held onto Blake, the heat of his body calling to me like a furnace.

"C'mere," he murmured, taking my hand and pushing through the door to the barn.

We slipped inside and found the place full of sacks of some crop, stacked high around the wooden walls. It was dark, but there was a skylight in the roof that allowed the moonlight to spill inside. Without the wind biting at me, it wasn't too cold and I wasn't going anywhere until Blake felt ready to come back inside anyway.

He started climbing up the sacks towards the roof and I followed him, clambering up to where he laid down beneath the skylight. He tugged me to his side and tucked me under his arm, his muscles folding around me. I snuggled against him, gazing up at the sea of stars above and the half moon which glowed so bright it cast a halo around it in the sky.

"I've never been this far out in the mountains," Blake murmured. "Mom and Dad took me camping at Lake Kahuto in the summer when I was a kid, but that's about as close I ever got to roughing it. And we had blow-up camp beds, a TV and a barbeque, so it wasn't exactly the bare essentials."

I snorted. "Try going wild camping in winter in bear season."

"You're a fucking badass." He chuckled, kissing my hair as he pulled me closer.

"Yeah," I sang teasingly. "I've got my dad to thank for that."

"I wish I'd met him properly," Blake said gruffly and my heartbeat faltered for a whole eternity.

"Me too," I breathed as tears stung my eyes. I'd cried so much over him, and I'd promised I wouldn't do it again, knowing it did nothing but cause me pain. But with Blake, sometimes I felt like he could see that grief in me so clearly that I didn't want to hide it. We recognised that part of one another just like we recognised it in Nash. Loss was like the rain. Sometimes it poured for days, other times there was a drought full of nothing but sunlight. But it always came back. It was inevitable.

"You know you can talk to me about anything, Blake. If you're angry or hurt or you wanna vent, I'm always here," I said earnestly.

"I know," he sighed. "Sometimes I don't think...my head gets so fogged up with rage, it's all I can feel."

"I feel that way sometimes," I admitted. "When I think of my dad and how he died at Mortez's hands. I replay it in my head over and over until it burns."

He held me tighter and I knew he knew how that felt without him even having to say it.

"It's like if you replay it enough, you can change it," he said, his voice laced with grief. "Every moment that led up to it and all the choices that could have been made which would have changed everything."

"Yeah," I agreed in a choked voice.

"Sometimes it's like that's all that's left of her," he said in a low voice.

"Like those final days have wiped away everything good before it. But I feel guilty as hell thinking that because there was so much good."

"Tell me something good," I urged and he fell silent for a moment, the wind howling somewhere off in the mountains.

He ran his thumb over the bracelet on my wrist that had belonged to his mom and I could almost feel a connection to her through it for a second. Like I knew her. Just a little bit.

"We used to make pancakes together every Sunday," he said at last. "Dad would get out of bed late and the two of us would make a complete mess of the kitchen before he came downstairs. We'd make everyone's favourite pancakes, always the same ones. Mine were chocolate and banana and hers were…cherries and maple syrup."

I turned my head to look at him as he said that, but he kept his eyes on the sky, his dark green gaze reflecting the sparkling stars. "But you always have cherries and syrup."

His throat bobbed. "After she died, I started eating it every day to remind me of her. To have something physical right in front of me first thing in the morning that would make sure I never forgot her. People always say they won't forget the dead, but they do. They move on. They get past it. They don't want to face the pain because otherwise it'll never leave. But if the pain leaves, doesn't that mean they leave too?"

I blinked back tears, looking up at the sky. "I don't know," I whispered because I struggled with that too. I didn't want to let go because what if I was the only thing still keeping them alive? Dad, Jess. If I forgot them, who else would remember them? But holding onto the pain didn't bring them back. It only made me suffer.

I reached up to brush my fingers over the necklace around my throat, trying to reach for some feeling of Jess lingering on it.

"Do you think they're somewhere out there?" he asked. "Do you think they miss us too?"

A tear slid down my cheek as I nodded. "I think we have to believe that, we have to hope they do. Because the alternative is too awful. But either way…they'd want us to stop hurting for them. I know I'd want that if things were the other way around. But that doesn't mean we have to forget them."

"You're right," Blake said heavily.

"It would hurt your mom to see you in pain. Just like it hurts me when I see you hurt yourself." I drew his bruised knuckles to my mouth and kissed them gently, working my lips across each one.

He rolled toward me, pushing a lock of hair behind my ear as he gazed down at me. "I never wanna hurt you again, Cinders."

"So don't," I breathed and he leaned down to kiss me, his mouth moving firmly against mine and I felt the depth of his words within it. Blake Bowman had once been my broken, vengeful monster. He'd hunted me, caged me, wounded me. But every blow he'd struck had really been against himself. Now, I treasured the scars he'd left on me, because through making each other bleed, we'd found a way to heal, to cope. He wasn't my monster anymore. He was my golden boy, my beam of sunshine in the dark. He shone so brightly, sometimes it was hard to believe he held anything but light in his heart. But I knew better. I knew that even the sun had scars beneath its blinding exterior. And that didn't make it weak, in fact, it burned all the brighter for them.

Saint's man showed up before dawn with almost everything we needed. He'd managed to get hold of the camping and trekking gear as well as the clothes and boots we'd need and he'd brought the guns and weapons Saint had requested too. Unfortunately, he hadn't been able to get hold of the Kevlar vests though and of course, Saint had lost his shit over it. It had taken me twenty minutes to talk him out of destroying the guy's entire life for failing him and in the end he'd finally given in so that we could head off. I didn't have high hopes for the guy's future though.

None of us were pleased about having to head into Troy's home without the bulletproof vests, but we couldn't waste any more time while Blake's dad was in trouble, so we just had to hope that we wouldn't need them.

So when we set off in our hiking gear as the sky began to pale, our packs were full of everything we'd need for the trek even if they were a little light on body armour.

There was an old path that led us out to the mountain we needed to cross but we were soon climbing through rocky terrain, our breaths misting before us as we marched on resolutely, wanting to gain as much ground as possible. We only paused briefly to eat lunch and drink hot coffee Nash had put in a flask, all of us lined up on a fallen trunk as the cold air whistled through the trees around us.

The forest grew denser as we moved on and occasionally I'd check the GPS with Saint to make sure we were still on track. My guys followed me, trusting me to guide them and by the time night was falling, I'd led us into a sheltered ditch between two huge rock formations and started teaching them how to pitch a tent. Monroe was the only one of them who had any real experience camping, so he helped me teach the others.

Kyan crouched down beside me with the hammer, excited to beat the tent pegs into the ground as I worked to get it in place.

"You have to do it at an angle," I told him before he went Rambo on the peg I was positioning at the side of the tent, the elastic wrapped around the end of it.

"Why's that?" he asked.

"Because if it's straight, the tension of the elastic could pull it back out of the ground. This makes it more stable." I held out my hand to take the hammer from him, but he clutched it to his chest like it was his new favourite toy. I snorted, rolling my eyes at him. "Fine, just hammer it in this way." I showed him how to hold the peg and he nodded, taking it from me and bashing it into the ground before looking to me for approval like a murderous little puppy dog.

"Perfect. Now do the rest of them." I kissed his cheek and stood up, heading over to help Saint who was laying out the pegs on the ground, adjusting them so they sat in a straight line. *Real helpful.*

I poked him in the back. "Do you wanna help me collect some firewood?"

He turned to me, looking so out of place here in the wild that I had to swallow a laugh.

"Alright," he said stiffly, and I sensed something was off as I took his hand and led him into the trees beyond the camp.

"Ahh! A peg just popped out and hit me in the eye, Kyan!" Blake shouted from behind us. "Put it in sideways like Tatum showed you."

"That's what she said," Nash joked and Kyan roared a laugh as I looked to Saint with a grin, but tension was lining his brow.

"Are you okay?" I asked when we got out of earshot of the camp.

"Yes," he growled, looking at the ground. "What's suitable for burning?"

"The dry stuff. There's usually some under the pines or any kind of tree that doesn't drop its leaves." I led him over to one and started piling branches in my arms beneath an old conifer.

Saint crouched down to help, examining each branch critically before building a pile of the ones which passed his assessment. We started making a good hoard, the light of the moon bright enough that we didn't even need to use our flashlights.

"These aren't dry enough," Saint snarled suddenly, standing up and kicking his pile so they scattered everywhere. "I'll start again."

"They're fine," I insisted, but he moved to examine another small branch with narrowed eyes and I sighed, throwing an armful of sticks onto the ground.

"Saint, what's going on?" I marched toward him and he stood upright, brushing down his knees before looking to me with the Devil in his eyes.

His jaw ticked and I could sense he was hovering on the verge of losing control. I hurried closer, cupping his face in my hands to get him to focus on me.

"I'm not used to this," he rasped. "It is one thing to be surrounded by my own things while we're moving from place to place. I can create some semblance of routine. But tonight, I will be sleeping on a roll mat in a tent which is hardly bigger than a janitor's closet and I – I-"

I dropped to my knees beneath him, bowing my head, my breaths coming unsteadily as I hoped this was enough to help him regain his feeling of control. We needed Saint more than ever right now and I wasn't going to let him slip into the chaos inside him. I was going to keep him here, keep him sane.

"You can do this," I told him passionately. "You can do anything. You're Saint Memphis."

He fisted a hand in my hair with a low noise in his throat.

Laughter and whoops carried from the camp and I knew the guys were messing around which gave me an idea.

"You need to get our camp in order, Saint," I insisted. "We need a fire and food and that tent ready to be slept in before a frost starts setting in."

"Yes…" he said thoughtfully. "Order. That's what we need. You'd best collect the firewood then, siren. Stand up and finish the pile."

I got to my feet and moved to do as he said, gathering up branches and he started pointing out more for me to collect. When the pile was big enough, Saint scooped it up and jerked his head in an order for me to follow him.

We returned to the camp, finding the other guys at war with three large sticks they were wielding as swords.

"You have dishonoured me, sir," Blake said in a posh voice, waving his sword at Kyan who smacked his with the full force of his strength, making both sticks split in half.

"Ha!" Nash struck Kyan on the back with his stick before hitting Blake across the arm. "Victory is mine!"

Blake and Kyan rounded on Nash, sharing a look before diving at him and knocking him onto the ground, trying to wrestle the stick from his hand. It was so good to see a smile on Blake's face again that one immediately split across mine. I knew this was what he did; he buried his emotions deep when they got too much and painted on a happy face. And if it helped him then I was all for it. At least he wasn't punching things anymore. I just hoped he wouldn't ever do that again after our chat last night.

"What in the name of all that is fucking holy is going on?" Saint snapped, pointing at the tent which had half fallen down.

The guys broke apart, looking over at us like guilty kids caught by their parents.

"Well...we got busy building the toilet," Blake said innocently, pointing at a tree where a hole had been dug in the ground and a branch was sticking up beside it with a roll of toilet paper perched on top.

I started laughing and Saint shot me an admonishing glare.

"Clean this place up," Saint hissed, smacking my ass hard as he encouraged me towards the others. *Damn that stings so good.*

I jogged over to them with a mischievous grin as Blake and Kyan got to their feet. Monroe held his hand out to me to help him up and I grabbed onto it. He smirked, tugging hard and I fell down on top of him with a squeal instead. He kissed me shamelessly, squeezing my ass where Saint had just spanked me.

"You look so fucking hot in all this hiking gear," he growled against my lips. "Like some sort of sexy mountain ranger. Have you come to punish me for setting a fire blazing in your panties?"

"Nash and Tatum, *desist,*" Saint snapped, but Nash drove his tongue into my mouth defiantly and I grinned as I kissed him back just as fiercely. Saint needed to be in control, so I was more than happy to give him a reason to punish me.

"Up." Saint caught my hand, pulling me off of Monroe and eyeing my mouth with a hint of lust in his eyes. "Both of you." He kicked Nash without tearing his eyes from me. "You will both be punished for disobeying me."

"I'm not being spanked like Blake was though, man," Nash said, and I looked over at him, biting my lip on a smirk.

"Are you sure? I'd really like to see that," I said seductively.

"No," Saint clipped. "You will both help to get this camp set up then report to me for your punishment." He pointed us over to Kyan and Blake as they struggled to get the tent back up without direction.

"Can you help them with that while I start a fire?" I asked Nash as we jogged away from Saint.

"Sure thing, princess." He knocked his arm against mine and we shared a mischievous grin before he headed over to the guys to help.

I built a fire in record time, falling into the familiar rhythm of it as I thought of my dad and tried not to let the memories get coloured by grief. I wanted to smile when I remembered him, not cry. I needed the good to burn brighter than the bad, because the final night of his life wasn't going to ruin every happy thing I had to hold onto about him. With a bit of effort, I managed to keep the dark thoughts at bay and by the time the fire was lit and the flames thawed out my cold hands, I felt like I'd taken another small step toward processing his death.

This was the kind of thing I'd always enjoyed doing with him and I wanted to be able to keep doing it in the future, taking trips out into the wilderness and letting my memories of him and Jess warm my heart rather than allowing them to fade.

I got the gas cooker going next, heating the five bean chilli I'd made last night before threading some slices of bread onto a stick and holding it over the fire to toast them.

I plated up the food just as Kyan, Blake and Nash appeared carrying a huge log out of the woods to place in front of the fire. Saint took my hand, drawing me away from the food and sitting me down at the heart of the log before wrapping a blanket around my shoulders. The rest of the guys scooped up the plates of food and handed them out, sitting down either side of me so we were snuggled together as we ate. Well, me, Blake, Kyan and Nash ate anyway. When I looked over Kyan's lap I saw Saint sitting with his plastic plate of chilli and toast laying untouched on his knees, his hands balled at his sides. I passed my blanket to Blake and tossed my empty plate onto the ground, getting up and moving to sit beside Saint at the end of the log, determined to get him through this.

"It's alright," he gritted out, but it clearly wasn't so I scooped up a forkful of chilli and held it to his mouth.

His throat bobbed then he opened his mouth and I placed it between his lips. He chewed it slowly then swallowed.

"How's that?" I asked, a smile dancing around my mouth.

"Surprisingly good," he said.

"The fire makes the bread smoky, right?" I said and he nodded, opening his mouth for more and I snorted as I continued to feed him.

"Nash and Tatum, you can report for your punishment now," Saint decided when he finished the last mouthful of food.

"You're not gonna get me to do shit, Memphis," Nash said as he got up and stretched his arms above his head.

"If you refuse, I will have Kyan and Blake keep you outside the tent tonight while you listen to us fuck Tatum without you," Saint said simply and my lips popped open.

Blake and Kyan laughed like they weren't gonna fight Saint on that and I punched Saint in the arm.

"What if I don't consent?" I said and Saint grinned at me.

"Are you really going to say no, siren? I'll make sure all the attention is on you. No work. Nothing. We will make you come so many times that you are blinded for a full day afterward."

I burst out laughing but heat rose in my cheeks too because I knew he damn well meant it. "Well okay, I'll play along. But I want the same punishment as Nash." I stood up, figuring Monroe might get off lighter if he only had to do what Saint wanted me to. Unless Saint wanted me to suck his cock, in which case, Nash was fucked.

"Are you sure, Tatum?" Saint purred darkly, his eyes glittering with amusement.

"Yep," I said, moving to stand at Monroe's side in unity.

"This is gonna be good," Kyan said with a savage grin.

"I think we'll have a little competition then," Saint mused, getting to his feet. "Move to the other side of the fire and turn around."

I glanced at Nash and we did as he said, standing with our backs to the flames opposite the others.

There was some whispering then the crunching of footsteps as they moved around the camp and I felt the three of them coming up behind us a minute later. Being stalked by the Night Keepers set my pulse pounding and I was vividly reminded of the way they'd held court as kings of Everlake Prep, punishing those who deserved their wrath. Monsters born to devour monsters.

Saint's hand ran down my spine in a fluid motion, applying pressure to make me bend over half way. Kyan shoved Monroe over less seductively and rammed his crotch against his ass, dry humping him and making Nash curse.

"Take it like a good little slut," Kyan joked and Monroe moved to stand up, but Blake shoved him down by the shoulders.

Kyan stepped away, laughing obnoxiously and adrenaline injected into my blood from that all-too-familiar sound. It always preceded him being an evil bastard.

Saint's hand slid around my waist, unbuttoning my pants and shimmying them down with my panties to expose my ass. I bit my lip on a gasp, not wanting him to know I was fazed. I glanced over as Nash cursed, finding Kyan doing the same to him and wondering what the hell they had planned.

"You guys are fucked up, you know that right?" Monroe growled.

"You're just as fucked in the head, Nash," Blake said, a grin in his voice. "You just prefer being on the side where the power lies."

"The game is this," Saint announced sharply to get everyone's attention. "We will place pinecones between your ass cheeks and the first one of you to drop one loses."

"Hang on, she's got a lot more cheek to hold on with," Nash complained and I burst out laughing.

"You've got two slabs of muscle for ass cheeks so I dunno what you're complaining about, Nash," I tossed back and he chuckled. "What's the prize for winning?"

"Loser goes down on the winner," Saint said without hesitation. "And as a sweetener for you, siren, if you win the rest of us will take turns going down on you too."

"Err, fuck yes," I agreed instantly. "You're going down, Nash. Literally."

Monroe barked a laugh, looking pretty excited about the prospect of winning now too. "Alright, game on," he said.

Saint placed his hand on my lower back, parting my cheeks with his fingers and positioning a pinecone at the top. "You've got this, Tatum," he said seriously which just made it all the more funny.

"Hey, that's favouritism," Nash growled competitively and I snorted. "You've got the King of OCD putting your cones in, you're gonna have an advantage."

"Don't worry, brother, I'll get yours in nice and deep," Kyan promised and Nash swore loudly as he shoved one between his cheeks.

I started laughing, losing it as Saint place another one between my butt cheeks. The prickly little thing was uncomfortable as shit, but I still planned on winning this game.

"Stop laughing, you'll drop them," Saint hissed, spanking the side of my thigh and I swallowed a moan as the pain flickered through my flesh and turned to pleasure. Was putting pinecones between your ass cheeks and being spanked by the Devil a kink? Because if it was, it was definitely one of mine. I really was as messed up as these beasts.

"How many has she got in now?" Nash asked.

"Five," Saint announced as he slotted another one in place and the pinch of pain made me shift from one foot to the other.

"Ha, Nash's got six," Blake announced.

"Hurry up Saint," I encouraged and he chuckled.

"Enjoying this, aren't you?" he taunted then added another. "Alright, that's enough, let them stand with their asses to the heat of the fire and see how long they can last without dropping one."

Saint moved away and the fire instantly washed over my exposed ass, making my skin start to tingle.

"Why's this turning me on?" Blake muttered to himself.

"Because everything turns you on when it comes to Tatum," Saint said simply.

"Oh yeah," Blake said with a snort.

"Jesus that fire is fucking hot," Monroe hissed.

"That's kinda the way of fires," Kyan taunted. "Oh by the way Saint, you see that nice juicy left ass cheek of Tatum's?"

"Mmm?" Saint questioned suspiciously.

"We've decided that's where she'll be getting her squid tattoo," Kyan said and I held back a snigger.

"That had better be a joke," Saint said icily.

"It's not," I played along. "I just feel like it's so personal to me and I want its meaning branded on me forever."

"Which is?" Saint hissed.

"You know what it is," Kyan laughed lightly. "Quit playing that game, man."

"I have no idea what it means," Saint snapped. "And I really think it's time you told me."

"It's what you think it is when you don't overthink it," Blake said. "Took me a while, but I got it now."

"You had better be joking, Bowman. I refuse to be the only one who doesn't understand it!" Saint balked.

"Saint's incapable of overthinking it," Nash tossed in.

My ass was getting seriously toasty and the pinecones were hurting like a bitch, but antagonising Saint was a good distraction. "I think once I have the tattoo it will make more sense to you."

"If Kyan marks your body with a squid, I will personally escort you to have it removed," Saint said sharply.

"I think you need to just embrace the squid, bro," Blake said. "It's much easier that way."

A pap sounded as a pinecone hit the ground and Nash groaned. "Fuck."

"Tatum wins!" Kyan crowed as Monroe shook out his butt crack ungracefully and I reached around, trying to rid myself of the cones with one percent more dignity. "I've got you, baby." Kyan's rough hands slid over my ass and he took out all the cones carefully. It was weirdly sweet before he leaned down to bite my left ass cheek hard.

"Motherfucker!" I gasped, standing upright and he yanked my panties and jeans up at the same time, grinning at me.

"Just so we remember where to put the squid," he purred into my ear.

I took hold of his arm, yanking his sleeve up and sinking my teeth into the squid inked on his flesh until he groaned. "Just so we remember where yours is, *baby*," I taunted then slipped away from him and kicked my shoes off before crawling into the tent. I had a prize to claim after all.

"Don't get too excited, siren," Saint called after me before I could strip off and lay back to await my first prize. "You're still undergoing your punishment. So you can spend the night dreaming about which of us will make you come the hardest in the morning. Until then, your panties are staying precisely where they are."

My lips parted in outrage and I was about to argue when Blake leaned down to speak into my ear. "Think about how hot you'll be for it after all of that anticipation," he purred. "And how well you'll sleep tonight knowing you'll wake up to one of us eating you out for breakfast."

I bit my lip and shrugged. That did sound like a pretty heavenly way to wake up after all.

My boys piled in after me and though it was made for six people, it was still a bit of a squeeze considering four of those people were built like shit brick houses.

They'd unzipped all of the sleeping bags and laid them out across the roll mats like one large bed and I wriggled out of my clothes down to my underwear before slipping under the covers. With a few grunts, accidental kicks and growls of frustration, the boys managed to strip off too and join me under the covers. Blake made it onto my right first and Kyan made it to my left, pressing close to me so I was pinned between two walls of warm muscle.

It was fucking heaven.

Saint made sure the tent was zipped up before lying down beside Kyan and taking up his Dracula stance on his back, closing his eyes, a crease between his brows.

"Tell us one of Poe's poems, Saint," I urged, sure he was still struggling with this situation. "It's almost midnight." I had no idea what the time was actually, but it was important he believed that right now.

He took a slow breath and recited a piece of a poem I'd heard him read before which made my heart fill with all the beauty and wonder of the world. "Thou wast all that to me, love, for which my soul did pine. A green isle in the sea, love, a fountain and a shrine. All wreathed with fairy fruits and flowers, and all the flowers were mine."

CHAPTER FORTY TWO

Hiking through the freezing forest between snow-capped peaks and towering pines was somehow liberating after spending so many months trapped in isolation one way or another. We'd had a lot more freedom to move around at Everlake Prep than most people in the world enjoyed, but just knowing I'd been confined within the walls of the school there had felt like being incarcerated.

This out here was pure freedom, nothing but us and the wilderness for miles on end, open skies above us and picturesque landscape all around.

And best of all, out here the rich boys didn't have the advantage. Tatum was the one with the knowledge of how best to traverse this landscape and I'd at least been camping several times in my previous life, so I knew the basics.

The others, not so much. I'd let Saint struggle with tent pegs for a full fifteen minutes before taking pity on him last night. It was too damn funny to resist the urge to video it though and I currently had a shiny new screensaver of his furious face when he'd caught me recording him.

It wasn't easy going by any means, but we'd made good progress, closing in on the fancy ass winter cabin Troy kept hidden away up here.

Tonight was the last night that we were going to have to spend out here though and when we woke tomorrow we'd be closing in on our destination, ready to end this. I'd been carrying this vendetta on my shoulders for far too long and it was beyond time I saw the man who had killed my family pay the price for his crimes.

"I think we'll be able to see it once we crest this ridge," Saint said as he strode up the trail behind me. Though trail wasn't entirely accurate as there certainly wasn't any real path here, just the odd track left by animals.

"You said that at the last ridge," I pointed out and he grimaced at that mistake.

"Yes. Well, it should be no surprise that I am not suited to mountaineering. But I recognise this view. It is very similar to the one you can see from the cabin and I have checked the GPS so this time I am almost certain." Saint scowled at the trees like he was daring them to disagree.

"Almost?" I teased and he ground his teeth as he stalked ahead, clearly needing to find out if he was right or not for himself.

"Tease," Tatum mocked as she appeared beside me, slipping out of the trees silently, like she'd been born to do it. She was like some little forest nymph at one with nature and I was loving getting a chance to see this side of her.

"He makes it too easy," I replied with a shrug.

The sun was low in the sky and we needed to make camp soon or we'd be stuck out here in the dark, scrambling to put everything together. I just hoped Saint was right about us seeing the damn cabin soon because knowing him, he'd insist we keep walking until we did.

"Ca-caw!" Blake's voice came from above us and I looked up to find him grinning down from the branch of a tree. The moment my gaze met his, he threw a pinecone straight into my face and I cursed him as I scooped it from the ground to return fire.

Tatum squealed as she ran for cover behind Kyan who whipped her off of her feet and threw her over his shoulder then ran on up the hill. "I'll save you, baby!"

Blake scrambled back out of the tree while I launched more pinecones at his ass and he cursed me as I took off after the others before he could make it to the ground.

We ran between the trees, launching more missiles at each other and laughing until we came up on a clearing at the top of the ridge where Saint stood smiling triumphantly.

"I see it," he announced, ignoring our game as Kyan set Tatum down on her feet and kissed her like it was the end of some movie from the fifties, dipping her low and hooking her leg into his grasp.

It was hard to make out in the dim light, but in the distance, I could just see an immense stone…castle. It was at least three floors high with smoke coiling from several chimneys. There was a dusting of snow on the roof of it and – *are those freaking turrets??* The thing looked like it had been built to look like Henry the Eighth's winter retreat and in no way resembled a damn cabin.

"I was imagining some little cosy cabin," I muttered, wondering why on earth I hadn't realised Troy Memphis would have built himself a freaking luxury escape out here.

"That was an absurd notion," Saint scoffed. "Though it looks like he's had an extension added since the last time I was here a few years ago, so it's a little bigger than I expected too."

"You called it a cabin!" I accused.

"Clearly that is just a mocking name my family uses for it. You can't seriously have expected to find Troy Memphis vacationing out here in some filthy shack, can you?" Saint looked at me like I was the one who needed his head checked and I just kind of stared back.

"Please tell me I'm not the only one who thinks this is fucking ridiculous?" I implored and Blake laughed.

"Nah, man, it's not insane. It's Troy Memphis. He's like Saint on steroids with a god complex. Nothing he does should surprise you," he said.

"Wait a minute, are you trying to say Saint doesn't have a god complex?" Tatum scoffed in disbelief and Kyan roared a laugh. "He literally set himself up to live in a church."

"Not to mention the fact that you enjoy worshipping me on your knees, siren," Saint teased, looking nowhere near embarrassed by the accusation.

I shook my head at him and focused on the 'cabin' once more. It was still a good distance away, but at least now we knew we hadn't fucked up and gotten ourselves lost out here.

The others all dropped their packs and started setting up the tent in the trees, but I found myself just standing there, staring across the forest that filled the valley and wondering if my fate awaited me beyond it.

I'd given up everything I'd ever been to get here. I'd sacrificed all I had left of myself after my family was torn from me that night. Sometimes I couldn't even remember the boy I'd been before my brother and mom were stolen from me, and the knowledge of that cut me deeply, because if he was gone then that was the last piece of them destroyed too.

Would killing Troy Memphis offer me a reprieve from all of this pain at last? Would I be free of it? Or was I always going to hurt like this? Would the sting of the injustice he'd served up to my family always be there? Was there any true hope of me making peace with this?

A hand slipped into mine and I looked down at Tatum as she stood there with the fading light reflecting off of her golden hair.

"Tomorrow we put our ghosts to rest," she said, knowing what I was thinking about without even having to ask. "We face the Devil and send him back to hell with our demons in tow. We need to let it go then, Nash. All of it."

"What if it isn't enough?" I murmured, my brow furrowing.

"It won't be," she replied, surprising me. "How could it be? Killing Mortez may have helped pay for my dad's death, but it didn't heal my wounds. Vengeance won't bring the people we love back to us. Our families are a piece of our souls which will always be missing. But they're not lost. They're here with us." She placed her hand over my heart. "They'd want us to find happiness. To live and remember them, but not to use them as an excuse to keep punishing ourselves. We let our anger die with the people who are responsible for the pain of their deaths. Then we focus on the love we had for them and they had for us. That's how we move on. By making peace with the way they were taken and holding on tight to the best memories we have of them."

"Tell me one," I prompted, and she hesitated a moment as she thought on that.

"When we were kids, this one time, Jess and I were camping with our dad and we played hide and seek with him. But he couldn't find us. We'd managed to wedge ourselves into the hollow of a tree and we must have stayed in there, silently giggling for half an hour or more. Finally, he started yelling for us with this fear in his voice, telling us the game was over and that he really needed us to let him know that we were okay. So we burst out and ran to him, finding him wild-eyed and worried, but the moment he spotted us his face split into the biggest smile you've ever seen. He wrapped us in his arms and squeezed us so tight that we couldn't breathe. I asked him what would have happened if we hadn't come out. Would he have given up on us and just gone home alone? And he told us that we were the only things in his life that truly mattered. That he would have hunted night and day for the rest of his life for us and never given up. I felt so loved when he told us that." Tears welled in her eyes, but she blinked them back and I tightened my hold on her hand. "Now you tell me one."

I hesitated for longer than she had and with a jolt, I realised that was because I never really let myself linger on my memories of my family. But that was making them fade and I couldn't bear the thought of that. I refused to allow it to happen. So I closed my eyes and submerged myself in a memory of Christmas Day, the scent of Mom making dinner in the air while me and Michael opened presents.

"Every Christmas, my mom would go all out with the dinner," I said with a smile. "She'd buy everything, even the stuff none of us liked and would slave away in the kitchen for hours - but she couldn't cook for shit." I laughed and Tatum smiled too. "Me and Michael would eat the lot anyway, scrape our plates and hide our grimaces while we crunched on burnt vegetables and devoured salty gravy. I kinda love the taste of badly cooked food because of those days. She'd ask us if we were enjoying it and we'd tell her it was amazing, and she'd smile because she knew damn well it was awful. But none of us would crack, keeping up the pretence of a perfect Christmas because it was our version of perfect and that was all we wanted. Then we'd crash out in front of the TV together and eat chocolate until we wanted to puke. We fell asleep like that every year, all of us together with Christmas movies playing on repeat."

"I can burn a Christmas dinner for you this year if you want to keep the tradition going?" Tatum offered as she reached up to cup my cheek in her hand and I smiled.

"Yeah. I think I'd like that. Saint probably won't though."

"I can handle him," she said, quirking a grin at me and I snorted because I knew damn well she could, even though I hadn't fully figured out how yet.

Tatum tugged on my hand and I let her lead me over to the others who were almost done with setting up the tent.

"Good boys!" Tatum said, praising them like they were dogs and clapping her hands in an over the top way.

"This shit is harder than it looks," Blake muttered as Kyan started rolling out sleeping bags inside the canvas space.

"Sure it is," she teased and Blake lunged at her with a playful growl.

Tatum ran for it, using me as a human shield while Saint rolled his eyes at us and started grabbing out food.

"Help me catch her, Nash," Blake urged as Tatum held onto me, making me move with her and keeping me between them. "Then we can pin her down and have our wicked way with her."

"Oh, is that the deal?" I asked, whipping around and catching Tatum by the waist.

"No!" she laughed. "I never agreed to that!"

"Come on, siren, we all know you can't resist us for long," Saint said, matter of fact, like he knew Tatum's libido better than she did.

Tatum ran past him, snatching one of the packets of dehydrated food and a bowl from his hands before hooking a bottle of water from Kyan's open pack which was sitting at the foot of a tree. Then she leapt up and managed to scramble into the branches above our heads before making herself comfortable sitting back against the trunk and smirking at us.

"Are you going to hide up there, princess?" I called as I looked up at her.

"I think I have to if I wanna protect my virtue long enough for me to eat," she replied with a laugh as she started making her food up in the bowl.

I chuckled and turned away to find her a spoon before tossing it up to her in her perch.

"I think we should forgo the fire tonight," Saint said as I took a seat on the ground beside him where he'd sat his ass on a fallen tree trunk. Far be it from Saint Memphis to ever sit in the dirt of course. "We don't want to risk the smoke being seen."

I looked over my shoulder in the direction of the monstrosity Troy Memphis called a winter getaway home even though I couldn't see it from this position.

"I guess so. But it'll be cold," I pointed out unnecessarily.

"We could gather the wood in case we get desperate enough to risk it," he said slowly. "But I think we can make do with body heat tonight."

A twitch of his lips was the only indication I got of his thoughts for how we could best make use of said body heat and I chuckled as I ate my food, having plenty of ideas of my own.

"It's hard to say exactly how things will go tomorrow," Saint said lightly. "And it may well be that we don't get much choice in how the events unravel. But if it comes down to a decision, would you like to be the one to finish my father?"

I raised my eyebrows at him discussing this so casually and tossed my now empty bowl down before us.

"Are you sure you don't need to do it?" I asked him. "To take back control and all that?"

Saint shook his head with that cunning little smile on his face. "I'll be happy just knowing he's gone. Besides, there would be a sense of poetic justice to it being you, Nash. You epitomise everything he thinks he is superior to. Your lack of good breeding, of money, the very fact that someone like you could be the end of him would never even cross his mind. And I think I'd quite enjoy the look on his face when it came to fruition."

"Ah, you want the token poor boy to do it and rub salt into the wound?" I joked.

"Don't take offence," he replied, catching my gaze and holding it. "I see plainly enough your value and I can assure you that I am well aware that money and position have absolutely nothing to do with the quality of a man's character. You are my brother. And yes, if you do it, it will cast an extra blow to him as we shatter his pride along with ending his life, but I also think you need this more than I do. He may have never offered me love, but he stole it from you in the most brutal of ways. So if you wish to be the one to see him ended-"

"Yeah," I agreed. "I think I'd like that. But when all is said and done, all I really want is to see him lying dead before me. If the chips don't fall in my favour for the task, then I'm not going to ask anyone to hold back on my account."

"Either way," Saint said. "Let's hope that tomorrow is the last sunrise that bastard ever lives to see."

"Agreed," Kyan said loudly as he finished laying out the bed inside the tent and came to grab his own food.

I started cleaning everything up as the light seeped from the sky, not wanting to be scrambling about for it in the dark.

The distant howl of a wolf caught my ear and I looked around with a shiver running down my spine.

Blake helped me to clean everything the way Tatum had taught us to and we walked out into the trees to rinse out the food bowls so that there weren't any smells lingering to attract a hungry beast in the night.

By the time we returned to everyone else, Saint was already inside the tent and Tatum and Kyan were packing the last things away.

The temperature was dropping with the setting sun and I noticed Tatum shivering as I closed in on her.

"Come on, princess," I said, winding an arm around her waist and drawing her towards the tent. "Let's get you in to the warm."

Blake and Kyan followed us into the fancy ass tent that Saint had bought and the moment Kyan zipped the thing closed, the wind was cut off, making us all feel much warmer.

Saint was sitting up on the heaped bedding, the glow of his cell phone lighting his face and bare chest as he checked the GPS for the hundredth time. He was damn good at hiding it, but I could recognise the signs that gave away his stress now, so I could see it in the tension of his posture.

We all kicked our boots off before moving closer onto the bedding and Blake switched on the little camp light which hung overhead, casting us all in a slightly red glow as the light reflected off of the canvas.

Tatum unzipped her coat, tossing it aside before peeling off her sweater too. Next she dropped her pants and kicked them away alongside her socks before taking her shirt off and moving towards Saint in a set of matching red underwear.

She lowered down to her knees before him and he slowly moved his phone aside, switching it off as he looked at her.

I exchanged a glance with the others and Kyan chuckled as he unbuckled his jeans and dropped them before ripping his shirt off so that he was left in his boxers. He moved to kneel beside Tatum, looking a lot less submissive even while he played the part and he smirked at Saint as he looked at him.

"Come on then, master," Kyan taunted. "Take control of us. You know it'll help with those Daddy issues that are plaguing you."

"Are we seriously doing this?" I asked, looking at Blake with a brow arched. "Just giving in to the will of the Devil?"

"I dunno about you, dude. But if the Devil is gonna command I make Tatum come, then I think I'm gonna have to go join the dark side." Blake grinned at me as he quickly stripped too and I rolled my eyes.

Tatum turned to look at me over her shoulder as Blake kneeled on her other side and my gaze slid over her near naked body in the red light as she bit her lip seductively.

"You're not playing fair," I groaned, my self-control losing a battle against my pride. We all knew I wouldn't just stand here and get left out, but fuck if I was going to kneel in front of that asshole.

Saint smirked at me over Tatum's head as he seemed to realise what my objections were to this and he jerked his chin my way, commanding her to move.

"Let's see if *you* can bring him to his knees then, siren," he suggested and my pulse picked up as her eyes lit with that challenge.

I stayed where I was, standing beside the large heap of sleeping bags as she crawled towards me and the others watched her with hungry eyes.

Her hands landed on my knees and I looked down at her as she ran them up my thighs until she found the solid ridge of my cock through my jeans. I groaned as she unzipped my fly, reaching out to run my fingers over her hair.

"Hands behind your head, Nash. But take your shirt off first," Saint commanded and Tatum actually fucking stopped what she was doing as she waited for me to comply.

I grunted something that may have included an insult for our evil overlord then fell into line like a good boy, yanked my shirt and sweater off and laced my hands together behind my head.

The moment I'd done it, Tatum worked my fly lower, pulling my boxers down too and freeing my cock with a sultry gasp that made me ache.

"Slowly," Saint said, and I almost groaned again as she followed his order to the letter, taking her sweet time wrapping the base of my shaft in her hand before running her tongue up the underside of it.

She continued to lick and tease me, tasting the bead of moisture that formed on the head of my dick, but not actually closing her lips around me until Saint commanded it.

"Now," he growled and her mouth closed over the head of my cock before she slid me right to the back of her throat, making me growl with the desire to grip her head between my hands. But I didn't, I kept to the game and my hands remained locked behind my head as instructed.

It was equally infuriating and exhilarating, never knowing what moment he'd pick to interrupt us or change what she was doing, and my muscles bunched with tension as I fought to keep my hands locked behind my head.

When I was certain I was about to come between those perfect lips of hers, he suddenly commanded her to stop and I couldn't help but lurch forward a step, reaching out and trying to stop her from retreating as she sat back onto her feet.

"If you won't kneel for me, Nash, maybe you'll do it for your queen?" Saint suggested and I gave up any pretence of fighting this as I shoved my jeans the rest of the way off and stalked her back onto the bed.

"Yes," I agreed. "For her."

Tatum took my hand and I let her draw me down as she smiled at me, pulling me into the middle of this little harem she'd claimed for herself as the others drew closer instinctively.

I caught hold of her and dragged her into my lap as I kissed those sinful lips and her hands roamed down my chest with the most delicious slowness.

I cupped her ass, not really listening as Saint started telling the others what to do, but Blake's hands brushed against mine as he took the job of peeling Tatum's panties off, drawing her up onto her knees to do it.

"I said, on your back, Nash," Saint growled.

I didn't move but Kyan suddenly grabbed my shoulders and forced me to lay down beneath Tatum and I would have cursed him for it if I hadn't been caught up in the taste of her lips against mine.

"If you won't listen, you'll have to be punished," Saint warned, sounding pleased about having an excuse for that, but if he seriously thought I'd let him spank me he had another thing coming. "Sit on his face, siren, take from him, don't give."

Kyan seemed to think he was the harbinger of Saint's commands because he instantly grabbed hold of Tatum and lifted her from my lap, moving her to kneel over my face instead. But if Saint really thought it was a punishment for me to get to devour her sweet pussy then he had me all wrong.

Tatum gasped as I gripped her ass and lowered her down onto my mouth, running my tongue up her centre and finding her clit with ease. I kept my eyes open, looking up at her as she pawed at her breasts and moaned for me, my tongue moving back and forth as I tasted her desire and sought out her pleasure.

Kyan moved in front of her, teasing her breasts free of her bra while leaving it on her so that the folded down cups pushed them up into prime position for his mouth and she moaned even louder as we worked on her together.

I kept my grip on her ass as I rocked her against me even more firmly, encouraging her to ride my face as I fucked her with my tongue, licking and devouring like I was starving for every taste.

Blake moved to kneel behind her, kissing her neck and reaching around to toy with the nipple which wasn't in Kyan's mouth as she moaned and fell apart between us.

My cock was straining with a desperate need and the louder she moaned, the harder I chased down her release.

"Open wide, siren," Saint commanded and her moans were muffled as Kyan stood in front of her, releasing his hard cock and driving it between her lips.

He gripped her hair, fucking her mouth as she dug her fingernails into his ass and dared him to do his worst, taking his cock to the back of her throat and moaning for more. And if our girl needed more then I'd happily give it to her.

I rocked her against my face again and pushed my tongue inside her sweet pussy, lapping and tasting her before returning to her clit and sucking hard.

I felt her come as she screamed around Kyan's cock and she ground down against my mouth as she rode it out.

"Take her first, Blake," Saint growled and she was suddenly lifted from my face, giving me a view of him as he watched us, his cock so hard in his pants that I could see the full outline of it straining for release. But the bastard was denying himself, watching the show and no doubt planning on stepping in at the last minute like the crescendo of this song we were writing. "On her hands and knees. Right where you are."

My eyes widened as Blake laughed, placing Tatum down so that her knees were either side of my hips and her hands landed by my ears.

She gave me a heady look as she was repositioned over me and I leaned up to kiss her as Kyan dropped down to kneel behind my head.

As Blake drove his dick into her, she cried out, biting my lip and making me groan before Kyan took hold of her hair and tugged her head back, breaking our kiss and giving her his cock again.

I dropped back down flat, looking up at the show as her tits bounced above me while Blake and Kyan spit roasted her right on top of me. Maybe I should have been pissed, but the sounds escaping her made that impossible as her ecstasy laced moans filled the air.

I arched up to suck on her nipple, my hand reaching down and finding her clit too, giving it some much needed attention while Blake fucked her hard and fast.

Saint got to his feet, moving to stand beside us, reaching out to caress her before striking his hand down on her ass. She came harder that time, her whole body tensing as Blake slammed into her harder and harder before finally coming too with a low groan.

Kyan being the asshole he was didn't give her a minute to catch her breath, still driving his cock between her lips even as Blake pulled out. I slid my fingers around her slick pussy, stroking gently and massaging her clit again.

"Enough, Kyan," Saint barked and Kyan cursed him as he withdrew his cock from Tatum's swollen lips, leaning down to kiss her roughly instead, his hand closing around her throat and making her moan again.

Saint moved behind Tatum, encouraging her to reposition so that she was straddling me as he drew her hair back behind her ear and ran his mouth up her neck.

"Do you want more?" he purred, holding onto her hips so that she couldn't sink down onto me.

"Yes," she gasped, her eyes on mine and full of need.

"Say it clearly," he commanded, and she bit her lip.

"I want Nash to fuck me until I can't breathe," she said huskily as Saint unhooked her bra and tossed it aside.

"And?" he prompted.

"And I want you in my ass," she added, her eyes flicking left and right to the other two while Saint tried to contain his grin. "And I want to satisfy Kyan and Blake again too. All of you. Together."

"Good girl," Saint growled, pressing her down to take my cock and I fisted the base of my shaft to position it for her as he moved away to find some lube.

Blake and Kyan drew in on either side of us, reaching for her breasts and kissing her neck while I teased her with my cock, rubbing the head back and forth along her entrance, rotating it against her clit and making her pant.

When she finally couldn't take any more, she caught my wrist to stop me and sank down onto my dick with a moan of pleasure.

Her fingernails bit into my chest as she started to ride me and I thrust my hips up to meet her, driving my cock in deep and loving the way it made her gasp every time I hit the right spot inside her.

Kyan and Blake continued to kiss and touch her, worshipping her like she deserved, and I loved seeing her like that, surrounded by us and overwhelmed with pleasure.

Saint returned, his pants finally gone as he slicked his hard cock with lube before moving behind her to give her what she'd asked for.

Tatum leaned down, kissing me possessively as he moved his dick between her cheeks, pushing into her with aching slowness and making her cry out as she adjusted to the fullness of the two of us inside her at once.

I could feel him too, the thin flesh dividing our bodies not disguising a thing, yet somehow I liked that, knowing that we were giving her so much at once, working together just for her.

"Look at you, baby," Kyan growled as he took in the sight of us. "You're so fucking perfect."

"*This* is perfect," she panted. "All of us."

Before any of us could reply to that, she pushed herself up and Saint leaned back to let her. Blake and Kyan moved either side of her once more and she moaned as she took each of their cocks in her hands and they began kissing her again, teasing her nipples and making her throw her head back in pleasure.

I started to move faster, finding the perfect rhythm with Saint to make her scream for us while Blake rubbed her clit and Kyan wrapped a hand around her throat, squeezing just enough to make her gasp.

We became this living, breathing embodiment of pleasure as we found a natural rhythm to each other's movements, each of us working to destroy our girl while she brought us to ruin in return.

No matter how much we gave, she just kept demanding more and soon I was fucking her deep and hard while she screamed an orgasm and her pussy clamped so tight I had no choice but to follow her into it.

Saint pounded into her a few more times before snarling like a beast and thrusting in deep as he finished and Blake groaned as he came too, capturing her lips in a lingering kiss while she rode out her orgasm.

Kyan laughed like a triumphant douchebag as he snatched her out from between the lot of us and placed her down on the bed to our right. He tossed her leg over his shoulder and drove his cock into her with one hard thrust that made her cry out again.

He was an animal like always as he claimed her roughly, slamming into her faster and faster until he was spanking her ass hard enough to leave a handprint and the two of them were coming loudly while the rest of us just watched.

Kyan kissed her almost sweetly as he took her leg from his shoulder and she smiled in that sexy, satiated way I fucking loved as she looked over to the rest of us too.

He rolled off of her and we all moved together, pulling bedding in around us as each of us found a way to touch her in our tangle of limbs. We drifted off beneath the stars, safe in each other's company for the final time, because I got the feeling that tomorrow was going to be the end in so many ways. I refused to believe we wouldn't survive it, but I knew everything would change because of it. And though I was more determined than I'd ever been to make certain those changes were for the best, it was hard to fully believe that there wouldn't be at least a little bad.

CHAPTER FORTY THREE

I groaned as I woke up, the obnoxious sounds of birdsong ringing out all around us and something hard driving into my ribs.

"I swear, if that's your dick, Kyan, I'm gonna punch it," I mumbled as I pushed myself up and found that it had actually been Nash's elbow. *Cock crisis averted.*

I snorted at my own internal joke and swiped a hand over my face as I looked around at the sleeping Night Keepers and our girl. My eyebrows went up as I found Saint still asleep in the centre of the group. Tatum had her head laid on his chest and his arm was curled around her as he held her close. I wasn't sure I'd ever woken up before him until this moment and he looked weirdly peaceful in sleep, despite the fact that he'd told me more than once that his demons haunted him most during the night. I was certain he hadn't been lying about that. Which left only one possibility for his current contentment and that was the girl wrapped tight in his arms.

I wondered if she even knew how much we'd all needed her. Probably not, because we hadn't realised it either, but now that she was here, rooted so deeply into our lives that I knew we'd never be able to untangle her again, I couldn't help but see it all the time. Our damage had been a potent, violent thing and though she clearly couldn't just come along and wave a magic wand to fix us, she'd given us something so much better than that. A future with light in it. Something to fight for. A love we couldn't have ever imagined and a bond we couldn't live without.

I made a move to get up, my knee knocking against Kyan's leg and he growled as he rolled over. "No, Davie. If you don't stroke its tentacles just right, that squid is gonna slither right up your ass and give you an enema to boast to your grandma about."

I had been going to let Saint sleep longer while I made a start on packing up our shit, but of course the meticulous bastard had set an alarm and bang on time, Claire De Lune by Debussy filled the tent, pouring from his cellphone. He'd brought enough charger packs to make sure the thing didn't die on him during our trek through the wilderness so I shouldn't have been surprised, but I probably should have found his phone and switched the damn thing off the moment I woke. That might have set him off though, so despite the fact that it was going to ruin his cute ass little snuggle with Tatum, I didn't make any attempt to grab it now.

Saint's eyes opened and Tatum groaned as she buried her face against his chest, trying to hide from the day.

"This is it then," Nash muttered as he pushed himself to sit up too.

"By nightfall, my father will be dead and yours will be safe," Saint said, looking me straight in the eye to show he truly believed that and I nodded.

"I hope so," I said, pinching the bridge of my nose as I forced my head into game mode.

I'd been tossing and turning all night worrying about what was happening to my dad, but now I just needed to focus. Freaking out about the situation wouldn't help him and it could just fuck everything up.

Warm hands slid around my neck as Tatum crawled into my lap and I opened my eyes to find her there, her hair all tousled from sleep and a grey t-shirt covering her slim frame which I was pretty sure belonged to Kyan.

"This is going to work," she swore with such certainty in her voice that I couldn't help but believe her.

"It's going to work," I agreed firmly, leaning forward to kiss her and seal that promise because she was right. It would work. I refused to consider any other outcome. I was born a winner and I wasn't going to start losing today.

Despite us seeing Troy's winter home before we camped last night, it had still taken us the full day to trek down into the valley and through the forest to reach it.

It had started to snow around midday and had slowly begun to settle all around us so that by now it was several inches deep. We'd stashed our camping equipment in the trees before closing in on the house and as we stood looking at it from the edge of the forest, we had nothing on us but our phones and weapons as we lurked in the dark.

"I still believe the wine cellar is the most obvious place for my father to be holding your dad," Saint said in a low voice as we looked at the dark building. Light spilled out from the edges of a few windows where curtains were drawn, but that was the only signs we'd seen to say anyone was in there.

"We get him to safety first then finish this," I murmured, saying the plan out loud for my own benefit. We'd gone over it plenty of times and I knew that we were going to prioritise my dad's safety over everything else. But I wouldn't be able to settle this frantic pounding in my chest until I was certain he was okay.

"Let's do this then," Kyan growled, his fingers curling into fists as the bloodlust in him showed.

"Follow me," Saint commanded and he took off without another word, slipping through the trees to avoid leaving footprints on the freshly fallen snow as we circled around towards the left of the house.

Tatum was right behind him and I moved to her left while Nash was on her right and Kyan behind her. We didn't need to communicate about our positioning like that. Each of us knew she was the most important piece to our puzzle and whether she liked it or not, we were always going to protect her in whatever ways we could.

It finally became impossible to stay off of the open ground which ran up to the rear of the property and Saint led the way out from beneath the trees and across the lawn. I just hoped no one noticed our footprints in the snow before we'd either done what we'd come here for or they were covered once more by the falling flakes to hide our passage.

We made it to a door partially hidden beneath a stone arch at the corner of the property. The wooden door was bolted and secured with a heavy looking padlock like Saint had predicted and Kyan pulled the handheld blowtorch from his pocket before lighting it and aiming it at the lock.

I looked around cautiously as the sounds of the dark forest behind us filled the night, listening out for anything unnatural amongst the call of owls and branches rustling in the wind.

"Are you sure this will work?" Nash hissed as the seconds ticked by and nothing but the low sound of the blowtorch filled the air.

"I've got it," Kyan growled.

"It will work," Saint added, his tone brokering no arguments.

"Shit, I love it when you guys go all criminal on me," Tatum purred and my lips twitched with amusement.

A click sounded from the lock and Kyan cursed as he used his hunting knife to move the burning hot metal off of the latch. As the padlock hit the snow, it hissed, steam rising around it and I stepped over it as I hurried to follow the others inside.

"This way," Saint murmured, leading us down a long, dark corridor which he'd told us was intended for use by the household staff.

Nash closed the door silently behind us and we were plunged into darkness so I had to squint to make out the shapes of my family around me.

After a couple of twists and turns, Saint pulled open another door and we headed after him down a set of brick steps. The scent of stone and dry wood filled my nostrils as we headed lower and lower and when we finally emerged in a huge wine cellar, Saint flicked on the lights.

I looked around at the oak barrels and racks of priceless wine and frowned. "I thought you said he'd be keeping my dad down here?" I demanded as my heart began to race. Because if he wasn't here then he could be anywhere in this fucking enormous place and I didn't like the idea of us making ourselves known before we could be certain he was safe.

"There's a room at the far end of the cellar," Saint said in a hushed tone, leading the way on as he pointed to the wooden door in question. "It's where he likes to sit and sample the wine when he selects a bottle."

"Fuck me, that might just be the most pretentious thing I've ever heard," Nash muttered and Tatum giggled.

"The point is, that room has a heavy door with a lock and can be heated, so I would hazard a guess that it's the most secure place to house a prisoner in the building. Not taking into account the extension my father had built, because I don't know the details of that." It was clear that fact pissed him off, but I wasn't going to get into it with him over that again.

I tried not to let his words worry me, focusing instead on the fact that my dad was most likely behind that door right at this moment.

I broke into a run, unable to hold back a second longer as the need to see him consumed me. I'd already lost one parent, there was no way I was losing another. No fucking way.

I swallowed thickly as I ignored Saint's warning growl, forcing the rest of them to keep pace with me or get left behind.

I reached the door, quickly unlocking the bolt on the outside, grabbing hold of the handle and wrenching it open, too excited to find it unlocked to even question it being so damn easy.

The others were right on my heels as I burst into the small room and a relieved laugh burst from my lips as I found my dad sitting there on a foldout bed.

But instead of him leaping up and wrapping me in his arms, his eyes widened in alarm at the sight of me and he shook his head.

"You shouldn't have come!" Dad gasped, his eyes full of regret and fear.

"It's okay," I promised him as I ran around the wooden table in the centre of the room and wrapped my arms around him. "We're here to get you out. We won't let that crazy motherfucker do anything to hurt you-"

"No, Blake, you don't understand. He knew you'd come. He set you up. It's a-"

The sound of a shotgun being cocked made my blood ice over in my veins and I whirled around to look back at the door where the others were still clustered.

"The fucking clock," Saint hissed in realisation. "I should have known it wouldn't be that easy."

"Don't do anything stupid," a male voice came from somewhere outside the room and my hand flew to the pistol at my belt. "Come on out. Do it quietly so that we don't have to open fire. The Grand Master wants to see you."

I made a move to draw my weapon anyway and my dad's hand clamped down on my elbow to stop me.

"Don't," he snarled in warning. "You can't beat him, son. That man is the Devil incarnate. We can't fight him and his people."

I wholeheartedly disagreed with that, but as I looked to the door where we'd entered, I saw the barrel of a gun pressed to the back of Tatum's head as she was forced to raise her hands in surrender. Rage pulsed through my chest and the urge to declare war filling every part of my being.

Saint caught my eye, shaking his head an infinitesimal amount. We couldn't fight our way out of this. But I swore on all I was, the motherfucker who had dared to threaten our girl would die at my hands today.

CHAPTER FORTY FOUR

The group of guards dragged us upstairs after they locked up Blake's dad again and panic rushed through me. We were taken to a long stone hall with flagstones and a huge arching window at the far end which snow was falling against.

My heart pounded unevenly as I tried to think up a way out of this, but the assholes had disarmed us, stolen any chance we had of fighting back. Now we were being thrown to Troy Memphis like were a meal for a rabid dog. And I didn't know what to do.

There was a large, circular table set up at the heart of the hall between two huge fires on either side of it. It was like something out of Game of Thrones but instead of the Lannisters sitting there, it was ten douchebags in robes, at the heart of which was Troy. He rose from his seat beside a woman with a bob of blonde hair and bright blue eyes which were wide and pinned on me. The rest of them were older men with sneering faces and grey or greying hair.

The guards released us, forming a line behind us as they held their guns ready to fire if we tried to run and my heart beat to a frantic tune. There was no way out. We were fucked.

"You took your time," Troy mused, a smug as shit look on his face as he clasped his hands behind his back and strode around the table to stand in front of us. His eyes moved over our clothes and his brow arched as he looked to Saint. "You came over the mountain? How positively uncivilised of you."

"You knew," Saint said in an empty tone as he kept himself entirely composed in the face of danger.

"Of course I knew you'd come. Do you seriously think I didn't stand near the old grandfather clock on purpose when I called you?" Troy asked coldly as he strode forward, his imposing height seeming to amplify the power radiating from him.

Saint ground his jaw and I could tell how much he was beating himself up over his father tricking him even if his eyes didn't show it. But he was going up against a man as smart as himself. He wasn't to blame for this. It was this evil prick standing before us.

"Well, you're finally here anyway," Troy went on when Saint said nothing in response. "You must be tired after such an arduous and pointless journey, it really would have been easier to walk through the front door and gives yourselves up."

His robed friends tittered, and my upper lip peeled back. "What do you want?" I snarled, though I feared I already knew. Troy had taken my blood once before and after the way he'd hunted for us, it was clear what he was looking for.

"You know what I want," Troy said simply, and my boys shifted protectively around me.

"Whoops, didn't you take one of those vaccines we stole from your company?" I mocked, wanting to poke at this asshole who dared to try and cage us.

"Unfortunately for you, no, I did not," Troy said and the air went out of me as he sized me up like an animal for slaughter.

"If you think we're going to let you take her anywhere-" Nash started, but Troy cut over him.

"Karen, come over here," Troy called, ignoring Nash entirely, making my blood burn.

The blonde woman floated up behind Troy and my eyes cut to her as she moved to stand before me, her head cocking to one side as she examined me. My throat thickened as a very real and disturbing feeling of recognition filled me. But I didn't know her. I was sure I hadn't met her before.

"Tatum Rivers," she breathed, shaking her head. "What a vile name."

"Excuse you?" I hissed and Troy watched me with amusement in his gaze, folding his arms as he looked from me to the blonde stranger, apparently enjoying something.

"It has nothing on your real name," Karen said, taking a step closer to me and my skin prickled all over. I suddenly felt the need to back up, to get as far away from this woman as possible, but I wasn't going to give her the satisfaction of seeing that urge in me.

"What's that supposed to mean?" Kyan growled beside me, but the woman ignored him, her eyes glued to me.

"You're Adriana Munt," she said.

"Um, no I'm not." I glanced at Troy who was eyeing me with interest. "Who is this?" I demanded of him.

"This is Karen Munt," he said.

"Your mother," she added, smirking at me and my heart locked up as I refused those words with every scrap of my being. What kind of sick joke was this?

"No," I said calmly, keeping my expression neutral as my Night Keepers stared at me from both sides. "My mother left when I was a toddler, she abandoned us-"

"Your father stole you and your sister from me," Karen snarled, her eyes flaring with anger and my pulse thumped heavily in my ears as I shook my head.

"Bullshit," I snapped.

"You're not really one for drama, Father," Saint cut in. "What is this about?"

"It's as she says," Troy replied with a shrug. "She is the girl's mother."

"Well, you know what?" I hissed at this bitch Karen. "I don't give a damn who you are. If you're standing beside that monster in those fucking robes, you're my enemy and nothing else." My heart pounded furiously against my ribs as I glared at her, rejecting her with everything I was. Even if what she said was true, I'd never had a care in my heart for a mother who'd walked out on me, so I wasn't about to start caring about one who was a part of Royaume D'elite.

Karen's nose scrunched a little as she regarded me. "You're not listening, Adriana-"

"Call me that again and I'll cut out your tongue," I spat as Blake shifted beside me, violence pouring from his posture alone.

"Fine," Karen sighed. "*Tatum*, then. Look, let's go and speak in private. I'll explain everything."

"I'm not going anywhere with you," I scoffed.

"And if you try and take her from us, I'll kill all of you," Kyan growled dangerously.

"And how will you manage that unarmed?" Troy asked as his creepy little friends released low laughs behind him.

"You'd be surprised what I'm capable of." Kyan took a step forward and I pressed a hand to his chest, giving him a firm look to hold him back.

We were unarmed and there was no way I was going to let any of my Night Keepers die for me. The others were all tensing and grouping closer to me too and I knew they were just as desperate to protect me. But I wouldn't see them throw their lives away. We couldn't fight, we had to wait for an opportunity to run and the only way to give us any chance of that was to stall them. Troy gave a sharp nod to the men behind us and they moved forward to restrain my boys.

"Tell me right here," I demanded of the woman who claimed to be my mother. "Tell me the truth."

She sighed and Troy checked his watch impatiently. "Five minutes, then we must move this along," he muttered.

Karen nodded, moving another step closer to me as she considered her words. "I have been working on projects funded by Troy and Royaume D'elite for years. Long before you or your sister were in my life. I fell for your father after we briefly worked in a lab together in Chicago. Of course, for the first few years of our marriage, he had no idea what my work really entailed, and I had no intention of telling him. He always thought of himself as so moral. He wouldn't have understood the need for the things I was working on."

"Like what?" I growled, forcing myself to tolerate this conversation as I glanced around, hunting for a way out, a gun, a plan.

"Biological weapons mostly," she said lightly like it was nothing and my attention was snared, a violent jolt running through my chest.

"Like the Hades Virus?" Nash gritted out and she cast him a fleeting glance before turning back to me.

"Yes, eventually I created it. Though not before I had my daughters. It was never meant to be used in this country, not initially anyway. But then your father discovered what I was doing. He broke into my lab, God only knows how long he'd suspected what I was up to. And when he found out the truth, he couldn't stomach it. He didn't understand the need for the bioweapons which my people and I made and sold on the black market. It was too much for him to handle apparently." Her nose wrinkled in disgust and mine did too but for completely opposite reasons. "For a man who seemed strong in so many ways, it turned out he was weak."

"He wasn't weak," I snapped, acid bleeding through my veins. "Morals aren't weak."

She raised a finger, pointing it at me as rage pinched her features and I hated how I suddenly saw some of myself in her face. "Morals are a concept created by the government, by religion and by people who want to control you. The only things that truly count in this world are money and power – and you can't have one without the other."

"Coming from a bitch who's a member of a disgusting club like Royaume D'élite," I growled. "Where people are controlled, chained and treated like less than animals. Like they mean nothing. Like they *are* nothing."

Karen started laughing. "A member?" she scoffed. "I am not a mere member, Tatum. I am one of the Grand Masters. As all ten of us are." She gestured to Troy and the creeps behind her and my jaw clenched at that revelation. Now they were all marked to die, because the club could be reborn through any of them. And we couldn't let that happen.

"If you're so against being controlled, then why do you do it to others?" Blake asked in a voice full of disgust.

"Because there are different classes of people," Troy answered coldly, and Karen nodded. "The powerful and the weak. We feed the weak to the powerful. We keep order. We define order."

I glowered at Troy before fixing my so-called mother in my stare. "So my father found out what a monster he'd married, took his children and ran?" I guessed and she bristled.

"He stole you both because he couldn't hack the real truth of this world. That there is no good and evil. That there is only power or the lack of it. And if you do not claim it, then you will be a slave to society and rules which were placed upon you without your consent! In this country, your life is decided for you before you're even born. I didn't want that for my daughters. I was building a new world for us. And your father ruined *everything*." Her lower lip trembled with fury and I could see she really believed the bullshit spewing from her mouth.

"Good," I snarled, hatred burning in my heart. "I'm glad he took us. I'm glad he kept us from you."

She had the audacity to look hurt by my words before straightening her spine.

"Your five minutes are up," Troy announced as he checked his watch once more.

Karen turned to him, raising her chin. "I wish to have a conversation with my daughter in private before we move her to the lab."

My heart splintered with fear at the word 'lab' and I looked to my Night Keepers in alarm, having no idea what to do. We were out of time and our fate was closing in on all sides.

Troy nodded to one of the guards behind me, his eyes void of all emotion as he wielded all the power in the room against us. And I knew we were going to be torn apart before he even opened his mouth. "Take her away."

CHAPTER FORTY FIVE

Karen grabbed hold of Tatum's arm, her pointed fingernails digging into the flesh hard enough to draw a hiss of pain from our girl's lips. She hauled her towards a door in the far corner of the room, a guard shoving her along from behind too and holding his gun ready to fire.

"Where are you taking her?" Blake demanded, moving a step forward and causing my father's goons to raise their weapons in our direction again.

"I'd be more concerned with your own fate if I were you," Father snarled, his lip curled back in distaste as Tatum cursed, trying to rip her arm back out of her mother's hold.

"Let her go!" I commanded, my voice cutting and firm enough to make the bitch pause as she looked my way, but only for half a heartbeat.

As Tatum tried to lurch out of her grip, the armed man behind her backhanded her hard enough to knock her from her feet.

A roar of rage escaped my lips as I lurched forward a step, but it was nothing compared to the animalistic bellow that escaped Kyan.

He lunged forward, ripping his arms from the grip of the man who had been restraining him and slamming his fist into the face of the asshole who stood pointing a gun at him.

"No!" I yelled as I tried to grab his arm, my fingers barely brushing against his sleeve as he leapt forward, his eyes set on Tatum as she screamed out a warning which came far too late.

The echoing bang of the gunshot blasted through the room and I swear that noise ricocheted right through my soul as Kyan was thrown from his feet, blood blossoming from the wound in his side, the bullet finding a home in his body and my world caving in around me as he fell.

Nash roared something incomprehensible as he lunged forward, reaching for our brother's hand as Kyan fell back to the floor, his head hitting the flagstones with a sickening crack.

Blake was screaming profanities as movement drew my gaze from Kyan to Tatum and the asshole who'd hit her wrenched her into his arms and dragged her out of sight while she screamed Kyan's name.

For a moment I was frozen, locked between the need to chase after her and the need to help my brother.

Kyan's blood spread out onto the floor as he lay there unmoving and as I lurched towards him, hands grasped the back of my shirt, clamping around my arms and heaving me away again.

He wasn't moving. Not a flicker of anything in his expression or powerful body to say that he was still with us, but my heart thundered in panic at the idea of such an unthinkable thing.

He wasn't dead. I refused it. I wouldn't allow the world to keep turning without Kyan Roscoe in it.

The world was a blur of motion as the remaining Night Keepers fought to get to him and the guards struggled to contain us. My foot slipped in blood as I managed to lunge between them for a moment.

I reached for him, my fingers grasping his and closing tight around them as an arm looped across my chest and tried to haul me back.

"Get up!" I yelled, my grip tightening as I yanked on his hand. "Your wife needs you! Kyan!"

He didn't respond in any way, not so much as a flicker of anything as his fingers stayed slack in my grip.

I was yanked back so hard that I lost my hold on him, a fist slamming into my side and forcing me to whirl on the men who were trying to restrain me.

The others were fighting too, Nash descending into little more than a beast while Blake hollered Kyan's name so loudly that it echoed around the room. But he still didn't move an inch.

"Let me go!" I roared as the rest of the guards converged on Blake and Nash and I lost sight of Kyan between the crush of fighting bodies, more and more hands grabbing me and forcing me away from the others.

"Get the body out of here," Father snapped, like Kyan was nothing more than an inconvenience to him. Some trash that needed to be discarded as soon as possible.

The pounding in my head was loud enough to tear me apart as I thought of that. Of my brother being gone and the hole he would leave in this world. It wasn't true. I wouldn't accept it. I'd chase him into hell and drag his ass back here if I had to.

I ripped my arms away from the men trying to hold me, losing all sense of myself as I fought with all the brutality of the man I loved who lay there on that floor, needing me more than he ever had. Bones crunched beneath my knuckles and blood flew, but as I was slammed back against a wall, I was overwhelmed by sheer numbers.

The men holding me were strong and even as I fought against their grip on me with all my strength, they refused to loosen their hold.

I was dragged from the room, pulled through a different doorway to the one where they'd taken Tatum and as I was wheeled around, I found my father's sneering face looking back at me with contempt.

"I tried my hardest to mould you into the man you need to be in a civilised way while you were a boy," he growled as the men hauled me after him down the cold hallway and I continued to kick and fight them.

"Let me go," I warned him in my most arctic tone while my heart raced in panic more potent than I'd ever experienced in my entire life. "This is your only warning."

"Says the man who has been outsmarted and restrained with little to no effort," Father scoffed as he opened a door and I was forced through it. "I think I'll take my chances."

My eyes widened as I was shoved into a room which was decked out like a fucking sex dungeon, though I seriously doubted I was here because anyone wanted to fuck me.

A black four poster bed hung with chains and manacles sat in the centre of the space and I fought harder as the men dragged me towards it.

I kicked and punched, hitting one asshole hard enough to knock a tooth out before one of my hands was locked into a leather cuff by the foot of the bed.

"What the fuck is this?" I roared, fighting savagely as two of them threw their weight on top of me and managed to pin me down on my back.

I bucked and kicked, my teeth sinking into a neck and ripping a chunk of flesh away, but it wasn't enough. Another cuff locked tight around my other wrist and my ankles were locked into the restraints on a spreader bar a moment later.

The guards scrambled away from me as I cursed and fought against the cuffs, tipping my head back to glare at my father as he narrowed his eyes at me, assessing me like I was a problem he needed to solve.

"Perhaps I should have taken a firmer hand with you before now," Father said, moving closer to me as the other men left the room.

I barked a humourless laugh because if he seriously thought he'd gone easy on me then he really was a fucking psychopath.

"Tell me what you did with the vaccines you stole from me," he said, his tone flat and icily cold. "Aside from the ones you wasted on those men out there."

I gave him my hardest, deadest look, not even bothering to reply. If he seriously thought I'd tell him that then he was insane. I would take the answer to that question to the grave. But of course he was going to try and force it from my lips anyway.

Father sighed as he turned away from me and for a few endless moments, I was left alone in the silence, straining my ears for some clue as to what was happening with Tatum and my brothers right now. Not that I heard anything, no matter how much I ached for some reassurance that they were close by. The stone walls didn't let any sound reach me before my father returned with a white dishcloth in hand.

Five men hurried in behind him, four of them placing metal buckets filled with cold water on the floor to the right of me. The last man placed a large copper trough at the foot of the bed behind my head.

Father calmly walked around the bed and tugged on something so that my legs were elevated, putting me on a slope and I slid down until I was hanging from the restraints by my ankles. My head hung over the end of the PVC mattress and I looked down at the copper trough as the guards left the room again.

"Last chance to make this easy," Father offered like he didn't have his only son strapped to a fucking BDSM bed in preparation for waterboarding him.

There was no way in fuck I was going to be giving him that answer, no matter what he did to me, so I offered him something else instead. Something which I knew would shatter all the illusions he'd ever had about me and the man he'd tried to carve me into with every single merciless act of fatherhood he'd bestowed upon me.

I spat at him, saliva landing on his perfectly polished loafer and actually making him flinch. For the first time ever, I saw his composure slip as his face crumpled with rage and disgust, but the vision was stolen from me as he dropped the washcloth over my face.

I barely had a moment to suck in a breath before the ice cold water crashed down over it and I fought against the urge to buck and flail as I held my breath and just tried to wait it out.

My lungs burned, my eyes scrunched shut and the cuffs on my wrists and ankles bit into my skin mercilessly. The sensation of drowning was almost overwhelming and when I had no choice but to try and suck in a breath, the feeling of it sent panic crashing through my chest.

But I didn't flinch. I didn't thrash or scream or beg. I didn't fucking break. And I wouldn't. No matter what he did to try and make me.

I was Saint-motherfucking-Memphis. I was born of the Devil and cast in the shape of hell. I'd never learned to bow, and I refused to bend. The only thing that would carve through my will was death itself. And if that came for me, I'd welcome it. Because my lips would never part on this secret and I would never cave to this beast who held me.

There was a time when Troy Memphis had ruled me with fear and the pathetic need to please him. But now the only one who held dominion over me was a girl with a heart too pure and a soul too good for me. Nothing else in this world could touch me now I was her creature. And I'd endure each and every ring of hell if that was what it took to return me to her side.

CHAPTER FORTY SIX

The asshole guard who'd hit me dragged me along behind Karen and pushed me into a room with a symbol on the door that looked like some sort of wheel. Grief slashed through my chest over Kyan and I was starting to spiral as I tried not to fall apart completely. I'd seen that bullet rip into him, seen him fall and heard the crack as his head collided with the ground, seen the way he'd gone so still. Too still. It was the exact way my dad had looked when he'd died. I was in shock, unable to fully process what had happened as I fought not to lose control. Because if I did, I'd never get back to my boys.

Silent tears tracked down my cheeks as my heart was carved up over Kyan, leaving it bloody and raw, the pain too blinding to bear. I had to fight for him. Because he would have brought heaven and hell to ruin if it had been me laying in his place. So I would do that for him. I'd find some lasting shard of strength in my soul to hold onto and I'd finish this war for my inked god. And when it was over, I'd let myself break and suffer in the wake of his absence until there was nothing left of me.

There were raised seats facing a red curtain inside the room and I was shoved down into one while Karen stayed on her feet.

"Thank you, Raul, you can go and dispose of the dead body now," she said curtly and a noise of utter grief left me before I lost it, lunging at her, wanting to tear her apart with my bare hands in the name of Kyan.

She grabbed a gun from inside her robes and shifted her finger onto the trigger as she aimed it at me, making me pause. "You may be important, girl, but if you fight me, I assure you I will shoot. So sit down."

The guard left and I gritted my teeth, staring at the gun and calculating the risk of attacking her, trying to pry it from her hand and turning it on her. If she got close enough, careless enough, I might just have a chance. But I couldn't give away that that was my intention, so I looked her in the eye and dropped back into my chair like I was admitting defeat. But hell if I was. I struggled to calm the shaking of my hands as I thought of Kyan and ached over his loss. *I'll burn the world down for you, my dark sinner, the fire will blaze so bright you'll see it wherever you are.*

"I know this is a lot to take in," she started.

"I can handle it," I said bitterly. "You're my mother? Sure, maybe you are. Do you think that earns you something with me? Because it doesn't. As far as I'm concerned, I have no mother."

"I did not abandon you, Adriana," she snipped, and I grimaced at that name. "But if you think I care what you think of me, you're mistaken. I gave you a chance a long time ago, both you and your sister. But I saw what you'd become."

"A chance?" I scoffed. "When was that then?"

"I found you eventually. It took years of searching, but I tracked your father down and followed you all to a mall in Atlanta. When he left you in a clothes store, I came to speak with you both. To see if you remembered me, to see what kind of people he'd raised you to be. You were ten and Josie was thirteen."

"That's not her name," I snarled, hating that her story sounded vaguely familiar. I remembered my dad making us leave that town when I'd really wanted to stay. Having to leave my friend Elle behind without any notice. Had he known Karen had tracked us down? "Her name was Jessica."

She waved a hand dismissively, irritation flashing in her eyes. "The two of you were riddled with your father's influence. He hadn't brought you up how I'd hoped. You were just pawns of society, just like every other child in the United States." She sneered in disgust, raising the gun a little and making me shift in my seat. "I knew then it was too late to save you from him, that you'd always see me as the big bad wolf. Your father ruined you both and then he went and killed one of you." She shook her head in irritation.

"Don't you speak about him like that," I snapped, my blood heating. "He was trying to protect us. That was all he ever did."

"Oh yes," she said mockingly. "I saw how frightened he was. I had my people watch him for a while, teaching you all of that prepper nonsense. And do you know why he did that?" She stepped closer, gazing down her nose at me. "Because he was afraid of me. Of what I was capable of. Of my power." She said the final word with reverence in her tone and it made me hate her with a fierce passion. "He had seen behind the curtain. He knew that the world could fall at any moment because of my inventions and those of my friends. So he tried to prepare you and your sister for the end of days. He made you afraid. He made you weak. He vaccinated you against any virus he could just in case that was the one that ended up out in the world. If you'd been at my side, on the side of the real power, you would never have been afraid a day in your life."

"My dad did not make me weak," I hissed. "He made me strong. Far stronger than you."

She tsked. "You know nothing of real strength. I have the whole country on puppet strings. I can make the great fall and the small rise. I am a goddess, Adriana. And you could have been one too."

I stood from my seat with my teeth bared and Karen raised the gun to aim it between my eyes. "I told you not to use that name," I warned. "I'm

Tatum Rivers. The daughter of Donovan Rivers. I'm not yours, I'm *his*."

"Sit down and listen to me," she barked. I hesitated before complying, the darkness in her eyes telling me she really would pull that trigger if she had to. And I was no good to my boys dead. "That wasn't even his real name you sad fool. So if you're his then you belong to a dead man with a fake identity," she laughed coldly and my breaths came frantically, though I was too proud to demand to know his real name. Because it didn't matter. He was my dad. He was Donovan just like I was Tatum and Jess was Jess. We were the Rivers family, and this bitch was not a part of it.

"He's dead because of me, you know?" she went on with a triumphant smile on her face and pain and rage spilled through my chest. I said nothing, containing my emotions as Dad would have instructed, waiting for the opportune moment to strike. I'd let her talk until I had that gun and was planting six bullets in her skull. "I set him up, I had the Apollo Company send him a letter to offer him a job there – a company that I own. I'd been working on a virus which would make an exceptional bioweapon. One that would wipe out the weak and allow the strong to rise. But when your father moved close to the California lab, I saw an opportunity for revenge against him. He accepted of course, considering the high salary included in the package, but then the dumb schmuck went and gave you a half-cocked vaccine for the damn Hades Virus years later."

Her whole face screwed up like she gave a damn about Jess and bile rose in my throat.

"Don't stand there and pretend she meant something to you," I growled, grief welling up in me over this bitch being responsible for the very virus which had killed my sister. "I've seen what people like you do at Royaume D'élite. I know the pain you cause, the blood you spill. You're not capable of loving someone other than yourself."

"You're wrong," she said with emotion in her eyes. "I loved you and Josie more than anything in the world. But you've been poisoned by society. It's too late for you to be like me now."

"I would rather die than be like you," I spat, disgusted at the mere prospect.

Her eyes darkened and she shifted the gun in her grip like she wanted to fire it. But she didn't. "I suppose I punished you all in the end. Perhaps you deserve the fate awaiting you, *Tatum*. Perhaps it will teach you the value of power. Because you hold all of it in your veins now."

"The vaccine you mean?" I growled.

"Yes," she sighed. "After I had your father tricked into stealing the virus and the new vaccine from his own lab and handing them over to one of Troy's contacts, Mortez, it soon became clear the vaccine wasn't entirely effective. But it wasn't a total failure. The security cameras caught him and voila, the whole world had a new enemy. An enemy I made of him," she purred. "In his final days, he was hated by everyone, he was shown for the weakling he was-"

"My father was not weak!" I roared and she stepped forward, pressing the gun to my thigh.

"We might need you, girl, but we don't need all of you. Watch your tone or I'll start your punishment now."

"What punishment?" I hissed.

She started smiling and I took a deep breath to stop myself from lunging for her, keeping my head level, preparing for my next move. But it was nearly impossible to remain within that calm place inside me. Because this bitch had been the cause of all of this. She was responsible for my dad's death, the reason he lay in ashes in a box, the reason he would never hold me again, the reason I'd never hear his voice or feel his touch. He was gone because of this atrocious woman. And I would make sure she bled out at my feet by the end of this night.

"We have until morning before my men arrive to take you to our new lab in the mountains so we can restart our work on creating a vaccine. I couldn't believe it when Troy discovered you and the secret you hold. Fate led you to bump into his own son and give the game away. I find it rather amusing that the very place your father tried to hide you led to me finding you again. And what a delightful surprise your miracle blood was. I guess your father did something worthwhile after all."

My breaths came heavily as my fingers bit into my palms. "I'm not going to some fucking lab again."

"You will. And you'll bleed for us in payment for your father's arrogance," she said, sounding disappointed. "Troy was in quite the rage when you were rescued from his lab the first time, so we'll be taking measures to ensure that won't be possible again."

"What measures?" I spat.

She tugged on a rope beside the curtains and they drew back, revealing a balcony that looked down on large room with two huge wooden crosses set up beside one another. Nash and Blake were strapped to them, stripped down to their boxers, their arms and legs locked in place against the wooden X. Nash had a bright red cross painted across his chest and Blake had a blue one, marking them out like fucking cattle.

"No!" I gasped in horror, leaping out of my seat as the loud music blared from somewhere below.

Anger and fear swirled in their eyes as they fought against their restraints, but I didn't think they could see me with the spotlights shining in their eyes, making my heart twist up into a knot of terror. "Blake – Nash!" I yelled and their eyes widened as they fought harder to get free, calling my name in reply.

"Let them go!" I screamed, rounding on Karen, about to lunge for that gun when the door opened and the other Grand Masters poured into the room, taking seats to watch the show though Troy wasn't among them. A guard stepped up behind me with his hand rested on a machine gun at his hip and jerked his head at me in a command to sit down.

"It's a dog-eat-dog world, Tatum," Karen said icily, taking her seat just as I was shoved down beside her by the guard. "And I'd rather be a pitbull than a chihuahua."

"If you hurt them, I will hurt you so bad that you'll beg me for death,"

I swore, fear sweeping through me in an overwhelming wave.

Karen smiled cruelly at me. "Or perhaps when they are dead and you accept that no one will come to save you ever again, you will realise that you never stood a chance of taking on a palace of gods."

CHAPTER FORTY SEVEN

The taste of blood flooded my mouth from my busted lip, and I spat a wad of it onto the floor as I squinted against the bright lights which were aimed right into my fucking face.

My muscles bunched as I tried to lift a hand to shield my eyes but the restraint on my wrist stopped me.

The giant cross I'd been strapped to was rough and hard against my spine and the metal cuffs that held my wrists cut into my skin painfully. My feet barely touched the floor and I muttered curses as I slipped an inch, making the cuffs bite into my wrists with a slice of agony.

"Nash?" Blake called from my right and I grunted, still squinting into the light as I tried to make out the figures in the room beyond it. Tatum was there somewhere, I'd heard her, I was certain of it.

But the figures were little more than indistinct silhouettes with the light shining so brightly, so it was impossible to put faces to the men I was vowing to kill.

"Where's Tatum?" I bellowed, my throat raw from the amount of times

I'd screamed those words at the dark room in the past half hour while we'd been left strapped here like this. "Is she up there?" I squinted up at the balcony, but it was no good, the lights were too bright.

I still didn't get any answers. They hadn't spoken a single word to us since we'd been dragged away from Kyan's body and hauled in here, strapped up like a pair of pagan sacrifices and left to fucking wait until now. The pain of his loss was like a shard of ice being driven into my heart and I didn't know how to handle it. He was my brother, my dearest friend, my family.

"Place your bets," a man called out as a door opened somewhere behind me and I cursed as my position made it impossible for me to turn and see him.

The most I could do was meet Blake's gaze as he strained against the restraints holding him to his own cross, his dark hair spilling into his eyes and sticking to his temple where blood trickled down his face from a wound in his hairline.

There was a big blue cross painted over his bare chest and I glanced down at the red cross they'd painted on mine, wondering what fucked up games they had planned for us.

Kyan had told us the stories about the things they did at Royaume D'élite and I had no doubt that this was likely to end really fucking badly for us if we didn't manage to escape.

"Red or Blue? Last bets now," the man called and the sound of something being wheeled across the wooden floor reached me just as he stepped into view, pushing what looked a bit like a roulette wheel into place between me and Blake on a large cart.

The bottom of the cart held a shelf filled with various things and I counted a knife, hammer, hacksaw and poker amongst them before he stepped into my line of sight and blocked my view.

"Let us go," Blake demanded furiously, rattling the metal cuffs that held his hands in place like he was aching to break free of them and kill this motherfucker here and now. *That would make two of us then.*

"You're going to wish for death before I give it to you," I snarled.

The man ignored us, taking a silver ball from his pocket and holding it up before setting the wheel spinning and tossing the ball inside.

The sound of cheering voices sounded beyond the lights and amongst them all, I thought I heard Tatum's voice raised in fear, shouting my name. But knowing she was close did nothing to comfort me, because if she was here then she was in danger. And I couldn't help her.

The ball rattled around in the wheel and I found myself holding my breath along with the crowd as I waited for it to stop.

"The winner is…Blue!" the man announced. "Bonus pay-out to anyone who had cattle prod!"

What the fuck did he just say?

The crowd were cheering again, some of them booing because they'd lost, but overall there was a lot of fucking noise. I watched as the asshole bent down and rummaged about in the bottom of the cart before standing again with a flourish, holding out a long, metal cattle prod and powering it up.

He strode towards Blake as I yelled curses at his back and the metal cuffs cut into my wrists hard enough to spill blood while I fought to escape with even more determination.

"Fuck you, you pig-ugly motherfucker," Blake spat half a second before the asshole slammed the cattle prod into his stomach.

I roared my fury at him as Blake's spine arched, his muscles tensing with the pain as he bit down on any noise escaping his lips in response to the shock and the crowd cheered for the game.

My rage blinded me as I fought and fought, my muscles flexing and my blood pounding with the desperate desire to get free and destroy every single monster in this room.

By the time I calmed down enough to pay attention, the ball was flying around the wheel again and Blake was panting in his restraints, his eyes blazing with pain and fury.

"Red!" the man cried in excitement and the first thing I felt was relief that at least it was me and not my brother this time. I would take every one of these losses over watching someone I loved suffer. "The brand!"

My eyes widened as he pulled a metal brand from the cart next and the crowd chanted encouragement as he moved over to heat it in the fire.

Fury pulsed through me along with the most crippling sense of uselessness. I couldn't break free of this. I couldn't escape. And I knew that this game wouldn't just end. They would keep playing, rolling the wheel and picking between me and Blake as the torture got worse and worse until one of us died. That was where the real money was being made here. They were betting on who would survive the longest. And either way I was going to be the loser. Not just because this would be my end and Blake's too. But because I knew that somewhere nearby, Tatum needed me. She needed me and I couldn't come for her. She was alone after we'd all promised that would never happen. And if the Night Keepers met their end here, then every oath we'd made would have been for nothing. And the idea of that failure hurt me so much more than any torture ever could.

The man approached again, the glowing hot brand with the Royaume D'élite symbol of a letter R inside a ring of fire on it held out before him.

I gritted my teeth before he pressed it to my thigh, biting down on my tongue as a roar of pain built in my throat and the scent of burning skin sailed beneath my nose.

It was agony unlike any I'd known before, blinding and unending and made so much worse by the stench of failure that accompanied it. Because I deserved this. I deserved all of it if I couldn't get to her. If she suffered because of my failure then I was owed this and more. And as the pain almost stole my sense of self, that was all I could hold on to. Our girl needed us. And we weren't coming.

Saint

CHAPTER FORTY EIGHT

It was never ending. This constant torrent of ice cold that made my lungs burn with the fires of hell.

My muscles tightened and strained against the cuffs holding me there, on some fucking sex bed which I seriously hoped had had a thorough clean, my biceps bulging to the point of pain as I tried to rip my way free of this torment.

Inside my head was nothing but white noise and the images I'd sealed away of her. Hot lips on my flesh and the bluest eyes I've ever seen staring right upon my blackened soul, seeing all of me and finding it enough. Finding it worthy. Impossible and yet true.

That was it. All I had left in the dark. Pain and panic, fear and misery and *her*. The rest paled into insignificance. Because every time a crack began to form in my flesh, she was there to soothe it away. She was there to whisper encouragement in my ear. She was there to pull me from the dark. I was her demon and I'd only ever break for her.

Not this monster. Not ever again.

The freezing water made me shiver violently as I bucked and thrashed, but I never made a sound. Not one.

The flood of water stopped, the washcloth which had been plastered across my face was tugged free and I looked upon the face of my own personal hell as he peered down his nose at me. No doubt he thought this position was fitting. Here I was beneath his heel. Below him. At his mercy. Under his control.

But I'd been wrestling control back from him for a long time now. Longer than he could ever fully comprehend. I'd been stealing it the day I'd taken that toy car to Spain when I was just a small child. I'd been claiming it every time I kept to my routine or played on my piano. There was music in my soul which he could never destroy, running thicker than blood in my veins.

I gasped, unable to help it as I choked down air and my lungs spasmed with pain, black spots dancing before my eyes as I fought to stay conscious.

"Where are the vaccines?" my father asked simply, smoothing down his shirt sleeve like the drops of water getting on his clothes were the biggest issue in the room right now.

I was panting in and out, my breaths coming harshly. There was no way to hide that as my raw throat and angry lungs fought for air and rejected it just as forcefully. Everything hurt. Inside my body, inside my head. I was getting delirious, my brain overrun with too much and too little and still that one fucking question was all he ever asked of me.

I looked him in the eye, let him see how fucking little I thought of him, how little I cared about him doing this. I let him see that he wouldn't break me, and I knew he understood.

His lips twitched with what I was certain was pride and I was pleased to say I didn't fucking want it. I didn't want his pride or his contempt, his love or his hatred. I wanted nothing at all from him aside from his death. And if I survived this exchange, I would deliver it to him on a silver platter.

The washcloth fell over my face again and my chest tightened in panicked anticipation of what I knew was to come as icy droplets of water fell from my hair into the trough beneath me while I listened to him scooping the water back into the buckets.

I would endure this though. I would endure it for my brothers and most of all I would endure it for *her*.

The water crashed down over me and inside my head I was screaming at the top of my lungs even while they burned, and I coughed and heaved uncontrollably. But not a sound left my lips in protest to the treatment. None would. I'd die first.

In the dark I sought her out again and I could almost taste her on my lips, feel the brush of her soft skin against my fingertips. That was all I needed to find my strength as the torture continued. It was all I needed to get me through anything.

I.

Would.

Not.

Break.

Kyan

CHAPTER FORTY NINE

Eternal darkness this was not. There wasn't a light at the end of the tunnel or a heaven full of naked Tatums begging for my cock. There were no fluffy white clouds or even the burning gates of hell for that matter.

No. Death for Kyan Roscoe felt a whole hell of a lot like being trapped in a vat of searing agony while unimaginable pain rocketed through my left side and the sound of All The Small Things by Blink-182 assaulted my ears.

Though I seriously doubted that was the soundtrack to hell and I got the feeling it might just be something a little more visceral as I listened to the lyrics and they drew me back to reality.

The back of my skull was banging like a goddamn drum and I had to assume I'd hit it really fucking hard, but I couldn't afford my injuries any attention right now. I needed to push them aside and figure out what the fuck was going on.

My eyes snapped open and I drew in a ragged breath as I squinted at my surroundings, taking in the clear plastic sheeting I was lying on over the cold, stone floor. The light overhead was bright and blaring off of white tiled walls and I spotted a little seahorse decal etched into them. There were no seahorses in hell. Fact. Squids clearly resided with the Devil, but there weren't any of them in sight. So I definitely wasn't dead. In fact, it looked like I was in a blandly decorated bathroom.

A man was humming along to the music which came from a portable speaker balanced on the toilet and I turned my head slowly just as he tipped a large blue barrel of liquid into the bathtub, his back to me as he worked. I narrowed my eyes at another barrel which lay on its side by his feet, reading the label and gritting my teeth as I realised this motherfucker was pouring me an acid bath.

Well fuck him. I didn't work this damn hard to paint my flesh in ink just to have it all dissolved in a fucking tub of sulphuric acid like some half rate gangster failure.

I rolled onto my side, sucking in a sharp breath as the pain of my bullet wound daggered into me like a pure shot of hellfire. Luckily, Blink-182 were loud enough to drown out the sound of me pushing up onto my hands and knees as I grunted against the pain in my flesh.

The asshole turned slightly and I stilled, waiting for him to see me, come at me, try and fucking finish me - but he didn't. He just leaned over to pour the last drops from his barrel of acid and offered a view of his profile for me. Which was all I needed to recognise the motherfucker who had laid his hands on my girl and fill me with a blinding need for vengeance.

I shoved to my feet, a furious snarl escaping me as I almost blacked out from the pain in my body, but I refused to let that stop me.

The asshole turned with a shout of alarm, grabbing a gun from his belt half a second before I collided with him.

My weight sent him crashing back into the wall beside the bathtub and I snatched the wrist of the hand holding his gun, slamming it back against the tiles with a furious roar.

He threw a punch straight into my side, agony tearing into me as he hit my bullet wound and stars burst to life before my eyes as darkness curtained my vision. Oblivion called for me and I told it to get fucked, throwing my forehead forward and smashing his nose, causing blood to splatter my face.

I drove a punch into his gut and slammed his wrist against the tiles again, forcing him to drop the gun which skidded away across the plastic sheet.

I wrapped my other hand around his throat, but his fist crashed into my side again and again and the pain was so blinding that I somehow found myself falling, my ass hitting the edge of the tub as I almost fell backwards into it.

By some act of God, or the Devil, or just fucking luck, I managed to grab the edge of the tub, my boot slamming into his chest as he lunged at me and knocking him away from me again.

I lurched after him, blood splattering the plastic sheet as I leaked worse than a faulty tap, but that didn't matter right now. What mattered was finishing this before my body gave up and I ended up taking a bath I'd never be getting out of.

I shoved myself away from the tub, coughing as the acidic scent caught in my throat and grabbing something from the top of the toilet to smash his head in with. Unfortunately, it was a fucking roll of toilet paper which just bounced off of his face as he lunged at me with a goddamn hunting knife. Not just any knife either - that was my baby, and he was turning it on me like some two-timing whore.

I ducked aside as he swung the blade for my throat, the backs of my knees hitting the toilet and making me fall back to sit on the closed lid and knock the speaker flying.

I grabbed the toilet brush holder from beside me and managed to smash it against the side of his head as he lunged at me again, the shitty brush side swiping his face and making him curse as he stumbled aside.

My body was screaming at me to stop, but I ignored it. No fucker told me what to do when I had my mind set on something, not even my own goddamn body and I slammed into his gut with my shoulder, knocking him from his feet. The knife went skittering away across the plastic sheet and the dumb motherfucker lunged after it, rolling away from me and exposing his back to me.

I threw myself after him, blood smearing across the polyethylene from my wound and soaking through my jeans as it painted everything in red.

I fell on him. Literally fell because I was pretty sure I blacked out again for a moment as a bolt of agony sliced through me so sharply that it stole my goddamn breath away. But the moment I blinked the darkness aside, my hand was fisting in his hair and I slammed his face down onto the tiles beneath us.

He reached for the knife as his blood flew, his fingertips brushing against the hilt while I slammed his head down again and again.

On the fourth strike, the tension went out of his limbs and I sucked in a breath through the pain that was consuming me, struggling to my feet as he twitched on the ground.

His fingers were still touching the knife and I kicked it away, swearing at the movement before gritting my teeth and hauling him upright in front of me.

I shoved him towards the bathtub, and he came to as I made him take a step over the slick plastic. He threw an elbow back at me but I was ready for him that time, blocking the strike with my forearm and kicking out the backs of his knees.

He screamed as he crashed into the side of the bathtub, his hands gripping the edge of it as I tried to force him closer.

For a moment, it seemed like my strength would give out and I'd fall back beneath his desperate attempts to escape me. But then I closed my eyes, the sight of him backhanding my girl flashing through my memory and a vengeful, furious beast awakened in my soul.

With a roar of effort, I gripped the back of his shirt and hauled him up and over the edge of the tub, his screams like the sweetest song in the world as he saw the inevitability of his fate coming for him and fell face first into the bath of acid.

I leapt back as the liquid splashed up around him, somehow avoiding every drop and he began kicking and flailing, desperate to get back out again before it was too late. But it was already too fucking late.

I slipped in the blood that coated the polyethylene sheet but managed to stay upright before ripping it from the floor and holding it up between me and the bath.

As the asshole scrambled upright, I slammed into him, knocking him back down into the acid and managing to place a hand on the back of his head as I forced him down beneath the surface.

He kicked and bucked, but I kept my weight on him, the plastic sheet protecting me from the acid as I silently thanked Niall for teaching me about fucked up shit like this. Polyethylene was immune to sulfuric acid, at least short term like this. This guy's body though? Not so much.

He finally stopped kicking and I stumbled back, falling on my ass as the energy was sucked from my limbs, my racing heart and the surge of adrenaline that had kept me going this long fading now that I'd won.

But I couldn't just let myself pass out again. For one, my girl and my brothers needed me. And for two, I was pretty certain that I'd bleed out soon if I didn't do something to stop this fucking hole in my side from leaking.

With a pained groan, I crawled towards the sink and managed to use it to heave myself upright. There was a mirror hanging above it and I looked at myself, taking note of how fucking pale I looked beneath the blood that coated my skin before ripping my ruined shirt off.

I looked down at the small, round hole in my side as blood ran freely from it and I bunched my shirt up to press down against it. I turned, looking for an exit wound in the mirror, but didn't find one. So the little metal fucker was still in there then. Good. I wasn't going to be taking it out myself either. I just needed to stop the bleeding for long enough to help the people I loved.

I turned and looked around the bloodstained bathroom, spotting a bag by the door and limping towards it. Inside, I found the weapons that had been taken from us when we were captured, and the corner of my mouth lifted into a smirk as I took the blowtorch from the middle of the guns before turning to hunt for my knife.

It had ended up in a corner and I stumbled towards it with more grunts of pain. I swear the bastard bullet hole hurt more now than it had while I was fighting for my motherfucking life.

I managed to grab the knife, kissing it for staying faithful to me before returning to my spot by the sink.

This was going to hurt like a bitch.

I lit the blowtorch and lifted the blade of my knife to the flame, heating it and sanitising it in one. I was practically a full-blown surgeon. Who needed some fancy degree and years of training?

When the blade was hot enough, I took a deep breath, pulled the bloodstained shirt away from the bullet hole and gritted my teeth.

This was either one of the worst or one of the best ideas I'd ever had. Only one way to find out for sure though.

I came damn near to screaming as I pressed the burning hot blade to my flesh, cauterising the wound and clenching my jaw so hard I was surprised I didn't bust a tooth.

It hurt. No, fuck that, hurt wasn't close to what it felt like. It was an exquisite kind of agony reserved only for the foulest of demons who resided within the deepest depths of hell. And I must have been one of them because somehow, I'd earned their pain too.

I held on for as long as I could before my fingers seemed to spasm of their own volition, the knife falling from my grasp and clattering loudly into the sink. I grasped the edge of the porcelain basin as I panted, my eyes clamped shut as I waited for the agony to fade and fought against the urge to black out again. The speaker was playing Numb by Linkin Park now and I couldn't help but wish for some numbness of my own to get me through this.

But I didn't need that. I had the best motivation in the world to keep moving, keep going, keep living. She had hair that shone like sunlight and wouldn't for one second put up with me bitching out and giving in now. And I wasn't going to let her down.

I opened my eyes, glaring into the mirror and looking at the darkness in them, seeing the monster in me more clearly than ever before as I gave myself to that part of my soul and let it take over. My gaze fell to the bullet hole and I was pleased to find I'd stopped that fucker in its tracks. No more blood. Which meant it was time to go.

I took a deep breath, grabbed my knife and turned for the exit. The bag of guns was too much for my weakened body to deal with and I cursed as I grabbed a couple of pistols, shoving them in the back of my pants before opening the door.

The room outside was lit up though thankfully empty and I could see it was a games room of some kind with poker tables laid out and unused.

I stumbled through the wide space, trying to hear beyond the pounding of my own pulse to anything that might help me find the others.

I was breathless by the time I made it across the room, and I stumbled before I made it to the door, smacking into a panel on the wall which popped open as I pushed myself upright again.

I looked inside at the circuit breaker, my eyebrows going up as I searched for the main power switch. I may have been all kinds of fucked up, but I was still a predator. And I had to think I'd hunt best in the dark.

My lips twitched as I reached out and flipped the switch, knocking the lights and every other electrical item in the building out of commission in one fell swoop.

I was plunged into darkness and I laughed to myself, a bitter, broken sound which was all threat and no joy.

I was coming for them now. And Lord help them when I arrived. Assuming I made it to them before my body gave out for good.

CHAPTER FIFTY

I was plunged into darkness and I didn't waste a single second to act as I latched onto this moment of potential salvation.

I dove out of my seat, leaping in the direction of the guard, my hands locking around his machine gun as fury carved a line through my chest. I got my finger on the trigger before he could even try and stop me, twisting the barrel towards him blindly and squeezing my finger on it.

An explosion of gunfire ripped through my ears and the man fell with a dying scream as hot blood splattered me and I was pulled down to the floor with him by the strap on the gun which was latched around his body. The sound of panicked shouts and people running for the door told me I had just seconds to act. Seconds to kill. And there wasn't a chance in the whole universe that I was letting any of these murderous fuckers escape.

I twisted the gun upright as best I could and started firing back in the direction I'd come, the rat-tat-tat of bullets drilling into my head as the sound filled up the small space and made a song with the gargling screams of my victims. The flare of fire from the gun barrel lit them up in a strobe effect as they died, and I grinned as I enjoyed this bloody disco of my own creation.

I managed to find the clip on the strap and released the gun from the guard's body as shots were fired in my direction. But I just kept my finger on the trigger as I sprayed my enemies with as much death as this gun could deliver until all movement in the room ceased.

A burning sensation along my temple said I'd come closer to death than I'd liked and as blood slid down my face from the bullet graze, I wiped it away.

I pushed to my feet, trembling in the dark as I hunted for anything to use as a light. I needed to be sure there was no one else alive in this room. That every last one of them no longer existed in this world.

My foot bumped into a soft body and I reached down, hunting through their robes and pulling out a phone, my ears ringing heavily from the gunfire. I switched on the flashlight, shining it over the massacre as my heart beat unevenly. I'd never killed on a level like this. And as hard as my breaths were coming and as shocked as I was by the blood painting the walls, I revelled in it too. Because each bastard in this room had unspeakable crimes to answer for. And now I hoped they were standing before the Devil in hell, all power stripped from their hands as an eternity of suffering began.

Karen's blonde hair was spilled out across the floor where she lay beneath one of the other Grand Masters, blood wetting them both and I couldn't find it in myself to feel even the slightest hint of regret over her demise.

I turned to look out over the balcony, seeking out Blake and Nash beyond it as panic gnawed at my chest. I could just make them out through the gloom and Nash's voice suddenly called to me in desperation. "Tatum! Tell me you're alright!"

The guy who'd been spinning the roulette was gone and I guessed he'd seen the fate that had befallen his friends. I'd sure like to fucking find him and make him suffer for what he'd done to my boys.

"I'm okay! I killed the lot of them," I cried back. "I'm coming. Hang on."

"You fucking angel," Blake said with a manic sort of laugh. "Hurry your sweet ass up."

I turned to the door and my heart jolted as it opened and a woman flew out of it, a whip of blonde hair making me snarl furiously. *Fucking Karen.*

I took chase, tearing after her into the hall and opening fire, but the goddamn ammunition belt was out. I'd shot every bullet in it and not one had secured her death.

She ducked her head, firing blindly behind her with her handgun so I was forced to take cover back in the observation room. She dove around a corner and out of sight, but my gaze fell on a bloody trail she was leaving behind and a cold, calm decision fell over me. *I'm coming, bitch. But not yet.*

I ran along the hall and down some steps, finding the door which must have led into the room where Blake and Nash were being kept and trying the handle. Locked. I stood back, angling the butt of the gun down at the lock and smacking it as hard as I could. It broke off and I shoved the door open, running inside and using the phone flashlight to find my boys as I tossed the empty machine gun away.

My hands shook as I twisted the locks on Blake's cuffs first, helping him down. He winced and I reached my fingers towards the burn on his side from the cattle prod and the bloody whip marks over his chest.

"It's alright. I'm okay," he growled, but this would never be okay. The sight of his blood was like a red rag in front of a bull to me. And my horns were sharp, ready to kill in penance for this.

I ran to Nash and let him down next, my heart clenching into a fist as he groaned his relief. The brand on his thigh was bad enough, but I'd had to watch as the guy beat him with knuckle dusters until his body was battered and bruised too. It was almost too much to see his beautiful body marked and branded with pain and a noise of anguish left me.

He moved in front of me as I checked over his wounds, my fingers grazing his ribs and he winced.

"I'm fine, princess," he ground out.

"Nothing about this is fine," I choked out.

Blake moved behind me and I pulled them close, allowing myself a moment in their arms as I just comforted myself with the knowledge they were here. They were still alive.

For a moment my mind fell on Kyan, but the chasm of grief laying in those thoughts was too deep to lose myself in now. I had to focus. I had to finish this.

"We need to kill that fucking bitch who gave birth to me," I snarled.

"We need clothes and weapons," Blake growled.

"They made us strip off out there," Nash said darkly and I followed him through to an adjoining room which looked like a metal cell, all of us freezing as we spotted the roulette spinner cowering at the back of the room.

"Oh no," he squeaked, pointing at us with a knife he must have grabbed from his sick cart of torture devices.

We moved toward him like the horsemen of the apocalypse and as he swung at me with the blade, I grabbed his wrist, twisting sharply and making him drop it. Nash pinned him to the wall by the throat and Blake grabbed the blade, driving it into his gut again and again until his screams fell away and the life flickered out of his eyes. Nash dropped him, sneering at his corpse and I turned my back on it with a ripple of satisfaction.

This place was primed to become a new kingdom of death. But there weren't going to be any royal assholes to fill it by the time we were done. They were going to pay for killing Kyan. I wouldn't rest until it was done. It was the only thing keeping me together, and I knew the second it was finished, I'd crumble over his loss and struggle to ever move forward.

The guys quickly got dressed then I led them out into the hall, eyeing the blood Karen had dripped all along the plush cream carpet in the dim light.

"The other Grand Masters had guns," I said before leading them to the observation room where I'd had to watch my boys be hurt.

Monroe led the way inside and let out a low whistle. "Ho-ly shit, princess. This is killing at its finest."

Blake tugged me close as we stepped inside, kissing me roughly on the top of my head before running his thumb beneath the cut on my temple to wipe the blood away. "If they weren't dead already, I'd murder them all over again. Slowly, so they pissed themselves as they begged for mercy. But I wouldn't offer any of them that for this mark on you alone, sweetheart."

"They got too quick of a death," I agreed. "For all they did to so many people, to Kyan, to you both, they didn't deserve a bullet, they deserved blades and fire."

"They were afraid at least, they knew what was happening," Nash said as he grabbed four guns and handed two to Blake before passing another one to me which I tucked into my waistband. He pointed to the crowd of bodies which had all clearly been running for the door before they died. He was right, but it still didn't feel like enough.

"We'd better make sure they're all dead," Blake said grimly. "We can't let any of these fuckers come back to rebuild Royaume D'élite."

"We do it for Kyan," I said, my voice breaking. "Then I need to catch that bitch Karen and make her scream." She might have been injured, but I didn't know how badly or how far she could have gotten.

"You two go ahead, I'll catch up," Nash urged before moving to press his newly acquired handgun to the back of one of their heads.

"No, we can't split up," I growled and Blake nodded firmly.

"Then let's make it quick," Nash said with a grimace and fired the shot into the man's skull, the sound seeming to ricochet through my whole body. The work was dirty, but we managed it in under a minute and were soon racing down the halls after my whore of a mother.

The lights suddenly flared back to life and I glanced at the others as we froze in the long hallway.

"Hey!" a guard shouted at us from the end of the corridor.

A loud bang rang in my head and my breathing stalled as the guard flew backwards, falling stone cold dead onto the floor with a heavy thump.

Blake's gun was raised and his jaw ticking, his eyes blazing with hellfire. He shone like a fucking star right then and I could barely tear my eyes away from him. I blinked and we were running again, following the bloody trail across the gleaming floorboards.

I turned the flashlight off and tucked the phone into my pocket as we turned down an opulent staircase to our right, following the blood to the ground level.

A cold breeze wafted against my cheek and I turned toward it, finding a door ajar with a bloody handle, the snow beyond it splashed with red under the moonlight.

A dark hunger pulled at my gut as I stalked toward it, hunting my prey with two of my wolves at my sides. I could scent her death on the air. And it was *mine*.

CHAPTER FIFTY ONE

The water stopped rushing over my face but the washcloth remained as I heaved and panted. My lungs were so desperate for pure air that I didn't realise my hands were being untethered before I was shoved upright and they were locked together behind my back.

I shook my head to dislodge the cloth, shivering uncontrollably from the freezing water that was running from my head down my back and over my shoulders, soaking into my shirt. I sucked in breaths as my racing heart thrashed like a trapped animal in a cage.

"Up," Father snapped. "Get up, Saint."

I blinked at him through the fog of my thoughts as I tried to align them and fully comprehend what was happening. The torture had left me short of oxygen and disoriented and I needed to get my bearings fast.

Loud blasts rang out, seeming to echo around the inside of my skull before I finally realised what I was hearing were gunshots.

A laugh tumbled from my lips as my ankles were freed from the cuffs on the spreader bar and my father dragged me off of the BDSM bed and onto my feet.

"What's so funny?" he demanded and my smile widened because despite all of his efforts to hide it, I could see that he was rattled and the taste of that was so sweet on my tongue that I couldn't help but gloat.

"I think you're about to realise exactly what my family are made of," I said in a low voice. "You said you couldn't understand what I saw in those people when I chose to align myself with them. Well, now you're about to find out. You set the hell hounds loose and they've got the scent of your blood."

Father scoffed, grasping my arm and dragging me towards the door. I let him pull me along, not wanting to stay in this fucking room anyway.

"Don't romanticise things, boy," he said dismissively. "Even if your friends have managed to cause some form of havoc, it won't last long. They can't possibly stand before the might of Royaume D'élite and survive. Just ask the dead O'Brien boy."

Those words hurt like a blow to the heart and I sucked in a sharp breath at the thought of Kyan lying bloody and still on the floor. But I couldn't allow myself to focus on that. I needed to stay sharp for the people I could still help.

"Where are you taking me?" I demanded as he hauled me along a corridor towards the stairs.

Three armed guards hurried to surround us and I sneered at them openly, not caring to hide my contempt from them as a gun was pointed at my head and they made me walk with them.

We moved quickly, Father's brusque pace enough to let me know that he wasn't as calm as he was trying to pretend, and I tipped my head back as I shouted at the top of my lungs. "I am the dark in the dead of the night!"

The asshole with the gun hit me in the temple and I hissed a curse at him, but I was almost sure that I heard the reply to those words shouted back to me from one of my brothers somewhere. It was impossible to be certain of who it had been, but just the suggestion that they were close, fighting, battling on, had my strength returning to me and hope swelling in my veins.

I was shoved down the stairs with Father's fingers biting into my arm as he forced me to move faster and faster. The echoing sounds of gunshots chased us out of the building and I took great joy in seeing him scurry like a rat from a flooding drain.

As we made it to the foot of the stairs by the front door, more gunshots sounded from even closer, making my ears ring as the sound resounded off of the brick walls.

Father turned to look between the guards, a momentary slip in his composure showing real panic in his eyes and I grinned at him like a savage.

"The three of you stay here and hold off anyone who tries to follow me," he barked, and they agreed instantly like the mindless goons they were, turning to stand their ground before the door.

Father dragged me outside, taking the gun from the asshole who had been holding it to my head and jamming it against my skull in his place.

"I want an heir, Saint," he growled as I dug my heels in. "But don't think that means I won't kill you. If you prove yourself beyond redemption by trying to escape me now, then I will put a bullet between your eyes and find a woman to cook me up a replacement in her womb. Don't test me on that."

"I wouldn't dream of it," I replied, my voice thick with disdain as I allowed him to march me out into the snow where his Bentley was parked up before the house.

Father wrenched the back door open as the sound of gunfire drew closer and he shoved me into the back seat before slamming it again and getting into the front.

A shot was fired from somewhere much closer just as he pulled away and I whirled around, my eyes widening in surprise and utter fucking joy as I spotted Kyan lunging out of the bushes and firing at us.

"Hear me roar!" Kyan bellowed, his bloodstained chest gleaming in the headlights as Father twisted the car towards him and slammed his foot down on the accelerator.

I lunged forward between the seats, head butting the side of my father's skull as the way my hands were tied made it impossible for me to do anything better, and he swerved violently as he fought to turn his gun on me.

I threw myself down just as he fired a shot and the back window was blasted apart in a shower of shattering glass.

"I warned you, Saint," Father growled as he yanked the wheel around, half concentrating on driving and half on trying to look back to aim his gun at me. "Mixing with low blooded heathens was never going to end well for you."

A violent roar came from the rear of the car and I whirled around in time to see Kyan grab hold of the headrest as he leapt onto the trunk, firing wildly towards my father in the front of the car as he clung on for dear life.

Windows shattered and the car swerved left and right in vicious motions that had me slamming against the door and smacking my head hard enough to make it spin.

I pushed myself up onto the chairs, keeping low out of Kyan's way as the car swerved over the icy tarmac.

Father whirled around in his seat, lifting his own gun, aiming right for my brother's head and I lunged towards Kyan. My shoulder collided with him, knocking his grip loose and making him fall back onto the drive as the shot was fired and missed him by next to nothing.

I leapt after him, diving headfirst out of the rear window and closing my eyes as I hit the ground hard, tumbling over and over as pain ricocheted through my body and the car slammed to a halt ahead of me.

My pulse thundered as I tried to scramble back to my feet, but I was unarmed, tied up and stuck here like a sitting duck.

Kyan groaned where he'd fallen, his gun nowhere in sight as he half pushed himself up while clutching a wound on his side and it was easy to remember that he'd come damn close to death already tonight.

And unless the tide suddenly turned in our favour, I had the horrible feeling that my father was about to win this part of the game.

CHAPTER FIFTY TWO

"Troy! Wait for me!" Karen's voice reached me from up ahead as we sprinted around the castle, hugging the wall to give us cover from any guns that might be pointed our way.

Panic tugged at my lungs and I ran faster through the mounting snow beneath my feet, my breaths misting before me as I carved through the bloody trail ahead of us.

We made it around to the front of the house where Troy was stepping out of a Bentley, raising a gun to point at two people on the paved driveway while Karen staggered toward him.

"Troy!" she cried and he looked up in surprise.

My gaze focused on the men on the ground. Saint. *Kyan.*

My world slowed, my head spinning, my heart swelling as I felt my connection to my husband more assuredly than ever before. My beautiful, dark sinner, pale and bloody but alive. Totally fucking alive. I was so overwhelmed by the sight of them and the love in my heart for both of those boys that I was momentarily frozen to the spot. But I had one task left to fulfil. I couldn't let

Karen or Troy get away. They were the last pieces of this horrible puzzle. Their deaths would fill the final slots and we could all finally wake up from this nightmare.

I raised my gun, aiming it at Troy with a sneer before pulling the trigger. He lurched sideways and the bullet went fucking wide. He turned his gun on me and Saint kicked his shins hard as his weapon went off. Strong hands pulled me back, dragging me behind the cover of the wall and I found Blake there, giving me an anxious look.

"Jesus, Cinders," he cursed. "That was too close."

"You're dead – our fucking queen is here!" Saint snarled and I struggled my way free of Blake to look around the wall.

Troy was back in the car, pulling away down the drive, clearly deciding he'd rather save his own ass than risk it going up against us in a shoot out. Karen had ducked down behind a boulder that flanked the drive and I growled as she darted out from behind it, clasping her side with one hand, blood oozing through her fingers as she ran as fast as she could to catch him.

"Wait!" she shrieked as the Bentley accelerated away.

Saint tried to get up, but his hands were bound behind his back and Kyan was struggling too, clearly in agony as he pressed his hands to the ground to push himself up onto his hands and knees.

A shot cut through the air and Nash suddenly threw his weight at me and Blake, flattening us to the wall once more as the bullet narrowly missed us. I turned back to see where it had come from as frantic breaths left me, finding a guard following us, panicking as he struggled to reload his gun.

Nash drew away from me and he and Blake ran at the guy full speed, firing their guns and taking the man down in a spray of bullets. But as the guard hit the ground, he started rising once more, clearly wearing a goddamn bulletproof vest as he raised his own gun to fire. My boys collided with him before he could, crushing him to the ground. And I knew they'd win that fight as the man started screaming beneath them and they worked together to pin him down and finish him.

I turned back to face Karen as she stumbled down the drive toward the car and Troy slowed to a halt for her. Kyan was on his knees, reloading his weapon as Saint fought against his restraints.

"Fuck," I spat, taking chase after Karen and raising my gun.

The passenger door was shoved open and Karen grasped the side of the vehicle, staggering toward her only chance of escape.

I stopped running and raised the handgun, levelling it on her, aiming down the sights and not moving a single inch as I held my breath. I had to do this right. Aim well and hit my target dead on. And for that, I had to remain still.

She kept moving jerkily as she grasped the door of the car, her head bobbing in and out of my shot as I growled under my breath.

I pictured my dad and Jess, I pictured the people she'd hurt, the chained and caged men and women I'd seen at Royaume D'élite. I pictured that virus sweeping through the world killing innocents without mercy. I pictured Blake's mom meeting her end and Kyan lying in his bed at The Temple barely able to draw breath.

An emotion welled in me so fiercely that it was all I could feel. One single defining emotion that was all projected towards these weak, cowardly human beings trying to escape justice in that car. It was hate in its purest form.

I pulled the trigger and Karen was thrown onto the ground in a spray of blood.

I released a heavy breath of satisfaction as a single tear tracked down my cheek, before I levelled the gun on the back of the car and started firing again. Troy took off with a roar of the engine and I realised the Night Keepers were firing too, bullets carving holes into his fancy ass car as he raced toward the exit. But he didn't slow. He kept going and going, making it out of sight until there was nothing left in his place but gas fumes and failed dreams.

Gone.

We'd lost him.

I turned to look at Saint in dismay, my heart sinking and his eyes pooled with a bitter disappointment. Then his features twisted with hate as a groan sounded from my mother on the ground, her body twitching with life.

Kyan untied Saint's hands for him and then Saint helped him to stand.

"You're alive," I choked as I lunged at Kyan, wrapping my tattooed monster in my arms, knowing he wasn't anywhere near okay, but he was still breathing. And that was what counted right now.

"Yeah," he saw gruffly. "Bullets are like candy to me, baby." He winced as I drew back and he looked over my shoulder, his breaths coming out in heavy pants. "Let's deliver Maren Kunt to Satan personally."

I nodded, savouring the closeness of him as I breathed in the scent of leather and blood on him, assuring myself he was really here. Then I turned and started marching toward Karen with purpose and felt my boys following me until we were all circling around her in a ring. Blake and Nash joined us, spattered with blood and looking thirsty for more death.

Saint kicked Karen to roll her over and she gazed up at us as she choked on her own blood, my bullet having blasted through the centre of her throat.

"Who's weak now?" I hissed at her and her eyes glistened with anger, defeat, fear.

"It's you," Saint supplied in an arctic tone. "You're the dirt at our feet."

"You're going to go into the ground and become a feast for the worms," Nash said chillingly.

"You're not going to be missed by anyone on this entire planet," Blake added with a taunting smirk.

Kyan shook a little as he leaned on Saint for support, his eyes hollow as he gazed down at our kill. "You're nothing…and no one…and nobody."

I crouched down as she started to jerk, the last of the life leaving her as I angled her face towards mine with the tips of my nails.

"I won't think of you after this day," I promised. "Not a soul in this world will." I leaned down to whisper in her ear. "And do you know what's weaker than the weakest woman on earth? The weakest woman on earth when she's dead."

A rattling, gargled breath left her and she fell still, her eyes locked on me, a permanent shadow of regret, defeat and failure stamped into her irises.

I got to my feet, sharing a look of relief with my boys, but it was short-lived as Kyan cursed and fell to his knees, dropping back onto the ground and sending a spray of snow out around him.

I threw myself down at his side with a panicked scream, clutching his hand as he gazed at me for barely a second with a thousand desperate words burning in his eyes.

"No," I gasped in fright.

"Was I a decent husband, baby?" he rasped and tears splashed down my cheeks in a torrent as his hand rested against my cheek, feeling all too cold.

I cupped it to my face as panic clutched every piece of my heart and wouldn't let go. I couldn't lose him. My dad had taught me to face the end of the world, but had never taught me how to make it through this. Because Kyan Roscoe's death was an apocalypse of its own kind. And I wouldn't be a survivor.

"You're the best kind of husband, Kyan. One who'd do anything and everything to save me," I choked. "And I promise your wife will do the same for you."

"The rest of you assholes better look after her," he breathed, his voice seeming to fade away. "Make her smile every damn day."

They all started making complaints, commanding him not to give up and swearing to look after me for the rest of forever with him at their sides. But I got the awful feeling he didn't believe he'd be there for forever with us and the thought of that was tearing me apart.

Peace filled his features then his eyes fell closed and I frantically tugged the phone out of my pocket as I started to call for help, yelling at him to stay right here with us.

Saint plucked it from my fingers as Blake and Nash knelt down either side of me in the snow. "Just keep talking to him," Saint commanded me. "Your voice will keep him here."

I started saying Kyan's name and begging him to stay, telling him about the life we were going to make together, all five of us.

"Hold on, brother," Blake growled passionately as Nash checked his pulse then started performing CPR.

Oh god, oh god.

It was all happening too fast and terror was thumping through my veins. I gripped Kyan's hand, holding onto him as my tears started to flow and a real sense of terror encompassed my heart.

I couldn't lose him. I needed him as surely as I needed the sun to rise. There was no us without Kyan. No Night Keepers, no anything. But as Nash worked to keep his heart beating, and Blake breathed air into his lungs for him, I felt death leaning over my shoulder, daring to come for the man who feared nothing. Not even the Grim Reaper.

"You can't have him!' I screamed from the depths of the nothingness in my chest. And I held onto him tighter, refusing death itself. Because no force in this land could take one of my Night Keepers from me. I was their protector, their saviour, their queen. And they were my kings of the dark, my immortal beasts. So if death was here to claim one of us, it had better take us all.

CHAPTER FIFTY THREE

ONE WEEK LATER

The four of us sat in silence as the time ticked by, none of us wanting to say or do anything other than just feel the emptiness of the space that Kyan should have resided in.

I felt hollow without him here. Like this barren space in me would never quite be filled again. It wasn't like when my mom had died. Though I'd never get over losing her, I was fairly certain that I'd finally come to terms with it. What had happened to her wasn't right and it hadn't been her time, but she'd at least lived. She'd known love and family and had seen her dreams come to fruition. But Kyan...he'd barely even begun to find out who he was without his family's shadow hanging over him. He'd barely even gotten a taste of love. It wasn't his fucking time.

I blew out a slow breath as I looked at the unfamiliar view outside the window, open planes coated in snow looking back at me blandly. None of us had been home in the week since it had all happened. Since we'd gone up against Troy Memphis and lost.

Saint had thrown himself into trying to track his father down, but it was no use. He'd even admitted so himself. Troy had run far away and put himself out of our reach. Saint had even pulled the plug on his assets, locking off his access to most of his money, calling in all of the favours he'd accrued with the powerful people Troy may have tried to turn to for help. And with Royaume D'élite gone it seemed like the last of his contacts should have been gone too. But apparently not. Someone must have helped him. Either that or he'd had an escape plan in place for a situation like this and there was nothing but dead ends left in his wake.

He was gone.

His reputation was in tatters, his companies sold off, liquidated or now under the control of his son. He was wanted by the FBI, his face plastered all over the news and the most wanted lists and yet he'd just up and vanished. Like a ghost.

I guessed ruining his life was something. But it wasn't enough considering all he'd done.

Saint had sworn he'd never give up the hunt, but I wasn't sure what the point of it was. I needed to let it go. We all did. If we wanted any hope of moving on and building...something.

I ran a hand down my face and sighed, turning my gaze to Tatum and offering her a hand as her tearstained cheeks hurt my soul.

She accepted it, her fingers curling around mine as she let me draw her from her chair and pull her into my lap.

"I don't want to live in a world without Kyan Roscoe," she breathed. "I need him darkening my doorway. I need him riling me up and fighting with me. I need him being the worst kind of asshole and laughing while he does it. I just...need him."

She looked up at me like I might be able to offer her some kind of fix for this, but how could I? There was nothing I could do but share in her grief and try to figure out what the fuck we were going to do without him, how the hell we were supposed to do anything at all.

My throat thickened and I leaned down to kiss her, tasting our grief between our lips as I wrapped my arms tightly around her and tried to draw her pain and fear into me. I wished I could make it all okay. I wished I could do something to change fate or bargain with it.

Saint was silent, glaring at the door like it had personally offended him, his posture rigid and jaw tight. He was going to break. Not in the ways he had before. Without Kyan he would break in a way I knew he'd never come back from. It would destroy him. It would destroy all of us and I didn't see how we'd ever recover.

"I can't just sit here," Nash growled, standing suddenly and knocking his empty coffee cup flying. "I'm going to go for a run."

None of us replied. He'd been doing that a lot, even though the doctors had told him it would aggravate the healing brand on his thigh. I guessed he just needed the oblivion of real exhaustion. The kind you could only get from pushing your body to its limits and beyond. Maybe I should have been taking a leaf out of his book, but I hadn't been able to do it. I didn't want to be away from Tatum. Not now. I couldn't.

I didn't think I'd slept more than a few hours this entire week and my heart hadn't stopped pounding since we'd been forced to watch Kyan collapse in the snow, see his body fail him and were left helpless at his side while his life faded.

It wasn't right. He'd been so strong, so solid, so freaking permanent that I hadn't even contemplated a world without him in it. Yet now that was all I could think of. This endless abyss of time that stretched out before us which should have been so full of joy and possibilities and now held no appeal at all. What was the point to it without him to share in it with us? After everything we'd survived together, didn't we deserve a happily ever after?

The door opened before Nash could reach it and Tatum sucked in a breath as she turned to look at the man who had just stepped into the room with us. Her hand locked tight around my fingers and I held my breath as I waited to hear what he had to say. Whether he was about to end the world or save it.

The doctor's face split into a tired smile and hope blossomed in my chest like the rising sun.

"He survived the surgery. We stopped the bleeding. I can't even begin to explain how unlikely..." He trailed off, shaking his head in disbelief. "Truly he should be dead. In fact, he *was* dead - *twice*. But by God, he's one stubborn bastard. His heart just kept coming back to life. He must have something he really wants to live for because I've never seen someone fight so hard to stay with us."

"Oh thank fuck," Tatum gasped before descending into sobs as I hugged her close and a relieved laugh fell from Nash's lips.

"When will he wake?" Saint demanded, getting to his feet and only looking marginally relieved. I knew he wouldn't believe it was true until he was looking Kyan dead in the face and seeing it for himself.

It had been a week of agony, waiting for him to wake up since his surgery to remove the bullet that was lodged in his abdomen. It had taken them hours to repair all the damage that had been done by it and pull it out of him, and he'd been in a fucking state afterwards. Then this morning he'd started bleeding internally again and they'd rushed him in for emergency surgery.

We'd endured seven days of hell while they'd kept him in an induced coma and monitored him constantly, warning us about how bad the odds were and encouraging us to say goodbye while we had that chance. Like hell we had. None of us had said a single goodbye to him. All he'd heard from the four of us all week were demands for him to fight this, stay with us, come back swinging like he always did. And it looked like the asshole had been listening. Though when they'd rushed him into the ER again an hour ago, I could admit that I'd been freaking the fuck out.

"Soon. If one of you wants to see him now, then-"

"We'll all go," Saint said forcefully, giving the doctor a look which was clearly aimed to remind him of who exactly was paying his wages here.

Tatum didn't wait for the doctor to agree, leaping from my lap but keeping hold of my hand and dragging me after her as she ran for the door.

Nash and Saint swept past the doctor too and we practically charged down the corridor to Kyan's room.

The place had been cleaned and aired out while he was in surgery, but he lay there now in the centre of the large hospital bed with the IV hooked up to his arm and more colour in his cheeks than I'd seen all week.

Tatum hurried to his side, smoothing his hair away from his face and leaning down to press a kiss to the corner of his mouth. His eyes flickered beneath the lids and I grabbed one of the chairs, dragging it right up behind her so that she could curl herself into it while staying right beside him.

We pulled the other chairs close to the bed too, all of us crowding around him, watching him sleep and waiting for the drugs to wear off while Tatum held his hand.

"I feel like our future just opened up before us again," I murmured, breathing a sigh of relief.

"We just got our life back," Nash agreed, clapping a hand on my shoulder and squeezing tightly.

We shared a look, and I knew he was thinking of how it had felt to be chained up on that cross waiting to die just like I was. Everything had come so close to falling to shit yet somehow, here we all were, alive, free. My dad was safe back at our family home, nothing but a few scrapes and bruises to show for his time held captive at Royaume D'élite. And the club itself was gone. We'd killed all of the major players aside from Troy and Saint had officially handed over every bit of evidence he had on the club of horrors to his contacts within the FBI yesterday so that they could take down the rest.

It was all over the news, but there wasn't so much as a peep about any of us. Nothing. We were ghosts who didn't exist so far as the reports went, and it would stay that way too.

This morning the news had broken about Tatum's dad being framed and she'd sobbed in relief for almost an hour before giving her attention back to Kyan's recovery. It had filled me with relief too, knowing the man who had worked so hard to protect his daughters was now exonerated. And his death had not been in vain. I just wished I'd gotten the chance to know him. Because from what Tatum had told me about him, I was sure we would have gotten along. And I wished I'd had the chance to thank him for bringing the love of my life into the world.

Everything was coming together. It was over. And even if Troy had managed to escape death at our hands, he was still ruined, gone, run away never to return. It was good enough. It had to be. We couldn't dedicate our lives to hunting a ghost. We needed to live.

We sat there and waited as Kyan breathed in and out slowly, his face more peaceful than I'd ever seen it.

"He's waking up!" Tatum gasped, pointing to Kyan's hand where she held it, his fingers now tightening around hers.

"Don't make me find your granny and force her to eat the kitty litter," he mumbled without opening his eyes. "Her dentures aren't strong enough for that and she'll break 'em on the granules while trying to choke the shit down."

I barked a laugh and suddenly we were all laughing together, relief and joy falling from us in a wave that became hysterical as Kyan opened his eyes and smirked at us even while he was clearly trying to figure out where the fuck he was. But I guessed it didn't matter. Because we were here with him. Tatum's hand was in his and we were laughing, smiling, just waiting for him to complete our tribe.

I didn't know what we'd do once he was allowed to leave the hospital. I didn't know where we'd go with the country still in Lockdown and Everlake Prep in our past. But it didn't really matter. Because wherever we went and whatever we did, we'd be together. I didn't even need to ask the others to know that that was the truth. We belonged together now and always. That was never going to change.

In years to come, people would look back on this time of wearing masks and social distancing, of missing people and enduring lockdowns, of the fear of the virus and the hope for an end to it and no doubt there would be a lot of mixed emotions about what we'd survived. But wasn't that the point? We *had* survived. And that was all that truly mattered.

Because my family was here, and we had a life ahead of us now. One where the Hades Virus would become a thing of the past and we could look back on our time in quarantine and at least say we'd found this.

Love.

Family.

Life.

And really, what else could anyone ask for that was more important than that?

CHAPTER FIFTY FOUR

ONE YEAR LATER

Dear Jess,

I'm sorry I haven't written to you for a while. The world got chaotic. Things were frightening, uncertain and I didn't want to write you letters full of all that. For a minute there I couldn't see the other side of it. It just looked like a tunnel of darkness stretching out endlessly. But there's always light on the other side. I'll remember that in future.

You'd totally laugh at me right now if you could see me. I kinda enrolled at YALE – I know, I know! I'm not the college type. But there was a Women's Studies class which seemed right up my street so Saint pulled a few strings to get me on it. It's not like I'm getting a degree or anything. I'll leave that to him, Blake and Nash. Honestly, I swear I'm getting a second-hand degree from Nash anyway because he loves telling me about the Greek *history he's learning. Which is pretty funny considering he said he'd never follow a future laid out for him by Saint Memphis. But when he looked at that Ancient Greek programme, I guess it got him hard because he's not stopped talking about it since. Did you know some ancient Greeks wouldn't eat beans because they thought they contained the souls of the dead?? If that's the case, I've eaten several towns worth of souls and I'm sorry if one of them was you. Though I'm pretty hopeful you didn't get to live on as a bean. That would be a shitty fate. No one wants their afterlife to end in a burrito.*

Okay, I've totally circled the point here but if you are watching me from a bean somewhere in this house then you probably already realised I'm dating four men including my husband. Weird, right? You should see the faces of the sorority girls who show up here daily looking to party with my boys. Kyan put a sign up on the door once with a filthy picture of me naked on a throne between all of my guys with the words: a queen with four consorts lives here. They definitely think I'm some kind of witch, but most of them think I'm the boss kind. I even made a few friends out of them who I get to do girly shit with.

OMG I didn't even tell you. So Saint bought a whole frat house for us and named it Nu Kappa, it was legit set up and decked out with everything we needed when we arrived. And he totally let a load of guys pledge themselves to the fraternity too and then the Night Keepers put them through the most insane hazing you could ever imagine – and to top it all off, Saint didn't offer a single one of them a place in the house. He said he didn't want anyone else living with us, so he clearly just went through with the whole thing so that he could haze those guys!

Honestly? I think it's overkill. Especially the super super super king bed he got specially made for all of us. I have no idea how they got it in the house, it takes up a whole room. But it's sooo comfy. And yes, I'm a total whore who sleeps with four guys every night and yes I let them do all kinds of crazy shit to me. Okay that was TMI. But there it is. And I've never been happier.

"What are you up to, baby?" Kyan's mouth pressed to the scar on my temple as he leaned over me, resting his tattooed hands either side of my letter on the desk as his bare chest brushed my shoulders.

"Writing to Jess," I said, tilting my head all the way back to look up at him.

He smirked as he dropped his head and kissed me upside down, his tongue stroking the roof of my mouth in the weirdest fucking way. When he pulled back, he snatched my pen and wrote underneath my last paragraph.

Hey Jess! It's Kyan here. The psycho husband. If you're a ghost, I strongly encourage you not to haunt this house when I'm around your sister. She can't help but take her clothes off and throw herself at me whenever she sees my massive c

I snatched the pen back, elbowing him in the gut and writing on below his words.

Sorry about him. I had to buy him a neck brace to help support his big head.

Kyan started kissing my neck. "I wanna show you something…"
I smiled, leaning into his touch and finishing up my letter.

I've got to go now but I promise I'll write again soon. Oh and…I wanted to tell you I'll be scattering Dad's ashes today. He'd have wanted you to be there and I know in some way you will be. But just in case you didn't get the memo. Here it is.

Love you forever,

Tatty xxx

"Tatty," Kyan murmured into my neck. "I like that."

"You can't call me it, it's sacred," I laughed as his mouth tickled my neck.

"Damn, you shouldn't have said that. Now I have to defile it." He nipped at my flesh and I batted at him as I got out of my seat. I was in pink yoga pants and a white sports bra. It was only spring, but I was tempting fate by dressing for summer, begging it to come to Connecticut soon.

I ran my fingers down Kyan's chest, following the lines of the ink to the raised scar on his left side. He'd tattooed the word 'bulletproof' along the length of it and it made me wish he was.

"Why'd you have to go and make a memento out of one of the worst moments of my life?" I asked, looking up at him and batting my lashes.

He rested his forehead to mine and smiled darkly. "Because I like to remember that even a bullet can't take me from you, baby. I'm here to stay."

"Well, that's a cute answer." I smirked.

"Come on." He caught my hand and towed me through the beautiful office which had a world map on the wall and little markers of all the places we planned on visiting.

We'd already ticked off Mexico after our vacation last summer and plenty of places around the States. I was excited to see more of the world. Especially after living through a time where travelling had seemed impossible for a while. But like the seasons, winter always turned to spring and spring to summer. It was inevitable. Even if it didn't seem that way at the time. The flowers would bloom, the leaves would grow green and lush and life would continue, even if a few scars of winters past remained.

There were still trials going on over the huge scandal caused by us exposing Royaume D'élite and witnesses had slowly crept forward among those who'd escaped. I'd watched every news report since it had happened, cursing the faces of those convicted and toasting with my boys every time another asshole was locked behind bars. The whole thing had caused such an uproar that new laws were being petitioned in Sequoia to have government officials to be more closely assessed during their time in power.

Dr De La Cost had turned out to be the best investment Saint had ever made and the vaccine had been distributed by Rivers Pharmaceuticals all throughout the world within a year.

Slowly, little by little, life had returned to normal. And nowadays, it all seemed like a dark nightmare we'd been stuck in for a while. Now we were awake and grasping life by the balls every day. There was a sense of freedom and hope in everyone I met, like they were out cherishing each day as deeply as I was. So maybe the dark days had been good for that one thing. Life tasted sweeter than before because we all understood the brevity of it now. And we knew what it was like to have our privileges stripped away, our doors shut and locked, our days lived in fear.

But as amazing as this new life was, there was always going to be a part of me that hated the fact that Troy had gotten away scot free. Saint still spent time hunting for him and I knew it had taken a toll on his heart to know his father was still out there. On Nash's too. I wanted Troy's death for them even more than I wanted it for myself. But all trails were cold. And if Saint couldn't find him, no one could.

Kyan towed me down the long landing with thick cream carpet through to the huge room that overlooked the woodland at the back of the house. The floor length windows of the balcony doors let light stream in and gild the room in deepest amber, highlighting his workspace. He had an artist's desk beside his easel, all kinds of paints and charcoals, pencils and chalks in a granite holder I'd bought for him alongside the little potted plants I'd got him too. I'd planned to keep them alive for him, but he'd watered them every day like a total cutey and had even drawn a couple of them once.

On the walls were his favourite pieces, a lot of them of me, and my personal favourite which was at the far end of the room, taking up a huge portion of the wall. It was a charcoal sketch of me standing between my boys as we looked out over a calm sea, all of us leaning close together and each guy's stance so distinguishable that I knew all of them by that much alone.

Kyan led me to his workspace and showed me his latest piece of a detailed octopus with its tentacles wrapped around a squid in an embrace.

A laugh escaped me as I picked it up. "I love it!"

He grabbed a white frame from his desk and grinned mischievously at me. "I think Saint would like it sitting on his piano, don't you?"

"I can't think of anywhere better," I chuckled and he fitted it into the frame before we ran out of the room, jogging downstairs into Saint's music room which was a perfectly organised space with a black grand piano at the heart of it. Kyan placed the picture on top of his piano, spending a moment positioning it just so before stepping back to admire his work.

"Perfect," I announced and he grabbed a handful of my ass, tugging me toward him and kissing me hard.

Saint had tried to insist he take the art course at Yale but like me, Kyan hadn't wanted the academic life. So Saint set him up his art studio instead and every now and then we all rented a stall at a market in town to sell some of his pieces. It wasn't about the money. It was about the greasy breakfast, the coffee, the sea air and passing on his incredible work to some of the locals.

"Oh shit," I cursed as I broke away from him and glanced at the clock on the wall which told me I only had ten minutes to get to work. "I've gotta go."

Kyan groaned, tugging me flush to his body again and trailing his mouth down to my neck. "Call in sick, it's not like we need the cash."

"That's not the point," I laughed breathily, kissing him hard before darting out of the room, grabbing my light blue coat from the rack by the door and pulling it on. "Love you!" I called to Kyan as I kicked on my sneakers, threw my phone into my grey handbag and darted out the door.

"Love you harder," he growled, catching the door before I could tug it closed. My eyes widened as he knocked it open, following me onto the porch in his boxers and grabbing me by the throat as he dragged me into a filthy kiss that sent heat skittering everywhere through my flesh.

"Fuck," I breathed as he released me, my gaze dropping to the huge bulge in his boxers.

"That's what we're gonna do when you get home. I'll pick you up at six," he said with a wink.

"I'm taking my own car, I don't need a ride home."

"I'll pick you up anyway. I wanna take you for a spin, baby," he said with mischief in his eyes.

"You know Saint hates you taking me on the bike," I said with a teasing grin, trying to push him back into the house, but he wouldn't go.

"Which is why I'll tell him I'll take the Hummer," he said with a smirk then released me.

I turned away, missing his touch already and my cheeks blazed hotter as I spotted a group of girls across the street who'd stopped to stare. I recognised them as some of the hopeful students who were always eyeing up my men. *They better not have been eyeing up my dark sinner's monster dick.*

I flipped them the finger and jogged over to my shiny white Audi, taking my car keys from my pocket. But before I got there, a car horn sounded and I looked around to find Blake flashing his lights at me and speeding down the road toward me in his fancy ass blue sports car.

He pulled up in front of me with his window down, his hair swept back and still looking damp from a shower, his grey sweatshirt taut against his muscles and a pair of dark aviator sunglasses in place. "How much for a night in your company, sweetheart?" he purred.

"You can't afford me." I smirked and kept walking toward my car while he drove along beside me like a stalker. *Joe Goldberg eat your heart out.*

I noticed the girls had stopped to watch again, whispering between each other, my life apparently far more interesting to them than their own. Which was kinda sad really.

"I'd pay top dollar for those lips alone," he purred and I shook my head at him as my smile grew wider.

"They're not for sale. They belong to someone else. Four someone elses actually," I said lightly.

"Lucky guys," he said. "Is there room for one more in your harem? I've got a big dick and know how to wash dishes good."

"Your dick does the dishes?" I teased.

"No, I do, sweetheart," he said with a low laugh.

"Well I have four big dicks and a dishwasher to keep me happy, so I'm good." I tossed my hair and he reached out of the car, hooking his fingers into the back of my yoga pants to make me stop.

I looked around at him, biting my lip as he slid his aviators down his nose to look up at me with his hungry green eyes.

"I can wash and iron clothes too," he offered with a wink.

"I've got a cleaner who does all that, thanks though." I tugged his hand out of my pants and took off toward my car again, my heart starting to flutter. It was crazy how much my guys still affected me on a daily basis. I didn't think I was ever going to stop feeling this insane, loved up way about them.

"I'll eat your pussy for three hours straight if you get in the car with me!" Blake shouted at the top of his lungs and the girls across the street gasped, staring over at me with parted lips and jealous glares.

I glanced back at Blake, stifling a laugh then shrugged casually and jogged to get in the car, slipping into the passenger seat. He dropped his hand between my thighs, tugging one leg open as he encouraged me toward him and I kissed him greedily, tasting all the light in the world on his tongue.

"Fuck you," I breathed against his mouth and he chuckled darkly.

"Yes please," he growled, pulling on my leg like he wanted me to get into his lap.

"You're an animal." I sat back in my seat and clipped my belt in place. "And I'm late for work. There's far too many dicks trying to stop me from getting there this morning, it's like a cock obstacle course."

Blake barked a laugh, jamming his finger on the dashboard and Something Just Like This by The Chainsmokers and Coldplay started playing as he took off down the road, leaving the gawping girls in his dust.

It was only a five minute drive to the harbour and as Blake drove like he owned the roads, we actually made it with one minute to spare as he parked up outside the boxing studio that overlooked the sea. It was a perfect spring day, the air cool but the sun gleaming down on the boats in the harbour and the water perfectly calm.

Blake walked me inside and we headed upstairs to the studio where my first class was gathering for their self-defence lesson. It was mostly kids and women, but a couple of guys attended too with their wives. I wasn't totally convinced that my guys hadn't warned every frat boy at Yale to keep fifty feet away from me at all times unless I was with one of them, but none of them would confirm it. They sure as shit didn't deny it though.

Blake drew me in for a heart-pounding kiss goodbye and I lingered in his hold for ten seconds I didn't have to spare, dizzy as I finally pulled away.

"Can I stay to watch?" he asked but I shooed him back toward the stairs.

"No, go home and relax. Oh and check out Kyan's new addition to Saint's music room," I added with a smirk and Blake grinned, waving as he walked back down the stairs. My gaze stayed on his broad shoulders for a moment. Since he'd joined the football team at Yale, I swear he'd put on another ten pounds of muscle. He was the quarterback, of course. That was probably why cheerleaders kept sniffing around our house like vermin. I found one lurking in the backyard once like a hungry racoon. She damn well didn't come back again after I was through with her though.

I stepped into the studio, the sun spilling through the room like molten gold and I smiled at the familiar faces surrounding me. I waved at my new friends Kayla and Dione who'd been attending my classes for the past few weeks and they smiled brightly at me.

"Hey guys," I said to grab everyone's attention. "Who's ready to become a savage?"

The sun was sinking over the sea as I stepped out of the boxing studio and locked up for the night. I only did day classes as I liked to spend my evenings and weekends with the guys, so the gym tended to attract students and moms. I swear the kids showing up with them were making me broody too, which I'd never really given much thought to before. And after I'd seen Emily Shaw's new baby, I'd legit got a weird feeling in my tummy which I'd never experienced before. Not that I was ready to start planning a family. I was way too young and I didn't want anything changing what me and my guys had. Not yet anyway.

Nash and I used the boxing gym whenever we wanted and he trained me for the odd local fight. I'd won my first three so far and there was nothing quite like the thrill of beating my opponent while my four Night Keepers stood beside the ring, roaring my name.

Kyan was waiting for me in jeans and a leather jacket, leaning against his motorcycle while some college girl in short shorts asked him directions, batting her lashes at him profusely.

He had a bored expression on his face as he answered her but when his eyes slid over her head to me, he stood upright, is mouth pulling into a slanted grin.

"Hey, baby," he called, brushing past the girl and leaving her pouting after him, her face falling as she spotted me.

Kyan grabbed me by the waist, lifting me up and making a cocky show of laying his claim on me while I laughed into his kisses.

"Take me home, big man," I insisted. "I'm gonna die of starvation if I don't get some pizza in my belly." Pizza night was still officially in place and I'd been hungering for it all week.

"Nash already put the order in," he announced, carrying me to his bike and planting my ass on the back of it.

"Did Saint see the drawing you made him?" I asked excitedly.

"Yup. He smashed it and threatened to cut me with the glass if I didn't tell him what the squid meant."

I laughed. "And you didn't?"

"No way," he said, grinning like an asshole.

"I hope you salvaged that drawing, I loved it," I said.

"Sure did, baby. I'll frame it for you again and you can put it wherever you like."

"I'll protect it from Saint with my life." I grinned.

He made a fuss of putting my helmet on and I placed his on his head too, snapping down the visor. He got on the bike in front me and I gripped his waist, locking my thighs around his as he took off down the street away from the harbour.

"Saint saw me take the bike," he called back to me as we closed in on home. "He's gonna be pissed."

"I'll handle it," I replied.

"I bet you will." He dropped his hand to squeeze my knee then turned down our street, passing all the other frat houses on the road and pulling up at the one on the far end.

Kyan rode into the garage and I jumped off the bike, pulling my helmet off and we were soon heading inside where I followed the delicious scent of cheese and tomato into the dining room. The white curtains were open either side of the window which looked out over our backyard. Monroe was often out there at the weekends mowing the lawn shirtless and looking hot as shit. He was pretty domesticated due to the fact that he'd lived alone for so long and he was fast training up the rest of my boys too. Not Saint, obviously – he just got the new version of Rebecca to do all of his chores. He called her Rebecca too, claiming that it made sense because it had always been a false name and it suited him to keep to it. Fuck knew what the girl thought of that, but I was guessing for the salary he paid, she'd decided not to give a shit.

Nash rushed at me as I entered the room, picking me up and spinning me around, claiming a kiss that made me heady. Saint grabbed me from him next, drawing me close and gripping my chin hard as he kissed me slow and deliberately like he was trying to mark me more permanently than Nash had.

"You're in trouble," Saint's voice dipped to a deep, threatening tone that made my heartrate spike.

"Well how about you take control in the bedroom tonight as a peace offering?" I arched an eyebrow and looked to the others as Kyan entered the room, stripping out of his leather jacket and tossing it on the back of a chair.

"Seems fair," Saint decided, his eyes glinting with all the bad things he had in mind already. Since we'd moved here, he'd purchased so many sex toys, whips, floggers and BDSM shit that we'd had to use the spare room to store it. It was definitely becoming something of a sex dungeon, but I wasn't complaining. Saint was exploring his need for control and I was exploring my need to be spanked like a bad girl in every dirty way he could think up. It was the best kind of adventure and we were all on it together. Kyan had added his own additions to the room too, including a bench he could tie me down on and some handcuffs he made regular use of. I swear Saint had been teaching him how to do all kinds of knots too because the last time Kyan had brought me in there, he'd bound my hands and feet so well he could barely get me out of his own trap when he was done with me.

Blake and Nash didn't tend to end up in there with us unless the drink was flowing and we all got pissed enough to be extra experimental. The weirdest night so far was when Blake had let Saint tie him up and used the flogger on his ass while I sucked his dick. Good fun though. I was all for them trying new things. Nash refused to let Saint do shit to him like that very often, but he'd once gotten so drunk he'd agreed to wear a ball gag so long as I wore one too. He'd fucked me so hard the next morning that I got the feeling trying to make him submissive only made him more dominant when he was let loose again. So I was all for encouraging Saint and Kyan to tie him up just to see how explosive he could get later.

Saint pulled out a chair for me and I dropped into it as Nash took the seat opposite and Kyan sat on his right. Blake and Saint sat down either side of me and I grabbed a box of margarita pizza excitedly, bouncing in my seat.

I took out a cheesy slice, my mouth watering but I offered it up to Saint first. He gripped my wrist, turning it forcefully towards my lips instead.

"You look like a ravenous beast, siren. I won't eat until you've had a least two slices," he insisted and I wasn't gonna complain about that.

I devoured the pizza and we all fell into conversation about our days while I fed Saint and he soon pulled me into his lap.

Nash fascinated us all with more facts he'd learned in class while Blake acted out a touchdown he'd scored in training which his coach had said was the best one he'd ever seen. With a little probing, Saint told us succinctly about his Classical Music class followed by his complaints about the people on his Political Science course who were constantly licking his ass to try and gain a new powerful friend for their future careers. An effort which was clearly wasted.

My phone buzzed and I took it out, smiling at the sight of Mila's name.

Mila:

Hey, girl! I'm home in New York for a couple of weeks. Me and Danny thought we could drive down to Connecticut for a few days to see you guys?

xx

I squealed excitedly and Saint frowned in surprise. "What is it?" he asked as everyone's eyes laid on me.

"It's Mila. She wants to come visit with Danny," I said with a grin.

"Hell yes!" Blake whooped.

"We can put them up in a hotel, I suppose," Saint said with a shrug and I smacked his arm.

"They'll stay here, Saint Memphis. They're our friends. You'd better not forget they saved our asses," I said and he considered that for a second before nodding.

"Alright, whatever makes you happy." He kissed my cheek and warmth spread through me as I replied, telling her to come as soon as she could.

The light pouring through the window started turning to a deep orange glow and I jumped up from my seat in alarm. "The sun's setting," I gasped.

"We can do it another day if it's too late?" Nash offered.

"No," I said firmly. "I want to do it today. I've already left it too long and today just feels…right." I took a deep breath as I mentally prepared for what I had to do. I knew I'd been avoiding this. But it was time. And it wasn't fair to leave my dad in that box on the mantelpiece any longer just because this was difficult for me.

"Then we're doing it, princess." Nash got up from his seat, offering me his hand and I took it, letting him guide me from the room as the others followed. We all put our coats and shoes on before I grabbed the box with my dad's ashes and we headed into the garage, piling into Saint's mom car. I'd told them all a long time ago where I wanted to do it. Dad and I had stayed in New Haven a couple of years back and we'd taken a walk together in East Rock Park every lunchtime while he was working. It had been our favourite spot and it was such a peaceful place that I knew it was somewhere he would have liked to visit again.

Saint drove us there in under five minutes and we all spilled outside, hurrying through the gate then I ran ahead toward one of the bridges that crossed the river. I made it to the middle and looked down into the water just as the dying sunlight poured through the sky in huge strokes of pastel colours. The clouds were so still they looked painted onto the colourful canvas of the atmosphere. It was picturesque and painfully perfect.

My boys moved to stand either side of me as I held onto the box, afraid to open it and let go. But I had to. I couldn't hold on forever.

"He won't ever leave you," Nash said in a low voice in my ear as tears burned my eyes.

"I know," I whispered as my heart began to ache. "It's still hard though."

"When I said goodbye to Michael and then to Mom, I made myself say it out loud so I could process it better, I guess. Do you think that would help?" he asked gently, his arm sliding around me as Blake pressed close to me on my other side.

I sniffed as I held back my tears, knowing they were inevitable, but Nash was right. I needed to say this out loud. And I didn't want to do it while I was crying.

I brushed my fingers over the box, gazing down at it and taking in a shaky breath. "I never pictured my life without you, Dad. You were the only constant I knew. My rock, the man who taught me to be brave and strong and to never back down from a fight. No matter how big the enemy." Nash laid a kiss in my hair as a razor blade seemed to lodge in my throat. "You said once that the kind of man you wanted me to choose as my own would look at me like he'd kill for me. I just happened to choose four who literally would, and they got the chance to prove it too." I released a breath of amusement as my guys chuckled.

I looked to the sky, knowing in my heart that my dad wasn't really in this box. That it was just what remained of him on Earth. But somewhere, somehow, I felt sure he was watching me with Jess at his side. And they were smiling.

"Goodbye, Dad," I breathed to the box, pressing my lips to it as the first tears began to fall.

I opened the lid, holding it out over the railing as a fierce wind picked up, blowing from behind us. Then I turned the box upside down and released the ashes into the air, an arc of grey dancing away from us through the sky, scattering in the river, the trees, the sky.

Dad was free. And finally, so was I.

CHAPTER FIFTY FIVE

FOUR YEARS AFTER THAT

"Well, shit," Blake said, reaching out and flipping the tassel of my graduation cap out of my face. We were headed out of the ceremony and looking for Tatum and Kyan in the crowd of people who had come to watch it. "We actually did it. And you don't even look *soooo* much older than the rest of us dressed up like this."

"Fuck off," I said, shoving him so that he stumbled away a step and his own cap fell off.

Saint caught it before it could hit the ground and turned it over in his hands thoughtfully. "This means everything is going to change again," he said seriously, though he didn't seem as thrown by that as I would have expected.

"There's a huge party being held tonight on the far side of campus," Blake began, but Saint cut him off.

"We won't be attending."

"Why?" I asked as we stalked through the crowd and everyone got out of our way as fast as they could. Even here, everyone knew who the Night

Keepers were - including the staff and parents. Maybe I should have felt bad about causing fear wherever we went, but there was something about the power in it that was kind of a rush.

"Like I said: everything is going to change." Saint placed Blake's cap back on his head and turned away like that was all he would say on the matter. *Fucking power hungry asshole.* Not that I minded that so much these days.

He strode ahead of us and me and Blake exchanged a look which encompassed our feelings towards him pulling that crap before we followed on after him. It wasn't like I was just happy to fall into line with his bullshit, I'd just learned that with Saint it was all about picking your battles. I didn't sweat the small stuff, then if I felt passionately enough to go head-to-head with him over something, I had a better chance at getting him to back me. It wasn't a fool proof method, but it worked often enough to keep us all happy.

"Where are they?" Blake muttered, looking around the thinning crowd as we still failed to spot Tatum or Kyan.

His Dad had been there to congratulate us the moment the ceremony ended and we'd spent a few minutes talking with him before he'd headed off to catch his flight, needing to get back for a game tonight.

"They're here somewhere," I muttered, searching too. "They were cheering me on when I collected my diploma on stage."

"And Kyan was catcalling during Saint's speech," Blake added with a snort of amusement.

No doubt Saint already had a punishment lined up for Kyan when he got his hands on him. Saint had been awarded a bunch of accolades and awards and had been asked to speak as one of this year's outstanding graduates. Some of the pomp and posturing had been lost though when Kyan decided to start whooping with excitement and fist pumping at the end of every sentence Saint read from his speech. It had been pretty over the top and I personally found it really fucking funny, but I was guessing Saint had ideas about spanking him for it which he wanted to play out.

"Where have they gotten to?" Saint demanded, turning back to face us and I shrugged.

"They'll be doing what they always do when they go missing," Blake said with a smirk and Saint narrowed his eyes.

"You're right," he growled, looking around slowly before stalking away towards the far side of the building, cutting a path right across the freshly manicured grass.

We followed him, letting him do his Sainty senses thing as he rounded a corner, and the soft sound of a moan reached my ears.

"They'll be looking for us," Tatum gasped, her point very much diminished by the gasp of pleasure that followed her words.

"Then come for me quick, baby, and we won't have to face the wrath of the Devil," Kyan growled.

The sounds of heavy breaths and barely stifled moans followed and as we stepped around another corner, we found them in a stone alcove. Kyan had Tatum pinned to the wall, her blue dress hitched up and his pants hanging from his ass as he fucked her like a man possessed.

Tatum's eyes flew open and she spotted the three of us just as she came for him, her moans mixed with a gasp of, "Oh, shit." As Kyan slammed into her a few more times before finding his own release.

"What a surprise," Saint drawled, folding his arms. "The drop-out delinquents are around here fucking like rabbits while the scholars accept their diplomas."

"We watched the ceremony," Kyan argued as he lowered her to the ground and fastened his fly. "At least we did until you three had your shiny little scrolls. Then we got kinda bored and Tatum begged me to give her my dick. You know I'm not going to say no to my wife when she requests cock."

"Shut up," Tatum hissed at him, slapping his chest as she righted her dress and moved past him to us. "I'm sorry, we meant to get back before it was over," she added to us, looking kinda bashful and there was no way in hell I was going to be mad at her over it.

"You watched the bit that counted," I shrugged. "But if you really wanna make it up to us-"

"No," Saint snapped. "There's no more time for fucking. We have a plane to catch."

"A plane?" Blake asked with a frown.

"Yes. And if we don't leave now, the flight will have to be rescheduled." Saint grabbed Tatum's hand and towed her away from all of us as he headed for the parking lot.

"Am I the only one who is totally lost here?" I asked, frowning as I tried to figure out what the fuck was going on.

"He's gone all Saint," Blake groaned while Kyan chuckled.

"Hey, I'm not complaining. If there's a plane then you know it'll be one of those fancy jets he loves. The real question is, who wants to join the mile-high club?" He stuck his hand in his pocket and pulled out a lacy black thong which he'd clearly stolen from Tatum and I grabbed it before Blake could.

"Mine," I growled, claiming that prize more than happily.

"Asshole," Blake muttered.

"I'm okay with that," I assured him.

Saint had already made it to his black mom-mobile which was parked up at the front of the lot in the special parking place he'd had arranged for himself when we started attending college here. He'd said something about a sizeable donation and that had been explanation enough for his entitled treatment. Saint might have learned some of the errors of his ways, but he was always going to be a stuck-up prick. Leopards didn't just change their spots and all that. But I liked to think the good in him made up for the bad. Most of the time.

We piled into the car and before long we were pulling up at the private airport, all while listening to Blake lament the fact that we were missing the party tonight and that he hadn't been allowed to say goodbye to anyone. Saint explained that no one was really important enough to warrant a special farewell and we all grumbled about that, texting the friends we'd made and promising to meet up with them over the summer or whenever. We couldn't exactly set any definitive dates tough. Who fucking knew what Saint had planned?

The private jet was ready and waiting on the runway like Saint had said, all of our luggage already onboard and I just gave in to his insanity as I boarded, not caring enough to argue over it. For someone who hated surprise changes of plans, he sure liked springing them on the rest of us.

The flight took five and a half hours, during which time I managed to join the mile-high club twice, much to my pleasure. Blake and Saint had also spent time alone in the rear cabin with our girl, but Kyan had been forced to sit his turn out in his seat as punishment for his earlier stunt with a ball gag in his mouth. Saint had spent an hour giving Tatum her punishment in private and the look on her face when he was done said she didn't exactly feel all that chastised.

Fuck knew what the flight crew thought of us, but I was well past giving a shit about judgemental assholes. We were the kings of the world worshipping our queen. No. Better than that: we were the Night Keepers satisfying our Night Bound. It didn't need to make sense to anyone aside from the five of us.

Following the flight, we piled into yet another brand spanking new mom-mobile of the exact same make and colour and Tatum insisted we leave all of the windows down so that we could enjoy the west coast heat as the sun started its descent towards the horizon.

We'd all given up on questioning Saint on our destination and I let my head drop back against the headrest, holding Tatum close as I fell asleep and she leaned her head against my chest.

"Keep your eyes closed," Saint's voice jolted me awake and I almost didn't do as he asked, but Tatum's hand moved over my eyes to stop me from opening them.

I still peeked out from beneath her hand, though all I could see was her looking cute as hell, her eyes shut tight as she leaned on me, clearly knowing I wouldn't have played along if she didn't force me to.

The car came to a halt and Saint got out before opening my door and tugging on my arm to make me step out too.

"No cheating," Tatum warned before taking her hand from my eyes and I sighed as I did what they wanted, letting Saint walk me over a stone pathway before he stood me next to Blake, my arm brushing his.

Kyan moved to stand on my other side next and finally the sound of Saint and Tatum's footsteps approached us last.

"Tell me what you feel, siren," Saint encouraged and she laughed lightly like she was enjoying herself, so I held my tongue and waited for her answer.

"The sun on my face," she breathed. "A sea breeze, waves lapping against a beach. It's...so quiet here. I feel calm, safe. Happy because I'm here with all of you. What's this about, Saint?"

"We needed somewhere to live now that we've graduated," he replied simply and that really got my attention. "And I remembered all of the things you told me about your idea of a perfect home, Tatum. As well as considering everything the rest of us require."

"What does that mean?" she breathed.

"I asked you to tell me what you feel here, siren, because I'm sincerely hoping, you feel at home. Open your eyes."

I took that instruction to be for all of us and did as he said. I opened my eyes as he took his hands from Tatum's too, so that all of us could see this place for the first time together.

My eyebrows rose as I looked out over perfect golden sand to a narrow jetty that ran into the blue ocean with little boats docked at the far end of it. The sun was setting over the sea and the sky was blazing with orange and pink as the balmy air wrapped around us like a warm embrace.

To our right, an enormous, white stone church towered over us, blotting out the damn sky and was no doubt even bigger than the freaking frat house we'd been occupying back in Connecticut.

"Come on," Saint urged as he took Tatum's hand and tugged to get her to follow him towards the church, beckoning the three of us after them.

I glanced around, noticing a huge gate at the far end of the long drive and a tall, white wall stretching out away from it, secluding us here from the world.

I shook my head at the insanity of this place as he led us inside and a huge open space unfolded before us. It was stunning, fucking perfect really which shouldn't have been a surprise. Everything was decorated in white and blue and something about the sapphire colour on the walls instantly made me think of the colour of Tatum's eyes which I knew was no freaking accident.

There was a whole wall of glass doors which looked out over that stunning view with access straight onto the beach and beside it the most expensive looking grand piano I'd ever seen sat ready and waiting for Saint's attention.

"Won't we get people looking in at us all the time?" I teased as I tried to wrap my head around the beauty of this place.

"Obviously that's a private beach," Saint tutted. "No one will be out there to see us if they know what's good for them and I made sure to check out the local area to be certain that those rules will be upheld."

I got the feeling this place had been built entirely for our purposes because it may have looked like a church from the outside, but the inside was like something from Million Dollar Decorators. And Saint had spared no goddamn money. The whole back wall was an arching stained-glass window which depicted five demons crawling out of hell to reach the shining queen with golden hair who stood at the surface of the world. The sunset spilled through the multi-coloured glass, casting a ripple of light across the flagstones.

Holy fucking shit.

I shared a look with Tatum as she gawped at it and Kyan started laughing.

"Where are we?" Blake asked, his eyes wide with awe. "I mean I know vaguely, but-"

"The closest town is called Sunset Cove," Saint explained dismissively. "There's enough there to entertain us if we want to spend an evening having a nice meal in the upper quarter and a much less appealing lower quarter beyond that if we require less civilised distractions."

"Tell me more about this unappealing area," Kyan said instantly, his head snapping around and I knew Saint had mentioned it for his benefit. "Is there somewhere I can fight there?"

"I'd be down for that," I agreed. It had been slim pickings for us to find good fights while we were at college, but there had been a few underground cage fighting joints we'd managed to frequent when we got the time.

"Count me in too," Tatum said with a grin.

"You could still go pro, you know," I reminded her and she shrugged.

"Maybe I will now I'll have the time to dedicate to that."

"There's a fully equipped gym downstairs in the crypt," Saint said nonchalantly. Of course he'd had a motherfucking crypt built here. There were probably sarcophaguses in there too just for authenticity's sake. "But I have also made contact with the relevant players locally. The leader of the Harlequin Crew is a badly bred ruffian with all the decorum of a crab in a bucket of lobsters, but he seems like a man of his word. I can put you in contact with him about any illegal activities you insist on taking part in. He has already accepted that we are going to be living here and knows exactly who he will be dealing with if any of his lackeys try to cause us trouble. Suffice to say, we have struck an accord, and I don't think the local criminals will cause us any issues."

"You're such a psycho. I've heard all about the Harlequin Crew, they're a bunch of lawless savages, suspected of putting more bodies in the ocean than the police can keep track of. And you just stroll on up to one of their most notorious members and 'strike an accord,'" Blake laughed and Saint smiled like that was the greatest compliment he'd ever received.

"Yes, well, I suppose Fox Harlequin scented another shark in the water and realised it would serve him better to befriend us than make us his enemies. Needless to say, he is aware of what I am able to achieve if he has a need for any such services and I now have a bunch of cutthroats to call on in a pinch. Everyone wins."

I shook my head at his back in disbelief as he shrugged that insanity off like it was nothing while Tatum grinned at me as she clearly agreed.

Saint continued to lead us through the countless rooms in the church, pointing out a studio for Kyan, an office for him, a dining room, home cinema room, games room and a huge pool which was in a courtyard to the side of the building complete with hot tub, sauna and steam room. The place was insane. It was The Temple on fucking speed. More than anyone could ever want or need and yet I couldn't take the fucking grin off of my face while we explored it, finding most of our stuff already here, packed away in closets as if we'd been living here for years rather than minutes.

When we headed upstairs, Saint showed us four individual bedrooms which ran along the rear of the church and at first I thought we all had our own rooms. But when he opened the final door to a massive room that ran the whole length of the house, that idea crashed and burned.

In the centre of the space, set up with a view looking right out over the ocean was an enormous bed. Even bigger than the one we'd had at the frat house. It must have been custom made and fuck knew how the hell the sheets were changed because it looked bigger than two super kings bolted together, and I had to believe he'd had everything about it made to order.

Tatum squealed as she kicked her shoes off and raced towards the bed, leaping up onto it and jumping excitedly.

"Do you like it?" Saint asked, looking between her and all of us, a flash of vulnerability in his gaze that halted any mocking comments on the tip of my tongue. He may have been socially lacking a lot of the time, but he really did care, and I couldn't imagine the amount of time and effort he'd put into this place and organising everything that came along with it. "There's a property close to town which would be perfect for you to hold your classes in, siren. And I've lined up football try-outs for you locally, Blake. There's a potential art studio I've seen as well and there are promising job prospects here for-"

"Shit, you really do think of everything, don't you?" I asked and he shrugged as if he wasn't well aware that he was insane.

"I try," he admitted.

"Sun, sea and sex? Yeah, it gets my vote," Kyan agreed with a laugh.

"Me too," Blake added. "But I'm gonna want a closer look at that gym you mentioned."

"I'll show you now," Saint agreed, glancing over at me and I couldn't keep him hanging any longer.

"You know I would have been happy in a two-bed apartment somewhere half decent," I said slowly and his face fell a fraction. "But, if I have to live in an obnoxiously big church with way too much space and more shit than I could ever need, then I can't imagine one that was any more perfect than this."

"Good," Saint said, his chest puffing out a little. "And call me affected by the pandemic, but I've also taken care to stock a secure section of the crypt with all the food we'll ever need if the world goes to hell again."

"Toilet paper throne included?" I asked with a snigger.

"Obviously." He smirked then turned to Tatum with hope in his gaze. "Is the new Temple to your liking, siren? If not, I'll have it burned to the ground by morning."

"Are you kidding me? I freaking love it!" Tatum exclaimed as Saint broke a smile and she leapt off of the bed again, jumping on him and kissing him hard as her smile blazed bright enough to express what we were all feeling. "Just so long as you're not expecting me to fill all of those other bedrooms with babies any time soon."

"Of course not, siren," Saint said, placing her down and kissing her softly once more. "You can have a couple of years before that."

"That's up to me, not you!"

She smacked him as he headed for the door again, taking Blake and Kyan to see the gym and he laughed like he didn't agree with that statement at all.

I headed over to the sliding door, opening it and stepping out onto the balcony to get a clearer look at that view as I let the idea of this place being our new home settle over me.

The sun had almost disappeared beyond the horizon and I leaned my forearms on the white railing as I looked out at it, releasing a slow breath and inhaling the sea air.

"Are you okay?" Tatum murmured as she followed me out, coming to stand beside me and taking my hand.

"Yeah," I said, watching the sunset as I ran my thumb over the back of her hand. "I'm just...letting go."

"Of what?" she asked curiously.

"Troy," I admitted, the sound of the waves on the shore calling to me like the softest lullaby. "I guess I just thought that we'd still get him. One way or another. But it's been years and even Saint can't find anything. I need to just accept that he's gone and move on from it."

"Easier said than done though, right?" she murmured, and I nodded, thinking about my mom, Michael, everything he'd stolen from me and how much I'd hungered for his death in return.

"Yeah," I agreed. "But I think they'd want me to let go of the idea of revenge. It's not like he has what he used to. I mean sure, I wish he was dead or at least locked up somewhere. But he lost his money, his power, his reputation. He'll live out the rest of his life alone and in hiding. And it might not be all that he deserved, but I think overall I can make my peace with it. I think I have to. Because we aren't going to find him, and I don't want him having that hold over me for the rest of my life."

"I love you, Jase," Tatum breathed and I looked at her with a soft smile as she used the name of the man I used to be.

"I love you too, Tatum. And I want to move on. Let this be a fresh start. All of us can make a real life here and I want to live it. Troy can get fucked, I don't care. All I care about is you, me and my brothers. It's more than enough."

I leaned down and kissed her, so much love and depth to that exchange that I knew letting go of this vendetta was the right thing to do. I was done living for hate. I had something so much better than that now.

And as we turned to watch the sun sinking beneath the horizon for the first time in our new home, I was happy to turn a new leaf, start a blank page and just live. Because there was one hell of a life waiting for me right here, and I didn't want or need anything else in the world. Only this.

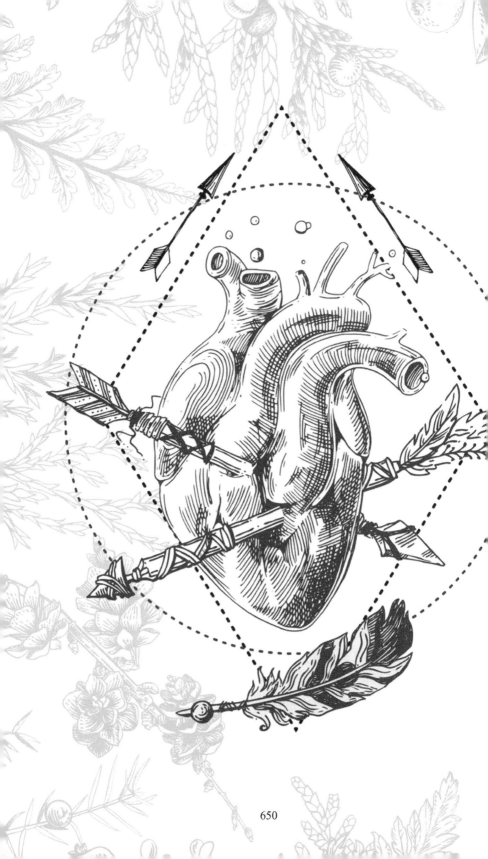

Troy

CHAPTER FIFTY SIX

ANOTHER FIVE YEARS AFTER THAT

I sat back in my chair, my gaze scanning the documents I'd been sent as I tried to track my son's movements. I had to admit, he was good. Better than I'd probably given him credit for. And though I'd found things here and there about the fortune he was amassing over the years, I still hadn't been able to pin him down yet.

He didn't make any purchases under his real name and I hadn't even been able to uncover any of the pseudonyms I was certain he must be using. Because there was no way I would believe he was out of the game. That boy had my blood whether he liked it or not and I knew he would be buying and selling, seeking out power like he needed it to live. But he was holding his secrets close to his chest and I just hadn't caught him yet.

With a mixture of irritation and pride, I placed my tablet down on the metal table beside me, looking up beyond the white parasol I sat beneath towards the blaring sun. It was always hot in this part of the world and I'd grown tired of the lack of variation to the climate soon after arriving here.

But I was stuck without alternative. It wasn't safe for me to travel while so many authorities hunted for me. And though I'd isolated myself in a country without an extradition agreement with the US in the ten years since I'd fled, I was certain bribes would be made or special operatives sent in to retrieve me if my location was discovered.

So I was left a prisoner in my own meagre, twelve bedroom home. In comparison to what most people had, I supposed it was somewhat luxurious, but when I tallied it against all I used to own, it felt awfully flat.

"Branston?" I called, placing down my empty scotch glass and looking around for my man servant to bring me another.

He wasn't anywhere in sight and when he didn't arrive after I called for a second time, I released a frustrated breath and rose from my chair to fix my own glass.

Honestly, what was the point in keeping house staff if they couldn't even keep a glass topped up?

I strode into the house, walking into the wide living area with the vaulted ceiling and the mezzanine level above it. I was bored of this place. Bored of existing in stasis with no power and even less friends. I needed to be free of this prison I'd built for myself and the key to that was in finding my son's money. In fact, I hadn't even been able to lock his location down since he'd graduated from Yale. It was infuriating.

I walked across the white marble floor towards the drinks cabinet, but fell still before I reached it as the large armchair placed by the window came into view and I found a woman sitting there. She held a glass of my favourite and most expensive scotch in her hand, the bottle on the floor beside her as she looked away from me out at the view.

She was wearing a white dress and was sitting sideways in the chair, her long bronze legs hanging over the arm of it with black stiletto Louboutins on her feet. She must have heard my approach, but she didn't turn as she continued to look out of the window, a cascade of blonde curls hiding her face from me.

I fell still, the hairs along the back of neck prickling as I looked at her. This compound was utterly secure. There was no way she'd just wandered in here past the ten foot walls and guarded gates. No way any of my men would have just let her in either. So how in the hell had she-

"Hello, Troy," the woman purred, turning her head towards me and my composure almost slipped as my gaze fell on the face of the Rivers girl.

The one who had corrupted my boy, the one who had taken everything I'd built and twisted it against me. She should have been dead a long time ago, but there she sat, drinking scotch worth more than she could possibly guess and looking me dead in the eye like she thought we were equals. Or worse than that, like she thought she was better than me.

"Saint?" I asked, knowing he must be here too, my voice cold and flat, nothing at all to show that I had been taken off guard by this arrival in my home.

My son stepped out from the doorway in the corner, his face harder than I recalled, features stronger now that he was older. There wasn't a trace of the weak child I'd once known in him and as I watched him approach me at a casual pace, I saw the man I'd always hoped he would become looking back at me and a smile touched my lips as I looked him over.

"I see you took my advice," I said as I adjusted my watch, pressing down on the emergency alarm which would activate silently and bring my men rushing to my location.

It was a shame, but I had come to the conclusion a few years ago that my son would have to die if I ever wanted to reclaim my empire. Once I'd achieved that I supposed I'd have to work on creating another heir, though the tedium of taking a new wife had slowed my progress on that idea.

"What advice was that?" Saint asked curiously, coming to stand behind the black widow who had lured him to her side.

But perhaps I had been wrong to balk against the idea of him aligning himself with this girl. The look in her eyes said she was just as determined and dangerous as him, so despite the weakness I knew this *love* he claimed to feel for her caused him, it was possible she provided some strength too.

"To always go after what you want and never give up until you have it in your grasp," I supplied.

"Well, he has a point there," Tatum said as Saint took her hand and lifted it to kiss the back of her knuckles. "You *are* very tenacious."

My son smiled as he pulled her to her feet and my skin prickled as I watched them together. Whatever they'd done to get in here, they certainly didn't seem in any hurry to achieve their goal. Which only gave my men more time to get here. In fact, I was surprised they weren't rushing into the room already.

"I always get what I want," Saint agreed with her, grasping her throat in his hand as he drew her close and kissed her hard.

The heel of her designer shoes bumped against the bottle of scotch, knocking it over and my gut dropped as the priceless liquid spilled out across the tiles.

"I assume you didn't just come here to paw at the girl who destroyed my club?" I asked in a bored tone, my fingers twitching with the desire to pick that damn bottle up while they just left it there to empty out.

"Of course not," Saint said, slipping his arm around her waist and ignoring the ever-growing puddle of scotch between us even as the thought of it made my jaw tick. "But I thought you might appreciate the time to realise your men aren't coming."

"What men?" I asked, my gut dropping as I resisted the urge to press the button on my watch again.

"It's actually rather simple to jam the signal from a panic device such as yours," Saint said, lazily reaching out to arrange a lock of blonde hair over Tatum's shoulder while she smiled at him with a dark hunger that made me wary.

"I don't know what you-"

"And hired thugs are all well and good," he went on, talking over me like I hadn't spoken at all. "But in the years since you ran away like a frightened rat down a storm drain, it has only become more and more clear to me that you had a fatal flaw in your grand design."

"What's that?" I asked, the accusation rankling me. There were no flaws in anything I did or created other than *him*.

"Would you like to tell?" Saint asked, and it took me a moment to realise he was addressing the girl and not me.

My upper lip twitched with the urge to peel back at that insult, but her sapphire eyes had moved to capture my gaze and the smile on her red painted lips made me hold my tongue on insulting her. I may have despised his feelings for this girl, but I couldn't deny the strength of them and I would have been a fool to bait him over her now.

"A bear may surround himself with coyotes," she said slowly, taking another sip of my scotch as she held my gaze without so much as the sign of a flinch. "But their loyalty will only ever be bought by the scraps they can steal from him."

"A bear is still the most powerful creature in the forest," I replied calmly, realising what she was saying. My men weren't coming, they'd been bribed into betraying me and letting these rats into my home.

"And yet, it can be taken out by a wolf pack," Tatum said, smiling predatorily.

"That's where you went wrong," Saint added, pausing to take a drink of the scotch as Tatum lifted the glass to his lips and I couldn't help but stare at the way they moved together, like two parts of the same being, utterly in sync. "You believed that ultimate power was something to be held by you and no one else. But look at you now, all alone in the world with not a person to care. Your name splashed all over the headlines labelling you as the man responsible for releasing the Hades Virus into the population. You're hated by more people than I could possibly count, responsible for so many deaths that the world could drown in all of that blood if it was spilled at once. Not to mention the rest of the atrocities you committed at Royaume D'élite. Everyone on this planet aches for your death. The only feelings anyone has towards you are those of hatred."

"In fact," Tatum added conversationally, running her hand down Saint's arm and looking at him like he was the reason the sun rose in the mornings, while he stared back at her like she was the reason it existed at all. "A lot of people would probably kill themselves in your position, unable to bear the burden of having done so much evil and of being hated by so many."

"Well, a lot of people are sheep," I sneered, unable to help it in the face of this emotional bullshit. "And the only cure for such idiocy is death."

"Funny you should say that," a rough voice came from behind me, but before I could whirl around, a hand closed tight around my neck. I was yanked backwards against a hard body as a second tattooed hand clamped around my jaw and gripped me firmly, immobilising me as the man behind me spoke. "Because we feel the same way about you."

"Father, you remember Kyan, don't you? Turns out, O'Briens really aren't all that easy to kill after all," Saint smirked at me like some gloating buffoon and I bared my teeth as I lunged for the flick knife I always kept in my pocket.

A gun pressed to my temple and I froze, wheeling my eyes to the left as the hammer was drawn back loudly, my gaze falling on the third of my son's little group of lackeys. The footballer. I'd been able to track some of his movements due to his professional career, but I still hadn't been able to trace my son via him. In that moment, his gaze was so dark and expression so cold that I was certain I was seeing exactly what appeal my son had found in him. That was the way of powerful men; we were always drawn together, but no true bond could form between us the way Saint tried to claim, because our struggle for supremacy would never end.

"I wouldn't try that if I were you," Blake said simply and my heart raced as I hunted for the route out of this. It was just another puzzle for me to solve, a game for me to win. There was a way. There was always a way.

The hand around my neck gripped tighter suddenly and I choked as Kyan forced my chin up and made me look to the balcony on the second floor where a man stood looking down at me, his dirty blonde hair falling in his eyes as watched me with a deadly look in his gaze.

Kyan's hand flexed as he adjusted his grip and for a moment I was certain he was about to break my neck. "Wait," I gasped, stalling for time.

"I think Nash has waited long enough," Tatum hissed, stepping closer to me with her high heels clicking on the marble. "It looks like the wolf pack just caught up to you." There was a pure and venomous hatred in her gaze which sent a shiver down my spine. But I wouldn't give up, I wasn't built that way. There was a way out of this, I just had to grasp it and then-

"My brother had his entire life ahead of him," Nash snarled from above me, his face the only one I could see which showed all of his emotions plainly. He was enraged, bloodthirsty, aching for vengeance and hungry to claim it. He nodded at Kyan and the oaf's hands tightened around my throat, cutting off my breath and making me buck and kick in fear.

He was taller than me so he heaved my weight backwards and panic washed through me as I was wrenched off of my feet, my hands clawing at his fingers desperately as I tried to prise them off.

I began to kick and thrash, grasping for my pocket in hopes of hooking the flick knife free as the very real prospect of my death flashed before my eyes.

But before I could succumb to it, I was thrown down into a wing backed chair with a thump, the hand was removed and the pressure released from my neck so that I could suck in a gasping breath. My pulse thundered with fear, but I forced it aside, refusing to allow them to terrorise me in my own home.

I panted heavily, trying to regain my composure as I looked between the people who had broken into my safe haven and Blake kept the gun trained on me to stop me from moving.

Kyan slung a heavily tattooed arm around Tatum's shoulders, his black wifebeater offending my eyes with its terribly casual appearance in my home, and as he placed a kiss to the top of her head, a thought occurred to me which tore into the fabric of the legacy I had hoped to leave upon this planet.

To further confirm my fears, Blake moved to her other side and ran a finger along her jaw in a clear caress, though his aim with the gun never wavered. It wasn't just my son. They were all beguiled by the beautiful girl before me. All fallen prey to her whims.

"Who said taking on Troy Memphis would be difficult?" Blake asked and Kyan laughed loudly while my son just kept on smirking, drinking in the sight of me brought to his mercy like this.

This was what he wanted, to prove that he could beat me, to bring me beneath him and make me fall to his command.

Footsteps thumped down the wooden stairs behind me from the mezzanine level and the group of savages before me all looked beyond me to the imposter in their midst. The poor man who'd come seeking vengeance, no doubt being used by my son purely to bait me. But I refused to rise to that.

Jase Harrington strode around me and came to stand close enough for me to smell the scent of pine and testosterone oozing from his skin. There was a roughness about him that spoke of his poor breeding, his white t-shirt clinging to his muscular frame and a fine lining of stubble coating his jaw. He didn't belong in this world of power and prestige. He was a bug that should have been squashed alongside his worthless family all those years ago instead of left to grow into this attack dog with a grudge to bear. That wasn't the kind of mistake I'd make again.

"Tell me," he said, his voice a growl as he looked at me like I was somehow beneath him despite the clear evidence to the contrary. "Do you think about them? The child you killed and the mother you murdered?" he asked and I scoffed.

"I barely even recall them," I spat, my voice a harsh whisper as the rage in me bled beneath my skin. No doubt he was drinking in the sight of me here, brought to heel beneath him but I would take great pleasure in paying him back for this offence. Then he'd learn to stay in his damn place at the bottom of the food chain where he belonged. "If it wasn't for your resurrection in my life, they would have been forgotten entirely."

A low growl rippled through him, echoed by the men at his back which to my horror included my own flesh and blood. Was my son seriously upset over something so trivial?

"Are you even sorry for it?" Blake demanded and I narrowed my eyes.

"I've never been sorry for anything a day in my life," I hissed. "You don't get to where I am by wasting time on regrets."

"He isn't capable of feeling anything, let alone remorse," Saint supplied, stepping to Nash's side and looking down at me with interest. "Although I think I see some fear in there now."

"What are you talking about?" I asked him, forgetting about the others as I focused on the power in the room.

Whatever my son had to say was the real reason for this. He would make his point then we'd figure out where to go from there. Though I doubted anything he could say to me now would make me reconsider my decision to kill him, no matter how much he might be impressing me.

"I was just thinking," Saint replied slowly, his gaze sliding over me critically. "How very human you are in reality. In the mind of a child, you were an unconquerable monster. But look at you now, just sitting there at our mercy and still incapable of any true and meaningful kind of feeling. I pity you."

"Pity?" I scoffed. "I was the most powerful man in our state. Possibly the most powerful-"

"*Was,* being the operative word," Kyan cut over me with a snigger. "But you don't look so badass now."

I adjusted my position, pushing my hand into my pocket, reaching for the flick knife just in case one of them lost their temper and tried to take this further before me and my son had finished this conversation and gotten to the point of it.

"Looking for this?" Kyan asked, smirking as he lifted my knife up before him, waving it at me tauntingly while my fingers closed on nothing and a spike of fear washed through me. I hadn't even noticed him taking it from me.

"This is a waste of time," Tatum said with a sigh as she pushed her way into the gap between Saint and Nash, her hands brushing against both of them lightly and as they turned to give her their full attention, I realised something far more terrifying than the gun which was pointed at my skull.

She slipped her fingers into Saint's pocket and took a pill from within it, smiling as she held it over the empty glass in her hand and dropped it inside.

The man who had renamed himself Nash stooped and picked up the near empty bottle from the floor before topping the glass up with scotch for her.

"Cyanide," Tatum explained as she slowly swirled the glass and the capsule dissolved. "I suppose some might call it the coward's way out."

All four of the men standing before me were watching her with a heated kind of devotion which shone brighter than the midday sun. They were enraptured, enamoured, totally beguiled and under her spell. My son included.

Saint wasn't the king of this tribe of heathens. They were ruled by a queen. And the look in her eyes said my death was already dealt. Panic came for me then as I considered that fully for the first time, wondering if I really might be staring my death in the face right now. But that couldn't be. I refused to be remembered as some coward who killed himself over the deaths of a bunch of nobodies and a virus that should have made me a fortune.

"There's no point in dragging it out. He won't ever understand the depths of his evil." Her gaze moved from them to me, her head tilting to the side and those blonde curls spilling over her shoulder. She looked almost angelic standing there, made up to perfection in that white dress with the sunlight from beyond the window casting a haze of light at her back. But the look in her eyes held nothing of heaven in it. They were filled with the fury of hell. "Unless you have any last words?"

"Saint," I snarled, looking at my son and urging him to take his place in command of this farce. "You can't seriously mean to end my life for the likes of-"

Nash lunged at me with a furious snarl and my gut lurched as I was shoved back against the chair.

Kyan moved to help him as I fought, grabbing my arms and pinning them at my sides as Nash knelt on my lap and wrenched my chin up, his eyes full of fury and wrath as he forced my mouth open.

Tatum stepped closer once they held me still like that, looking down at me with interest. I fought to speak, barking my son's name, but he gave no reaction at all.

Nash took the glass from Tatum's hand and poured the contents into my mouth before slamming my jaw shut again and clamping his hand down over my lips to keep them closed. He grasped my nose tightly as I bucked and fought, but between him and Kyan, I has helpless to escape.

I fought the urge to take a breath for as long as I could, refusing to swallow so much as a drop of that foul concoction, but soon my lungs were burning, and I had no choice.

I swallowed despite every desire in my body to do the opposite and the moment I did, the two of them released me, backing away.

I fell forward, sucking in air as pain blossomed within my body.

I tried to stand but fell back in my chair, my gaze moving wildly between them as the five of them stood there watching me, perfectly still with fire and sin in their eyes and not the slightest indication that they had any regrets about this.

"This is for the people you thought were worthless when they were really worth a million of you," Nash growled.

"Goodbye, Father. And just so you know, I found the secret will you made where you tried to cut me out of my inheritance and had it destroyed. A new, entirely authentic looking will leaving everything you own to me has now been produced in its place. I just didn't want you to go into death believing you'd gotten one up on me," Saint added coldly and from those words, I realised that this was no game. There was no end to it beyond my death. They really had poisoned me. No one was coming for me. And nothing I did could stop this fate now.

I began to twitch and flail where I sat, foam bubbling between my lips and darkness pressing in on me from all around.

Tatum stepped forward, smiling cruelly as she watched me dying right before her eyes.

"I am the dark in the dead of the night!" she cried as her pack of heathens closed in beside her, all of their eyes on me, hungering for my end.

"Hear me roar!" they bellowed, the noise of their cheers echoing on into death with me as I fell away from them. Into the void of the dark and beyond. Into a place without position or power or wealth. Into the depths where no light could find me. And I was cast adrift forever into nothing. Where no one would remember my name. And I would eternally be alone.

CHAPTER FIFTY SEVEN

TWO DAYS AFTER TROY MET HIS DOOOOOOM

I sipped freshly squeezed orange juice as I sat on the veranda of the most beautiful resort I'd ever visited in my life, reading a reverse harem book on my Kindle. Turned out my situation with my boys wasn't totally unheard of. At least not in fiction anyway. And I was more than happy to blaze a trail in real life. Why be worshipped by one guy when you could be worshipped by four?

We were visiting the Marquesas Islands in French Polynesia after flying here as soon as Troy Memphis had stopped kicking. We were owed a celebration, but this place was flashy even by Saint's standards. And it felt like a whole world away from anywhere I'd been before.

Our balcony overlooked our private infinity pool which sat above the tropical rainforest, sweeping down to a beach just for us and the purest blue water of the sea beyond.

Saint had disappeared before we all woke up and I lounged on the decking in the shade of the awning, my feet up in Nash's lap as he massaged them. His trunks were short, showing the tattoo Kyan had inked there to cover up the brand on his left thigh. It was of five wolves with their snouts raised as they howled to the moon above a snow-capped mountain. And I'd spent time kissing it more than once since he'd had it done.

Kyan was swinging in a hammock to my right and Blake was back inside the suite ordering more pastries from the reception desk.

The warm air floated around me and brushed against my bare skin, my little pink bikini feeling like too many clothes with the humidity pressing in. But all the heat in the world couldn't dislodge the peace washing through me as I bathed in the afterglow of Troy's death.

I got out of my seat and dropped into Nash's lap, pushing my fingers into his hair. We'd all stayed up half the night drinking, dancing and fucking. There were scratches along Nash's shoulders which I'd left there when he'd claimed me in the early hours of this morning with the fury of a beast and I scored my thumb across them as he smirked.

"How are you today?" I murmured in his ear as his hand ran up the length of my spine.

"Never better, princess," he sighed and I leaned back to look at him. I could see the weight lifted from his shoulders like it had been a physical thing he'd carried around all this time. He'd tried to let his need for vengeance go when it had seemed like we'd never find Troy, but I knew what a relief it had been to finally pay him back for all he'd done to his family and rid the world of him for good. His eyes held a sea of light and there was a permanent smile on his lips. Lips that had done a thousand filthy things to my body last night as he celebrated his victory. "But I'll be even happier when you let me finish that foot rub."

He lifted me by the ass, dumping me back in my seat before dropping into his and grabbing my foot to run his thumbs up the centre of the sole. It was fucking incredible.

I released a long breath, unsure I'd ever been this relaxed before as I watched my gorgeous dark angel over the top of my kindle.

"You're staring," he teased.

"You look so fucking hot when you're worshipping me, Jase," I said and he smirked at the use of that name.

"When I'm finished here, I plan to get down on my knees between the legs of my goddess and pray for rain."

"You're a savage," I laughed and he grinned wolfishly to confirm it.

Blake marched out onto the deck in his blue swimming trunks, his skin kissed deeply bronze by our days in the sun. He'd gotten the best tan already and he was a smug bastard about it too.

"Who's up for snorkelling today?" he asked, dropping down beside Nash and stealing one of my feet into his lap. I grinned at them, placing my Kindle on the table and leaning back in my seat.

"I'm in. I'm gonna bring my phone to get some pictures," I said. Saint had bought us all the latest iPhones which were completely waterproof and had pro cameras. He made us upgrade to the latest model every time a new one was released even though year old phones worked just fine. But that wasn't the point apparently.

Our pastries arrived and the maid laid them on the table before hurrying away again. I nabbed myself a croissant and picked it apart, sighing as I pushed a piece into my mouth and the buttery goodness melted on my tongue. "Where the hell has Saint gotten to?"

"He's probably gone to war with that seabird who shat on him yesterday," Kyan called over with a snort, his inked arm falling out the hammock and his fingers grazing across the wooden floor.

"Well he's going to miss out on the fun," I said with a laugh as I remembered Saint's horror at the bird shitting on him. He'd lamented over his ruined Ralph Lauren shirt and cursed the creature and several generations of its family.

I tugged my feet out of the grip of Nash and Blake's hands and used my toes to caress their dicks. They grinned demonically at me as I bit my lip, but before I could get carried away with that idea, the door banged and Saint came striding out onto the veranda. He leaned down to press a kiss to my cheek then swept past me to the edge of the balcony, looking like he had some announcement to make. He was dressed in chinos and a white shirt which brought out the rich, earthiness of his eyes. Saint made dressing down look like he was on an expensive photoshoot at all times.

"Where have you been hiding?" I asked, sweeping my hair away from my shoulders so it hung over the back of the chair.

"I've been finishing up the final arrangements," he said, his eyes dancing with some secret and I frowned.

"For?" Nash pressed.

"For our wedding day," Saint announced, grinning at me.

"What?" I laughed in confusion as Kyan sat upright in his hammock and nearly fell out of it.

Blake and Nash shared a look as I drew my feet out of their laps and gave Saint my full attention. If there was one thing I knew about Saint Memphis, it was that he didn't joke about matters to do with our relationship. If he said there was a wedding organised, there was a freaking wedding organised.

"I spent some time researching where we could have a wedding which would cater to our needs. A few countries in Africa were an option for a while, but I would have had to pay off too many corrupt people to allow a woman to marry multiple men rather than the other way around. So I decided that route was too complex. That was when I discovered the polyandrous laws on these islands where a woman can lawfully wed several husbands if she is of higher status than the men. Which of course, was easy to prove as our girl is a queen and the Marquesans seemed more than happy to accommodate our situation without very much persuasion at all."

"Are you serious?" I asked, hope filling my voice. "I can have all of you as my husbands?" The idea made me so freaking giddy that I got out of my chair and ran over to grab Saint's arm, waiting anxiously for his answer.

He cupped my cheek, his thumb carving a line up to the scar on my temple. "Yes, siren. You can. And I truly beg that you do." He dropped down onto one knee suddenly and I gasped as he took a white ring box from his pocket, popping it open. The sun flashed on the most beautiful round cut diamond I'd ever seen sitting in a delicate clasp with a vintage design. It was huge, a fucking boulder of a diamond and I was utterly speechless as Saint offered it to me, his eyes full of hope and happiness.

"I'm a commoner before a queen," he rasped. "Begging to enter her palace and lay all he is at her feet. I am yours whether you accept this ring or not, but if you were to wear it, I would want for nothing more in all the years left to me in this lifetime."

"Hang the fuck on," Blake balked before I could answer, my heart pounding as I got lost to the question Saint had sprung on me. "You can't just show up with a ring looking like a damn prince while we're sitting here half-naked with nothing to offer her but goddamn pastries."

"I'm hardly responsible for if or when you decide to propose to Tatum," Saint said dismissively.

"You planned our wedding without telling us," Nash interjected. "You could have given us a heads up and maybe we all could have a ring to offer her today."

"You also need my permission," Kyan tossed in.

"Don't even try it, Kyan," I growled then beamed at Saint, holding out my left hand. I still wore the skull ring Kyan had bought for me, so I didn't really have room for the meteor Saint was offering, but we'd figure that out later. "Of course I'll marry you." He slid the ring onto my middle finger and I realised the sneaky bastard had already planned for the issue of me wearing more than one as he stood up, pulling me to him and kissing me with leisurely strokes of his tongue as the others were forced to watch. I smiled my head off as I turned to them, bouncing on the balls of my feet.

"I don't need a ring from you guys," I said seriously as I took in Blake and Nash's sad expressions. "And you don't have to marry me if you don't want that. Don't let Saint make the decision for you. But…" I stepped away from Saint and dropped down to one knee in front of them and their eyebrows shot up. "I want you both. There isn't an us without you, Blake and Nash." I looked between them intently. "Will you marry me? Make me the happiest woman in the entire world, make me whole. Because each of you hold a piece of my heart and it can't be held together without us all as one."

They shared a look then both of them reached for one of my hands and pulled me up. They stood, hugging me between them, taking it in turns to kiss my mouth then my neck until I was sighing and arching between them.

"Is that a yes?" I begged.

"Yes, princess," Nash growled against my ear while Blake murmured it against my lips.

"I consent," Kyan said, pushing out of his hammock with a smirk as the guys parted from me.

"We do not need your consent," Saint growled. "We will marry her because she wants it, regardless of what you want."

"I still give my agreement, just so you know. And technically I'll be marrying her twice now, so I'll be the official head husband," Kyan taunted, catching my hand and eyeing the ring that sat beside his with a low whistle.

Saint barked a laugh. "You will be the page boy at the wedding, not a groom. You cannot marry her twice even here."

Kyan's jaw ticked. "I'm not gonna be the fucking page boy."

"Nah, he's the best man," Blake announced with a grin. "Aren't you, brother?"

"Kyan?" I whispered, looking up at him as I rested a hand on his chest. "Don't ruin this."

Kyan sighed, gripping the back of my neck and drawing me closer. "Never. In all seriousness I want you to have them. Because we're equal. And I'm gonna be right there cheering you on because this makes our family official. We'll all be Roscoes-"

"Rivers," Saint cut over him, raising his chin in a challenge. "We will all be a Rivers."

My brows lifted and I looked to Nash and Blake who beamed, seeming happy with that idea, but they couldn't possibly be as thrilled as I was. *Oh my god, this is one of the best days of my life and it's barely even begun.*

"Then I'm changing my name too," Kyan growled furiously.

"Of course you will. I already have the paperwork ready for you to sign," Saint said with a smirk. "Now everyone go and shower and get changed, we only have two hours until the ceremony."

I started to jog away with my boys, but Saint caught my arm. "Not you, siren. You need to go down the hall and open room five-oh-two." He slipped a key into my palm and my lips parted as he kissed my cheek, giving me an intense look before directing me away.

I did as he asked, slipping out of our room and heading down the long hall, unlocking the door at the end and stepping inside.

"Surprise!" a group of girls screamed and Mila suddenly dove on me, squeezing me tight. Dione and Kayla from college were there too and I nearly burst into tears at finding them all here together. They were wearing beautiful flowing, pale pink gowns and I gazed at them in awe as excitement blazed through my chest.

The whole room was decked out for me with hair stylists and a makeup artist as well as ten goddamn designer wedding dresses hanging in bags along the rear wall for me to choose from.

"Time to get ready, girl." Mila beamed as she led me toward the bathroom. "It's your freaking wedding day!"

I wore a white dress which had delicate straps, a lace bodice and a skirt which flowed out around me in several layers of soft material. It split up the thigh and when the wind blew, my garter peeked out and I imagined the guys would be fighting over who got to take it off later. *Lucky I'd secretly put another three on my other leg to stop them fighting over it then, isn't it?*

I was led down to the beach by my beautiful friends in their dresses with lilies clasped in their hands. We wore sandals and mine had diamonds on the straps which wound around my ankles and between my toes. As we made it to the white sand, I was guided into a marquee so I couldn't see my boys beyond it and they couldn't see me.

Inside, I found Kyan waiting there in light grey trousers, loafers and a white shirt. His hands were in his pockets, his hair styled back and his head cocked to one side as he took me in. Hell he looked good all done up like that. But nothing could hide what he was, no matter how many fancy clothes he wore. He was my monster through and through. And that outfit could just as easily be stained in blood and I'd still want him as my husband. Maybe even more so.

"Fuck, baby, you look like a fallen star. The heavens are gonna want you back when they realise you're missing."

"Well they can't have me," I said with a smile that had been permanently stitched into my cheeks since Saint had announced the news.

"I wouldn't let you go even if they did," he purred.

Mila stepped in front of me, checking over my dress, adjusting the glittering tiara in my hair and the veil which trailed down my back. "You look fucking perfect, girl," she said, her eyes glistening as she squeezed my hand. "Are you ready?"

I nodded, taking a shaky breath. I wanted this more than anything. All of us joined as one, bound in every way we possibly could be.

"You're gonna be fine. Just don't fall over your own feet, kay?" she laughed and I did too, then she moved to the front of the marquee with my friends just as music started up out on the beach. A harp was playing a beautiful tune as the girls stepped out, disappearing from sight and I gasped as I recognised the song Saint had composed for me all those years ago. He'd written me many more since, but that one would always hold a special place in my heart and of course he knew that. He was Saint Memphis. Though I guessed he was about to become Saint Rivers.

Kyan moved to my side, offering me his arm. "I know your dad should be the one walking you to my brothers today, but would you be happy for your husband to do it instead?"

I blinked back tears at the mention of my dad, nodding firmly and taking his arm. "He'd have chosen you in his place, Kyan."

"You reckon so?" he asked hopefully and I leaned up to kiss his cheek.

"I know so," I said and he beamed as he led me to the exit. The music changed to Baby Mine by Betty Noyes and my heart squeezed at the familiar tune my dad had sung to me when I was a child, the same one Saint had hummed to me in my time of need a long time ago. Kyan led me out onto the beach and the midday sun poured down on us, making my white dress gleam.

My breath caught at the sight of the rows of chairs in the sand covered in white cloth and wrapped with pink bows to match the bridesmaids. I'd never spared much thought to what my wedding day would be like. I hadn't ever imagined I'd get married before Kyan and now I was finding myself about to walk up another aisle with three more men at the end of it.

Saint, Nash and Blake wore outfits which matched Kyan's and my heart fluttered wildly at the way their eyes raked over me with a fierce desire.

I remembered the first time I'd seen my Night Keepers all together at Everlake, their eyes filled with a hunger I'd felt deep in my soul too. It was the same look they gave me now, and I realised the five of us had always been inevitable. Fate had woven our destiny and there wasn't a regret in my heart over how we'd come to be here. The good, the bad, the dark days and the light. They were each threads in a tapestry that was uniquely us. And I'd treasure it always.

Nerves warred in my stomach as I moved through the aisle of chairs. The back rows were filled by locals who seemed as pleased to be here as if they really knew us. At the front was Blake's dad with his girlfriend, Christina, a redhaired woman who'd been his housekeeper back in the days of the pandemic. She'd brought him meals every week and ensured he made it through, being there for him when no one else could be. He'd introduced us to her as his close friend, but after a few months Blake had finally called him out on it and said he loved Christina and was just happy his dad wasn't lonely anymore. Not long after that, Cooper and Christina had moved to Sunset Cove to be closer to us and I adored them both now like they were blood.

Sitting beside them was Danny in a pair of smart cream trousers and a white shirt, his eyes flicking from me to Mila who was standing at the front with the other bridesmaids. The two of them were more in love than ever and a little birdie had told me (AKA Blake) that Danny was planning on proposing soon. It was so freaking exciting.

All of the faces of the people I loved were angled toward me as I walked up to the arch of delicate pink flowers which my boys were standing under. A Marquesan man stood in white robes beside them, smiling kindly at me as I approached. I was so ready to be joined to them like this, I was practically bursting with excitement.

Kyan released me and squeezed my hand in goodbye before moving to stand beside the Night Keepers. My throat thickened with emotion as I gazed upon each of their faces, unable to believe I was lucky enough to claim one of these men as my own let alone all of them.

We'd fought battles together, spilled blood for one another and I knew we would cross any ocean in any land to be together if we had to. We'd proved that there was no force in this world which would keep us apart. So now there was just an eternity of life waiting for us to come and claim it. And I couldn't wait to answer its call.

CHAPTER FIFTY EIGHT

ONE YEAR AFTER THE WEDDING

"Oh fuck, fuck, Jesus, shit," Blake muttered, carving his hands into his hair as the midwives flapped their arms at us and made us all get out of their fucking way for the hundredth time. They weren't pleased about there being four of us in here, but every time they demanded to know which one of us was the father, we adamantly told them that we all were.

And of course Saint had gone all Memphis on them over it, insisting they let us stay under threat of ruining their careers and personal lives. Though I had to admit, the midwife in charge of Tatum's delivery was the closest person I'd ever seen to matching Saint in pure fucking balls as she glared him down and told him to check his damn privilege. He actually did it too, though he clearly had no intention of being chased out of the room, but he was willing to let her call the shots in here aside from that.

This time, as the others were forced to retreat, I was the one who stayed by Tatum's side, tugging her hair away from her sweaty forehead and squeezing her fingers tightly while she panted and groaned on the bed.

The midwife did her examination in the few seconds between contractions and I swear my heart was racing even faster than the baby's which we could hear over the monitor that they'd strapped around Tatum's swollen belly.

We'd been here for sixteen hours and I had never in my life been as fucking worried as I was right now. I didn't know what to do or the right things to say and every time any of us tried to make a joke to lighten the mood, Tatum went all Satan eyes on us and we shut the fuck up sharpish.

"I'm sorry to say this sweetheart, but you're still not ready to push," the midwife announced and Tatum groaned in pain, crushing my fingers as another contraction overwhelmed her.

"Do you want some water?" Nash offered.

"Or a cold compress?" Blake added.

"Or a scone?" Saint suggested.

"No I don't want a fucking scone!" she yelled and I was pretty certain she broke my finger as her grip impossibly tightened.

"Maybe you should re-think the pain relief?" the midwife suggested kindly. "We could be in for a long wait here and an epidural-"

"Yes," Tatum gasped, nodding her head. "That. Do that-"

"Are you sure?" I asked her, leaning down to speak into her ear. "Because when we did all those classes you were pretty fucking adamant you wanted to do it naturally without drugs and-"

Tatum snatched hold of the front of my shirt and dragged me down so that we were nose to nose and she was glaring into my eyes with the rage of the Devil himself.

"Don't you talk to me about a natural fucking birth when you're just standing around watching this happen!" she snarled. "The Tatum who said those dumbass things was a fucking idiot who had no idea what hell this would be. She was a naive bitch and she's dead now, just like you'll be if you try to talk me out of taking pain relief again. When you have to push a watermelon out of your fucking vagina you can come back to me with your no drugs bullshit, but until then just shut the fuck up and help the woman give me the drugs."

I swallowed thickly and nodded, kinda afraid of the demon who lived inside my wife and wondering if this really was Saint's baby after all, because she definitely had something pure evil inside of her that hadn't been there before.

"Yeah, okay, whatever you need," I agreed quickly and she released her hold on me as she dropped back against the pillows.

"Alright sweetheart, I'll get the anaesthetist and sort you out pronto," the midwife said loudly, ignoring us like we weren't involved in this. And as I was without a vagina, I could concede that this probably wasn't my place to start arguing, so I did as requested and shut the fuck up.

The midwife left the room and Tatum lunged forward so suddenly that I had to catch her to stop her from falling out of the bed. She glared at me like I should have guessed she was going to do that, and I apologised as I shared a glance with Blake over her head while mouthing 'holy shit' to him.

"Maybe you should stay in bed?" Blake suggested, reaching for her then drawing back like he wasn't sure how to help.

"I can't lie down. It's worse if I lie down," she panted, reaching out for Nash and digging her fingernails into his bicep as she gritted her teeth against the pain of another contraction and he just let her draw blood from his flesh without a word. *Probably for the best.*

Saint had gone very still, his eyes on her like he was assessing everything, calculating odds and trying to work this out like a math problem. But the way he was locking up told me just how much he was freaking out inside and I knew he was on the edge of breaking over how useless this whole thing was making him feel.

"No," Tatum snapped, pointing at him. "You don't get to lose your shit today. It's not about you, so lock that shit down. Buck the fuck up or get out."

"I'm not going anywhere," Saint growled in response. "I'm just trying to think of all the things that might help you."

"Oh, are you going to reach up into my vagina and take this baby out of me nice and gently?" she asked and yeah, I was officially terrified of her. And impressed. And kinda hot for her. Not that I'd dare suggest anything to do with my dick right now, but Tatum going all badass just did things for me and seeing her couple that with this momma bear psycho shit... Yeah. I was here for it. Terrified, but here for it.

"Why don't you try the bouncy ball thing again?" Nash offered and the scowl she threw him could have cut glass.

"You were keen on doing that hands and knees thing," Blake added, moving to the bed and jumping up onto it on all fours. "You know, like that woman from the classes said about the gravity helping and shit. Kinda like it does for animals in the-"

"Do I *look* like a wild animal to you, Blake?" Tatum hissed, her fingers crushing mine again as another contraction came for her.

The four of us looked at her, wearing nothing but a stretched out men's t-shirt with bare feet, her blonde hair sticking up in every direction and her blue eyes scarily wild and we all shook our heads.

"Fuck no," Nash said. "You look stunning."

"Gorgeous," Blake added.

"Beautiful," Saint said.

"Ferocious," I added, and I was pleased to see she took that as the compliment it was meant to be.

She broke a laugh for a brief moment. "Sorry, I'm being a total asshole," she gasped. " I just- *holy mother of fuck*, whichever one of you put this fucking thing inside of me is going to be getting a dick kick every day for a fucking month!"

Okay, yeah, she was insane, I was scared for all of our lives, but I was also staying right here beside her until this was over anyway.

I less than subtly shielded my balls with my free hand and luckily, we were saved by the midwife reappearing alongside the anaesthetist.

Saint nudged me aside as he and Blake helped her onto the bed and Nash clapped his hand down on my shoulder, exhaling sharply and glancing at me with a *what the fuck* look which I definitely gave back to him. They did not mention this in the antenatal classes. *Maybe I should tell them to add it – Class Nine: how to cope when your wife is possessed by the devil during labour and you're reduced to a useless as fuck punching bag who can't do anything beyond just staying strong and letting her abuse you as much as she likes in hopes that it helps a bit.*

I just hoped that this epidural was like a freaking magic potion, because I wasn't sure I could watch her in pain like this for much longer. Shit, how did anyone go on to have more children after surviving this? I'd lived through a death game, the Hades Virus, brought down an elitist organisation, escaped from my Irish mob family and survived a gunshot wound against the odds and I didn't think I'd come close to enduring the way Tatum was feeling now. She was a fucking goddess, and I was going to make certain I told her that every day for the rest of forever to make sure she never forgot.

Blake moved to stand in front of Tatum, holding her hands and murmuring to her about how amazingly she was doing while the anaesthetist sorted out the epidural for her.

The midwife wafted the rest of us back into the corner for the hundredth time and I reluctantly accepted that, moving to stand with Nash and Saint as we watched.

"Why doesn't anyone tell you this is fucking terrifying?" Nash muttered, swiping a hand down his face as he looked between us for an actual answer.

"That crazy bitch at the prenatal classes made this sound like a magical experience," I growled, wondering if I should sneak over to her house at night and give her a really good fright to teach her a damn lesson. "This is about as magical as the Texas Chainsaw Massacre."

Saint punched me in the arm and I didn't retaliate because I probably shouldn't have said that so loudly where Tatum might hear. Luckily, she seemed to be fully focused on Blake and her breathing, so I seemed to have gotten away with it.

"What did we decide about the paternity test in the end?" Nash muttered and I shrugged.

"I don't give a shit about that. I'll love it the same whether it's got my blood or not."

"You can't call a baby 'it'," Nash hissed but we'd been having this conversation since it was conceived so he needed to let it go.

"Well until I know if it's a boy or a girl, I'm gonna keep doing it. And seeing as you assholes all voted with Tatum against finding out the sex-"

Tatum let out a pained growl and we all paused to look at her, each of us leaning forward like we wanted to run over there and hold her, but Blake had it and the doctors were still doing their shit, so we made ourselves stay back.

"We can do a paternity test before we decide to have another child," Saint said. "That way we can make sure each of us has a child with our genetics and-"

"You seriously think you're going to convince her to have more babies after this?" Nash hissed and Tatum turned to look at all of us, her eyes narrowing like she knew what we were saying. Shit, she was scary right now.

Saint swallowed thickly and shrugged. "Maybe not," he conceded.

"I'm more concerned about her surviving this one," I growled, wondering why the hell we'd even decided to have a baby. I mean yeah, I was pretty fucking excited about having a little dude or princess to run around with and get into trouble, but if I'd known what would happen to our girl to get it here, I wasn't so sure I'd have gone along with it. "Shit, this baby had better be really fucking cool or I don't think I'll ever forgive the little bastard."

"We are all married to her," Saint replied. "So it won't be a bast-"

"There we go, it'll kick in shortly," the anaesthetist announced and we stampeded out of our corner to get to Tatum's side first.

She dropped back down onto the bed, some of the pain already seeming to slip from her expression as she looked between the four of us with the hint of a smile on her face.

"I'm never having sex again," she whispered and a laugh spilled from my lips as I leaned down to kiss her forehead.

"You've got this, baby," I growled, knowing in my heart that it was the truest thing I'd ever said to her. "You're a fucking queen. You can do this. And we'll be right here beside you the whole time."

The room was strangely silent following the panic of the delivery. This odd kind of calm dropping over all of us beneath the weight of this utterly life changing event.

Something had shifted in me the moment the baby had been born, this sense of purpose that I hadn't had before. I didn't know how to properly put it into words, but I just felt overwhelmed with it all.

Tatum lay in her bed, nursing the healthy baby boy and watching him with this serene look on her face that I just couldn't help but sketch. Nash and Blake had already taken about a million photos of the two of them in the twenty minutes since he'd come into the world screaming like a banshee and ready to take on everything and anything that came his way. But I just needed to capture this feeling. And as the sketches came together, I couldn't help but be proud of my work.

My favourite was the piece I was just finishing, Tatum sitting in bed between the four of us as we looked down at her, the baby cradled in her arms and that freaking smile on her face which I just wanted to devour. It was almost certainly worth all of the agony it had taken to bring him into the world. She certainly seemed to think so anyway and as she was the one who had endured it, I was willing to take her word on it.

"Do you want to hold him, Kyan?" Tatum breathed and I looked up as I finished my sketch, wetting my lips and placing my sketchbook aside.

I was the only one who hadn't yet, but for some reason, I was hesitating.

It wasn't that I didn't want to, more that I wasn't sure I was cut out for taking hold of something so precious and fragile without tainting it. I'd already had to accept that I'd corrupted Tatum, but a baby was just so pure and innocent, and I was everything but those things.

I hadn't even been the least bit pissed when it had been clear from his skin tone that I wasn't the bio dad. Because deep down in my gut I couldn't help but feel that my blood was a form of poison and giving it to a child would be akin to cursing them.

In hindsight, I should have known full well this kid would have Saint's genetics. The bastard had planned a romantic weekend away for him and Tatum precisely when he'd figured out that she'd be ovulating, then spent the entirety of it buried inside of her to make sure he'd be the one who impregnated her first. I hadn't even thought about that freaking trip until his smugness forced him to admit to it ten minutes after Caesar was born.

Blake had punched him, and Nash had cursed him but I'd just laughed.

I didn't even care. It was so fucking Saint of him and too fucking funny. Of course he'd known Tatum's menstrual cycle better than she had. The rest of us had just had a perfectly normal, 'shall we stop using contraception and try for a baby' conversation and had been content to let nature take its course from there. He'd been charting periods and working out dates until he knew the exact time she'd release a freaking egg. *Asshole.*

In reality, I knew that none of us gave a shit who shared DNA with the little creature who had just become the centre of our universe. It didn't make a blind bit of difference. We would love him just the same. That was how it was in our family.

"He looks happy with you," I told Tatum slowly, closing my sketchbook and laying it down on the little table beside me.

"He wants a cuddle with his daddy," she insisted, seeing right through me as always and I pushed my tongue into my cheek as I looked at the tiny little thing in her arms, both aching to pick him up and afraid of fucking it up if I did.

"I'm pretty sure *I'm* his daddy," Blake teased, leaning down over Tatum's shoulder and kissing the tiny human on the top of his soft, dark hair.

"How do you figure that out?" Nash asked.

"Because I'm clearly the fun one. So I get to be Daddy, you're Dad, Nash. Kyan is Pa and Saint is... Father."

I snorted a laugh as Saint scowled, folding his arms. "Why do I have to be the formal one?" he asked with that rich boy lilt to his tone which clearly answered his damn question for him.

"Watch out, Father's in a mood again," I hissed, cupping my hand around my mouth as if I was trying to make sure Saint didn't hear, even though he clearly could.

"Fuck off," he muttered, his brow pinching in a way that actually made me feel a little bad. I knew that the last thing he wanted to be was a figure of fear for our son and that he worried about having too much of his father in him to stop that from happening.

"Alright," I said, standing up and clapping my hand down on his shoulder, leaving charcoal marks on his skin. "How about you can be Papa? That's cute. Big old papa bear."

I nudged his arm and a smile touched his lips.

"I don't hate that," he admitted, and Tatum beamed at me. Maybe I had this dad stuff down already - I was breaking up fights and making Saint happy, a kid couldn't be harder to manage than him...right?

I shifted closer to the bed and Tatum adjusted her hold on the little fella, moving him towards me in his snuggly blue blanket - Saint had packed two entire bags for the baby, one for if it was a boy, the other for if it was a girl. Not that I'd be letting him toss that pink blanket. Caesar was comfortable enough with his masculinity to pull off pink.

I reached out to brush my fingers over the baby's head, but Saint caught my elbow before I could do it.

"Wash your hands," he ground out and I might have taken offence if my fingers weren't stained black from the sketches I'd been doing, so I just rolled my eyes and crossed the room to do as he instructed.

I turned back towards the bed and found Blake in my way, grabbing the hem of my shirt and tugging. "You need to hold him skin to skin," he said. "For the bonding and shit."

Apparently he'd swallowed the fucking guidebook we'd been given during those antenatal classes and was going to micromanage everything we did with Caesar now to make sure we all got the full baby experience so he got the best possible start in life. I couldn't really voice any complaints about that, so I just tugged my shirt over my head and tossed it down on the chair I'd been sitting in before approaching Tatum in the bed again.

"Why is it that even after all of the things we've survived, I feel totally out of my depths with this tiny little person?" I muttered as I came to stand over her, stroking my fingers through her hair and placing a kiss on the top of her head.

"I think we're all pretty overwhelmed," she said, smiling tiredly. She'd been a freaking warrior throughout the twenty-seven hours Caesar had taken to come into this world and I would never forget it. This woman right here was so much more than a queen. She was a damn goddess. In fact, I was pretty sure all women were. They could create life and survive the process of bringing a perfect little creation into this world. Meanwhile, here I was with a cock that basically just planted the seed and then hung there waiting for another round of seed planting. Why was it that men thought they ruled the world? It was pretty clear to me that women deserved that accolade. "But I know you're going to be an amazing father, Kyan. All of you are. And how lucky is Caesar to have so many of us all for himself?"

I could feel the others watching me as Tatum shifted the blanket away from him and lifted the little bundle of trouble towards me. I reached out for him, cradling his little head in one of my hands and drawing him into my tattooed arms, letting him rest against my chest as I just stared at him.

Something in my soul expanded as he shifted and made little noises, his mouth opening and closing like he was hoping for some more milk and I bounced him just a bit to settle him down.

I turned away from the watching eyes of the others and walked towards the window, moving so that the soft sunlight spilled down on us and stealing a moment alone with our son as my heart swelled with emotion and love and everything just kinda shifted in my mind.

"Hello, little hell bringer," I murmured, stroking that soft hair and watching as he cracked his eyes open. I knew he couldn't really see me properly yet, but as I looked into those familiarly blue eyes and he wrapped his tiny hand around my thumb, I knew that I would tear the world apart for him. He was something utterly pure, untouched and more loved than he could possibly comprehend yet.

But he would come to. I'd been worried about the fate of a baby who was raised by monsters before this moment, but as I looked down at our boy with his warm, brown skin and the cutest fucking button nose I'd ever seen, I knew that was so stupid of me. He'd just been born into a family without limits or boundaries who could offer him the world and protect him from the dark. He would know more love than he could cope with and be strong and powerful in all the ways that counted.

We might have been a bit fucked up, but that was okay. Because our form of chaos was the very best kind. And we were about to embark upon the greatest adventure we'd ever known.

"You see that out there?" I asked Caesar as he just kept looking at me. "That's the world you were born to rule. You'll grow and flourish and learn to master it. You'll be a king among the masses. Don't you worry, my boy. You're going to be a damn natural. And if anything ever tries to hurt you, you'll have a pack of monsters at your back. What better life could there be for you than that?"

CHAPTER FIFTY NINE

AAAAAND ANOTHER FIVE YEARS LATER

"Caesar Donavan Rivers!" I shouted as my little monster of a five-year-old pushed his younger brother into the sea and sat on him. "Kyan!" I called in desperation as I stood up with Beau clutched to my breast as he fed. The blanket covering him flew off in the wind, exposing my other boob to the world. Thankfully, the rest of the party guests hadn't arrived so it was just my children and my husband I was flashing right now.

Chaos. My life was chaos. And it was fucking beautiful.

Kyan charged away from the buffet table with a cocktail sausage in his mouth, the poor guy only having looked away for ten seconds to feed himself, but those ten seconds had been too long. Because Caesar could go rogue in under three.

Kyan scooped the two boys into the air, Caesar by his leg, and he crushed Rowan to his chest as he checked he was okay. The kid laughed his head off as he soaked his Pa's nice blue shirt and got it all sandy too. He was as hardy as his tattooed daddy that one. Rowan had taken a full on punch right in the face from Caesar the other day and started laughing. It was kinda scary how thick Kyan's blood ran in his veins. He was only three and he was already giving Caesar a run for his money.

I sighed my relief, dropping back into my deck chair under the shade of the parasol just as Blake came running out of the house. "Everything okay? Oh shit, you know your tit's out, right sweetheart?" He moved to stand before me and I gazed up at him with a grin.

"I'm aware, golden boy," I purred and he gazed at my exposed breast for a long moment before leaning down to kiss his son's raven hair.

"Is it weird to be jealous of my own kid?" he murmured as he lifted his head to kiss me too.

"Weird is kinda our middle name so I wouldn't worry about it." I smirked and he headed off to chase down Beau's blanket.

Kyan placed Caesar down in the sand by the buffet table and pointed at him. "Five minutes in the naughty corner, hell bringer."

"That's not fair!" Caesar yelled, slamming his fists down into the sand in fury.

"You nearly drowned Rowan, it's perfectly fucking fair," Kyan warned and Caesar gasped dramatically.

"Pa swore!" He pointed accusingly, looking to me for justice. And I'd sure as shit bring it.

"Well you'd better join Caesar in the naughty corner then, Kyan," I said with a grin playing around my lips as Blake reappeared with my runaway blanket, draping it over me and I tucked it around Beau as I cuddled him closer. The kid loved his food as much as Blake did. He wouldn't have unlatched from my breast if that blanket had flown away mid snowstorm. I wouldn't have bothered with it at all only that Cooper was going to arrive any minute and he always used the side gate since Blake had given him the code. I didn't wanna flash him my boob; that was no kind of greeting for my father-in-law and his new wife.

Blake sat down in the deck chair beside me, pushing his fingers into his dark hair and flexing those glorious muscles of his. He looked a little tired considering he'd been up a few times in the night. Since the very first day we'd brought Caesar home, my boys had helped in any way they could with the night shifts, feeding our babies my expressed milk and rocking them down when they wouldn't settle. Saint had devised a rota which meant that the five of us all got plenty of sleep and no one got too exhausted. When we'd first arrived home from the hospital with Caesar five years ago, I had never in all my life been so happy for his organisational skills. Or the willingness of my boys to do any and everything they could to keep both me and our baby content. And they'd never complained a single day about it since.

Kyan placed Rowan in Blake's lap before heading over to sit beside Caesar in the sand, my husband's clothes officially ruined for the party. But as he pulled his shirt off and the sun gleamed on his inked skin, I didn't think that was such a bad thing. And I wasn't even gonna bother getting the kids changed as they were only in beachwear anyway.

"Now why did you try to drown your brother?" Kyan asked Caesar in a growl.

Caesar gave him an indignant look worthy of Saint. "He was a shark. I had to kill him before he ate mommy."

"Shark, shark!" Rowan grinned as Blake bounced him on his knees, apparently agreeing with Caesar's story.

"You can't kill sharks," Kyan warned and Caesar rolled his freaking eyes.

"He's not *really* a shark, Pa," Caesar said like Kyan was the one who believed he was. "And what if a real shark did try to eat mommy? Can I kill one then?"

Kyan considered that with a frown and I smothered a laugh as I watched, waiting for his answer.

"Well your daddies will do that," Kyan decided.

"What if none of you are there?" Caesar tossed back. He had an answer for everything, just like his Papa. "I'm the oldest. I should kill the shark if none of you are there."

"No, because then your mommy will kill it. She's a savage." He threw me a dark grin and I bit my lip.

"Well what if the shark has tied mommy up?" Caesar pressed. "And what if his shark friends have got my brothers? Am I not allowed to kill sharks then?"

"That's a tough one, brother," Blake sniggered before blowing a raspberry on Rowan's neck and making him giggle wildly.

Kyan considered that then sighed, scruffing Caesar's hair. "Fine, *then* you can kill a shark."

"Yay!" Caesar jumped up and Kyan caught him by the back of his shirt, yanking him back down into the sand before he could escape.

"One more minute. And you need to apologise to Rowan too," Kyan said sternly, that fierce expression of his making me all tingly inside.

Caesar groaned, throwing himself down in the sand. I reckoned our family photo was gonna be interesting today. I didn't think we had a single one where we all looked presentable. Saint hated that, but I freaking loved it. My children looked wild like the wolf pups they were. And I couldn't be prouder.

Beau fell asleep and I pulled the blanket off of him, placing him in his cot which set up in the shade beside me and finding my dress was now wet with milk.

"Dammit," I muttered, trying to wipe it off but it was no good. "I'd better change."

Blake nodded as I got up. "Fetch the birthday boy while you're at it." He pinched my ass as I walked past him and Rowan reached out to try and do the same.

"You're teaching him bad habits," I sang and Blake grinned, leaning down to talk in his ear.

"Lemme teach you about a little word called consent…" Blake whispered.

Rowan threw his head forward and headbutted him in the face and I snorted a laugh as I left him to deal with that drama, walking into The Temple through the wide open glass doors.

I jogged upstairs and grabbed a white sundress, exchanging it for my ruined blue one before heading back down to the kitchen. The sound of the front door opening made my heart leap and I jogged along the hall. The tinkling of Saint's piano carried to me from his music room, the beautiful piece filling the house.

I made it to the front hall just as Nash stepped inside with MJ in his arms looking like a mini version of me and him. He had bright blonde hair and blue eyes which shone like sapphires, his skin a deep golden colour. I ran forward to hug Nash and my little two-year-old, squeezing them tight and kissing my husband on the lips.

"Kees, kees, mommy," MJ begged too and I leaned down to kiss his chubby little cheek.

"Hey baby, did you have fun with Dad?" I asked then looked to Nash when he nodded. "Was he good?"

"Well…he begged for an ice cream so we grabbed one from the surf and turf, then he ate it too fast and threw up everywhere."

I laughed, looking to MJ who grinned cheekily. "Oh no."

"Yeah, I had to do an outfit change in the trunk of the car then the little guy almost pissed on me, but I swerved so he pissed on a woman's shorts who was passing by instead. She didn't notice so…I'm calling it a win." He smirked and I kissed him again as I laughed.

"Sounds like a success to me." I grinned.

"Yeah and wait until you see the cake, princess." He lifted the paper bag in his hand with a grin and I bounced on my toes excitedly.

"He's gonna freak, isn't he?"

"Yeah, it's the best one yet. We'd better wear some of Blake's football gear when we show him."

We headed through to the kitchen and I pulled MJ into my arms as Nash took the cake out of the bag and placed it on the white marble counter. It was a huge red squid, each layer of the cake covered in iced tentacles that looked pretty damn realistic. Across the bottom of it were the words *Happy Birthday Squid.*

"I roared a laugh and MJ giggled too, pointing at the cake. "Skid!"

"No, MJ. That's Papa," Nash corrected with a wicked grin.

"Papa," MJ corrected, giggling again.

It was the cutest damn sound. It almost made me broody for another one. But then I remembered that giving birth was an utter bitch and I'd sworn not to forget that again. Four was enough. Four boys of course because what this house had needed was more testosterone – not that I would have wanted it any other way.

Somehow the memories of labour seemed to fade each time until I was tempted to do it all over again. It was like there was a fertile little witch living in my head casting spells on my mind to make me think labour might just be bearable the next time. If I did get pregnant again, I was absolutely having a C-section. But I wasn't going to do it again anyway so that was irrelevant. We had four beautiful children and that was plenty to fill my heart to the brim.

"You'd better hide it, I'm gonna go and get Saint," I said with a smile. We'd banished him to his music room while we set up the party and he was more than happy to comply. He'd probably have stayed in there all day if I didn't fetch him. He was about as keen on us making a fuss over him as he was about poor grammar. But I just pulled the 'kids love a birthday party' line on him and he had no choice but to accept it.

Nash put the cake in the fridge and I placed MJ down so he could toddle after him outside. I jogged away through the halls and made it to Saint's music room, listening to him play as I waited for a lull before I disturbed him. I knew he wouldn't mind me walking in, but I also loved to bathe in the pure peace of his music, knowing he was lost to its embrace.

The music stopped and his voice rang through the room. "I know you're there, siren. Don't keep me in suspense."

I released a breath of amusement, pushing through the door and stepping into the beautiful room. He'd drawn the black-out curtains and a single candle was lit up on top of his piano, our black cat Debussy just a shadow beside it, her eyes shimmering like a demon's. She mewed in greeting as Saint turned to me and patted his knee. Besides Saint, I was the only other one of this household she tolerated and I guessed that was because us girls had to stick together. Although I was pretty sure she'd steal my devil boy from me in a heartbeat if she got the chance. The girl was smitten since she'd shown up on our porch and Saint had taken her in, and I guessed I couldn't really blame her.

"Shut the door and come here," he commanded.

"But everyone's waiting for you to join the party," I said teasingly and he groaned.

"Yes, I am well aware. Now do as I ask. It's my birthday after all."

I kicked the door shut with a smirk, moving over to perch on his knee and his hand skimmed up my thigh as he leaned into my neck and breathed in deeply.

"You are looking edible as always." He kissed the soft spot behind my ear, tucking my hair away to give him more access as he nibbled along my flesh.

"Come and join us outside," I urged.

"Are you all going to make a spectacle of me?" he asked, tilting my head around to steal a kiss.

"Yes," I purred, running my hand down his black shirt to feel his heart beating powerfully under my palm.

"I detest fuss," he said and I laughed.

"You don't seem to mind it so much when *I* fuss over you." I ran my hand lower and he chuckled darkly before capturing my wrist.

"Well you are the exception to every rule I have ever lived by, siren, so that does not surprise me."

My heart fluttered as Saint's fingers moved further up my thigh but Debussy jumped on my lap right on top of his hand and nuzzled her head into his chin.

"Pussy blocker," I laughed, stroking her and she mewed innocently. "She wants you to herself."

"Well the chances of a cat killing you are low, Tatum, but never impossible," he said with a smirk then tilted Debussy's chin up to look at him. "If you must murder someone, make it that nosy neighbour along the street who always stares at our girl."

"Mr Newton is in his nineties," I laughed.

"Then no one will suspect a thing when he dies in his sleep," Saint said and I smacked his arm.

"You're the Devil," I breathed.

"In the flesh," he agreed, flashing me his teeth in the dark.

A pounding of little footsteps pattered this way and the door swung open, revealing Caesar there, looking like the embodiment of mischief.

"Caesar!" Kyan's booming voice sounded through the house. "You're in trouble when I find you."

"Uh-oh, what did you do?" I asked as he scampered forward and crawled under the piano.

"Shh, mom," he whispered.

"Caesar?" Kyan growled, his footsteps pounding in this direction.

I opened my mouth to call out to him then Saint's hand closed over it to silence me. The door kicked open a second later and Kyan folded his arms as he stood in the doorway, arching a brow at us.

"Yes?" Saint inquired, his hand sliding from my mouth as he pulled me tighter against him.

For someone who liked keeping order, he sure didn't do it with his kids. I was pretty certain he thrived on the carnage in this house when the kids were running wild. I kinda did too.

"Have you seen Caesar?" Kyan asked, his eyes shifting to the piano where a smothered laugh sounded from beneath it.

"No," Saint said simply and I snorted a laugh.

"What did he do?" I asked, because if Caesar had been really bad, I was gonna have to hand him over to Sheriff Kyan for another punishment.

"Rowan slapped him with a bag of frozen peas and Caesar drop kicked him. It was kind of impressive if it hadn't been such a dick thing to do," Kyan said with a snigger.

"It was a bag of frozen *beans*, Pa," Caesar's voice came from under the piano in annoyance and Kyan ducked down, hauling him out with a chuckle of triumph. He started tickling him as he fought to escape and Caesar's laughter filled every corner of the room, making my heart expand.

"Seems like tit for tat to me," Saint commented as I dropped out of his lap, kneeling down to tickle Caesar too.

"Rowan hit his head when he fell. I mean, he took it like a fucking warrior but still," Kyan growled.

"Pa swore again!" Caesar cried and I turned on Kyan, tickling him instead. Caesar laughed wildly, jumping up to help me as Kyan fell down beneath us. Saint was suddenly above his head, yanking his arms up so we could tickle him more easily.

"Alright, alright," Kyan choked out as we showed him no mercy, but we didn't stop.

He yanked a wrist free of Saint's hold and suddenly he was free. Caesar caught my hand to tow me out of the room to safety and I laughed as I chased after him.

We ran down the hall with Saint behind us but just as we made it to the kitchen, a huge thump sounded followed by Saint cursing. I twisted around, finding Kyan on top of Saint on the floor, wrestling him down and planting a wet kiss on his mouth.

"Oh for fox sake, Kyan," Saint spat, keeping to his no swearing rule in front of the kids even now which was just too cute.

"Happy birthday, brother." Kyan grinned.

"You heathen, you're not even wearing a shirt. What kind of hillbilly event is this?"

Kyan laughed as he got up, pulling Saint after him and clapping him on the shoulder. Rowan came running in from the beach suddenly with a stick, his hazel hair sticking up in every direction as he charged down Caesar with a roar.

"Woah, woah!" I scooped Rowan off the ground, wrestling the stick from his surprisingly strong grasp before he could spear his brother on it.

The doorbell rang at that moment and my heart pounded excitedly. "That'll be Mila," I said with a grin.

"Ope!" Rowan said excitedly.

"Yes, baby, Hope's here too," I said, surprised he remembered their little girl.

Mila and Danny still lived in Sequoia but we visited each other as often as we could. Hope was the same age as Rowan and the two of them had taken to each other the last time they'd met a few weeks ago.

I carried Rowan to the door as Saint tried to talk Kyan into putting a shirt on, smiling to myself at the madness of this party already. I opened the door and Mila squealed as she ran in with Hope in her arms, the two of them wearing pale yellow summer dresses which matched.

"Hey girl!" We wrapped each other in a hug full of babies and kisses before I stepped back to let them in, hugging Danny too.

"It's so warm here," Danny said with a grin then whispered to me, "I'm trying to convince Mila we should move here too, but she won't have it."

"Keep trying," I said with a grin and we all headed through the house and out to the beach.

We took seats on the deck chairs and Cooper and Christina soon arrived, fussing over the kids while I caught up with Mila and Danny.

At the earliest opportunity, Nash headed off to fetch Saint's cake, tossing me a mischievous wink as he headed into the kitchen.

Saint sat in a deck chair beside me, smiling as he watched the kids play with Cooper and Blake. Beau was still sleeping serenely in the cot between us and Saint had his hand hanging down into it, his fingers brushing over our youngest's hair absentmindedly.

When Mila and Danny went off to play with the kids, I reached under my chair to where I'd stashed one of Saint's presents, holding it out to him in the glitzy silver wrapping paper. "I got you this."

He arched a brow, taking it and picking gently at the cellotape instead of tearing into it. "Is this something I can open in front of the kids?" he murmured.

I laughed, nodding. "They'll probably try and steal it from you though."

"Well that doesn't mean it is suitable for them. Do you remember last Christmas when MJ found that new dildo I bought you and used it like a chew toy?"

"*Saint*," I hissed, glancing at the in laws as laughter burst from me.

He smirked like the devil then opened the present and took out the Action Man figure inside which was just like the one he'd told me he had as a kid. One that Troy had taken from him. It had a car and a gun and I'd written the name Clive on the box with a kiss.

His eyes widened and his lips parted. "You bought me Clive?" He looked to me in adoration as I smiled.

"Yep. Do you like him?"

He nodded, his throat working as he stared at it. "Yes, siren, it's perfect. Thank you."

A shriek came from Hope as MJ dumped a bucket of sand over her head and Rowan dove on him like a little beast. Before he could land the first punch, Blake whipped him into the air and gave him a stern look while Mila laughed, working to get the sand out of her baby's hair.

MJ ran away from the scene of the crime, the sun glinting off of his golden hair. He ran to Saint who scooped him into his lap, not seeming to care at all about how sandy he was as he placed a kiss on his forehead.

"You're such a softy," I teased, reaching over to squeeze Michael Junior's pudgy arm. He was so damn squishy.

"Happy birthday to you," Nash started singing and we all joined in as

Kyan came running out in a white shirt which was on backwards, clear Saint bait. He was such an asshole. Why did I love it so much?

Everyone joined in singing while Saint stiffened in his seat, despising this custom as everyone sang out of tune and stared at him. But the kids loved it so he accepted it for their sake.

Nash presented the squid cake to him as the song came to an end and Saint's eyebrows descended.

"Oh for the love of Christ," he muttered. "Must we do this rigamarole every year?"

"It's tradition," I said with a smirk.

"Skid, skid, skid!" MJ started chanting as he reached for the cake and Saint shook his head and cracked a smile.

"You'll be in trouble later, all of you," he warned, giving Nash a pointed look and I chuckled as Saint lifted MJ up to let him blow out the candle on top of the cake.

"Ohhhh, *I* wanted to blow out the candle," Caesar complained as he crowded closer with the others.

"Well we can light it and do it again," I suggested just as Rowan ducked between Nash's legs and shoved his hands into the icing at the back of the cake. It toppled forward and I gasped, lunging desperately to try and catch it but it was too late as it smashed all over MJ and Saint's lap.

Rowan burst out laughing as MJ squealed in delight and the rest of the kids dove on them to grab a piece of the exploded cake. Saint grinned at the carnage and I picked up a piece of cake, holding it to his lips.

"You look good in red," I purred and he took a savage bite out of the cake as Nash snapped a photo.

"I want some!" Blake pushed to the front, grabbing a handful off of Saint's crotch and he cursed.

I gazed around at my family as Blake pushed a piece of sweet strawberry cake between my lips and I was sure my life couldn't possibly get any sweeter than this.

"You know what would balance out our family?" Kyan mused as he lifted me out of my seat, dropping down into it and placing me in his lap.

"What?" I asked, smearing some cake over his lips and he sucked my fingers, cleaning up the four rings which represented each of my husbands. Nash had bought me a silver ring with a sparkling blue sapphire and Blake had bought me beautiful platinum band engraved with the words *our love, our life, our queen*. I wore one on each of the fingers on my left hand and never took them off.

"A little baby girl." Kyan patted my belly and my eyes narrowed.

"Ooh, I'm down," Blake agreed.

"Hell no, if you want another one, one of you can give birth to it," I growled, going full devil woman and they shrank away fast, clearly reminded of my four labours. I was not a princess when I gave birth and they knew it all too well. Nash still had crescent shaped scars on his arm since MJ.

"I'm just saying, it would even out the testosterone levels a bit," Kyan went on.

"Do you wanna die today or something, bro?" Nash mocked, grabbing my hand and pulling me out of his lap.

He drew me back against his chest, wrapping his arms around my waist and I leaned on him with a sigh as I watched the others all wrestle over cake and Saint laughed like there were no demons living inside him anymore. At least not ones that couldn't be tamed.

Everyone looked so damn happy and there was really nothing more I could ask for in the world than that. My tribe had grown and was so full of love that it could fill the entire ocean. I was the luckiest girl on earth, surrounded by a family of warriors who squeezed every drop out of life.

We'd built our own Temple where we worshipped all forms of chaos, and I was going to thrive in it for the rest of forever with my monsters at my side.

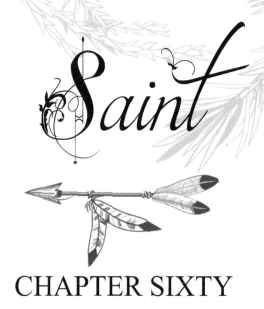

CHAPTER SIXTY

Getting the kids to bed was always a mixture of routine and carnage, but at least the party had thoroughly worn them out. Mila, Danny, Blake's dad and Christina had left us to it while we were battling tiny people into pyjamas and the five of us had all gathered out on the deck to see out the last of my birthday.

There was something special about the silence that followed a day full of children's screams and as much as I loved the chaos the boys created, I always savoured this moment of peace once they'd settled for the night.

"I have one request," I asked, stroking my fingers through Tatum's hair as she leaned back against me where we sat on the steps of the wooden deck, her toes in the sand, looking out over the beach as we all watched the sunset.

"Just the one?" she teased.

"Yeah, yeah, we get it, man," Nash said, knocking his shoulder against mine in an affectionately mocking kind of way. "You wanna boss us all around in your sex dungeon tonight."

I rolled my eyes, objecting to the word dungeon but it hardly seemed worth mentioning if he hadn't stopped calling it that after all these years.

"I'll agree so long as you do that thing with all the ropes again," Kyan said, grinning at me as he slung his arm around my shoulders.

"Oh, you mean that Japanese thing?" Blake asked from his position laying in the sand before us, his hand sliding up Tatum's leg as he grinned at the memories of the last time we'd played with that.

"It's called shibari," I muttered, wondering why I bothered - I was fairly certain that they chose not to learn the proper name just to infuriate me.

"Is that a yes then, birthday boy?" Tatum teased and I smiled as I drew her blonde hair over her shoulder, giving me access to kiss her neck where her Night Bound tattoo sat on her skin.

"If you're certain you want to be bound at the mercy of monsters?" I replied and she moaned softly as I kept kissing her.

"It's a little late to go back on that decision now," she replied, wiggling the fingers on her left hand so that the rings she wore caught the light of the setting sun and Kyan chuckled darkly.

"So can we go now, or-" he began.

"The sun's still going down, asshole," Blake protested, thumping him in the thigh. "Tatum wants to watch it."

"Oh yeah, *Tatum's* the one who dragged us all out here like a puppy who wanted to go play with a new ball," Nash mocked and Blake shrugged as he continued to caress Tatum's leg and she shifted as she leaned back against me.

"What was your request, Saint?" Tatum asked, as she gave Kyan a playful smack to his arm, making it clear we were staying for the sunset.

"It's a simple one," I said. "Or at least I hope it is. And after all of these years, I think it's time I got it."

"Intriguing," Nash said and I huffed out a breath because I still expected to get nothing out of asking this question, but it was like an itch in my damn brain that had been haunting me for far too long. I needed the answer. The internet wouldn't provide it, no one I had asked had been willing or able to give it to me straight, but there were people sitting here with me now who knew. And it was past time they told me.

"I just want to know," I said, stealing myself for their bullshit but pressing on all the same. "What does the squid mean?"

A beat of silence passed before all of them fell about laughing and a flash of irritation drove its way right through the fabric of my being.

"Forget it," I growled, moving to push myself out of my seat, but Tatum caught my wrist and held on tight, refusing to let me go.

"Don't run off," she pouted.

"Yeah, there's no need to go getting your squid in a twist," Kyan added, smirking in that way that made me want to punch his damn face in.

"You wouldn't want to get your tentacles tangled," Blake added and I narrowed my eyes on him. There had been a time when he'd been as in the dark about all of this as me so either one of them had spilled or he'd figured it out years ago and I'd been left alone in my quest for this knowledge.

"Jesus, Saint, you look like you might bust a nut if you grind your teeth any harder," Nash joked, nudging me playfully and I huffed out a breath.

"Is that really your birthday wish?" Tatum asked, turning so that she could look at me and I narrowed my eyes as I looked back

"You have no idea how infuriating it is for me not to grasp something the rest of you share," I replied evenly. "Even the kids seem to understand it. And I just…it's not…I don't fucking get it!"

She glanced between the others and my phone buzzed in my pocket. One look at Kyan as he shoved his own phone back into his pants' pocket should have been enough to tell me what it said, but of course, I couldn't resist the urge to look.

Kyan:
squid emoji

Saint:
It's not funny. It hasn't been funny for sixteen years. It never was funny.

Blake:

It's like when you *onion emoji* in your pants, but you get a little teared up so you *otter emoji*

Nash:

Kinda like *flamingo emoji* but with more *crab emoji* and a little *salt emoji*

Saint:

I hate all of you.

Kyan:

There you go, being all *squid emoji* again. It's tiring, dude. Why don't you just *squid emoji*?

Saint:

I AM SICK OF THIS SHIT!

Tatum:

Okay. I'll tell you x

Tatum:

squid emoji

I looked up from my phone as Tatum tossed hers down on the steps and turned to climb into my lap, straddling me and pushing her fingers into my hair while the others all chuckled.

"Truly?" I asked and she nodded, smirking at me like this joke had never once gotten old for her.

The bright orange rays of the setting sun gilded her hair with a halo of light and I wound my fingers around her waist, the soft material of her white dress slipping against my skin as I looked at her. I loved this colour on her, fucking adored it and I swear she knew. That was why she'd worn it today, the light to my darkness.

The others were still laughing, their arms brushing against us as they pressed close, the five of us always gravitating together like that, especially when Tatum was at the heart of us like now. Where she belonged.

Despite everything we'd been through, the good and the bad, the fucked up and the feral, we really were happy. Our little family against the world. And I wouldn't change a damn moment of what we had or what we had to come for anything.

Tatum leaned in and placed her lips against my ear as she spoke to me in a breathy voice and my heart actually raced as I realised she really was going to tell me what it meant. The mystery would be over, the plague of not knowing would finally be lifted from me.

"The squid means…"

AUTHOR NOTE

Well slap my ass and call me Tallulah, we just went and finished a motherfucking series! Did we pass the test? Do you hate us? Love us? Fall into the confusingly terrifying middle ground of understanding that we're bad for you and yet you still keep on finding yourself coming back for more?

I feel…well shit, I feel all kinds of things, happy, sad, a little confused over the squid (I'm glad we could clear that up for you), relieved and yet kinda empty too as these characters have finally finished telling us their story. I'm gonna miss them, but I'd like to think we did good by them and set them up with a life that they can really live to the fullest.

How did we do without a cliffhanger? I have to say it was hard not to leave you all hanging by your fingertips and cursing our names there, but don't worry, there is plenty more of that planned for this year. Did you hate us when Troy escaped? I kinda loved that he did that, sorry, not sorry. It just made that revenge taste so much sweeter in the end for us…

On a slightly more serious note, you probably picked up on the fact that some of the themes of this series were loosely based off of events going on in the world right now with the-virus-that-shall-not-be-named. This year has been…well, let's go with *interesting*. The kind of interesting like when you step on a Lego with a bare foot, fall down the stairs and land in dog shit, only to wonder why the hell there's dog shit in your house when you don't have a dog and then realise that you can't visit your friends or family for a year, so you just lay there in agony, covered in the shit screaming at the windows WHY DID YOU EAT A FUCKING BAT???

Ahem.

I know that lockdown has looked different to all of us and there have been plenty of lows to dwell on, but I'd like to think there have been some highs too. We all got to spend more time with the people we love and focus on the things that are most important to us while also getting the opportunity to think on the things we miss the most and can look forward to reclaiming as this crisis finally comes to an end. Plus books. Books, books and more books. Were any of us really in lockdown when we could escape into another world with the flick of a page? How damn lucky are we to have that?? I mean, it's not quite the same as being able to go out and leave the damn house but it is pretty freaking awesome in my opinion.

    Shout out to all of the badass hospital and essential workers who showed up every damn day throughout this as well. Without you guys on the front line, this whole thing could have been a lot worse and we have so much love and respect for you guys. If you're reading this and our books brought you even the slightest bit of joy and respite between shifts, then we're so glad to have been able to offer you that.

    So, Tatum and her Night Keepers have made it to the finish line, me and Caroline feel like total zombies – these books were thiccc. Blood, sweat, tears, a little crazy and a lot of badass went into these books and just maybe, they will keep a place in your heart long after The End like they will in ours. And maybe they'll live on in the world of say…Sinners' Playground. Where they may or may not show up in Sunset Cove with Rogue and her harem of dark and dirty gang members. Haven't started that series yet? Well you can dive in right now if you're ready to face the gritty underworld of the Harlequin Crew.

    Stay safe, wear a mask and take joy in only having to put makeup on the top half of your face. Keep your toilet paper game forever strong - may you never go without a wipe again. And for the love of fuck, please don't eat any bats!!!

    Love,

    Susanne & Caroline xxx

    P.S.

    If you do find yourself obsessing over this series and wanna come stalk us, send us abusive messages for all the heartache or even some love (love you too, boo) then why not join the best group of people we know in our Facebook reader group? I promise that the answer to Saint's question will be in there *squid emoji* …maybe. xx

ALSO BY CAROLINE PECKHAM & SUSANNE VALENTI

Brutal Boys of Everlake Prep
(Complete Reverse Harem Bully Romance Contemporary Series)
Kings of Quarantine
Kings of Lockdown
Kings of Anarchy
Queen of Quarantine

**

Dead Men Walking
(Reverse Harem Dark Romance Contemporary Series)
The Death Club
Society of Psychos

**

The Harlequin Crew
(Reverse Harem Mafia Romance Contemporary Series)
Sinners Playground
Dead Man's Isle
Carnival Hill
Paradise Lagoon
Gallows Bridge

Harlequinn Crew Novellas
Devil's Pass

**

Dark Empire

(Dark Mafia Contemporary Standalones)

Beautiful Carnage

Beautiful Savage

**

Forget Me Not Bombshell

(Dark Mafia Reverse Harem Contemporary Standalone)

**

The Ruthless Boys of the Zodiac

(Reverse Harem Paranormal Romance Series - Set in the world of Solaria)

Dark Fae

Savage Fae

Vicious Fae

Broken Fae

Warrior Fae

Zodiac Academy

(M/F Bully Romance Series- Set in the world of Solaria, five years after Dark Fae)

The Awakening

Ruthless Fae

The Reckoning

Shadow Princess

Cursed Fates

Fated Thrones

Heartless Sky

The Awakening - As told by the Boys

Zodiac Academy Novellas

Origins of an Academy Bully

The Big A.S.S. Party

Darkmore Penitentiary

(Reverse Harem Paranormal Romance Series - Set in the world of Solaria, ten years after Dark Fae)

Caged Wolf
Alpha Wolf
Feral Wolf

**

The Age of Vampires

(Complete M/F Paranormal Romance/Dystopian Series)

Eternal Reign
Eternal Shade
Eternal Curse
Eternal Vow
Eternal Night
Eternal Love

**

Cage of Lies

(M/F Dystopian Series)

Rebel Rising

**

Tainted Earth

(M/F Dystopian Series)

Afflicted
Altered
Adapted
Advanced

**

The Vampire Games

(Complete M/F Paranormal Romance Trilogy)

V Games

V Games: Fresh From The Grave

V Games: Dead Before Dawn

*

The Vampire Games: Season Two

(Complete M/F Paranormal Romance Trilogy)

Wolf Games

Wolf Games: Island of Shade

Wolf Games: Severed Fates

*

The Vampire Games: Season Three

Hunter Trials

*

The Vampire Games Novellas

A Game of Vampires

**

The Rise of Issac

(Complete YA Fantasy Series)

Creeping Shadow

Bleeding Snow

Turning Tide

Weeping Sky

Failing Light

Printed in France by Amazon
Brétigny-sur-Orge, FR